Rainy Days

LORY LILIAN

Rainy Days

ISBN: 978-1-936009-18-3

Book and cover design by Ellen Pickels

To my friends Monik and Elsa,
my love and heartfelt gratitude
for their help, support and encouragement
in my first attempt to write about
Darcy and Elizabeth.

Special thanks to Margaret Fransen and Ellen Pickels
for their support and assistance in publishing this book.

Chapter 1

After three full days of rain, the sky began to clear, and the sun finally seemed tempted to show its face. It was early morning, and everyone in the house was still in their rooms — except her.

Elizabeth Bennet was having another sleepless night, no doubt caused by the long period of time she had to stay indoors and the fear of hearing Mr. Collins address her with an unwelcome proposal.

Almost from the beginning, her cousin seemed determined to favour her. Of course, her dear sister Jane was his first choice, but thankfully, Mrs. Bennet told him about Mr. Bingley's attentions towards Jane, and Mr. Collins turned — quite naturally in his opinion — to the second in age and beauty.

As the weather was so inviting, Elizabeth decided not to let another moment pass without taking advantage of the beautiful November day, so she donned her outerwear and went outside.

By breakfast time, I shall return and, hopefully — being tired — spend the morning in my room, reading or talking with Jane about the upcoming ball.

The dance was another delicate matter; its beginning would be a disaster as Mr. Collins had asked for her first set. However, she was happy with anticipation, thinking of the pleasurable evening she would spend in the charming company of Mr. Wickham. With the militia in town, there should be enough gentlemen in attendance to guarantee her a partner for every dance. She shuddered as she recalled an assembly wherein she had been left without a partner, which had prompted derogatory comments from a *certain* gentleman regarding her being *"slighted by other men."*

Of course, Elizabeth liked *him* too little to value his opinion. She remained with no cordial feelings towards Mr. Darcy since that night, and furthering their acquaintance during the days spent nursing her sister at Netherfield, she had easily read his character: a clever man, well read and well bred, who cared for his sister and his friend.

Perhaps too caring. *I hope he will not discourage Mr. Bingley in his attentions toward Jane; no doubt Miss Bingley and Mrs. Hurst would welcome such a gesture,* Elizabeth thought bitterly.

Nevertheless, the time spent at Netherfield also confirmed for her that he was a proud and disagreeable man — haughty, reserved and fastidious — who considered all of them beneath him and treated them accordingly. Furthermore, Mr. Wickham's sad recounting of mistreatment by the gentleman confirmed her earlier suspicions about his lack of integrity.

Her friend Charlotte Lucas believed Mr. Darcy had every reason to be proud, but Elizabeth disagreed; surely, there could be no basis for such behaviour. And even if it were justified, his pride did not entitle him to disregard his father's will and reduce to comparative poverty a good, sensible man like Mr. Wickham.

Strangely, a brief meeting she had witnessed in Meryton between Mr. Darcy and Mr. Wickham still puzzled her exceedingly. Though he was blameless, Wickham appeared embarrassed and uncomfortable — and a little alarmed — while Mr. Darcy seemed surprised, hurt, and definitely angry. The former turned white, while the latter became alarmingly red-faced.

Of course, she knew too little of either gentleman to be certain her observations were well founded or to understand their reactions. *Papa would have read them in an instant just looking at their faces…*

However, Mr. Bennet showed little interest in the two gentlemen or, for that matter, in any other people or events around him. His constant preoccupation was his books, which always keep him company in the solitude of his library; the only person admitted whenever she wished was Elizabeth.

Improving my mind by extensive reading… That was Mr. Darcy's definition of an accomplished woman. Poor Miss Bingley. She went to so much trouble to prove she was a great reader.

With these thoughts on her mind, Elizabeth walked quickly. She enjoyed the feeling of the wind on her face and the smell of fresh air after the rain. She preferred an alternate path she knew well and walked for a time through the wooded area till she reached a small hill near a stream — deeper than it had been in some time — and began to climb.

Suddenly, she saw the little cottage — a place dear to her heart.

It had been built at Mr. Bennet's request after he and his brother Gardiner spent a day fishing — with little Lizzy accompanying them — and they all had been caught in the downpour from a terrible storm. By the time they reached Longbourn, they were soaked; all three suffered terrible colds and remained in bed for almost a fortnight.

Mrs. Bennet demanded they swear never to repeat their irresponsible actions and forbade all from fishing ever again. After talking to Mr. Gardiner and deciding that Mrs. Bennet had a certain point to her argument, Mr. Bennet made certain the dangerous event would never occur again; they built a small lodge for shelter in time of need.

The cottage had three rooms. The main room had a fireplace with a comfortable armchair nearby, and close to the window — convenient for reading — were a table and chairs. The second room, smaller, contained an iron bed in which Mr. Bennet could rest from time to time while his companion, Mr. Gardiner, oversaw the fishing tools. The third room was a small kitchen, and a closet held the most urgent necessities. The cottage always contained blankets, towels and the material for starting a fire.

The last time Elizabeth was in the cottage was about five years earlier — before the Gardiners' fourth child was born; however, she knew a servant checked the cottage from time to time.

She had no intention of going inside. She planned just to look at it and pass on by. *How strange... Suddenly I find myself missing my childhood.*

She walked a little further but suddenly felt a powerful chill. Recovering from her thoughts, she looked around and saw the sky filled with heavy clouds. Her surroundings were becoming black and cold, and she was suddenly in the midst of frigid darkness.

Elizabeth was wearing naught but a muslin gown, Spencer, cloak, bonnet and gloves, but none was made from substantial fabric. Certainly, nothing she wore would protect her should the weather become treacherous.

I had better hurry home before the rain begins, she mused silently.

However, it was too late; in a few moments, a heavy rain began to fall steadily until all she could see was a curtain of water in front of her. *I must get back to the cottage; it is my only chance. I shall freeze to death trying to get home in this driving rain.*

The more Elizabeth attempted to quicken her pace, the more slowly she seemed to move. The field was mostly slippery mud; her clothes were soaked and began to feel colder and heavier. She was stumbling blindly.

I do not want to sprain my ankle just before the ball... or perhaps it is not such a bad idea, considering the fact that I must dance the first two with Mr. Collins... but then I shall not be able to dance at all, not even with Mr. Wickham! That would be a tragic event, indeed...

She tried to laugh at her situation, but she became frightened and extremely worried about what her family would think when they discovered her missing. Surely, they would fear the worst.

She wrapped her arms around herself and rubbed up and down as feverishly as she could, trying to keep to the correct path leading to the cottage. Suddenly, she stopped at the sound of a horse's galloping hooves and the deep, strong voice of its rider.

He must be mad to ride so on a nearly invisible road; it will lead him and his horse unerringly into the stream. I must warn him.

She ran to her right and, lifting both her hands, began to yell.

She startled; the rider was closer than she thought, and she found herself directly in the path of his mount. The man saw her, too, and pulled the reins with all his might, causing the horse to rear; its legs slipped and it fell. The rider was about to be caught underneath, but at the last second, he threw himself clear and landed in the mud — well away from his horse. The animal righted itself and ran into the dense woods.

Elizabeth was too terrified to move or breathe. Her whole body trembled. She watched the man on the ground and tried to speak to him to see whether he was hurt. She attempted to approach him, but her feet would not move, which was for the best, because in the next second, she heard a well-known, unpleasant voice growling at her.

"Are you out of your mind to yell like that? What on earth were you thinking to scare my horse and make him throw me to the ground?"

It was obvious he had not recognised her, but Elizabeth was quite cold, scared — and now angry.

"I am terribly sorry, sir, for upsetting you so. I was trying to stop you from running directly into the stream. If I had known it was you, Mr. Darcy, I should have thought twice before acting so impulsively."

In a second, Darcy was on his feet. He was wet, his hat was lost somewhere, and his fine coat and gloves were covered in mud.

"Miss Bennet! May I ask what you are doing here?"

She glared at him, her 'fine eyes' casting daggers.

"Besides scaring you and your horse, sir? Well, I can no longer deny it. That was the precise purpose of my morning walk."

"I am sorry for offending you, Miss Bennet. I only meant that I was surprised by your sudden appearance, and I was equally surprised at my horse's reaction to the situation. I have never been thrown from a horse in my life."

Really? What a stunning event: Mr. Darcy in the mud at my feet. What an extraordinary experience.

"Oh, it is quite all right, Mr. Darcy. I am becoming used to it. Offending me appears to be a regular pattern of our meetings whether they take place in a ballroom or in the woods."

He froze, furrowing his brow. "Miss Bennet — " he began, but she cut him off fiercely.

"Mr. Darcy, this is hardly the time or place to talk. I was attempting to find refuge from the storm before we met, and I intend to continue doing so. Good day, sir."

She began to walk at a quicker pace, but he was behind her in an instant.

"Miss Bennet, you are perfectly right; forgive me for my thoughtless behaviour. If I may be so bold, might you consider allowing me to accompany you? I confess I am not familiar with these grounds, and I should be most grateful to you for any help you can offer me in finding my way. On the other hand, I hope to be of assistance should you need it."

Elizabeth hesitated only a moment before answering. She could not leave a man alone in the woods in such awful weather, even if that man *was* Mr. Darcy. He was correct; she might need a man's hand if only for assistance in opening the old cottage door.

"Of course you may join me, Mr. Darcy, and I hope, despite the fact that we are not friends, that we might help each other to pass this difficult time."

She continued to walk as Darcy trudged closely behind, lost in his own intense thoughts.

DARCY WAS STUNNED. HER WORDS resounded in his mind, but he was unable to comprehend their meaning. '*Offending me appears to be a regular pattern of our meetings whether they take place in a ballroom or in the woods.*' Had she heard his indiscreet remarks about her at the assembly where they first met? She said she would have thought twice before rescuing him if she had known who he was, and she was continually offended by him. How could that be?

He was convinced that he had given her more attention than any other young lady. From almost the beginning of their acquaintance, he had come to admire her. He was deeply attracted by the beautiful expression of her dark, sparkling eyes, her wit and liveliness, and her open, unaffected manners. He had already confessed to himself that, if not for the inferiority of her connections, he would have been in real danger.

The inferiority of her connections — and the complete lack of propriety of her mother and younger sisters — was his best defence against this dangerous attraction. He could never consider connecting himself to a woman whose situation in life was so beneath his and whose family was in such need of a sound education. The mere thought of Mrs. Bennet and her daughters running and yelling around him at Pemberley was enough to diminish the ardour he felt every time Elizabeth was in his presence... or in his mind... or in his dreams... Diminish, yes — but it did not make the attraction vanish.

However, it did not take him long to understand fully that he *was* in danger, no matter how inferior her situation might be, and he had spent the past couple of weeks in an exhausting torment, trying to fight against the most frightful feeling he had ever experienced.

Every day he waited for an opportunity to see her and speak to her, and every night when sleep evaded him, he blamed himself for his fickle obsession and his weakness. When they happened to meet, her presence made him tense and dizzy at the same time. He desperately watched her every move, smile and lively conversation but never interfered in any of them.

He was astonished at the way he reacted to her. His heart pounded wildly, his eyes sought a sign of recognition from her, and he shivered any time she was close or spoke to him. He tried to convince himself that it was nothing more than the physical attraction he felt for a handsome woman, and he forced himself to censure and control his reactions.

Never had his body responded in such a powerful and disturbing way to a woman's presence, and this weakness ashamed him. Moreover, he could not remember whether he ever truly had been attracted to any woman before meeting Elizabeth.

So, reluctantly, he admitted to himself this failure and lack of self-control, trying to release his distress with reasonable explanations.

First — it had been a few years since he was in a woman's intimate company; his duties — to his sister and to all those who depended on him — left him little time to think of selfish pleasures. Even if he did occasionally think of them, he was always a man of great self-control and a strong will that induced him to do only what was proper and what was demanded.

Secondly, Miss Elizabeth Bennet was not only a handsome woman but singularly different from all the ladies he had met before; she had a witty mind and uncommon intelligence.

Therefore, he *allowed* himself to be attracted to her.

Nevertheless, he understood he was deceiving himself — with little success. He might be telling himself that what he felt was mere attraction, but he *knew* it was more — frighteningly more. He understood this during the time she stayed at Netherfield tending her sick sister — the most wonderful, trying and tormenting days he remembered enduring in years.

Yes, her appearance was always a most pleasurable and delightful sight, but it was equally pleasant to talk to her, to listen to her bright answers to Caroline Bingley's vicious attacks, and to witness her determination in expressing and sustaining her own opinions.

Every time she spoke to him, there was a mixture of sweetness and archness in her response; he never knew whether he should feel offended or admire her even more for her wit. Her soft lips were always twitching in a most tempting way, her eyes sparkling and her eyebrow deliciously rising in challenge. He was convinced beyond any doubt that she understood his feelings, reciprocated them, and was waiting for his attentions. However, he could not offer her that. He could not fancy himself offering her anything more than a simple acquaintance. His duties and his family's expectations forbade any other intentions or thoughts regarding Elizabeth Bennet. She was to remain a pleasant memory — a most pleasant memory — but nothing more.

Therefore, not wanting to trifle with her or her feelings, he decided to avoid any further attentions to her that could raise expectations impossible for him to fulfil.

Consequently, he withdrew even more, content to admire her from afar. He talked to her less in her last days at Netherfield and tried to avoid her company. He even spent more than half an hour reading in the library while she was in the same room without addressing a single word to her.

That morning, as with many other mornings, he awoke after only a few hours of restless sleep — another disturbing matter. Every time he closed his eyes, she appeared in his mind; never before in his life had he dreamt of any woman. Now, his dreams were filled with Elizabeth Bennet, and they were the sorts of dreams he could not even allow himself to remember. It would not do!

He had fetched his horse and thrown himself into a long, wild ride in dreadful weather precisely to clear his mind of her image and forget about the ball that, no doubt, would bring her again to Netherfield. Nothing could be worse than seeing her dance with other men.

Now, here they were together, alone — dangerously alone. He followed her, watching from behind. Her hair was in great disorder and soaking wet. Her dark curls had escaped their hairpins and lay in heavy waves about her shoulders and back. Her dress and shoes were mud-soaked, and yet he was sure she had never looked more beautiful.

What a simpleton I am! While I tried to conceal my preference for her, I was never in any danger of raising expectations; she simply hates me —

"Mr. Darcy! Mr. Darcy!" She tried to catch his attention, but he was so involved in his thoughts that she had to shout at him several times before he heard her.

"I am so sorry, Miss Bennet... I was distracted. Is there anything you want me to do?" He looked at her intently.

That look again, she thought. *Well, this time I cannot blame him; I must look simply horrendous. At least I do not have to worry for my safety in being alone with this man. If he did not find me handsome enough to tempt him at the assembly when I looked my best, God knows what he thinks of me now when I am such a mess.*

"Mr. Darcy, this is the place. Will you be so kind as to try opening the door?"

"Of course, Miss Bennet. Allow me, please."

He tried the iron doorknob, but the door was tightly closed; meanwhile, the weather was getting worse. He forced the door with his shoulder — once, twice, and the door gave way.

"Come, Miss Bennet."

She entered with a great sense of relief as she was feeling increasingly chilled. She felt her lips trembling as her body was shaking. Darcy followed her in and glanced about the first room.

"Miss Bennet, do you know this place?"

"Yes, I know it very well."

"Do you think I could find something useful for us — something to start a fire, perhaps? Or some blankets?"

"I know with certainty that we shall find all those things; this cottage was built precisely to offer shelter for a short period of time in situations like this. They must be in the main room near the fireplace."

They entered together, finding everything located precisely as Elizabeth remembered. She went directly to the closet in the adjoining room and found a towel. It was obviously a long time since it had been laundered, for it smelled quite musky indeed; but it was, nevertheless, dry, which was what they needed beyond all else. The first thing she did was put the towel to her head to wipe the dripping water from her face; she put a blanket around her shoulders to warm herself a little. Mr. Darcy was gazing at her from the door.

"Mr. Darcy, please came in and take one of these towels. You are all wet."

"Thank you, Miss Bennet; I appreciate your concern. It will be very useful indeed."

He took one of the towels. "In the meantime, I shall try to set the fire."

"Set the fire? By yourself, sir?" Elizabeth's voice was full of irony.

His lips twisted in a hidden smile. *Indeed, I usually do not do such things for myself, but in this, I shall amaze you, Elizabeth . . .* He did not even turn to face her. He just left the room while drying his hair with the towel. *Oh, what a smell! I shall have to take at least a two-hour bath to clean myself. And Elizabeth will need one, too.*

Suddenly, the image of Elizabeth in a bathtub fully occupied his mind, and he stopped for a second to enjoy his fanciful imaginings; in the next second, he censured himself. *She is here with me alone in a sorry situation, and I am such a poor excuse for a gentleman that, instead of doing all I can to protect her and assure her of her safety, I am thinking such vile things. No wonder she hates me!*

Darcy set the fire with relative ease. He had done so many times in his youth. His excellent father always told him he must be able to look after himself and his family in any circumstances, no matter how difficult or how unlikely they might be. *Well, Father, this is certainly a difficult and unlikely situation in which I now find myself.*

"Miss Bennet! The fire is ready."

In the next room, Elizabeth tried somehow to arrange her hair, which she knew was an absolute disaster; she caught it together on her back, dried her face and wrapped herself tightly in the blanket. Although there were several more, she decided this one would absorb most of the water from her clothes, after which she could take another. She also considered saving a dry blanket for Darcy. *Miss Bingley would kill me if something happened to him.*

She heard his voice calling and was sure he was asking for help. Quickly, she appeared in the doorway, and the first thing to draw her attention was a strong, welcoming fire.

"Mr. Darcy, I must confess I am all astonishment. I never would have imagined that the master of Pemberley — "

While speaking in her usual teasing tone, she looked toward him and suddenly stopped in astonishment; she began to chuckle. She put her hand to her mouth in a futile attempt to stop her laughter, but her eyes betrayed her, and she could see that she was offending him.

"Miss Bennet, may I inquire as to what you find so amusing about the fire I made? Does it not please you?"

"Of course, sir. I am most grateful for your trouble in making the fire, I assure you. It is just that..."

She could not contain her mirth any longer and began to laugh openly. His face was streaked with brown smudges! She knew what had happened; the heavy dust on the towel had combined with the rainwater on his face and turned to mud, which was now covering most of his features.

With his dirty face, no hat and gloves, and his hair in disorder, he looked more like a mischievous boy than the proud, unpleasant man who always made people feel uneasy and intimidated.

Oh my, what a wonderful sight! I must share this with Jane and Charlotte as soon as possible. How I should like Miss Bingley to see this, too. He is, all of him, six inches deep in mud!

Darcy was watching her intently as she laughed heartily, unaware of the arousing sight she presented with her wet, muddy gown adhering to her legs and the Spencer moulding to the curves of her body. He needed all his strength to control his desire to take her into his arms and kiss those soft lips and laughing eyes.

He allowed himself to relax and join Elizabeth in her amusement. Pursing his lips, he tried to keep his countenance, but his eyes and the corner of his mouth betrayed him. Thus, Elizabeth saw with wonder for the first time a full view of his dimples when he began to speak again.

"As you seem unwilling to reveal the reason for your amusement, I shall try to puzzle it out. Might it be the fact that my face is covered in dirt?"

Elizabeth was startled, and a surprised gasp escaped her lips.

"Indeed that *is* the reason, Mr. Darcy, and I must apologise for my manners, but I simply could not help myself. I never would have imagined seeing you... Please, forgive me."

He gazed steadfastly into her eyes and smiled at her, an open and sincere smile that gave her an odd combination of chills and warmth. It was the first reaction of that kind Elizabeth had experienced in the company of a man.

"There is no need to apologise. If you will just assure me of your secrecy about this situation, I shall go outside and wash my face in a moment."

"Of my secrecy, sir, you can rest assured. But how did you know what roused my amusement?"

Darcy looked at her again, his smile growing larger until he began to laugh in spite of himself.

"Miss Bennet, we are both wet and used the same set of towels. I shall find something for you to clean your face, as well."

Elizabeth became flushed with mortification and was at a loss for words as she caught his meaning. She could think of nothing to say and cast her eyes down, imagining what she must look like. She felt suddenly even more ashamed of her behaviour compared to Mr. Darcy, who graciously said nothing about her appearance until she began making fun of him.

Darcy opened the cottage door, took the rainwater in his hands and began to wash his face. When he was done, he took off his neckcloth, folded it as a handkerchief, kept it in the heavy rain for a few seconds, and then handed it to Elizabeth who was staring at him mesmerised.

Never before had she seen a man do something as intimate as cleaning himself or removing his neckcloth, and never had she held a man's garments. She took it, afraid to touch it, embarrassed that she would have to clean her face with something that had been in such close contact with his body. The thought made her tremble, sending cold shivers down her spine.

Darcy was watching her and finally comprehended her uneasiness. He smiled to himself at her innocence; she looked so young, fragile, and uncomfortable that all his other feelings for her were put aside. He felt overwhelmed by a tender need to take care of her, protect her, and keep her safe.

"Miss Bennet, I am deeply sorry I cannot find something more adequate to clean your face. If it is not comfortable for you to use my… this, I shall try to find something else in the closet, or perhaps you would prefer to remain as you are until you return home. After all, there is no one here to see you —

"No… no… I shall use it. Thank you, sir. I am just afraid I shall spoil it forever," she answered, not wanting to appear ungrateful for his efforts.

"As for that, you must not worry at all."

She began to clean her face as well as she could without thinking of anything else.

A few moments later, her face was clean; she could see that from the approving smile on his lips, but at the same time, she felt increasingly chilled even though she was near the fire.

"I must get another blanket. This one is completely wet. And Mr. Darcy, you should do the same. There are a few more blankets in there; you look very cold yourself."

"Yes, I think I shall do that. But please, rest near the fire. I shall bring the blankets for both of us."

Elizabeth followed him with her eyes and could not cease to wonder at his transformation. He is being kind and attentive. Who is this man? This cannot be Miss Bingley's Mr. Darcy.

He was back with the blankets immediately and helped replace her wet covering with a dry one. He stood in front of her and put his arms lightly on her shoulders to adjust the blanket, allowing his hands to linger only a few seconds. Facing him, she felt as if she were wrapped in his embrace. He kept gazing at her, his countenance worried. She was not looking well at all. She was clearly chilled through.

"Miss Bennet…" He hesitated a few moments and then continued, "I know it is highly improper for me to ask you this, but you must find a way to dry your clothes before you put the blanket around you."

She raised her eyes at him incredulously as if she could not believe he was suggesting such a thing. "I am afraid I do not fully understand your meaning, sir," said she soundly, wrapping the blanket forcefully around her body and trying to protect herself.

The rain was becoming more intense; she could hear it beating on the roof like a wild animal.

"I shall explain myself. Your dress is soaked, and no matter how many blankets you use, they will soon become wet; you will never manage to keep yourself warm. Staying near the fire might help, but there is a great risk of catching a dangerous cold. I am suggesting that you…remove your dress and put it near the fire to dry, and to…twist and drain your other clothes…and after that to cover yourself in one or two blankets to warm yourself and — " He twisted his signet ring. He did not know what else to do. His voice was trembling a little; he could not believe he dared suggest such a thing. His face was flushed — as was Elizabeth's — and neither of them could look at the other.

"Mr. Darcy, I thank you for your concern, but you are perfectly right; it is completely improper for you to suggest such a thing. You could not possibly believe that anything would convince me to remove my clothes in here while I am alone with you."

Darcy knew he had no right to insist, but he also knew how to have his way; he felt responsible for her safety.

"Miss Bennet, I know I have given you no reason to trust me since we have known each other, but you have my word as a gentleman that neither you nor any other woman would be in any danger in my presence. I have a young sister who is under my care. Please believe me when I say I have always treated young ladies with the same respect I expect other men to show towards my sister. When I asked you about drying your clothes, I thought only of your welfare. You look truly ill, cold and tired."

He never took his eyes from her, and Elizabeth held his gaze for a moment, lost in its intense expression. Unexpectedly warmed, although water was dripping from her dress below the blanket, she averted her eyes, suddenly feeling flushed and shy.

"Mr. Darcy, indeed I know you are a gentleman, and I did not think I would be in any danger from you, sir. In any case, I should rather stay like this a little longer, hoping the rain will stop shortly and I shall be able to run home rather than put both of us in an awkward situation."

"I do not think the rain will stop soon. I shall respect your wishes, but you must allow me to insist on putting one more blanket around you at least. I am perfectly fine; I do not need any."

"That would be a good idea, thank you, but you must take another blanket to cover yourself. In this matter, I also insist, sir."

"Well, then thank you; I shall do that." He stopped and then turned to her.

"Miss Bennet, would you mind if I took off my coat? I should like to put it near the fire..."

"No, sir... Of course not."

She was upset with herself for being so uncomfortable near him; after all, he had been all kindness and goodness and done everything in his power to make her feel easy, something she would have thought impossible only an hour ago. *What is it about him that makes me feel so strange? Then again, I have always reacted strangely in his presence.*

He took off his greatcoat and coat, remaining as suitably attired as Elizabeth had seen him once in the billiard room at Netherfield.

Well, not exactly. The last time I saw him dressed so, he was not wet. But then, neither was I.

He was far better protected from the rain than she was; under his thick, black greatcoat, he was wearing a coat and a waistcoat. In fact, his waistcoat and shirt were barely wet.

He squeezed his coat thoroughly until much of the water from it dripped on the floor. Then he put it on the chair as near to the fire as possible; she knew he was trying to suggest what she should do with her own clothes.

"Will you consider at least taking off your cloak and doing the same with it? You must be even wetter than I since evidently my coat is much thicker."

"No, thank you, sir. I am perfectly fine."

His insistence made her uneasy, and trying to protect herself from the strange feelings he aroused in her, she became defensive, her voice teasingly sharp as in many of their previous conversations.

"I am sure I look very ill, and it must be an unhappy, uncomfortable situation for you. You have likely never been in the company of a lady looking as poorly as I."

Darcy turned around and stared at her; he saw her eyebrow rising in challenge as it had many times before. On this occasion, he knew very well that she was not flirting with him but trying to tease and punish him for his conduct. Happily, as no Miss Bingley was there to disturb them, he could finally answer her as he pleased.

"This *is* a peculiar experience for me, but you must not feel uneasy. I have the highest opinion of you, and I find you as charming as ever."

Elizabeth started to laugh nervously. "Yes indeed, I can easily believe you find me as charming as ever."

"I am afraid I do not follow you. Did I say something to offend you?"

"No, you did not, sir. I thank you very much for saying you have the highest opinion of me, but we both know what you think of my appearance. You made that perfectly clear when we first met at the assembly in Meryton."

Darcy froze; this was the second reference she had made to being offended by him.

Now having the confirmation that she heard his remark, he quickly tried to find an apology, but her eyes were wearing a daring expression filled with mischief, and he could tolerate it no longer.

Holding her gaze, he answered in a deep, serious voice. "Miss Bennet, you could not be farther from the truth. My behaviour that night was unpardonable, and I made an unfair comment about you, which I regretted almost the following moment. Since then, having been in your company many times, I have found nothing wanting in you. For some time now, I have considered you a remarkable young lady, truly accomplished and equally charming."

She looked at him incredulously, her eyes wide and her mouth half-parted. She was not sure whether he had spoken in jest or was trying to flatter her to take advantage of their situation. However, his eyes and face appeared set in stone. He was not only serious but almost grave, and his voice was calm and even. He was not paying her a compliment or trying to flatter her; he was merely stating a fact.

Seizing the opportunity arising from her sudden silence, he continued. "If I appear insistent insofar as your removing your clothes, I assure you it is not because your appearance is unpleasant, but rather that I am concerned for your well-being. I also find you to be absolutely charming but perhaps not entirely proper in that wet dress."

He cursed himself for speaking so to her; he knew she would be frightened by his presumption, but if she could be persuaded to remove her cold, wet clothes, which were a threat to her health and even to her life... well, that was all that mattered.

Elizabeth remained stunned for a few moments; her mind could not comprehend what she had heard. Did Mr. Darcy just say he found her... tempting? Was that not the meaning behind his reference to her wet dress?

Darcy searched her eyes and face a little longer. It had been less than an hour since they entered the cottage, though it seemed longer.

"Miss Bennet, I shall allow you full privacy to decide what is best for you. I shall go to the next room and remain there as long as necessary. Or, if you prefer, I am willing to remove myself from the cottage and stay outside near the door until we can each return to our homes safely."

He bowed to her — a formality that looked decidedly silly in his present state — and left the room.

"Mr. Darcy!" He turned to her, and she continued with a barely audible voice. "There is no reason — no need for you to stay outside, sir. The other room will suffice, thank you."

He bowed again and closed the door after him; Elizabeth followed him with her eyes, still under the shock of his revelation.

As soon as he was gone, she hurried to check that the door was locked. She fixed it with a chair but then laughed bitterly. If he were a threat to her or had any wicked thoughts, he would not be stopped by an old door. That was obvious from the ease with which he had opened the cottage door. All she could do was be civil to him and hope he would be the same to her.

Breathing deeply, she began to wonder what she should do. Was she in any real danger being in the cottage with Mr. Darcy? He was indeed disagreeable, but he never gave her any reason to think him improper. She clearly remembered his words about his younger sister — about being worried for her well-being.

Although she was trembling, she began to think rationally now that she was away from him. *Would he take advantage of a woman with whose family he was so well acquainted? Would he risk his reputation just to . . . ? In any case, he probably can have any woman he chooses. He surely does not need to . . . Why on earth am I thinking this way? Am I losing my mind?*

The next moment she was ashamed of herself. No, in no way would she be in any danger from him. He told her as much, and she knew it for herself. Even if she found him to be a hateful man, she knew he would not harm her. And his reference to his sister . . . she was quite impressed, considering how reserved he usually was. No, she would surely be safe with him.

She unwrapped the wet blanket from around her body and laid it down; then she looked carefully at herself for the first time that morning. *What a mess. Covered in mud and soaking wet . . .*

Suddenly she froze and blushed deeply. Her dress was white, quite wet and very revealing. Fortunately, she was wearing her spencer, but it was not enough to cover her. *Oh my goodness! What must he think of me? I cannot entertain any hope that he failed to notice how transparent this material is when it is wet. He told me as much.*

She was mortified at the thought of seeing him again, walking with him more than three miles home, and perhaps even encountering someone else! Drying the dress and top as soon as possible was not just a good idea — it was something she had to do without delay!

She took off her shoes, removed her dress and stockings, squeezed them as Darcy had done with his coat, and put them on a chair; she did the same with her Spencer. She hesitated only a moment before she removed her petticoat, squeezed out the water as well as she could, and put it on again; she did the same with her undergarments. Elizabeth shivered feeling the damp fabric on her skin; nevertheless, it was better than before.

She wrapped herself in the blanket so that only her head remained uncovered and gathered the second blanket around her as well. She then sat in the armchair close to the fire, her feet tucked under her.

Yes, this is definitely better; I must thank him for his advice. Now I can see why Mr. Bingley always applauds his cleverness and asks for his opinion.

She smiled to herself at the thought, but in the next second, she found herself wondering what Mr. Darcy was doing.

In the other room, Darcy was trying desperately to comb his hair with his fingers; he knew how untidy he must look. He took a blanket and put it over his shoulders while thinking of Elizabeth.

This time spent with her alone was a blessing, a precious gift; not only had he the chance of learning her true opinion of him, but he was provided ample opportunity to change that opinion. He would be a fool not to take advantage of it. *Now I know what I must do.*

A second later, however, he changed his mind. *What exactly are you thinking? You cannot possibly have any serious design on her! You must consider your duty to your family, to Georgiana, to Pemberley, to all the people who are in your care who deserve a perfect mistress…*

He was abruptly roused from his thoughts by a gentle knock at the door.

"Mr. Darcy, you may come in if you wish…"

Chapter 2

Darcy did not expect any further invitation, but he knocked a few times before entering. He tried not to stare at her, and she tried to avert her eyes, but neither of them could avoid looking at the other.

So she did change, finally.

"Sir, you had better take a chair near the fire to warm yourself."

"Thank you, Miss Bennet."

He sat near the fire, close to her. *Too close.* He could not decide whether the sudden heat that enveloped him was from the fire or from her undressed, wet, shivering body in need of being held and warmed — and caressed. He wanted nothing more at that moment than to hold her tightly in his arms and be cold no longer.

Darcy sat with his back to the chair that held her wet dress; he was deliberately trying not to embarrass her further. Elizabeth was eminently aware of his efforts and grateful to him for attempting to make the situation less awkward for her. They were both uncomfortable, given their unfortunate predicament and the awareness of the other's proximity, so neither knew how to begin a neutral conversation.

Allowing some further minutes to pass and desperately trying to regain her spirits, Elizabeth grew determined not to let his presence intimidate her.

"Mr. Darcy, I think we should try to make some conversation."

"I shall be most happy to talk with you about any subject you desire."

"I shall think of something… "

She saw him looking intently at her and could not help teasing him lightly. "Sir, I certainly hope you will not dare to say again that I look charming, for now I shall be absolutely certain you are mocking me." Her voice was the same as the one he knew so well from their past debates, and he saw her right brow rise charmingly; he quickly understood her attempt at conversation and was pleased by her efforts.

"Miss Bennet, I am deeply sorry, but I cannot find you anything other than charming. On the other hand, that garment… That is the most dreadful dress I have ever seen in my life and not at all attractive on you." She began to laugh heartily.

Can it be true? He is teasing me and enjoying it. Who is this man? "Thank you, sir. You look less than perfect, yourself." *Oh lord, he is smiling at me!*

A little distressed by the new display of his dimples and open smile, she teased him further. "And you must have noticed, Mr. Darcy, that this is not a real dress. You are, after all, very perceptive, as I was told by a certain young lady."

"Miss Bingley," said he, trying to appear quite serious, "always gives me credit for more than I ever can be. However, I know it is not a real dress, and I am quite relieved, because it would have been the ugliest dress in the whole world."

"Oh, I would not be so sure about that. The servant women wear similar clothes all the time, and they often look quite tolerable in them. I am certain that your servants are no different." *But, of course, you cannot consider servants to be human at all.*

"Miss Bennet, I must confess I never look closely at my servants' clothes — men or women. But I promise I shall check, and if what you say is in fact true, I shall pay them additional wages so they can afford better clothes," said he, smiling.

"But sir, if you increase their income, perhaps they will prefer to spend it for extra food or to save for their children rather than buy finer clothes for the sole purpose of pleasing you." Her tone was by now fierce. *Why am I so angry with him? Perhaps because of what he did to poor Mr. Wickham?*

In fact, speaking about servants reminded her of that gentleman's sad story, and she felt guilty for forgetting about him and almost allowing herself to be deceived by Darcy's pleasant manners. His countenance suddenly became serious, and his tone lost all its playfulness, but he answered her less severely; he seemed conciliatory and willing to get along well with her, reminding Elizabeth she must keep her temper under control.

"Miss Bennet, I hope none of my servants or tenants is in need of anything and surely not of food or comfort for themselves or their families. It is my custom to treat them with all the respect and care they deserve and to compensate them fairly for their work."

"I am sure that must be right, sir." After a moment she continued, "Indeed sir, that is quite remarkable. You must have many people depending on you, and it must be difficult to do what is right all the time."

"It is difficult sometimes; nevertheless, I consider that to be one of the most important duties I have. It is equally true that doing the right thing can be uncertain and depends very much on those who are involved."

"And you never let other feelings come between you and that duty?"

"What other feelings could there be?" Darcy's face had become as dark and stern as it used to be.

"I do not know — vanity, pride, a bad temper. After all, you yourself told me that your good opinion once lost is lost forever. It is easy to be blinded by prejudice when those feelings overwhelm you."

"Perhaps, but I am careful not to allow that to happen."

She grew more and more annoyed. *How cynical you can be, Mr. Darcy. I liked the old, rude Darcy better than this insincerely charming and cruel man; how dare he consider himself so correct after effecting such a great injustice on Mr. Wickham.*

"Well, it is good to see that you are so confident in your judgment. But certainly you are aware that some people might contradict you." *Let us see how you defend yourself.*

"Again, you are absolutely right, Miss Bennet. But may I enquire as to what these questions tend?"

"Merely to the illustration of your character," said she, endeavouring to shake off her gravity. "I am trying to make it out."

"And what is your success?"

She shook her head. "I do not get on at all. I hear such different accounts of you as to puzzle me exceedingly."

"From whom could you hear such different reports if I may be so bold as to enquire? Or do you know, by chance, many other acquaintances of mine?" His dark eyes were on fire while searching her face, and he knew the answer long before she spoke it.

"As a matter of fact, I recently met on old acquaintance of yours — Mr. Wickham." *There, I am not afraid to defend my opinion or my friend.*

A deeper shade of hauteur overspread his features.

"Mr. Wickham is blessed with such happy manners as may ensure his making friends. Whether he may be equally capable of retaining them is less certain."

"He has been so unlucky as to lose your friendship," she replied with emphasis, "and in a manner from which he is likely to suffer all his life."

Darcy made no answer for a while, and Elizabeth was convinced he was desirous of changing the subject; she was wrong, for he spoke again.

"Am I correct in assuming that Mr. Wickham told you of our past dealings?"

"Yes, he did me the honour of trusting me enough to tell me about his misfortunes."

"Am I to understand then that you and Mr. Wickham are old acquaintances?"

"No indeed, sir; we met just a few days ago."

"I see..."

"Why would you presume otherwise?"

"I... I just find it hard to understand why a gentleman would talk of such a delicate subject with a young lady who is not a relative or an old friend."

For a moment, his words struck her with all their hidden force, but she continued to defend Wickham and, at the same time, her conduct toward him.

"I understand from your words that you consider such a discussion highly improper, both from Mr. Wickham for starting it and from me for listening and accepting it."

"Miss Bennet," Darcy's voice again became forceful and at the same time soft, and his eyes met hers, trying to tell her more than could his words. "Since the first day I met you, I have never found anything improper in your conduct. Unfortunately, I hardly can say the same about Mr. Wickham."

That shiver again! Why do I shiver when he looks at me?

"I think you are aware, sir, that Mr. Wickham easily could have said the same about you."

"I am sure of that, Miss Bennet. In fact I am positive he frequently says something akin to that."

Elizabeth became uncomfortable at his statement but said nothing, allowing him to speak further.

"Miss Bennet, I should not expect you to believe me, considering our short acquaintance and the fact that my behaviour toward you was not what it should have been, but as I said before, I consider you one of the most intelligent people I have ever known. I trust you will use your intelligence, your knowledge and your wit to search for evidence, proof or witnesses before believing anything that I, Mr. Wickham or any other man whom you scarcely know might tell you. It would indeed be marvellous if all young ladies were as cautious as you when dealing with men who may be unscrupulous."

While he was speaking earnestly and without the anger or pride Elizabeth had expected following her attack, his gaze never left hers. She could see no insolence or sign of the impenetrable mask that used to cover his face. She became increasingly flustered by the intensity of his look and equally shocked by her own reaction to it.

The compliments he gave her conspired to make her feel equal parts pleasure and embarrassment — along with some degree of shame, knowing that his praise was undeserved.

"One of the most intelligent people . . . " That is the greatest compliment any man — except my father — ever gave me.

"I thank you sir, but I am afraid you give me too much credit. To be honest, it would be difficult for me to do as you suggest since Mr. Wickham was kind enough to trust me with his version of the story while your opinion is still unknown to me."

"Miss Bennet, it is not a matter of trust but of respect. I do not know what Mr. Wickham has told you — though I might easily guess — but my dealings with him were very unpleasant. Normally, I would never burden you or any other respectable young lady with such a narrative unless it was absolutely necessary. Nevertheless, I shall be more than happy to answer any questions you may have, giving you the proof you require."

By now, Elizabeth was stunned. The sincerity in Darcy's face was not to be doubted, and the confidence he showed could be generated only by the truth. But how could that be? Mr. Wickham was such a pleasant man; he also seemed sincere. It was impossible to fathom he could be a liar.

Then what could have happened? Perhaps there was some altercation between them — one of a serious and passionate nature — that caused Mr. Darcy to disregard his father's wishes. Being unshakable and proud men, both certainly believed they were in the right.

From Mr. Darcy's features, she was now convinced he was telling the truth, but she was not ready to consider — and even less to admit to herself — that Mr. Wickham had told her lies; she had believed him so readily.

"Thank you for your offer to answer my questions. I shall remember it."

"And, Miss Bennet, please do not try to sketch my character at the present moment, as there is reason to fear the performance would reflect no credit on either of us."

"But if I do not take your likeness now, I may never have another opportunity."

"I would by no means suspend any pleasure of yours," he replied smiling. "I hope we shall be in each other's company on future occasions and you will be able to make a better evaluation of my character in ... a few weeks perhaps?" She was happy for the opportunity to change the subject.

"So you are to be in the neighbourhood for some time?"

"I really do not know for certain. Mr. Bingley is the master of the house, and I am totally at his disposal. I am attempting to help him with estate business."

"Mr. Bingley must be very grateful to have a friend not only experienced but also willing to help him."

"Mr. Bingley is a remarkably good man but perhaps not as confident in his own abilities. Nevertheless, he deserves all the good friends he can get."

She was pleased to hear him speak kindly of Bingley, and she was amazed at how the tone of the conversation between them changed in only a few minutes to a light and pleasant one.

While speaking, he looked at her with an openness she never would have thought he possessed before that day. She liked that very much but could not lose the opportunity to tease him.

"Indeed, sir, it is difficult for him to be confident when he is constantly reminded of the perfection of your house and your extraordinary library. How can he grow more confident when he must stand against the expectation of a man without fault?"

A moment after she finished, she was afraid she had gone too far and that he was offended; she diverted her eyes from him. "Miss Bennet ... "

She raised her eyes and met his gaze, which was as reproachful as the tone of his voice, but he did not seem displeased or angry. Actually, a tentative smile was lifting the corners of his mouth.

"I have never said such things about my home, my library or myself. I have never compared Mr. Bingley to anyone and certainly never to me."

"I know you did not, sir. In any case, you did not have to. The praise around you is continuous, and everyone can hear it; it must all be true, as it comes from someone who is such an intimate acquaintance of yours."

She knew it was improper for her to speak in such a manner. Mr. Darcy was a friend of the Bingley family, and he was probably displeased by remarks concerning Miss Bingley, but the impulse to tease him and Miss Bingley at the same time was too strong. "'A man without a fault,' 'a man you cannot laugh at.' Were not those Miss Bingley's words?"

His reaction stunned her. There was Darcy, staring at her and trying vainly to hide the smile that was threatening to overspread his face. He was biting his lower lip and attempting to divert his eyes from her. His whole face seemed brighter and younger than ever.

"Miss Bingley is very generous in her praise of my home; nevertheless, she is not an intimate acquaintance of mine or of my home and most assuredly not of my library."

"Of that sir, I can easily believe."

"But I must confess, I pride myself on both my home and my library. They are the work of many generations, and I consider them indeed wonderful."

"So am I to understand, sir, that you are a great reader yourself?"

"No, Miss Bennet, if I remember correctly, you are the great reader, although you find pleasure in many other things."

Elizabeth began to laugh heartily, and Darcy soon followed her in a more reserved manner. Suddenly, the room became warm and comfortable.

THEY BEGAN TO TALK OF books they recently read, of those they liked or disliked most, amazing each other by the revelation of their tastes and opinions — though not always alike — in literature, poetry, history and theatre.

She was full of admiration for his great understanding and knowledge, and he was amazed at how passionate she was in expressing her opinions. He was restrained and calm, searching for arguments to sustain his ideas; she was impetuous and lively, filling the room with joy. He spoke with wisdom and prudence about what he thought regarding a certain subject. She answered him with wit and teasing, expressing her own opinion.

Their feelings were different but similar at the same time. They were like fire and ice, melting together to find the perfect mix. They were enjoying each other's company, amazed that they could spend a pleasant time together without an argument but rather filled with challenging debates. Delightfully, they were discovering one another.

Never before had Elizabeth had the opportunity for such a conversation with any gentleman except her father. She had met many charming young men, both in Hertfordshire and in London while visiting her relatives. She had spent many hours in pleasing conversions with some of them, perhaps flirting a little and being courted occasionally.

But this was so different. Darcy was neither flirting with her nor courting her; he was actually talking to her! He was treating her as his equal, respecting her opinions even when they differed from his, asking for her point of view, and challenging her to defy him.

And all the time he was smiling and wrapping her in tender looks, raising in her sensations that frightened her by their novelty and overwhelming strength. Cold chills were travelling over her arms, down her spine to her legs, up to her neck and back again. Her body was shivering though she felt such warmth, as if she were not merely near the fire, but in it.

More burning even than the fire were his closeness, his intense looks, and the things she saw in his eyes. Not even Elizabeth could misunderstand the nature of his gaze this time, and that, combined with the situation in which they found themselves, gave her a strange feeling. It was the first time in her life that a man had seen her in such an intimate state. She was without her dress, though she was fully wrapped in the blankets. Her hair was down and she was without her shoes. She always believed that only her husband would ever see her so — and maybe not even him. The unknown and ambiguous sensations in her made Elizabeth more flustered and emotional; and, because she worked hard to conceal it, she became more voluble and talkative, to Darcy's great delight and enjoyment.

His feelings were not different from hers but were stronger and more difficult to control; he was neither afraid of them nor surprised by them. He knew well the kind of sensations she aroused in him, and it was not difficult to recognise her own reactions to him. He was more bewitched than ever and could not take his eyes off her, even though he realised he made her uncomfortable and caused her to blush constantly. He only hoped it was not a completely unpleasant discomfort for her.

He began talking to her again, listening to her carefully, admiring her wit, her liveliness, her passion in expressing her beliefs, the sparkle in her eyes, and her smile. This time they were all directed at him.

How could I ever believe she was welcoming my attentions before and flirting with me? That is just her way. But still… she is acting differently than she did before. Is it possible I have improved, in some way, her opinion of me? Could I be so fortunate?

Her beauty was greater than ever, precisely because she was so natural. Her hair was almost dry, and her heavy curls spread around her beautiful face and fell onto her back and shoulders.

He felt almost overwhelmed by the desire to thrust his fingers through that wonderful, silky hair and caress her.

He had been with women in more intimate situations, but he had never felt anything similar. He had never been in love before, and the feelings for the young woman in front of him were so powerful that he was afraid they would burst forth from his chest.

Darcy unconsciously found himself praying for the rain to last a few more hours so he could remain a little longer in her company. He was afraid that, if they left the cottage now, she would remember his previous treatment of her, how much she disliked him, and what Wickham told her of him.

He heard her asking his opinion about some book, which was her father's favourite, and he could not pull himself together enough to give her a coherent answer. Therefore, he pretended not to remember details about it, and she began to explain the particulars. This led to Elizabeth's opening a new topic of conversation that she considered safe: her father's care in guiding her into the world of books. He watched her with admiration and approval as she spoke affectionately of her father.

"So do I understand you spend many hours in the library with your father? Do any of your other sisters share your passion for books?"

"Mary reads a great deal and equally gives a great importance to improving herself in music. And my sweet Jane likes to read, but none of them shares my taste in books. It was just something between me and my father."

"That must be wonderful."

"It is, but I also like to spend as much time as I can outdoors, walking through the fields. I am afraid Papa spends too much time in his library, and it is not good for his health. I try to take him out whenever I can."

"I, too, like to spend time outdoors when at Pemberley. It is a fortunate thing that my sister, Georgiana, shares the same pleasure. We spend as much time as possible taking long rides or walks together when we are at home."

As he spoke of his sister, his eyes became even warmer, and the tone of his voice grew softer although a little sad.

"You seem to be quite close to your sister, Mr. Darcy."

"Yes, I am. How could I not be? We are the only two left in our family."

"It must have been difficult for both of you to lose your parents." *What a stupid thing to say. Of course it was difficult.*

Before answering, Darcy looked at her soundly. He had not talked to anyone about his parents for so long that he almost forgot how painful their deaths had been for him. Still, he felt a strange impulse to do so at that moment as Elizabeth seemed sincerely willing to listen to him.

"It was difficult, especially for Georgiana. My mother died many years ago when Georgiana was only an infant, and my excellent father died five years ago. Since then, we have had only each other. Of course, we have close relatives who are attentive to us and give us all their support, nevertheless..."

"And you are taking care of Miss Darcy alone? That is indeed an extraordinary thing."

"No indeed, Miss Bennet, I do not deserve such praise. I am her guardian together with my cousin, Colonel Fitzwilliam, and I have the best masters at my disposal to give Georgiana a proper education."

His tone remained soulful and melancholic. Elizabeth missed the lively conversation they were enjoying a few minutes earlier and could not help sharing his sadness. She was pleased by his talking about his sister but would have preferred to do so in a more easy and friendly manner.

Thus, hoping to cheer his mood, she began to tease him gently. "Two guardians for Miss Darcy? Hmm… Is your charge giving you so much trouble already? Young ladies of her age are sometimes a little difficult to manage, and if she has but half your spirit, she may like to have her own way — not to mention the fact that she is such an accomplished young lady and must have many admirers around her."

The moment she finished, she knew she had made an unforgivable mistake. His face instantly became stern, livid and pained; his eyebrows knit together, and his eyes opened widely in disbelief while searching her own eyes, trying to discern the meaning behind her words.

He stood and answered coldly, full of repressed rage and disappointment at what he thought to be the revealing of her opinion about his sister. "Miss Bennet, my sister is still almost a child. I know that your opinion of me is very low, and I can accept your reproaches as being correct, but my sister does not deserve to be spoken of in such terms. I shall not allow that from anyone — not even from you."

He turned his back to her, glaring at the savage rain outside the window, unable to breathe because of the knot in his throat. He would have killed Wickham if he could. To spread false stories about him was one thing, but to expose Georgiana in such a way? To whom had he also been speaking?

Too hurt and angry to think clearly, he paced the room like a caged animal, intent on calming himself while deciding upon his next course of action.

Chapter 3

Darcy's unexpected and violent reaction was a complete shock to Elizabeth — and a frightening one. His rage was so evident that, for a moment, she was afraid he would physically harm her.

She followed his movements, not daring to meet his eyes. What could make him react in such a way? She forced herself to remember her exact words and determine what might have affected him so completely.

His pacing did not cease. The blanket was falling from his shoulders, but he did not seem to notice. He appeared oblivious to anything except his thoughts — and his anger. The pleasant gentleman with whom she had recently been so delighted had disappeared.

He was so attentive, so considerate toward me, and I somehow offended him deeply. But what did I say? I must apologise, but for what?

Elizabeth's opinion of Darcy had drastically altered in the last few hours. She had appreciated his efforts to make amends for his previous behaviour and to demonstrate an easiness that was not characteristic of him — or of the Mr. Darcy she had thought she knew until that morning. Moreover, she was grateful for the kindness and protectiveness he had shown in his dealings with her. He tried diligently to make their horrific situation as bearable and easy as possible under the circumstances.

Nevertheless, she could not truly know him well in such a short time. He had tried to infuse more civility into his manners, but he was still a complete stranger to her. Her remorse for the offence she had apparently given was still mixed with fear. She was trapped alone with him and could not be sure what to expect. Allowing her eyes to rest on him, she was unable to understand everything she read in his face, but one thing was clear and impossible to ignore: Grief and intense pain had changed his entire countenance.

She knew she should do something; she needed to do something. She could not bear the thought of him thinking ill of her.

Even a few days ago when his manners were proud and unpleasant, and her opinion of him low, she would have done something to amend the pain she had involuntarily inflicted on him and — more importantly — on his young sister. It was her mistake, and she had to find a way to fix it though it meant she must face his anger.

"Mr. Darcy," she said softly. He was still not responding; in fact, he seemed not to hear her. Elizabeth got up from the armchair and drew near him. He stopped and looked at her — a stern, icy look she recognised from the early days of their acquaintance.

"Sir, please allow me to apologise for everything I have just said. I beg you to believe that it was only an unthinking jest meant to release the tension of our conversation. Your openness caused me momentarily to forget propriety. I cannot express enough my regret for the offence I unwittingly gave to you and your sister. You must believe me, sir, that offending you was not my intention. How could I intentionally insult someone I do not even know?"

Elizabeth felt a lump form in her throat and tears sting her eyes. She was unaccustomed to begging, but she desperately wanted him to believe her. She searched his face and locked her eyes with his, attempting to plead her case. Perhaps he was unable to believe her words, but he must see the sincerity in her eyes.

She was very close to him, and the blanket that covered her had slipped, exposing her neck and shoulders. Her feet were bare on the cold floor, and the repentance that saddened her face made her helpless and vulnerable. Darcy felt torn between a desire to wrap his arms around her, and an impulse to flee and never see her again. How could she have believed Wickham?

Clearly, her intention was not to offend. As she said, their open and easy manners had made her forget the proper rules of behaviour. The comments about Georgiana in all probability had slipped innocently from her lips. But the thought of her chatting with Wickham about him and his sister, or laughing with him… The impropriety of her behaviour could not be forgotten so easily — or forgiven. What a disappointment! Above everything, a tremendous sense of guilt overcame Darcy as he remembered Georgiana's sweet face — hurt, disappointed, and tearful.

He looked down at Elizabeth, her face lifted to his, waiting for him to say something. She was trembling, perhaps from the cold, perhaps from other causes, clearly affected by their disagreement. Seeing her like that was too much for him to bear. The remorse in her eyes seemed so sincere that he could not refuse her. He hated himself for it — for the weakness he felt for her and for everything this country girl had been doing to him, his character and his personality in the last month — but at that moment he could not allow her to suffer any longer.

"Miss Bennet, I must apologise for my ungentlemanly reaction. I know I must have appeared a savage to you. Please forgive me. I have no other excuse than my protective nature and my affection for my sister."

"I am the one who owes you an apology, and please believe me — "

"Come; let us go back near the fire. You are cold."

He put one arm around her shoulders and guided her to her chair.

He helped her resume her seat and wrapped the blanket more securely around her shoulders, trying not to notice that as he did so, their fingers touched briefly. After assuring her comfort, he took his place in his own chair, steadily holding her gaze. They finally spoke in unison.

"Mr. Darcy... I — "

"Miss Bennet, I — I am sorry, please continue"

"No, please, sir, I have nothing important to say."

"Miss Bennet, I shall ask your forgiveness if my words cause you pain, but I beg you to be very careful in Mr. Wickham's presence and not to give credit to everything he might do or say."

Elizabeth's astonishment increased at this change of topic, and she was not sure she took his meaning correctly.

"Mr. Wickham? What do you mean, sir?" she exclaimed. Then recovering a little, she continued, "I thank you for your advice. I am sure it was kindly meant. But I cannot quite understand, sir, how Mr. Wickham could be involved in our present conversation?"

"Miss Bennet, I know that he was your source of information regarding both myself and my sister. Truth to tell, I never would have thought him capable of spreading such words about Georgiana. God knows what he might have said and to how many other people."

His last words were voiced almost in a whisper, and Elizabeth could hardly hear them, but she immediately realised that his response had been caused by a misunderstanding. Because of her thoughtless, frivolous remark, he had assumed Wickham had told her something that could harm his sister!

She felt relieved. Now that she understood the reason for his strange reaction, she knew what to do. Of course, that only gave rise to many other unanswered questions and thoughts about Wickham, Miss Darcy, and Darcy himself. What could Wickham possibly have to say about such a young lady?

However, it was not the proper time to let herself be overwhelmed by those questions. She needed all her self-confidence and determination to say what needed to be said.

She leaned toward him, coming even closer, and looked daringly into his eyes as she began. "Sir, earlier you accorded me praise that was largely undeserved. May I speak to you frankly?"

"Of course, Miss Bennet. I should not want it any other way."

"Thank you... As I already confessed to you, Mr. Wickham did tell me of your past dealings with him and of what he considered your unfair treatment of him — and I must confess I believed him."

She paused for a moment, seeing the deep furrow that suddenly appeared between his brows. He started to play with his signet ring as she continued her confession.

"I never, not once, did what you implied I should have done. I did not ask for proofs or witnesses. I never bothered to consider rationally what he told me. I was not in the slightest as intelligent or wise as your compliments would indicate." She averted her gaze and blushed crimson. "Mr. Wickham's countenance, voice and manner established him at once in the possession of many virtues, and I gave him full credit for them."

His countenance became even more severe as his jealousy of Wickham increased. He stared at her in disbelief, almost shocked by her words. *Why is she telling me all of this? Does she enjoy torturing me? How can she be so cruel and so... unladylike as to tell me directly that she likes that scoundrel?*

"I do not know whether Mr. Wickham told me the truth or not. I do not know whether I was wrong to trust him and form a favourable opinion of him. I have no tangible reason to doubt his words or his intentions."

Darcy was beyond the limits of his patience. He could not keep his eyes on her, nor could he tear them away. He simply could not tolerate any more and was about to rise from his chair when her voice and tentative touch on his arm stopped him.

"What I do know is that now, after all the unexpected things I have discovered, I shall reconsider everything I have been told in the last few days, and I hope to reach a better understanding of Mr. Wickham's character — and yours."

She smiled, but his face remained severe, waiting for her next words.

"But Mr. Wickham said not a word about Miss Darcy until the moment I asked him about her. We did talk about your sister, but the fault was mine more than his, and I am full of remorse for having indulged myself in that sort of conversation. I beg you to believe me that the only unfavourable thing Mr. Wickham mentioned regarding Miss Darcy was the fact that she is very much like yourself in the matter of pride."

She held his gaze steadily, though she was deeply mortified by the admittance of her own faulty behaviour. She wanted him to see the truth in her eyes. In shouldering the blame for having initiated the conversation about Miss Darcy, she hoped to convey to Darcy that Wickham was not likely to approach the subject with anyone else without encouragement. She wished to assuage any fears that malicious gossip would be spread through the neighbourhood: besides, she did not believe Wickham able to do such a thing.

Finally, Darcy understood the meaning of what she had told him. Her confessions of gullibility and her favourable opinion of Wickham had been meant to prove her complete honesty and assure him that his sister's reputation would not be sullied. She had selflessly put herself in an awkward and embarrassing situation to ease his discomfort.

He could not help feeling deeply impressed by the sincerity and care she showed for his wounded feelings and by her remarkable courage.

He breathed deeply and closed his eyes for a moment. When he opened them, her eyes were before him, sparkling and smiling as if to say, *"Now do you believe me?"*

He felt mortified by his own behaviour, harsh words and unkind thoughts about her. He had hastily judged her once more and could think of nothing that would undo the damage to her already poor opinion of him.

"Thank you for letting me know that, Miss Bennet," was all he managed to say. "And I know there is nothing I could do to win your forgiveness for having offended you again with my poor manners and callous behaviour. Nevertheless, I dare to ask you for the opportunity to apologise — "

"Mr. Darcy!" Her tone was lively and cheerful, and he quieted. Elizabeth was not formed for ill humour. Their unpleasant misunderstanding, once clarified, could not have dwelt long in her spirits. She soon found her lively disposition and was determined to make him do the same.

"As a matter of fact, sir, there is something you could do that will secure my complete forgiveness."

He looked at her quickly, only to see her right brow raised in an arch manner. She was teasing him, and he could see it but did not dare to presume she was no longer upset. Still, he tried to answer in an equally light manner, hoping for reconciliation.

"Please tell me, Miss. Bennet, and I shall do so at once."

"You could put some more wood on the fire because it is a little cold."

She paused and waited, smiling until he did exactly that. *Seeing him obey me with such alacrity is not at all unpleasant,* she thought, smiling to herself.

"Is it better now?"

"Yes, sir. Thank you."

"Can I give you my blanket, Miss Bennet? My clothes are almost dry, and I am rather comfortable."

"No, thank you, sir. But there is another thing I should like you to do, if you would be so kind."

"Anything."

"Could we just… resume our conversation from where we were before my silly and very poor jest interrupted it?" She became more serious, choosing her words carefully and blushing as she spoke.

His countenance changed, and a smile overspread his face. "Gladly, Miss Bennet." He took his place in the chair, close to the fire and close to her.

"Let us try to remember where we were. Of what were we speaking?"

"I believe we were speaking of Miss Darcy. I should be very happy if you would tell me a little more about her."

When she finally managed to lift her eyes, she saw him looking at her seriously — neither stern nor upset but rather delighted by her request. She indeed wanted to know about Georgiana, and he could not miss her intentions or her interest. "I would be most happy to do so, Miss Bennet."

He began to speak, his voice soft, the smile never leaving his face. "My sister has a specific gift for the piano, but she is not as accomplished as you may have heard, regardless of certain people's praise; however, she is still young and, hopefully, someday will be a remarkable lady as you said. But she is not at all proud, Miss Bennet, only quite shy. And she is sweet and kind, I might add — very much like my mother."

"Those are indeed wonderful qualities, Mr. Darcy, and if I may say so, they are much more important and rare than a thorough knowledge of music, singing, drawing, dancing and modern languages."

"I completely agree with you, Miss Bennet."

"Still," continued Elizabeth, "I hope she is improving her mind by extensive reading in order to be truly accomplished."

He pursed his lips, trying to check a laugh.

"I am glad to be able to say that she is. I have always taken great delight in seeing a lady not merely reading but also finding pleasure in doing so, rather than, let us say, playing cards perhaps?"

No, this cannot be; he is flirting with me! thought Elizabeth in disbelief.

"So, Mr. Darcy, am I to understand that the ability to play cards is not included in your idea of an accomplished woman?"

He was about to answer her in the same teasing manner when he suddenly rose from his chair and went to the window. Deep in conversation, neither of them had realised that their surroundings were silent, and all they could hear, besides the sound of their own voices, was the fire.

"Miss Bennet, the rain has stopped. I think we must leave at once before the weather worsens again. I shall let you prepare yourself. Please let me know if you need my help in any way."

"I… I shall, sir." With a quick bow, he left the room and closed the door behind him.

Elizabeth was taken by surprise at his words, and a strange sense of sadness and regret overcame her. She had anticipated an unbearable morning in the company of this disagreeable man; instead, it had turned out to be some of the most charming, challenging, and enlightening hours she had ever spent. Now she understood, regretfully, that this was assuredly an event never to be repeated. She already felt the loss of his company. Mechanically, she began to dress herself.

In the next room, Darcy was desperately trying not to entertain the image of Elizabeth unwrapping the blanket from herself, her undergarments still wet and clinging to her body, and then putting her dress on and trying to set it to rights. *You are completely losing your mind, man,* he censured himself.

Presently he heard a knock on the door and hurried to open it, only to see Elizabeth standing there properly dressed, including her bonnet. The only things missing were her gloves, still wet and muddy — not that their other clothes were completely dry. In fact, everything, including their coats, was still wet and uncomfortable to wear, and hers even more so; he was well aware of that. Darcy went to douse the fire and then opened the front door, inviting her:

"Shall we?"

THE COLD AIR STRUCK THEM forcefully, seeming to freeze their clothes to their bodies and causing Elizabeth instinctively to ease closer to Darcy for protection. She was extremely cold already. He was pleased by her gesture and was tempted to wrap her in his arms to warm them both, but he controlled himself, offering her his right arm instead.

"Miss Bennet, it is indeed terribly cold. We must walk as quickly as we can or else I am afraid you will become ill. Take my arm; the ground is muddy and slippery. We must be careful not to fall."

Her left hand clutched at his right arm, and they began to walk at a quick pace. Darcy was careful not to hurry her too much, as she almost lost her balance on a few occasions. Finally, she tightened her grip on his arm and, searching for as good a support as possible, put her other hand on his arm as well. However, the sensation of his wet coat was unpleasant and only succeeded in making her colder. She tried to cover her discomfort by clasping her hands together in order to warm them a little.

They were neither talking nor looking at each other, but Darcy noticed her gesture.

"Miss Bennet, I am so very sorry you have to bear my wet and dirty coat; if I could do something for your comfort..."

He suddenly took both her hands in his and covered them, offering warmth and protection. Her hands were now in his open left hand, cradled in his palm.

Elizabeth was startled at his gesture and was held breathless for several moments. For the first time in her life, she felt the touch of an unrelated man's bare hand, and she never would have imagined the feeling could be so overwhelming. His touch was not at all tentative; he was holding her hands with determination, stroking them gently to warm them. Protectively and tenderly, he was taking care of her.

"Is it better now?" he asked innocently, as if he had not the slightest idea how improper his gesture was. He seemed only worried about her well-being.

"Yes it is, thank you," she murmured shyly.

She knew she should have removed her hands from his, but she could not, nor did she want to. Her attention was divided between the road and the warmth of his hands as he settled her left hand in his palm and caressed the back of her right hand with his thumb.

Actually, Darcy knew very well the effect his gesture was having as his feelings were much the same as hers.

From her reaction and the deep blush suffusing her face, he guessed it was the first time she had been touched in such a manner. This thought delighted him. He was flattered by her responsiveness to his light touch but not content; he wanted more than that. He had not yet decided exactly what he wanted from her regarding their future, but he knew he wanted more.

At last, Longbourn came into view, and Elizabeth was relieved by the thought that she would soon be securely home and that her family would no longer worry; yet, once again, a feeling of regret pervaded her consciousness. She knew they would never have the opportunity to repeat that day's events, and she felt the loss in a strange way. Unconsciously, she returned the grip of his hand as though wanting to be assured of his continued presence.

Darcy was dealing with the same feeling of loss as Elizabeth. He experienced the bliss of having her near and holding hands in such an intimate manner and was desolate at the thought of losing that closeness. He began to grasp the truth he had been seeking for so long. He felt her tighten her grip and looked down at her, scrutinising her face.

Suddenly, he knew what he wanted from her.

His duty, his sister, his responsibilities — none of them would be disgraced by having a woman like Elizabeth as his wife. Her situation in life and lack of connections — all those things that had weighed so heavily on his mind a few days ago — were forgotten. They were nothing compared to the happiness he felt in her company and the joy that filled his soul. If only she could improve her opinion of him and accept his attentions — his courtship… *Courtship? Am I already courting her?* he asked himself, amused and worried about the rapidity with which everything was happening and about his complete turn of mind. He had never been an impulsive man, and his own reaction frightened him.

"My family must be terribly worried by now. They must be thinking that something horrible has happened to me," said she in a hushed voice.

Yes, her family… they are still a vivid memory.

He tried to cover this unpleasant thought, while replying teasingly, "Well, something horrible did happen to you. You were forced to spend many hours in my company. What could be worse?"

For the first time since leaving the cottage, Elizabeth lifted her eyes to meet his gaze and held it, smiling. *Well, if you hope I shall contradict you, you will have to wait a little longer, Mr. Darcy. I still remember your words at our first meeting.*

He did not give her time to form a proper answer before he took her by surprise with another question. "May I be so bold as to ask you a personal question? If you find it improper, I shall not insist upon your answering it."

"By all means, Mr. Darcy, please ask your question. I find it hard to believe that you could ask an improper one."

"Would you truly have let me fall in the stream this morning had you known I was the rider?"

She gazed at him in disbelief, but seeing his light countenance and a hidden smile at the corner of his mouth, she gave him the answer he was looking for. "Mr. Darcy, I actually thank you for your question as it gives me the opportunity to answer your previous questions as well. I would not let you — or any other person — fall into a stream. However, when we met this morning, I must confess that there were few people of my acquaintance whom I preferred less than you. And I did then consider our encounter a horrible thing to have happened."

Darcy felt her painful words like a knife twisting in his heart, but the pain faded instantly as he remembered her hands in his and met her laughing eyes, fixed on his face.

"I see... and that being the case, Miss Bennet, may I hope that, perhaps, your opinion on the matter has altered in the last few hours?"

"Indeed it has, Mr. Darcy," was her very short answer, giving him a degree of joy he had not felt in quite some time.

Longbourn was very close, and they continued to walk at a quick pace as the rain had resumed. Darcy did not release her hands but loosened his grip so she could choose the moment to remove them; she did so, slowly and reluctantly, and only when they were close to her home. Even then, she kept her left hand on his arm.

AT LONGBOURN, THE AGITATION WAS beyond all limits. Since early that morning, the discovery of Elizabeth's absence and the dreadful rain that followed had induced Mrs. Bennet to act more irrationally than usual. Mr. Bennet tried to calm her, explaining that no one knew the woods better than his Lizzy. He reminded his wife that their daughter might well have gone to Netherfield to rest until the rain stopped or taken shelter in the cottage nearby.

However, such assurances could by no means tranquillize Mrs. Bennet as her worry was not for Lizzy's safety; she knew her husband's arguments were rational. She was more concerned about the possibility that Mr. Collins would see how wild the girl was and turn his attentions elsewhere.

Indeed, during the first hours of Elizabeth's absence, Mr. Collins held forth with numerous moral extracts, sermons and, more importantly, quotes from Lady Catherine, all regarding the importance of a young lady's proper behaviour, especially one intended to be a parson's wife.

As Elizabeth had predicted, the person most worried, though apparently calm, was Jane. Her heart was overcome with grief, and tears were about to spring from her beautiful, blue eyes. Mr. Bennet noticed and invited her into his library. He asked her to sit and gave her a glass of wine, embracing and trying to comfort her. However, his gestures of concern were so unusual that they merely confirmed to Jane the gravity of her sister's situation. Father and daughter remained together as Jane began to cry in earnest, knowing there was nothing they could do until the rain stopped or lessened in intensity.

John was dispatched to Netherfield to make inquiries, and Mr. Bennet prepared to leave with him to begin the search. Just as they exited Longbourn, Lizzy, together with Mr. Darcy, appeared before them.

Mr. Bennet's relief was beyond anything he had experienced in a long while. He walked towards them, relieved to see his favourite daughter back home, safe and sound. However, a question arose instantly in his mind: What was Lizzy doing in the company of Mr. Darcy?

Mr. Bennet had met Mr. Darcy only once at Lucas Lodge. However, he had heard at least a dozen times the story of his slighting Lizzy at the Meryton assembly.

Another oft-related story of the gentleman's rude behaviour concerned Mrs. Long, who had stood near him for almost half an hour without his addressing her. Mrs. Bennet seemed to find great pleasure in reminding them constantly of these particular events.

Truth be told, Mr. Bennet was not deceived that his Lizzy was the most beautiful girl in the world, and her teasing manner might prevent some gentlemen from thinking her unfailingly amiable. Therefore, the information that Darcy had thought her *'merely tolerable'* was not enough for Mr. Bennet to form a sound opinion of the man. He was certain of two things: Darcy was extremely rude to voice his thoughts of Elizabeth aloud, and he clearly had unaccountably bad taste for not liking Mr. Bennet's favourite child.

However, Darcy's refusal to address Mrs. Long directly was something Mr. Bennet could easily understand.

Another thing of which Mr. Bennet was certain was Lizzy's dislike of Mr. Darcy. So what was she doing in his company?

To secure an answer before everyone else surrounded the newcomers, he walked directly to them. However, before he could reach them, Jane ran past him, and shortly the girls were in each other's arms, Jane crying from happiness and Lizzy trying to comfort her.

"Lizzy, are you well? I was so worried. I thought that… Oh, thank you, Lord!"

Elizabeth felt tears in her own eyes as well, moved by her sister's tenderness, but tried to laugh. "Dearest Jane, please do not cry. I was in no danger; I simply took a walk, and I was caught in the rain. It is not the first time and probably will not be the last."

The shrill voices of Mrs. Bennet, Lydia, and Kitty, who now came running, turned all attention toward them.

"Oh Lizzy, you ungrateful child! You delight in vexing me! How can one expect my poor nerves to resist such a shock?!"

"My dear," Mr. Bennet's calm voice cut her off. "Let us be grateful that nothing bad has happened. And let us go into the house as quickly as possible before we are all soaked."

He did that, taking his wife's arm and inviting everyone to follow him.

"Oh, Mr. Bennet, just look at her wild appearance; she is like a savage. What will Mr. Collins say? And in front of Mr. Darcy! No wonder he did not want to dance with her! I wonder if any man will ever want to dance with her again, not to mention make an offer to her . . . "

It cannot be said who was more mortified at her words, Elizabeth and Darcy — who were exchanging embarrassed glances, their cheeks deeply flushed — or sensitive Jane. However, it *is* certain that Mr. Bennet was extremely diverted by his wife's words and the reactions they produced.

In those few minutes, he made some interesting observations. Both Lizzy and Darcy looked uncomfortable but in no way irritated or displeased with each other's presence. Furthermore, from time to time they exchanged stolen glances. They were wet but not wet enough to have stood in the rain for long; the gentleman was obviously dressed for riding, but his horse was absent. He could hardly wait to learn everything, but this was not the proper moment, and he kept any questions to himself.

Suddenly, Mrs. Bennet — of all people — realised the import of the situation and turned to them, making her husband do the same.

"And Lizzy, what are you doing in the company of Mr. Darcy? Mr. Darcy, where did you find her? Sir, it would be very ungentlemanlike of you to tell anyone about what appears to be an unfortunate incident. I assure you Lizzy is not always so wild and — "

Darcy bowed deeply and spoke solemnly to her. "Mrs. Bennet, please rest assured of my secrecy; indeed, it was a fortune circumstance that I met Miss Bennet since my horse had just escaped, and I was completely lost in the woods in the midst of the storm."

Hastily, Elizabeth interrupted him. "Indeed ma'am, I managed to find shelter from the rain in the cottage for a while, and on my way home I was fortunate enough to meet Mr. Darcy, who was so kind as to accompany me so that I could return quickly and safely."

She gave Darcy a pleading, embarrassed glance while Darcy responded with a wondering glance of his own. Not for a moment had it crossed his mind not to tell the truth regarding their meeting. All saw their exchanged looks, but only Mr. Bennet and Jane gave them any weight.

The gentleman addressed his wife calmly. "As you see, my dear, they both seem to be very fortunate in meeting each other, and they managed to come home safely. That is good enough for me; let us not delay in this weather."

"Well, I suppose we must thank you, Mr. Darcy," said Mrs. Bennet coldly.

Saving her second daughter was not enough for her to excuse him completely for his previously rude behaviour; nevertheless, his promise not to reveal to anyone what had happened was certainly a point in his favour.

"Let us all go inside. The two of you must change out of those dirty clothes. We have not yet breakfasted and will surely starve to death if we do not eat something immediately," added Mr. Bennet.

Darcy felt he had endured enough of the Bennet family for one day, and the sight of a strange-looking gentleman in the doorway, expressing his happiness at the arrival of his fair cousin Elizabeth, was too much for him.

"Mr. Bennet, I do not want to impose on you and your family. If you would be so kind as to lend me one of your horses, I shall leave for Netherfield without delay. My friends must be concerned about my absence."

They had reached the main door, and everyone else entered.

"Mr. Darcy, the rain has started again, and you are in no condition to travel, not even for a distance of three miles. You are wet through and almost frozen, and the main road is very bad indeed. I shall send John — properly dressed for the weather — to Netherfield to inform everyone you are safe. Perhaps you would like to write a note yourself?"

"Thank you, Mr. Bennet. I am grateful for your concern but — "

"Mr. Darcy… " Elizabeth's voice from the doorway made them both turn to her. "I beg you to accept my father's suggestion, sir. You saw for yourself how dangerous it could be outside in this weather. After all the help you offered me, I could not forgive myself if something happened to you."

Their eyes met and held briefly, forgetting they were not alone.

"Lizzy! Where are you now, child? Come here at once! You will become ill, and your nose will be red at the ball!" Elizabeth turned to attend her mother, giving Darcy a last glance before disappearing through the door.

"Well, Mr. Darcy? Shall we go in? Or would you prefer to have Mrs. Bennet begging you as well? That is, of course, if you do not find it insupportable to spend more time with us. If that be the case, I should be more than happy to lend you a horse to return to Netherfield."

Mr. Bennet's tone was very polite, but the subtle irony was not unnoticed by Darcy. He tried to keep his countenance while answering, "Thank you, sir, for your hospitality."

"Well, good then. Let us enter."

Chapter 4

Mrs. Bennet was turning the house upside down, giving orders and asking for a supplementary course on the table in order to satisfy as pretentious a man as Mr. Darcy. The gentleman tried valiantly — though in vain — to assure her that the meal was undoubtedly admirable as it was until Mr. Bennet nodded to him not to insist on the subject and showed him to a guest room.

After leaving Darcy in John's care, Mr. Bennet retreated to the serenity of his library. The day had been exhausting for him, and considering the things he would need to find out from both Lizzy and Darcy, the next day was not likely to be any more restful.

Mr. Bennet's most vivid recollection was the look his daughter and Darcy had exchanged when she related their meeting. Darcy's surprise was obvious while she had looked at him as though pleading for his help. Even more, the fact that he had decided to remain and join them after Lizzy requested it, though he seemed not at all inclined to prolong his visit at Longbourn, roused his curiosity further. It was clearly a concession against his will, and he had done it for her. Apparently, the last few hours had brought about a significant alteration in their relationship. A gentle knock on the door took him from his thoughts, and he called for John to enter.

"Yes, John, come in."

"Sir, Mr. Darcy has been taken care of. He wrote a note for Mr. Bingley and is currently enjoying a glass of wine. Is there anything else I should do before departing for Netherfield?"

"No, John. Just be careful, and do not hurry yourself in this bad weather."

"Thank you for your concern, sir. I shall leave immediately."

When John left, Mr. Bennet rose from his chair, took a bottle of his finest brandy, and went to Darcy's room. He knocked and waited until he heard Darcy's grave voice in answer. Entering, he found his guest clad in a robe, standing near the window with a glass in his hand and looking preoccupied.

"Mr. Darcy, do you mind if I disturb you? I thought you would like something stronger to drink."

"Of course, Mr. Bennet. Thank you again for your consideration."

The older gentleman poured a glass of brandy for each of them and handed one to Darcy.

"I would have invited you to my library, but as you might have noticed, we have another guest in the house, and I wanted to be sure we would have the opportunity to speak without interruption about an important matter."

Darcy looked at him expectantly, suspecting he knew what the 'important matter' was.

"Mr. Bennet, I am at your disposal. Again, I should like to thank you and to apologise for the trouble I have caused."

"Well, Mr. Darcy, no thanks or gratitude are required. But speaking of gratitude, I understand that you were a great help to my Lizzy, so it is I who should thank you."

Darcy took a deep breath and looked at Mr. Bennet determinedly. His countenance grew sterner, and he began to pace the room, finally stopping in front of Mr. Bennet, who was watching him with great interest.

"Mr. Bennet, I can no longer continue speaking of this subject, however important it might be, without revealing to you a significant fact."

"Mr. Darcy, you sound quite ominous. What could be the matter? Did something happen?"

Darcy began to pace again as he spoke.

"If something improper did indeed occur, it is not for me to say. Perhaps you could make such an assertion after my confession, sir. I simply wanted to say that I have the highest opinion of Miss Elizabeth and would never do anything disrespectful toward her or against her wishes. Nevertheless, I cannot ignore the fact that you are the head of this family and deserve to be informed about everything that passed this morning between your daughter and me. I know only too well how important it can be to know the truth in order to be able to protect your family."

He paused again, making Mr. Bennet — who was unprepared for such a beginning — most impatient and equally curious.

"Please do not delay your confession, sir. I am all curiosity."

"Mr. Bennet, the circumstances of my meeting with Miss Bennet today were different than you were given to understand. I can only guess that, in misrepresenting the situation, Miss Bennet was trying to save your family from any unpleasant moments."

Mr. Bennet stared at him for some time, pleased and relieved by what he had just heard. Apparently, the gentleman was about to offer answers before he asked the questions. The fact that Darcy had decided to disclose such information and put himself in an awkward position was proof of his honesty and deference towards the master of the house. It spoke well of his character, and Mr. Bennet added it to his developing opinion of the gentleman.

"So, Mr. Darcy, am I to understand that you intend to relate to me the true circumstances of your meeting?"

"Of course, sir. As I said previously, I met Miss Bennet while I was trying to find my way out of the wood. The rain was dreadful, and my horse ran away after unseating me. Fortunately, Miss Bennet was kindhearted and allowed me to accompany her to the cottage for shelter."

Darcy cast a worried glance at Mr. Bennet, and then continued with alacrity.

"I give you my word, Mr. Bennet, that my decision to join Miss Bennet was made not only for my own safety but for her protection as well. I could not allow her to remain alone in that fearful storm so far from home and unchaperoned. I now understand that, in doing so, I did not take into consideration all the elements and consequences of my actions, and I put Miss Bennet in a most improper position. I should have found another, more acceptable way to ensure her safety and mine."

"Mr. Darcy..."

Darcy paused, and turned inquiringly to his companion.

"I think you have taken far too much responsibility upon yourself. I do not believe there was any possible alternate solution for you and my daughter."

"Yes there was, sir. I should have left her safely alone in the cottage and come directly here to inform you."

The elder gentleman could not hide a smile and shook his head.

"Indeed, that would have been a partial solution but not easy to accomplish and perhaps a little foolish. You would have put your own safety and health in danger."

"I know, sir," answered Darcy simply and without hesitation.

They gazed searchingly at each other for some moments. Mr. Bennet was disconcerted facing a man who had just admitted he would be ready to risk his own well-being in order to offer the best protection for his daughter. Finally, he took his glass and smiled openly at his guest.

"I am glad you did not do that; it would have been an unnecessary risk. Now pray tell me, how did you find the cottage? Did you approve of it?"

Darcy stared at him, not comprehending the question. "The cottage? Umm...quite pleasing and useful, sir."

"I am glad to hear that. Could you start the fire?"

"Yes I could. Everything necessary was at hand."

"May I inquire how exactly you put my daughter in an improper situation as you said? Did anything in particular occur between the two of you?"

The quick changes in topic were disturbing. Darcy had the feeling that Elizabeth's father was trying to take him by surprise in order to catch him in a wrong answer. Darcy was not accustomed — and even less pleased — at such treatment. But what could he do? He was at Mr. Bennet's disposal.

"Nothing particularly, sir, except that Miss Bennet was alone with me for many hours, and her reputation — "

"Mr. Darcy, you told me previously that you understand my position as the head of this family and the importance of my knowing the truth. I hope I am right in believing you to be a trustworthy man. So I am going to ask you a direct question: Did anything happen between you and my daughter that compromised her virtue or her reputation?"

"No, sir."

"Thank you, Mr. Darcy. Now let us enjoy this brandy, shall we?"

They breathed deeply, both relieved by the understanding they had reached. Darcy was surprised that Mr. Bennet trusted him. He knew he would not have been so easily satisfied with simple answers if something similar had happened to his sister.

After enjoying another glass of brandy, Mr. Bennet continued.

"Mr. Darcy, I am not comfortable about being forced to tell you this, but I imagine you are already aware of its possibility. If the circumstances of your meeting were to become public knowledge, my daughter's reputation would be damaged and certain measures would be required."

"I perfectly understand that, sir, and I constrain myself by a bond of honour to do what is rightly needed."

"Well, let us hope it will not come to that. I should not want you to be forced to make such a sacrifice after your honest confession."

"Mr. Bennet I am sure any man, in marrying your daughter, would find it not a sacrifice but an honour."

"Is that so? I must confess I am quite surprised to hear that from you, Mr. Darcy. From my previous information, I was more inclined to believe the opposite. Well, well... And do you happen to know my daughter's opinion on this subject by any chance?"

"I do, sir," answered Darcy with apparent bitterness. "In the course of our conversation, I learned that my manners and behaviour had fairly induced Miss Bennet to have a poor opinion of me."

"Indeed?" Mr. Bennet looked at him sympathetically. "Well, if that was previously the case, after today I am sure my daughter has found many reasons to improve her opinion. I know I have!"

"Thank you, Mr. Bennet."

"Well, I shall go now and tell a servant to bring you some clothes; I shall meet you in the dining room later."

John had not travelled halfway to Netherfield before he met Mr. Bingley, the Bennets' servant, and several other men, all of whom had formed a search party. Bingley's sanguine disposition was much affected by his friend's disappearance, especially after Darcy's horse reached the stable alone.

Finding that Miss Elizabeth was missing as well only increased his anguish, first because he was fond of Elizabeth, and second because he knew how affected his 'angel' would be. Not for a moment could he have conceived of the idea that Darcy and Elizabeth would be found at the same time.

When John told him the particulars of their meeting, he was gratified that everything had turned out well. He sent his men back with a message for his sister — Miss Bingley had been hysterical all morning — and continued on his way to Longbourn with dry clothes for Darcy.

The reunion at Longbourn was a happy one, Mr. Bingley's presence giving pleasure to Jane and even more to Mrs. Bennet, who immediately extended an invitation for breakfast.

In less than half an hour, Darcy had briefly described the whole situation to Bingley, and then, dressed properly in dry clothes, entered the dining room where the Bennet family was already seated.

Normally, Mr. Bennet had Lizzy on his right and Jane on his left. However, considering the situation, he had saved those places for the two gentlemen. Since Bingley was the first to appear, he, without a second thought, took the place next to Jane. Darcy — pleased by the arrangements — found himself happily situated between Mr. Bennet on his left and Elizabeth on his right. Mr. Collins, with great determination, occupied the free chair next to his fair cousin Elizabeth.

Mr. Bennet's interest resided mostly in Darcy, since he knew everything he need know about his eldest daughter's admirer. Unfortunately, as they began the meal, the conversation was monopolised by Mr. Collins. While Mr. Bennet and Lizzy previously had been diverted by his stupidity, his long, ridiculous lectures were now annoying. Bingley's light remark about the bad weather, the rain and the poor state of the roads gave Mr. Collins the ideal occasion to perform.

"I must say, my dear Mr. Bennet, that perhaps the roads could have been better maintained by certain personages in order to avoid this unfortunate situation. This never would have happened at Rosings Park. My noble patroness, Lady Catherine de Bourgh, always speaks about the importance of having a perfect road under any circumstances. The roads at Rosings are never in bad condition, no matter how inclement the weather."

"That is a ridiculous thing for you to say, Mr. Collins! The roads at Rosings are as bad as any others in such weather."

Everyone stared in disbelief at Darcy's harsh words, but he paid no attention. He knew he had been rude, but he had never claimed to have much patience, and the insipid parson was insufferable.

Mr. Collins turned red with indignity, not because he himself had been censured but because of Darcy's flat contradiction of a compliment to Rosings Park. Even

Elizabeth cast a reproachful glance at Darcy, but he continued unperturbed.

"I have visited Rosings every spring for the past ten years, and more than once the carriage has been mired down because of the impassability of the roads." Every pair of eyes around the table was now turned to him in wonder, so he felt obliged to continue, addressing Mr. Bennet especially.

"Oh, I neglected to mention that Lady Catherine is my aunt."

The effect of his words was extraordinary, so great was the general surprise. They had heard for many days of Lady Catherine and the grandeur of Rosings. That Darcy was so closely related to her made his importance, and consequently his worthiness, all the greater in the eyes of Mrs. Bennet.

Not surprisingly, the greatest reaction stemmed from Mr. Collins, who could not breathe for a few moments, his face turning from red to white and back again. A mix of absolute happiness and deepest humility caused him desperately to search for air along with the proper words.

Mr. Bennet took another sip of wine, his amusement increasing. *That was a very big mistake, young man, and you will pay dearly for it!*

Darcy felt the consequences immediately as Mr. Collins suddenly rose to his feet and made an enormous bow, so close to him that Darcy could feel his breath.

"Mr. Darcy, I cannot express in words how exceedingly gratified I am by this extraordinary discovery! To have the happiness of meeting a nephew of Lady Catherine de Bourgh! I am most thankful that my discovery was made in time for me to pay my respects to you, and I trust you will excuse me for not having done so before. My total ignorance of the connection must plead my apology — "

"Mr. Collins, I am pleased to meet you as well, but please sit down, sir, or I shall be forced to stand myself."

"Oh, do not disturb yourself," said he in haste, afraid of displeasing Darcy. Mr. Collins resumed his place at Elizabeth's right but could not stop speaking to the newest object of his adoration. He leaned toward Darcy, causing Elizabeth to move out of the way, his breath obviously disturbing her.

"Mr. Darcy, I am in the most fortunate position of being able to assure you that her Ladyship was in the best of health — eight days ago," he said, a huge smile covering his face.

"Thank you, Mr. Collins. I am happy to hear that."

From that moment, all attempts at conversation between Darcy and Mr. Bennet were in vain as Mr. Collins had only one purpose: to express his approbation for everything Darcy said.

Soon, Darcy was once again at the edge of his tolerance. He had been delighted to be situated between Elizabeth and her father. Though a brief acquaintance, he found Mr. Bennet to be an unexpectedly pleasant conversationalist with a wit and subtle irony similar to Elizabeth's. He was more than willing to establish a closer relationship with Mr. Bennet, but the presence of Collins was ruining everything.

What bothered and disturbed Darcy most was that, every time Collins addressed him, he was leaning in front of Elizabeth, touching her arm shamelessly and forcing her to pull back to avoid his undesirable closeness.

He was sure the man did it on purpose. Moreover, Darcy could swear that Collins was losing no opportunity to stare at Elizabeth's décolletage.

Elizabeth's face coloured highly, her embarrassment increasing with each passing moment. She discreetly tried to move closer to Darcy and further from her cousin to avoid his breath and improper touch on her arm, but the problem remained. Her discomfort affected Darcy more than his own annoyance, and he could tolerate it no longer.

"Mr. Collins, I shall be very happy to continue this conversation with you. However, I am afraid that in doing so, we shall disturb the others. Miss Elizabeth, would you oblige me and change places so I might be closer to Mr. Collins? I have many questions to ask him about my aunt." Then he turned toward Mr. and Mrs. Bennet, apologising.

As improper as such a gesture might be, no one dared to say anything. On the contrary, Mr. Bennet's opinion of Darcy improved still further — as well as his amusement — as he witnessed the exchange. Darcy's putting himself willingly at Mr. Collins's disposal in order to protect Elizabeth from embarrassment was a sacrifice indeed.

Half good-humoured and half-preoccupied, Mr. Bennet wondered about the possibility that such an important man might have serious designs on Elizabeth. Was he wise enough to look beyond her lack of fortune and connections — beyond her situation, so far beneath his?

Moreover, was Elizabeth aware of any of this? He decided that a long, serious talk with her was essential.

Elizabeth, too, was startled by Darcy's request and only nodded her approval at changing places. She was utterly surprised and delighted that Darcy had noticed her discomfort and tried to alleviate it, but she was also mortified to be the subject of such improper behaviour from Mr. Collins.

Her cousin was displeased at the new arrangement, but it had happened too quickly for him to protest. In any case, what could he say? Contradicting Mr. Darcy was not an alternative. He convinced himself that it was proof of Mr. Darcy's appreciation for him, so he continued to display his admiration for the nephew of his patroness until the gentleman made his farewells.

Elizabeth had no opportunity to talk privately with Mr. Darcy, and she considered it for the best. His closeness made her senses respond acutely, and her expression was continually flustered. She was concerned that her family would notice something she was yet afraid to accept, so she kept her gaze mostly on her plate. Nevertheless, her eyes were constantly attracted by the movement of his hands on the table, while the recollection of those hands holding and caressing hers sent shivers up and down her arms.

She could scarcely think of anything else, but she was able to see in amazement that the change in Darcy's manners lasted a few more hours indeed. She could not help but ask herself what made him behave in such a way. He was more agreeable and willing to please than she had ever seen him before. He was polite to her mother and even to Mr. Collins. As for her father, Mr. Darcy seemed to enjoy discussing various subjects with him from books to estate management.

His manners were nothing but amiable. Occasionally, when the comments or the shrill tone of the conversation became too intrusive, Darcy cast a glare at the other end of the table where Mrs. Bennet and the youngest misses sat. From time to time, he seemed to look with great interest in the direction of Jane and Mr. Bingley. Elizabeth did not know whether he was displeased by his friend's open display of affection, but he was clearly preoccupied.

Overall, the late breakfast was a pleasant affair. Taking advantage of a momentary break in the rain, Mr. Darcy nudged Bingley, suggesting it was time to take their leave and expressing his gratitude toward Mr. and Mrs. Bennet for their hospitality. He felt slightly disappointed at not having the chance for another private conversation with Elizabeth, but she did hold his gaze for a moment, even managing to smile at him until her cheeks turned crimson and she averted her eyes. Before departing, the gentlemen promised to call the next day.

As soon as they left, Elizabeth excused herself, claiming exhaustion.

"Lizzy, after you rest I should like to talk to you privately in the library. Will you oblige me?"

"Of course, Papa. Would you rather speak to me now?"

"No, indeed; it is nothing so urgent. Take your rest. I shall see you later."

Bingley and Darcy's way back to Netherfield was relatively quiet. From time to time, Bingley expressed his pleasure at seeing both the elder Miss Bennets so well and of his anticipation for the ball.

Darcy was enjoying the memory of Elizabeth's beautiful face and the recollection of her proximity. He decided that later, after taking a long, hot bath, he would have a glass of wine and further consider the day's events.

They reached Netherfield quickly only to meet an agitated, even hysterical, Caroline Bingley. She had been worried earlier, but the revelation that Darcy and her brother had tarried so long with that dreadful family only magnified her jealousy of Eliza Bennet.

Darcy thanked her for her care and sincerely apologised for worrying her. He even tried to explain the reason for their delay at Longbourn, but Miss Bingley's vicious comments, directed at the Bennets generally and Eliza in particular, were too much for Darcy. His patience had been tried sufficiently for one day by Mr. Collins.

"In any case, Miss Bingley, it was fortunate that I did not come here directly. My appearance was barbaric; my cloak was six inches in mud — not to mention my hair, which was in significant disarray. I should not have wished to frighten you."

She quieted immediately, looking at him wide-eyed. He took the opportunity to excuse himself, went directly to his room, ordered a bath, and relaxed. Miss Bingley, on the other hand, was so enraged that she could not speak for many minutes.

WITH A KNOCK ON THE door, Bingley entered Darcy's room.

"Darcy, may I keep you company for a few minutes? I am sorry for Caroline. She can be quite trying at times."

"No, Bingley, I am sorry for losing my temper, and I shall apologise to Miss Bingley; it is just… It was a very difficult day."

"Yes. It was very fortunate that you and Miss Bennet met, was it not?"

"Yes — very fortunate indeed," Darcy hid a smile behind his wine glass.

"I must say, I can hardly wait for the ball. I hope that the time will pass quite pleasantly in the company of Miss Bennet. I have already asked her for the first two dances."

Darcy only looked at him without answering, so Bingley continued. "Do you still disapprove of Miss Bennet, Darcy? I could not help noticing your displeased looks during our stay at Longbourn."

"I do not disapprove of Miss Bennet at all, Bingley. She is indeed very beautiful and seems to display a pleasant disposition and proper behaviour."

"Then what is it, Darcy? I should like to hear your opinion."

"Bingley, I did watch you at Longbourn, mostly because your preference toward Miss Bennet was… clearly expressed."

"I see. And, in your opinion, how should I have expressed my preference?" Bingley's voice became a little irritated.

"I think you should act according to your intentions regarding Miss. Bennet. I am sure you understand that this kind of attention will raise the expectations of Miss Bennet and her family."

Bingley looked thoughtful for a while. Then turning to Darcy, he asked, "What if my behaviour *is* in accord with my intentions? What if it is my desire to raise those expectations? What would you think in such a case?"

Darcy took a deep breath before answering. Only that morning, he would have strongly advised Bingley against such a union, not only for the Bennets' lack of connections and fortune, but also for their improper behaviour — not to mention his conviction that Jane was indifferent to Bingley and would accept him only for financial reasons. But now, what answer could he give?

"Bingley, my opinion is not important. But if you want my advice as your friend, I shall tell you this: Before making any decision, be sure of the seriousness of your feelings and of Miss Bennet's affection."

"I know my feelings to be very serious, Darcy."

Darcy started to pace the room, searching for the right words.

"Bingley, we have been friends for many years, and please do not be upset with me for saying this: I have seen you in love many times! Miss Bennet is very beautiful; it would be easy for any man to become infatuated with her."

"I am not merely infatuated; I am deeply in love with her. But perhaps you are talking about yourself! Perhaps you also have intentions toward her!"

"Do not be ridiculous, Bingley. I have no intentions towards Miss Bennet. At least not towards the eldest one…" he whispered.

Bingley was taken aback by this assertion.

"Darcy, what did you just say?"

"I did not say anything of importance, Bingley."

"Yes you did! You said you had no intentions towards Jane. It is Miss Elizabeth, is it not?"

"Bingley, I do not wish to have this conversation. You asked my opinion, and I gave it to you; now if you will excuse me — "

"No, Darcy, I shall not be dismissed. Now I understand everything; your behaviour toward Miss Elizabeth is in accordance with your intentions. You are restrained toward her because you do not want to raise expectations you are unable to fulfil."

"Bingley, I do not want to continue on this subject for the moment. Nevertheless, when I have something to share with you, I shall. Trust me."

Bingley gave up and returned to the subject of his angel. "So, Darcy, about my problem… You said earlier that you have nothing to reproach in Miss Jane Bennet — well, except for the fact that she smiles too much, of course. Do you have any reason to believe she has no affection for me?"

"I do not know Miss Bennet well enough to form an opinion. However, I must say that I did not see any special display of affection, although she receives your attentions with pleasure. Her countenance is always so serene that I do not think it is easy to reach her heart. But that might just be her character; you should trust yourself to be a better judge in that regard."

"But surely, Darcy, you cannot believe her to be a fortune hunter."

"No, not a fortune hunter… However, you must admit that Mrs. Bennet can be very persuasive if she chooses. That is precisely why I suggested you not be hasty; be sure before taking a decisive step."

Then, trying to lighten the mood, he added, "And Bingley, about Miss Bennet smiling too much… It is odd that I ever said that, having you around! No one smiles more than you."

"Yes, you are right, Darcy. So you see — we are a perfect match. But Darcy, by your reasoning, you and Miss Elizabeth are totally unsuited for each other; she likes to laugh, and you are serious all the time."

Darcy stopped a moment and then turned toward Bingley with a mischievous glint in his eyes. This only fuelled Bingley's curiosity further.

"Maybe so, but you see, Bingley, I laugh enough when I have good reason, and Miss Elizabeth knows to be serious when necessary."

A few minutes later, Darcy's valet announced that his bath was ready. Once alone, he slipped into the tub and let the warm water envelop him, his eyes closed, wondering what Elizabeth was doing. Unlike other times when thinking of her had been a painful struggle, his thoughts now brought a new, pleasant state of contentment. For the first time, his own feelings, desires and needs were not the subject of his reverie.

Instead, he tried to remember — word-for-word and minute-by-minute — the time they had spent together, searching his memories for some hint of her feelings for him. The question he asked himself most often was whether she was thinking of him — at least a little.

AT LONGBOURN, ELIZABETH COULD DO little except think of Darcy — the time they spent together, his voice, his face lightened by his smile, all the things he said and did, his hands holding hers and lingering on her shoulders…

She felt so much and feared the feelings that had overwhelmed her in such a short time. Even more, she was afraid of her reactions when he was near her and the loss she felt when he left. Was it possible to long for a man she had disliked so profoundly until that day? And all the sensations aroused in her the last few hours… Could she feel that way toward a man? Could she feel that way toward Mr. Darcy of all men?

Her distress was deepened when she considered other aspects of the situation, especially the two things that had bothered her most.

First, Darcy's intentions toward her were a source of painful wonder. Elizabeth could not — and dared not — believe that a man of his importance could have any serious designs on her or want to be connected with her family. She tried not to allow herself to dream of impossible outcomes.

The second was Mr. Wickham's story. Was it true? Had Darcy done such a horrendous injustice to his old friend and the favourite of his late father?

Now, at a distance from Darcy's distracting presence, she understood there could be no justification for such cruel behaviour, and the confirmation of this story would throw a deep shadow over Darcy's whole character.

She decided to share her uncertainties and fears with Jane immediately. Her sister's kindness and gentle wisdom often helped to clear her thoughts and find the correct answers to difficult questions.

Then she would have to talk to her father, who, no doubt, would demand some honest answers himself.

Chapter 5

After a warm bath, Elizabeth nestled in the comfort of her bed, suddenly tired and dizzy. Though she covered herself in blankets, she could not stop herself from trembling and laughing at the same time. Her mother was right after all: she would have a red nose at the ball.

Hill entered with her special tea, and after a cup of it, sleep finally overcame Elizabeth, closely watched over by a worried Jane.

A couple of hours later, she opened her eyes — or tried to — hardly noticing Jane and Mr. Jones standing near her bed. She heard them talking but could not understand their words. Her head was aching, and even opening her eyes required far too great an exertion. She felt warm — very warm — and waves of cold perspiration soaked her gown, causing her to shiver. *How can this be? How can I be so warm and yet shiver so violently?*

She could not find an answer to her silent queries, but vague recollections played in her sleepy mind — recollections of *that* day when she frequently had felt the extremes of burning heat and freezing chills. His eyes, his hair — wet and curled — his lips pursed together in a smile or in anger, and his hands lingering on her shoulders as they wrapped her in a blanket. His hands were so strong yet gentle; never had she thought those long fingers could caress her cold hands so tenderly. She knew the feeling of his thumb on the back of her hand, and her palm resting within the gentle grasp of his — skin against skin. How could a man's hand trouble her so? Every man's hand was the same, was it not? Yet, his hand alone made her shiver and burn.

Then there was the expression on his face, lightened or darkened by so many feelings. Feelings? What kind of feelings did he possess? His dark, staring gaze — it was not disdain with which he looked at her; she knew that now, but she did not know what else he felt for her.

She had been so cold, and he was correct in insisting that she remove her wet clothing. She felt only a little better afterwards. Her skin was wet, cold, and scratched by the dusty blanket. How would his hands feel on her skin? Would he caress it as tenderly as he had caressed her hands? She was cold and could not find the warmth she longed for. His hands would warm her, no doubt. If he burned her through the blanket in only a few moments of resting his fingers on her shoulders, how could she abide his hands on her bare skin? They would burn her; she knew that. They already did. Her whole body was on fire. Suddenly, with these thoughts raging through her fevered mind, she was no longer cold.

THAT WHOLE AFTERNOON JANE DID not move from her sister's bedside.

Mr. Jones said he could not be certain whether it was simply a cold or something more grave. They would have to wait until the next day for him to confirm his diagnosis. He gave his patient some draughts and insisted she be supervised. He warned that her fever could become dangerous.

Jane's desperation reached its peak as she watched her beloved sister remain barely conscious — mumbling, trembling and sweating profusely. Many times she and Hill changed Elizabeth's clothes as they became drenched in the fever's grip, and to Jane's utter surprise as she leaned her ear near to her sister's lips, she could hear Elizabeth whispering Darcy's name.

Before dinner, Elizabeth finally awoke. She seemed to feel somewhat better, even managing to smile, and asked for water. She was given soup — with great insistence that she eat it — and another cup of Hills's tea together with the draught Mr. Jones had prescribed. She fell asleep again, and this time her sleep was restful. Jane remained close to her as did Hill. Mary joined them quite early in the morning and insisted that both her sister and Mrs. Hill retire for at least a couple of hours before breakfast.

The long rest, the draughts, and Hill's tea proved effective as the patient awoke completely recovered in the morning.

Elizabeth was almost fully dressed when Jane entered, gasping with pleasure at the image of her sister looking so healthy.

"Good morning, dearest Lizzy. Are you alone? Mary promised to stay with you when I left a couple of hours ago! How are you?"

"I am very well, Jane. I sent poor Mary to her room. She looked exhausted while I slept very well and feel quite rested."

"Thank the Lord. I was so worried! You had been feverish since yesterday afternoon and were largely unconscious. I was so afraid… "

Jane embraced her sister warmly, grateful to see that her worst fears were unfounded. She kissed Lizzy's cheeks, smiling with relief.

"You should remain in bed; you need rest. You cannot feel well so soon, especially after such an awful time yesterday and so many trying hours."

Elizabeth returned her smile, blushing. "Well, Jane, to be honest it was not such an awful day — I mean yesterday."

"No, of course not, you are right. You were very lucky meeting Mr. Darcy when you did."

"Yes, I was very lucky, Jane; if you only knew — "

"Knew what, Lizzy? Is there something you want to tell me? You know, dearest, last night you mentioned Mr. Darcy's name a few times."

"I did? Oh dear! Did anyone hear me?"

"No, only I heard; do not worry. But Lizzy, I shall ask you again: Is there something you want to tell me? You seemed to be on friendlier terms with Mr. Darcy yesterday. I hope he did not hurt you in any way."

"Oh no, dearest. And yes, there is something I should like to tell you! To be honest, I shall die if I do not tell you. But please promise not to be upset."

"Lizzy, how can you even say that? Please tell me. I am so curious."

"Well, Jane, Mr. Darcy and I did not meet on my way home; you see..."

Elizabeth recounted for Jane the entire episode, focusing on every detail and every word Darcy had said to her. Poor Jane listened in astonishment and concern. Being taken by surprise, she could not hold back a gasp when she heard about her sister being alone with a man in such an improper situation. She suffered for both of them when told about their misunderstanding. She was mortified, thinking only of what discomfort her sister must have experienced.

"Oh, Lizzy! I am so grateful to Mr. Darcy for all his care. But I can very well understand why you did not reveal the truth earlier."

"Yes, Jane, only think of what Mama would do! Poor Mr. Darcy would have been tied up and dragged to the church in no time — some reward for his chivalry," said Elizabeth, laughing a little nervously.

"I am afraid he would have been. Dear Mama can be so determined and a little trying at times. Lizzy, you seem to be more inclined to think well of Mr. Darcy after everything that happened."

"Yes I am. I must confess that I saw a part of Mr. Darcy's character that I could never have guessed before. He was so caring, so very kind and amiable. Oh Jane, you would not believe what I found out! Mr. Darcy told me directly that he admires me greatly. Can that be true, do you think?"

"Dearest Lizzy, do be serious! No, it cannot be! Or can it? I do not mean to imply that Mr. Darcy could not admire you, but I know he was not partial towards you, and I know how much you dislike him. Are you trying to laugh at me by deceiving me, Lizzy?"

"I am not deceiving you, Jane. He told me that much himself. You can well imagine my surprise on hearing him. And I was amazed at his gallantry and his changed behaviour. Did you notice it?"

"Mr. Darcy was indeed very pleasant and polite yesterday except, perhaps, for that comment directed towards poor Mr. Collins."

"Yes, Jane, poor Mr. Collins! If I still had a remnant of disapproval toward Mr. Darcy, it was all gone the moment he changed places with me at breakfast. Now I am sure he must love me madly, for what man in his sane mind would have put himself willingly next to Mr. Collins?" Lizzy started to laugh heartily, and Jane could only join her.

"Lizzy, what of Mr. Wickham's story? Do you still believe Mr. Darcy capable of such injustice, or have you discovered more about that subject?"

"I confess I did reconsider the whole story, Jane, though Mr. Darcy did not really say anything about the matter. He did offer to answer any question I might have. Dearest Jane, do you remember when you tried to defend the conduct of each of these men and presumed a mistake or misunderstanding between them occurred? Well, yesterday morning I recalled your words. What puzzled me exceedingly was Mr. Darcy's reaction when I mentioned Miss Darcy. He seemed to believe that Mr. Wickham would spread malicious words about him and his sister. I must confess, it gave me great discomfort. I never would have thought Mr. Wickham capable of that."

"Well, Lizzy, I think we should remember that we have known Mr. Wickham only a short time. While he is a very pleasant man and his preference for you is plain, it would be wise to enjoy his company but not trust him implicitly. After all, we do not know anything of his former life."

"Yes, my sweet Jane, you are wise as usual."

"Oh, Lizzy, you are teasing me again. I know you have more quickness of observation than do I, but sometimes you are so passionate in your judgments. Now I may confess that I have been a little concerned about your previous decision to favour Mr. Wickham so completely after only two days' acquaintance." She blushed saying that, afraid to offend her sister.

Elizabeth began to laugh and was just about to answer her sister when Lydia boisterously entered the room. "Lizzy, come down at once; Denny, Sanderson, and Wickham are here to call on you. Apparently, they found out about your mad escapade and want to be sure you are all right. Oh, you are so lucky! You will be the centre of their attention at the ball."

"I sincerely hope you are wrong, Lydia. I have no such aspirations. I should be pleased to have no more attention than usual."

"Lizzy, are you well enough to meet them?" asked Jane. "It is a little too early for a proper visit. If you do not feel fully recovered, I shall make excuses for you, and I am sure they will understand."

"Of course, I am well! In fact, I am quite anxious to see Mr. Wickham and talk to him. I made a promise, and I intend to keep it."

"What promise, Lizzy? To whom?"

"To Mr. Darcy and to myself. Come, Jane, let us go downstairs."

By the time the eldest Miss Bennets entered the salon, the gentlemen had been invited by Mrs. Bennet to stay for breakfast. They readily expressed their delight in seeing Miss Elizabeth looking so well.

Mr. Wickham was as charming as ever, and his preference for Elizabeth was displayed clearly enough to make her slightly uneasy and raise Mr. Bennet's sudden curiosity.

The visitors inquired about Elizabeth's little adventure, and while she tried to explain the circumstances, Lydia, who had been as noisy as possible in order to attract the gentlemen's attention, interrupted.

"Yes, and on her way home she met Mr. Darcy! Mr. Darcy, of all people. What a joke! You could only guess what he may think of her. But I must say he looked quite a mess himself, all wet and muddy."

"Really?" inquired Mr. Wickham. "That is indeed odd. It is unlike him to be out in such weather. It must have been horrible for him to spoil his fashionable clothes and endure contact with the muddy world."

All three officers laughed, accompanied by Mrs. Bennet and her youngest daughters. Pleased by the attention, Mr. Wickham continued. "Or perhaps he is a friend of the family and was coming precisely to call at Longbourn?"

"Oh no," cried Lydia. "He is not a friend at all. In fact, we all hate him. He is such a rude and disagreeable man."

To everyone's utter surprise, Jane commented first. "I do not know what reasons brought Mr. Darcy on the same path as Lizzy, but I am most grateful to him for taking such excellent care of my sister and helping her to arrive home safely. I am sure all our family is equally indebted to him, and I should be very happy indeed to call him a family friend."

"Yes, Jane is right," accepted Mrs. Bennet. "We should be grateful to him for his assistance, though he is indeed very much as Lydia said. We can hardly tolerate him."

"My dear Mrs. Bennet," her husband interjected, "could you allow me the free use of my judgment on this subject? I did spend some time with Mr. Darcy yesterday, and I dare say I tolerated him well enough. In fact, we had quite a pleasant conversation on a variety of subjects, and Mr. Darcy's taste in books is very much to my liking."

Mr. Bennet's unexpected appreciation of Mr. Darcy impelled Mr. Wickham to display his irritation. "Indeed, sir, I find it difficult to believe that you and Mr. Darcy could have similar taste in anything."

Mr. Bennet raised a brow in wonder at such a statement.

"Pray tell me, Mr. Wickham, why you should find it so? Books are my passion, and from what I could learn in our limited time together, Mr. Darcy is a great reader himself. Be kind enough to enlighten me on how you could possibly know my tastes or Mr. Darcy's.

"I beg you will excuse me, Mr. Bennet. I do not know anything about your preferences, but I am sure they are exquisite. However, I know a great deal about Darcy's. I have known him for many years."

"Really? How have you come to know him so intimately?"

"My father was old Mr. Darcy's steward. The late Mr. Darcy was also my godfather and excessively attached to me. He took good care of me and even paid for my schooling. Mr. Darcy and I grew up together as boys."

"Indeed? How interesting." Mr. Bennet's curiosity was growing with every minute of this conversation, and he began to scrutinise Mr. Wickham, listening carefully to everything he said.

"Yes, sir. That is why I cannot say for sure that Mr. Darcy is a great reader. I know that he prides himself on being an educated man and seeks to improve his library constantly, but I dare say not for the pleasure of reading itself but perhaps for the pride of being well-read and informed."

Mr. Bennet was trying to remain amused and avoid becoming annoyed; he continued his inquiry with a slightly sharper tone, but Mr. Wickham did not notice the irony in his words.

"Come now, Mr. Wickham! I know Mr. Darcy is not half so charming or pleasant as you are, but give the fellow a little credit! I have always considered reading to be food for the mind and the soul. To say he reads not for his pleasure but for his pride, is like saying he eats not because of hunger but from his pride in his chef!"

"Well, I can very well imagine Mr. Darcy doing just that!"

"I shall not contradict you, Mr. Wickham. Apparently you do know the gentleman better than do the rest of us, and I am convinced he may claim the same for you."

"Indeed I do, Mr. Bennet. Unfortunately, Mr. Darcy did me a great injustice without my having done anything to deserve it. I have a warm, unguarded temper, and I may sometimes have spoken my opinion of him and to him too freely. But the fact remains that we are two very different sorts of men, and Darcy hates me."

"You poor man!" cried Lydia. "How can that be? What did he do to you."

Elizabeth was shocked that Mr. Wickham would tell her family his story using almost the same words he used with her two days earlier. She could not believe he dared bring up such a subject publicly. She was now struck with the impropriety of such communication to strangers and wondered that it had escaped her notice when he first told her. She wanted to say something but did not trust herself to curb her tongue or her temper.

With his usual smile and confident demeanour, Mr. Wickham continued, "Well, I have already had the pleasure of relating this story to Miss Elizabeth, and she was so good as to give me her attention."

"Indeed? How fortunate, Mr. Wickham," Mr. Bennet intervened before any of his daughters could speak. "If that is the case, we shall ask Lizzy in the event we require further details." With a pointed look, he added, "And allow me to express my surprised satisfaction at the great faith you have in our family — following such a short acquaintance — as to share the private business of your past with us. But let us move to the present; please tell us, how did you find yourself in our town?"

Elizabeth was relieved by the sudden change of topic and asked the gentlemen if they planned to attend the ball. Mr. Wickham, eager and happy to answer, considered the question a sign of Elizabeth's interest in him. She dared a glance in her father's direction, but instead of seeing the well-known ironic smile in his eyes, which usually expressed his delight in making fun of follies and nonsense, she met her father's stern expression.

Such a rare expression on his face could not be misunderstood. Mr. Bennet was intensely displeased.

THE DAY WAS BRIGHT AND sunny, and after discussing the weather, the gentlemen proposed a short walk in the park around the house before they departed, which was gladly accepted by all the ladies.

As always, Mr. Wickham showed his preference by offering his arm to Elizabeth, who coldly accepted it. The discussion inside the house had left a bitter taste and many doubts about Mr. Wickham's appearance of goodness and the integrity of his character. She remembered Jane's words about being too passionate in her judgments and felt inclined to agree with her sister.

She perfectly remembered everything that had passed in conversation between Mr. Wickham and herself that evening at her Aunt Philips's house. He had assured her that respect for old Mr. Darcy would always prevent him from exposing the son, and now, only four days thereafter, he was more than willing to relate the story to her whole family and openly laugh at Mr. Darcy.

This inconsistency between his stated professions and his conduct was too obvious to remain unnoticed. She made an effort to participate in his conversation and even to smile at him — he was still charming and pleasant — but how differently did everything now appear where he was concerned.

As they walked, Elizabeth could not fail to notice that he was attempting to put a distance between them and the rest of the party, and she became irritated at his presumption that she would agree to such a scheme. She pretended to be fatigued and insisted on returning to the house, a suggestion accepted, albeit reluctantly, by her companion. Still, he continued to make lively conversation, and Elizabeth continued to smile pleasantly and give the outward appearance of approving of what he said.

The moment they reached the corner of the house, both startled in utter surprise — for there stood Mr. Darcy, an unmistakable expression of shock darkening his already severe countenance.

Elizabeth was mortified, her heart in her mouth. She could only guess what he might believe on seeing her walking alone with Mr. Wickham in what appeared to be a cordial state. She cast her eyes sideways, smiled shyly and spoke uneasily to him. "Mr. Darcy, what a pleasant surprise."

BEFORE DEPARTING FOR LONGBOURN THAT morning, Darcy had prepared himself with such extraordinary care that it might have embarrassed him had he been aware of it. He changed his coat twice and seemed displeased with his valet's every move. Though surprised, the servant remained unruffled, only stepping aside and allowing his master to finish for himself the last small details of his appearance. He had never done that before.

The ride to Longbourn was silent. Neither Darcy nor Bingley seemed inclined to polite conversation. However, while Bingley was easy and joyful, Darcy's demeanour was less certain. Despite Mr. Bennet's politeness and Elizabeth's changed attitude, he could not be sure of his reception. After discovering Elizabeth's previous opinion of him, he could not put aside the regret for his formerly rude behaviour, nor could he chase away the fear that Elizabeth's opinion of him was beyond repair. The thought troubled him, and unconsciously he pulled on his neckcloth in an attempt to loosen it; the gesture only constricted it more.

His other neckcloth was safe, locked away in a drawer. He had dried it but had hidden it so it would not be laundered or even touched by anyone else. He wanted to keep unaltered Elizabeth's touch, her scent, and the trace of her hands and skin.

He remembered her expressions of surprise, embarrassment, and vulnerability when he handed the fabric to her. Her reluctance to wipe her face with it and her attempt to turn her back to him — as though hiding some improper gesture — had melted his heart. He had needed all his strength at that moment to fight a desire to clean her face himself — first with the soft, wet fabric, then slowly with his fingers, and finally with his lips dropping light kisses over her eyes and cheeks, and then lowering to her slender neck before returning to her lips. Those lips, which could smile in a thousand ways, would surrender, trembling, soft and delicious, under his caress. Irrationally, he felt himself jealous, envying that small piece of linen, the first thing that had ever touched both his bare skin and hers.

However, he also felt contentment, for he did touch, hold and caress her hands. He could feel them — and her whole body — shivering, warming, and responding keenly to his closeness. Even more, he vividly remembered her tightening the grip on his hand when they reached her house. Was it possible that she experienced the same sense of loss when they had to unclasp their entwined hands? After all, she insisted he remain and have breakfast with her family. Was she merely being polite? Did the new light he saw in her eyes when they glanced at each other mean something more?

He was roused from his reverie by Bingley's voice the moment they arrived at Longbourn. They noticed the Bennet ladies walking in the garden in the company of some officers, but while Bingley hurried toward Jane, Darcy remained behind, searching for the lady he wanted to see. Elizabeth was not among them, and he presumed she had remained indoors. He approached the main entrance, anticipating the pleasure of seeing her again.

This happy thought was dashed at the shocking sight of Elizabeth appearing around the corner of the house on Wickham's arm, separated from the others and talking privately, her shy smiles directed toward the officer. The distress he felt threw him into despair. All his hopes were in vain; he had misunderstood her once again. She had been polite to him the previous day, but her preference for Wickham remained unmoved. Though he was rational enough to notice her distress and embarrassment when they faced each other, it was small consolation for his disappointment!

He saw her tentative smile directed at him and heard her words.

"Mr. Darcy! What a pleasant surprise!

Darcy was grateful for a lifetime of education and self-control, which saved him from completely exposing himself to ridicule. He succeeded in keeping his countenance and bowed in her direction, acknowledging Wickham with only a slight nod of his head. Elizabeth continued to speak and offer an explanation in an obvious attempt to ease the situation.

"Mr. Wickham, Mr. Denny, and Mr. Sanderson were kind enough to call on us after finding out about my little adventure yesterday."

She looked into his eyes, but Darcy was too affected to react properly; his face remained stern, his pained countenance betrayed only by his eyes.

Growing more embarrassed and diverting her gaze before returning it to him, she spoke further. "We were taking a stroll in the garden before Mr. Wickham's departure. Would you care to join us?"

"No thank you, Miss Bennet. I came with Mr. Bingley, and we will stay only a few moments. I am very pleased to see you are well."

"I am. Thank you."

The situation was intolerable. Darcy and Wickham did not speak to each other, and neither of them looked at the other.

Elizabeth was still holding Wickham's arm, and Darcy's gaze was repeatedly attracted to that spot. *She was holding my arm only yesterday. Her hand was in mine a few hours ago.*

Darcy's only desire was to pull her away from Wickham. He knew he could not do that. He had no right to command with whom she could and could not walk or talk, or whose arm she could hold. He felt desperately helpless — trapped with no way out. He stood there, knowing that he should depart and attempt to retain some dignity, but he could not leave her with that man. He was overwhelmed by a desire to protect her, though he knew she was in her own garden, surrounded by her family.

The grief that pierced his heart was so powerful that it made him falter.

He was incredulous as he watched her continue to accept and seemingly enjoy

Wickham's company after all he had told her. Unfortunately, Darcy knew too well that women more experienced than Elizabeth had done the same and fallen for Wickham's charms. Still, he had hoped Elizabeth would react differently. Suddenly, Wickham broke the silence.

"Well, Miss Bennet, it is time for me to go, but before that, may I ask a personal favour of you?"

Saying this, he took Elizabeth's hand in his, kissed it, and then spoke in a tone that expected no refusal.

"Miss Bennet, I would be very happy if you would reserve two sets for me at the ball tomorrow! Perhaps the first and the supper set?"

Elizabeth's cheeks became dark red, not from pleasure, as Mr. Wickham seemed inclined to believe, but from the deepest embarrassment. The last few minutes had been the most unpleasant and difficult she could remember. From her position, she could see both Mr. Wickham and Mr. Darcy; while the former was smiling in delight and awaiting her answer, the latter was very much as she had seen him in the cottage when they had argued about Georgiana.

She was mortified by the liberties Mr. Wickham had taken, not just in front of Mr. Darcy but also in full view of the house. She could swear she saw her father watching from the window and was angrier with herself than with Mr. Wickham for letting him believe she would welcome such behaviour.

She recollected herself and slowly began to withdraw her hand from Mr. Wickham's. "Your request honours me, Mr. Wickham; unfortunately, I am in no position to accept it. My cousin, Mr. Collins, has reserved the first set."

"Then the last set will be acceptable," he interrupted her confidently.

Really? Acceptable indeed? Well, you are too hasty, sir, she thought, angry at his presumption.

"Mr. Wickham, I shall be happy to secure you the second set, if *that* is acceptable to you! As for another... well, I know there are many young ladies desirous of having the pleasure of dancing with you. So let us remain with only one set for the present." She smiled so pleasantly that Mr. Wickham could do nothing but accept her offer.

Content with herself, she dared a glance in Mr. Darcy's direction, expecting to see an amused and pleased expression on his face. Instead, she saw only the same grief and sadness, his jaw clenching and his eyes even darker. She did not know what to do next.

Why is he acting like this? He should be pleased with the way I refused Mr. Wickham those dances, keeping them available for... someone else. Perhaps I was mistaken, and he has no interest in this matter after all.

The only thing Darcy understood was that Elizabeth already had most of her dances secured and thus she could not oblige Wickham's requests.

The rage and pain he felt clouded his mind; moreover, as her hand was still held by Wickham, a completely new sense of jealousy arose within him.

He suddenly made an excuse, pretending he wanted to pay his respects to the rest of the Bennet family. When he was about to enter the house, Elizabeth's determined voice stopped him.

"Mr. Darcy!" He turned to her, waiting. "Sir, I wanted to thank you again for the advice you gave me yesterday. Be assured that I did not forget and am trying to follow it."

He looked at her, incredulous at his incapacity to understand her correctly. Slowly, he began to take control of his temper and apprehend her meaning. Relief instantly spread over his face, lightening his countenance; the trace of a smile raised the corner of his mouth.

If he still had any doubts, they vanished when her open smile parted her lips and her right eyebrow rose in a well-known gesture. Though Wickham was still present, Darcy forgot about him.

Feeling like a fool in front of Elizabeth, he admitted with inner happiness and admiration for her brightness, "I should have known you would do no less, Miss Bennet. I must apologise for failing to see that immediately."

Perhaps you are not as perceptive as Miss Bingley thought you to be, after all, Elizabeth teased him silently.

With another bow and a smile lingering over his lips, Darcy entered the house, leaving Elizabeth in the company of Wickham, this time without fear, knowing she could fend for herself.

I am such a ridiculous fool. He smiled to himself at the otherwise unpleasant thought. He allowed himself the pleasure to act foolish in front of her.

As Bingley was accompanying Miss Bennet in the garden, Darcy spent the next half hour in the library in Mr. Bennet's company. The older gentleman was pleased by the opportunity, but little conversation was possible between the two gentlemen, Mr. Collins being present and bestowing continuous praise upon Lady Catherine's nephew.

Shortly, Mr. Bennet brought up the subject of Mr. Wickham. Darcy's reaction was swift and forceful, confirming for Mr. Bennet the tension between the two gentlemen, but he offered only kind words for Mr. Wickham's late father and a brief comment about how he and Mr. Wickham had become strangers in the last several years. As they were not alone, there was no opportunity to speak further on the subject.

The return of the ladies brought them to the drawing room. Refreshments were offered and accepted, and the conversation became easy and animated.

After a few minutes, Darcy mustered the courage to secure a chair close to Elizabeth, and she greeted him with obvious pleasure. They talked about the weather for a while, but their voices soon were overshadowed by those of the younger Miss Bennets and their mother as they voiced their eager anticipation of the upcoming ball.

Wary at having been refused twice before when he had ventured to ask Elizabeth to dance, Darcy whispered, feeling more embarrassed than he could remember in years,

"Miss Elizabeth, speaking of the ball, might I be so bold as to ask for your hand... for a set? I mean... if you still have a set available and if you might feel inclined to dance with me..." He looked and sounded most uncomfortable, almost shy, like a young, insecure lad.

Elizabeth would have laughed had she not been so surprised and thrilled. She felt her heart beating so furiously that she was afraid he could hear it.

"Mr. Darcy, I think I shall be very much inclined to dance, thank you. Would you prefer a particular set?" She tried to sound teasing and smiled at him, but she knew her voice was trembling a little.

"No, indeed. I understand that most of your dances are secured, so I should be happy to be accepted for any of them."

She looked at him, raising her eyebrow in wonder.

"Where did you hear such a thing, sir? Indeed, you are mistaken. I have been asked only for the first set by Mr. Collins and for the second by Mr. Wickham."

"But..." He searched her sparkling eyes in confusion, making an effort to remember what he had heard in the garden and to understand why she denied something she said earlier.

Elizabeth could perceive his struggle, and the feeling of having such power over him delighted her profoundly; she could make him happy or miserable with only a word. She preferred the former, so she added in a playful manner, "If I remember correctly, I told Mr. Wickham earlier — if that is the circumstance to which you are referring, sir — that I was already engaged for the first set and would be happy to secure the second for him. Did you hear me say something different, Mr. Darcy?"

She was shamelessly flirting with him in front of her entire family and knew she would be embarrassed later at her behaviour, but for the moment, she simply could not restrain herself. From his reaction, she could see that at least he was not displeased with her.

Darcy was not at all displeased; in fact, he was more delighted than he had been in a great while. Only an hour earlier, he was miserable at the thought that she still preferred Wickham to him, only to discover that she not only refused that man but also offered him the very thing Wickham had requested.

"No, I did not hear anything different, Miss Bennet. I was just not attentive enough to understand the true meaning of your words. Happily, it is now I who have reached a clearer understanding."

They were speaking only to each other, their gazes steady, ignoring everyone else. Her eyes sparkled and her lips tightened in an attempt to stem her laughter while he needed all his strength to fight the desire to take her into his arms. For a second he considered doing just that in order to compromise her and be forced to marry her, but he censured himself for his thoughts.

I am definitely losing my mind. With a discreet smile on his face, Darcy leaned slightly towards Elizabeth, continuing to seek the desired answer.

"Miss Elizabeth, if you are not otherwise engaged, may I ask for the supper dance?"

"With pleasure, Mr. Darcy." *Finally, you have understood!*

To her utter surprise, however, he continued his inquiry. "And, as I am such an unpleasant fellow and there are no other ladies desirous of dancing with me, may I dare ask for the last set as well?"

Elizabeth stared into his dark eyes a moment, her surprise obvious.

To be invited to dance by Mr. Darcy was a pleasant thought for her and quite amazing, as he made it well known that he disliked such activity. But being invited by him for two sets was unbelievable, and so it would be for everyone in the neighbourhood; the gossips would have ample ammunition for several days! Was he aware of the implications? She could only hope he was.

Not wanting to show her dismay, she answered teasingly, "You may dare ask, Mr. Darcy, and yes, I shall accept, thank you, but only if there are no other ladies desirous of your company and no other gentlemen ask me for the favour of that set."

He lowered his voice, clearly flirting with her.

"This is not at all fair, Miss Bennet. You put my request under a condition impossible to achieve. It is very likely your card will be filled before the ball begins, and that is precisely why I ask the favour a day before the event."

She held his eyes briefly, blushing from his closeness. In order to conceal her emotion, she answered in the same whispering voice while lifting a flushed and smiling face to him. "It is not at all an impossible condition, sir. As we both know, I was slighted by other men on a previous occasion, so it is likely to happen again."

Darcy took the hit as well as he could, knowing he deserved the reminder of his outrageous words against her. He searched her eyes to be sure she was not upset, and she was not; the laughing sparkles were still there, and he breathed in relief.

Putting aside his usual reserve, he allowed himself to take full delight in her company. He even enjoyed being teased and found great amusement in teasing her back, so he responded before fully pondering his reply.

"Your harsh words are well deserved, Miss Elizabeth, and I shall do everything in my power to make amends for my comment on that dreadful evening. Perhaps 10 or 15 years of proper behaviour will be sufficient finally to obtain your forgiveness."

Before Elizabeth could completely grasp the import of his words, they were interrupted by Mr. Bingley who had just declined Mrs. Bennet's invitation to stay for dinner. He explained that he had much unfinished business as he was forced to leave for London the day after the ball.

Mrs. Bennet's disappointment was at least as great as Jane's was, but she expressed it in a far more blaring and inarticulate manner. She became somewhat calmer when Bingley explained that he was hoping to resolve his business in town within a week and that neither his sister nor Darcy would accompany him. He also promised to accept a dinner invitation for the first evening of his return, indicating that it was time for them to take their leave.

A few minutes later, both gentlemen departed for Netherfield, content with their day and leaving behind the two eldest Miss Bennets: one smiling sweetly to Mr. Bingley and the other still trying to recover from the shock of Mr. Darcy's words and the implication of what he had said to her.

After a glance toward his daughter, Mr. Bennet went directly to the library; understanding the message, Elizabeth followed him only a few minutes later.

"Sit down, my child. Would you like a drink? We have much to discuss, and it might take a while."

"Is there something particular you would like to ask me?"

"Yes, there are many particular subjects I want to ask you about. For instance, I understand there is a story you should share with me."

"I do not exactly know what you mean, Papa."

"Really? So there is more than one story you should share with me?" She did not answer.

"Well, let us start with the end. Would you be so kind as to tell me the story involving those two gentlemen I had the pleasure of meeting today? That is, if you trust your father well enough to reveal such a secret."

Elizabeth hesitated a few moments before she finally began to relate what she heard from Mr. Wickham. She was displeased about having to tell her father such a disadvantageous story about Mr. Darcy precisely when she was so uncertain of her own feelings regarding both gentlemen. As she spoke, she watched Mr. Bennet, but his countenance was unreadable; when she finished, he looked at her silently for some time and then finally spoke.

"Well my child... that is quite a story, is it not?"

"Yes, indeed. However, Papa, as Jane said, it is possible that a great misunderstanding provoked the story."

"Aha. Jane said that? But what do you say, Lizzy?"

She looked at him and blushed deeply. "I must confess I did trust Mr. Wickham implicitly. I never questioned the veracity of what he told me — at least, not until very recently."

"I see... My child, are you involved in some sort of relationship with Mr. Wickham?"

"Papa, how can you imply such a thing? Of course not! I met Mr. Wickham only four days ago!"

"Well, you could have misled me in this as well. Considering your private discussion with the gentleman, I should say you were intimately involved."

She looked at him gravely and lowered her eyes.

"Mr. Darcy asked me the same question. He, too, implied that I must have had a close acquaintance with Mr. Wickham, or he would not have trusted me with such a private matter."

"He did, did he? So you discussed the subject with Mr. Darcy? You truly amaze me, my child. And pray tell me, what did Darcy have to say?"

"Not very much, in fact. To be honest, I reproached him for his mistreatment of Mr. Wickham, and he said the story was too unpleasant to inflict it upon me. He offered to answer any questions I might have on the subject."

"And did you have any questions?"

"No, sir."

"Well, I might have some. But we were talking of Mr. Wickham, not Mr. Darcy. Now please help me to elucidate that problem, for I am afraid I do not have the pleasure of understanding you. You said you met Mr. Wickham four days ago. Would you tell me exactly how that happened?"

"It was the day we all walked to Meryton with Mr. Collins. There we were introduced to Mr. Wickham, and while we talked to him, Mr. Darcy and Mr. Bingley appeared. I could not help but notice the odd reaction between Mr. Wickham and Mr. Darcy."

"I see. And then ... ?"

"Well, I met Mr. Wickham again a day later at my Aunt Philips's, and he told me his story. That is all."

She looked at her father, waiting for his reaction, but he was only searching her face with great interest.

"So am I correct in assuming that Mr. Wickham knew little of you on your second meeting? He could not have known what kind of person you were nor could he possibly have reason to trust you."

"You are correct, sir."

"All right, now I come to the point: If he did not have any reason to hold you in special regard, why did he choose for you to hear his story? You were no different to him from any other young lady. Then why precisely you? Were you the only one available? Were all the other ladies dancing or otherwise occupied? I must confess I do not understand."

"I ... I do not know, sir." She was embarrassed by now, and those thoughts, loudly expressed by her father, made her feel the weight of her blunder.

"And how could he know you were not a friend of Mr. Darcy?"

"I ... I might have mentioned my dislike for Mr. Darcy."

"Aha ... now I think I understand. Mr. Wickham asked your opinion of Mr. Darcy, and after you expressed your dislike for the man, he began to tell you the story. Is that correct?"

"Yes, sir. I suppose it is."

"I see. Well, my child, I can see only two reasons for Mr. Wickham's acting in such a manner. Would you like to hear them?"

"Of course, Papa."

"Well — either Mr. Wickham was deeply and totally in love with you from the first moment he saw you and instantly decided to put his whole life history in your hands — in which case I can only wait for him to come to me and ask for your hand — "

"Papa!" Lizzy's serious voice interrupted him. "I beg you not to say such things, not even in jest, sir!"

"So that cannot be the truth?"

"No, sir!"

"Well, that is a relief, because I should have been forced to refuse him my consent in any case."

"And the second reason, Papa?"

He looked at his beloved, witty daughter and smiled. "My dear girl, I am sure you can apprehend for yourself the other reason. You have sense and judgment, and I expect you to use them."

"Well, Papa, Mr. Darcy expressed that opinion, as well!"

"Really? And what exactly did Mr. Darcy say? He also called you *'my dear girl'* I presume?"

"Papa! Now I understand what Mama means when she says you delight in vexing her!"

They laughed, but Mr. Bennet was by no means finished with her.

"So, my dear, Mr. Darcy told you pretty much the same things as I did. And pray tell me, when did you have the opportunity to talk about such a delicate subject — on your way home in the rain?"

Lizzy, stunned in front of her father, her eyes and mouth opened wide, was attempting to find something to say. "I… We… "

Then, mortified at being caught in a lie like a child, she decided to tell her father the truth. "Papa, I am truly sorry I concealed the truth from you. You have every reason to be upset, but please believe me; I did it only because I did not want to give Mama any mistaken ideas."

"Well, I am ready not to be upset and to hear you out if you decide to tell me the truth."

Still embarrassed, she told her father everything he needed to hear. When she finished, she expected to see her father displeased, but to her great surprise, he was merely serene.

"Lizzy, I have a question, and I want a truthful answer. Did anything happen between you and Mr. Darcy? Did he compromise you in any manner?"

"No, Papa! How can you say that? He was a perfect gentleman and exceedingly helpful, even though I must confess I was quite rude to him at times. I reproached him for so many undeserved things."

"Well, that is another surprise. Your opinion of Mr. Darcy seems to have improved. Did you forgive him for not wanting to dance with you? Perhaps he decided to pay for his fault by asking you to dance tomorrow night?" He was teasing her, expecting her to be embarrassed, but she returned his smile.

"You are correct, sir. Mr. Darcy apologised for his comments on that evening, and since my own behaviour toward him was not above reproach, I did forgive him. And my opinion towards him has indeed improved."

"Well, my child, in that case it is my turn to confess something to you: Mr. Darcy already told me the truth about your meeting. He considered that I, as your father and the head of the family, had the right to know what transpired. I must say my own opinion of him is quite high at the moment!"

Lizzy watched her father in disbelief. Was he only making fun of her all this time? She grew furious with him and with Mr. Darcy for not respecting her decision to keep the truth of their meeting private as she had asked him to do. She was about to leave the library when her father stopped her once more.

"My dear, do not be upset, and I beg you not to be angry with Mr. Darcy. What he did was indeed proof of his worthiness. He seems to be a very responsible and honest young man! Come, Lizzy, let your father kiss you before you go to bed. You must be very tired."

Elizabeth turned, smiled and embraced her father who kissed her forehead.

"Papa, after hearing everything, would you tell me your opinion of the story between Mr. Wickham and Mr. Darcy? Is one of them deceiving us?"

Mr. Bennet waited a few seconds before answering. He was not able to form a sound opinion yet and did not want to influence his daughter in any way. He wanted her to find her own answers.

"My dear, I cannot tell for sure. As I said, Mr. Darcy seemed to be very honest, and it is hard for me to believe that he would intentionally disrespect his father's wishes. On the other hand, Mr. Wickham could not have invented such a story without there being at least some truth in it. So if you want a guess, perhaps the living was left to Mr. Wickham by the late Mr. Darcy but only under some conditions that were not fulfilled. That might very well explain the present tension between them."

Thinking of Darcy's reaction in the cottage, Elizabeth knew it must have been more than that, but she could not discuss the matter any further, not even with her father — at least not for the moment.

"I could not help but notice that you seemed to disapprove of Mr. Wickham this morning."

"My dear, I do not disapprove of Mr. Wickham. He is a pleasant fellow, and your younger sisters seem to be very desirous of dancing with him at the ball! And certainly he has good taste in liking you. However, Lizzy, if I were you, I would keep the conversation with Mr. Wickham to less exciting subjects... like the weather or dancing perhaps?"

"I shall do that, sir. Thank you!" answered Lizzy, smiling at her father.

She kissed him once more and went to her room, eager to be alone and put her thoughts and feelings in order for the next day.

What will happen tomorrow? she mused.

Chapter 6

The prospect of the Netherfield ball was extremely agreeable to every female in the Bennet family. Mrs. Bennet chose to consider it as given in compliment to her eldest daughter and was particularly flattered; Jane pictured herself having a happy evening in the society of her two friends and the attentions of their brother. The happiness anticipated by Catherine and Lydia was as great as for any other event of that kind, and even Mary could assure her family that she had no disinclination for it.

Elizabeth thought with pleasure of dancing a great deal with a certain gentleman and of seeing a confirmation of everything she believed in both Mr. Darcy's and Mr. Wickham's looks and behaviour.

The time spent with both gentlemen and the discussion she had had with her father the previous day had been most enlightening for her. She could see very clearly now that, even if Mr. Wickham's story was — totally or partially — true, his motive in addressing her and narrating it to her on their second meeting was not at all honourable, and she had been a simpleton to accept such an intimate conversation with him.

She prepared herself for the ball with extra care and was delighted to see that the dress she had ordered — a cream-coloured one — was very flattering to her figure. Annie, her maid, had arranged her hair masterfully with small, white flowers plaited into it, leaving a few heavy curls of her dark hair to dance freely on her nape. Even her mother complimented her, and Mr. Collins was more attentive to her than ever, obsessively repeating how anxious he was to have the pleasure of their first set together.

By the time of their departure for Netherfield, the whole Bennet family was exhausted from enthusiasm and agitation, but none more so than Mr. Bennet, whose only hope was for as quiet and peaceful an evening as was possible at a ball. Even more, he seriously considered feigning a sudden headache in order to remain at home, but the prospect of a noisy fight with Mrs. Bennet was even more appalling, and he finally resigned himself to the task and entered the carriage.

DARCY WAS DRESSED LONG BEFORE the first guests appeared but did not descend to the ballroom in order to avoid Miss Bingley as long as possible. He knew he would have to dance with her eventually, but he would not ask her for the first set; he refused to pay her that compliment.

He smiled to himself at the boyish eagerness with which he was waiting to see Elizabeth again, hear her voice and enjoy her sparkling eyes; he was certain he had never before awaited a ball with such happy anticipation. *Well, truth be told, it is not the ball that I am waiting for.*

After a month of inner torment and struggle against his own feelings, Darcy had at last surrendered to what he felt and what he wanted. The result was an amazing sense of peace — a joy and liveliness long forgotten. He remained wholly aware of the considerations against her family — chiefly the lack of decorum and propriety in the youngest girls and their mother — but he was relieved that at least one of her parents was quite to his liking.

He knew Mrs. Bennet to be on a desperate quest for rich gentlemen for her daughters, and he was pleased to discover Mr. Bennet's differing opinion on the matter. The indubitable proof had been that gentleman's reaction when he discovered the truth about the time his daughter had spent alone with Darcy in the cottage. Most fathers — those with greater wealth, connections and positions — would have asked him immediately to marry the lady for less compromising situations. Mr. Bennet, however, had merely expressed his hopes that such a sacrifice would not be necessary, relinquishing the prospect of future wealth far above his present situation. In doing so, he had stated clearly that his second daughter's well-being and happiness were his main concern. Darcy could not help wondering — and a smile spread over his face at the thought — how Mrs. Bennet would react if she knew the particulars of the situation. He could well imagine himself shackled and married the following day. *Considering that the next step would be the wedding night, I would not mind. I could bear the sacrifice well enough.*

With such thoughts in his mind, he stared from the window at every carriage; finally, his wait ended as he recognised the Bennets among the first guests arriving.

Elizabeth descended from the carriage and, as if attracted by a spell, looked up and saw him at the window. His breathing stopped and then his heart beat wildly when he saw her smile tentatively at him; oblivious to all others, he hurried downstairs to greet her.

WHEN THEY REACHED NETHERFIELD, ELIZABETH'S impatience and eagerness to see Mr. Darcy made her feel ashamed of her lack of restraint. His appearance at the window and the smile directed at her filled her heart with an overwhelming exultation and an even more pleasurable anticipation of the night's events. Only a moment later, she saw him disappear and hoped — knew — he would come to meet her.

The whole family entered the main hall, greeted with a polite and apparently kind welcome by Miss Bingley and Mrs. Hurst. Elizabeth passed near them, smiling politely but coldly; she could still hear Mr. Collins's compliments on their elegance when a well-known voice startled her.

"Miss Bennet, what a pleasure! You look wonderful tonight!"

"Thank you, Mr. Wickham. You are very kind."

She was so disappointed that she could not hide the bitterness in her voice.

"May I accompany you inside, Miss Bennet?"

"In fact, I — "

"Are you waiting for someone specific?"

"No, indeed — only for my family."

"I just saw them entering, so shall we?"

She had no other choice but to accept his arm and walk into the ballroom with him. As she feared, Mr. Darcy appeared in the doorway, instantly checking his rush to her side and restraining his obvious desire to approach her.

He greeted her properly and politely, bowing to her, and Elizabeth answered elegantly with a timid smile, her eyes searching his face with worry. She was mortified at the thought that he would be angry at seeing her with Mr. Wickham and that the unfortunate event would spoil their evening.

However, Darcy had learned his lesson from the previous day; he knew her preferences well enough to keep his jealousy and displeasure under control. He felt tempted to pull Wickham away from her — or even to order the servants to throw him out — but such a conflict would certainly embarrass her and possibly ruin the time they could delightfully spend together. That was a prospect he rejected utterly. Nothing would come between them that night; it was a promise he made to himself, sealed by a barely noticeable smile meant only for Elizabeth. Her lips turned up slightly in response, proving to him that she understood his silent assurance.

He did not speak to or even look at Wickham, but addressed Elizabeth directly. "I just met Mr. Bingley and your sister, and they asked me to look after you and see that you are well."

Her smile grew and brightened her countenance.

"Thank you, Mr. Darcy, I am perfectly well. Mr. Wickham has very kindly offered to escort me inside."

"Then I shall meet you again later. Now, if you will excuse me… "

He departed without haste, and a moment later Mr. Wickham turned to her, smiling ironically.

"I notice that Mr. Darcy has become quite a favourite of yours lately. I was surprised to see some members of your family having amiable rapport with him."

"You are correct, sir. Mr. Darcy seems to be the kind of man who improves on better acquaintance. Quite different from others, I might say."

Wickham did not quite know how to respond to her statement; something in her countenance alarmed him, and he was almost relieved when Elizabeth excused herself to talk with Charlotte Lucas, allowing him time to think on what he should do with this unexpected development. Slightly afraid of Darcy's reaction, he had decided to attend the ball regardless, confident that his old acquaintance would do nothing to provoke a scandal in his host's home. Moreover, Wickham was certain he had a far better position than Darcy in the neighbours' esteem — especially in the Bennets' opinion — but his worry grew as he came to understand he had been wrong in his assumptions. He had noticed on the previous day that his presence near Miss Elizabeth was annoying Darcy though he could not guess why. Perhaps Darcy was a friend of Mr. Bennet. However, annoying Darcy was enough of a reason for him to defy prudence.

Darcy took a glass of wine as he stared at Elizabeth. She looked beautiful! Her dress faithfully followed the curves of her body with every move. The low neckline revealed the creamy skin of her long neck; her only jewel — a garnet cross necklace — drew his gaze obsessively to that spot. *She is more beautiful than I ever saw her before... in company.*

He hid his smile behind the glass, afraid someone would guess the improper thoughts aroused by his recollection of their precious moments spent alone together with only the rain for company. He was almost ashamed of the wanton desire he had for her, barely within control, but his sense of guilt was somehow diminished by the certainty that his intentions toward her were nothing but honourable. He wanted much from her — he wanted everything from her — but he desired nothing that she was not willing to offer him.

Darcy noticed that her charming appearance drew the attention of many other gentlemen, and he felt a sharp stab of jealousy, angry with himself for being so irrational. Stronger than jealousy, however, was his worry, which increased as he watched Elizabeth talking with Wickham. He wondered how that scoundrel dared to come to a ball in the house of his friend. He soon put aside any attempt to understand the limits of the man's impertinence, relieved to see Elizabeth moving away from him and joining her friend Charlotte.

Both ladies began to talk cheerfully, and from time to time Elizabeth's eyes turned in his direction, holding his insistent gaze for a few moments and then averting her eyes, blushing. He saw her wrap her arms around herself as if she were chilled, and he smiled again, recognising her gesture.

Is it my gaze that makes you shiver, Elizabeth? Can you feel my eyes caressing you from afar?

He wished to be near her and envied everyone who was so fortunate as to be in her company. He tried to remain patient until an opportunity arose to approach her properly or until they danced together. And then the supper... and then... He must have a second dance — no question of that.

It was still early, and some guests had yet to arrive. Darcy decided to take a stroll about the room with the intention of greeting Miss Lucas properly; that Elizabeth happened to be near was only a happy coincidence. At that moment, he was intercepted by Mr. Collins who bowed as low as possible without toppling over.

"My dear Mr. Darcy, it is a great honour to talk to you again."

"Good evening, Mr. Collins. In truth, I am a little surprised to see you here; I had thought that dancing was not the proper way for a clergyman to spend an evening."

"No indeed, sir, I am by no means of the opinion, I assure you, that a ball of this kind, given by a young man of character to respectable people, can have any evil tendency." Then he leaned in and continued in a lower tone, "And sir, I must confess to you that I am here on the advice of my noble patroness, your aunt, Lady Catherine."

"Really, sir? And what advice was that?"

"To find a wife, sir! 'Mr. Collins,' her ladyship said, 'you must marry. Choose properly, choose a gentlewoman for my sake; and for your own, let her be an active, useful sort of person, not brought up high, but able to make a small income go a good way. This is my advice. Find such a woman as soon as you can, bring her to Hunsford, and I will visit her.' And, since I shall inherit Longbourn at the death of my honourable cousin Mr. Bennet, I thought it proper to choose a wife from among my cousins. Do you not think it a thoughtful gesture, sir?"

Darcy stood still for a few moments, trying to understand what the parson had said. He generally gave little consideration to Collins, and he had barely been listening to him, but his last sentence surely caught his attention. Suddenly the revelation struck him; this silly man had chosen Elizabeth to be his wife! He was grossly appalled by the thought, but, happily, he knew for certain it would never come to pass — *not if I can do something to prevent it* — but he was still in disbelief at Collins's presumption. He tried to recollect himself enough to continue the conversation.

"Indeed, a very thoughtful gesture. And may I ask whether you favour one of your cousins in particular?"

"Sir, I should be happy to answer any question you might do me the honour of asking... and yes, I have decided in favour of my cousin Elizabeth."

"Really?" He breathed deeply a few times, trying to control himself. Then he looked with great preoccupation from Elizabeth to Collins. "I congratulate you, Mr. Collins, on your choice. Miss Elizabeth is indeed a very charming young lady, although I must say I am a little surprised."

"Oh, thank you, Mr. Darcy; I am honoured by your approval."

"Am I to understand, Mr. Collins, that you have already reached an understanding with Miss Elizabeth and her father?"

"No sir, but I have every intention of proposing tomorrow morning. However, I do expect success. My situation in life, my connections with the noble family of de

Bourgh, and my relationship to her own family, are circumstances highly in my favour. And however charming my cousin may be, she must take into consideration that it is possible she might not receive another proposal, considering her lack of dowry."

"I see. Mr. Collins, when you have everything settled, let me know. I promise you my full support. In fact, if you find it agreeable, I shall write a letter to my aunt myself in order to declare my good opinion of Miss Elizabeth. Happily, by the time my aunt meets her, she will have become accustomed to the idea." Then he bowed and took his leave, adding, "You are a very courageous man, Mr. Collins. I never should have thought you capable of contending against Lady Catherine to defend your choice."

For a few seconds, Collins did not fully understand Mr. Darcy's meaning. All he knew was that Mr. Darcy approved his choice and offered his support. His support for what? Trying to remember this, moment by moment, the words came into his mind and began to make sense. A cold sense of panic spread throughout his body, and he hurried after Mr. Darcy, stopping him in a very ungentlemanly manner by grabbing his arm.

Mr. Darcy looked evidently displeased. "Is there a problem, Mr. Collins?"

"Certainly there is, sir. I must have a few words with you, Mr. Darcy, I beg you! Our conversation requires me to ask. Sir, am I mistaken or did you imply that Lady Catherine would be displeased by my choice of Miss Elizabeth Bennet as my wife? Why would her ladyship disapprove of her?"

"Mr. Collins, I shall not talk with you about Miss Elizabeth or any other young lady in particular. You know your cousin better than I do, and if you believe Lady Catherine would consider Miss Elizabeth the proper wife for you, then it must be true. And, if you are determined in her favour, the opinion of Lady Catherine or me should be insignificant."

His eyes opened widely at such a statement. "Mr. Darcy, I beg to differ, sir. Lady Catherine's opinion is the most important thing to me, and any advice you might give me would be much valued."

Mr. Collins's gaze turned to Elizabeth who was talking with Miss Lucas and two officers. She was laughing — a little too loudly for his taste — and she... Was it possible? Was she flirting with those men? He quickly remembered her escape in the rain and her appearance — so wild and muddied — her many improper comments, and her obvious preference for Mr. Wickham. He froze and turned to Mr. Darcy, panic evident in his eyes.

"Mr. Darcy, I might have been imprudent and hasty in my choice. I shall be forever grateful to you for your valuable advice. Indeed, a clergyman cannot be too prudent in this matter, especially one who is so happy as to have Lady Catherine's protection."

Mr. Darcy only nodded, seeing that by now both Elizabeth and Mr. Bennet were looking curiously in their direction.

"Mr. Darcy, I would be more than grateful to you if you would not mention this conversation to anyone and particularly not to your aunt."

"You may be assured of my secrecy, sir. Do not distress yourself."

"Thank you, sir! Happily, this ball could be an excellent opportunity to meet other charming young ladies, and happily during the dances I shall — "

Suddenly he stopped and cast another frightened glance at Darcy.

"Oh my! I have already invited my cousin Elizabeth for the first set, and now my preference for her will be evident to everyone. I could never bestow my favours on another young lady this evening."

He looked ridiculously upset, shifting from one foot to the other as Darcy bit his lower lip, fighting desperately the laughter that wanted to burst from his chest. *This cannot be! I cannot be tempted at this level and still be forced to keep my countenance.*

Every proper manner would forbid his doing such a thing, and he knew it was preposterous, but he could not be rational in anything regarding Elizabeth, so he took the opportunity.

"Mr. Collins, I do not see a cause for such distress. Indeed, sir, one might feel indisposed and not inclined to dance at times. I am sure Miss Elizabeth would understand a sudden indisposition. And since I promised you my support… I am not engaged for the first two sets and could offer to dance with her in your stead to avoid putting her in a disagreeable situation."

The relief Mr. Collins felt at that moment would be difficult to describe. He was convinced once more that all the great qualities possessed by Lady Catherine resided equally in her nephew. He approached Elizabeth, followed closely by Darcy, who was not only amused but a trifle worried at Elizabeth's reaction to his involvement. His sense of honour made him feel guilty at what he had done, but he knew he was right. Elizabeth could not welcome the parson's attention.

The music was about to begin for the first set, and Elizabeth was still talking with Charlotte. She introduced her cousin to her friend and then waited for Mr. Collins to claim her hand for the dance.

"My dear cousin Elizabeth, a temporary indisposition prevents me from honouring my previous promise, and unfortunately I will not be able to enjoy your company for the first set."

Elizabeth stared at him in astonishment.

"I am afraid I do not follow you, Mr. Collins. Are you unwell, sir? Shall I fetch my father?"

"No, indeed! Your care does you honour. However, I have only a slight indisposition which will prevent me from dancing this set."

"Well, do not trouble yourself, Cousin. It is of no consequence. I shall simply enjoy my conversation with my friend."

"Miss Elizabeth?" Darcy's deep voice startled Elizabeth, and she turned her eyes to him, only to be riveted by his gaze. It was the first time he had addressed her since their meeting in Mr. Wickham's company.

"Would you do me the honour of dancing this set with me? I hope it would not be an inconvenience, either for you or for Miss Lucas..."

She frowned and remained unmoving, looking at him incredulously. What was happening? His face appeared as stern and unreadable as ever, his playfulness betrayed only by his eyes. He was pleased with himself, but Elizabeth was not diverted. She felt he had somehow convinced Mr. Collins to feign illness so he could have his second dance. In her heart, she was pleased by the thought that he had acted so improperly simply to gain one more dance with her, and she was infinitely happier to have his company than that of Mr. Collins. Still, his actions disturbed her; she remembered that he was a proud man, accustomed to having his own way.

"Of course, Lizzy, go and dance; do not worry about me," said Charlotte.

He was waiting, and not wanting to create a scene, she finally agreed. "Thank you, Mr. Darcy. I shall be happy to dance with you."

He offered her his hand, and she took it reluctantly, but his slight touch made her tingle; the vivid memories of their ungloved hands held together rushed into her mind.

He tightened his grip and led her to the floor.

"Miss Bennet, allow me to tell you how wonderful you look this evening."

"Thank you, Mr. Darcy," was her polite answer.

The music began and they started to dance; every movement that drew them closer or parted them aroused a variety of feelings. Elizabeth tried not to look at him but could not stop her cheeks from colouring crimson at his closeness. A quick glance around the room proved that, as she had anticipated, most of the assemblage was staring at them in wonder. That she had been asked by Mr. Darcy for the first set did not go unnoticed.

Darcy searched her face with close attention and great amusement. He could tell she was displeased, but he was not worried as the reason was not a serious one. However, she looked amazingly beautiful when angry, and he was enraptured watching her bite her lip and hurl sharp looks from her sparkling eyes.

When their hands touched during the dance, she scarcely held his, but he was more than happy to hold hers as tightly as propriety allowed. Eventually, he broke the silence.

"Miss Bennet, may I be so bold as to ask the reason for your obvious displeasure? Do you find my company disagreeable, or is my dancing not to your liking?"

"Mr. Darcy, I do not find your company disagreeable, and your dancing style is exquisite." She stopped for a few seconds, arching her right brow as if challenging him to answer. "And I am not displeased; I am only worried for my cousin's health. Could you enlighten me as to his problem? You seemed to spend a good deal of time talking to him immediately before his indisposition."

She tried earnestly to censure him for his behaviour, but her amusement was obvious, and she tried diligently to maintain a serious demeanour. However, she had to make him understand that she did not approve of being forced into anything and would not allow him to treat her as a simpleton to be toyed with. To her utter surprise, Mr. Darcy answered with no hesitation or attempt to conceal the truth.

"Yes I could, Miss Bennet, since I am familiar with Mr. Collins's indisposition. Do not worry; it is nothing serious."

Shocked by his open admission, she almost forgot the steps of the dance. "And do you know, by chance, what caused his indisposition?"

"Yes I do, but since I promised my secrecy, I cannot relate any details."

They were dancing in perfect harmony, looking into each other's eyes as if trying to intimidate and dominate, duelling with wit and liveliness. Darcy enjoyed it immensely and did not even try to conceal his feelings. A smile appeared at the corner of his eyes and lips, and he continued, "However, I can say that Mr. Collins's indisposition is a result of his acknowledgment that he had made a choice contrary to his situation and the advice he previously had been given."

"I see… And may I ask how he reached that understanding? Did he perhaps ask your opinion?"

"He did."

"And am I to understand that you disapprove of his choice?"

"Not at all, Miss Bennet. In truth, I approve of his choice very much. I only pointed out to him that such a choice was perhaps not the most appropriate one for *him*."

Elizabeth's surprise at hearing his words was matched only by that which she had felt when he had spoken of "10 or 15 years of proper behaviour" being enough. She understood too well that *she* was the choice to which he was referring! She could not believe the proper Mr. Darcy would make such a suggestion to her — and more than once. Whether or not he was serious, it made her uneasy. She was only beginning to know his character, and her feelings toward him remained ambiguous. She averted her eyes, blushing and warming at the feeling of his hand taking hers again.

Suddenly he changed his tone and said quite seriously, "Miss Bennet, I have a confession to make."

She looked at him and was relieved to see a well-known expression of easiness on his face. "Really? I hope it is not a frightening one."

"Hopefully not, Miss Bennet. I took advantage of Mr. Collins's indisposition and offered to take his place in this set with you. I must say that I was happy to do so and I might have encouraged him a little in that regard. I am sorry if I created any inconvenience for you."

His confession was sincere, and she was pleased to see that he genuinely respected her as evidenced by his insistence that she know the truth of even this preposterous situation. However, she was not about to let him off so easily, so she answered in her teasing manner, "Well, Mr. Darcy, my cousin's company is very much missed, but I hope I shall become accustomed to yours without any great inconvenience."

Her eyes were laughing, and the next time the pattern of the dance brought them together, she took his hand with confidence. The rest of the set passed with only a few remarks and many exchanged smiles. They were content in their closeness and the touch of their hands, lingering only a moment more than necessary, each lost in the depths of the other's eyes, and both hoping for this set to last longer and for their next one together to come sooner.

The amazing event of Mr. Darcy's dancing the first set with Elizabeth Bennet brought the couple to everyone's attention as the gentleman's dislike for such frivolous activities was generally acknowledged. Mr. Darcy himself had told Sir William Lucas that dancing was a compliment he never paid to any place — not even to St. James's — if he could avoid it. The reason for the miraculous change in Mr. Darcy's opinion quickly became a topic of general wonder.

In a corner of the ballroom, Mr. Bennet watched his favourite daughter partnering with Darcy. He was amused by their obvious argument during the first half of the set but somewhat worried about the way they looked at each other later. Something seemed to have developed between them in only three days, and it was too much and too hasty for Mr. Bennet.

Mrs. Bennet was not of the same opinion. When the first dance began, she was talking with Lady Lucas and Mrs. Long about how fortunate Jane was to be the object of Mr. Bingley's admiration. However, the unexpected vision of Elizabeth standing up with Mr. Darcy was such a great surprise that she remained silent, watching them incredulously for many minutes, accompanied in her astonishment by the other two ladies. An unexpected, new prospect — more advantageous than others — seemed to arise before them.

From another corner of the room, imbibing freely from a glass of wine and with a singular frown upon his face, Mr. Wickham also fixed his gaze upon Miss Elizabth and her companion.

The set ended, and Mr. Darcy led Elizabeth to her father, bowing to Mr. Bennet, as he had not had an opportunity to greet him properly that evening.

The elder gentleman met them with a smile and, after the proper salutation, wasted no time in saying, "Mr. Darcy, you seem to be enjoying the ball, I should say."

"I must confess I am, sir."

"I am glad to hear it. Lizzy, where did you lose our cousin Mr. Collins?"

"He was indisposed and could not dance, Papa."

"Indeed? Well, I must confess I am very disappointed. I was looking forward to your dancing and quite prepared for considerable entertainment."

Seeing Mr. Darcy's uncomfortable fidgeting, he added, "I mean no offence, Mr. Darcy, but you dance so well that I was not at all diverted. To see Mr. Collins exhibiting — now that would have been a spectacle."

"Papa! I never should have thought you capable of finding amusement in your daughter's discomfort."

Lizzy's reproach only brought laughter to her father, and she was about to say something more but was stopped by Mr. Darcy's sudden chuckle. She looked at him reproachfully, trying to restrain herself from joining them; more than one person was looking at their little group. They had clearly become the centre of general observation — and gossip, no doubt. She quickly excused herself, saying that she wanted to talk to Jane; before Mr. Darcy could apologise for his behaviour, she was in the middle of the room near her sister, whispering something in Jane's ear and casting furtive glances in their direction.

"I am sorry for my reaction, Mr. Bennet. I hope I did not offend Miss Elizabeth. I shall go and apologise at once."

"You will do no such thing, Mr. Darcy, for it will put me in an even worse position. You laughed with me, thus you will have to suffer the punishment with me."

"As you wish, sir." Darcy smiled, his enthralled gaze following Elizabeth around the room.

Mr. Bennet's voice stirred him from his reverie. "Mr. Darcy, am I wrong in saying that you and Lizzy seemed to get along quite well?"

Darcy looked at him, slightly embarrassed, but said lightly, "No, sir, you are not wrong. I mean... I believe you are not wrong. I can only hope Miss Elizabeth's opinion is the same."

"Well, I dare say it is the same. Apparently, I was correct the other day in assuming that Elizabeth's opinion of you would improve."

"Yes, sir, I hope so."

"However, Mr. Darcy, we must discuss another matter since it seems that things have changed a little in the last couple of days."

"Certainly, sir."

"I could not help but notice that your attentions toward Elizabeth are quite obviously and openly displayed."

Darcy felt again like a young boy caught doing something wrong and began to fidget with his wine glass, obviously embarrassed.

"Mr. Bennet, do you consider my behaviour toward Miss Elizabeth in any way offensive?"

"No, sir. And I am sure my daughter would let you know if something improper had occurred. Mr. Darcy, my good opinion of you has grown consistently since our last meeting. I believe you to be a responsible man but also a young one as I myself was once. I just want to be sure that you are aware of your behaviour and of the possible consequences in terms of gossip and expectations raised."

How strangely amusing. He is telling me exactly the same things I told Bingley! Nevertheless, he knew the answer perfectly well and gave it, looking the elder gentleman straight in the eye.

"I am fully aware, sir, and I assure you my behaviour is in accordance with my intentions."

"I see. And have you and Elizabeth come to an understanding?"

"No, sir. Miss Elizabeth and I have not discussed anything of this sort."

"And you have no intention of discussing the matter anytime soon?"

Darcy was trying diligently to find the proper words, but he finally decided on honesty.

"Mr. Bennet, if I were to consider only my wishes, I would immediately ask for a private audience with Miss Elizabeth and then with you. However, although I have reason to believe her opinion of me has lately changed for the better and hope it will grow more favourable in time, I believe such a discussion at this moment would, unfortunately, give Miss Elizabeth great discomfort and would not assure me of a favourable answer."

He stopped a moment without averting his eyes.

"That is why I ask your permission to call on you for the next several days on my own — and with Mr. Bingley after his return from town — in order to become... better known to your entire family."

Mr. Bennet smiled at his choice of words.

"I am sure my entire family will be more than pleased to know you better, especially Mrs. Bennet and Lydia."

His obvious amusement made Darcy gulp violently from his glass. He could accept Elizabeth's teasing, but being the object of such sharp irony from both her and her father in one evening was somewhat overwhelming.

Their conversation was interrupted as the music for the second set began, and he was forced to go in search of Miss Bingley. He knew that Elizabeth had accepted Wickham, and it was the perfect time for him to fulfil the obligation to dance with his friend's sister.

Chapter 7

When the music started, both Elizabeth and Darcy took their places with their partners, exchanging glances and smiles — gestures that did not escape either Miss Bingley or Mr. Wickham.

"I must say, Mr. Darcy, I was quite surprised to see you dancing the first set with Eliza Bennet. I had no idea your admiration for her fine eyes went to such lengths." He merely looked at his dance partner and made no answer.

"When I heard you saying one night, *'She, a beauty? I should as soon call her mother a wit,'* I never should have imagined you would suffer such a change of opinion."

Still Darcy made no answer. He allowed her to speak as he followed Elizabeth with his eyes. Miss Bingley easily noticed the direction of his gaze and, enlightened by a sudden idea, began a new topic.

"I see many other gentlemen seem to be enchanted by her fine eyes and other charms, particularly the officers, and she seems to enjoy Mr. Wickham's company very well indeed. These country girls so easily fall for a uniform and the dashing man who wears it."

Darcy tried to compose himself before answering.

"Miss Bingley, I should be very grateful if you would change the topic of conversation. I shall not discuss Miss Elizabeth Bennet with you or any other person. However, I am at your disposal to spend the remaining time in pleasant conversation about any other subject you choose."

His voice was calm, but a brief glance at his expression convinced Miss Bingley not to continue, and in order to show her disapproval, she said not another word for the entire length of the set.

Though Elizabeth did not find Mr. Wickham's company as pleasing as she had previously, she still could enjoy a dance with him. He was skilful and easily conducted a diverting conversation. However, she frequently looked in Mr. Darcy's direction, occasionally meeting his gaze and observing his stoic attention to Miss Bingley's conversation.

"You seem to be deep in thought, Miss Bennet."

"I beg you will excuse me, Mr. Wickham; it was very impolite on my part."

"I was surprised to see you stand up with Mr. Darcy for the first set! If I remember correctly, you told me that Mr. Collins had secured it."

"Indeed he had, Mr. Wickham, but my cousin had a sudden indisposition, and Mr. Darcy was kind enough to request the set in his stead."

"Yes... Mr. Darcy is all politeness."

Elizabeth changed the topic and began an easy conversation about the ball and the number of couples. From time to time, she looked into Wickham's face, only to glimpse an expression that gave her some alarm. She was relieved that the dance was approaching its end.

"To be honest, Miss Bennet, I can understand your feelings. Darcy is a very important man and knows how to please a lady once he has decided in her favour."

"Mr. Wickham, I do not have the pleasure of understanding you."

"I am sure you do, Miss Bennet. You are an intelligent lady."

"Thank you for the compliment, but it is undeserved, I assure you."

"It usually takes him some time to decide as his pride always takes the lead, and as far as I know, he chooses only women of remarkable beauty with the highest position in society." Taking advantage of a movement in the dance, he leaned towards her, whispering, "Did you hear of Miss Alton?"

"No, Mr. Wickham, I did not, and I do not think it is proper to — "

"Miss Alton, the famous actress... You must have heard of her; she has been the most popular of her generation. All the royal courts of Europe were competing to have her as a guest. She is now married and retired, but she and Darcy had a... very interesting relationship some years ago — not to mention that her husband is an earl many years older than herself and a close acquaintance of the late Mr. Darcy. Very convenient, is it not?"

The music ended, and Elizabeth endeavoured to control herself in the face of Mr. Wickham's impertinence. Talking of such things with a lady was unthinkable for a gentleman, but he seemed at ease as he smiled intimately at her. Her indignation and anger were roused to such an extent that she was tempted to apply her hand sharply to his smirking face.

Charmingly, Mr. Wickham took her hand and led her from the floor. "I hope I have not offended you; 'twas only a harmless comment. We are good friends, are we not, Miss Bennet?"

She stopped in the middle of the room and turned to him.

"Mr. Wickham, I should hardly call an acquaintance of six days a friendship. If I led you to believe I should welcome such a discussion, it is entirely my fault, and

I apologise for it. However, no friendship — not even that of a lifetime — will ever persuade me to talk about the private life of either Mr. Darcy or any other ladies and gentlemen. And now, if you will excuse me, sir, I need some fresh air and solitude."

She departed from him at a rapid pace and went onto the balcony, but Mr. Wickham quickly followed. "Sir, I thought I made it clear to you — "

"Miss Bennet, just one moment, please. I honestly do not want you to be upset with me. I just wanted you to know the truth. And speaking of the truth… I do hope you know that Mr. Darcy will marry no one but his cousin, Miss de Bourgh; it is a match arranged when they were infants."

The shock Elizabeth felt stopped her breathing. She stared at him, her eyes wide, unable to move. Taking advantage of her stillness, he took both of her hands in his and put long and repeated kisses on the backs of her gloved hands. She recovered and removed her hands quickly, censuring him in a steely voice. "Mr. Wickham, you forget yourself!"

She returned to the ballroom, leaving Mr. Wickham alone on the balcony. She immediately saw Mr. Darcy coming directly towards her, his expression anxious and his eyes asking a silent question.

He obviously intended to address her, but she could not bear to speak with him at that moment; in great haste, she turned and left the room. Once she was out of sight, she began to run, not stopping until she reached the library. She closed the door behind her and sat down heavily on the sofa. She was afraid she would start to cry, and she could not let that happen. She would give neither Mr. Darcy nor Mr. Wickham that satisfaction.

Steps could be heard in the hall, and even before the door opened, she knew who it was.

"Miss Bennet… are you unwell?"

Darcy moved closer as the room was lit only by the moonlight through the curtains, and he could barely see her. His worried gaze fell upon her sitting on the sofa, her eyes downcast and her hands trembling.

"Good God, what is the matter? Miss Bennet, what has happened? What did Wickham do to you?"

"Mr. Darcy, I have had more than enough of both you and Mr. Wickham. If you would be so kind, I should like to be alone for a while. Your company is neither needed nor desired, sir, but thank you for your concern."

Darcy was shocked by her harsh words. He first took offense and was about to leave her but immediately changed his mind. He had been worriedly watching her exchange with Wickham on the dance floor, but he had not seriously determined that something was amiss until Elizabeth's escape to the balcony. He had decided to go to her immediately, but Sir William Lucas had detained him for some minutes. Upon seeing Elizabeth's hasty exit from the balcony — followed by Wickham's smug departure — he could wait no longer. He left Sir William in the middle of a florid sentence and followed her, sure that Wickham had hurt her in some way.

Now he was here with her, and she was close to tears and undoubtedly upset with him. *What could that devil have told her?*

He moved closer and knelt near the sofa. "Miss Bennet, I shall leave you alone if that is your desire, and if I have done anything to offend you, I shall accept my penance, but please, tell me whether Mr. Wickham did or said anything to you. Do not allow him to distress you; I beg you, Elizabeth."

She finally lifted her eyes and met his; she was not crying, but her pain was evident. In an icy tone, she censured him. "Mr. Darcy, I should be most grateful if you would not use familiarities in your address to me."

He stared at her, realising what he had said, and then quickly rose to his feet.

"I am sorry, Miss Bennet; I should not have addressed you in such a way, and I beg your forgiveness. My only excuse is my concern for you."

"You must not concern yourself about me, Mr. Darcy. I am not your sister. There is no need for you to protect me." She knew her words would pain him, but she wanted him to suffer.

She turned to him and continued, "And if you were the respectable gentleman you pretend to be, you would not act in such a manner toward me, knowing full well that you are soon to marry Miss de Bourgh. But perhaps you consider all of us of so little consequence that we do not deserve to be treated with respect by such an important person as yourself."

Her eyes were filled with rage, and she held his incredulous gaze for a few moments, hoping that she could transmit to him all of her outrage. Darcy, however, merely breathed deeply, closed his eyes, and then opened them with relief, his countenance suddenly more serene. *So that is why she is so angry; Thank God she is not hurt!* He could see her suffering, but he could not help but smile at her, increasing her anger as she turned her back to him.

"I see Mr. Wickham continues to favour you with stories about me. However, I had the pleasure of hearing you say only yesterday that you would follow my advice about searching for proofs and evidence of anything he might say." She glanced toward him briefly and then averted her eyes.

"I hope you will believe me when I say that I am neither by honour nor inclination bound to my cousin or to any other young lady. As I said before, I am more than willing to answer any questions you might have, including questions about my relationship with my cousin Miss de Bourgh. However, more important to me is your accusation that I have not treated you and your family with respect; you must allow me to defend myself on this count."

She still was not facing him, and he respected her wishes, continuing to speak to her back.

"Miss Bennet, I know that in the past my manners toward you were not as they should have been, but I was hoping that had changed in the last few days. If I still gave offence, it was done most unwillingly, I assure you."

He paused. "The only thing for which I can reproach myself is that I selfishly bestowed my attention upon you without any consideration for your feelings. Although I know my intentions toward you to be nothing but honourable, I can now understand that you have not received those attentions with equal pleasure and that I have only made you uncomfortable. I beg you to excuse me if this was the case and please accept my assurances that I shall restrain myself in the future. Furthermore, I should understand if you do not want to dance another set with me."

He waited for her answer in silence, maintaining the small distance between them. Darcy knew she received his attentions with pleasure, but he also could understand her embarrassment and uncertainty about him. However witty and intelligent she might be, she was still young and undoubtedly inexperienced in dealing with men. *She probably imagines I was only trifling with her, and maybe she is a little jealous, too.*

Strangely, though his heart ached to see her suffering, he was also happy and satisfied to know she was suffering because of him. He hated himself for having such vain and selfish feelings, but it was the truth. He was tempted to take her in his arms, kiss her, comfort her, whisper in her ear everything he felt for her, and tell her that, if she wanted, he could protect her and bind himself to her and only her from that moment on. He knew, however, that this would only frighten and embarrass her further. The moment for such a declaration had not yet come. He could only put himself at her disposal and let her choose for herself what she needed and wanted from him.

Elizabeth closed her eyes, trying to calm herself and form rational thoughts, but she simply could not think of anything. Her head was spinning and her heart aching; Mr. Darcy being so close was not helpful.

"Mr. Darcy…" Her voice was barely audible. "I do not think there will be a need to change the dance arrangements. However, I should like to spend some moments alone if you do not mind."

"As you wish, madam."

"Thank you." Although she could not see him, he bowed to her and left the library, remaining outside at the door in case someone should disturb her.

Hearing Mr. Darcy's strong pace as he departed, Elizabeth turned her head, looking after him. She was grateful he had respected her wishes and gone, but at the same time, she felt a sense of disappointment. She had held an impossible hope that he would put his arms around her, or at least that he would take her hand in his to comfort her. She knew that such behaviour would be highly improper and that it was ridiculous for her to feel that way only a few moments after she had accused him of not respecting her. She had never been embraced by a man who was not family, so she did not really know what she wanted, but the feeling was stronger than her reasonable thoughts, and her body ached for the comfort of his arms. She breathed deeply, trying to remain calm. *You are ridiculous! You are behaving like a child and making a fool of yourself. Regain your composure, Elizabeth, and think.*

She closed her eyes and remembered everything that had happened in the last half-hour as she began to pace the room. *Why am I so upset? Because of Mr. Wickham's impertinence and forwardness or because of what he told me about Mr. Darcy? And what did he tell me? Is there some truth in what he said?* Soon she admitted that what had upset her most and made her almost burst into tears was Mr. Wickham's suggestion that Mr. Darcy could not seriously pursue her as he would marry Miss de Bourgh in any case. But now, after the moments of anger had passed, she knew that could not be true.

Mr. Darcy had told her that he was not to marry Miss de Bourgh, and despite the hard words she had thrown in his face, she knew he would not lie regarding such an important matter. But as her father previously said, neither could Mr. Wickham have fabricated such a thing without there being at least some truth in it. And that remark about Mr. Darcy favouring other ladies... She took Mr. Wickham's comment, weighed it rationally, and finally accepted that it was also probably true in some way. *I am neither by honour nor inclination bound...* Perhaps so, but Elizabeth was not so naïve as to be ignorant of a few things about the world and gentlemen of the world.

After a few minutes of deliberation, fighting for the first time against the bitter taste of jealousy without even knowing what it was, she grew upset with herself. *I indeed have no sense! Until three days ago, I hated Mr. Darcy and acted in a despicable manner toward him. Surely, I have no right to be bothered by anything he might have done in the past that has not involved my family or me!*

Towards her, his behaviour had been nothing but gentlemanlike. He had told her his intentions were honourable, and she wanted to believe him. Besides, she could not forget they had spent many hours alone, and she had been completely without protection. It would have been a perfect opportunity for a man at least to try to... if he had wanted. The most powerful proof was that he had told her father the truth about their meeting in the cottage. She knew that in doing so he had exposed himself, for Mr. Bennet could have forced him to marry her at that moment.

All those thoughts warmed her toward him, and she decided she had no reason not to enjoy his company for the time being as long as he acted respectfully toward her. She arranged her dress, pressed her palms to her burning cheeks, and opened the door to leave the library.

She found Mr. Darcy in the hall by the door, waiting, looking so strong, protective and obviously worried; the sight of him made her heart beat faster.

And I hurt him again, abusing him so abominably with my cruel words.

In that moment, she decided what she should do to avoid any misunderstanding in the future. Approaching him, she smiled shyly, self-conscious of her impulsive reaction and what she intended to ask.

"Miss Bennet, are you feeling better?"

"I am now, Mr. Darcy. Thank you for your patience."

"Shall we return to the ballroom then?"

"In fact, Mr. Darcy, I must confess I am not inclined to dance at the moment. However, I should be grateful if you would do me the favour of answering a few questions about a common acquaintance as you previously so generously offered to do.

Darcy looked at Elizabeth with obvious surprise.

"You want to talk about… ? Now? I am afraid a ballroom would not be the proper place for that kind of talk, Miss Bennet."

"Perhaps not, but what about the library? That is… if you think it would be acceptable for you to reveal these things. I do not want to impose on your private matters." She was a little distressed by his apparent reluctance and was prepared for him to maintain his secrecy.

"Miss Bennet. I am the one who offered to discuss this with you a few days ago. Do not feel uncomfortable asking for what I offered you. I was just surprised by your sudden decision to hear me. Shall we enter then? It should not take long."

He opened the door and entered the library again, hurrying to light the candles. Being alone in the same room with her was bad enough, but being alone in the dark was unacceptable and dangerous in every sense.

"Please sit down, Miss Bennet. Would you like something to drink?"

"No, thank you. Mr. Darcy, I am sorry for any inconvenience I might be creating with my curiosity. It is just that… Mr. Wickham has indeed told me many things tonight as he did a few days ago, and I should like to know your opinion about them."

"I understand you, and truth be told, I am happy you decided to listen to me although I am not quite sure about the time and place for this discussion. Should someone find us here, the situation might be misunderstood."

He was indeed worried that they could be found there alone. Of course, the worst that could happen would be that he was forced to marry her as soon as possible. However, he did not want her to be forced into marrying him and would not allow a scandal to mark the beginning of their relationship.

Elizabeth blushed violently and rose to her feet, suddenly understanding his reason. "You are perfectly right, Mr. Darcy. I was impulsive and thoughtless. I do not want to put you in such an inconvenient position, so dangerous for your name and reputation. Let us go back."

"Miss Bennet, it was not about *myself* that I was thinking. It is not *my* situation or reputation that concerns me. If you want to talk, we must do that."

He smiled lightly and encouragingly, inviting her to return to the sofa while he took a chair. He was tempted to sit next to her, but he knew that would be a very imprudent move. Having her close without being allowed to touch her was a torture in itself, and it need not be amplified.

"Miss Bennet, do you have some particular question?"

"No sir, I thought it would be better that, perhaps... you would tell me what you consider necessary for me to know... so I should not interfere in something that is not my concern."

"Very well then. Before going further, I should like to clarify Mr. Wickham's statement about my cousin, Miss Anne de Bourgh."

"No, really, sir, that is not necessary — "

"I think it is; please allow me to explain. My cousin Anne is indeed a very pleasant young lady, but her health is not good; consequently, she does not travel much. That is why Colonel Fitzwilliam and I are careful to make annual visits in order to spend some time with her. Although I am very fond of Anne as my cousin, let me assure you that neither she nor I intend to be connected in any other way. However, my aunt insists upon this, and she can be very demanding; she never accepts opinions other than her own."

"Like my mother," said Elizabeth, trying to lighten the atmosphere.

"Oh, no, Miss Bennet, her vehemence is much more so. Trust me as I am now acquainted with both the ladies in question."

She smiled, and he was about to resume his story when the heavy door of the library opened and a well-known voice startled them.

"Elizabeth, may I inquire what you are doing here alone with Mr. Darcy?"

THEY HURRIED TO THEIR FEET, seeing an agitated Mr. Bennet in the doorway. The tone of his voice left no room for misunderstanding regarding his opinion about the situation in which they found themselves.

"Mr. Darcy, allow me to say that this is indeed a situation that would bring harm to my daughter's reputation. To be honest, I am very disappointed; I should not have expected such behaviour from either of you."

"Mr. Bennet, if you would allow me to explain, sir — "

"I do not think any explanation would be satisfactory, sir. Lizzy, let us return to the ball this instant. Your mother asked insistently about you — "

"Papa, I shall go, but before I do, I beg you to listen to me."

"Say what you have to say quickly, and let us be done with this."

"You have no reason to blame Mr. Darcy. Nothing improper happened."

"How can it not be improper to be alone in the middle of the night with a man in an isolated room?"

"I am the one to blame, because I acted childishly. I was upset by something Mr. Wickham told me, and I ran in here. Mr. Darcy was only too kind to try to comfort me."

"Did Wickham harm you in any way, Lizzy?" asked Mr. Bennet, suddenly worried.

"Not really, father. He just upset me."

"I see; then I am at a loss to understand why, if you were upset, you asked Mr. Darcy to comfort you and not me or your sister, for instance."

"Mr. Bennet, the situation is not what you have been told, and Miss Bennet is only too kind to take the blame upon herself. She did not require my help. In fact, she told me that my presence was not welcomed. It was only my selfish and prideful nature that led me to the presumption that I could be of some help, and in doing that, I created an awkward situation."

Elizabeth's father looked from his daughter to Darcy, struggling to keep a serious countenance while they were trying at once to excuse each other. *Now, that is some loyalty.* He was much diverted.

He was also quite disapproving of the situation in which he found them. Not for a second did it cross his mind that Elizabeth and Darcy were doing anything improper. His guess was that they wanted to have a private conversation and searched for a secluded place, but for anyone else who might have seen them alone, it was as improper as any other frivolous activities. He decided to chastise them a bit longer.

"Well, apparently we can argue until morning trying to decide which of you has the greater part, but neither of you is without blame. So let us return; I hope I made myself clear in saying that I will not tolerate this kind of behaviour again. I do not want this situation ever to be repeated. Dancing is what I remember one must do at a ball."

They were deeply embarrassed; Darcy had little to say — firstly, because the gentleman was Elizabeth's father and secondly, because he knew very well that Mr. Bennet was right.

Both men were surprised to hear Elizabeth's determined voice.

"Papa, I do understand you perfectly. But I beg you to allow me a few more minutes to speak with Mr. Darcy. I was just asking him about an important and private matter — "

"Lizzy, I cannot believe my ears! What important and private matter can that be? Do you and Mr. Darcy have some secrets to share that cannot be revealed to your father?"

Again, Darcy intervened. "Mr. Bennet, it is not actually a secret. I was about to tell Miss Bennet about my past dealings with Mr. Wickham."

Mr. Bennet's first reaction was one of boredom. *Ahh... that Wickham story again! Oh my, not before dinner...*

In truth, Mr. Bennet had real interest in few things in his life, and Mr. Wickham was not one of those things. However, looking at the two young people in front of him, he was surprised to see them very affected and preoccupied with the subject. Mr. Bennet was at a loss as to why his normally witty and bright daughter would react in such an uncharacteristic way and waste her time at a ball speaking of Mr. Wickham. The fact was more surprising as her opinion about the fellow obviously had lowered in the last couple of days. *In truth, she seems to have reacted strangely since the very beginning in any matter concerning these gentlemen.*

Although he wanted to assure his daughter's tranquillity, he could not decide to make such a concession and risk prolonging their present improper situation. "Lizzy, I am sorry to disappoint you, my child. I respect your wish, but it is unthinkable to leave you here alone."

"Mr. Bennet, I had the privilege of your trust on a very delicate matter three days ago when you hardly knew me. I am sure I can depend on your secrecy with this unpleasant story. So if you could spare a little more time, I should have no objection to sharing it with both you and Miss Bennet."

Darcy's tone was full of deference, but he was insistent, and Mr. Bennet understood that this was something of importance. "Very well, Mr. Darcy, let us hear you out once and for all."

They sat on the sofa while Darcy began to talk with obvious distress.

"Miss Bennet, I do not know what Mr. Wickham told you, so I shall start from the beginning. He is the son of a very respectable man who had the management of all the Pemberley estates for many years, and whose good conduct in the discharge of his trust naturally inclined my father to be of service to him. On George Wickham, who was my father's godson, his kindness was likewise liberally bestowed..."

By the time he finished the story, Elizabeth's torment had grown considerably. She was mortified at how despicably she had acted three days ago; upon neither Mr. Wickham nor Mr. Darcy could she think without being ashamed of herself. She could not reconcile herself with the benevolence she had bestowed upon Mr. Wickham from the first moment of their meeting and the injustice she had heaped on Mr. Darcy — and would have continued to heap on him if not for their accidental meeting three days earlier. She could not meet Mr. Darcy's eyes, but she braved a quick glance in her father's direction in order to read his reaction to the gentleman's tale.

Mr. Bennet, however, was not in the same way impressed. As his opinion about either man was never as bad or good as was Elizabeth's, this revelation was not a surprise to him. Yes, Wickham proved to be a cheating scoundrel who tried to deceive them all and mostly tried to deceive his Lizzy, but that was something Mr. Bennet would think about... tomorrow in his library. For now, he was pleased to be done with this.

However, Darcy continued to speak, pacing the room, and Mr. Bennet followed him with his eyes, impressed by the young man's changed appearance. Clearly, he was burdened by an immense weight and had more to tell.

"Last summer Wickham again most painfully gained my notice as he tried to impose himself on a young lady of my family who was then but fifteen. Wickham persuaded her to believe herself in love and to consent to an elopement. His chief object was unquestionably the young lady's fortune, which is considerable, but I cannot help supposing that the hope of revenging himself on me was a strong inducement.

Had he been successful, his revenge would have been complete indeed."

He again stopped for few moments, breathing deeply in an attempt to calm himself. "Mr. Bennet, Miss Bennet, of everything I have said I can put at your disposal proofs and documents to attest to their veracity."

Darcy's latest part of the story affected Mr. Bennet more than he would expect. He fully remembered Darcy's words from three days earlier about the necessity of knowing the whole truth in order to be able to protect one's family. For the first time, Mr. Bennet began to think of the burden that must have been on this young man's shoulders since his father died five years before. He could not help but go to him and stroke him on the back in a show of support. "That will not be necessary, Mr. Darcy. We are very grateful for your trust in us and assure you of our secrecy."

Then, without completely understanding why he was making such an unthinkable gesture, Mr. Bennet went slowly to the door, looking pointedly at both Elizabeth and her companion.

"Well... I am quite illuminated for the moment. Lizzy, in case you have further questions, do ask them quickly. Supper is about to start, and I shall wait for you at the table shortly." With that, he left the library, closing the door behind him.

Elizabeth and Mr. Darcy remained behind in amazed silence, hardly believing that they were left alone. Finally, she succeeded in recovering and broke the silence, her voice trembling, barely daring to hold his gaze.

"Mr. Darcy, I cannot tell you how sorry I am for what I said before and for believing Mr. Wickham so unconditionally when he first told me his story. I shall never forgive myself for being so — "

"Miss Bennet, I shall not hear any of this." He smiled warmly in order to reassure her and moved closer. "It would be very sad to know that what I revealed made you uneasy. I just hope that knowing the truth will help you to protect yourself better. Mr. Wickham has always tried to hurt people who are important to me."

He took her hands in his, gazing deeply into her eyes. Startled by this new indirect declaration, Elizabeth lifted her flustered face to him and unconsciously responded to his grip with her own. He whispered, although nobody was in the room but her.

"There is something more I must tell you, Miss Bennet. The young lady I was talking about... it was my own sister, Georgiana. About a year ago, she was taken from school, and an establishment was formed for her in London. Last summer she went with a Mrs. Younge — her companion — to Ramsgate. There also went Mr. Wickham, undoubtedly by design, for there proved to have been a prior acquaintance between him and this Mrs. Younge, in whose character we were most unhappily deceived. Happily, I joined them unexpectedly a day or two before the intended elopement, and Georgiana, unable to support the idea of grieving and offending a brother on whom she looked almost as a father, acknowledged the whole of the matter to me.

You may imagine what I felt and how I acted. I wrote to Mr. Wickham, who left the place immediately, and Mrs. Younge was of course removed from her charge. For months, my major concern was Georgiana's disappointment and despair, the many nights she spent without sleep, crying... I tried earnestly to be of help to her, but I am afraid I did not have much success. She is a little better now and, I hope, will recover completely in time. I pray daily for that."

His grief was so obvious that Elizabeth felt a strong urge to wrap her arms around him and hold him tightly. She knew she could not do so, but she slightly tightened the grip on his hands in compassion and understanding, their gazes steadfast. Slowly, he lifted her hands without loosening the grip and pressed them against his chest.

Elizabeth could feel his chest moving with every breath, every beat of his heart: regular and strong. She desperately tried to say something. Her lips parted to let the words out, but the lump in her throat stopped them. Unconsciously, her breath and her heart changed their rhythm to match his. A soft whisper finally emerged. "I am so sorry..."

Their faces were so close that each could feel the other's warm breath. It made her tremble, and cold shivers froze her neck and travelled wildly down her spine and arms. Her stomach was in a knot. Her breath stopped, waiting.

She was certain he would kiss her and did not know what to do. She could not move — nor did she want to. As if by itself, her flustered face lifted to him a little more; her dry mouth waited, eager to feel for the first time a man's lips on hers — Mr. Darcy's lips. Instead, he inclined his head with the obvious intention of kissing her hands.

She suddenly, hastily withdrew her hands. "No... do not do that!"

At his wondering look, she whispered her reason, mortified. "Earlier, on the balcony... Mr. Wickham kissed my hands. I do not want you to..."

She could not continue; hiding her eyes, her head down, timid and unsure of what to do next, she waited for his reaction.

At first, under the power of his own emotions, Darcy failed to see the meaning of her words as rage and jealousy defeated him. A moment later, her reaction brought him the understanding he needed to know what to do.

He took off his gloves and reached for her hands again, bringing them back to their position near his heart, caressing them lightly with his thumbs. Slowly, never ceasing to search her eyes for a sign of disapproval and prepared to stop if she wanted him to, he nestled her two hands in his left one. With a gentle touch, his right hand slowly removed her gloves, one finger after another with continuous care until her hands were free, uncovered, and bare in his — skin against skin. Her fingers — cold, trembling, and shy — against his — strong, warm, and daring.

Though Elizabeth had memories of their holding hands on the way home three days before, the feeling at this touch was so powerful that it made her knees grow weak, and she almost lost her balance.

Then, while she could do nothing but stare mesmerised at him, his head lowered slowly, and his lips, soft and tentative, pressed against the back of each hand. His eyes searched her face, but nothing there told him to stop. He licked his lips to collect her scent, and then, tenderly, his thumbs never ceasing their strokes, he bestowed a lingering kiss in her palms.

Elizabeth felt she would faint. His lips were wet now yet burning, soft yet strong and gentle yet daring — not just pressing this time but kissing her palms. She closed her eyes, and the last thing she saw were his — also closed. She was now certain she would faint. Desperately seeking support, Elizabeth leaned against him — body against body, but instead of wrapping her in his arms as she expected and desired him to do, he withdrew, putting a little distance between them.

Darcy's emotions were even stronger than hers were — stronger than he had ever experienced before and more difficult to restrain. He had touched, held, and kissed other women's hands before — bare hands — a simple gesture that never aroused any sensation in him except, perhaps, a slight pleasure. He had touched and held Elizabeth's hands just a few days earlier on their way back from the cottage, but then the gesture was mostly protective.

But what had just passed between them was pure, blissful intimacy. He had crossed the limits of propriety, and he was fully aware of it; astonishingly, she had allowed it. She trusted him enough to allow this breach of propriety, and he did not fail to understand the meaning of her acceptance.

The taste of her skin on his lips aroused the most exquisite sensation in him — passion, desire and need of a kind that could take full control of him were his honour not strong enough to resist. It was his duty and responsibility to control himself and his feelings; he could not betray her trust. Darcy separated from her reluctantly, every fibre of his body screaming for her closeness. He knew only too well that, if he did not stop that instant, he would have a difficult time maintaining proper behaviour.

"Miss Bennet, I think we should go now; your father is expecting us shortly." He smiled, trying to ease the tension.

She only nodded as Mr. Darcy began to put her gloves back on with caring, protective and lingering moves, their hands touching. It was as though they did not want to separate from each other. The intensity of the moment and its meaning evaporated Elizabeth's every rational thought. She watched their joined hands as though she were hypnotised, happy but embarrassed, pleased but deeply ashamed by what had just passed between them.

Before Mr. Darcy released her hands, he added softly, "Miss Bennet, I should like very much to call on you tomorrow if that would be acceptable to you."

She knew her face was red with pleasant anticipation at his request, and she liked so much the feeling of his hand holding hers. She could not conquer her nervousness enough to face him, though she was attempting to regain her composure.

She whispered, "I should like that very much, Mr. Darcy."

They walked together to the door, their arms brushing lightly.

"Thank you. I shall look forward to it. Shall we return now?"

"Yes, thank you. I shall go into the ballroom first."

She cast a last glance towards him and left the room. Darcy breathed deeply and smiled contentedly to himself, suddenly anxious to see her again. *Hopefully, this will happen very soon.*

On her way to the ballroom, Elizabeth met her father.

"Are you all right, Lizzy?"

She looked at him, blushing. "Yes, I am. Thank you, Papa."

"Very well then; let us enter. And I am begging you, Lizzy: no more stories tonight! I am an old man, my child." She began to laugh, grateful to her father for his understanding and attempt to cheer her.

Mr. Bennet and his daughter entered the dining room, searching for their names on the cards. Elizabeth was happy to find herself situated near Jane, who was at Mr. Bingley's right. Across from Jane were Sir William and Lady Lucas and then her parents, followed by Mrs. Long and Col. Forster. On her side of the table were a few empty chairs, and then, toward the middle of the table, Lydia, Kitty and Maria Lucas were across from some young officers — Mr. Wickham among them — all of them already improperly talking and laughing quite loudly. From the opposite end of the table, Miss Bingley and Mrs. Hurst were watching the whole exchange with a superior dignity and great enjoyment.

Elizabeth took a glass of water to cool herself and began to speak with Jane, flustered and embarrassed by the feeling that everybody knew what had just happened between her and Mr. Darcy.

Her uneasiness increased on seeing the man himself enter only a few minutes later and taking the chair to her right.

"I believe this is my place."

Chapter 8

He bowed politely to everyone in attendance and took his seat while asking for a glass of wine. Elizabeth turned her head to him and dared to lift her eyes to meet his.

"This is indeed a surprise, Mr. Darcy."

"Yes, it is, Miss Bennet, and a very fortunate one, I might add."

She raised her brow at him questioningly, but Mr. Darcy kept his usual countenance, exchanged a quick glance with Mr. Bingley, smiled politely at her, and then turned his attention to his plate.

Elizabeth gradually succeeded in regaining her composure. She was acutely aware of Mr. Darcy's closeness, and initially every move he made seemed to be intentionally in her direction. She startled each time, afraid that he might touch her hand or lean closer to her.

But of course, Mr. Darcy did none of this. They were at the table under the scrutiny of many eyes, and he could not possibly do anything to precipitate gossip about them. His responsibility and sense of protection over her were as strong as his tender feelings.

If not for some light conversation and tentative smiles between them and their previous dance together, everyone at the table would have been of the opinion that Mr. Darcy's behaviour towards Elizabeth was the same as ever, if perhaps more polite. Even Mr. Bennet, monitoring them closely at the sight of their being seated together — and certain that this could not have been a coincidence — found nothing wanting in Mr. Darcy's proper behaviour.

The first course was served, and while they enjoyed the meal, a light and agreeable conversation ensued. On the other side of Darcy was Miss Charlotte Lucas, a very pleasant companion even for Darcy; unfortunately, near her was situated Mr. Collins, grateful for the good fortune of being so close to both Lady Catherine's nephew and such a charming young lady as Miss Lucas. Darcy was at least content that Wickham was too far away to address Elizabeth directly. He was paying diligent attention to his plate of food while listening to Elizabeth talk with her sister and her friend.

Sir William began a detailed story of his presentation at the Court of St James's, and Darcy was sure the display was mostly for him. As proof of this, a moment later Sir William asked whether Darcy went often to St James's and how he enjoyed life in town. He also pointed out to Darcy that he also would have liked a house in town but was not sure this would be good for Lady Lucas's health.

As much as Darcy's mood might have changed in the last days, he was not a social person and did not want to be engaged in such a conversation with Sir. William. In truth, he did not want to be involved in any kind of conversation except with Elizabeth and perhaps a few other people in the room. Still, he tried to give a neutral answer, saying he did not spend much time in town.

"And when I am in town, I do not attend many social events," he added as politely as possible.

"That is true," agreed Bingley. "We can hardly convince him to leave his house, and if he does leave, it is only to go to the theatre or the opera."

"We also enjoy going to the theatre when we are in town visiting our aunt and uncle," said Jane in a low voice, trying to join Mr. Bingley in the conversation. "And they always gave us so much joy by taking us to premieres or other important events."

"Yes," added Elizabeth, eager to encourage a topic in which Darcy would be comfortable participating, "but unfortunately we are rarely in town and miss the many wonderful spectacles I should very much like to see."

"Well then, Miss Bennet, Miss Elizabeth, if I should happen to be in town, I should be more than happy to escort you to the theatre or to any other event you wish to attend," offered Bingley charmingly.

"Thank you, sir," was Jane's shy answer — actually more of a whisper.

"Indeed, Mr. Bingley," Mrs. Bennet intervened, "we all thank you. We are more than grateful to you. Do you happen to have a box of your own?"

"No, Mrs. Bennet, but Darcy has one, and I am sure he will oblige us."

"Of course, Mrs. Bennet, I should be delighted to have you as my guests when you are next in town," offered Darcy politely, but he could not help picturing himself with the noisy Bennet family in his box.

Well, if Elizabeth and I can be in some other place, I should not mind.

"Oh, Mr. Darcy, that is very gentlemanlike of you, too, sir," exclaimed Mrs. Bennet enthusiastically enough to be noticed by the whole room.

The discussion continued about the subject of art with little input from Darcy — who was only too happy to be close to Elizabeth — until they both startled at the sound of Mr. Wickham's loud voice, which drew the attention of all those around him.

"Miss Elizabeth, as you are so fond of theatre and have missed so many plays, you should ask Mr. Darcy for more details about this pastime. I have heard that he is a great expert on the subject, although I am not quite sure that you both would share the same tastes."

Darcy nearly choked on his food. He remained stunned for few moments, unable to decide whether he should respond or merely strangle Wickham that instant. He was inclined to do the latter, but before he could react, he heard Elizabeth answering sharply while she smiled charmingly.

"Thank you very much for your advice and for your concern regarding my improvement, Mr. Wickham. I shall do that, and I can only hope that Mr. Darcy will have enough time to spare for answering my questions." Having said that, she turned to Darcy and waited for his answer.

"I shall be more than happy to do that, Miss Elizabeth. And, after having the pleasure of talking to you previously, I trust I can safely say that indeed we do share the same tastes regarding our passions for art and culture."

Not for a second did Darcy look in Wickham's direction, although he could feel his impertinent gaze. He swallowed more wine, trying to calm himself, and Elizabeth's composure gave him a little comfort. She seemed quite relaxed and smiled at him. Darcy was content to see her pleased.

But Elizabeth was neither calm nor relaxed. In fact, she was full of rage in the face of Mr. Wickham's new proof of unworthiness and ungentlemanlike behaviour toward her by his insistence upon a subject she had told him specifically she did not wish to discuss. He was offending not only Mr. Darcy — who was the primary target of his attack — but also herself by broaching such an outrageous subject, which no gentleman should discuss in front of a lady.

She was also bothered by Mr. Darcy's reaction, which only confirmed that her suspicions were correct and that perhaps some truth did exist in Mr. Wickham's story. Nevertheless, considering the difference between what he had told her about his relationship with Mr. Darcy and what was actually true, she drew the conclusion that Mr. Wickham once more was trying to transform the situation into a villainous attack on Mr. Darcy. With these thoughts in mind, she managed to maintain her good spirits, deciding to enjoy as much as she could the remains of the evening and the pleasant company around her. She smiled at Mr. Darcy and tried to look as serene as possible.

Mr. Bennet watched the entire exchange and the reactions of the three participants. He began to wonder what it was about, but stopped after only a few moments, conceding that he really was not interested. *What if, heaven forbid, there is another story?! I do not want to hear another one! Two stories in one night — and a ball — are much more than I can bear!*

He took a gulp of wine and began to scrutinise Mr. Wickham more carefully. Mr. Bennet did not give much consideration to Mr. Wickham's behaviour toward Mr.

Darcy — that was Mr. Darcy's business to take care of — but that man had constantly been upsetting his Lizzy lately. That *was* his problem, and Mr. Bennet suddenly decided that some inquiries over the next days about Mr. Wickham — in town and in the regiment — were in order.

As supper progressed, Elizabeth grew more uneasy and less capable of enjoying herself; her family appeared to have made an agreement to expose themselves to ridicule as much as they could. Lydia and Kitty were laughing and flirting shamelessly with the officers, and Mrs. Bennet was talking far too loudly with Mrs. Long and Lady Lucas, while Mr. Bennet only smiled ironically at them from time to time.

If the exhibition had escaped Bingley's notice, the same could not be said for Darcy, whose gaze was drawn to them in a silent contempt that Elizabeth easily read on his face. Even if Darcy considered Mr. Bennet an educated man and very agreeable company — and was grateful to him for his understanding and support — he could not agree with him about the way he was treating his family, content to laugh at his silly, youngest daughters and exuberant wife without making any attempt to correct them. In Darcy's opinion, it was not a marriage as it should be, and his was not proper behaviour for a father and head of the household.

A very annoying moment occurred when Bingley asked for some music and Miss Mary Bennet offered herself. She finished the first song without any indication of freeing the place at the instrument until she was stopped by her father as she started a second selection. Then, when Mrs. Hurst began to play shortly thereafter, Mrs. Bennet engaged Mrs. Long in a shrill conversation about Miss Bennet and Bingley, stating overtly that an alliance between them would expose her girls to other gentlemen of fine breeding and wealth.

Darcy attempted to ignore the scene before him as he could see from the corner of his eye how Elizabeth cast worried glances in his direction. Indeed, thought Darcy, she had every reason to be embarrassed as Mrs. Bennet's behaviour was completely improper, and though he could understand her efforts to find proper husbands for her daughters, her lack of sense and decorum could not be forgiven so easily. He leaned slightly towards Elizabeth, smiling, and was about to ask her something — anything — just to distract her and show her that he did not blame her for her family's behaviour.

Yet, in the next second, Elizabeth's already crimson face turned from red to white when Mrs. Bennet declared how nice a man Mr. Collins was and how much he admired her second daughter.

"However," continued Mrs. Bennet, "Lizzy seems to favour Mr. Darcy more, which is a very wise turn: such a tall and handsome gentleman... and ten thousand a year! Lizzy was always very clever."

Elizabeth was so shocked and startled that her reaction made Darcy lose the hold on his glass and, as a result, he spilled the wine on himself. He rose to his feet instantly, while Elizabeth, not daring to look at him, was wishing and praying she could disappear into the floor forever.

Darcy tried to calm her, assuring her gently that there was no reason to worry, as he would simply change his clothes. He retired as discreetly as he could, but the damage had been done; there were few among the guests who had not noticed the scene, a fact that made Miss Bingley deeply satisfied with the evening.

Darcy felt angry, offended and humiliated by Mrs. Bennet's outrageous behaviour. He had been pushed beyond any acceptable limits of civility. He could well imagine that this was the way she spoke and thought about him within her house, but to speak aloud in that manner while he was within hearing was unthinkable!

In any other circumstances, he would retire and never accept that person's company again. *Unfortunately, she is Elizabeth's mother,* he thought with chagrin. Elizabeth's embarrassment and consequent grief pained him even more than his own distress.

This supper, which he had waited for with pleasurable anticipation, turned out very badly indeed; Wickham's impertinence, Sir William's boring conversation, everybody's eyes scrutinising his behaviour and, finally, Mrs. Bennet and her comments, ruined what could have been a most delightful and agreeable time for both him and Elizabeth.

Thinking of her, he put his own hurt feelings aside, imagining how dreadfully she must have felt with all the laughter around her and Miss Bingley's contemptuous, self-satisfied smile; no doubt her tongue was already spreading sharp comments about the Bennet family. He knew all too well that his prolonged absence would only raise more talk and increase Elizabeth's embarrassment, and she did not deserve that. In a great hurry, he called for his servant and changed his clothes as quickly as he could, intent upon returning downstairs for the remainder of supper.

Before re-entering the supper room, he decided to escape for a few minutes outside the house in order to calm himself and regain his stoic patience before having to face his table companions again. The night was serene, and he took a few steps into the yard, remaining there to admire the stars. *I should bring Elizabeth to see these wonderful stars; she would be enchanted.*

Suddenly, his attention was caught by male voices piercing the night's silence from the corner of the house. He turned to leave, in order not to intrude on someone's private conversation, until he recognised the voices.

"Wickham, you are becoming quite boring with all your talk of Miss Elizabeth. Can you change the subject to something more interesting?"

"You are a fool, Denny! Miss Elizabeth is a very interesting subject, but you are not clever enough to understand it."

"Oh, spare me! She is handsome, I admit, but not the handsomest woman around.

And she is far too outspoken, has a terribly sharp tongue and no dowry at all. I would never marry a woman like her."

"Neither would I, Denny. On that, we are in complete agreement. However, a man can have many other interests in a woman apart from marriage."

"Well," added Sanderson, "Darcy seems to find her interesting, too. There must be something about her — "

"Exactly, Sanderson," answered Wickham more to himself. "Never in my life have I seen Darcy show such attention to a woman and accept so graciously the offences associated with her. You know," continued he, as though he were telling a good joke, "there have been so many young, pretty ladies around him who tried to gain his attention since he was 18, but he only looked at them to find fault. He was so ridiculous with his solemnity and sense of honour. One might suspect he has no interest in women at all."

"Well, maybe he has not," laughed Denny. "I have heard about some gentlemen having other... preferences in this area — "

"Oh, that is not his case, as far as I know. He is too ridiculously moral to enjoy all the pleasures his situation and fortune offer him. Would I have been in his place... So you see, Denny, there must be something very special about Miss Elizabeth Bennet to make Darcy act so... lively. She is charming and witty, and her figure is very attractive and no doubt tempting, but she is just a country girl. I have seen him surrounded by far more beautiful women with better connections and fortunes, but he showed merely the slightest interest. So what is it that is sustaining his attention?"

"Perhaps he just wants to have some diversion with a pretty girl. Maybe her lack of connection is precisely what is appealing for him. He can take his pleasure with her and then leave," said Denny, laughing again.

"Yes, perhaps; thinking back to that story about him encountering her in the storm, I am tempted to agree with you. Meeting in the wood in the storm and, according to Miss Lydia, with their clothes muddy... I would wager that Darcy just discovered how delightful nature can be if one has the proper company." All three burst into laughter so loud that Darcy was certain that, were it not for the music, they would have been heard from inside the house.

"Still," continued Wickham, "if that is the case, could he be so stupid as to accompany her home afterwards? I doubt that very much. And let us think of this evening; he certainly would not show such an obvious and public interest in her in a room full of people — not to mention in front of her family — if all he wanted was some pleasurable private time with her. I am sure there is something more, and that makes Miss Elizabeth Bennet all the more interesting to me in many ways." They began to laugh together and added something in a lower voice that Darcy was unable to make out.

As disturbed as he was by all he had overheard, his calm almost at the edge of his limits, Darcy felt an overwhelming rage take control of him. He felt a savage need for physical release — a wild desire to cause pain to those men. The feeling was so powerful that it frightened him; these men pushed him beyond the limits of his civility. He breathed deeply a few times, clenching his jaw and his fists in an effort to calm himself; he could not allow himself to be drawn beyond those limits. He moved forward until he appeared within sight of the three men, his voice reverberating like thunder.

"Good evening, gentlemen!"

His sudden appearance was such a shock that they instinctively reacted by taking a few steps backward. Though his face was lighted only by the moon, Darcy's countenance projected a dangerous disposition that none of them could fail to notice.

"Good evening, Mr. Darcy," answered Denny, obviously embarrassed, wondering how much of their conversation Darcy had overheard.

Wickham's shock was even greater, and he could not articulate a single a word; that Darcy was outraged was obvious to him. It was the first time since the Ramsgate incident that Darcy was actually addressing him. In their previous encounter, not one word had been directed to him. He shortly regained his composure though, and when he spoke, his response did not hold any trace of embarrassment

"Mr. Darcy, what a surprise. Do you want to join in our conversation? We were just talking about the lovely Bennet family."

"Wickham, I have no desire to join you in any conversation you may be having, especially one that dishonours your positions as officers and as men."

"Mr. Darcy — " Denny tried to interject, but Darcy stopped him fiercely.

"Lieutenant Denny, do not insult me more by presuming you could possibly find an excuse for your offensive words. And I strongly advise you not to trifle with me. I am not a patient man. Your friend, Mr. Wickham, should have told you that. I have a disagreeable temper and a resentful character. I should not hesitate to use my wealth and connections to ruin you all for far less than what you have done. At the end of this ball, I can easily have you lose your present commissions and be unable to secure others anywhere in England. Then you would have plenty of time to spend in moronic jokes and dishonourable gossip."

His cold, poignant words were spoken neither in anger nor in haste. He was not especially menacing, but simply informed them of what they could expect as a result of his ire. None of them doubted the solemnity of his statement. An evening of high jinks could cost them more than Sanderson or Denny was willing to lose. Sanderson decided to make any effort required to repair their earlier mischief.

"Mr. Darcy, you are correct in everything you said. Our behaviour has been unacceptable, and our only excuse might be that we overly indulged ourselves in Mr. Bingley's fine wine. I hope I have my friends' consent when I say we are ready to apologise and offer you any satisfaction you might consider appropriate. We acted preposterously and are ashamed of that, I can assure you."

Darcy stared at him a few long moments, making Sanderson shift from one foot to the other, like a child waiting for his punishment. He had acted like a boy, and Darcy had treated him like one.

"Mr. Sanderson, you should not speak for your friends; they seem to have tongues — which are quite poisoned, I might say — and can speak for themselves. Or am I wrong?"

"Come, Darcy, you cannot talk to us in this manner! We are officers in His Majesty's militia, not children to be censured!" Wickham's voice lost none of its initial impertinence, as he knew Darcy incapable of any indiscretion leading to public scandal.

"Are you really officers, Wickham? If not for your uniforms, your complete lack of honour and morality would have deceived me. If I had considered you gentlemen and officers, I should have treated you honourably and solved the problem in a gentlemanly manner. But your behaviour proved to me that you are indeed nothing more than boys in need of discipline, and I am considering the best way to teach you respect and manners."

"Wickham, please! Mr. Darcy, I beg you to tell us what we can do to end the unpleasant situation we have created, here and now. You must believe that, though our words have been outrageously offensive, our intentions are nothing but honourable."

"Mr. Sanderson, again I advise you to speak for yourself; for your friends' intentions you should not wager. Fortunately, your ridiculous, childish jokes and thoughtless words cannot offend. I have too little respect for you to be offended." He was insulting and humiliating them, as he had never done to anyone before, but he still thought it was too little.

"But you deliberately offended a young lady with irreproachable character who has never been other than kind to you. You were guests in her father's house, and I trust you have been welcomed there every time. You were treated as friends, and yet you repay their affability by maligning Miss Elizabeth. What would you call such behaviour, Mr. Sanderson? And what would Colonel Forster call it? Should we perhaps ask his opinion?"

Sir—?"

"However, as I have no desire to waste any more time with you, I shall attempt to forget everything I heard, as long as no vile talk tarnishes Miss Elizabeth's reputation. However, at the first malicious word against her, you may as well start looking for another way to support your existence."

"But sir…" Denny tried at that moment to intervene. "You cannot hold us responsible for every rumour! It is possible that rumours or gossip may be spread without our even knowing it."

"I can and will hold you responsible. I shall not trouble myself overmuch to search for the truth. These are my conditions. I shall not show you any more consideration than you have shown me."

"I see…" Denny looked from Darcy to his companions and back again to Darcy, but it was Sanderson who spoke again.

"Very well, sir. I beg you to accept our sincere apologies and be assured that none of us would ever repeat these unhappy remarks about you or Miss Bennet, whose behaviour indeed has always been honourable and polite."

Lieutenant Denny nodded his agreement and started to formulate his own excuses, but Darcy interrupted him harshly.

"Let us not waste our time with this conversation. I should like to speak privately with Mr. Wickham if he would indulge me."

"Well, I am afraid that will have to wait. I have no wish to abandon my friends." He was smiling recklessly at Darcy, made confident by being three against one and knowing Darcy to be incapable of either using physical violence or making a public spectacle, despite his just threatened menacing.

But neither Denny nor Sanderson were in the mood to meddle in the conflict between Wickham and his old acquaintance or to raise Darcy's anger more than they already had.

"Do not mind us, Wickham. In any case, we were about to enter the house."

They hastily left, and Wickham, shocked at being abandoned, tried to follow them; he was stopped by Darcy's firm grasp of his forearm.

"Not so hasty, Wickham! We have to discuss an interesting subject as you yourself said before."

"I do not know of what you are speaking, Darcy. And now if you will excuse me, I must return — "

"You will go nowhere, Wickham, until I am done with you. Do not make me lose all my patience and force you to stay," whispered Darcy harshly, without loosening his grip on Wickham's arm.

By now Wickham was indeed shocked; he had known Darcy for many years but had never heard nor ever seen him behave in any way other than entirely proper and composed, no matter how upset or angry he might have been. An aggressive Darcy was something new and disturbing, and he made Wickham most uncomfortable. A direct confrontation between them was not wanted and could be dangerous.

"No need for that, Darcy. I will listen to you if you will release my arm."

Darcy did so reluctantly and posted himself in front of Wickham, obstructing his path back to the house. The two men merely looked at each other a few moments in silence. Darcy knew that, if the smallest part of what he was feeling was visible on his face, he must appear quite savage.

Finally, Wickham diverted his gaze and began to formulate an explanation, but Darcy fiercely cut off his words.

"I have no desire to listen to your lies, Wickham, but you should listen to me carefully because I shall only say this once. I do not want to see you anywhere near the Bennet family; I do not want you to speak a single impolite word about Miss

Elizabeth, and I do not want you to address her further except to show her the usual courtesy. Do you understand me?"

He was not angry, but he spoke with a cold, calm voice. He was steady and determined, standing very close to Wickham and looking directly at him.

"I am still indebted to you Wickham — not with the living you implied I owe you, but with the proper reward for what you did last summer. You should know me well enough by now to realise that I — unlike you — always pay my debts. Do not make the mistake of increasing my ire with your improper behaviour. Do not make me impatient to pay you back."

For the first time in his dealings with Darcy, Wickham felt a shiver of fear. His only thought at that moment was to extricate himself from Darcy and return safely to the house full of people.

"Darcy, do not be so upset. We made some comments about Miss Elizabeth, I will admit, but it was all harmless. You know how men talk — "

"I know nothing about the kind of men of whom you speak, Wickham, and I have no interest in knowing them. I just want to know if you accept my terms."

"Yes, yes, Darcy, I accept. Now may I go inside? I am freezing out here! It is almost winter for God's sake."

Darcy made a slight gesture, indicating he could proceed, and followed Wickham's quick pace with an incredulous glare. He knew very well that Wickham could not be trusted, but at least for that evening he would behave himself. As for the next day... Measures would indeed be required.

As soon as he entered the house, Darcy realised he had been absent for almost an hour, and Elizabeth's lovely presence was exactly what he needed to calm himself. However, she seemed quite dispirited at the moment and, after he resumed his place by her, continued to eat the last course in silence. She was not desirous to speak with or even look at him. After supper, Elizabeth retreated to a corner, still grieved, mortified with shame, and anticipating nothing more for herself. She knew that, had Mr. Darcy any serious intentions toward her earlier, all hope must surely be lost after the last horrible hour.

Jane drew near, attempting with little success to comfort her. A few moments later, to Elizabeth's utter surprise, she saw both Mr. Bingley and Mr. Darcy moving in their direction, smiling politely. A pleasant conversation arose about the dinner, both Jane and Mr. Darcy congratulating Mr. Bingley on the evening's arrangements.

Gaining her courage, Jane asked Mr. Bingley about his imminent departure for London. Elizabeth took the opportunity of relative privacy and turned to Mr. Darcy, barely daring to lift her eyes to him.

"Mr. Darcy, I am so sorry for what my mother said! I can only imagine how offended you must have felt. Please allow me to apologise on her behalf as I am sure she meant no harm."

He looked at her intently until, finally meeting her eyes, he answered her cogently with no attempt to conceal his opinion.

"I shall not deny that Mrs. Bennet's remarks were offensive to me although it is not the first time I have heard something of the kind. I am somewhat accustomed to being talked of in that manner."

Elizabeth's embarrassment was beyond anything she remembered having experienced in her life, and she could only guess what he might think about her and her mother. She tried to be brave and hold his gaze, but her cheeks burned red. When she thought that nothing could be said to make her more self-conscious, she heard him lower his already deep voice.

"However, I must confess it was comforting to know I was preferred to Mr. Collins after you told me only two days ago that there were few people whose presence you would not prefer to mine."

She gaped at him open-mouthed, too shocked to speak. *He is teasing me! And more, he is flirting with me again when I thought he would be upset and never speak to me again.*

As if entirely to confirm her thoughts, he added, "But I do have a question, Miss Bennet. While you obviously favour me for my ten thousand a year, could the fact that I am tall and handsome — as Mrs. Bennet kindly pointed out — have influenced you in any way?" He arched his brow, and Elizabeth quickly covered her mouth to prevent a peal of laughter from escaping.

A small grin was hidden at the corner of his mouth, his eyes betraying his merry disposition as he awaited her answer. She coloured further but decided to accept his challenge and gave a small, shy smile. Biting her lower lip, her eyes sparkled with mirth.

"Indeed it has, sir, together with the fact that you are such a skilful dancer and a man without fault."

"I am pleased to hear that, Miss Bennet. And dare I hope for the favour of a second dance? The last set, perhaps?"

"It would be a pleasure, Mr. Darcy. Thank you."

Elizabeth knew that his manner of speaking to her was not an impertinent display but an effort to overlook the appalling moment created by her mother, and she was deeply grateful to him. They stared at each other, their eyes speaking of the mutual support and help they had shared that eventful night. No words were needed; their silent understanding was complete.

Elizabeth and Mr. Darcy spent the remainder of the night in close company whenever they had the opportunity, mostly with Jane and Mr. Bingley, and occasionally with Mr. Bennet. She danced another two sets, one with Mr. Bingley and the other with Charlotte's brother, while Mr. Darcy asked Jane and Mrs. Hurst to stand up with him.

When it was time for the last set, Darcy was anxious to enjoy the pleasure of her exclusive company once more. He could talk to her, touch her slightly and hold her hands a moment longer than he should. To his delightful surprise, Darcy began to understand what it meant to feel alone with a woman in a room full of people. He saw her blushing under his gaze and knew she shared the same feeling. They were solitary figures in the midst of the crowd. No one and nothing else mattered at that moment — only the music, which enveloped them and wrapped their senses in its spell.

When the ball ended, the Bennets were the last guests to leave, and Mr. Bingley and Mr. Darcy helped the ladies into their carriage as raindrops once more began to fall. Mrs. Bennet expressed their hope that Mr. Bingley would have a safe journey, and Mr. Bennet renewed an invitation to Mr. Darcy for dinner.

As soon as the guests departed, both gentlemen excused themselves and retired directly to their rooms, avoiding Miss Bingley's constant tirade about the Bennets and how tiresome the ball had been.

From their windows, Bingley and Darcy each tried to catch a final glimpse of the carriage departing through the rain for Longbourn.

Chapter 9

Elizabeth Bennet thought November 27 would be one of the happiest days of her life. She woke quite late for her, smiling happily, her soul full of joy.

A rude blast of rain hit her window with frightening power, and she hid herself under the blankets, while pleasurable memories of the hours spent in a cottage four days earlier overtook her.

With a gentle knock on the door, Jane entered smiling at her. "Good morning, lazy one. I cannot remember when you were last in bed at this hour. Did you sleep well?"

"Good morning, my sweet Jane. No. Truth to tell, I did not sleep very well, for I have dreamt all night long. But they were wonderful dreams."

She indeed looked very pleased, and it was not difficult to imagine the reason for her happiness. "I am glad to see you so happy, Lizzy."

Her voice immediately caught Elizabeth's attention. "Jane, is something wrong? You seem upset."

"I am not upset, it is just that ... "

"What is it, dearest, please tell me?"

Jane tried to avoid a direct answer, but a new inquiry from her sister convinced her to reveal the truth. "I was looking at this dreadful rain and could not help being worried about Mr. Bingley. I know London is not far away, but the weather is so bad and the roads ... Something horrible might happen."

"Oh, Jane, please do not think like that! I am sure Mr. Bingley will return very soon, and all your worries will make his coming back to you even more wonderful."

Jane blushed deeply at her sister's words and closed her eyes for a second to imagine that so-awaited moment. "I hope you are right, Lizzy. You know, the road to our house is already awash."

Elizabeth jumped off the bed and went to the window; the view of the road under water made her heart throb. She suddenly understood better her sister's fear for Mr.

Bingley's safety. As Jane left the room, Lizzy began to dress herself; she soon joined her family at the breakfast table where everybody was in animated discussion about the ball. As soon as she entered, Mrs. Bennet's attention turned to her.

"Lizzy, my child, I must confess I was very proud of you last night. You looked so beautiful and danced so well. Your whole appearance must have been suitably fashionable for a man like Mr. Darcy to notice you and bestow such particular attention upon you."

"Mama, I thank you, but I am sure you are exaggerating. I looked just as I always do, and Mr. Darcy was only being nice to dance with me."

Elizabeth blushed at her own lie and dared a glance at her father, only to see him hiding a wry smile behind his napkin. She turned her attention to her plate and began to eat in silence.

The hours passed, and the weather seemed to turn even worse.

With every minute, Elizabeth became more restless. From the moment she departed Netherfield after the ball, she was anticipating seeing Mr. Darcy again at dinner and was already fantasising about their exchanged glances, smiles, and teasing conversation. With her book open in her lap, she allowed her thoughts to fly back to the Netherfield library, almost feeling his touch on her hands and his lips on her palms, and the simple memory made her heart leap.

She remembered how he flirtatiously teased her about why she was favouring him while they danced together. She remembered his voice whispering to her, *"Wickham always tries to hurt people who are important to me…"*

Feeling her cheeks becoming red and warm, she excused herself, retired to her room and threw herself onto the bed, embracing the pillow. She could allow herself, finally, to admit that she was infatuated with Mr. Darcy! The thought of him brought forth feelings she had never known before, sensations she experienced not only when he was near her but also when he was far away. His presence and his absence made her equally unsettled, and his features, touch and smell were deeply embedded in her mind and soul. Was this love? She could not be certain after only a few days, but she knew she could think of nothing except him.

She hoped that he would come to call despite the horrible weather, but she prayed that he was wise enough *not* to come and put himself in danger.

He did not come, and soon the road to Longbourn was entirely submerged. The rain eventually stopped the next morning, but the muddied road remained impassable for another day. At last, on November 29, carriages could reach Longbourn with minor difficultly, and while John prepared for Mr. Bennet to go to Meryton, the Bennets received callers.

The first to arrive were Charlotte and Sir William to spend several hours with the Bennets. Charlotte's company was a balm to Elizabeth and helped her pass the hours easily until Mr. Darcy would call.

Elizabeth knew, without any doubt, that he would call for dinner as he had been expressly invited to do so, so she prepared herself with extra care as she breathlessly anticipated his arrival.

In Mr. Bennet's absence, Sir William engaged himself in conversation with Mr. Collins and graciously invited the parson to dine at Lucas Lodge. As the prospect appealed to him, Mr. Collins secured an invitation for himself for that very day, and Elizabeth did all in her power to encourage him to accept the invitation, thinking Mr. Darcy would be more pleased without his fawning presence.

It was soon afternoon, and they were having refreshments and sharing opinions about the weather when a letter was delivered to Jane. It came from Netherfield, and she opened it immediately. The envelope contained a small sheet of elegant, hot-pressed paper, well covered with a lady's fair, flowing hand. Elizabeth saw her sister's countenance change as she read it and saw her focusing intently on some particular passages.

Sensing her sister's eyes scrutinising her, Jane soon recollected herself and put the letter away. She tried to join in the conversation with her usual cheerfulness, but anxiety affected her ability to attend to the discourse, and she paid little attention to her guests.

Sir William and Charlotte, accompanied by Mr. Collins, took their leave shortly afterwards, and a glance from Jane invited Elizabeth to follow her upstairs. When they were in their own rooms, Jane took out the letter.

"This is from Caroline Bingley. Its contents have surprised me a good deal. The whole party has left Netherfield by this time on their way to town — without any intention of returning. You shall hear what she says."

The shock of this news was so powerful that Elizabeth was forced to sit down and look at her sister in disbelief. Jane read the first sentence aloud, which included the information that Mr. Darcy had left Netherfield together with Mr. Bingley the day following the ball, of their resolution to follow their brother to town directly, and of their intent to dine that day in Grosvenor Street where Mr. Hurst had a house.

While Jane continued to read, Elizabeth forced herself to form no expectation at all of its contents, considering the source of it, but the news did cause her heart to shatter.

She seized the letter from Jane quite roughly and began to read it herself. With amazement did she first understand that Mr. Darcy left together with Mr. Bingley without believing any apology or acknowledgement — if not for her at least for her father — to be necessary.

"As you see, Lizzy, Caroline decidedly says that none of the party will return to Hertfordshire this winter." But Elizabeth did not hear Jane, continuing to read the passage that drew her attention most:

Mr. Darcy is impatient to see his sister, and to confess the truth, we are scarcely less eager to meet her again . . . "

"And, Lizzy, did you read the paragraph about Miss Darcy? Does it not expressly declare that Caroline is perfectly convinced of her brother's indifference to me and of his preference for Miss Darcy and she means to put me on my guard? Can there be any other opinions on the subject?"

"Yes there can be. Will you hear them?"

"Most willingly."

"You shall have my opinion using very few words. Miss Bingley sees that her brother is very much in love with you and wants him to marry Miss Darcy. She follows him to town in the hopes of keeping him there and tries to persuade you that he does not care for you. Indeed, Jane, we are not rich enough or grand enough for them, and she is all the more anxious to get Miss Darcy for her brother, hoping one intermarriage would bring a second. But, my dearest Jane, you cannot seriously imagine that Mr. Bingley is less sensible of your merits than he was three days ago when he took leave of you."

Elizabeth was firmly convinced of what she told her sister, and to Miss Bingley's suggestion that her brother soon would be involved in a relationship with Miss Darcy she gave no consideration. Beyond Mr. Bingley's obviously strong attachment and admiration towards Jane, the way Mr. Darcy spoke of his sister never led Elizabeth to understand such a thing. Events of the recent past at Ramsgate were her strongest proof that Miss Darcy had no tender feelings for Mr. Bingley, or she never would have considered eloping with Mr. Wickham. She tried to represent to her sister as forcibly as possible what she felt on the subject and soon had the pleasure of seeing its happy effect. Jane's temper was not despondent, and she gradually let herself hope that Bingley would return to Netherfield and answer every wish of her heart.

But Elizabeth's conviction of Mr. Bingley's return could bring no balm to her own distress and suffering. She still could not believe and even less understand that Darcy also had left and why he would have done such a thing when he explicitly asked for permission to call on her and openly accepted Mr. Bennet's invitation for dinner. She was childishly hoping that Miss Bingley was grossly deceiving them and that Mr. Darcy had never left Netherfield and would still come to call.

Lizzy and Jane agreed that Mrs. Bennet should only hear of the departure of the family without being alarmed with the news of their uncertain return. But even this partial communication gave their mother a great deal of concern, and she bewailed it as being exceedingly unlucky that the ladies should happen to go away just as they were all becoming so intimate. After lamenting it, however, at some length, she had the consolation of thinking that Mr. Bingley would soon come down again and bring Mr. Darcy with him to dine at Longbourn The conclusion of all was the comfortable declaration that, though the gentlemen had been invited only to a family dinner, she would take care to have two full courses.

Mr. Bennet treated the matter quite differently upon hearing the news. Calmly, he expressed regret that he could not have the pleasure of intelligent male conversation at dinner soon and his hope that the business that caused Darcy's departure was not of too serious a nature.

Over the next few days, Charlotte Lucas called again with a new invitation for Mr. Collins, showing an amiable attention to the gentleman to the relief of all his cousins.

But Charlotte's kindness extended farther than Elizabeth had any notion of; its object was nothing else than to secure Mr. Collins's addresses for herself. Such was Miss Lucas's scheme, and appearances were so favourable that, when they parted after the second time Mr. Collins dined at Lucas Lodge, she felt sure of her success. Indeed, his newfound passion led him to escape Longbourn House the next morning and hasten to Lucas Lodge to throw himself at her feet. His reception was of the most flattering kind, and in a short time, everything was settled between him and Miss Lucas to the satisfaction of both. Sir William and Lady Lucas were speedily applied to for their consent, and it was bestowed with a most joyful alacrity.

Charlotte resolved to give the information personally to Elizabeth. She valued her friendship beyond that of any other person and knew Elizabeth probably would not understand her decision. Therefore, on the following morning, Miss Lucas called soon after breakfast and, in a private conference with Elizabeth, related the events of the day before.

For Elizabeth at the age of twenty, the days following Miss Bingley's letter were the most difficult and painful she could remember. She had not slept more than a few hours each night as Mr. Darcy's spectre appeared every time she closed her eyes. Her dreams brought the exquisite and painful feeling of his touch, his lips, his scent, his voice and the intense, dark stare that made her dizzy and sent shivers through her body.

After reading Miss Bingley's letter repeatedly, Elizabeth found that, instead of answers, there were thousands of questions spinning in her head. What possibly could have happened? She perfectly remembered every word between herself and Mr. Darcy from the first day in the cottage until their separation after the ball. She spent hours contemplating what could have made him change his mind so drastically as to forget proper manners — not paying even a short, polite, last call to the family or leaving a departure note for Mr. Bennet.

Each recollection of her family's impropriety in Mr. Darcy's company and every reproach she directed toward him brought memories of his previous contempt, causing her more grief as she came to accept that there were indeed plausible reasons for him to reconsider his intentions towards her once the excitement of the ball had passed. She was fighting both the regret of what she had lost and the vexation caused by his furtive departure, leaving her in a state of depression beyond anything she had known before.

A gentleman who had respect for a lady would never act in such a despicable manner. He would at least announce his change of plans. But he was probably anxious to put as much distance as he could between himself and Hertfordshire.

She did miss him deeply; never could she have imagined that love and longing for a man could be so fierce or that a heart could truly be broken. For indeed, now, when all her love must have been in vain, she understood and accepted with her eyes and her soul weeping, that the feelings that burdened her must have been love.

She dreamed, her eyes open, of his taking her hand again and whispering into her ear. She could smell his scent and feel his nearness... and all she could do was cry in frustration. Though she had not shed tears since she was a child, she felt a need to do so at that moment. She felt desperately alone as she had no one in whom to confide, not wanting to add grief to Jane's suffering or bring additional worry to her family. She came to desire as much as Jane did for Mr. Bingley's return, with or without his friend. She needed to understand what had happened to Mr. Darcy, and if she could not get the answer from the man himself, she could accede to hearing it from his friend.

Elizabeth was in such a poor state of mind and heart that, when Charlotte came to share the news of her engagement to Mr. Collins, Elizabeth's reaction was not what it should have been.

"Engaged to Mr. Collins! My dear Charlotte, impossible!"

The prospect of Mr. Collins's fancying himself in love with her friend had occurred to Elizabeth within the last few days, but that Charlotte would encourage him was unthinkable, and her astonishment was consequently such as to overcome the bounds of decorum.

Elizabeth quickly recollected herself and was able to assure her friend with tolerable honesty that the prospect of their relationship was highly beneficial and that she wished her all imaginable happiness. She had always felt that Charlotte's opinion of matrimony was unlike her own. She could not have supposed it possible that, when called into action, she would have sacrificed every sincere feeling for worldly advantage. Charlotte as the wife of Mr. Collins was a most humiliating picture!

Elizabeth's disappointment in Charlotte made her turn with fonder regard to her sister, of whose rectitude and delicacy she was sure her opinion could never be shaken. Mr. Darcy and Mr. Bingley had now been gone for a week, and nothing was heard of their return; Jane had sent Miss Bingley an early answer and was counting the days until she might reasonably hope to hear from her again.

Day after day passed with no other tidings of the gentlemen than the report, which shortly prevailed in Meryton, of Mr. Bingley's coming no more to Netherfield the whole of that winter.

Almost three weeks after her first, Miss Bingley's second letter arrived and put an end to any lingering doubt. The first sentence conveyed her assurance of their being settled in London for the winter and concluded with her brother's regret at not having had time to pay his respects to his friends in Hertfordshire before he left the country.

Hope was entirely over, and when Jane could attend to the rest of the letter, she found little except the professed affection of the writer that could give her any comfort. Miss Darcy's praise occupied the chief of it. Her many attractions were again dwelt upon, and Caroline boasted joyfully of their increasing intimacy, venturing to predict the accomplishment of the wishes she had unfolded in her former letter. A day passed before the sisters had the courage to speak to each other of their feelings, and each heart was divided between concern for the other sister and her own grief.

Of course, Mrs. Bennet and everyone in town were sensible of Jane's anxiety and could presume how painful it must have been for her. But things were quite different in Elizabeth's case. Except for Jane and Mr. Bennet — if he decided to give the thought any consideration — no one suspected Elizabeth's misery and suffering.

If at the ball everybody could see Mr. Darcy's partiality for her, it was such a brief encounter that it was forgotten at once. No one found it strange that Mr. Darcy had left with his friend, for no one could imagine any reason for Mr. Darcy to remain in the neighbourhood. A preference shown at a ball for a young lady would mean little to a man of his consequence and position in society. Moreover, should the gentleman have had an inclination toward her, Miss Elizabeth Bennet's open dislike for Mr. Darcy was publicly acknowledged for many weeks before the ball, so a change of heart was unlikely; consequently, her feelings on the subject were not considered.

Mr. Wickham was never again a guest at Longbourn nor did he encounter Elizabeth after the ball. Lydia and Kitty met him occasionally in Meryton and brought reports of him back to Longbourn.

Shortly after Mr. Darcy left the neighbourhood, Mr. Wickham's misfortunes were openly acknowledged and publicly canvassed, and Mr. Darcy was condemned as the worst of men. Moreover, a rumour began to circulate that Mr. Darcy was rejected in his attention by Miss Elizabeth for his repulsive behaviour toward her favourite, Mr. Wickham. Meryton was divided into two camps: one applauded Elizabeth's courage in rejecting such an important man despite his fortune and position in society, and the second considered her quite a fool for not taking the opportunity to increase her family's situation substantially. Shortly, these rumours came to Mrs. Bennet's ears.

While Jane used her steady mildness to bear these attacks with tolerable tranquillity, Elizabeth did not. Her passionate nature and sense of guilt intensified her grief more than she could have imagined.

Mrs. Bennet returned from Meryton one morning, shrieking for her smelling salts and demanding Lizzy tell her what she did to Mr. Darcy that made him leave. When she accused her of ruining Jane's happiness and the whole family's well being, Elizabeth could hardly keep her countenance in the face of such a preposterous accusation.

She resigned herself to enduring her mother's diatribe, and when the lady finished, Elizabeth expressed a wish for a short walk. No sooner had she left the house — fighting the cold wind and praying the frozen blow would cool the wound in her heart — than thousands of thoughts started to spin in her head, making her wonder whether her mother was right. Perhaps something she did or said had made Mr. Darcy change his opinion of her, take his unexpected leave, and convince Mr. Bingley to do the same.

Unconsciously, her steps led her to the cottage, and she found herself again before the heavy, old door. She entered and looked around, memories overwhelming her, and she sat in the same armchair as she had days before. She sobbed uncontrollably until she had no tears left and returned only in time for dinner, completely frozen and wanting to see and talk to no one. The person she most longed to see might never cross her path again.

DURING THAT MONTH, MR. BENNET saw the distress of his eldest daughter and the turmoil in the family caused by the departed Netherfield party and some letters sent by Miss Bingley, to which he gave not the slightest consideration. He could easily imagine that Jane and Lizzy felt crossed in love. The idea was highly entertaining and provided an opportunity for constant teasing, he being most amused by his second daughter's behaviour. He never would have imagined his witty, high-spirited favourite to act so foolishly; he joked with them several times, saying it was time for them to be heartbroken and "next to being married, a girl likes to be crossed in love a little now and then."

He had given little thought to the situation and never considered their suffering and distress to be serious as he found nothing alarming in Mr. Darcy and Mr. Bingley's departure and delay in town. However, that evening at dinner was too much for Mr. Bennet with Lizzy's red, swollen eyes, pale face and trembling hands and his wife's continuous complaints about what his favourite daughter did to ruin the entire family.

"Mrs. Bennet, of what are you talking?"

"Oh, about Lizzy and Mr. Darcy, of course. And about Mr. Bingley and Jane. They will all die old maids, and Collins and Charlotte will take our house after your death," she yelled hysterically.

He looked austerely at his wife before speaking in a severe tone.

"Today I have the definitive proof that my dear wife at her age is akin to our youngest daughters, not only in beauty but also in spirit and sagacity! Mrs. Bennet, what were you thinking to spout such nonsense and bring Lizzy to this state of distress? Have you all lost your minds since the ball?"

His angry voice made all the ladies attend to him with great surprise. Lydia could never remember her father speaking before in such a firm manner.

"My dear husband, I was just worrying about our daughters' happiness and well-being. I never meant to offend Lizzy, but she is such a headstrong, wild girl and never listens. And all Meryton talks about — "

"Mrs. Bennet, enough of this! If all Meryton speaks such nonsense, it is immensely comforting to me, for it proves there are many older people even sillier than Lydia and Kitty. Consequently, neither you nor the girls will go to Meryton again soon and certainly not without my consent. And I forbid any of you to spread gossip or speculation about Mr. Bingley or Mr. Darcy. What are you women thinking? Is not a man allowed to go and look after his business and return when and if he chooses without being talked of? From now on, I shall not hear a word of this, do you understand me?"

Six ladies approved silently, none daring to contradict him. With a last disapproving look, he returned to his plate and wine, exhausted but content with his decisiveness. Mr. Bennet was reluctant ever to disturb his peace and tranquillity with a high tone or harsh manners toward his family.

But apparently the situation required it!

The next day, Elizabeth awoke feeling unwell with a bad cold and high fever that lasted the entire week. It was nothing especially serious but, selfishly — and uncharacteristically cowardly — Elizabeth found her illness quite convenient; she could be alone in her room and her bed without calls or reproaches from her mother. She had only her sorrow for company. She and Jane tried to comfort one another, and in a mutual understanding, neither gentleman's name was mentioned between them.

One morning, as Lizzy was in bed and Jane was brushing her hair, Mr. Bennet made his appearance, his countenance jovial and humorous, in one of his obviously teasing dispositions.

"Girls, I wanted to talk to you. I hope I am not interrupting you."

"Of course not, Papa," answered Lizzy. "Please enter and sit down."

He took a chair and searched their curious faces for a few moments, deeply satisfied with the anticipation of his disclosure. "I have received a letter this morning that took me quite by surprise. As it could be of some importance for you, I thought you ought to know some of its contents."

The colour now rushed into his daughters' cheeks, and they moved uncomfortably in anticipation, scarcely allowing themselves to presume or hope.

"You look eager, I must say. Do you have enough sagacity remaining to discover the name of its sender?" He smiled in pure enjoyment at their embarrassment, and as they chose to cast their eyes down at their hands, he put the envelope in front of them, declaring:

"By all means, do not be missish; it is easy to guess. As your fair cousin, Mr. Collins, would have said, such elegant handwriting and superior paper could belong to none other than a nephew of the noble Lady Catherine de Bourgh."

Chapter 10

Elizabeth and Jane stared at their father in utter silence, waiting for him to continue and fearing the worst.

"Well, well... not a word? Am I then to understand that you are not in the least interested in the letter's contents?"

"Papa!" Lizzy's voice was reproachful and impatient. "I beg you; this is not a proper moment for teasing. Read the letter, please."

"Well, if you insist, I shall oblige you this time. Let us see... He begins with apologising and expressing his regret for not being able to attend the dinner invitation after the Netherfield ball... what follows should not interest you... And... yes, this is it:

> *The situation is not yet of a nature to allow me to leave London for the next few weeks, and as Mr. Bingley chose to remain and offer me his support, it is probable that his return to Netherfield also will be delayed for an uncertain amount of time.*

"Then," continued Mr. Bennet, "the next passage again does not pertain to you... And Mr. Darcy ended the letter by expressing his best wishes for our family on behalf of him and Mr. Bingley."

The girls remained unmoved and in disbelief until Elizabeth finally burst out, "That is all, Papa? That was the news you wanted to share with us? What you read explains nothing more than we already knew. Please let us read the whole letter! I can see two whole pages."

"I shall do no such thing, young lady! How can you even suggest it? This passage should have explained many things to my witty Lizzy and my sensible Jane, but apparently neither of you could fathom anything from it."

"Papa!"

"No 'Papa!' Lizzy. I am speaking the truth. Neither of you are being at all clever!

I can understand your distress — I was young once, you know — but can you not apprehend some reason for this situation? Did it never cross your pretty heads that perhaps there was an explanation — a serious one, not the nonsense your mother talks about — that caused the gentlemen to leave in such a hurry?" He arched his eyebrow at his daughters in the same manner that Lizzy so often did.

"You might find this difficult to believe, but even the most deserving and charming gentlemen sometimes have other responsibilities besides entertaining young ladies at dinner."

With that, shaking his head and smiling wryly, he left the room.

The girls remained in silence for a few moments and then began to talk at once. Finally, they concluded that their father was right, and indeed a few morsels might be gleaned from the short passage in his letter.

First, Elizabeth regained a modicum of tranquillity after a month of torment, seeing that at least Mr. Darcy wished to maintain a correspondence with her father, and apparently a private one. It was true that he did not say a word about the cause of his precipitate departure from Netherfield, but he did mention that Mr. Bingley would be delayed a few more weeks, not that he was established in town for the whole winter as Miss Bingley suggested in her letters. They were interrupted by Annie, who asked Lizzy if she felt well enough to join the family downstairs. Lizzy was feeling better than she had the whole of the last month. It was three days before Christmas.

MRS. BENNET HAD THE PLEASURE of receiving her brother and his wife who came to spend Christmas at Longbourn.

Mr. Gardiner was a sensible, gentlemanlike man, superior to his sister in both nature and education. Mrs. Gardiner, who was several years younger than Mrs. Bennet and Mrs. Philips, was an amiable, intelligent, elegant woman and a great favourite with her Longbourn nieces. Between the two eldest and herself there existed a very particular regard.

The first part of Mrs. Gardiner's business on her arrival was to distribute presents and describe the newest fashions in London; when she finished, Mrs. Bennet had a surfeit of grievances to relate and much to complain of.

"I do not blame Jane," she continued, "for Jane would have got Mr. Bingley if she could. But Lizzy! Oh, sister! I do not know what to think..." She continued to relate — in hushed tones so as not to be heard by her husband — that Lizzy's rudeness to Mr. Darcy made him leave.

Mrs. Gardiner, to whom this news previously had been given in the course of Jane and Elizabeth's correspondence, offered her sister a brief answer and attempted to shift the tone of the conversation.

"Oh, dear sister, I am sure that cannot be. Lizzy is a remarkable young lady and never would do something improper or offensive. But let me speak to her, and I shall see what is to be done."

As soon as she was able to secure some time alone with Elizabeth, Mrs. Gardiner brought up the subject again with tender understanding.

"Lizzy dearest, now do tell me everything I should know, will you? I must say I never saw you in such low spirits. I never should expect that of you. I have always thought that, if anything of the kind should happen to you, you would laugh yourself out of it directly."

Lizzy tried to smile, but the sadness in her eyes was so obvious that Mrs. Gardiner caressed her hair in a loving, motherly gesture that caused Lizzy to fall into her arms sobbing.

She held her niece in silence, continuing to stroke her hair until Elizabeth felt calmer and began to talk. For more than an hour, she revealed everything to her aunt: Mr. Wickham, the cottage, the ball, and Mr. Darcy's story. Only her private moments with Mr. Darcy in the library, when he took off her gloves and kissed her hands, were kept in deepest secrecy.

"Dearest, that is quite a story. The Darcys are well known in Derbyshire and much admired; it seems likely to have been a desirable match for you and also for Jane to marry Mr. Bingley. And from what you have told me, there were some most promising inclinations from the gentlemen. I am sorry it went off badly, but these things happen so often! Inconstancies of this type occur frequently in courtship."

"Yes, Aunt, but what gives me the deepest grief is Mr. Darcy's leaving so unexpectedly. He was so kind, so gentlemanlike" — *and so tender* — "and so pleasant until the end of the ball."

"That is indeed surprising."

"You know, Aunt, I have told this to no one, but" — she blushed and cast her eyes down — "I had begun to believe that Mr. Wickham was right and Mr. Darcy never had serious intentions towards me."

"I see... and did you have any reason to believe that? Did Mr. Darcy suggest something improper that prompted you to refuse him?"

"No, Aunt," cried Elizabeth. "Never!"

"Then, from what I have heard, I can only conclude that Mr. Wickham is not a man to be trusted. I advise you to put all his stories aside and think of something else."

"Papa just received a letter from Mr. Darcy, you know..."

"Really? Well, I believe that is indeed good news. What did he say?"

"I do not know for sure; Papa just read us a short passage, but there were some apologies, mention of a situation that would keep him in London for some time and some good wishes to our whole family for Christmas. And apparently he wrote another two pages intended only for Papa."

Mrs. Gardiner took a few moments to think, looking at her beloved niece. She did not want to give Lizzy any false hopes, but neither did she want to see her in such a state and would do anything to cheer her up. "Lizzy, pray tell me, what did my brother

Bennet think about this matter?"

"Papa is constantly teasing us; he said we are neither witty nor sensible."

"I see… Well, dearest, for the moment I would wager this: whatever the reason Mr. Darcy left in haste will be revealed to you in time. He seems to be an honourable man, as was his father, and his current close acquaintance with your father will oblige him to behave honourably at the very least."

She paused briefly and then continued, "Lizzy, I have a proposal, but please do not expect too much from it. Could you and Jane be prevailed upon to come back with us to London? A change of scenery might be beneficial — until your mother calms herself a little about this whole affair."

Before Lizzy could form an answer, she added, "However, I want to remind you that we and these gentlemen live in very different parts of town; all our connections are vastly different from theirs, so it is unlikely you should ever meet them at all unless they specifically call at our home."

"Call at your home? Mr. Darcy may, perhaps, have heard of such a place as Gracechurch Street, but he would hardly think a month's ablution enough to cleanse him from its impurities were he once to enter it. Depend upon it, Mr. Bingley never stirs without him."

"Lizzy, you deal too harshly with him. I must say such comments are mean and petty, and certainly not proper for you."

Elizabeth felt her cheeks turn red and started to form an explanation, but her aunt stopped her. "Pray do not worry, my dear. I perfectly understand you. I just wish that all this might come to a better ending than can be hoped for at present. Speak with Jane and let me know what you both decide, will you? And now let us join the others, for my children may be in need of me."

"Aunt, I cannot thank you enough. You are such a joy and comfort for us every time we are in need. We could not hope for anyone better."

"Oh, you are welcome, dear," she answered, kissing Lizzy's cheeks.

After a few days of deliberation and additional teasing from Mr. Bennet — "You may go girls, and I promise you that, should someone return to the neighbourhood, I shall send you an express to come at once; your mother will go and tie them up just in case they choose to venture away again." — the eldest Miss Bennets accepted their aunt's invitation with pleasure.

The Gardiners stayed a week at Longbourn, and the whole party returned to London on December 29. Despite their aunt's advice, Lizzy and Jane could think only that they were in the same town as the two gentlemen who most occupied their thoughts, and to neither of them did sleep come easily. Overnight, it began to snow peacefully.

The following morning after breakfast, Mr. Gardiner left to take care of business that required his attention before the New Year. Thus, the ladies made plans for a short walk in the park, together with the children, as the snow had covered everything around.

All were gathered in the dining room when the servant entered to announce: "Two gentlemen are here to see Miss Bennet and Miss Elizabeth... Mr. Darcy and Mr. Bingley, ma'am."

Lizzy and Jane sat in shock for a few moments, one turning red and the other white, appearing distressed and bewildered. "Thank you," said their aunt. "Please wait a few more minutes before inviting them into the parlour."

The presence of Mr. Darcy in Cheapside was something Elizabeth would not have considered when they were on the best of terms; that both gentlemen would call so early and on the second day after their arrival in town seemed incredible.

"Lizzy, Jane, could you please try to recollect yourselves? I shall need one of you to be sensible enough to make the introductions, so try to behave normally," said Mrs. Gardiner, shaking her head.

The gentlemen entered and made significant, elegant bows, each attempting to catch the eye of a particular young lady but with little success. The smile Darcy hoped to see on Elizabeth's face and the sparkle in her eyes were not there; he noticed that her countenance seemed different while her eyes purposely avoided his. Finally, Elizabeth gained her courage and carried out the introductions, her embarrassment making her insecure.

She dared not stare at Mr. Darcy but managed to cast a furtive glance at his face as she introduced him to her aunt. Their gazes locked for a second, but she averted her eyes quickly, leaving Darcy surprised and wondering at her unexpected reaction. *He looks tired but also serene, as if nothing has happened between us. He acts as if he has done nothing wrong. If he has not come to apologise, why call on us?*

Bingley could not take his eyes from Jane and tried to catch hers for a moment — with little success as her gaze was quite fixed on her hands.

Darcy decided that polite conversation was required. "Mrs. Gardiner, please allow me to apologise for this impromptu visit. I hope we do not intrude at an inconvenient moment."

"Do not trouble yourself, Mr. Darcy, Mr. Bingley. You are not intruding, although I must say — and I know I speak for my nieces as well — that this is indeed a surprise. We only arrived yesterday, and it is astonishing that you already have heard of our arrival and honoured us with a visit. Did you have any difficulty finding the house?"

"Not at all, I assure you. I received a letter from Mr. Bennet last night in which he was kind enough to answer some questions for me. He mentioned that Miss Bennet and Miss Elizabeth were in town, and we decided to make a brief call today."

"I see! I am glad you did. Please sit down gentlemen."

Mr. Bingley took a seat close to Jane, but even his less than perceptive nature could register that she did not appear as pleased and easy as she used to be in his presence.

However, he was so happy to see her again that he decided to put aside the uneasy feeling and deal with it later.

Indeed, Jane felt no happiness, only a tremendous sadness at being so close to him and knowing that he was merely being polite and wanted nothing more from her. Her hands were trembling, and she pressed them together to conceal her emotions.

For Lizzy's part, if in Darcy's absence her suffering was silent and painful, his presence made her spirit rise more daring than before, determined at least to satisfy her numerous questions and demand explanations. She was angry with him, not just for leaving a month earlier but also for coming to see her as though he were not to blame. She was especially furious with her father for toying with her and Jane.

Mrs. Gardiner, a woman of refinement and an excellent hostess, sensed the tension in the room and, after ordering some refreshments, began a light conversation, pleased to have an opportunity to judge for herself the two gentlemen who brought so much grief to her favourite nieces and so much torment to her sister-in-law. She only smiled, imagining what Mrs. Bennet would have said if she knew both of them were in her house. *Well, apparently Lizzy was wrong in assuming Mr. Darcy did not know where Cheapside is and would not come around. That is a good sign.* "Mr. Darcy, it is an honour to meet you; I have known and respected your family for a very long time."

"Indeed, Mrs. Gardiner? I thank you; I am delighted to hear that. Are you acquainted with any of my family members?"

"No sir, I have not had that pleasure. But I grew up in Lambton, which is very close to Pemberley."

"That is indeed a remarkable surprise, Mrs. Gardiner. Lambton is a delightful village, and I have many fond memories of it from when I was a boy."

He then turned to Elizabeth and Jane as much as to Mrs. Gardiner, asking, "I hope you left the Bennet family in good health."

"Yes, they were all in excellent health," Mrs. Gardiner answered.

"Was the weather tolerable when you left Longbourn?"

"Yes it was; thank you."

Elizabeth finally spoke. "Unlike the day you departed from Netherfield, Mr. Darcy, when, if I remember correctly, the weather was dreadful! I am happy to see that you arrived in London safely." Her harsh tone and sharp gaze left Darcy bewildered.

Mrs. Gardiner and Jane startled at her daring and reproachful statement. The hostess looked with censure at her niece to remind her of civil behaviour, but Elizabeth kept her eyes locked with Darcy's in a silent battle of wills, full of unspoken questions.

At this, Bingley's attention was caught, and he intervened genially. "Thank you for your concern, Miss Elizabeth. Fortunately, we left immediately after the ball before the weather worsened, and we arrived quite safely."

Elizabeth turned to look at him, displeased by his easy tone, and missed seeing Mr. Darcy's frown though it did not escape Mrs. Gardiner's notice.

"However," continued Bingley, "Louisa and Caroline arrived with great difficulty two days later. They were forced to change carriages twice."

"I am sorry to hear that," offered Jane, hardly able to lift her eyes.

"Oh, do not distress yourself, Miss Bennet. It was their impulsive decision that put them in a difficult situation. They had no business in town."

"I hope Miss Bingley and Mrs. Hurst are in good health," continued Jane.

"Yes, they are. They will be happy to learn of your coming to town.

Jane exchanged a quick glance with her sister and then looked uncomfortably at Mr. Bingley again. Elizabeth could take no more and, ignoring her aunt's earlier silent reproach, interrupted again in the same brash manner.

"Mr. Bingley, as far as I know, your sister has been informed already. Jane wrote to Miss Bingley about our arrival in town several days ago."

"Oh really?" Bingley's eyes widened in astonishment. "I wonder why Caroline failed to mention such an important thing to me."

Yes, Mr. Bingley. I wonder too! thought Elizabeth.

"Perhaps she did not receive the letter?" tried Jane timidly, embarrassed by the conversation.

"Yes, perhaps, or perhaps I did not listen carefully. I must confess that in the last weeks I have spent most of my time at Darcy's townhouse and have not paid much attention to my sisters. I think she at least told you about that."

The force of his statement made so openly and easily proved Miss Bingley's assertion of his attentions to Miss Darcy. Jane felt dizzy, and her face went white. She was compelled to grasp the couch and close her eyes for a moment; her reaction did not go unnoticed by everyone present. With an extraordinary effort, Jane continued, as her heart was breaking.

"Yes, Miss Bingley did mention you were closely engaged with Mr. and Miss Darcy. I hope Miss Darcy is in good health?"

Both Darcy and Bingley looked at her in astonishment, turning their gaze to Elizabeth and then to each other. Mrs. Gardiner had the oddest sensation that they were having a conversation in a foreign language she did not entirely understand. She was about to put an end to the charade by intervening with some direct questions, but Darcy's deep, grave voice restrained her.

"No, she is not yet fully recovered, Miss Bennet, but she is improving. Of course, she is not in any condition to leave her room yet, but this morning she was considerably better, which is why I decided to leave the house for a few hours and seize the opportunity to call upon you."

Jane raised her head and looked at him in surprise, while Elizabeth, with little control over her words, burst out, "What is wrong with Georgiana?"

Four pairs of eyes stared at her, and she blushed and tried to form a more proper inquiry; happily, her aunt was perceptive enough to save the situation.

"I can understand Lizzy's precipitate question, Mr. Darcy, as we are all surprised by this revelation. Is Miss Darcy unwell, sir?"

Mr. Darcy shifted his gaze from Mrs. Gardiner to Elizabeth and then to Jane, the intense set of his brows revealing his wonder.

"I am sorry, Mrs. Gardiner; I did not mean to burden you with our family problems. I dared to speak of it only because I presumed you were already aware of my sister's accident."

"It is not a burden, Mr. Darcy, I assure you. But as far as I know, neither I nor my nieces are aware of any misfortune suffered by Miss Darcy."

"I understand that now, and I must say I am quite surprised; Miss Bingley assured us that she explained the whole thing very clearly in her letters to Miss Bennet."

Bingley's voice was as serene as usual. "Oh, who knows what Caroline was thinking? She can be so forgetful sometimes. I am sure she wrote about some fashionable things, omitting what was really important."

"Yes, I am sure it was an omission," accepted Mrs. Gardiner, as the tension between Mr. Darcy and her niece was difficult to ignore.

"Mr. Darcy," she continued, trying to draw their attention, "I hope the accident you spoke of was not serious and Miss Darcy is now recovered."

"Oh, she is better, but she was indeed very ill," replied Mr. Bingley, and his answer finally aroused Mr. Darcy's attention.

He began to speak to Mrs. Gardiner, all the time feeling Elizabeth's eyes burning his profile. "The accident was not very grave, but unfortunately, its consequences were quite serious. It happened on the 24th of November; as you remember, there was a terrible storm."

He addressed Mrs. Gardiner, but his words were for Elizabeth alone, and he was keenly aware of her movements and almost felt her tense on hearing the date; it was the one they had spent together in the cottage. Mrs. Gardiner only nodded, encouraging him to continue.

"She went to call on our aunt, Lady Matlock, together with her companion, Mrs. Annesley. Unfortunately, my aunt was not at home, and Georgiana decided to return home. Although the distance was not very great, the storm soon intensified. Nobody really knows what happened. Apparently, thunder frightened the horses, and they bolted and began to run, colliding with everything in their way. A wheel of the carriage broke and the carriage rolled on its side. Nobody was badly hurt, but Georgiana's left leg was caught under the seat and was broken."

A gasp escaped both Jane and Elizabeth as he resumed his story, obviously living through the horrible moments once more.

"Of course, the footman went for help immediately, and Mrs. Annesley did all she could to protect Georgiana from the rain and cold but with little success. Help came as quickly as possible, but she was more than half an hour in that cold rain, and with her fragile constitution, she fell very ill."

He rose from his seat and took a few steps across the room, followed by the worried eyes of the occupants.

"An express was sent to me that day; apparently it reached Netherfield in just a few hours but was put near my other correspondence. I was not very… attentive to my duties on those days," said he, with an unconscious glance at Elizabeth. Her cheeks reddened from the implication of his words, and a shiver spread down her body as she remembered her own confused feelings during that time.

He stopped pacing and sat again. "I am sorry. It is still not easy to talk about this. After the ball, when looking through my desk, I finally saw the envelope and recognised Mrs. Annesley's handwriting. Of course, I opened it instantly, and you must imagine how I felt. I left within half an hour, and Mr. Bingley was good enough to join me. We came straight away, reaching London at dawn. When we arrived — "

He stopped; his embarrassment was apparent at displaying his feelings openly. Mr. Bingley continued somewhat more calmly.

"When we arrived, the doctor told us there was little hope of her recovering. Darcy never left her side for a moment; I practically fought with him to sleep a few moments from time to time while I took his place. Of course, the entire time more than one nurse and at least one doctor were in the house, but Darcy did not trust anybody enough to take care of her."

Jane put her hand to her mouth to stop another gasp, her eyes by now brimming with tears, as were those of Elizabeth and their aunt. Mr. Bingley's devotion to Miss Darcy was only one more proof of his affection for her, but Jane could not be jealous; all she felt was sorrow for Mr. Darcy's suffering and his sister's illness, and pride at Mr. Bingley's loyalty towards the woman he loved. The sorrow of not being that woman was painful but no stronger than the other feelings. Her goodness and gentleness of heart would not allow her to feel any other way.

Many minutes passed in silence, everyone's emotions so similar and yet so different. Each of them felt a great disturbance, not only for themselves but for the others as well.

Thousands of thoughts spun in Elizabeth's head, trying to find a balance between the unexpected happiness arising from her sense of Mr. Darcy's worthiness, and the great sorrow Jane would suffer at this confirmation of the affection between Mr. Bingley and Miss Darcy.

Through it all, she remembered her father's hushed but deserved words: "Did it never cross your pretty heads that perhaps there was an explanation that caused the gentlemen to leave in such a hurry?"

After a few moments, Mr. Darcy regained his composure.

"Three days before Christmas, a miracle happened, and she slowly began to recover."

And that very day he took the time to send a letter to my father, thought Elizabeth in astonishment, growing increasingly ashamed of herself for her frequent lack of trust in the gentleman.

"We were so happy and grateful that our prayers had been heard," added Bingley, looking to Jane and hoping to evoke a relieved expression on her face, but all he could see was the deepest sadness.

"It was indeed a Christmas miracle, sir, and please believe me that, had we known, Miss Darcy also would have been daily in our hearts and prayers," added Mrs. Gardiner.

Her nieces only nodded, and Darcy, recovering from the emotion of his story, thanked her heartily, moving his eyes to Elizabeth and then to Jane. The change in Elizabeth's countenance made his heart soar; yet, at the same time, he felt bitter disappointment as he understood that she was still inclined to believe him capable of mean and purposeful deception. His strongest feelings, however, were against Caroline Bingley, and he was relieved that she was not anywhere around him as he doubted he could control his rage. But Jane Bennet… Darcy thought he had never seen her in such a state before; she was normally so serene, calm, polite with everyone and pleasant to Bingley, but now…

She cannot even look at Bingley… And she hardly spoke at all. All she said was… His eyes moved from her to Elizabeth as Jane's last words came back to him; suddenly, a revelation struck him. *Oh my, how stupid we have been…* and his heart ached for the young lady and her undeserved sorrow. He took a deep breath, allowing a tiny smile to grace his countenance, and turned to Mrs. Gardiner.

"The comfort and help of a loyal friend is indeed priceless at such a difficult time, and I deeply felt that in the last month when Bingley was my most reliable support. He was like the best of brothers for both me and Georgiana." He knew he was right in his assessment the next moment when Jane startled and looked at him, her beautiful blue eyes filling with unshed tears.

"Oh, your praises are undeserved, Darcy, I did nothing more than any friend would do at such a moment," answered Bingley, puzzled by Darcy's unexpected statement and Jane's unusual reaction.

"No, Bingley, you did infinitely more, although, poor Georgiana has had to pay a high price for his devotion. The minute she began to recover, all she heard from Bingley were stories about his friends in Hertfordshire and his eagerness to return there. Even my cousin, Colonel Fitzwilliam, declares he knows everything about the county now."

When he finished, Jane Bennet's eyes were indeed full of tears, but her beautiful face revealed a true expression of happiness. She was glowing, and Darcy's heart melted with brotherly tenderness.

He allowed Jane to enjoy Bingley's closeness and attentions fully and returned his gaze to Elizabeth, relishing in the depths of her sparking eyes, full of mirth and gratitude; his reward was there.

Chapter 11

Mrs. Gardiner felt utterly ignored by her nieces and the two gentlemen but also pleased at the favourable resolution of their annoying uncertainties. She was not insensible to the great compliment of Mr. Darcy's attention toward Elizabeth, knowing better than did anyone the extent of the Darcys' influence and station in life. After this unexpected and not quite proper visit, she gained the conviction that neither his feelings nor the respectability of his intentions could be questioned.

After a few moments of watching both couples in silence, she reminded them of her presence by starting a new topic of conversation.

"Mr. Darcy, Mr. Bingley, I am very sorry that Mr. Gardiner is not at home to welcome you. I hope he will have the pleasure of meeting with you soon."

"Thank you, Mrs. Gardiner," answered Mr. Darcy. "Perhaps, if you will permit it, we could call next at a more convenient time of day to find him at home. As for now, I am sorry to say we must depart."

"It will be our pleasure, Mr. Darcy, I assure you. In fact," added Mrs. Gardiner, seizing the opportunity, "if you gentlemen are not otherwise engaged, it would be an honour to have you as our guests for dinner."

"Thank you, Mrs. Gardiner," Bingley hurried to answer, bewitched by Jane's delightful smile. "If we would not be intruding, it would be a delight to accept your invitation. We have no fixed engagements."

Unlike Mr. Bingley, Mr. Darcy looked uneasy and hesitated to give an answer

"I thank you, Mrs. Gardiner, but for the moment my time and my actions depend upon my sister's state of health. I confess this is the first time since the accident that I have been absent from her for so many hours."

His dark eyes searched Elizabeth's, and he could see that she was disappointed, despite her understanding smile. He tentatively smiled back.

By now, Elizabeth understood how wrong she had been not to trust him and appreciated the degree of distress he was enduring. The fear of losing his beloved sister, the only member of his immediate family, must have been more painful than she dared imagine. Not without shame did she comprehend that her own torment — which, though not unreasonable, seemed somehow selfish — paled in comparison to his. She could not resist harbouring unkind, resentful thoughts toward Caroline Bingley — and herself as well for allowing the woman to succeed so easily in her deception.

As for Mr. Darcy's refusal — while her present desire was indeed to be in his company, the knowledge that her distress had been baseless allowed her to be patient. She could wait for him as long as necessary — all her life if need be. Her eyes fixed with his and told him as much.

Their hostess broke the silence. "Mr. Darcy, we do hope you will find Miss Darcy improving, and we are grateful you took the opportunity to call on us. And, if we do not have the pleasure of seeing you again tonight, I am sure another opportunity will arise."

"Thank you, Mrs. Gardiner. However, even if I cannot stay for dinner, I hope to be able at least to call this evening and meet Mr. Gardiner."

"That would be lovely. I am sure my husband will be honoured."

"As will I," he responded politely.

The gentlemen soon bid their good-byes with the pleasant anticipation of their next visit. As soon as they were out of hearing, Elizabeth and Jane burst into joyful conversation. Their display of unrestrained emotion was watched closely with motherly love by Mrs. Gardiner.

"Oh, Lizzy, did you hear what Mr. Darcy said about Mr. Bingley and Miss Darcy? Can you believe it? Oh, Lizzy, I am so happy. I am sure he did that on purpose, but it is so amazing. How could he know? Mr. Darcy is such a clever man, is he not, Aunt?"

Not to mention exceedingly handsome when he smiles and enchanting when he kisses my hand, thought Lizzy, her spirits fully recovered; she closed her eyes for a few seconds to embrace her memories in precise detail. When she opened them, she faced her aunt's penetrating gaze. She blushed and smiled at Mrs. Gardiner. Yes, Elizabeth was pleased, and she had no fear or shame in showing it.

Mrs. Gardiner expressed her good opinion, confessing she liked them both very much indeed. She left the room to give specific orders for dinner preparation, while Lizzy began discussing Miss Bingley's deceitful behaviour with such vehemence that Jane could do nothing but agree that Caroline Bingley was not the honest friend she had believed her to be. While that admission caused Jane a great deal of grief, Lizzy was relieved that her sister would not be misled easily by that lady again!

As THEY ENTERED THE CARRIAGE, Bingley's enthusiasm was boundless. Darcy was as reserved as ever, staring out of the window to conceal his anger.

In the past month, his thoughts had constantly been divided between Elizabeth and his sister. He longed for the former — desperate to be close to her — but his heart ached for Georgiana's injury. His memories of that fateful, stormy day in particular were acutely divided between the ecstasy of his precious time with Elizabeth in the cottage and the agony of knowing that his sister, at that moment, was lying hurt.

When he remembered their dances together — her smiles and sweet flirtations at the Netherfield ball — he could not dismiss the thought that his sister was fighting at the same time for her life. It was as though the happiness he had finally achieved in acknowledging his love for Elizabeth had come at an unbearable price. His greatest comfort, which soothed the intolerable pain of seeing Georgiana unconscious, was the memory of Elizabeth's eyes, her smiles, the gentle touch of her hand, and the teasing words that twisted her lips with such aching sweetness. He desperately wanted to take her hand and hold it, just to feel the warmth of her presence.

He had come to know her well enough to be certain that she would generously share his worry and grief; she would stay with him near Georgiana and would give them both strength and liveliness if she could. Though she was far away, he was certain she was keeping him and his sister in her thoughts and in her prayers. Every time he closed his eyes and every time he fell asleep, Elizabeth was there — in his thoughts, in his dreams, in his mind, and in his heart. He could almost feel the gentle, comforting touch of her hand on his shoulder when exhaustion and despair overwhelmed him.

He could recall vividly the relief he felt when Georgiana began to recover; he felt he had been brought back to life when she first recognised him. Then, the amplified joy of hearing only a few days later about Elizabeth's unexpected arrival added to his blessings. But his anger grew as he thought back to the moment he had entered the Gardiners' house and had seen her acting so strangely, worse even than in the first days of their acquaintance. His heart had ached with fear that something had happened to change her feelings, only to discover that the reason was the intentional deceit of Caroline Bingley.

How could I ever have trusted Caroline? Did I completely lose my mind? My only excuse can be my lack of sleep and preoccupation with Georgiana.

"Darcy, I cannot tell you how grateful I am to you for bringing me along to make this call. It was the most wonderful morning I have had in quite some time; I cannot remember the last time I was so delighted. Oh yes, I can: at the Netherfield ball!"

"Yes, we had a pleasant time indeed, and I must confess I admired the Gardiners' home. I found Mrs. Gardiner to be unexpectedly amiable and fashionable. I can only hope Mr. Gardiner is the same."

"I am sure he is, but Darcy, I must confess I could pay attention to nothing else around me except Jane. She is so much more beautiful than I remembered. I can scarcely wait to return for dinner."

"I am very pleased for you; I am sure you will have a delightful time." His tone was not at all enthusiastic, so Bingley restrained his joviality.

"I say, Darcy, you do not seem to be content although I am sure you were equally pleased to see Miss Elizabeth."

"Indeed I was, Bingley."

"Then what is it? Are you still concerned for Georgiana? Perhaps I should remain with you tonight; I can dine with the Gardiners some other time."

"Please do not trouble yourself. There is no need for you to postpone the dinner; I am sure Georgiana is well.

"Then what is it? Come, Darcy, do not dissemble; I deserve better. You are quite upset, and you should trust me enough to tell me why."

Darcy turned to his friend and, seeing his serene countenance, could restrain himself no longer.

"If you insist on knowing the truth, you will. Yes, I am upset, Bingley. I am extremely upset with your sister."

"My sister? Which one? I am guessing it is Caroline. Why?"

"Why?! Why?! Bingley, I am sorry to say it, but sometimes you just —! How can you ask such a question? Were you not in the same room with me? Did you not hear what Elizabeth said? Did you not see Jane Bennet?"

His violent reaction disturbed Bingley greatly; he concluded that Darcy was merely fatigued and irrational.

"I was in the room and I heard, but— Oh... you are referring to the fact that Caroline did not tell the Bennets of the accident. Am I correct?"

"Yes, Bingley, I was referring precisely to that."

"Oh, you should not be so harsh on her. I am sure she just forgot. She is not such a bad person, you know. She did care for Georgiana, and she was greatly distressed by the whole situation."

"Bingley, my respect and gratitude for you cannot be expressed, but you are too good and most naïve. I can accept that she forgot to mention it in the first letter — although it was precisely intended to explain the reason for our departure — but what of the second? Did you not ask whether she wrote about that subject, and did she not specifically reply in the affirmative?"

By now, Bingley's countenance had darkened, and he was looking at Darcy with great attention.

"And what about not informing you regarding their coming to Town? Do you really think the letter was lost as Mrs. Gardiner politely suggested? Or perhaps Caroline forgot again! However, as Miss Jane herself pointed out, your sister did not forget to mention to her that you were closely engaged with Georgiana and me. Can you not understand the true meaning of that?"

He looked pointedly at his, by now, thoughtful friend and shook his head.

"Moreover, we must take into consideration a further effect. After our open display of preference at the ball, our sudden departure and failure to return without any proper explanation no doubt exposed us to the censure of the whole neighbourhood for caprice and instability, and probably left the ladies to its derision for disappointed hopes. I can only imagine what gossip was spread through Meryton!"

As Darcy spoke, Bingley's face expressed a tumult of feelings he had never experienced in such depth. Every moment of their visit replayed in his mind, and he at length correctly interpreted what he had seen with his own eyes but failed to comprehend.

"What a simpleton I have been; I cannot believe it! I am a stupid, stupid man; I do not deserve Jane Bennet! All this time Caroline made her believe that I had abandoned her and was now engaged to Georgiana! How will I ever face her again? Not only did I stupidly trust Caroline without question, I could not offer Jane the smallest consolation or comfort, as I was not perceptive enough to understand her distress. It was you, my friend, who better understood the woman I love. How can that be?"

He was so furious, that his face had turned completely red, a state in which Darcy never had seen him in the whole course of their acquaintance. His own rage quite vanished in the face of his friend's distress.

"Bingley, calm yourself. All is arranged now, and you will be able to face Miss Jane quite well, I should say. And she will be equally pleased to see you again, I am sure."

Bingley just shook his head and ran his fingers through his light hair. "I cannot control myself, Darcy. I am so hurt by my sister, disappointed in myself, and ashamed for what I made the Bennets endure."

"Bingley, no one blames you. You are one of the best and most considerate men I have ever known. But it is true that your sister has gone too far this time; she intentionally deceived us all, and that is not acceptable."

"I agree with you, Darcy, and I shall not try to excuse her. I am sure we both know what her motivation has been, but no motivation could justify such outrageous behaviour," said Bingley in complete embarrassment.

"We are in full agreement, Bingley. Happily, everything turned out well before any permanent damage occurred."

"Yes, Darcy, and that is only thanks to you."

The carriage stopped at Darcy's house, but Bingley refused the invitation to enter, promising he would stop to collect Darcy for their visit later that evening. Presently, he was extremely anxious to speak to his sister.

BINGLEY REACHED HIS OWN HOUSE and with dispatch inquired after Caroline, finding her in the dining room with Louisa.

Good, this is even better, thought he, entering slowly and endeavouring to maintain a serene countenance.

"Charles, what a surprise! I am so happy to see you! How is dear Georgiana? I hope she is well?"

"Yes, thank you, Caroline, she is acceptably well and improving."

"Well, I am sure your presence nearby was greatly appreciated by her and Mr. Darcy, Charles. I would have been close to her, too, if Mr. Darcy had allowed me to be. However, curiously, he refused to admit me. That must have been because Georgiana was more desirous to see you than me."

She exchanged an insinuating glance with her sister, and then turned to her brother, only to find a stern face in the place of his typically joyous smile. "Come brother, we all know how fond you are of Georgiana, and from what I saw, both families are pleased by the attachment."

"Caroline, I cannot believe how superficial you are to think such a frivolous thing while Georgiana was dying! I was not escorting her to a ball, for heaven's sake!"

Both women looked at him, shocked by his tone. He tried to calm himself, poured a glass of wine, and then took a place on the settee facing them.

"Caroline, I have wanted to ask you for some time now. Has there been any news from Hertfordshire?"

The sisters exchanged a glance, but Caroline quickly regained her usual spirits. "No Charles, not a word. Jane never replied to my second letter."

"I find it unusually curious that not a single word of compassion or support has been sent for Darcy's sister; after all, the Bennets were quite closely acquainted with him."

"Well, Charles, perhaps they were not in the least interested in the poor girl's suffering, or maybe they have found another subject of interest in the neighbourhood. As for what would be politely required, even you must have noticed that the Bennets were not very proficient in that respect."

Both she and Louisa began to titter, making Bingley's glass tremble in his hand with a rage that overwhelmed him. He looked at them as though seeing them for the first time in his life and then leaned back in his seat. His face wore an unusually harsh expression, and his eyes were dark-blue steel.

"But, Caroline, you did explain to them about Georgiana's accident, did you not? Darcy specifically asked me, and I told him you did so."

"Yes, of course I did as you required. I am a woman of my word."

"That is indeed very odd, because you see, dear sister, both Darcy and I just paid a delightful visit to the Gardiners' house in Gracechurch Street, and we spent a few pleasant hours with Miss Bennet and Miss Elizabeth!"

His sharp, mocking voice alone would have been sufficient to worry Caroline, but his revealing words caused her to choke on a slice of teacake. She began to cough, her eyes widened in shock. Her face grew red in a desperate attempt not only to breathe but also to find a proper answer.

Bingley watched her with an unfeeling, ironic glare, making no move to help her as Louisa rose hastily to bring her sister a glass of water. Eventually, taking a few violent gulps of water, Caroline stopped coughing and opened her mouth, attempting to utter a few words, but her brother continued.

"You can imagine our surprise when we heard the Bennets were completely unaware of the accident and their surprise when Darcy related the whole story to them."

His countenance was such as his sister had never seen before. For the first time, both Caroline and Louisa were aware of who was the undeniable master of the house and that he was greatly displeased.

Swallowing more water, Caroline finally found speech.

"Charles, that is indeed a surprise. When did dear Jane come to town?"

"Yesterday, Caroline, as she announced to you in her last letter — the one you did not receive, as you just assured me."

"Indeed, I did not receive it. What delightful news. I shall go and pay her a visit today, I long to see my dear friend again. She is such a sweet, dear girl."

"Caroline, do not toy with me a moment longer. Your behaviour was below anything I ever could have imagined, and I shall never forget it. You have deliberately disregarded my wishes and intentionally deceived Miss Bennet and her family, as well as Darcy and me."

His voice was so strong and intense that even the servants were startled; it was the first time they had heard their master's voice raised in anger.

"Charles, you forget yourself! How dare you speak to your sister in such a manner?" Louisa interrupted, but Bingley's eyes were full of rage, and she almost felt a blow from the force of his angry countenance.

"Not a word from you either, Louisa! I am convinced you were fully aware of everything! And if Caroline is displeased with my manner, she is free to leave this house at any time."

He turned his gaze from one to another, furiously clenching his fists. "How dare you? This is beyond imagination." With that, he went to the door, turning his back on his sisters.

"Charles, please allow me to explain. You must know how much I love you and that everything I have done was for your benefit. I shall speak to Jane Bennet. It was just a misunderstanding; I am sure she will understand."

"No explanation is possible, Caroline. Indeed, Jane Bennet will forgive you, for she has the most generous and kind nature. You would do much better to prepare a brilliant explanation for Darcy — that is, if he ever allows you near his person." With that, Bingley strode briskly from the room.

Caroline trembled in panic as she saw her many, well-prepared plans ruined in an instant. She was convinced once more that it was entirely Eliza Bennet's fault. As soon as her brother was out of hearing, her rage burst forth: "I hate her, I hate her . . . " causing the servants to shake their heads in shocked wonderment.

Darcy entered his house half-pleased with his day and half-afraid to hear unfavourable news about his sister.

He went directly to her room and found her sleeping, her maid in one chair and the nurse in another. After the fresh perfume of the winter air, Darcy could sense the heavy smell of sickness. A wave of grief washed over him as he regretted his sister could not enjoy the refreshing weather outdoors.

He approached the bed and looked at Georgiana, breathing peacefully; she appeared childlike, her pale face thin, still bearing the evidence of illness. Darcy leaned closer and put the back of his hand to her forehead. He was relieved; she had no fever and seemed to be sleeping peacefully.

At his tender touch, she opened her eyes and smiled at her brother. "William, I am so happy to see you!" she breathed in deeply, closing her eyes in pleasure. "Brother, you smell like winter! Did it snow?"

"Yes it did, sweetling," Darcy said as he returned her smile, placing a kiss on her forehead. "How are you feeling today?"

"Oh, I am better — so much better! I have anxiously awaited your return, so tell me everything about your call. Did you have a pleasant time?"

"Yes, we did, dearest — a very pleasant time, indeed."

"And Miss Bennet and Miss Elizabeth? Are they well, I hope? Oh brother, do not make me ask so many questions, I beg you. Tell me everything."

He was happy to see her so animated and described to her how delighted he was to meet Elizabeth and Jane Bennet and their aunt. His voice was calm and tender as if telling a story to a child, and he was content to see his sister listening with great pleasure. He truly cherished such moments, especially after seeing Georgiana through her battle against a dreadful illness. It had brought them together in spite of the grief and pain; they had the opportunity to spend more time together and, as she had begun to improve over the past fortnight, to become even closer. Their bond of affection was further strengthened by an earnest trust in each other despite the difference in their ages. That trust allowed them to bypass their usual reserve and share their private thoughts — even about such topics as George Wickham and Elizabeth Bennet.

"William, I am happy to see you so content. I am very sorry I shall not have the opportunity to meet Miss Elizabeth . . . and Miss Bennet, of course."

"You will, I promise, as soon as you have fully recovered."

"Oh, but that might take several weeks, and I am sure they will not remain in town for so long." Her weak voice was filled with regret, and Darcy caressed her cheek gently.

"Dearest, please do not be sad. The only important thing now is for you to be well, and I promise I shall do everything I can to help you recover."

"I know, William. Oh, but I forgot to ask. Where is Mr. Bingley? I cannot wait to hear his story. I am sure it will be even more detailed than yours."

"He had some pressing matters of business, and then he is returning to the Gardiners' for dinner, so I do not think he will come to see you today."

"I am so happy for him! He must be full of joy to be receiving an invitation so soon!" Then, she turned to her brother, looking at him earnestly. "But were you not also invited?"

"Yes I was, but I have declined for this evening."

"You have declined? Why would you do that?"

"Because I want to have dinner with you, here, as we do every day," he answered, smiling at her.

"Oh no, William, you cannot do that. You must go, please; I should feel so badly if you lost this opportunity because of me. Please say you will go."

In an instant, he became serious, and his mood was reflected in his answer.

"Georgiana, there is nothing more to say on this subject. I shall be sure to watch you eating as the doctor specifically advised us. You will oblige me, for this is the only way you can fully recover and accompany me on my next visit to Miss Bennet. Do we have an agreement?"

She withdrew in her shyness, intimidated by his words, and nodded in silence, but she saw him smiling again as his hand caressed her hair.

"Thank you, my dear sister, for your concern and support. You are a blessing to me, you know?"

She tried to regain her smile and dared to answer boldly. "There were many moments when I was more a burden than a blessing, Brother. I know that. That is why I shall always listen to you."

"Good, I shall retire now. Try to sleep a little more; I shall see you later. And... Georgiana... if you eat satisfactorily, you will perhaps truly feel a little better... and if you can do without me, perhaps I might go out for a few hours later in the evening."

WITH GREAT EFFORT AFTER A long hot bath, Charles Bingley succeeded in regaining a part of his usual cheerfulness. The thought of seeing Jane Bennet again soon helped him in this achievement. He did not wish nor did he expect to have another conversation with either of his sisters that day, and he left the house eagerly, hurrying to Gracechurch Street.

He was somewhat worried about his hosts' opinion of him and his sister, considering the afternoon's revelation of Caroline's behaviour. But his reception was so gracious, Jane's beautiful eyes so welcoming, and the smile on her face so radiant, that he forgot almost everything, even to express his friend's excuse and promise to call later that evening, only remembering after Mrs. Gardiner's specific inquiry.

Mrs. Gardiner placed both nieces on either side of her with Mr. Bingley sitting near Jane and Mr. Gardiner at the other end of the dinner table.

Though Mr. Bingley was seated near Mr. Gardiner and anxious to make the best impression on that gentleman, he proved to be a dreadful conversationalist that evening. In truth, the constant smiles and blushes exchanged between Mr. Bingley and

Jane, the regretful glances towards the empty place at the table by Elizabeth, and the understanding smiles of Mr. and Mrs. Gardiner made the conversation at the table rather sparse.

Happily, after the second course was served, the servant entered and announced Mr. Darcy, whose presence was received with great interest and no little pleasure. Unconsciously and completely impolitely, his eyes rested on Elizabeth's glowing face the moment he entered the room, ignoring the rest of the party. Quickly regaining his composure, he was introduced to Mr. Gardiner. Darcy expressed his apologies for disturbing them at dinnertime and received hearty assurances that he was most welcome.

He was invited to take his place next to Elizabeth and Mr. Gardiner, a situation that pleased him exceedingly; he answered their compassionate questions about Georgiana with sincere gratitude. With Mr. and Mrs. Gardiner fulfilling their duties as hosts with elegance and with Darcy's surrender of his usual reserve, the dinner became more animated and pleasant.

Elizabeth did not often turn her eyes to Mr. Darcy, but she listened most attentively to all that passed between him and her uncle, and gloried in every expression and sentence of her uncle that marked his intelligence, his taste, and his good manners. She saw Mr. Darcy desirous to please and more animated than she had ever seen him in company. Elizabeth felt relieved, happy and contented — though not particularly relaxed — and was completely unsuccessful in concealing the blushes caused by Mr. Darcy's close proximity.

After dinner, the gentlemen retired to Mr. Gardiner's library but soon joined the ladies again. Mr. Gardiner seemed in particularly good spirits and went directly to his wife.

"My dear, I have delightful news: Mr. Darcy has invited us to dinner at his home the day after tomorrow on the first day of the New Year. I must confess I did accept as I knew we had no other fixed engagements."

Mrs. Gardiner looked at Elizabeth, desirous to know how she, whom the invitation most concerned, felt disposed as to its acceptance, and seeing her evidently very pleased and her husband so fond of the gentlemen's society, she expressed her delight and acceptance.

"Mr. Darcy, this is indeed a pleasant surprise, and we would accept your invitation, but are you sure we would not be intruding, considering the particular situation of your family?"

"Mrs. Gardiner, please be assured that it would be an honour to have you as my guests. There will be no other guests except Mr. Bingley and his family; my aunt and uncle had other plans that could not be cancelled. Your presence would be a welcome addition to our little party."

Elizabeth could not help but be pleased and triumphant; she said nothing, but it gratified her exceedingly, for she knew the compliment was mostly for her sake.

The rest of the evening passed in the same pleasant manner, Mr. Gardiner finding many reasons to be pleased with both gentlemen, especially upon realising their mutual pleasure in the sport of fishing.

If for Mr. Bingley and Jane the evening was everything they could have hoped, being perfectly content to be in each other's company, the same could not be said for Elizabeth and Mr. Darcy. Although both were enjoying the company and the evening, they were hoping eagerly for a few moments alone together to put behind them a long month of grief, sorrow and misunderstandings. However, no opportunity of the kind arose until the last moment of the gentlemen's departure.

ALL FOUR GARDINER CHILDREN, TWO girls and two boys, were excessively attached to their older cousins although their various personalities led them to express their affection in different ways.

Thomas, aged nine, and Henry, seven and one-half, were very gentlemanlike and well mannered when in company. The two were attracted to books and everything new but also restless and willing to play. Their quick minds and overflowing energy more than once made for hard times for their governess, Mrs. Burton, and many of their mischievous practical jokes were sources of anxiety for their mother and younger sisters.

While the boys were much alike, the girls were a different matter entirely. Margaret at the age of six was already a complete young lady, attentive to her looks and clothes, inclined to try her mother's jewels and reticules, and exceedingly talented at the pianoforte.

The youngest, Rebecca, only four and one-half, was a bittersweet mix of all the children: intelligent, precocious, pretty like her older sister but full of energy like her brothers and equally inclined to join them in their play, from catching frogs to climbing trees whenever the opportunity arose. She had been scolded more than once by Mrs. Burton and Mrs. Gardiner, but the most difficult task for both ladies was to explain to her why she was not allowed to do such things. Her astute mind and young age made it difficult for the ladies to offer her proper and understandable answers to her endless questions of 'why' and 'what is this,' but made her the favourite of her father and cousin Lizzy and, consequently, spoiled by them both.

The day after Mr. Bingley and Mr. Darcy's visit, the children were hoping to have a chance to spend more time in their company. An extraordinary event had occurred; that night it had snowed again. Everything was white as in a fairy tale, and they prepared themselves more quickly than ever for their daily walk in the park, reclaiming their cousins' company.

Elizabeth was always happy to spend time out of doors, and the weather was so magnificent that she accepted without hesitation. The excitement of Becky, who was able to play in snow for the first time in her life, was so overwhelming and contagious that Jane agreed, too.

Though it was early, several couples were enjoying a walk through the streets, rejoicing in the beauty of pure whiteness. The Gardiner children had no restraint in playing and running about, throwing themselves to the ground and fighting with snowballs — except Margaret, of course, who was holding Jane's hand — in spite of Mrs. Burton's horror and her vain attempts to demand proper behaviour. They became quite noisy, and Elizabeth joined them in their play, allowing them to hide behind her in their fight, laughing and falling down together until their cheeks became red with cold, their eyes were brightened by the effort, and their clothes were in great disorder.

Jane, holding Margaret's little hand, watched from afar, smiling understandingly. Mrs. Burton, however, tightened her lips in gentle disapproval of such bizarre behaviour — and from such a lovely lady as Miss Elizabeth.

No more than half an hour after their arrival in the park, they were surprised by the unexpected appearance of Mr. Bingley and Mr. Darcy. While Jane managed to meet them with her usual graciousness and elegance, Elizabeth stared at them in shock, deeply embarrassed by her doubtlessly unladylike appearance. So abrupt was their appearance that she could not recollect herself soon enough; self-consciously, she joined them with little Becky holding tightly to her pelisse and the boys following along.

She greeted the gentlemen properly, and while they bowed elegantly to her, she sought a way to hide her hands in their now dirty-white gloves, a gesture that made Darcy's lips twist in a smile. Both gentlemen politely greeted Mrs. Burton and the children, who responded seriously and graciously. Elizabeth, blushing from the effort and the cold as well as the pleasure of seeing Mr. Darcy again, offered them an open smile.

"Mr. Darcy, Mr. Bingley, what a pleasant surprise. We did not expect to meet you today and especially not in the park."

"It was a surprising decision for us, too," answered Bingley. "We had some business to attend to in this part of town and decided to make a short call; as you obviously were not at home, Mrs. Gardiner was so kind as to tell us your location."

"We hope we did not interrupt you," Mr. Darcy intervened, a hint of a smile in the corner of his mouth.

"In fact you did, sir, but the interruption was not at all unpleasant," answered Elizabeth teasingly and slightly flirtatiously. She had regained her cheerfulness, but Mr. Darcy's intense gaze was making her a bit flustered.

"However, I am afraid we have stayed too long in the cold weather and it is time to return home. Would you not agree, Mrs. Burton?"

"Indeed I would, Miss Elizabeth," was the lady's answer. She discreetly signalled to the children to stand next to her, and they obeyed in an instant.

"We were wondering whether you would allow us to keep you company on your way home?"

Mr. Darcy's voice and his insistent gaze were enough for Elizabeth to feel she lacked strength to refuse him even had she wanted to. However, refusing his company was the furthest thing from her mind; his closeness was what she most desired to enjoy fully the wonderful morning's walk.

Mrs. Burton and the young maid walked slowly in order to allow some private space for the couples, while the children chased each other a bit more before exiting the park. Both gentlemen offered their arms to the young ladies, and while Jane accepted Mr. Bingley's arm graciously, Elizabeth had a moment of hesitation as she looked ruefully at her dirty, wet gloves, not daring to put them on the sleeve of his elegant coat. She directed a shy, apologetic look to Mr. Darcy, peeking at him through long lashes that tried to cover her laughing eyes.

Darcy understood her perfectly but, careless for the state of his coat and bewitched by her overwhelming liveliness, was only afraid he would not be able to overcome the powerful impulse to kiss her bright eyes. His desire was so strong that he could almost feel the softness and the taste of her skin tantalising his lips. What would she say if he simply lowered his head and touched her crimson cheek with his lips? He did not dare discover the answer, but boldly, allowing a smile to spread over his lips, he grabbed her reluctant hand and brought it to rest on his forearm. He could barely restrain himself, thinking how much he wanted to take off those useless gloves and warm her hands with his. Holding her hands was still an incredibly vivid memory, one he dearly wanted to experience again.

She blushed even more at his gesture — he was afraid she understood his thoughts — but she finally took hold of his arm, and his other hand came up quickly to cover hers, protectively and warmly. They exchanged a quick glance — enough for him to perceive her acceptance of his boldness — and her little hand moved slightly under his. Almost unconsciously, they entwined their fingers — not completely, just enough to avoid notice by anyone else. His eyes were fixed upon her beautiful profile, but though his intense stare was burning her, she did not dare to lift her eyes from the ground. Instead, she started to walk, seeking a way to begin the conversation properly.

"Mr. Darcy, I am so sorry for my appearance, I was caught up in my little cousins' game and almost forgot myself. Apparently, I have made it a habit to show myself in front of you in the most disadvantageous circumstances—" began Elizabeth.

A habit indeed… So she remembers what she told me that day in the storm

"Do not worry Miss Bennet, it is not yet a pattern as it has happened only three times before today. And I should not call this circumstance disadvantageous but rather unusual and quite charming,"

She laughed. "You are teasing me, Mr. Darcy, and that is not very gentlemanlike. I cannot possibly believe you find anything charming in my playing with the children and dirtying myself or in seeing me covered in mud as has happened previously," she said, trying to tease him back.

"I am not teasing you, Miss Bennet, but speaking the absolute truth; the last time I saw you covered in mud — as you said — is a treasured memory."

He lowered his head a little, enough to see a blushing wave spread over her face and neck, and he knew she could feel his gaze. She kept her eyes on the ground but unconsciously brought her hand up to his arm and joined it with the other, so both her hands were now resting under his protective palm: another movement of their fingers, another tightening of their touch, another slight caress of the other's hand. Her gesture was as eloquent as a tender answer, and he did not fail to understand it.

Darcy stopped, looking somewhere far away as if admiring the view and then made a step forward to face her.

"Miss Bennet, I must confess that I came here today not by a fortunate coincidence but with the precise purpose and hope of finding a few moments alone with you as I wanted to tell you a few things."

She finally raised her eyes to his, waiting and never releasing his arm.

"I know I cannot possibly find the words to express my deepest regret for our inconsiderate behaviour in departing from Hertfordshire. I can only imagine how it appeared to the whole neighbourhood and in what light the whole event — deservedly — appeared. Please allow me to apologise and — "

"Do not apologise, Mr. Darcy. You did nothing wrong; you simply acted as any gentleman in your situation would have acted."

He wanted to say something, but she continued, looking deeply into his eyes, blushing while making her confession. "I shall not deny that we were... worried and surprised by your departure, but the fault was not yours. I... we understand perfectly what happened."

Her voice barely audible, she added, "Miss Georgiana's accident... occurred the same day that..."

"Yes."

She wanted to continue but found nothing to say. What words would have been proper at such a moment?

"Miss Bennet, I should like to ask you a personal favour." His voice sounded grave, and she nodded without hesitation.

"If I am not asking too much, would you allow me to introduce Georgiana to you tomorrow? She truly regretted that she could not come to visit you, and she expressed an insistent desire to meet you."

"It would be an honour, Mr. Darcy. But is she recovered enough to entertain guests? I was under the impression she was still in bed."

"No, she is not well, and she is still keeping to her bed, not just for her illness but for her broken leg as well. But if you would agree to... just visit her briefly in her room. Please believe me, Miss Bennet, there is nothing contagious in her disease at the moment. I would never jeopardise your safety if that were the case."

His caring words melted her heart. He looked so unsure of himself, so troubled, and so much in need of tenderness that she raised her hand to caress his face before realising what she was doing. She stopped in the middle of the motion, suddenly realising their location and their companions, and returned her hand to his arm, resuming their slow walk.

The gratitude on his face proved to her that he understood her gesture, and she felt embarrassed but did not avert her eyes. She was no longer unsure — not of herself and not of him. Her eyes and her smile were telling him, "Yes, I confess I wanted to touch you, but I stopped because we are in public."

Her voice a little shaky, she finally found the words to continue. "Mr. Darcy, my only concern was for Miss Darcy's health. I should be truly delighted and honoured to meet her if it would not be disturbing to her rest."

"I confess I am overly protective towards her, Miss Bennet, and no visits have been allowed since the accident except for our closest family and friends: my aunt Lady Ellen, Bingley, and Colonel Fitzwilliam. They have been close by all this time and have helped me. Nobody else is admitted."

Except me, thought Elizabeth, her heart full of joy at the hidden implication of his words.

"Except you," continued Darcy with a low, deep voice, reading her thoughts and tightening his grip on her hands.

No other gesture or words were needed.

Chapter 12

Mr. Darcy and Elizabeth, arm in arm, continued to walk in pleasant silence, keeping their distance from the others in the party until both were startled to hear the children's heightened voices and then Rebecca's loud cry.

Elizabeth left Mr. Darcy's arm and hurried to her cousin although Mrs. Burton, Jane and Bingley were already there. The girl had fallen down in the snow, and the boys were denying any blame for what happened. Jane caressed Becky and lifted her up on her feet. But when Elizabeth approached and knelt near her, the girl threw herself at her neck and continued to cry in her arms.

"It is all right, my love, don't cry… Tell me what happened." Lizzy's voice was sweet and comforting, and she wiped the little girl's tears, shaking the snow from her clothes and the curls of her hair.

"Thomas and Henry pushed me and I fell. They are always so unkind to me — "

"Now, sweetie, you know that is not true." Lizzy tried to calm her while her brothers were formulating different excuses and explanations for Mrs. Burton. "Are you hurt?"

"Yes I am," she cried. "I hurt my hand so bad that I cannot move my leg."

"I see. Show me where you are hurt." After a short inspection, it was clear nothing harmful had occurred.

"We will take care of you at home, dear. Let us go now, for it is very cold."

Mrs. Burton was about to take her little hand gently, but the girl protested. "I cannot walk so far; I am hurt."

"Oh, yes you can, little missy," answered Mrs. Burton. "And it is not too far. You walk this distance at least twice every day."

"Yes, but now I am hurt and I am cold and I am so upset, and I cannot possibly walk with all those three problems." Her eyes again filled with tears, and her lower lip trembled.

She turned her sad, little face to Lizzy and begged her, "Please Lizzy, can you carry me home?"

"Miss Rebecca, if you will agree, I shall carry you," offered Mr. Bingley, but the girl shook her head. "Please, Lizzy?"

"Aha, now I understand," answered Mrs. Burton in a more severe voice. "What you really want is for Miss Elizabeth to pay you more attention. I am completely against this kind of spoiled behaviour."

"Sweetie, I cannot carry you. You are a big girl now, and you are too heavy to be carried."

Becky wiped her tears with her sleeve and took a few steps, obviously upset, and then suddenly she turned and addressed Mr. Darcy. "Can you carry me, please? You look much stronger than Lizzy."

Her request, after so decidedly refusing Mr. Bingley's offer, took everyone by surprise, Mr. Darcy most of all. Until that moment, he had retreated somewhat from the group, watching them a little detached and selfishly hoping everything would be resolved quickly so he could resume his walk with Elizabeth. He had never been in the close proximity of little children, except his sister, and he never really knew how to act around them.

When Becky addressed him, so small at his feet, he almost did not even hear her. Somewhat confused, he lowered his eyes and saw her small face lifted to him and waiting, and he simply did not know what to answer. He looked at Elizabeth, silently asking for an indication, but she did not understand the meaning of his gaze and thought he was displeased.

"Becky, it is very impolite to bother Mr. Darcy with such a request — not to mention that you are so dirty and wet. Please, be a nice girl and we will walk slowly home."

Finally, Darcy passed his initial surprise and reacted as he should, forcing a gentle smile to his face. "Miss Bennet, she is not bothering me. I shall carry Miss Gardiner — no trouble at all."

"Are you sure, sir? Believe me, it is not necessary — " But the girl quickly threw her little hands up to him.

"Thank you, Mr. Darcy! Now we can all walk together — the three of us."

He held her in his arms, and with everyone finally calmed, the whole party resumed the walk to the Gardiners' home, Mr. Darcy and his two companions a pace behind. She encircled his neck with her little arms, her head very close to his and began to search his face with great curiosity.

"As you can see, sir, Mrs. Burton was absolutely right earlier when mentioning that this disobedient, little girl only wanted to remain close to me. It is my fault; I have always been too indulgent with her."

As much as she loved her cousin, Elizabeth was troubled by the thought that Mr. Darcy would be displeased at being forced into such familiar behaviour in a public place.

However, he leaned his head to her and whispered with the hint of a flirting smile at the corner of his mouth, "A very strong reason not to refuse her, Miss Bennet, as I can easily understand her wish."

Although she should have been accustomed by now — from the Netherfield ball especially — to those little hints of his preference toward her, she could not cease to be astonished every time she heard such things from the man she always thought to be austere and reserved. She preferred not to respond, looking carefully at the ground until the silence was broken by Becky's cheery voice.

"Am I too heavy, Mr. Darcy?"

"No, you are not, Miss Gardiner," he answered, very politely, making the girls chuckle.

"You called me Miss Gardiner?"

"Yes, I did. Are you not, by any chance, Miss Gardiner?" Mr. Darcy was determined to participate in the girl's game to please Elizabeth.

"No, I am not Miss Gardiner. Margaret is Miss Gardiner; I am a spoiled, naughty girl," she answered seriously as an introduction to herself, making him suppress a laugh.

"Spoiled and naughty is not good, you know," Becky explained most sincerely in a low voice. "Mama and Mrs. Burton call me that when they are angry with me."

"I see. And how should I address you?"

"Oh, you can call me Becky."

"All right then, Miss Becky."

She shook her head, discontented with his lack of understanding. "Not Miss Becky — just Becky."

"I am sorry; now I understand. Just Becky." He cast a quick glance toward Elizabeth, content to meet her merry eyes watching them approvingly.

"You are very tall, Mr. Darcy — taller than Lizzy and Papa. I feel like I am in a tree." He did not really know what to respond, so she continued.

"My Aunt Bennet from Longbourn said you are tall and handsome and have ten thousand a year. I do not know what ten thousand is, but I think she is very fond of you, for she speaks about you all the time."

Elizabeth lifted her eyes to her, mortified and alarmed at what she might say next. She opened her mouth to stop her, but Mr. Darcy quickly interceded.

"Thank you, Becky, and to Mrs. Bennet, too."

He was smiling, amused not just by the little girl's honest, unrestrained chatter but by Elizabeth's obvious distress; she probably knew her cousin very well and was expecting additional surprises to be revealed.

Breaking all the rules of proper behaviour, he could not help inquiring of Becky further, taking Elizabeth quite by surprise.

"And did Mrs. Bennet say anything else about me?"

"Mr. Darcy! You should not encourage her in this improper discussion! Perhaps a more neutral subject could be found?"

She was openly censuring him. Mr. Darcy, however, was not desirous to lose such an unexpected opportunity of enjoying himself.

"I am sorry we upset you, Miss Bennet. We were only talking about — "

Becky leaned her little head closer and whispered into his ear, though loudly enough for anyone nearby to hear.

"I cannot tell you for sure what else she said, for I am not supposed to listen to the grown-ups talk."

"I see. That is very proper indeed; I am glad you obeyed."

He looked to Elizabeth, silently saying, *Do not worry; I shall not ask anything to embarrass you further,* and she relaxed a little.

Nevertheless, paying more attention to them than the path, her foot slipped and she was about to fall; at the last moment, she grabbed Mr. Darcy's arm.

"Miss Bennet, are you all right?"

"Yes, sir, I am perfectly fine."

"Please take my arm; it will be safer that way."

She could easily see the wisdom of his advice and kept her hand under his arm, her closeness making him feel a delightful sense of completion. But his moments of silent enjoyment disappeared in no time when Becky, helpfully, offered them a much better solution.

"Mr. Darcy, you should carry Lizzy, too. It would be safer that way!"

Elizabeth felt not only her cheeks but also her whole body blush violently. Her embarrassment grew beyond limits as the conversation continued.

"I am afraid I cannot do that, Becky."

"Why not? Is she too heavy?"

He turned his head, looking at Elizabeth earnestly and intently as though measuring her, while Elizabeth, mortified and red-faced, desperately tried to hide her eyes and control the sudden shiver that overwhelmed her whole body under his stare.

"No, I do not think she is too heavy, but it would not be proper for a gentleman to carry a lady."

Becky remained silent a few moments, thoughtful.

"Are you certain about that, Mr. Darcy? 'Cause I am sure I saw Papa carrying Mama to her room one evening after we were all gone to bed and I woke up to ask for a cup of milk."

It was too much for him, and all he could do was look at the little girl in his arms, speechless, his eyes wide, as she obviously was expecting his opinion on the subject. He dared to cast a glance at Elizabeth, and to his surprise, this time she was amused and smiled ironically at him. Her expression said, *I warned you not to encourage her.*

"Uh... I am quite certain it would not be proper to do such a thing in public, but

I am sure your father had a very good reason to do so. Perhaps your mother was not feeling well; and it was not in public, was it?"

She nodded her agreement, but her face still expressed puzzlement as Mr. Darcy noticed a moment later.

"So it would have been proper for you to carry Lizzy if not in public? And if Lizzy felt unwell and still in public, would it then be proper to carry her?"

Mr. Darcy's jaw opened visibly at these new questions, whose answers he would not attempt to voice, and he could hear Elizabeth chuckling at his right.

A new question came forcefully. "So, Mr. Darcy, it is proper to do some things only when not in public and when someone is ill?"

"Uh ... yes, some things, yes," he admitted reluctantly, though fearful of what she would ask next.

"I see ... " She seemed pleased with his answer, and a light glinted in her eyes as a new idea crossed her mind.

Without any connection to the previous topic, she continued, "You are not scary at all, Mr. Darcy!"

He furrowed his brow and looked at her. "Did you believe I was scary?"

"Yes I did! We saw you when you left yesterday, and we all believed you looked scary and Mr. Bingley looked nice."

"Becky! You are being unacceptably rude. Apologise to Mr. Darcy immediately!" Elizabeth bore the offence in his stead; however, he seemed not affected, even managing to smile.

"Do not worry, Miss Bennet. I am accustomed to the fact that everyone likes Mr. Bingley better than me and understandably so. He is indeed much more agreeable."

"Oh, but I do not like Mr. Bingley better. I like you better," was the girl's reassuring answer.

"Thank you." He decided it was best to say as little as possible and not to encourage her further.

"I do not like Mr. Bingley at all."

"Why not?" he answered, utterly surprised.

"Because he has blond hair," whispered the girl.

"Uh, I see. And blond hair is not good?"

"No, it is not, because he looks just like my brothers, and I am upset with all of them."

Mr. Darcy could not remember the last time he was so amused.

"Well, Becky, I am happy you do not think me scary anymore, but I am sorry you do not think Mr. Bingley is nice, because he is indeed."

"Oh, but I do think he is nice. I just don't like him."

After a short pause, she looked attentively at his face and then continued.

"He is nice, but you are very pretty."

All Mr. Darcy's self-control vanished, and he could restrain his laughter no longer, desperately hoping no acquaintance was around to see him.

"Well, Becky, I have been told many things in my lifetime, but I have never been told I am 'pretty'."

"But pretty is good, you know?"

"Yes, indeed," he answered, laughing, but he stopped, feeling her little finger pressing his cheek.

"What is this?"

"I do not know. What does it looks like? Is my face dirty?"

"No, it is something very funny indeed. What is it?"

Clueless, he turned to Elizabeth, asking her opinion, Becky's little finger still puncturing his face, but Lizzy was flustered and tried not to look directly at the spot to which the girl pointed.

Eventually, she managed to articulate an answer, wondering if she could possibly be more embarrassed. "It is a dimple," came the answer that took him quite unprepared.

Becky was only half content, though, and needed further explanation.

"Dimple is good?"

"I do not know," laughed Mr. Darcy again. "It is not for me to say."

She turned naturally to her cousin. "Lizzy, dimple is good?"

She closed her eyes, breathing deeply and, trying to avoid his eyes, suddenly she looked straight at Becky with Darcy in the corner of her eye.

"Yes, Becky, dimple is very good," she responded emphatically, causing Mr. Darcy to redden unexpectedly.

"Becky, I am afraid you have distressed Mr. Darcy more than is acceptable with your questions. I do not think he will ever call on us again," said Elizabeth, more to Mr. Darcy than to her cousin, but the little girl became alarmed.

"Did I distress you, Mr. Darcy?"

"I confess you did, but it was a pleasant distress, Becky. I do not think I have ever received so many compliments in one day."

She smiled contentedly. "A compliment is when you say something nice about someone, is it not?"

"Yes, it is."

"Well, if you come to visit us again, I shall give you even more compliments, Mr. Darcy," concluded the girl, happy to find a way to tempt him not to leave forever as Lizzy had implied.

Both Elizabeth and Mr. Darcy chose not to say anything, relieved that they had reached the Gardiners' house.

The gentlemen declined to enter and bid their good-byes, Becky bestowing a sweet kiss on Mr. Darcy's cheek. Then, politely, under Mrs. Burton's vigilant eyes, she took a very nice farewell from Mr. Bingley, too, and entered the house.

Elizabeth and Jane remained outside a few moments to see the gentlemen into their carriage, still marvelling at their present bliss. A mere two days before, both of them were heartbroken and hopeless. They could not believe their happiness and good fortune.

THE GENTLEMEN SAT COMFORTABLY IN the carriage.

"Darcy, you seemed to become a favourite of another young lady."

He looked at Bingley and a huge smile spread over his face.

"Well, Bingley, what can I say? Your misfortune is that you have blond hair, and blond hair is not good."

"I beg your pardon? Darcy, are you all right?"

Bingley was concerned by his friend's shocking peals of laughter, not ever remembering such a sight. Eventually, Darcy regained his control.

"Oh my, Bingley! I absolutely have to tell you this in every detail! And tell my cousin and Georgiana, as well. By the way, Bingley, did you ever notice that I am pretty?" Bingley's eyes and mouth flew open.

As Darcy related his talk with Rebecca, Bingley's laughter brought tears to his eyes. It was indeed fortunate that none of their acquaintance encountered the carriage and heard them express their amusement in such an ungentlemanlike manner.

THE NEXT DAY, MR. DARCY arrived at the Gardiners' house to escort them to his home. It was still early for dinner, but the hour had been established previously as Mr. Gardiner was desirous to consult a few books in Darcy's library; a short visit with Miss Darcy was also scheduled.

For two days, Darcy was preoccupied with making sure everything was perfect for the dinner as it was Elizabeth's first visit to his house. His agitation transferred to Georgiana — worried that the state of her health was not proper for such an important event — and then to the staff. He knew he was irrational, for Elizabeth, Jane and the Gardiners were not the kind of people to be impressed by richness or greatness, but he continued in the same manner until his cousin Colonel Fitzwilliam, the younger son of Lord Matlock — coming for his usual visit with Georgiana — could take no more.

"Darcy, for heaven's sake stop commanding others about; you are driving your servants to distraction. Let them do their jobs; they are exceedingly well trained as far as I know. Sit down and tell me about this dinner — to which, by the way, I was not invited."

"I am sorry, Cousin. I am completely irrational today. You are right, of course; let us drink something, and I shall tell you the news."

As with Georgiana, Darcy also had become more open and close to his cousin during the last trying month, so close that he dared to talk with him a little about Elizabeth Bennet. However, until that moment, the colonel never considered how determined Darcy was toward the young lady or how anxious to make his intentions known. As Darcy related Miss Bingley's deceit, his two meetings in as many days with the aforementioned lady, and the invitation to dinner, the colonel began to worry. He was fully aware of Miss Bennet's family, and while he was not so rigid as to despise or disregard her for her lack of fortune or connections, he was fully aware that, for a man of Darcy's situation and expectations from family and society, it would not be an insignificant problem.

He looked contemplatively at his cousin who seemed not to consider how this news would spread through town, not to mention the storm that would brew when their aunt Lady Catherine found out. *Nor will my parents be at all pleased. I can only imagine my father's reaction.* Determined to be well informed and have the most accurate personal opinion on the matter, he invited himself to dinner, already formulating a credible excuse for leaving a party hosted by his parents.

Elizabeth's trepidation exceeded Mr. Darcy's, and though both her aunt and Jane agreed she looked splendid, she was still worried about her appearance and about the entire evening's events.

At last, Mr. Darcy arrived, and as soon as he entered the room, their eyes met; each thought the other looked extraordinarily well, but their anxiety only increased, causing them, quite naturally, to appear impolite and somewhat peculiar to the other members of the party.

Mr. Darcy handed all the ladies into the elegant carriage. There was little talk during the ride, and shortly they arrived at the Darcys' townhouse.

The moment she was in front of the impressive entrance, Elizabeth could not help being overwhelmed by the elegance and magnificence of the house, 'ten thousand a year' resonating menacingly in her head. She closed her eyes in an attempt to control her emotions before entering, having the first material proof that Mr. Darcy was not just the man with whom she had danced, walked, flirted and held hands, but master of all this and so much more. The thought gave her little comfort.

"Miss Elizabeth?" His voice was low but warm, his worried eyes studying her and his smile tentative. He understood her; she was convinced of that. As at other times, he understood her uncertainties and was ready to relieve them.

"Shall we enter? I cannot tell you how thrilled I am finally to have you here." She blushed, smiling at him.

As they walked arm in arm, he leaned closer and whispered, "Thrilled is good, you know?"

Elizabeth only managed to whisper back, "Yes, I know," as thrills diffused in a warm-cold wave inside her body, weakening her knees as the couple entered the main room to join the Gardiners and Jane.

They were expecting to see the Bingleys and Hursts, but they had not yet arrived. Both Elizabeth and Jane anticipated their meeting with Caroline Bingley with little pleasure. They were happy that Mr. Darcy was so thoughtful as to invite them earlier in order to become better acquainted with his house before the imposing Miss Bingley came to reclaim her rights as his intimate friend.

Mr. Darcy was everything charming, his wish to please them so obvious that it was touching. Refreshments and drinks were offered as dinner was to be served somewhat later.

"Mr. Darcy, is Miss Darcy feeling well today?" asked Mrs. Gardiner.

"Yes she is, Mrs. Gardiner, and I must say quite eager to meet you. I was just about to ask you to accompany me to her apartment for a few moments."

Mrs. Gardiner, a wise woman, knew when she was actually desired.

"Mr. Darcy, I should also like to meet Miss Darcy, but I shall await another opportunity; I do not want to fatigue her, and I know that I am not the one she wants to see at the moment."

He started to protest, but then understanding her meaning and the fact that she was honest and caring in her offer, he only bowed respectfully to her.

"Mrs. Gardiner, I want to assure you that you will be welcome any time in our home; please consider this an open and permanent invitation. Now, if you would allow, I shall guide your nieces to my sister, and later I should be honoured to show you the house."

Chapter 13

The preparation for the Bennet sisters' visit proved to be an opportunity for genuine improvement for Georgiana. Consulting the doctor and having his approval, Darcy transformed Georgiana's dressing room to host this visit so she could leave her bedroom after more than a month. The servants took the opportunity to clean the room and, especially, to open the windows, allowing the fresh winter air to enter.

The most comfortable settee in the house was brought and transformed into a resting place where she could recline among the elegant pillows to keep her warm and cosy. She insisted on having her hair arranged as she would for a special occasion. She was prepared in a snug sitting position even before Darcy left to retrieve their guests, and she employed her time reading Shakespeare — which she knew almost by heart but was proper to conceal her emotions — with Mrs. Annesley watching her carefully.

For the Bennet sisters, the moment was no easier. Jane, though she knew her worry was unfounded, still harboured mixed feelings and was uncertain about the introduction while Elizabeth was distressed by her desire to make a good impression. The moment they entered the room with the anticipation of the formidable presentation, they almost gasped in amazement at seeing, in an improvised bed, a pale young girl, obviously more intimidated than they were. They expected to see someone much like Mr. Darcy, and it surprised them to be proven wrong.

"Miss Bennet, Miss Elizabeth, allow me to introduce my sister, Georgiana. Georgiana, may I present Miss Bennet and Miss Elizabeth Bennet."

"How do you do?"

"Very pleased to meet you, Miss Darcy," they answered warmly.

She tried to return their smiles. "Would you like to sit down?" She indicated various places around a small table arranged for the purpose of their visit and positioned near the settee.

Elizabeth agreed and took the place nearest to Miss Darcy.

Darcy returned to the drawing room after a few minutes, not wishing to leave the Gardiners alone too long. Once he was gone, Georgiana became even shyer and seemed frightened.

However, Elizabeth did not allow her to feel that way for long.

"We are very happy to finally meet you Miss Darcy. We have heard so many things about you from both Mr. Darcy and Mr. Bingley."

Georgiana blushed.

"And I about you both, Miss Elizabeth. You are very kind to come to see me under these unpleasant circumstances."

"No indeed, Miss Darcy, we are happy to be here. And I must say I am pleased to see you so well."

"Thank you. I hope to have the opportunity to see you again very soon."

"And perhaps then," said Jane, also shyly, "we shall have the pleasure of hearing you play, Miss Darcy. We have also heard you are fond of music and very accomplished at the pianoforte."

Georgiana blushed even more and with difficulty tried to find a proper answer to such a compliment but could say no more than, "Thank you."

Elizabeth, with sympathy for this young girl — so timid and painfully shy — tried to remember what Mr. Darcy had told her in order to find a comfortable topic. Happily, she saw the book on her left and took the opportunity.

"Am I to understand you like Shakespeare, Miss Darcy?"

"Indeed, I do."

"As do I — very much indeed. I also enjoy any play I can attend."

"I share the same passions, Miss Elizabeth. My brother introduced me to Shakespeare's work when I was very young and also took me to every new performance. We saw many plays more than once as I was too young to understand some of them fully."

Masterfully, Elizabeth encouraged her to talk about various things she seemed to enjoy, not ceasing to wonder at how thin and pale she looked. She had pleasant features, though different from her brother, and her eyes were incredibly blue, perhaps, thought Elizabeth, more accentuated by contrast with her pale skin.

Jane entered little into the conversation, but whenever she did, she was kind and gentle, which increased Georgiana's comfort. Her easiness grew as Elizabeth continued to ask questions she knew would give her pleasure, and the girl indeed answered with great delight.

From books to music and theatre to opera, Georgiana began to relate to them her tour of Italy and the extraordinary spectacles she saw there. Both sisters seemed pleased and surprised by her stories, which give her more encouragement. Though still reserved in expressing herself, her intelligence and education were evident and greatly appreciated by both her guests.

They were in the middle of a pleasant, animated conversation when the door opened, and Mr. Darcy and Mr. Bingley entered. The moment he saw Jane, Mr. Bingley's face began to glow, and he went directly to her, smiling, his happiness apparent. Then he greeted Elizabeth, moved near Georgiana, kissing her hands tenderly, and asked how she was feeling.

Both Mr. Darcy and Elizabeth looked at Jane with worry at the same time, but she appeared serene and not unpleasantly affected by Mr. Bingley's familiarity toward Georgiana. When their gazes met, they smiled at one another, amazed once more at how their thoughts seemed to coincide.

"Miss Bennet, Miss Elizabeth, your presence is required downstairs. Miss Bingley and Mr. and Mrs. Hurst have just arrived and were asking after you," said Darcy, fully aware that this was the least reason to make Elizabeth desirous to leave her present company.

"So soon?" asked Georgiana without considering her words and trying to conceal her disappointment.

"Not so soon, dearest, a half an hour has passed since I left you, and we want to begin a tour of the house as I promised Mr. and Mrs. Gardiner."

"You are right, of course," she agreed, obviously in low spirits.

Suddenly Elizabeth interjected cheerfully, "Actually, Mr. Darcy, I must confess you were interrupting us precisely in the middle of a very interesting story. If Miss Darcy is not fatigued, I would be grateful if you allow me to stay a little longer."

Her request took the others quite by surprise, and Darcy was about to protest — he truly wanted to show her the house — but then he met her eyes. How could he refuse her when all she wanted was to please Georgiana?

"As you wish… I will return to escort you to the dining room later."

"Thank you, sir."

Jane bid goodbye to Georgiana and, supported on Bingley's arm, was followed closely by Darcy, who turned to cast a last glance at them. As he exited the room, he could hear his sister's shy voice.

"Miss Bennet, I am indeed grateful for your decision to stay a little longer, for I know the meaning of this. But I know you would prefer to be with the others from the party, and I do not want to keep you from the enjoyment and their pleasant company. So please do not feel obliged to stay with me."

Elizabeth was not to be discouraged so easily and decided to be honest.

"Miss Darcy, although it is true that I remained to keep you company, it is equally true that I enjoy talking to you, and I infinitely prefer your company to Miss Bingley's, whom I am not desirous to meet at the moment."

Georgiana's eyes and mouth opened in great surprise at such a statement, and she did not know quite what to do or say, but she ceased feeling guilty for prolonging Elizabeth's visit. "Thank you," was her whispered answer.

Elizabeth resumed their previous discussion, asking for more details, and was amazed at the number of places and countries Georgiana had visited, despite her young age. More than once, her questions were directed to something related to Mr. Darcy, and his sister was only too happy to answer, careful to present her brother to his best advantage, although soon she could see there was no need to improve Elizabeth's opinion of him.

As their conversation became more animated, Elizabeth asked Georgiana not to address her as Miss Bennet any longer but by her given name, and when the girl accepted under the same condition, they soon ceased the formal manner of addressing each other.

An hour later, which passed unnoticed, Mrs. Annesley entered with two maids who were carrying a tray full of various courses of food and fruits; she apologised for disturbing them, but it was dinnertime for Georgiana.

"Mrs. Annesley, please postpone it a little longer. I am not hungry, and I could not eat in front of Miss Bennet."

Mrs. Annesley remained disconcerted.

She knew it would be impolite to interrupt the visit, but the doctor and the master were very strict regarding her mistress's meals, and she was diligent in respecting their directives as it was in Georgiana's best interest.

"Mrs. Annesley," interrupted Elizabeth, "I do not think you should change dinnertime for me. I will stay only a few more minutes; you can leave the tray on the table."

The maids did as she required and left while Mrs. Annesley took a seat in a corner as discreetly as possible, waiting to see whether her help was needed. Elizabeth cast a quick glance toward the plates.

"Georgiana, I cannot believe how much food is here. Are you eating so much at one meal?"

"No, of course not," she answered, a little uncomfortably. "But my brother has ordered that all the types of food that I favour be sent to me, even Italian or French food so I can choose."

She blushed and continued, feeling quite guilty.

"I am not a very good patient, and I always upset William by not eating enough. The doctor said I will not recover if I am not well fed."

Elizabeth tried to lighten the tone of their conversation while she was inspecting the tray with great interest.

"Georgiana, this smells delicious." She leaned closer and whispered, "You know, I must confess I was so excited about Mr. Darcy's invitation that I did not eat anything today, and now I am feeling quite hungry."

"Oh, I am sorry! I am sure you will be invited to dinner very soon."

"Yes, but until then, would you mind if I join you and eat a little now?"

"Of course not, Elizabeth, but what about dinner?"

"Oh, do not worry. I will just taste a very little now to temper my hunger so at the dinner table I will be able to eat no more than a proper lady should."

"A proper lady should eat little? I did not know that."

"Oh, yes. It is a well-kept secret among ladies and one of the most powerful arts and allurements in finding and securing a husband. Apparently, it is not appreciated by a gentleman if a lady eats too much, perhaps because a wise gentleman is sensible not to being forced to spend extra money for his wife's food in addition to her jewels and gowns." She started to laugh in the face of Georgiana's incredulity, and the girl smiled back at her.

"Elizabeth, you are just teasing me."

"Well, maybe yes, maybe no. Let us see what we have here. Oh, that looks wonderful. Let us try it, and tell me what it is." Her joy and vitality were contagious, and Georgiana could do nothing other than oblige her.

Neither of them really ate much, but at Elizabeth's impulse and repeated inquiry about one course or another, Georgiana ate a little of everything as Elizabeth was sampling the various dishes prepared for each course.

So pleased was Georgiana to have Elizabeth in her company that, as timidly and obviously unaccustomed as she was, she invited her to call again the next day, an invitation accepted without a second thought. Elizabeth also was delighted with Georgiana's company and, more than anything, was desirous to help in any way she could for the young girl's improvement.

As they ate, Mr. Darcy entered the room silently and stopped at the door, looking at them in amazement. They were not facing him and did not notice his entrance, but he could see their profiles.

His sister, a slight smile on her lips, was eating with more appetite than she had in a long time, but his eyes were fixed on Elizabeth's lips as she licked them, pleased with the taste of her food. This simple, natural gesture made his own lips dry, though he thirsted not for water but for her.

Mortified, he recovered a few moments later while desperately trying to shake off those oh-so-improper thoughts. He hesitated as he tried to gain control of himself, taking a few more steps into his sister's room and approaching them slowly.

The ladies finally noticed his presence; Elizabeth startled and quickly covered her mouth with her napkin, whispering to Georgiana, "I am afraid Mr. Darcy has caught me, and now he will understand my deception."

Georgiana answered daringly in the same jovial manner, "Do not worry. My brother is a rich man; he can afford a wife who eats quite a lot!"

The innocent statement stunned both of them and seemed to hang in the silence. One was shocked for what she had inadvertently implied, the other — not unpleasantly— was unsure of how to react. They looked at each other for a moment, embarrassed, but a moment later Elizabeth burst into laughter under her napkin, and

Georgiana joined her timidly, happy to see she was not upset.

"May I inquire as to the reason for your amusement, ladies?"

"Yes you may, Mr. Darcy, but we will not answer, for it is a private matter. Not to mention that the answer would likely place me in an unfavourable light," Elizabeth replied, making his sister burst into another peal of laughter.

"Georgiana, I am pleased to see you eating a little more than usual," said he, amazed to see them looking at each other and smiling again.

"Well, Brother, Miss Bennet's company was very stimulating."

"Yes, I know. Miss Bennet's company is always very stimulating." Mr. Darcy smiled, making Elizabeth blush again. "I am sorry to interrupt your visit, Georgiana, but your room is ready, and it is time for the doctor to check on you. Our guests are expecting Miss Bennet downstairs as the *other* dinner will be served very soon."

"Oh I know! Elizabeth, I am so sorry for having selfishly detained you so long. I had a very pleasant time, but I am afraid it was not very polite of me."

"It was a pleasure for me as well, Georgiana, as I have already told you. I am sure the doctor will find you quite well."

"Thank you! Shall I see you again tomorrow?"

"Yes, you may depend upon it."

Both of them looked at Mr. Darcy for his consent, only to see the hint of an approving smile on his lips. He addressed Elizabeth with warm politeness that perfectly matched his smile.

"Miss Bennet, if you will excuse me for a moment, I will take my sister to her room and return."

With her maid's help, he lifted Georgiana in his arms, one hand supporting her back, and entered the bedroom.

Mr. Darcy returned a few minutes later and gently took Elizabeth's elbow, directing her to the door. However, it was not the same one by which they had entered but the door that led to Georgiana's small study — another beautiful room, smaller and illuminated gently by a few candles.

His gesture caused Elizabeth to cast a wondering glance at him, but his countenance was light, and a smile twisted at the corner of his mouth.

"Miss Bennet, I understood you will call again tomorrow?"

"Yes, sir, if you approve. If you consider it too tiring for your sister, I will postpone the visit."

"No indeed. I approve of it very much indeed." He stopped before opening the door, forcing Elizabeth to do the same.

"Miss Bennet" — she turned to him — "please allow me to thank you and to tell you how grateful I am for your kind attention toward my sister."

"Sir, please believe me, there is no need to thank me. I spent many pleasant moments with her; she is indeed a remarkable young lady."

"Yes, she is, and I was amazed to see her so animated and happy in your presence. You seem to have a power over the Darcys, Miss Bennet," said he, his voice deep and gentle while reaching for her hands and holding them tenderly. They were close to each other, and both moved even closer until their bodies almost touched.

For Elizabeth it was as astonishingly pleasant as she remembered — the feel of his strong but tender hands holding and stroking hers — but now she knew what would come next, so she was not surprised. She allowed herself to enjoy fully all the sensations his caressing fingers and overwhelming nearness aroused through her and inside her. Although she felt her knees weakening, she still could smile as her gaze was locked by his; she was even able to tease him.

"What power do I have over the Darcys? The power to make them eat?"

He brought their joined hands close to his chest, caressing the backs of her hands with his thumbs while Elizabeth boldly began to move her fingers over his, fondling them, instinctively wishing to return the astonishing sensation that was sending thousands of thrills along her spine.

Her tender but obvious response made Darcy's heart almost burst with happiness, and he leaned closer, his forehead almost touching hers, amazed to see that, from so close, the sparkle of her eyes was brighter and more radiant then ever — and different from what he had seen before. Could there be... passion in her eyes? And desire? Or was it only his imagination deceiving him — his own desire intoxicating his senses? But he knew he did not misunderstand her when he felt her trembling, though she could not possibly have been cold. In truth, her whole body was radiating warmth.

His thirsty lips hardly managed to whisper, "No, Miss Bennet — the power to bring joy into our lives."

It took all of his restraint and the proper manners ingrained by years of education to maintain tenuous control over his overwhelming passion. His mind was clouded by the urge — the desperate need — to touch her, taste her, and devour her. After the long, dark month of painful longing, to know that it was not a dream, that she was there, so close that he could feel her breathing, tensing, trembling, waiting...

Her hands were in his, their fingers entwined — hers almost as daring as his — tantalising, caressing each other as if all sensation began and ended in their hands, in that spot where their flesh was joined.

Never releasing her gaze, he lifted her hands until his impatient lips reached them and bestowed a lingering kiss on each of her wrists. Tracing his way down to her palms and back, his soft kisses, warm and wet, left Elizabeth dizzy and breathless.

Elizabeth gasped when she felt his lips for the first time — not just touching her bare skin but moving, pressing against it, his mouth half parted, warmer, bolder and more impatient than she remembered, taking from her and demanding still more. She could think of nothing other than that she wanted to give him more and wanted more from him. Unconsciously, her flustered face moved closer to his and her dry lips parted slightly… waiting.

He was aware of nothing except her intoxicating closeness — just the two of them, alone — her soft, unadorned lips: a homage offered to him. The shiver struck them both in the same moment in anticipation of what would come next, their faces drawn to each other until their lips almost joined.

But he withdrew a few inches, just enough so as not to be touching her anymore. He remembered he had something to do first; he could not think coherently enough to recall what, for his brain seemed to register nothing but her warm closeness, but he knew it was something important and must be done before letting himself throw away all the restrictions of propriety.

"Miss Bennet, I must — "

Though deeply disappointed by the interruption, she tried to regain her composure and enlarged the distance between them.

"Mr. Darcy, we both must remember we are in your sister's apartment, and my relatives are waiting for us downstairs." Her voice was in no way reproachful but sweet and teasing; however, her words made Darcy conscious of his duties and responsibilities as a host and master of the house.

"You are right, of course. Miss Bennet, I am very sorry. My manners were unpardonable. I am again in the position to beg your forgiveness. My behaviour was intolerable."

He hastened to release her hands, but she deliberately delayed him, clasping his hand between hers more tightly.

"Sir, I can only hope there was *nothing* intolerable or regrettable in our behaviour, for if that were the case, I am equally to blame. As shameful as it might sound, you did nothing that I did not accept and welcome."

Even in the relative darkness of the room, her eyes seemed like diamonds, and her teasing but slightly embarrassed tone, as well as her flustered, smiling face, were the sweetest reward for his distress.

"No indeed, Miss Bennet, there is nothing for which to be sorry. And certainly you are not to be blamed for anything."

She blushed, smiled sweetly, and then turned to the door without a word, still holding his hand in hers; this time he stopped her.

"Miss Bennet, please allow me only one moment. Tomorrow, when you visit Georgiana, could you reserve a few minutes for me? I have a very important question I have been meaning to ask you for quite some time. And while I do not want to hurry you in any way, for I am not expecting an immediate answer, I can go no longer without addressing the question."

Her whole body was thrown into an amalgam of fire and ice as her heart seemed to stop and then started to beat so wildly that it threatened to break through her chest; she could hardly find the proper words. When she met his eyes, she could see his pleading gaze, full of uncertainty, obviously as full of emotion as she was, and she did not delay her answer.

"Of course, Mr. Darcy! However," said she, smiling and hoping to put an end to the unbearable wait, "if the question is so important and you have wanted to ask it for some time, could you not do it now? After all, what will a few more minutes do?"

He returned the smile but offered her his arm. After she took it, he led her outside the room to the stairs.

"No, I cannot, for it is a very important question, and I need time to ask it properly."

He could feel the tightening of her hand on his arm and knew she understood; for a few seconds, his heart seemed to stop in anticipation, waiting for a sign of her own wishes and intentions.

"I see... but I must confess I am confused. As you have wanted to ask it for quite some time, one would believe you have had time enough to prepare it."

"Yes I have, Miss Bennet, but I do not like to hasten such important matters. I would prefer to take time to do them properly, slowly and with care as I want them to be perfect."

"I see..." another shiver ran up her spine, though she did not quite understand why. She felt more than understood that his innocent statement was hiding other meanings, and more than his insinuating words, his pointed look and deep, almost whispering voice, made her tremble again.

"Then I shall have to wait until tomorrow. But did you not mention you will be out tomorrow, sir?"

"I did, Miss Bennet; however, there are occasions in which I prefer to take my time, and occasions in which I prefer to make as much haste as possible, and tomorrow's business will be in the latter category, I can assure you."

They stared at each other a few more moments, until their attention was drawn by voices in the dining room and Mr. Darcy remembered his duties as a dinner host.

"Miss Bennet, forgive me. I forgot to mention that I welcomed a last-minute guest. My cousin, Colonel Fitzwilliam, has just arrived and joined us. I hope you will not be displeased."

"I am sure I shall not, Mr. Darcy. It would be a pleasure and an honour to meet your cousin." In fact, she was quite happy that something had come up to distract her attention until the momentous 'question' could arise, and such a long wait she had to bear: a whole evening, a night and a morning — an eternity.

Chapter 14

The party that gathered in the dining room could not have been more diverse in thoughts and hopes for the evening.

Darcy was still exceedingly angry with Miss Bingley, blaming her for the distress Elizabeth and Jane Bennet had endured and especially for her deceptive suggestion regarding a relationship between Charles and Georgiana. However, Darcy never retracted the dinner invitation for Miss Bingley or the Hursts because they were his friend's family, although after Bingley related to him his tempestuous discussion with her, he concluded that Miss Bingley had received a well-deserved reprimand.

Bingley, directly involved and still resentful, more or less purposefully forgot to mention to his family that the Bennet sisters and their relatives from Cheapside were also invited. However, in order to avoid a violent reaction, he told them the news in the carriage, and Caroline was choked with anger. Louisa reproached him — a good opportunity for Bingley to suggest that they could return home if they were displeased.

No matter how angry she was, Caroline never would have allowed Eliza Bennet to be near Mr. Darcy an entire evening without her strict supervision. Entering Mr. Darcy's house, Caroline was uncomfortable at his possible reaction — perhaps he would ask her to leave — but also hopeful she would have a few private moments with him to explain herself and formulate a credible excuse.

Her fear only proved how little she knew Mr. Darcy; he was cold but polite—he never could mistreat a woman in his home—and acted with civil attention as a perfect host toward all his guests, cutting Caroline off at every attempt to approach him. His attitude of avoiding her, together with his easiness toward the Gardiners, made Caroline grow more indignant and revolted by Mr. Darcy's sudden lack of pride and self-respect; to be on friendly terms with such people was unthinkable!

When she discovered that Eliza and Jane Bennet were admitted to see Georgiana, her anger was beyond limits, and it took an extreme effort to maintain her decorum.

To make matters worse, as she tried to be polite to those people, a shock struck her: although Jane Bennet had returned, Eliza remained above stairs with Georgiana. This was most humiliating, considering that Caroline never had been invited to Georgiana's rooms.

Both Caroline and Louisa greeted Jane with their usual insincerity of friendship, and Caroline went so far as to reproach Jane for not having notified her of their arrival in town, thus leaving it to be understood that Jane's letter was lost. Nevertheless, even they could grasp the change in Jane; she was as sweet and gentle as before, but her attitude toward them and their brother was different. She was more attentive than before to Charles — her smiles and glances open and inviting — but she exhibited a cold, distant politeness towards them. It was obvious she knew the truth and would allow herself to be deceived no longer.

Caroline dared to ask about Elizabeth and received the communication that she was with Miss Darcy and would join them later. With that statement, Jane closed the subject and resumed her conversation with her aunt and Charles. She simply dismissed his sister with a determination that infuriated both Caroline and Louisa beyond the limit of their patience but brought a smile of approval to Mrs. Gardiner's lips.

Soon, Colonel Fitzwilliam appeared, and he was a welcome addition to the party; his happy manners, pleasant conversation and unpretentious behaviour made him delightful company for everyone.

Another hour passed before dinner was announced, and Mr. Darcy went himself to escort Miss Eliza Bennet to the dining room, something that, Caroline Bingley reflected, he never would have considered doing when they were in Hertfordshire.

ELIZABETH AND MR. DARCY ENTERED the dining room arm in arm, her cheeks flushed and his face lightened by an open smile; no one who saw them earlier when they left the drawing room doubted that something had changed in that short time. The connection between them seemed altered.

Elizabeth greeted Bingley's sisters elegantly but coldly, and after Mr. Darcy introduced her to his cousin, the whole party proceeded into dinner. Mrs. Gardiner was watching her niece with pride and joy, more certain than ever about the future of the relationship that seemed to blossom.

Similar thoughts crossed the colonel's mind as he watched them; he was struck by Elizabeth's luminosity — as though the air were glowing around her — and by Darcy's serene countenance. They indeed looked stunning together, and the colonel was not a man easily impressed.

Mr. Darcy took his place at the head of the table with Elizabeth on his right and his cousin next to her; on his left were Mr. and Mrs. Gardiner and then Jane and Mr. Bingley, Miss Bingley and the Hursts.

Shortly after making Elizabeth's acquaintance, Colonel Fitzwilliam understood why Darcy was attracted to her. Very attractive, though not as beautiful as her sister, she was bright and clever in a pleasant, friendly way unlike Miss Bingley's sharp, aggressive intelligence. Moreover, Elizabeth Bennet had vitality, liveliness, and brightness. She was more restrained, however, than the colonel expected after Darcy had admiringly related to him some of their verbal duels of the past. *Well, maybe she is not as witty as Darcy said, but she definitely has the most remarkable eyes,* thought he, sitting near her and having the opportunity to admire her profile, her long lashes and the diamond gleam in her look at close range.

Nevertheless, he was astonished that his cousin could appreciate Miss Elizabeth Bennet's charm and openness, for she appeared to be more his type than Darcy's. *Then again, nobody ever seemed to be Darcy's type until now.* The colonel was not displeased with his observation regarding the Gardiners — the infamous part of Miss Elizabeth's connection. Mrs. Gardiner was a beautiful and fashionable woman, obviously accustomed to polite society; her manners and the way she annihilated Caroline Bingley's attacks proved that.

In the few hours since they had met, the colonel saw that Mr. Gardiner seemed to be unusually well informed about almost every aspect of London's business life. The colonel had no adequate information about the other members of the Bennet family, but the fact that Mr. Bennet was a respectable gentleman — as Darcy informed him a month earlier on his return from Hertfordshire — was a good sign. So too was Jane Bennet, not just for her remarkable beauty, but also for her sweet countenance and pleasant manners.

As for Elizabeth Bennet — obviously, her situation in life required prudence in marriage, and Darcy was by far more than she ever could have hoped to attain. The colonel was convinced everyone would consider her a fortune hunter; he himself had considered the prospect likely. However, though he could not form an opinion from being in her company for only a couple of hours, he could not deny the attraction between her and Darcy.

Oh, for heaven's sake, he is more ridiculous than Bingley, just staring at her and smiling like an old tomcat.

She in turn was glowing every time she looked at him — or every time he looked at her, *which is pretty much all the time.* A sudden revelation struck him: the bond between the two subjects of his observation was stronger than he imagined! And the way they entered the dining room together, and the fact that she had spent so much time with Georgiana... *Has he already proposed to her?* He gulped down the remaining wine in his glass, even more troubled. He had to find a way to speak with Darcy as soon as possible.

If he were in a position to give Darcy advice, Colonel Fitzwilliam certainly would recommend to him more patience and prudence before entering into such an engagement; but he did not consider even for a second trying to persuade Darcy against Miss Elizabeth.

First, having known Darcy intimately for a lifetime, he knew such an attempt would not be met with success, and no other result than a quarrel would ensue. Darcy never made a decision in haste and, before deciding, always considered and analysed all the implications and outcomes.

Furthermore, seeing Darcy so altered and serene was a joyous sight — especially after the past weeks of sleeplessness and torment caused by Georgiana's illness. *If this is the doing of Miss Elizabeth Bennet... well, she has my approval, fortune hunter or not. Darcy, no doubt, is much taken by this country girl.* The colonel was not reconciled to the fact that the dutiful, proper Darcy would decide to marry someone so beneath him. He wanted most of all to be sure that his cousin was rationally considering what he was doing and not merely experiencing a blind interlude of wild passion for a woman's charms. For if that were the case, the passion — and the colonel knew about passion — would slip away, but the regrets and bitterness would remain forever. It would be disastrous for not only Darcy but also for Elizabeth and both their families.

So CAUGHT WAS THE COLONEL in his meditations that he barely noticed his other companions.

Caroline Bingley's rage, carefully hidden for a while, escaped her control when she heard Mrs. Gardiner speaking about the gentlemen's visit a couple of days before. "Mrs. Gardiner, from what I hear, Gracechurch Street is quite far away; it must have taken you a great deal of time to cross town today."

"No indeed, Miss Bingley, we arrived in a short time, I might say. But of course, we had the advantage of Mr. Darcy's excellent carriage."

"Ah..." continued Miss Bingley, "well, it is understandable you do not have your own carriage, for it is an expensive investment."

"Miss Bingley, you do not need to worry," interrupted Darcy, addressing her for the first time. "Mr. Gardiner possesses quite a fine carriage, but it was my pleasure to escort them personally to my home."

"But is that area quite safe?"

The question was so rude that Bingley startled and cast a meaningful glare at his sister, who decided to ignore it, looking expectantly at Mrs. Gardiner. The answer, however, came from Elizabeth's mocking voice.

"Indeed it is, Miss Bingley; thank you for your concern. We have been visiting our aunt and uncle many times a year since we were children and have never had any reason to complain. But, of course, for someone like yourself, accustomed to high society and more fashionable locales, perhaps it would be preferable not to venture into that precinct."

The colonel smiled behind his napkin *Hmm... That was harsh but deserved. Well, it seems this is the first sign of the real Miss Elizabeth...*

"It is more than safe; it is quite a delightful area, I assure you," replied Mr. Darcy.

"I am particularly fond of the park near the Gardiner's house... charming."

Elizabeth could not help blushing as did Jane when Charles agreed, full of enthusiasm. In the next moment, Elizabeth startled, feeling Mr. Darcy's foot slowly touching hers under the table — or rather, his boot touching her shoe! It was not an insinuating touch, seeming more like an accidental movement of his long legs under the table than a purposeful sign, but still she felt a sudden need to swallow some cold water.

After a few moments, she dared to glance at him and saw a small, comforting smile on his lips; she was assured that his touch was not accidental. She smiled in return without moving her foot from his. Miss Bingley continued, knowing she made a mistake but growing angrier as she understood she had nothing more to lose.

"Well, I must believe you, Mr. Darcy, but I have to say your tastes seem to have changed dramatically in the last months in more than one respect."

The allusion touched everyone at the table, and a moment of silence followed until Bingley answered with a determination that made Jane gaze at him with growing admiration.

"Really? And how can you tell that, Caroline? I am sure you never knew Darcy's true tastes — or mine for that matter." His remonstrance was rude, especially as it was made in public, but his sister seemed determined to offend everyone and ruin the evening; he would not allow that.

His success was complete as Caroline was briefly lost for words, allowing the colonel to take control and direct the conversation to a more neutral topic until dinner ended. As no lady of the house was present to do the honours as hostess, Darcy proposed — and it was accepted — that they forego the separation of the sexes after dinner, and they all moved together into the drawing room to enjoy their after-dinner drinks.

As the evening progressed, some music was requested by the gentlemen, and all the ladies in the party agreed to favour them. Mrs. Hurst began the entertainment, and the colonel took the opportunity to join Darcy, who was in the corner with a glass in his hand.

"Well, Cousin, I must thank you for this dinner. It was enlightening as well as entertaining."

"Yes, I saw you truly enjoyed yourself."

"No more than you, I am sure. I was just wondering... is there some news you wish to share with me, Cousin?"

"About a particular subject or you are interested in any kind of news?"

He was hiding a satisfied smile while teasing his cousin.

"Well, any kind of news... about the war, the economic situation, Miss Elizabeth Bennet..."

"Ah... I understand. No, there is no news for the moment. But I hope that will change tomorrow."

"I see... Are you sure, absolutely sure about this, Darcy?"

"Cousin, I never have been more certain of anything in my life. Trust me, I have thought about every aspect of this... situation... for the last two months. I know her connections and fortune are not what our family and relatives would expect and desire. I have no doubt your parents and Lady Catherine will be resentful and disappointed, as I am also fully aware they will express strong arguments against this alliance with much eloquence and indignation. Nevertheless, my decision is made. If I should be so fortunate as to secure Miss Elizabeth Bennet's hand and affection, I shall be the happiest of men."

His tone was almost a whisper, but his voice was determined and fervent as the colonel had never heard him speak. In fact, he never before had heard Darcy speak of happiness — of his own happiness. He patted Darcy's arm.

"Well, Cousin, if this be the case, call me when the storm begins. I shall be there for you; you may rely on me."

Then he leaned his head toward Darcy and whispered, fighting his own mirth.

"You looked so ridiculously lost during dinner, looking only at her like a puppy... and... did you by any chance make her a sign under the table?"

Darcy looked at him questioningly, only to amuse the colonel even more. "Oh, don't worry, it was not noticeable, but I was very attentive to you both and observed the moment. I must confess I have done it so many times in the past with many charming ladies that I could recognise the reaction."

Darcy cast him a serious and reproachful glare, censuring his words.

"Cousin, I hope you are not implying anything improper. I have never done such a thing before with any other lady, and nothing disrespectful happened between Miss Elizabeth and me."

"I know, I know, I was just teasing you, but, Darcy, do you not know that she will have you eating from her palm in no time? She will do anything she pleases; you will never be able to refuse her anything if she knows how to ask... appropriately! You will be hopelessly at her mercy."

"I am already at her mercy, Cousin, and trust me, I will be happy to refuse her nothing."

"Yes, I am sure you will. Oh my — I never would have thought that you, of all our acquaintances, would make a love match."

Mrs. Hurst's performance concluded and then Miss Bingley's; it was then Elizabeth's turn. She took her place at the pianoforte and began to play, blushing and trying to control the trembling of her hands as she felt Mr. Darcy's ardent gaze bestowed on her. She lifted her eyes from time to time, meeting his and smiling tentatively.

Her performance was not as masterful as the others were, but it was pleasant and unpretentious. When she finished, the colonel approached her and requested another song, offering to turn the pages for her, so Elizabeth was obliged to continue. Casting another glance at Mr. Darcy, she could see that he looked content, and that simple fact made her happy.

During Elizabeth's second song, the butler approached his employer and whispered to him; Mr. Darcy left the music room without a word, a gesture that worried both the lady and gentleman at the instrument. With a strange sensation of fear, Elizabeth managed to finish her song and return to her aunt on the settee, escorted by the colonel.

As Darcy entered the main hall, he was shocked but pleased when he recognised the guest who had interrupted his party.

"Mr. Bennet!"

"Mr. Darcy..." came the reserved and reluctant answer.

"Please excuse me for bursting into your home in such a manner, but I understand my brother Gardiner is here, and there is an urgent situation that requires his immediate assistance."

"Of course, sir. Please do not make yourself uneasy. Would you care to join us? The entire Gardiner family is here, together with Miss Bennet and Miss Elizabeth."

"No, sir, thank you. I understand you have other guests, and I do not want to disturb them. In fact, I do not want the reason for my visit to be known at all, if possible."

"Then let us go into the library; I will have Mr. Gardiner fetched at once."

He sent the butler to summon Mr. Gardiner as discreetly as possible while they entered the library and Darcy poured each a glass of brandy. He watched Mr. Bennet carefully and was worried by his unusually distressed and grieved countenance, wondering what could have happened to reduce him to such a state. It could not be something regarding the family's health, or he would not have left them but sent an express instead.

"Mr. Bennet, I know I have no right to insist in a private matter but I beg you, let me know if there is something I can do to relieve your present state. I hope you know you can rely on my help and secrecy, sir, whatever the situation might be."

Mr. Bennet breathed deeply, unable to bear Darcy's inquiring look.

"I would have told you in any case, sir, and asked for your help with any information you might have. It is my youngest daughter, Lydia. Last night she ran away... she eloped... with Wickham."

Darcy was stunned into silence and could not react for a few moments, staring mutely at his companion. When he finally found words, he could not formulate a reply, for Mr. Bennet continued pacing the room restlessly, his fatigue making him almost at a loss for words.

"It never crossed my mind that something like this could happen. I have found out so many things about Wickham lately. I spoke with Colonel Forster, and he promised he would make inquiries about the man's previous activities, and then last night he just disappeared, taking Lydia with him."

Darcy violently swallowed the rest of his brandy. "But, sir, are you sure? Absolutely sure?"

"Yes, my foolish daughter left a note to her sister Kitty in which she explained they went to Gretna Green to marry, but we both know that will never happen; she has no money, no connections, nothing to tempt him. He is merely hiding from his creditors. Most likely he will abandon her somewhere on the streets and —"

Mr. Bennet could not continue but poured himself another brandy; at that moment, the door opened and not only Mr. Gardiner but Colonel Fitzwilliam as well entered the room, asking what had occurred.

Darcy had no alternative than to introduce his cousin to Mr. Bennet and was about to ask the colonel to leave when a sudden idea stopped him. He approached Mr. Bennet, who was about to start speaking with his brother.

"Mr. Bennet, I hope you will accept my entire help in this situation. I have to confess I am very selfish in asking this because I have more than one reason to want the problem solved as rapidly and conveniently as possible. Moreover, I know it is mostly my fault; I should have known better than to expose you and your family — "

"Thank you, Mr. Darcy. How could I refuse such an offer when I am lost and do not know what to do? You, of course, are taking too much upon yourself; the fault is entirely mine. I was not wary enough and never very diligent in protecting my family."

"Gentlemen," interrupted the colonel almost rudely, "this is a fascinating discussion but perhaps you could delay it? It seems to me something very serious and urgent has occurred, and it might be more useful to seek a solution and debate the laying of blame a little later."

"The colonel is right, Brother. For God's sake, tell me what happened!"

Mr. Bennet looked uneasily at the colonel and then at Darcy, who in turn finally came to the point. "Sir, my cousin is indeed the most trustworthy person we could hope to find, and his help could be priceless in this situation. If you will permit me, I would suggest confiding in him."

The gentleman silently agreed; Mr. Bennet was tired, dejected, and full of remorse, and the two glasses of brandy had made him light-headed.

"Do as you wish, Mr. Darcy."

"Very well then. Mr. Gardiner, I do not know how much you are aware of a certain Mr. Wickham, an officer who was in residence in Meryton with the regiment." He nodded as the colonel looked at Darcy, his brows furrowed.

"This man is an old acquaintance of mine, and when I met him in Hertfordshire, it was indeed the most unpleasant surprise. Being a few times in his company, Mr. Bennet was not deceived by Wickham's pleasant manners and decided to make inquiries about his activities in the neighbourhood; when we shared our opinion—during the Netherfield ball—I considered the plan very wise. Unfortunately, Georgiana's accident demanded my sudden departure, but as soon as I had the opportunity, I wrote

Mr. Bennet a letter, and we began a brief correspondence during the last two weeks. Imprudently and without proper consideration, I suggested that he try finding any debts Wickham may have procured in Meryton and in the regiment, for I confess I intended to redeem his bills and promissory notes in order to control him and, eventually, force him to leave the neighbourhood. It was, of course, a mistake — the result of my selfish desire to have him gone as soon as possible as it was convenient for me at that moment. What I should have done was to expose him long ago so he never could deceive another honourable person. Wickham indeed left but convinced Miss Lydia Bennet to elope with him, apparently to Gretna Green, but... "

Both Mr. Gardiner and the colonel were obviously taken aback, but while the former continued to ask his brother-in-law questions, the latter paced the room thoughtfully, shaking his head and whispering to his cousin.

"Darcy, what you really should have done with Wickham is what I suggested you do the first moment he approached Georgie, and I still think it is the best solution! But now, enough with talk and remorse — let us find a way to solve this matter as soon as possible. Mr. Bennet, are you sure they went to Scotland?"

"No, I am not. I asked in every village and postilion from Meryton to London, and they had last been seen entering town, but the location will be impossible to establish."

"Yes, it was very wisely done and very helpful. Darcy, we need men to follow their trace from London — although I doubt very much they have gone further — and other men to discreetly search inns and houses with rooms for rent, and not the fashionable ones, for he is without any money or resources."

"Yes," agreed Darcy, "and where is the first place he would go?"

"Edward Street — to Mrs. Younge," said both in unison.

Less than half an hour after they had gathered in the library, the plan was fixed and appeared to have a good chance of success. First, Darcy insisted that Mr. Bennet remain and rest, but he declined — upset and somewhat offended.

"Mr. Darcy, I know you are doing more than you should and more than I would dare to hope, and I am deeply grateful; but please, at least allow me to pretend to myself that I am useful to my family, even if it seems I am not especially needed."

Eventually, every detail of the plan was established and it needed to be followed immediately; any delay would diminish the final, desired outcome. The dinner party was over.

Mr. Bennet remained in the library, and the gentlemen returned to the other guests. Miss Bingley and Mrs. Hurst openly displayed their displeasure with the fact that their hosts left them for so long, and Mr. Darcy apologised, explaining that a matter of great importance and urgency had just occurred.

He tried to respond silently to Elizabeth's worried and questioning gaze, especially when, after a few more minutes, the colonel announced that he had to leave the party for he was expected elsewhere. Mr. Gardiner joined him, insisting they also had to depart, leaving the Bingleys and the Hursts no other alternative than to do the same, though it was undoubtedly obvious to everyone that something grave had occurred.

"Bingley, I need your complete discretion. Please take your sisters home now and meet me later in..." whispered Darcy to his friend in the main hall before he left; the answer he received was a silent nod of agreement.

Elizabeth and Jane, still shocked at the sudden change of plans and trying to understand but not daring to ask directly, only exchanged worried glances between them and their aunt until Mr. Darcy finally addressed them.

"Ladies, Mr. Gardiner will escort you to the library and I will come to you very shortly. Please follow him."

Darcy joined them about fifteen minutes later, clothes changed, and what he saw literally broke his heart. He never believed he would see Elizabeth's beautiful face so darkened by grief or her eyes red and swollen with tears. Mrs. Gardiner was trying to comfort both her and Jane, and while Jane seemed to be somehow reasonable, Elizabeth's reaction was stronger than expected, almost violent.

"But Papa, how could this happen? You knew what kind of man he was! Our eyes were opened to his true character by Mr. Darcy so many weeks ago! Why was Lydia allowed to be in his company? Poor, poor stupid girl! Wickham will never marry her; we all know that. And even if he does... such a man! She is lost forever and our whole family ruined with her —"

"Lizzy dear —" tried Jane, but Elizabeth would not be stopped.

"And how could she leave the house in the middle of the night without any of you seeing her? Did anyone ever oversee that girl?"

She knew she was selfish and unfair and that her words were hurting her dear father, but she could not control herself. She was deeply sorry for her sister and would have done anything to help her, but she was also burdened by her own pain and despair. Everything was lost; she knew that now.

Her power was sinking; everything must sink under such a proof of family weakness — such an assurance of the deepest disgrace.

Mr. Darcy never would ask his question under these circumstances, and she could very well understand why. All her hopes vanished; all her happiness was doomed to end before it started, and all her love was in vain.

Hearing the man entering, she bit her lower lip until blood appeared in an attempt to stop her words and her weeping, but the tears continued to roll down her cheeks; she buried her face in a handkerchief to conceal her sobs.

Darcy came closer to them, looking intently at Elizabeth, grieved to see her so affected by the news. He wanted so much to hold her, wipe her tears, and comfort her. He restrained the impulse, instead concentrating on the best way to finish what must be done to regain her tranquillity.

"Miss Bennet, Miss Elizabeth, did your father inform you of our plan?"

"Yes, sir."

"Unfortunately, we must hurry; my carriage is waiting to take you all back to Gracechurch Street. Or, if you prefer, I would be honoured to have you all as my guests here until tomorrow."

"Thank you, Mr. Darcy, we will leave in an instant," answered Mrs. Gardiner, as her nieces were unable to articulate a single word.

They all went to the door silently through the main hall, Mr. Bennet leading the group to the carriage, Elizabeth trailing behind — unconsciously trying to prolong as much as possible her last moments in his home — her eyes and head downcast in shame and humiliation.

She could feel Mr. Darcy close behind her but dared not face him, even for a moment. She only hoped she could hold her tears long enough for him not to witness her weakness and despair. She had almost reached the door when she heard him call her as his hand touched her arm gently.

"Miss Elizabeth… "

Her name on his lips had such a sweet and tender resonance that her heart ached at the thought that he never would address her by her given name again. She kept her eyes to the ground without any answer. So he turned her to him, placing his hands on both her arms, barely touching her in a gentle embrace, without considering that her father and her other relatives were expectantly waiting for them only a short distance away.

"I do not want to make vain promises, but please trust me when I say I will do everything in my power to bring all this to a better resolution than seems possible at the moment. You must have faith and trust me, Elizabeth."

She finally dared to look at him closely as he lowered his head to hers; there was no disdain or pity in his eyes. Nevertheless, there was pain; she recognised it and was content in her selfish grief to know that he too was suffering along with her. She was certain that he understood the gravity of the situation and its impact over their lives — their lives that could not be joined as they both desired, not after what happened. To share that burdening grief with him brought her pained heart a little comfort, but so very little.

Fearful that no other opportunity would likely present itself, Elizabeth did what she so often longed to do. She lifted both her hands to stroke his face with tentative, cold, trembling fingers and with all the tenderness in her heart; her eyes, moist with tears, were staring deeply into his, as she tried to discover the most hidden part of his soul. Then, standing on her toes, she touched his lips with hers in the slightest, most tender kiss imaginable… and in the next instant she was gone, not a glimpse of her appearing from within the carriage, which had departed in haste.

Chapter 15

Darcy remained stunned, in disbelief, following her with his gaze. Her luscious scent still hung in the air, and the traces of her delicate fingers still warmed his face.

That gentle caress had washed over all his senses. Unconsciously, he licked his lips to taste her delicious flavour and closed his eyes to prolong the moment. His shattered mind still could not comprehend what had happened and could not believe she dared to do what he so wanted but had dared not do. "I am completely at her mercy."

The happiness he felt was something so new and powerful that all other thoughts vanished, and he forgot about Wickham and Lydia Bennet or her father and uncle waiting for him outside. After a few minutes of total stillness, the unpleasant reality invaded him again when he remembered Elizabeth's pained and grieved countenance, and his anger was directed more violently than ever toward the man who had caused it.

The worried voices of the two gentlemen and their request to leave as soon as possible gave him the last needed impulse; the most important thing for the moment was to put an end to the reason for Elizabeth's pain, and then he would see her again, feel her again, and touch her again. When that moment came, it would be his turn.

Elizabeth saw and heard nothing during the short ride home.

She wondered how one could fall from the highest cloud to the deepest abyss within seconds and without even knowing when it happened.

She was still frightened by her own daring gesture to Mr. Darcy and the breaking of every propriety of ladylike behaviour. Never had Elizabeth been kissed or caressed on her face, and the thought that she had done so mortified her and made her whole body burn. The shame and remorse overwhelmed her; while her younger sister was passing through the most difficult time of her life, all she could think of were her own wanton desires.

She knew — she could feel — that he also wanted to close the gap between them that night in Georgiana's study, but he was a proper gentleman and treated her with respect. Not like her. If he had any remaining doubts regarding the end of their connection, her wanton behaviour surely convinced him she was as improper and wild as her sister.

Elizabeth did not notice when the carriage stopped, so she listened, as if in a dream, to her aunt and Jane talking between themselves and to her, but she paid little attention. She finally reacted when they spoke about the possibility of returning to Longbourn immediately and about how poorly their mother would deal with all that was happening; Kitty and Mary had no real support and probably wished for the help of their older sisters. Of course, no decision could be made before speaking with Mr. Bennet on his return.

Mrs. Gardiner proposed that at least an express should be sent to Longbourn, and Elizabeth offered to write it herself, but when her aunt returned ten minutes later, the paper was still blank. Mrs. Gardiner sent her to bed and accomplished the task herself with all the tact necessary.

Elizabeth took her aunt's suggestion heartily and ran into her room, wanting nothing more than solitude and seclusion. Jane visited her a little later, offering to stay with her and talk. They did so for about half an hour even though Elizabeth would rather have been left alone with her thoughts and grief to try to put together the broken pieces of her heart. Her sister's company was not as welcome as it once was.

Apparently, Jane was oblivious to the deeper implications for all of them of Lydia's unfortunate situation. She continued expressing her opinion that Mr. Wickham must have known Lydia had no money, and if he had decided to elope with her, perhaps it was because he really loved her. Elizabeth could only respond with a bitter, incredulous smile to such kind naïveté, but she did not contradict her too strongly, thinking that maybe it was for the best not to burden Jane with more grief.

Despite the ultimate outcome, she hoped Mr. Bingley's affection for Jane would overcome the obstacle; moreover, he had no history with Mr. Wickham and could not be as affected as Mr. Darcy was by the connection.

Soon after Jane left, the whole house went silent; darkness surrounded it. Fighting fatigue and the sorrow that threatened to defeat her, Elizabeth began to rationalise, seeking the slightest hope, but she could find none. The small and acknowledged unrealistic one was that nothing improper had happened and, despite the scandal that would follow her irrational gesture, that Lydia could return home without being forced to marry Mr. Wickham. Otherwise, even if they married, having such a husband would assure Lydia an unhappy future.

Sleep mercifully put an end to her torment near dawn, but it only threw her into strange and frightening dreams — dreams of Mr. Wickham hurting her sister in the most horrible ways, and dreams of Mr. Darcy caressing her, kissing her, holding her in his arms and then leaving without a word. The impression was so real that she could sense his touch and scent as if she were allowed to steal a glimpse of something she could never have. She awoke terrified and trembling, her nightgown soaked with perspiration and her heart beating violently. Daylight invaded her room, but darkness filled her soul.

What good could a new day bring? The previous evening, she was hoping and praying for this day to come sooner. It was the day meant to open the gates of happiness for Elizabeth — the day Mr. Darcy would ask his question, and she would say, "Yes." The day had come at last and brought nothing but painful suffering and despair.

She was ready to go downstairs when Mrs. Gardiner knocked at her door.

"How are you, dear?"

Her eyes surrounded by dark rings spoke for her.

"You did not sleep at all, did you?"

"Very little... I found little peace or sleep."

She tried to conceal her sadness but with little success; her eyes, red and swollen — unmistakable proof of a tearful night — betrayed her and worried Mrs. Gardiner even more.

"My dear, I do not want to deceive you with false hopes, but I gave it a lot of thought last night, and it appears to me unlikely that Mr. Wickham would form a dishonourable design against a girl who is by no means unprotected or friendless. Could he expect that her friends and family would not step forward? Perhaps he is indeed fond of her and intended to marry her as Lydia said in her notes."

"Do you really think so?"

"I do, upon my word. And, my dear, no matter what happens, I think you are reacting a little too strongly. You should try to be more calm; your family might need to depend on you."

"I know, Aunt, and I do not deserve your kindness and patience. I am ashamed to admit it, but I am a horrible person — selfish and inconsiderate."

"How is that, dearest?"

"I am concerned not only for Lydia but for my own selfish reasons. I am not as good a sister as Jane is. I mean... I would do anything to have Lydia safe, it is just that... " Her voice became barely audible as tears threatened her eyes again, and she was fighting heartily to stop them.

"Now, now, calm yourself; do not talk like that. None of this will be needed, I am sure. What selfish reasons make you a bad sister?" She smiled a little and tried to comfort her as she did her own children.

"I did not mention this to you but... last night... I believe Mr. Darcy intended to... he said he wanted to ask me a question today. But now that will never happen! And I cannot stop blaming Lydia for this. My only hope is that at least Mr. Bingley will continue his attachment to Jane and his intention will bring a happy conclusion for them. And I fervently pray that Papa will find Lydia and she will be safe."

"I am praying for this, too, Lizzy. Fortunately, Mr. Darcy and Colonel Fitzwilliam offered their help. I have great hopes that everything will be as well as can be expected under these circumstances."

Mrs. Gardiner stopped a few seconds and looked thoughtfully at her niece, carefully choosing her words.

"As for Mr. Darcy... Did he give you any indication that his intentions toward you changed after he learned of the news? I do not want to be indiscreet, but I could not fail to notice you delayed a little with him when we departed."

"No, Aunt; he was very nice — very gentle — and he told me he would do everything in his power to bring the best resolution to the situation. And he said I must trust him and have faith."

"Well... that sounds very promising to me. I think you have little reason to be upset and disappointed."

"But, Aunt, how can I not be so? What resolution can be achieved so I could preserve some hope? If Mr. Wickham does not marry Lydia after eloping and spending time together in God knows what sordid inn, the scandal will ruin the whole family, and our name will be compromised forever. No honourable man will want to have anything to do with us and surely not Mr. Darcy. The duty to his name and to his family would forbid it, and I could not blame him."

Mrs. Gardiner shook her head in disagreement, but Elizabeth continued, more animated. "And even if they finally marry, how can anyone expect Mr. Darcy to overcome a sentiment as natural as abhorrence against any relationship with Mr. Wickham? Brother-in-law of Wickham! Every kind of pride must revolt from the connection!"

"My dear, sit down here by me and try to calm yourself. There... Now, Elizabeth, listen to me; you are an intelligent young woman, and I will not deny that everything you said is just. Moreover, I am sure you are aware that, even without this unfortunate occurrence, the differences between our family and Mr. Darcy's cannot be ignored, and a union with you — even under the most honourable circumstances — would bring little pleasure or contentment to his friends and relatives. And Lydia's unfortunate situation will indeed not favour any of us — not our good name nor our reputation."

Elizabeth remained in grieved expectation a while longer, considering her aunt's just but nevertheless painful words, wondering why she was trying to amplify her grief by presenting so clearly how beneath him she had ever been and how much that gap had grown.

"However, Lizzy, I cannot help remembering that only a few days ago, before our arrival in town, you were devastated by Mr. Darcy's departure from Hertfordshire and by his unjustified neglect and abandonment, only to discover how little trust and understanding of his true character you have had. This time he did not leave without a word or with an unknown reason, so perhaps you should do as he asked you — to have faith and trust in him, at least until he proves unworthy of that trust and affection."

"Aunt, I know he is worthy of my trust and my affection; he is truly the best man I have ever known. My suffering is so deep because I know the value of my loss."

"Elizabeth, I do not know the nature of Mr. Darcy's feelings or intentions toward you; I can only suspect them from my observation. And I can state that I never saw a more promising inclination or a more eloquent display. Considering Mr. Darcy's private and restrained nature, that fact is most astonishing. Let us wait a little longer and see if his feelings and attachment toward you impel him to find a solution without any loss for any of you."

Elizabeth remained in silence, calling for hope to come back to her and ease her soul of the great burden of despair. How could love give her such bliss and anguish? Before she could answer, the maid entered and handed her a letter, which was opened with no little anxiety while Mrs. Gardiner left the room to give her privacy.

Dear Elizabeth,

Yesterday you had to hurry away, and we failed to establish an hour for your call today. So I sent the carriage for you with Molly to accompany you, and it will wait until you are ready.

I must confess I am anxious to see you again; I spent delightful time in your company yesterday, and I look forward to doing the same today. I can only hope the feeling is mutual.

Unfortunately, my brother sent word he was detained for an indefinite period of time and not expected to return home soon, but I hope we will have a pleasant day together. I asked Mrs. H. to prepare a special meal for today, and I am confident you will enjoy it.

Oh, I forget to mention — if Miss Bennet is willing to accompany you, please extend the invitation to her as well. It would be a pleasure to see her again.

— Georgiana Darcy'

Elizabeth, who in the torment of events completely forgot about the visit due to Georgiana, felt her head spinning. Could she keep her promise of calling? Would Mr. Darcy approve under these new circumstances her close association with his sister? Apparently, Georgiana knew nothing of what occurred, and justifiably so. Mr. Darcy never would bother her fragile constitution with such a story.

On the other hand, was it possible to refuse her when she promised so solemnly the day before to call? Then again, how could she dare return to his house alone after her display of improper and shocking behaviour? She would die of shame to meet his eyes again.

She went downstairs, found her aunt and sister with the children, and asked their opinion. They were both quite surprised to hear about the invitation, but once she told them all the details, they immediately agreed only one response was possible.

"My dear, of course you must go. I know you are not in the mood for a visit and anxious to wait for news, but remaining at home will not help either."

"Yes, Lizzy dearest, and if you refuse, poor Miss Darcy would be so disappointed. I will stay home with aunt and the children, and if you are needed, we will send for you immediately."

"But what if Mr. Darcy should be displeased? He could not desire to prolong our connection after what has happened, and he would be right in feeling so."

I was difficult for Jane to understand Lizzy's reasoning. She knew — vaguely — of Mr. Darcy's past relation with Mr. Wickham, but not for a second could she imagine that Mr. Darcy would hold Elizabeth responsible for something that was not her doing or her fault. Her sister's questions and behaviour puzzled her exceedingly.

"My dear," Mrs. Gardiner again broke in, "I think you give Mr. Darcy considerably less credit than he deserves. However, even if you are correct about his future intentions, he could not possibly blame you for keeping your promise toward his sister, especially when you said he seemed so pleased and encouraging yesterday. If not for anything else, at least for the tranquillity of Miss Darcy, he would be content with your visit. I am sure of that."

Reluctantly, Elizabeth prepared herself for the call, her heart still fearful of having to bear the rejection and disdain of the man whose approval she wanted most in the world. She asked Jane once more to accompany her, but the elder Miss Bennet declined, secretly hoping that in doing so she was allowing her sister to find a way to improve her intimacy with Miss Darcy for the benefit of both.

All the way to the Darcys' house, Elizabeth exchanged only a few words and polite smiles with Molly. She retained the dread of being an unwanted presence in his home, and every moment increased her grief.

When the carriage reached its destination, it was early, shortly after breakfast. The butler and Mrs. Hamilton, the housekeeper, greeted Elizabeth with a familiar but respectful politeness and showed her to Georgiana's apartment.

Mrs. Hamilton carefully scrutinised with the greatest interest the young lady who had been invited to visit for the second time in two days, though she tried to hide her curiosity. There were all the signs that her master found this lady worthy of his admiration, and for the first time in her 15 years of service in the house, she noticed his openly expressed interest for a lady. The gesture of allowing her to spend time alone with Miss Darcy was final proof that this lady was held in the highest esteem.

The fear below stairs that Miss Bingley was rumoured to be the future mistress had vanished the previous night when the amiable Miss Bennet entered the house.

However, Mrs. Hamilton was not persuaded by a gentle smile; Miss Bennet was a changed person from the night before. Her confidence, serenity, and loveliness had disappeared, and dark rings shadowed her eyes. Could this be related to the master's sudden, extended absence?

Georgiana's face brightened with pleasure on seeing Elizabeth enter. Elizabeth smiled and approached the bed, taking the girl's hand and expressing her delight in seeing her again, but Georgiana saw and felt the changes in her and watched her companion with no little worry.

"How are you Georgiana? You look very well indeed."

"Yes, I feel well, thank you. And you?"

"I am well." She met the girl's eyes and blushed with shame, seeking an excuse for her appearance. "I had a sleepless night and feel a little dizzy, I suppose. But it is a pleasure to be here with you."

Miss Darcy smiled back and did not insist on the matter, evidently not a pleasant one for her visitor. She offered Elizabeth coffee, tea and cakes, masterfully arranged on a small elegant table near the bed, and they talked calmly. Georgiana tried, shyly and tentatively, to refer to the previous night and to her brother, but to her astonishment, Elizabeth's reaction seemed to be more of embarrassment and grief than pleasure. The younger girl was left not only surprised and confused but also worried that something dreadful had happened. Finally, she found a safe topic.

"Elizabeth, I have a surprise. As I will probably stay at least a fortnight in bed, I asked Mrs. Hamilton to have my little piano moved into my room here. So when you visit again, you will be able to play for me."

"Georgiana, I would be happy to do that, but unfortunately I am afraid there has been an unexpected change of plans. I think we will return home very soon, possibly even today or tomorrow."

"Oh, dear! Did something bad happen? Is someone ill?"

"No — just an unfortunate situation that requires our presence."

"I am so sorry! But can I hope… Will you agree to write to me while you are gone?" She sounded shy and hopeful at the same time. "I would like to continue our acquaintance if that is agreeable with you."

"I… I think it would be better if you ask for your brother's opinion on this matter, too. If he approves, I would be happy to correspond with you."

"Surely you cannot think my brother would be against it!" She stopped when Elizabeth averted her eyes. "Is my brother aware of your problems?"

Elizabeth nodded in agreement.

"Is… is that the reason for his being gone today?"

"Yes, but please do not ask me anything. Mr. Darcy will tell you if he considers it appropriate. I am truly sorry for causing these troubles to you both. I am afraid I am not a good companion for you today, and instead of comforting you, I only upset and grieve you."

Georgiana's voice became more serious and grave in a moment. "Elizabeth, I am not a child, you know. I do not need to be entertained, and I hope I would understand if you are distressed and in need of comfort."

Georgiana breathed deeply, overwhelmed by her daring speech. "I do not know what happened between you and my brother since last night when obviously... But I am sure nothing can change his opinion of you — or mine. I know I am considerably younger, and you could not possibly trust me, but at least you must know there is no need to conceal your distress. I know so much about anguish myself, Elizabeth."

Both of them seemed desirous to speak more on the painful subject, but neither of them dared to do it. Mrs. Annesley's entrance and amiable greeting to Miss Bennet provided a good opportunity for the change to a lighter topic of conversation.

Mrs. Annesley did not remain long in their company as she left to call upon one of her friends. After her departure, both Elizabeth and Georgiana attempted to continue the conversation and not allow sadness to overcome them again, but the words came with difficulty, and the awkwardness of their situation proved a difficult obstacle to overcome.

A STRONG KNOCK AT THE door startled them both, and Elizabeth felt she would faint on hearing Mr. Darcy's deep voice.

"Georgiana, may I enter?"

"Yes, William, of course."

The girl looked briefly at her visitor and saw her face turn white as she twisted her hands in her lap.

He entered and moved closer, greeting them with a reasonably pleasant countenance; Elizabeth did not fail to notice that he appeared tired, but he was shaved and dressed in different clothes than he wore the previous evening. He must have returned some time earlier, and Elizabeth was dying of anxiety and curiosity to ask him about Lydia, but she could find no way to do such a thing in Georgiana's presence. He leaned to kiss his sister's forehead and then turned to Elizabeth, whose embarrassment had turned her into a statue.

"Miss Bennet."

"Mr. Darcy."

"It is fortunate I still find you here, for I have some positive information to share with you. I just left Mr. Gardiner's house a little more than half an hour ago, and I came directly, taking only a few moments to adjust my appearance because I indeed looked very 'scary,' as Becky would say."

She opened her eyes widely at him, failing to notice his small joke about her little cousin, only begging for any news, inconsequential though it might be.

"Sir, my uncle and my father... Are they well? I must return home as soon as possible. Georgiana, please forgive me; I cannot delay a moment longer."

She rose, but Mr. Darcy stopped her, heedless of his sister's presence.

"Miss Bennet, please allow me to detain you for a few more minutes. The situation has been taken care of in as satisfactory a way as possible under the circumstances. All three of them are at the Gardiners' house for the time being, and I think I am correct in saying they are in good health but very tired, and without any doubt, they must be sleeping now."

Her astonishment was beyond measure: "All three? Is it possible?"

He smiled comfortingly and nodded in agreement.

"Of course, I would ask the carriage to be prepared for you as soon as you want, but I do not think they are in need of any urgent help at the moment. Mrs. Gardiner and Miss Bennet seemed very efficient in taking care of everything. And Mr. Bennet sent an express to Longbourn to announce the latest news. So I trust nothing more can be done at this time."

"I thank you, sir. My gratitude cannot be expressed, I am so..." She could not finish, as tears overwhelmed her. "But, if it is not too much trouble for you, I would want to be with my family as soon as possible."

"Of course. If you will allow me a few moments, I will make the arrangements for your departure." He tightened the grip of her arm a moment, wrapped both women in a warm, affectionate gaze, and then left the room. Elizabeth could barely look at Georgiana, but the young girl understood the delicacy of the moment and did not inquire further. Instead, she smiled.

"Elizabeth, did you see? William said everything is well now. You do not need to worry anymore."

She reached her hands toward her, and Elizabeth sat on the bed and embraced Georgiana, their heads resting on each other's shoulders.

At about the same time, Colonel Fitzwilliam, the second son of Lord Matlock, entered his parents' townhouse, tired, dirty and seething with repressed anger toward Wickham.

The man's profligacy and licentiousness had always been outrageous, but the night before, he had overstepped all acceptable limits. Wickham's demands had been not only ridiculously high but had been made with such impertinence that the colonel was tempted several times to solve the problem more efficiently at the cost of a bullet — as he had desired ever since he had first learned of the scoundrel's scheme against Georgiana.

He was at a loss to understand how Darcy was capable of keeping his calm countenance and dealing with him in a determined but elegant manner, though the colonel could tell that more than once Darcy had been as tempted as he was to use a more efficient method than mere persuasion.

At least now, everything was done, and he hoped his new commission would be far enough away so as not to see Wickham more than once in ten years. As for that stupid, silly girl, mindless and imprudent... he did not want to imagine what kind of life they would share, and happily, he had no interest in knowing.

He tried to sneak into his room before anyone saw him but with no success. Lady Ellen was waiting for him.

"My dear son, would you do me the honour of spending one minute in my company before disappearing again?"

"Of course, Mother, please forgive me. I only wanted to refresh myself a little first."

"Well, do not worry; I know how you look after a night spent who knows where and in whose company. Come and sit a moment; have a glass of wine and tell me how dinner was last night and why you mercilessly abandoned me without an explanation. Everybody asked about you, especially a few handsome young ladies."

He laughed, kissed his mother's hand, and poured some brandy, knowing there was no escape. Moreover, conversations with her had always been a pleasure as she had an amazing understanding of things of which many ladies would not dare to think.

Lady Ellen had been one of the beauties of the *ton* in her time, her lovely face matching a sharp, witty mind and a fortune that gave her a comfortable independence in every aspect of her life — from choosing her husband to doing what she wanted, before and after her marriage.

Lord Matlock had been the fortunate man who was rewarded with her affection and hand — an honour desired by many others. His reckoning had been his wife's continual contradiction and disobedience for thirty-five years, creating as many battles as any war, although their mutual affection remained strong and assured them a happy marriage and a happier parenthood.

Their two sons each inherited the character of one of their parents, and a fragile balance existed in the family on every important matter. However, the balance did not exist where the colonel's life and future were concerned, the other three members demanding that he seek a proper wife and settle down in his own home. His absence for an entire night was the incentive for his mother — who had a clear but undeclared partiality for him and had never refused him anything — to demand another discussion on the subject of his adventurous life.

"Well? Will you tell me the truth about dinner the other night? Your father will return soon from his club, and I would like to learn the true version of the story, not the one created for him."

"My dearest mother, there is not much to tell. I confess I was curious to attend because Darcy invited some unknown guests — his and Bingley's acquaintances from Hertfordshire."

"I see… And among those guests were there, by any chance, any attractive ladies to arouse your interest? I find it difficult to believe you were merely there to make new acquaintances."

"You are right; as a matter of fact, there were two beautiful young ladies: Misses Jane Bennet and Elizabeth Bennet. The other guests were their relatives — an aunt and uncle."

"Why do you stop, young man? You must know I want more details."

"Well, there is not much to say. Miss Jane Bennet is the young lady who stole Bingley's heart — you remember Bingley, do you not? — and he has never ceased talking about her these last two months. But I can find no fault in this, for she is indeed remarkably beautiful and has a sweet disposition. I am sure she will be the perfect wife for him if he ever gains the courage to ask for her hand."

"She sounds lovely, and you know I like Bingley very much, especially when he is without that sister of his. By the way, did Darcy manage to eat or breathe, or did Caroline hinder him completely?"

"To be honest, in that respect it was a most entertaining evening. I am sorry you missed it; you would have adored seeing Caroline Bingley reprimanded more than once, not only by Darcy but by her own brother — and deservedly so, for she had been quite impertinent and offensive to the guests."

"Oh dear, what a loss indeed. So are you saying that little puppy, Bingley, has become a full-grown guard dog?"

He could not restrain his laughter.

"A very inspiring metaphor but true nevertheless. He is quite proficient in protecting Miss Bennet — Miss Jane Bennet, I mean, for the other one does not seem to need protection. She is quite capable of biting by herself — elegantly but efficiently."

"That sounds interesting. Do I detect the beginning of admiration here?"

"Maybe, my lady, but not the kind of admiration you think. Miss Elizabeth is a remarkable young lady, and I indeed came to admire her after a short time in her company. But I have every reason to believe her affection and hand are already secured — or very soon will be."

"Well, that is a relief. I would not want you to trifle with a gentleman's daughter, but I would also want you to remember that a country girl is not what you need in a wife."

"There is no need to remind me, my lady, you must grant me that. However," continued the colonel, seizing the opportunity, "Miss Elizabeth Bennet appears to be much more than a simple country girl. In manners, wit and quickness of mind, she reminds me very much of you, or rather of how you must have been some years ago — except that she is not as beautiful as you were and certainly not as wealthy."

"Well, dear son," answered Lady Ellen, half in jest, "few women are as beautiful as I was! But I must confess you have made me quite curious about this lady. If your statement is correct, then the man who secures her affection is indeed a fortunate one. I hope he will be worthy of her."

"I dare say you are correct in every aspect, Mother; he is a fortunate man, and he will be worthy of her." He hid a smile behind his glass.

"Is that so? My interest is now completely engaged. I am determined to ask Darcy to host another dinner without delay so I can have the opportunity to meet both Miss Bennets. But I will insist that Caroline Bingley be invited, too. Maybe I will be fortunate enough to have a repetition of the spectacle."

"Well, I am certain you will have the opportunity to meet them very soon, and I will be here to remind you of every word you said just now."

He smiled mischievously and kissed his mother's hand, asking to be excused. He climbed the stairs to his room, very pleased with himself, while Lady Ellen's lovely brows furrowed thoughtfully.

Several minutes elapsed — Elizabeth could not be sure how many — before Mr. Darcy returned. He lingered in the doorway; his face brightened and his heart melted at the sight of the women he loved most embracing each other. "Miss Bennet, the carriage will be ready in a few minutes. I will accompany you if you will allow me."

She rose and held Georgiana's hand tightly, whispering, "Thank you."

"Shall I see you again soon, Elizabeth?"

"I… I do not know. As I said it is possible that we — "

"I can assure you, Georgie, that you will see Miss Bennet again very soon. And do not worry, dearest; all is well. I shall return to you shortly."

They went down the stairs in grave silence, but Mr. Darcy did not lead her to the hall as she expected.

"Miss Bennet, until the carriage is ready, I was hoping we might speak privately for a few minutes. I know it is not entirely proper, and ordinarily I would not dare to suggest it…but there is a matter of great consequence I wish to discuss with you, and I do not know when such an opportunity will arise again. Moreover, I thought you might like to ask me more questions and details about Miss Lydia, and so I am at your disposal."

She nodded in agreement, grateful for his kindness and understanding; indeed, she was anxious to know more — to know everything — but did not dare to open that dreadful subject with him.

Mr. Darcy opened the library door as she wondered what important matter he could wish to discuss with her. She had neither the courage nor the energy to face his intense gaze. What would happen next? *Why did he say I would surely see Georgiana again? Doubtless he must be careful to avoid exposing his sister to scandal by allowing a connection with me, especially considering my new connection with Mr. Wickham, and then…* His voice, unexpectedly tender and as gentle as a caress, brought her from her reverie.

"Miss Bennet, please sit down."

She did as he said; her body obeyed his commands rather than her will.

He took a chair and sat by her, taking her hands gently.

"Mr. Darcy, you said that my sister is in my aunt's house? Is she unharmed? How did you find them in such a short time?"

"She... seemed to be in good health, although I do not believe she was at all pleased to see us."

Elizabeth started to ask another question, but he continued.

"We were very fortunate in our quest; we found them in Mrs. Younge's house, although she did not want to divulge their secret at first — not wanting to betray Wickham — and nothing we told her or promised her came to fruition in the beginning."

He was smiling tentatively, using a light, neutral tone as though relating a story, but Elizabeth could only imagine his aversion to being obliged to ask, insist, and even make promises to that despicable woman. Even worse was Lydia's wild reaction and Mr. Darcy's being forced to witness it.

"I am truly sorry; I know how Lydia can be — how much effort it must have cost you to find them and how unpleasant it must have been for you to attempt such a search."

He intended to say something, but she would not allow him just yet. "Mr. Darcy, I cannot express my gratitude for your help and the generous compassion that induced you to take so much trouble in order to discover them. My entire family and I will be forever in your debt."

"Please do not speak of gratitude; I did nothing to deserve it — quite the contrary. The entire situation was caused by my mistaken pride in not exposing Mr. Wickham when I first should have. Furthermore, finding them was not only my doing but also that of Mr. Bennet and Mr. Gardiner, together with the efforts of Colonel Fitzwilliam and Mr. Bingley. My only assistance was in knowing some of Mr. Wickham's habits and connections."

"And what happened with Mr. Wickham? Where is he now?"

"He will remain at the inn until the wedding — "

"The wedding? So they are to be married?"

"Yes, apparently that was the final solution. Miss Lydia was quite insistent on marrying him, and finally, Mr. Wickham also agreed."

"He finally agreed? He did not intend to marry her, did he?"

The subject was highly improper, and both were uneasy to speak of it, but Darcy was determined to tell her the truth. He trusted her good sense and judgment, and he knew that concealing the facts from her would not relieve her obvious distress. "I will not lie to you: no, he did not."

"And may I ask with what arguments he was convinced?"

"We... As I said previously, both Colonel Fitzwilliam and I know how to convince Mr. Wickham when necessary."

She regained her courage with the determination of one who has nothing more to lose and lifted her gaze to look deeply into his eyes.

"Mr. Darcy, you have just said you will not lie to me. I am begging you to answer truthfully: Did you offer him money to marry my sister?"

He wanted to avoid the answer but could not meet her intense, searching look; he averted his eyes, which was enough confirmation for her.

"Oh, dear Lord, what a shame, what a shame…"

Elizabeth was deeply mortified and humiliated on behalf of her sister before the man whose good opinion she wanted most. She rose in great haste, pulling her hand from his, and went directly to the door, not even trying to stem her tears; in a moment, he was by her side.

"Elizabeth, please do not run from me."

With her last fragment of rational thought, she noticed his addressing her by her Christian name and knew it was not right, but compared to her wanton behaviour the previous night, how could it be considered improper?

He firmly held her arms and turned her to him. Now they were alone with no one to interrupt them, and she needed to be comforted, caressed, and held; his arms knew best how to do it. She belonged in his arms.

"Please look at me and tell me what I can do to bring laughter back into your beautiful eyes."

Unexpectedly and shockingly, his fingers gently touched her chin, lifting her face until their eyes met and held — spellbound — his thumb tenderly stroking her face.

"The sadness and distress on your face has followed me every moment since we parted last night. I would do anything to see you smile again; you are the one who brings joy into my life, remember? Where is that joy and liveliness, my dearest, loveliest Elizabeth?"

Her heart threatened to stop beating, and her whole body melted under the warmth of his closeness and his burning touch.

"Elizabeth, I know how difficult these moments are for you and how you must have been suffering for your sister. That is why I will not pressure you in any way, so I will not ask my question today. I will wait patiently until you allow me to do it. But I am begging you — do not prolong my agony by making me wait too long."

Elizabeth's astonishment almost made her faint. She stared at him, doubting that she had understood his words, her face colouring crimson, fighting to regain her breath and to keep her heart from bursting. She could not think properly; she could not think at all. All thoughts and senses were concentrated on his right hand touching her chin and caressing her face, while her eyes were pleading with his to give her a confirmation of what she was afraid to admit she had just heard.

"Mr. Darcy, I am afraid I do not understand you. I… cannot imagine what question you are talking about."

Darcy smiled and intensified his caress.

He knew he was being more bold and improper than he should and that he might frighten her. But he was certain he had guessed her feelings correctly for some time, and the last days spent together, especially the previous evening, were certain confirmation. Her behaviour dissipated any doubts or misunderstandings; he was sure she understood him correctly.

"Yes you can, Elizabeth. You understood me last night when we talked before dinner, and later, when you did... what you did" — He took her hand and traced her fingers over his face, as she had the night before. — "so you certainly understood me when you did this... " He leaned his head and touched her lips with his own as softly and lightly as she had done. She watched him, mesmerised, waves of chills spreading through her rigid body, which seemed to have lost all power of movement. She began to tremble. Her lips were burning from his touch, and his scent was more intoxicating than ever — she had never been so close to him with her body and her soul.

She put her hands on his chest, leaning against him for support, for she knew she would fall otherwise. She needed his strength to compensate for her weakness. She needed him, utterly and completely, and did not dare to entertain the smallest hope that her need would be fulfilled.

"Sir, you cannot possibly refer to... you cannot consider... not after what happened with my sister, not after you know Mr. Wickham is going to be my brother... "

The tears flowed freely from her eyes and rolled over her cheeks; this time he wiped them away with his thumbs.

"And you, Elizabeth, cannot possibly consider that anything would prevent me from asking that question after I have been waiting for so long to do so. You cannot possibly believe I could be satisfied with the regret of letting you go when there is the smallest chance to obtain your affection and hand."

The happiness she felt at hearing his words was so powerful that she was certain her soul would not be able to bear it, but her sadness was not lessened. To know he truly loved her and wanted to marry her almost broke down the last vestiges of resistance that remained in her, and she could only articulate a few more words.

"But sir, surely you must be aware of the scandal that will be associated with my family. You cannot allow it to fall upon you or Georgiana. *I* cannot allow that." She was crying, her heart broken, as close to him as if they were one person.

Darcy only smiled and encircled her shoulders with one arm as he gently tilted her head to rest on his chest. Then he tenderly placed a few light kisses on her silky hair.

"What I cannot allow is that anything or anyone should make you cry ever again, Elizabeth. Nor can I allow you to leave my arms, unless I can be certain you know that this is where you belong. Can you not feel that your place is here — in my arms, in my home, in my life?"

She did not move, for never in her life had she felt so protected and complete as in that moment in his embrace, near his heart. She only lifted her face, now so close to his that they could feel each other's breath, her lips barely able to speak.

"But sir, are you sure you have taken careful consideration of all the implications of my family's situation and your own family's reaction?"

He gently stroked her hair, resting his chin on the top of her head, his heart melting at such proof of her own care and consideration.

"I did a long time ago. I will not deny that I struggled to repress my feelings for you for many weeks when we were in Hertfordshire until I came to understand that you were everything I wanted and had been looking for in my life. And since that moment, I only waited and hoped for a moment to speak of my love, a love that allowed me to think of no one but you."

He felt her startle in his embrace and then tremble as a most becoming blush spread over her beautiful face and descended to the soft, creamy skin of her neck, her eyes hiding behind her long lashes.

He smiled at her and cupped her face with his hands.

"However, I must say I am all astonishment that we have discussed all the details of the advantages or disadvantages of a possible alliance between us, but I do not recall myself proposing to you or your answering me. Perhaps it is, after all, an appropriate moment to do that, would you not agree?"

Elizabeth was too embarrassed to say a word — the happiest embarrassment she had ever felt — and tried to smile in his embrace while nodding silently and shyly.

"My affection and wishes cannot be a surprise to you. I know you understood them; you have felt them for a long time now. And if not" — he smiled, a hint of mischief twisting the corners of his lips — "my shocking, improper behaviour toward you should have been proof of how ardently I love and admire you."

With his voice as tender as his caress, he declared all that he had long felt for her, his adoring, rapturous gaze enfolding her and never leaving her eyes as he spoke. He could witness the brightness on her face and the twinkle in her sparkling eyes growing with every word, rewarding him with a happiness he never would have thought possible to feel.

"My dearest, beautiful Elizabeth, would you do me the honour of becoming my wife? I know I broke my promise of delaying this proposal until you were more tranquil, but in my selfishness, I cannot keep my word. If you have any doubts about me, if your feelings do not allow you to give me a positive answer, or if you need more time to be sure of your decision, tell me and I will accept it. I will not give you up, but I will wait for you and do everything in my power to prove myself worthy of your love. But I beg you not to give any thought to Mr. Wickham or the effect of this unfortunate situation on your family or mine. They are of no consequence to me. My only concern is to know your feelings and wishes."

She did not consider, not even for a second, thinking of anyone or anything except the two of them. The whole world vanished; their love was so powerful that she could feel it surrounding them. Her hands lifted to his face, and she fought against the lump in her throat that would not allow her words to give him all the assurance he needed.

"Neither my feelings nor my wishes should be of any concern to you, sir, as I am sure you have not failed to understand them for quite some time."

Pleased and encouraged by the expression of heartfelt delight that spread over his face, she continued teasingly, repeating what he had told her only a few minutes earlier, in a love game that could have only two winners.

"If nothing else, my shocking, improper behaviour should have been a proof of their nature, Mr. Darcy. I know you were sure of my feelings last night when we talked before dinner, or later when I did... what I did..." — She touched his face with her fingers as she had the previous evening.— "and when I did this..."

She intended to repeat that light kiss, but this time his daring, thirsty lips captured hers, savouring their sweet softness so long desired.

Chapter 16

It was more a tentative and gentle touch of their lips than a passionate kiss, but it was so intense in its meaning that time seemed to stop as the room and indeed the whole world spun around them. His right hand slowly glided to the back of her neck, his fingers joining a rebellious lock of her hair, and his left hand encircled her waist.

Darcy was desperately fighting against his passion. He knew he could not allow his hands to caress her as he desired, his arms to pull her as close as he wanted nor his lips to take possession of her mouth. He felt her lips shyly pressing against his and knew it would be easy for him to make them part and for her to surrender to him completely. He could feel her soft, warm body pressing against his as she stood on her toes, while her hands were encircling his waist; she was shivering slightly in his embrace and every fibre of his body could feel her tremor.

Many times — nights and days — he had dreamed of the moment she would be in his arms for the first time, about the pleasure he would feel the very first time. But pleasure seemed such a poor word to describe the sensations she aroused in him.

Yet, what other word could do justice to that utter, blissful happiness that enveloped him — that amazingly powerful storm inside of him, more powerful than anything he had ever experienced or imagined? *Love! That is the word!* The thought made his heart pound, and instinctively he pulled her even closer so he could also feel her heart beating against his chest.

Elizabeth did not dare — or know how — to breathe in that close embrace. But she needed nothing else — not even breath — only the warmth of his lips, the strength of his body against hers, and the comfort of his embrace.

Until a few minutes before, her soul had been buried beneath a burden of grief and despair, believing that she had lost him forever. Now she was so close to him — their arms wrapped around each other and their chests pressed against each other — that she could sense the wild beating of his heart. As for her own heart, she did not know whether it was still beating or not. Her head was swimming, causing every rational thought to vanish, and she was aware of nothing but his strong arms and the burning touch of his lips against her own.

A desperate need for air made her withdraw slightly without opening her eyes, amazed and overwhelmed by the exquisite sensation building inside her by the kiss — her first kiss. A deep sigh of contented pleasure escaped her lips, making Darcy smile, and she blushed, knowing he understood her. Her knees, like her entire body, melted and grew weaker at the revelation that his hand was still resting at the junction between her neck and her shoulder, his palm pressed gently and possessively against her bare skin. The gentle caress of his thumb seemed to tease her senses, burning that spot as cold shivers made her tremble more. She knew she was dangerously close to fainting.

"Elizabeth, are you unwell?"

"No, no... but I think I should sit." He directed her to the settee, never releasing her from his embrace, and they sat together. She still did not trust herself well enough to face him, and he became worried. "Elizabeth, will you not look at me?" His voice was tender, whispering close to her ear, which only increased her disturbance as one hand was still on her shoulder while the other was holding hers.

She finally lifted a flushed face, dared to meet his eyes briefly, and then averted her eyes as she tried to think of something sensible to say.

"I am not unwell; do not worry. It is just that — "

"Yes? Please tell me what is disturbing you?"

Your hands... your closeness... were the answers that burst into her head, but she searched for the proper words to explain her reaction to him. "I know I am reacting foolishly, and you must think me a simpleton indeed. Please forgive me. It is just that I have never... This is the first time that I... "

If her mortification had allowed her to look at him, she would have seen an expression of utter delight and a radiant smile lighting his face.

"And for what exactly should I forgive you? It is I who should beg your forgiveness for frightening you with my impulsive and improper behaviour."

She shook her head and attempted to gain a little more self-control.

"No, you are not to blame any more than I am. Sir, I am not frightened, though I must confess I am truly embarrassed. I never imagined that a kiss could be so... "

She had to stop, for she was at a loss for words again, but he continued, tenderly caressing her hands.

"So overwhelming?" She nodded in agreement, trying to stop her hands from trembling.

"Well, Elizabeth, I am happy to know I am not the only one feeling that way. At least we can be embarrassed together."

She turned her head to him in surprise, only to meet a smile hidden in the corner of his lips and eyes full of mirth. "I am silly, am I not?"

"No, you are not. Every moment spent with you is proof to me that you are even more wonderful than I imagined."

Her face coloured highly again, but this time she indulged herself in the pleasure of his confession and held his darkened gaze until he spoke again with a hint of mischief in his voice.

"Should I beg you finally to give me an answer?"

"Answer?" Her head was spinning, and she could barely think properly.

"The answer to my proposal."

"Oh, that answer… I am sorry; I am a little dizzy."

"I am very pleased to hear that," answered Darcy, with a cheeky smile that made his dimples appear in full view, suddenly bringing to her mind little Becky's words: *'Dimples is good?'*

"You are pleased that I am dizzy, sir?"

"Yes, I am…because your presence has always been intoxicating to me, and I feel dizzy whenever I am near you or even think of you, which has been most of the time this last couple of months."

His words and his gaze were so intense that another wave of warm redness spread over her face, and all she could say was a small, "Oh…"

"However, you must realise by now that you are already compromised and your answer does not matter; you have no other honourable alternative than to accept me."

"True, sir, I have no other alternative indeed. So I will say, 'Yes!'" Elizabeth felt her heart was melting, and her soul was full of tenderness seeing the relief and happiness lighting his handsome face. *Could he really believe I would say, "No?"* His delighted smile and intense gaze made her think he would kiss her again. Darcy leaned towards her, whispered in her ear, and then, to her utter surprise, suddenly exited the library. He returned shortly and resumed his place. Then he handed her a dark red velvet jewellery box.

She tried to maintain her breath at a normal pace while he helped her open the box and extract a ring. It was an exquisite piece with an oval centre diamond and a channel of many other very small diamonds placed in the gold band. It was impressive in its brightness but not ostentatious in its grandeur. Elizabeth thought she had never seen anything so beautiful.

"I know you cannot wear this gift until your father gives us his consent, but will you allow me to put it on your finger now as proof that we have taken the first step in our future life together?"

She only nodded, her heart throbbing wildly. He placed the ring on her finger and then touched it to his lips. "These diamonds sparkle like your eyes, and the ring is full of light as you are."

Mesmerised, barely knowing what she was about, she leaned her head and lifted their joined hands, kissing the ring in the same spot that he had. When their eyes finally meet, no words were needed to seal their complete understanding, and no words were possible as he claimed her lips ever so gently, with love and infinite tenderness, as were his feelings for her at that moment.

The time for passion would come later.

Mr. Darcy withdrew his face slightly but embraced her tightly, and Elizabeth put her head on his shoulder, remaining still for a few minutes until he heard her whispering.

"There is another thing I forgot to tell you."

"Oh? And what that might be?"

"I forgot to tell you how much I love you."

She felt him holding his breath as his heart beat so violently that she could easily hear it. "Ardently?" He tried to make a little joke, but his words came with difficulty.

"I do not know if 'ardently' describes it, but I love you so much that it is almost painful. I know that sounds odd, but I cannot find another word to describe how I feel."

"No indeed, my dearest Elizabeth, it does not sound odd; it sounds exactly the way I feel, too!"

The peaceful silence surrounded them a while longer, neither daring to speak or move, enjoying the moment of secluded intimacy, which likely would not arise again soon. His hand was resting on her shoulder, gently stroking; all her thoughts and senses were focused on that spot. They remained in silence, their eyes closed.

Placing light kisses on the top of her head, Darcy came to his senses first, remembering the world outside the library. "Elizabeth?"

"Yes?" She did not raise her head from the comfortable position.

"Did you say anything in particular to Georgiana?"

The question brought her thoughts painfully back to reality. "No, I did not tell her anything, but I am afraid I acted foolishly and selfishly, and I distressed her quite badly."

She suddenly stood, growing more agitated. "I must apologise to Georgiana, and then I must go home; the carriage is waiting for me. Surely Jane and my aunt need me."

"Elizabeth, please!" His voice was deep and calm but commanding, and its effect was immediate.

She lifted her eyes to him, unconsciously obeying. However, in a lower tone, she continued. "I have delayed too long; my family must be worried."

"Please sit down a moment, and let us talk about this." He gently pulled her back to the sofa and sat close to her, taking her hands in his left hand, as his right arm came to rest around her shoulders. "I understand that you want to be with your family, and the carriage is ready and waiting for you. But they will not be worried, and they are not expecting you so soon. In fact, Mrs. Gardiner insisted that I tell you there is no urgent necessity for your presence at Gracechurch Street."

"And my father?"

"Mr. Bennet, and also Mr. Gardiner and Miss Lydia, I suspect, took a warm bath and a well-deserved sleep after our long, tumultuous night."

She searched his face and then gently stroked his forehead and eyebrows. "You also deserve to sleep; you look very tired."

"I am tired, but I am also so very happy at this moment that I could not possibly find the peacefulness of sleep. These few minutes spent with you are what I needed most." He closed his eyes, enjoying her gentle caress until she spoke again.

"Sir, I must go and speak, at least briefly, with Georgiana and apologise for the distress I caused her. My father will likely want us to depart for Longbourn as soon as possible, and I will not have the opportunity to talk to her again soon."

"If you do not mind, I would rather speak to Georgiana myself first. I want to tell her the news personally."

"Do you think she will disapprove of our — "

"Our engagement? No, of course not." He tenderly kissed her forehead. "I want to tell her about Mr. Wickham."

"But, are you sure it is wise to expose her to such horrible news so soon? Perhaps you could wait a few more days until she is completely recovered."

He considered a few moments. "Yes, perhaps you are right. I will decide while speaking to her. But I will tell her our joyful news as soon as possible. She will be happy to have such a wonderful sister so soon."

"Thank you, sir," whispered Elizabeth, squeezing his hand.

He cast a short, mischievous glance at her. "Elizabeth, is there any possible way to persuade you not to call me 'sir' or 'Mr. Darcy' any longer?"

She lifted her head and stared at him as he was fighting with little success to hide a smile. She was still unaccustomed to this teasing man, so different from the aloof one she had known three months ago.

"No persuasion is needed, but how should I address you, sir? I do not remember your revealing your first name to me when we were introduced, or any time later. But then again, at that time you found me not tolerable enough to tempt you even for a dance and certainly not worthy of such a personal disclosure."

Even if her tone was light — and he could not doubt she was teasing him back — his reply was very serious.

"I know I offended you, and I cannot apologise enough for that, Elizabeth. As I told you one day at Longbourn, I hope that in 10 or 15 years I can make amends for my outrageous behaviour at the beginning of our acquaintance."

"Sir, I was only teasing you. I was indeed offended that night but not so deeply, for I cared too little of your opinion then to seek your approval. Besides, it matters not, since all is forgotten now, truly; however, I cannot promise I will not tease you again on occasion about that subject."

He kissed her hand once more. "You are too generous; I cannot forgive myself so easily. And I was indeed impolite about my name."

"Your name is Fitzwilliam, and your family calls you William. I have known that for quite some time."

"Really? And how did you come to know that? "

"I asked Jane to ask Mr. Bingley."

He laughed openly. "Of course — an easy answer. So dare I trust you will not call me Mr. Darcy, at least when we speak in private?"

They were so close that they could feel each other's heavy breath. She brushed her lips very briefly to his to seal her promise and then turned more serious.

"As much as I would like to stay, I must leave. I am anxious to speak to my father. Do you happen to know when he intends to return home?"

"All I can say is that you will not leave town for at least two or three days. A special licence must be secured, and then your father and Mr. Wickham will sign the settlement — most likely tomorrow or two days hence — then the announcements. If everything goes as planned, the wedding could take place in a week."

"I see… I know I should be grateful that everything has concluded better than we could have imagined yesterday and in such a short time, but I am so concerned for my sister! He has a great number of debts; as Papa said, how will he pay them? And how will they live after the wedding? Will they return to Hertfordshire? Will he be accepted back into the regiment after such a disgraceful escape? I do not think father will be able to support them both, and I do not think he would want to. And if not, what will happen to Lydia?"

She did not even try to hide her restlessness, for she knew he could understand and comfort her.

"Yes, I know you have many questions. No, he will not return to Hertfordshire. He — It is expected that he will be offered a commission in the regulars, most likely in the North. I think everything will turn out well indeed, and hopefully he will be wiser from now on as he has a family to support."

She paused a few moments, staring at him. "William, what kind of commission was he offered so suddenly? And what happened to his debts? How could such a dreadful situation be resolved so easily?"

"Elizabeth, I would rather not speak about that subject any further, and I am asking you to indulge me in my wish. Fortunately, everything was settled, and nothing else is of any consequence."

"It is for me. I know beyond any doubt that all this is your doing. You cannot deny it."

"I have no wish to deny it. I promised I would not lie to you. But as I told your father this morning, I have no further explanation to offer regarding this matter."

He caressed her hair, adding more gently, "My love, I did what was my responsibility to do. I will not deny, however, that the wish of giving happiness to you added force to the other inducements that led me on, and I would have done much more to see you smile again. Did I not tell you so?"

"Yes, you did." She gazed at him adoringly, and he felt his mouth become dry at the expression on her face.

"Elizabeth... I really think you should leave now. If you indeed want to leave..."

She felt her cheeks, neck and ears burn as cold shivers travelled wildly down her spine again; she could only nod in agreement. Reluctantly, they rose, and he instantly took hold of her hand, their fingers entwined in a tight grip as they approached the door.

"Will you come to speak with Papa today?"

"Yes, of course. Moreover, I forgot to mention that Mr. Gardiner invited Bingley, my cousin and me to have dinner in Gracechurch Street tonight."

"Indeed? I am so happy I will see you again so soon..." Her own enthusiasm embarrassed her a little, and she blushed, adding politely, "It also would be a pleasure to resume my acquaintance with your cousin. I hope he will allow me to express my gratitude for his assistance. We cannot repay his kindness — "

"No, he will not allow you to express any kind of gratitude — I am certain of that. But I will tell you that his assistance was indeed helpful. It is a good thing that we succeeded in finding them so soon. At least, we know Miss Lydia is safe now. Do not be distressed any more about what was done."

"Thank you, William."

They reached the door, but she stopped and looked at him uneasily.

"What if the servants see us leaving the library after more than an hour alone? I am mortified imagining what they will think of me — and with good reason! I would never be able to face them."

"Do not worry about the servants. First, only Miles knows we are here, and I trust him implicitly. And even if others should find out, after obtaining your father's consent, I intend to inform the staff so that at your next visit they will treat you as the mistress of the house."

She blushed with great emotion and no less pleasure, while he lowered his head and briefly touched her lips once more. "I will miss you very much."

"As I will miss you. I hope you will not be late."

"No indeed. In truth, I intend to come earlier, so I can have the opportunity to speak to your father."

"I will look forward to it."

They exited silently, and indeed no servant was in the hall except Miles.

"Miles, please fetch Molly and ask her to accompany Miss Bennet."

They went out, and Darcy handed her into the carriage, making a proper farewell before returning in haste to the house.

Darcy entered Georgiana's room and found her reading more calmly than he would have expected. "Please forgive the delay, dearest."

"No need to apologise, William. Did Elizabeth leave? Is she well?"

"She is very well, and so am I."

His countenance clearly expressed his happiness, and Georgiana could only smile in return.

"I am very happy that your delay was worthwhile."

"It was indeed; in fact, I have some wonderful news to share."

Georgiana's reaction was even more enthusiastic than he anticipated, and she impulsively threw herself on her brother's neck, kissing his cheeks — something she had not done in years — and thanking him for giving her a most wonderful sister. She asked for more details, insisting upon knowing when Elizabeth would pay her another visit, and they chatted cheerfully for almost half an hour.

"My dear, unfortunately, I must tell you another thing, which will pain you. I am sorry to spoil your pleasure, but I think you must be informed."

"What is it, Brother? Tell me, I am begging you."

"Georgiana, the reason Elizabeth was in such torment is that her youngest sister, Lydia, who is only fifteen, eloped the day before from her parents' home...with Wickham."

A loud gasp escaped her, and she put a hand over her mouth to conceal the shock. Only her incredible blue eyes remained wide open. "But how... how was that possible?"

He related to her with few details the reason for Wickham's presence in Meryton and his deceit towards the Bennet family, concluding with the upcoming wedding. Georgiana remained sullen for several minutes.

"Thank you for telling me, Brother."

"Would you like to ask me anything more? I promise you that man will no longer bother you, even though he will be part of Elizabeth's family. He will never be allowed in your company."

"I know that, William. If you will excuse me, I feel very tired now. I would like to sleep."

He stayed a few moments longer, but she closed her eyes.

Elizabeth's concern over her family increased on the way back to Gracechurch Street, but as Darcy presumed, her father, sister and uncle were sleeping while Jane was playing with the children. She asked to be told everything about Lydia, and Mrs. Gardiner, after assuring her that she seemed to be in good health, could not conceal her displeasure with her youngest niece's unchanged behaviour even after all the trouble she caused her entire family.

The report about her father and uncle brought nothing more than she already knew from Darcy; then it was Elizabeth's turn to inform them about her visit to Miss Darcy.

Elizabeth could keep her precious secret no longer; pleased to be able to bring a little joy after the difficult situation they went through, she shared her happiness with her sister and her aunt. Jane and Mrs. Gardiner embraced and congratulated her heartily while asking for more details, and she indulged them with all that could be revealed.

Only in the late afternoon did Elizabeth have the opportunity to speak to her father. She was already tired after her talk with Lydia, which had turned into a quarrel. Lydia did not attempt to listen to her, only saying how thrilled she was to be the first one in the family to marry, how much she loved her dear Wickham, and finally accusing Lizzy of being jealous, for Wickham had always been her favourite.

She was startled at seeing her father, for Mr. Bennet looked not only tired but also older from his stressful burdens. He was pleased to speak to his favourite daughter, but not even she was able to lighten his mood. No words could comfort him, and he accepted no excuse; it was his failure as a father entirely, and he was fully aware of it.

"But do not concern yourself, Lizzy; it will all pass soon enough. Everything has turned out well so far with little effort from me. My part of the settlement is to give Lydia her equal share of the five thousand pounds — secured for you girls — after your mother and I are gone and 100 pounds per annum during our lifetime. Can you believe Wickham would be such a fool as to take her for so little?"

She tried to interfere, but her father would not allow her.

"And he is no fool, you know. He did not intend to marry her. He told me he needed to make his fortune by marriage, for he was penniless, and I know well the amount of his debts — more than a thousand pounds. Mr. Darcy and the colonel talked a great deal with him privately while we tried to bring Lydia to her senses, and he apparently changed his mind completely."

"Oh Papa, must she marry him? She will be so miserable; there is not the slightest chance for her to be happy with him."

"We tried to convince her, but she would not heed us. And... they already... So you see, there is nothing else to be done. But what I would really like to know is how much money Darcy had to spend to convince him and how I will ever be able to repay him for the favour. He absolutely refused to tell me, but I can easily imagine just how much this has cost him. You know he even promised to obtain that man a new commission in the North after the wedding. Can you believe that?"

She embraced her father, pained by his grief but happy she could say something to please him.

"Dearest Papa, I have reason to believe that Mr. Darcy will come to speak to you today. And even if you are not able to return his money, it will be in your power at least to return him a favour."

"Is that so? Well, you appear to be fully aware of Mr. Darcy's intentions. Do you intend to reveal any more details to your old father?"

"I do not. You will have to wait until he meets with you."

"Then leave me alone to enjoy your uncle's library, teasing child."

It was only half past four when Mr. Darcy's presence was announced. He was greeted by Mrs. Gardiner, who welcomed him affectionately and invited him to join the family in the drawing room. He could hear Elizabeth and Jane playing with the children, obviously not expecting guests so early, but he declined joining them, instead asking whether Mr. Bennet were available for a private talk. She directed him to the library, and he entered without delay, finding Elizabeth's father alone.

"Mr. Darcy! This is indeed a pleasant surprise. Please come in."

"Thank you, sir. May I inquire how you are feeling, Mr. Bennet?"

"Well, how can I be? Like a father who witnessed his youngest child's ruin and knew he did nothing to prevent it."

"Mr. Bennet, you are too harsh on yourself."

"No I am not, and we both know that. But let us speak of this no more. Would you care for a glass of brandy?"

"Yes, thank you. Mr. Bennet, I have come early today with the purpose of asking something of you."

"I must confess I was waiting for you, sir. Lizzy mentioned that you might want to ask me something."

"So much the better then… Sir, I trust that my high esteem and tender regard for your daughter have not been a secret to you. I had the pleasure of speaking with you about this subject almost two months ago, both at Longbourn and then at Netherfield during the night of the ball."

"Yes, I do remember."

"From that moment, even though unforeseen situations forced me not to be in her company as much as I would have wished, my affections grew stronger and my intentions clearer than ever. To my surprise, in these last days I have been given many reasons to believe that Miss Elizabeth's opinion of me improved and changed favourably, more that I would have hoped. So today I made her an offer of marriage, and she consented to become my wife. What I would like to ask you, Mr. Bennet, is for your consent and your blessing."

Though tall and impressive in his stature and appearance, his countenance was insecure and uneasy; he was fighting his reserve, obviously unaccustomed either to speak about his feelings or to put himself at the mercy of others. His patience, fortunately, was not to be tried this day.

"Mr. Darcy, indeed I have known of your regard for Lizzy and of hers for you for some time now. It would be an honour for me to give you my consent and a joy to give you my blessing. I could not wish for a better husband for my Lizzy."

"Thank you, sir." He breathed deeply and swallowed a little more brandy.

"However, I am surprised that you decided to propose today; in fact, I am quite surprised that you proposed at all after what happened. I must remind you that, unfortunately, Wickham will be a part of this family, too."

"Sir, I will not deny that this fact is appalling to me, and I must confess now that I have no intention to keep nor maintain a relationship with him. Miss Lydia, as a member of your family, will be welcome in our home always, but I will never invite him or accept his company in town. Even if you disapprove, my intentions are not negotiable in this matter."

"Oh, I cannot argue with you, sir; in fact, I agree wholeheartedly. Now, if you will allow me, I would like to fetch Lizzy for a moment."

Mr. Darcy nodded in agreement, and Mr. Bennet left only to return a few moments later with a joyful Elizabeth.

The moment they saw each other, their expressions changed instantly, and they were drawn to each other as though under a spell. Mr. Bennet was more affected than he would admit by the expression of happiness displayed by both his daughter and the gentleman. However, trying to hide his emotions, he could not refrain from adding, "Well, it seems that my old cottage was useful to you in more ways than one — am I right?"

A wave of redness spread over their faces, amusing Mr. Bennet.

"You are right sir; it was most useful indeed."

"Well, it is good to know I contributed to the happiness of at least one of my daughters. Let us return to the others and tell them the news."

Elizabeth took Mr. Darcy's arm, and he was delighted to see his ring on her finger. They entered the drawing room together, children's happy cheers covering their entrance. Becky ran to Mr. Darcy; he lifted her in his arms, and she kissed his cheeks. Soon, the Gardiners joined them, and the happy news was announced. Words of congratulation flowed freely, and their joy compensated somewhat for the distress of the day.

At around half past five, the ladies departed to change for dinner; when they returned, the colonel and Mr. Bingley had already arrived, and both hurried to greet them and congratulate Elizabeth in particular. Instantly, Bingley exchanged a quick glance with Jane and saw her blushing but smiling sweetly and encouragingly to him.

Neither Elizabeth nor Mr. Darcy made any effort to conceal their wish of being together, causing Mr. Bennet and the colonel to amuse themselves on their behalf. It was particularly diverting for both gentlemen to see a man of Mr. Darcy's disposition allow his happiness to overflow in mirth. However, Mr. Darcy seemed completely oblivious to their amusement, his attention concentrated upon Elizabeth.

Lydia joined them for dinner, irritated that her sister's engagement overshadowed her own.

Her only revenge was that she would be married much sooner and her betrothed was more agreeable than the boring Mr. Darcy.

Dinner arrangements were made to everyone's comfort. Mr. and Mrs. Gardiner were seated at each end of the table; on one side was Mr. Bennet; Mr. Darcy was seated to his right, followed by Elizabeth and then Colonel Fitzwilliam; on the other side, sat Mr. Bingley, Jane and Lydia. Of course, Mr. Bingley paid attention to no one other than Jane, wondering how Darcy managed to propose and become engaged in such a short time while he had not even voiced aloud his admiration for Jane.

The first course was about to be served when the doorbell rang, and to the mortification of all but Lydia, Mr. Wickham appeared in the doorway, bowing to the host and moving to the table without hesitation.

"Mr. Gardiner, I apologise for my intrusion. I hope I am not disturbing you. You said earlier this morning that I could visit my betrothed whenever I pleased, and I take the opportunity to do so now."

"You could have sent your card first," answered Mr. Bennet harshly, but Lydia rose and ran to him.

"Oh my dear, I am so glad you came. I am so bored, and I have missed you. And you will never guess what has happened: Lizzy's got engaged to Mr. Darcy."

Mr. Wickham could not hide his shock at this revelation and moved his gaze to Elizabeth. He found her face red with mortification at her sister's behaviour and his own impertinent intrusion. He then moved to look at Darcy who only honoured him with a brief, cold glance.

Mrs. Gardiner invited him to join them and placed him near Lydia, facing the colonel.

"Mr. Darcy, Miss Elizabeth, allow me to congratulate you. This is indeed a surprise. I never should have guessed."

"Thank you, Mr. Wickham," answered Elizabeth, trying to sound polite.

Although dinner was not as pleasant as it should have been — everyone obviously uncomfortable with the uninvited presence — Darcy decided the day was too important to allow Wickham to ruin it. He tried to ignore the man, engaging in pleasant conversation with his future father-in-law and his intended, while the colonel enjoyed Mr. Gardiner's company.

But Lydia and Mr. Wickham interrupted every discussion without showing the slightest sign of remorse or decorum. He even dared to mention how honoured and grateful he was to be accepted into their family, a remark that forced Mr. Bennet to respond sharply.

"Well young man, we are all very anxious to see how you will express your gratitude, but for some reason, I do not expect to be surprised."

Elizabeth tried to enjoy the dinner and Mr. Darcy's nearness; on more than one occasion, their movements allowed brief touches of their hands or arms, and his eyes were fixed upon her lovely profile most of the time, making her blush continuously. However, she could not stop casting intense glances toward Lydia and Mr. Wickham, searching for any sign of affection in his attitude that might give her the smallest hope for her sister's future happiness. The only result of her observations was a deep shame with herself for trusting the man so readily in the past.

The separation after dinner was brief, and when the gentlemen returned to the drawing room, Mr. Darcy did not hesitate to secure a chair near Elizabeth. He wanted a few private moments with her before the evening came to an end, and she welcomed him with pleasure.

"Elizabeth, you look remarkably well this evening."

"Thank you, William. I wanted to ask you the moment you arrived: How did Georgiana take the news? Did you tell her everything?"

"Yes, I did. She was as happy as I presumed regarding our engagement, but as for the other subject, I must confess her reaction surprised me. She said nothing beyond thanking me for informing her. But it is precisely her lack of reaction that worries me.

"Was she well when you left the house?"

"I checked on her, but Mrs. Annesley said she was asleep, and I did not want to disturb her." After a short pause he continued, "Elizabeth, I was wondering… Could you perhaps pay her a short visit tomorrow? I will be out on business until late in the afternoon, and I intend to call on my aunt and uncle to inform them about our engagement. I know she would like to have your company again."

"Of course. I look forward to it."

"Thank you, my love. And I hope I will find you there when I return." The tenderness of his address in a room filled with her family coloured her cheeks highly. Moreover, he was discreetly squeezing her hand and caressing the finger wearing the ring. Elizabeth, though flustered and embarrassed, managed to squeeze his hand back briefly while whispering to him, "I will be waiting for you."

As everyone was in need of rest after the previous sleepless night, and the following day was announced to be eventful, the guests prepared to leave quite early at around nine o'clock without indulging themselves in any other pleasant evening activities.

The colonel and Mr. Bingley had shared the latter's carriage on their way to the Gardiners, but the colonel expressed his desire to return with Mr. Darcy as they had several details to conclude for the following day. Since Mr. Wickham was the only one without a carriage, and he was obviously hinting he needed a means of getting himself home, Mr. Bingley felt obliged to offer his assistance After all, no matter how little he enjoyed his company, if things progressed as Mr. Bingley was hoping, this fellow soon would be his brother-in-law.

In the privacy of the carriage, the colonel teased his cousin.

"So you did it, did you not? You simply could not wait any longer; I should have guessed that last evening."

Darcy laughed, well humoured. "Well, you may put it that way if you like. The truth is that the right moment came, and I could not let it pass."

"Yes, I am sure you could not. And I do not dare to ask about that right moment. So... when do you plan to inform the family?"

"No later than tomorrow. I will come to fetch you in the morning, and I think later in the afternoon would be a good time to tell them."

"I hope you know there is a great risk it will ruin your whole day."

"I am aware they will raise many objections, but I am prepared for that."

"Many objections? They will throw themselves on you like eagles. You know, I tried to prepare my mother today and told her some nice things about Miss Elizabeth."

"You did? And may I ask what nice things?"

"Well, it suffices to say that mother was so interested that she intends to meet the lady personally. But of course, I neglected to mention to her your romantic interest in the lady."

"Well, I am grateful for your preparatory work. Let us hope then that Lady Ellen will be softer hearted."

"No indeed, you cannot entertain such hope. You know how important to her are one's situation in life, wealth and connections. She explicitly gave us her opinion on the matter more than once."

"Cousin, I am sympathetic to your parents' wishes, and I know they will be disappointed by the news, but nothing will make me change my opinion no matter the consequences. I can only hope I will not be forced to make a choice between them and Elizabeth, for my choice is already made."

"Well, let us be optimistic. We shall find a way to conquer this. But Darcy, I think you might have another, more serious problem."

"Another? And what problem might that be?"

"Wickham!"

"That is not a problem, it is a— Do not make me say the word, Cousin."

"Oh, by all means, say the word! I did not like at all the way he was staring at you and Miss Elizabeth tonight. I am afraid he will reconsider his position now that he knows you are to be his brother-in-law."

Darcy let escape such a curse that the colonel started to laugh. "I thought about that, too. If I had known that rascal would appear, I would have kept our engagement secret until they had signed the settlement, but there is nothing to be done now. We will see what awaits us tomorrow."

"There is always something to be done about Wickham."

"Come, do not start again. And yes, I confess I was tempted many times today to wipe that impertinent, provocative smirk from his face! I only restrained myself because I did not want to ruin his pretty face for the wedding and thus cause more embarrassment to the Bennet family."

"If you put it that way, I see you have a point. I will not insist upon the subject." The carriage stopped in front of the earl's house.

"Well, Darcy, that is all for tonight. I had a very pleasant dinner. I truly like the Gardiners you know."

"I am glad, cousin. I will see you tomorrow at eight."

The colonel descended from the carriage when a sudden idea crossed his mind.

"I say, Darcy, since it is still early and my parents usually retire quite late, why not enter with me and talk to them now? Maybe they will be tired and not react too harshly. In any case, you will settle the whole affair tonight, and then you may go home, drink a bottle of brandy and sleep until tomorrow."

Darcy hesitated only a moment. "You are absolutely right. That is sound advice. I have no reason to delay until tomorrow. Let us go in and be done with this."

"Very well then, Darcy. And do not worry; I will not leave you alone with the eagles."

"I am truly grateful for your help, Cousin, but I am not in the least worried. I am perfectly capable of defending my decision to marry the woman I love."

Chapter 17

Lady Matlock was entertaining her husband in the music room, performing for him at the piano while the earl was savouring a glass of port. It was one of those rare, quiet evenings without any guests or event to attend.

Their elder son Henry had been wed for six months, and he was not visiting as frequently as he had in the past. As for their younger son — the colonel — when he was in town, he was usually engaged in evening entertainments, and he was not expected to return home until late. Thus, when he entered not alone but in Darcy's company, they greeted them both with great pleasure.

"Dear nephew, what a pleasant surprise to see you! How is Georgiana? I presume she is well since you decided to leave home."

"Yes, Aunt, thank you for your concern. She has been well for the last few days and is improving constantly."

"I am glad to hear it. I intend to visit her very soon. I long to see her and was troubled that I was not able to go and see her recently."

"She will be very happy to see you, I am sure."

The earl invited them to join him and poured them each a glass of port.

"So, Darcy, do you have a particular reason for this rather late visit, or had you just wanted to see us?" The earl sounded very happy; he, too, was delighted to see his nephew and hear such good news about his niece.

Darcy was the only one who remained standing. He took a few steps and then stopped in front of the sofa where his aunt and uncle were sitting.

"Actually, I do have a specific reason, Uncle. Truth be told, I have wonderful news, and I want to share it with you as you are my closest family."

They stared at him, waiting in wonder and quite impatiently, but nothing prepared them for his next words.

"I am very happy to tell you that I am engaged to be married."

Their eyes widened in surprise, and both exclaimed in a most improper manner, "What!?"

"Darcy, did you finally propose to Anne?" asked the earl quite incredulous.

"No, Uncle, I have never intended to propose to my cousin. The young lady to whom I have offered my hand in marriage is not acquainted with you, I believe."

The earl rose from the sofa in surprise and began to pace the room. "But who is she? And when did you meet her? When did you court her? You have barely left your house since Georgiana became ill."

"I met Miss Elizabeth Bennet more than three months ago while visiting my friend Bingley in Hertfordshire. Her father's estate is no further than three miles from Netherfield."

"Oh, her father owns an estate? Well, thank heaven for that!" cried the earl in jest. "Darcy, have you lost your mind and all good sense? Did you hear what you just said? Out of all the eligible young heiresses in the *ton,* you chose the daughter of a country gentleman from only God-knows-where?"

Before Darcy could formulate an answer, Lady Matlock suddenly addressed her son.

"Robert, would you accompany me to the drawing room? I believe your cousin and your father are in need of a private conversation about this rather delicate matter."

The colonel was trying to protest as he had promised Darcy his support, but Lady Matlock had already grabbed her son's arm quite forcefully and was directing him to the door. There was nothing left for him to do except exit the room with her after exchanging a brief glance with Darcy. Before closing the door behind him, he heard Darcy's low voice and the earl's insistent demand to be informed about all the particulars of the *affair.*

Upon entering the drawing room, Lady Matlock cast a quick glance around to be sure that no servant was within earshot. She then turned toward her favourite son and slapped him with all the force of her delicate hand.

He stared at her in shock; never in his life had his mother struck him in punishment, not even when he was a boy and his wild behaviour was worthy of parental censure.

"How dare you mock me? Do you think I am an old, mindless woman with whom you can play games? You should have learnt by now that I am not to be trifled with, and if you have not, I am most willing to teach you that lesson right now." She was intensely angry, and a look as sharp as daggers was levelled at her son.

A man in his early thirties and a head taller than his mother, the colonel was grieved and intimidated by her strong reaction and wounded countenance. "Mother, please allow me to explain — "

"Oh, I will allow you to explain this riddle to me, have no fear of that. In fact, I am quite curious to hear how you can explain that you deceived me on purpose about Miss Bennet, telling me what you believed I would like to hear but concealing the most important fact: her engagement to your cousin."

"My lady" — he began using his affectionate and respectful way of addressing her since he became an adult — "I trust that, after you are informed of all the details, you will find me not to be as guilty as I may appear to you at the moment." He paused a little, and Lady Matlock took a comfortable place on the settee.

"By all means, do tell me all the details."

"Mother, you must know that I would never dare be disrespectful to you, to wilfully deceive you nor trifle with you. It is true, however, that I tried, quite consciously, to present Miss Bennet to you as favourably as possible, for Darcy had confided in me his affection for her. But I did not lie, for I myself did not know that Darcy intended to propose to her today, and I did not deceive you; everything I said about Miss Elizabeth Bennet is true. And with all due respect and affection, I must say I am determined to support Darcy in his decision."

He stopped and searched his mother's eyes, but he could read nothing in them.

"Robert, how many times have you met Miss Bennet?"

"Only twice, my lady: today and last evening."

"I see. So would it be correct to state that you have only a brief acquaintance with her?"

"Yes."

"Then nothing you have told me about Miss Bennet can be considered 'true' as they are only your observations based on very little evidence. She might be handsome and charming; I will grant you that. As for the rest, I will restrain from expressing myself for the moment. Now come and sit down; you are making me dizzy with your pacing about the room. And please be so kind as to offer me a glass of wine." He did exactly as his mother requested.

"I must tell you, I agree with your father that Darcy has lost his mind. I cannot believe he decided to connect himself — and by implication our family — to someone whose situation in life is so far below ours. That Miss Bennet is beautiful and charming is of little consequence."

The colonel thought it wise not to contradict her.

"Are you not disagreeing with me?"

"No indeed, Mother. My own first opinion was no different from yours when Darcy confessed his interest to me. Moreover, I was convinced that he had finally fallen into the trap of a fortune hunter."

He knew his mother well enough to guess that she was thinking the same.

"And may I ask why you decided in her favour after only two days' acquaintance?"

"I witnessed Darcy's happiness in her company and the expression on her face while looking at him."

His simple statement caused Lady Matlock to look at him as if she did not understand the meaning of his words. She had no answer prepared for it and no argument against it.

Several minutes of silence passed before she spoke briefly. "After Darcy departs, I would like you to tell me everything you know about Miss Bennet. If you promise me honesty, I will promise you a fair judgment regarding the lady. At present, I can offer you no more."

"My lady, I would not dare ask for more than a fair judgment. I am confident you will come to the same conclusion I did."

"Do not presume too much, and do not hope for too much, son! I am not as easily charmed as you are."

Their conversation was abruptly interrupted by the sound of a door and Lord Matlock's voice.

"If you willingly accept becoming a stranger to your family, so be it. After a couple of years, when you are satiated and tired of the little lady's charms, you will realise I was correct and come to apologise. Until then, I have nothing further to say regarding this matter."

He entered the drawing room like a storm and, on his way to his library, stopped momentarily in front of his wife.

"He is completely unreasonable; I never would have expected this behaviour from him. That country girl has turned him into a bewitched fool!"

"Lord Matlock!"

She reproached her husband with a harsh tone as she had done with her son, and the colonel was sure she would have no scruple in also slapping her husband if need be.

"Language of that sort is unacceptable in my presence! I strongly recommend you partake of the solitude of the library and a glass of wine. I will talk to Darcy myself."

"Yes, by all means do that. Try to convince him. Maybe he will listen to you."

He disappeared through the library door, and Lady Matlock exchanged a brief glance with her son as they walked to the music room; she found Darcy pacing the room and breathing deeply, clearly affected by the confrontation. He looked livid, his eyes darkened by anger and by the evident effort of controlling himself.

"If you will excuse me, Aunt, I will leave now."

He bowed politely, clearly prepared to leave, but Lady Ellen put her hand on his arm.

"Darcy, please stay a moment. Please sit and allow Robert to pour you some brandy."

"I am afraid I have neither the disposition nor the desire to remain. I do not possess the ability to have further conversation in my present state."

"Please stay… as a favour to me." He hesitated a moment, enough for his aunt to seize the advantage.

"I know Lord Matlock has offended you deeply, and I apologise for his bad manners; I am sure he will apologise himself on a later occasion."

"Lady Matlock, offending me was of no great importance, but Lord Matlock offended Miss Bennet in a most outrageous manner, undeservedly and most unfairly. I cannot allow or forgive that, not even from my excellent uncle. I shall be forced never to visit this house again. I am sorry."

His aunt had never seen him so offended, and her heart melted for him as if he were her own son. They had always treated the Darcy siblings as their own children, and he had always held them in the highest esteem and regard. Under no circumstances would Lady Matlock allow him to leave her house in such a state and with the intention of never returning due to the nature of his disagreement with the earl. A few moments were enough for the lady to decide the best course of action, the most advantageous one for all the parties involved. She took his arm firmly.

"Darcy, of course you will do as you wish, but please give me a few minutes. Please indulge me in this?"

Tired and powerless to enter into another argument at the moment, he accepted and sat on the settee while the colonel poured him a glass of brandy. They enjoyed the drink for a couple of minutes before Lady Matlock spoke again.

"Nephew, I hope you know that, despite his inconsiderate words, Lord Matlock has the deepest affection and concern for you. His only excuse might have been that your announcement has astonished us both. You have never given us any reason to expect such a thing, and I must say that I too have some doubts regarding your decision. Also, be assured I have no intention of offending Miss Bennet in any way. I am sure she is everything charming and might be a good wife for you, but will she be a proper mistress of Pemberley? Will she be able to rise to the expectations of the position and to honour it as did your mother and grandmother? I am afraid it will be too difficult a task for the daughter of a mere country gentleman who may only be acquainted with the lesser responsibilities of a small estate."

"I can understand your surprise, Aunt, and I can also understand your disapproval of my choice. Moreover, less than two months ago, I myself would have been decidedly against the mere idea of such a union regardless of my admiration of her. I congratulate myself on being wise enough to understand, before it was too late, how mistaken I was. In truth, I have every reason to believe that Miss Elizabeth Bennet will be an excellent mistress of Pemberley. She is generous, kind and amiable and possesses an intelligence that I have not met with in any young lady before her. She is not merely witty and bright but pleasant, unpretentious and also accomplished in every way a proper lady should be."

"I see ... Well, I must say she sounds very impressive. If she is only half as you describe her, she must indeed be as no other lady I have met before. If she is also as beautiful as I imagine she is, it is no wonder she managed to charm you as not one of the ladies of the *ton* has succeeded in all these years."

Her tone was light and conversational, but Darcy could easily understand her hidden meaning and discreet allusion to a mercenary purpose.

"Indeed you are mistaken, Aunt. She made no attempt to charm me; in fact, it was quite the opposite. For as long as a month after we were introduced, our every encounter turned into a debate, she missed no opportunity to challenge and censure me, and I offered her numerous opportunities to do so. But she did all this in such a playful manner that I was never offended — quite the opposite, I might say. She refused to dance with me more than once, you know."

His every word made Lady Matlock knit her eyebrows in disbelief. She thought Darcy spoke in jest — and his voice indeed sounded amused as though he were telling a joke — because she could never imagine any woman would dare treat Darcy in that manner. His next words only increased her astonishment.

"And I, in my selfish pride, chose to see her behaviour as flirtatious. I was convinced she admired me and was seeking my attentions. Consequently, for many weeks I tried to treat her coldly, not to raise any expectations. Can you imagine me such a fool? I came to understand the truth only when she explicitly told me that I offended her every time we met and that there were few people whose company she would not prefer over my own."

"Oh dear — now I am shocked! The lady seems quite wild and frightful. That way of treating you was preposterous."

He began to laugh, quite relieved at the turn of the discussion. "No, believe me, I deserved every derisive word and poor opinion of me. For you see, Aunt, I deeply offended Miss Bennet the first moment we were introduced just because I was in a bad humour. Bingley suggested that I should ask her to dance, but I refused quite rudely, calling her 'not handsome enough' though I had not even looked at her properly. Alas, she heard me!"

"Oh, heavens! Now you cannot leave! Pour me another glass of wine and tell me all the particulars; I deserve at least that much."

Fatigue from the previous night, two glasses of brandy, and his aunt's encouragement made Darcy more talkative than usual. Lady Matlock wisely chose to let him speak and, instead of posing direct questions about Miss Bennet and her family, found her answers in her nephew's story. Another two hours passed before they finally ended their discussion and Darcy decided to leave.

"Well, Nephew, this was the most entertaining evening I have had in years. I never would have guessed at the behaviour you exhibit among strangers. Now you absolutely must bring Miss Bennet for tea as soon as possible so I can meet her. And then you must have another dinner and invite the Bingleys, too, for I understand I missed quite a spectacle a few days ago."

Though she spoke in a light, jesting tone, he bowed in front of her and kissed her hand formally.

"Thank you, Lady Matlock. I know Miss Bennet will be honoured to meet you. Please send me word when it would be convenient for you, and we will honour the invitation."

When Darcy reached his house half an hour later, he asked briefly about Georgiana, and he was told she was well. Then Miles assisted him in retiring for the night, and he fell into the deepest sleep.

At the same time, the colonel and Lady Matlock remained in earnest conversation while the earl, taking his wife's wise advice earnestly, found himself quite put out by one too many glasses of brandy.

Elizabeth had another restless night, this time from the unexpected and still not completely believable happiness that prevented sleep from claiming her for many long hours. Only when dawn appeared did she finally fall asleep. She woke a few hours later, not tired but with anxious anticipation of what the day would bring her. *The second day of my engagement.* If not for the ring that sparkled on her finger, she might fear it was only a dream.

An exquisite bouquet of red roses was delivered to her before breakfast, making her blush in front of her family. She took the card and gasped as her heart beat wildly on seeing her own earlier thoughts written by Darcy.

> *This is the second day of our engagement, and I love you even more than I did yesterday. The hours until we meet again seem an eternity.*
>
> *F.D*
>
> *PS. I have ordered the carriage to remain at your disposal for you to call on Georgiana.*

Elizabeth barely noticed the meal on her plate or the topics of conversation; after her father and uncle departed, she tried to spend some time playing with her young cousins, and she was more than pleased to tell them of her engagement and answer their questions.

Around half past ten, while Mrs. Gardiner and Jane were trying to persuade Lydia to demonstrate moderation in discussing all the things that needed to be purchased for her wedding, Elizabeth prepared to call on Georgiana.

She felt guilty for again not staying at home to help, but Mrs. Gardiner heartily encouraged her outing. Her aunt would have left Lydia alone herself, so much was she irritated and even revolted by her youngest niece's lack of judgment, but there was nothing to be done. Lydia was Lydia after all.

The next morning, Colonel Fitzwilliam found his mother in the dining room and greeted her affectionately and with no little admiration. They conversed until after midnight, but her appearance was as flawless as ever at that early hour of the morning.

He thought he had never seen his mother appear less than perfect in any situation. Her gowns, jewels, and hairstyle were of the highest possible fashion but never ostentatious; rather, she exhibited more of discreet elegance. Her adornments plainly spoke of her wealth and position in society but also her exquisite taste.

For more than thirty years, she had been one of the most admired ladies wherever she appeared, including St. James's Palace. Even now, at the age of four and fifty, her entrance into a room full of people made all eyes turn toward her. She had been — and still was — not only beautiful but also glowing, spreading light around her, a quality the colonel had never found in any other woman of his acquaintance.

They did not begin breakfast until the earl appeared, his countenance looking a bit the worse for wear. "Good morning, Father."

"Shhh... Robert, do not talk... I am afraid my head will explode if I hear any noise."

He took his place opposite his wife, asked for coffee, and gulped it all desperately under Lady Matlock's reproachful gaze.

"Am I to understand you were too fond of your brandy last night, husband? By the time I went to see you in the library, I was told you were escorted to your rooms and had retired."

He only nodded and poured himself another cup of coffee.

"Yes, I was trying to calm myself after my quarrel with that boy. I lost my temper completely with him."

"Yes you did; I grant you that."

"But how could one keep one's demeanour upon hearing such news? I do not want to imagine my sister Catherine's reaction when this report reaches her ears."

"Well, husband, I dare say she will react no differently than you. You both are under the impression that raising your voice and offending people are the strongest weapons in a battle. And you both should have learned by now how wrong you are, for neither of you have ever won a battle against me."

She was jesting, looking at her husband in a flirtatious way, her eyebrow raised challengingly, and the earl hid a smile at the corner of his mouth with obvious affection and admiration for her.

"You are right, wife, but then again I do not remember anyone winning a battle against you."

"True," she answered with no modesty, and all three smiled while enjoying their meal.

"So, tell me, my dear wife, did you also win the battle with Darcy? How were things settled?" asked the earl after a few more minutes had lapsed and he had poured himself yet another cup of coffee.

"Husband, I entered into no battle with my nephew. We did talk with admirable calmness for almost two hours, and I discovered many astonishing things. I must say, I have not seen Darcy so well humoured and open in his manner for years. The lady seems to have a good influence on him. I can only hope she is at least half as accomplished as he described her to be. I invited them to have tea with me in the coming days, so I can make my own judgment based on close observation."

The earl's face turned red at his wife's words. "Invited her to have tea with you? Ellen, have you also lost your mind? I sent you to bring him to his senses, and you said you would make him reconsider this ridiculous engagement — not share stories and schedule social calls."

She was stunned, turning white at his offensive speech in the company of their son; doubtless, the servants who served at table also heard him.

"Lord Matlock, you did not send me to do anything. I willingly offered to talk to our nephew, and I certainly did not say anything about my intention of convincing Darcy in any aspect of his decision."

Her voice was as low as possible, but her tone was steely. However, his anger, lack of concentration caused by a poor night's sleep, and a terrific headache caused the earl to react improperly, and he continued as he began.

"Well, apparently I was wrong in trusting your judgment and good sense in this matter. You are of no help to me; you have only worsened the situation. From now on, I forbid you to interfere, and I absolutely forbid you to invite that country girl here."

If a look could burn, Lord Matlock would certainly have been scorched in the next instant.

The colonel felt the tension and cast a quick, worried glance at his mother in time to see her rise from her seat and move slowly toward her husband, stopping only when she was close enough to speak to him almost in a whisper but still audible to their son.

"Lord Matlock, many times in my life I have questioned my wisdom in accepting you as my husband, but only at this moment am I strongly convinced that it was a great mistake and I should have chosen more carefully. Do not presume that you can forbid me anything, as no one has done so since I was eight years old. And if you are not willing to accept my guests and treat them with all due respect, you should consider removing yourself from this house, which I inherited from my excellent father."

The earl's eyes opened widely in astonishment as he attempted to comprehend his wife's statement. She turned majestically and, before leaving, threw her husband a last glance over her shoulder.

"And, Lord Matlock, if you decide to remain in this house, I strongly advise you to change your manner of addressing us and never again raise your voice to such an unacceptable level, or upon my word, I shall call you 'Lady Catherine' for the rest of your life."

Many long moments passed before the earl could understand fully that he was being punished for his behaviour and his language as if he were a boy of five. He gulped loudly and looked at his son, but the colonel had already finished his breakfast and excused himself, explaining he had urgent business. Alone in the dining room, the earl still could not apprehend his mistake. Only much later did he realise that, though his bad temper made him lose his calm many times in his life, for the first time in 34 years of marriage, he gravely and purposely had offended his wife.

All four gentlemen were to convene at the office of Mr. Darcy's solicitor as was agreed the evening before. The settlement was prepared as previously discussed, and it was expected that Mr. Wickham and Mr. Bennet would sign it. Afterwards, the day's schedule included Mr. Darcy assisting Mr. Wickham in applying for a special license, Mr. Bennet and Mr. Gardiner taking care of the announcements, and the colonel's settling the matter of the new commission for the soon-to-be bridegroom.

According to the plan fixed late the previous night, Mr. Bennet intended to depart for Longbourn as soon as possible. Despite the various express messages sent to her, Mrs. Bennet was expected to be past the limits of her nerves after more than two days of uncertainty. Moreover, he absolutely refused to return to town or give permission for any member of his family to attend the wedding.

At Mrs. Gardiner's advice and persuasion, he allowed his eldest daughters to remain in town until after the wedding to assist Lydia, to help Mrs. Gardiner control and chaperone her, and then to attend her wedding. After all, for Lydia, it was indeed one of the most important events in her life, and she should have at least two of her sisters with her.

The arrangements were quite satisfactory for Mr. Darcy as it secured him more time with Elizabeth. Not wanting to waste the opportunity to host his future father-in-law in his house, he extended a dinner invitation for that same evening with only the Bennets, the Gardiners and Mr. Bingley attending; the colonel, who was also invited, declined due to a previous engagement.

The gentlemen grew concerned about Mr. Wickham's arrival; he was not a man to be trusted, and every minute of delay induced more anxiety and reinforced the colonel's belief that he would not attend the meeting but increase his demands before agreeing to the marriage. However, to their utter surprise, the gentleman in question appeared very jovially, greeted them and apologised for his delay. No more than half an hour later, the settlement was signed. As the first task was resolved, everyone's attention turned to what remained to be accomplished. They separated as planned with an expected reunion later that afternoon.

Entering Mr. Darcy's town house for the third time, Elizabeth felt the difference as soon as she took the first step on the stairs. Her fears and uncertainties vanished, and everyone from the doorman to Mrs. Hamilton — who greeted her in the hall and asked if she would allow her to express her congratulations — was solicitous towards her. It was obvious that Mr. Darcy had kept his word and informed the staff of her new situation.

"Thank you, Mrs. Hamilton. Your kind words are most welcome and greatly appreciated."

"Mr. Darcy told us we were to be at your disposal, so please let me know if there is anything you need."

"I will, thank you, but for now I would only like to see Miss Darcy. She is well, I hope?"

"Mrs. Annesley complained to Mr. Darcy that she seemed to be in lower spirits than she was yesterday and that she did not eat satisfactorily. Except for that, she seems to be in good health. Please follow me, Miss Bennet."

Mrs. Hamilton entered to announce Elizabeth and then left quietly, but not without noticing Georgiana's distressed reaction as she put her book aside to greet her visitor. If Mr. Darcy had not told her how pleased his sister had been by their engagement, Elizabeth would have been justified in believing the opposite. She tried to maintain her countenance with a pleasant smile as she approached the bed.

"Good morning, Georgiana. I hope I did not intrude with this unannounced visit."

"No, Elizabeth, I am pleased to see you. My brother let Mrs. Annesley know that you might come, so it was not unexpected." Elizabeth sat in the armchair near the bed, and they both smiled shyly at each other.

"Elizabeth, please allow me to congratulate you. I was so happy when William told me. I could not have hoped for a better sister."

"Thank you, Georgiana. Your approval and good opinion are very important to me. I was afraid you would be... displeased with the engagement."

"Displeased? Why should I be displeased?"

Elizabeth blushed in embarrassment. "I thought that perhaps, after Mr. Darcy told you about the situation created by my youngest sister's thoughtless gesture — "

"Oh, Elizabeth, how could I be displeased with you for that? If you only knew... I was at least as thoughtless as your sister. I would have done even worse if not for my brother's help." She paled more than usual, and tears appeared in her blue eyes, ashamed of what she had just said. Elizabeth rose from the armchair and sat on the bed beside her, embracing her with affection. Georgiana only leaned her blonde head on Elizabeth's shoulder and began to sob. Gently stroking her hair, Elizabeth tried to calm her with kind words.

"Georgiana, Mr. Wickham does not deserve your tears. You should not suffer for him anymore."

She felt the girl startle as she lifted her eyes, glowing with tears on her pale face. "Elizabeth, do you know about — ?"

"Yes, I know. Mr. Darcy told me, and I must say that your courage and strength astonish me greatly. I admire you so much, Georgiana."

"I do not understand you, Elizabeth. What is there to admire? I acted foolishly; I deeply grieved my brother and almost dishonoured my name and my family."

Elizabeth held her trembling hands and squeezed them gently.

"Georgiana, if this is the reason for your distress, you are quite mistaken. You acted far more wisely than many older and more experienced women would have done. It was easy for Mrs. Younge and Mr. Wickham — two masters of deception in whom you had every reason to trust — to persuade you, to make you believe yourself to be in love, and even to consent to an elopement. It is not difficult for the kind and affectionate heart of a young girl to misunderstand a tender childhood regard for an old family friend. But you did not lose your wisdom and admirably chose to trust in your brother and tell him everything about the elopement. Your heart doubted that man, and your reason told you what was to be done. This is extraordinary for a girl so young under those circumstances."

Georgiana was listening to her new friend with astonishment. Never in those long, painful months had she interpreted her actions in that way, and the praise from her future sister buoyed her soul.

"And I can heartily assure you that your brother is only deeply concerned for you, for the grief and pain you have suffered. We were both worried that perhaps you are still affected by — "

"Oh no," interrupted Georgiana. "Please do not believe I have any other feelings for Mr. Wickham than anger for his ungrateful behaviour towards our family. And I am very sorry for your sister. I am afraid she will not be happy with him."

"Yes, I share the same fear, but there is nothing else to be done. All of us, including your brother, tried to convince her not to marry him, but she could not be moved. She is not wise and would not listen, and she will have to pay all her life for that."

They paused a few minutes, and then suddenly Georgian broke the silence.

"Elizabeth, is this your betrothal ring? It is so beautiful; I have never seen it before."

Elizabeth blushed and exposed the ring to be better admired.

"Yes, it is the most wonderful ring I have ever seen. I am almost afraid to wear it."

"Oh, but just wait. William will give you so many other jewels; they are all exquisite. Most of them are at Pemberley, and you must have a little more patience. I hope you will like Pemberley. It is the most wonderful place. You can ride for hours and hours and just rejoice in all its beauties."

Her enthusiasm and animation made Elizabeth laugh, thus lightening their conversation considerably.

"Georgiana, I am sure I will love Pemberley, though I hope to persuade Mr. Darcy to leave the jewels where they are. As for the hours of riding — I am afraid I will have to ask Mr. Darcy to give me a little phaeton to follow you slowly. I am not very fond of horses, but I do like to walk and spend as many hours as possible outdoors."

This statement greatly surprised Georgiana. "Elizabeth, you do not ride?"

"I am afraid not... and I have no desire to do it. I am sorry to disappoint you."

"Oh, this cannot be. Then you had better consider breaking the engagement this instant, for William would not accept this. Riding is his favourite sport, and I do not think he will accept your following him in a phaeton. That would slow him a little from his gallop." They both started to laugh, well humoured.

"Perhaps I should have mentioned that to him before accepting his proposal."

"Yes, perhaps, because you will have no alternative than to learn; trust me."

Their voices were cheerful and a little loud; the conversation became more and more animated and continued in the same manner without the two young ladies noticing the opened door and the unexpected and unannounced guest who entered and stopped to look at them in surprise.

DARCY LEANED BACK AGAINST THE carriage wall, staring out the window. Finally, he was relieved and content with that awful day's achievements, and he could relax a little, trying to ignore the man sitting opposite him. All arrangements for the unwanted wedding were fixed, and in few minutes, he would drop Wickham at his inn and continue the ride to his house where he hoped Elizabeth was waiting for him. He was a little worried about his sister with whom he had not spoken since the previous day, and he trusted that Elizabeth's care and open manners could bring Georgiana some relief.

An inner smile lit his face as his thoughts rested upon his intended. He could still smell her scent and feel the softness of her lips pressing against his, the skin of her neck shivering under his touch, her tentative but promising response to his caress. He could not help but wonder whether she had missed him and enjoyed the roses he sent her. Would she be as shy as she was the previous day when they were alone? Would she allow him to kiss her again? Without any consideration for propriety, he was determined to secure at least a few minutes with her in privacy if she would agree.

Darcy breathed deeply, almost frightened by his need to see and touch her again.

He startled at the sound of Wickham's ironic voice. "I say, Darcy, I would never have thought it possible for us to become brothers after all. It is the most astonishing event."

"Wickham, do not entertain any hopes of taking further advantage of the situation. You will never be my brother; in fact, you will never be my *anything* except the scoundrel who betrayed my father's trust and affection. In truth Wickham, I have no desire to speak to you anymore. I have had enough of you these last days and, quite honestly, these last years."

"I am truly sorry you harbour such harsh feelings toward me, Darcy. Say what you want; when the announcements appear for both engagements, the whole town will know that the master of Pemberley will be married into the same family as the son of his father's steward. What a joke!"

A defiant grin and a daring look concluded his derisive words, and he searched with satisfaction for the first signs of irritation on Darcy's face. He knew Darcy well enough to know what to say to get a reaction from him, and it was satisfying to see him struggle to keep his countenance, his decorum and his gentlemanlike manners.

He had always found great satisfaction in hurting Darcy since they were children. He never felt anything but resentment, jealousy and hate — yes, even as a boy he hated him! — for being his rich godfather's son and for being a boring, unpleasant boy whom everyone seemed to admire and praise.

Oh, it was true that old Mr. Darcy was kind to him, allowed him to remain in the family's company, and invited him to family parties when he grew older. Yes, everybody enjoyed the company of "*... the young Mr. Wickham — such a charming, pleasant gentleman, and very handsome too.*" However, the young Darcy was praiseworthy in everything, and though not fond of society — preferring studying and riding with his father to balls and parties — he was declared one of the most handsome and desired single young men in town.

Darcy's father was fond of his godson and enjoyed his company, but he always said how proud he was of his son. *"He is my pride,"* he used to say. Yes, he did buy his godson the finest clothes and pay for him to attend the best school — but for what purpose? The young master was always the best at school, the best at sports, *and the best at every damn thing.* Wickham never could win any praise when competing with him. Of course, his father — Mr. Wickham — always insisted that he needed to try harder and learn more if he wanted to be proficient in anything, but the extra work and hours of studying were not to his liking. He dreamed constantly of besting Darcy, but in truth, he wanted to *be* Darcy.

He had a bit of remorse at such feelings but was almost pleased when Lady Anne and then his godfather passed away. The Darcys were no longer happy.

What he did not take into consideration was that the young master of Pemberley was not easily deceived as the late one had been. Losing his benefits, rather than making him regret what he had and had not valued as they deserved, only increased his hatred toward Darcy. And after he failed to conclude the affair with Georgiana, he was certain — more than anything — that he would never be around any member of Darcy's family or even speak to one of them again.

Now they were to be brothers after all, and Darcy was to wed a woman who favoured Wickham first. For the first time, he felt he had a secret power over Darcy, and he intended to use it. Now it was indeed so easy to win, at least partially and for a short time. However, he wanted to savour the taste of Darcy's defeat.

"Come now, Darcy, do not be so harsh with me. Last night I was under the impression that Miss Bennet's charms improved your rude manners, at least to some degree. You seem... bewitched by her."

Darcy gave him a dark, warning glare and then turned his head to the window in an attempt to dismiss him, but with little success.

"You know, I must confess I did not guess the nature of your interest in Miss

Elizabeth at all. I had noticed your attentions toward her, but it never crossed my mind that you would be induced by her into matrimony. To succeed where so many young heiresses and their mothers failed year after year must be the supreme proof that Miss Elizabeth's qualities and accomplishments are above those of most ladies. You must feel very fortunate that she chose you to be the recipient of her... charms."

His insinuating tone was giving a twisted meaning to his words with their offensive implications while he impertinently held Darcy's darkened gaze.

"But Darcy, did you not ask yourself whether her preference toward you would have been the same if not for your financial condition? Surely, her mother had not failed to notice your attentions toward her and persuaded her to accept you. That woman would kill to secure a son-in-law half as rich as you are. Poor Elizabeth must not have stood a chance against her."

The effect of his words on Darcy was so powerful that Wickham could sense his whole body tensing, while his jaws clenched and a small vein pulsated violently at his temple. The carriage cabin was too small to hold the extraordinary tension, and Wickham knew he put himself in danger, but he simply could not stop — as he could not stop in a card game with an enormous stake.

"Oh, do not be angry with me; I only speak the truth! You surely must have been aware that she greatly disliked you at the beginning of your acquaintance. I know for sure that she did because she told me as much. We were always good friends, you know. She was very pleased to accept my attentions from the first moment we met, and we spent a very enjoyable time together, talking and... Well, let us say just talking, shall we? I mean, before you became intimate with her... I cannot condemn her for choosing you; she is a very smart woman, and she knows her own interests only too well."

Wickham's words sounded insulting even to his own ears, and he knew the danger of his daring speech, but the sudden change of countenance in Darcy — his frozen, wounded gaze — were worth any risk.

In the next moment, Darcy silently moved closer to him, his eyes fixed on Wickham's face, his eyebrows knit together menacingly; then his whole body moved suddenly in his seat, making Wickham startle and turn his head to avoid the blow.

What followed was more powerful and painful than a hundred blows; Darcy resumed his initial position, leaned against the back of his seat, and began to laugh — a hearty, unrestrained laugh, as though enjoying himself after a good joke. He cast a pitiful glance at his childhood companion, shaking his head at the sudden revelation that struck him.

"Wickham, I must thank you, for you have helped me finally understand the truth. I have known you almost my whole life, and until this moment, I never truly understood what a completely ridiculous fool you are."

"I... I do not know what you are talking about, Darcy."

"I can easily believe you do not understand me, which only proves that my statement was correct; you are stupid! Allow me to enlighten you. Only a fool would assume that I would consider marriage with Miss Bennet without being assured of her worthiness or her true feelings for me. And only a fool would purposely offend my future wife, knowing that his entire future is in my hands. Only a fool would try my patience, knowing that I can throw him in debtor's prison at the blink of an eye or have him dishonoured and begging on the streets whenever I please."

He paused a moment and then started to laugh again. "You know, I should kill you for your attempt to discredit Miss Bennet, but you are such a poor excuse for a man that you do not deserve to be taken in earnest. I shall tell the story to Elizabeth tonight so we can laugh together. I think Mr. Bennet, too, would be much diverted with my tale as new proof of his son-in-law's worthiness. And now, out of my carriage and out of my sight, Wickham, before I throw you into the street. I cannot bear your presence a moment longer."

He unlocked the door and pushed Wickham out unceremoniously, forcing him to jump from the still-moving carriage. "I should have thrown him out years ago..."

Relieved and contented with himself, he put Wickham out of his mind, all of his thoughts more pleasurably engaged in the anticipation of seeing Elizabeth again. *And hopefully not just* seeing *her*...

SHE REMAINED NEAR THE DOOR, watching the lively chat and Georgiana's delicate laugh for several moments. The last time she had seen Georgiana, the girl was just recovering from her dreadful illness and could hardly sit up in bed. *Could that have been less than a week ago?*

"Good day. I hope I am not interrupting your conversation."

Startled, both young ladies turned to the visitor who was moving toward them with superior elegance and a severe countenance, resting an intense gaze upon Elizabeth.

For the first time in her life, Elizabeth felt intimidated as she rose to her feet, blushing.

"Aunt Ellen! What a pleasant surprise!" cried Georgiana with as much joy as affection.

"How are you, sweetie?" A loving smile lightened Lady Matlock's face as she lowered her head and tenderly kissed her niece's cheeks. "You look marvellous, Georgiana."

"Thank you; indeed, I am feeling much better."

"You seem to be in a good disposition, as well."

"Yes, I am, and I must give thanks to my friend for that. Aunt, please allow me to introduce to you my dear friend, Miss Elizabeth Bennet; Elizabeth, this is my aunt, Lady Matlock."

"It is an honour to meet you, Lady Matlock."

"Well, Miss Bennet, I am glad to meet you at last; I have heard so many things about you lately, and might I say, they have been quite astonishing. But Georgiana, from what

I have heard, Miss Bennet is not just your friend but soon to be your sister; am I correct?"

"Yes, Aunt. I did not know whether William had informed you. Is it not wonderful? I am so exceedingly happy! I could not hope for a better sister."

"I can see you are happy, dear," answered the lady, turning to Elizabeth, who wore an embarrassed smile. She did not fail to notice that Lady Matlock neither expressed her own opinion nor congratulated her.

"I must say I am impressed, Miss Bennet, My nephew, my niece and even my son seem to hold you in the highest esteem and admiration. I have not heard such praise about a lady in quite some time."

"Thank you, Lady Matlock."

"Do not thank me; I only repeated what I have heard. However, I must say you seem to be... less talkative and voluble than I had expected. Are you as happy as Georgiana about this engagement? I can hardly imagine what a young lady of your situation must be feeling when she is honoured with a marriage proposal from such an illustrious gentleman."

The hidden meaning of Lady Matlock's words did not escape Elizabeth. She could not say whether Mr. Darcy's aunt was displeased about the engagement or disliked her personally, but it was certain that she did not approve of his decision or her. The lady's sharp, inquiring look could not be misunderstood. She was not rude but of a coldly superior politeness, all the more striking compared to her tender manner of addressing her niece.

After the first moments of confusion and discomfort caused by Lady Matlock's unexpected visit and the clearly negative impression she had formed of her, Elizabeth quickly regained her wit, and her spirits rose again as always when confronting a challenge. Lady Matlock was indeed Mr. Darcy's aunt and one of his nearest family, but she, Elizabeth, was the woman he had willingly chosen to be his wedded wife. She had every reason to feel proud and no reason to feel inferior in any sense. Quite daringly and looking straight at the older lady with a hint of a smile — much as she had when arguing with Mr. Darcy at the beginning of their acquaintance — she did not delay her answer.

"Lady Matlock, though I am grateful for all the praise that has reached your ladyship, I am sure much of it was biased by the partiality of Mr. Darcy, Georgiana and Colonel Fitzwilliam. However, if I might venture to guess what you have heard, I can confirm at least one truth — that I am indeed very talkative — but I am not sure whether this can be counted as a good quality!"

Lady Matlock's surprise was obvious, as her perceptiveness allowed her to sense the teasing riposte in the young woman's words. In a more serious tone, Elizabeth continued.

"But I am indeed happy about the engagement, Lady Matlock, and I thank you for asking me."

"Well, I am glad we clarified that. I do not want to impose upon you; I should leave and let you continue your conversation. Miss Bennet, I hope we will meet again soon, I asked Darcy to invite you to have tea with me one of these days."

Her voice was as impersonal as before, but Elizabeth became easier at this proof of amiability.

"I would be honoured, Lady Matlock."

"Oh, Aunt, please do not leave so soon. You have not even taken a seat since you arrived. Can you not stay a little longer? I have truly missed you. And I am sure Elizabeth would enjoy your company, too."

"Georgiana, I spoke in earnest when I said I did not want to intrude. You seemed to be having a pleasant and private conversation with Miss Bennet when I interrupted you."

"It was not at all private! In fact, I would love to share it with you. Would you mind, Elizabeth?"

Elizabeth coloured deeply, and she again felt ashamed and embarrassed. What had been a reason for amusement and jokes with Georgiana, suddenly turned into a failure when on the verge of being exposed to her aunt. She tried to keep her countenance and even to smile, making sport of herself.

"No, I would not mind. After having heard so much praise about me, it must be time for her ladyship to learn the truth about my lack of accomplishments."

For the second time, Lady Matlock's surprise was clear from her expression, as she looked at Elizabeth, intrigued. "Well, then I will stay a few more minutes."

"Lady Matlock, would you rather sit here near Georgiana? I trust it will be comfortable enough."

"Thank you, Miss Bennet. You are very kind."

Elizabeth offered her the armchair she had previously occupied and, since no servant was in the room, took another chair for herself and moved it closer to the bed. Though Lady Matlock never would have considered moving a chair around the room by herself, she was pleased with Elizabeth's doing so; it was a natural gesture, not humble, not meant to impress but to make the situation as comfortable as possible for all of them.

"We were talking about Pemberley, Aunt."

"Ahh...indeed not a private subject but an interesting one. And may I inquire what was so amusing about it?" She was delighted to see her niece so well recovered and lively after her dreadful illness.

"Georgiana was telling me about the beauties of Pemberley and about the pleasure of riding, and I confessed that I am not much of a rider. Moreover, I am not quite inclined to learn, as I prefer to walk whenever I have the chance." Though she tried to maintain a light tone, Elizabeth expected that Lady Matlock would not be amused by her deficiency. And indeed, when their eyes met, she could see she was correct in her assumption; however, the reaction was not at all what she expected.

"Well, Miss Bennet, I hope you are aware that, as Darcy's wife, you will have to learn many things, inclined or not, and quite often you will have to do what must be done instead of what you might prefer."

They held each other's gaze a few moments, searchingly, in a silent confrontation, and even Georgiana's face changed a little, sensing the tension.

"I am aware of that, your ladyship, but I am grateful to you for reminding me. However, I trust that, most of the time, what I prefer will not differ from what must be done."

Accustomed by her character and rank always to be in control, Lady Matlock was both disturbed and disconcerted by Elizabeth's tone and countenance; she could not be sure whether the girl was courageous and witty or merely impertinent. However, as a fair combatant, she could recognise that she herself had been the one to provoke the confrontation and consequently Elizabeth's reaction; she also noticed Georgiana's distress. She decided to change the conversation to a more neutral topic for her niece's benefit and to delay her evaluation of Miss Bennet's character for a later time.

The conversation, however, was not yet over as Elizabeth continued.

"Lady Matlock, I beg you to believe me when I say that I appreciate my good fortune and the honour of entering into Mr. Darcy's family. I fully comprehend that there will be many things I will have to learn, and I will spare no effort in my attempt to improve myself so as to be worthy of my future position."

A brief glance was enough for Lady Matlock to understand how sincere and respectful that statement had been, and she thought she recognised a trace of fear and uncertainty in the young lady's eyes; no impertinence was there — only dignity and determination. A hint of a smile lifted the corners of Lady Matlock's lips and brightened her eyes as she looked at Elizabeth.

"I am glad to hear you say that, Miss Bennet. However, you absolutely must learn to ride and very well indeed if only because Miss Bingley is a proficient rider, and she will not stop chasing Darcy if you offer her such an opportunity."

Elizabeth's surprise made her laugh at this unexpected change of topic and the evident change in her ladyship's disposition. Moreover, she was pleased that the lady took her hand gently, looking at the ring that was glowing on her finger.

"I assume this is your betrothal gift?"

"Yes." She turned her hand, allowing the ring to be admired, the emotion and pleasure obvious on her face.

"It is beautiful, would you not agree, Georgiana?"

From that point, the conversation went neutrally and pleasantly; Lady Matlock asked a few more questions about Elizabeth's sisters, her father's estate, and her aunt and uncle in town with the usual curiosity for a new acquaintance and never displaying any sign of disapproval or disdain, not even when it was mentioned that the

Gardiners lived in Cheapside. Moreover, the lady asked a few particulars about Mr. Gardiner's business as it appeared that the colonel had expressed a great enthusiasm for his abilities and knowledge.

Half an hour later, she rose, expressing her intention of leaving and, after she took her goodbyes from her niece in a tender and caring manner, turned to Elizabeth.

"Miss Bennet, would you like to take a stroll with me downstairs? I promise I will not detain you more than a few minutes, for I know Georgiana is desirous of your company."

"Of course, Lady Matlock, I would be happy to accompany you."

Before exiting the room, both could see an expression of distress and concern on Georgiana's face, and at the same time, they smiled reassuringly to comfort her.

"Miss Bennet, I am sure you know my reason for inviting you to accompany me," Lady Matlock began as soon as they left the room.

"I think I do. I assume your ladyship would like to speak to me privately."

"Well, then let us enter the drawing room for a few moments, shall we?"

Once inside the room with the door closed behind them, they sat on opposite settees, facing each other silently. "Miss Bennet, there are indeed some things I think are important that we address at the very beginning between us. Will you allow me to speak frankly to you?"

"Of course."

"Good. And will you promise to favour me with equal sincerity in your answers?"

"I will."

"Please believe me that I have no intention of offending you, none whatsoever, but my concern for both Darcy and Georgiana demands that I be sure of your intentions and interests. Anne Darcy was not just my sister-in-law but my best friend, and her children are as dear to me as my own."

Elizabeth only nodded in agreement, waiting for her to continue.

"Miss Bennet, when Darcy told us last night of your engagement, we were absolutely astonished and, I must say, not at all pleased. We never considered that he of all men — who always had an exceptional sense of duty and propriety — would decide to marry someone outside the circle in which he was born and raised. I myself never considered anything less than the daughter of a peer for him, but over the years he never showed any inclination for the young ladies of the *ton*, and you must know that he could have married anyone he chose. Under these circumstances, you surely understand our shock and disapproval when he informed us that he had chosen a country gentleman's daughter whom he had met three months ago and about whom we knew nothing. You cannot deny that securing the affection, and now the hand in marriage, of a man of Darcy's wealth and situation must be more than you ever would have dreamed."

She paused, searching Elizabeth's face and seeing a shadow of distress, but continued without any attempt to lighten her tone.

"However, my nephew's decision seems to be made and impossible to change. He seems to have an uncommon affection and admiration for you of which I never would have suspected him capable. What I truly want to know is whether your feelings for him are as strong and sound as his are for you. I must grant you that the changes in both my nephew and niece are quite impressive; I have not seen them in such good spirits in years. Moreover, I should be grateful to you if I can be assured that your intentions are honest and your affection for my nephew, and consequently for his sister, matches theirs for you. But I must say you seem just too good to be true."

Her words were, without doubt, offensive in their meaning, accusing Elizabeth of dishonesty and mercenary intentions. However, her tone was neutral; she stated from the beginning that she would speak without disguise of any sort, and she was doing no differently. Thus, for her own part, Elizabeth was rather pleased with the opportunity for honest talk; her reply was calm, and she spoke without taking her eyes from her interrogator.

"Lady Matlock, if my affections for Mr. Darcy, as well as for Georgiana, were less than they are, I would have been offended by your ladyship's speech; but since the well-being of Mr. Darcy and his sister is also my concern, I can understand your mistrust of my interests and the honesty of my feelings. However, I have faith that your ladyship will have no cause to complain regarding this aspect of our relationship."

"You seem very certain of yourself, Miss Bennet."

"I am very certain indeed of my feelings." She blushed a little saying that but continued. "But I must say that I am not at all 'too good,' your ladyship, and I have done nothing to deserve praise for the present state of Mr. and Miss Darcy. How could anyone not feel friendship and affection for Georgiana, not because she is Mr. Darcy's sister but because she is so kind and sweet; who would not love such a sister? As for Mr. Darcy…" She paused few moments to search for the proper words.

"It is true that gaining Mr. Darcy's affection and hand in marriage is more than I ever could have dreamed, but his situation in life and his fortune have nothing to do with this! I will not deny that my own lack of fortune demanded prudence in marriage, but I never would agree to marry a man only for his wealth. A marriage without mutual affection and respect is worse than a life of loneliness."

By that time, her voice had become not just determined but challenging, defying Lady Matlock to contradict her; her eyes were glowing with passion and fortitude when she talked about Mr. Darcy, which his aunt did not fail to observe. The force of her last statement changed the lady's countenance in an instant.

"Furthermore, Lady Matlock, I know that any young lady would be glad to accept Mr. Darcy because he is indeed the best man I have ever known. To have the admiration and affection — I dare say to have the devoted love of such a man — seems too wonderful to be true, and I am happy to respond with equal devotion... and love."

"Well... that was quite a declaration, Miss Bennet! Upon my word, you expressed your opinion very determinedly for someone so young. However, if you would allow me, I have one more question: do you understand exactly what it means to be Darcy's wife? Do you understand the responsibilities this implies? Do you understand that any failure on your part will ruin him in terms of reputation and respect, and will expose him to the censure of society?"

She was waiting for — nay, she was demanding — answers, and Elizabeth chose to give them, not with anger but with the honesty previously demanded, not allowing her pride to control her.

"Your ladyship is correct in saying that I am not prepared to be the proper mistress of Pemberley, but Mr. Darcy chose to trust me when he made me an offer of marriage, and I would do whatever is in my power to prove myself worthy of his trust. I am confident that I will succeed because I would do anything for him. I would — "

She blushed furiously saying that and averted her eyes, trying to find the proper words but not daring to speak further, instead trying to calm herself. Elizabeth startled almost violently when the lady stretched out her hand and gently touched her arm, smiling openly and calmly as if nothing had happened.

"Yes? Please continue, Miss Bennet... "

"I... I never would have imagined it was possible for a woman to love a man as much as I love Mr. Darcy. I am almost embarrassed and frightened of my own feelings. I —"

She was burning with mortification for making such an improper disclosure in front of a stranger, and not just any stranger, but the formidable aunt of the man in question; she did not dare to lift her eyes.

After a long moment, Lady Matlock started to laugh, making Elizabeth look up at her with shocked curiosity. "Oh dear, indeed we seem to have a problem here, and quite a serious one I might say!"

At that moment, Mr. Darcy entered the drawing room, a worried frown on his face as his eyes rested on Elizabeth, who was staring at her hands entwined in her lap, her face flustered, while his aunt was laughing, apparently quite amused.

"Lady Matlock, Miss Bennet, what a wonderful surprise to find you both here." He came closer, greeting his aunt and then his intended; Elizabeth only managed to answer with a shy smile to his short, inquiring look.

"Will you allow me to join you, ladies?"

"Oh, we certainly shall, as I was just talking with Miss Bennet about a very serious problem, which apparently must be solved without delay." Elizabeth turned to her, eyes wide in utter surprise that she could raise such a subject in front of her nephew.

He took a seat near Elizabeth, more curious than surprised, trying to determine how the conversation had gone and whether Elizabeth had been hurt or offended. "May I help you in any way?"

"Yes you may. We were about to discuss your wedding date; as I understand, it is not yet settled."

She smiled, satisfied at the looks of relief on both Elizabeth and Darcy's faces.

"Oh… We have not had the opportunity to discuss it, but I hope we can approach the subject today before Miss Bennet's father leaves town."

"Good! You must consider the date very carefully. The season begins in March, and it is important to know if we will introduce Elizabeth" — none of them failed to notice the change of address — "as your wife or as your betrothed."

Darcy let out a little laugh. "My dear aunt, I never have given any consideration to the season; you cannot possibly believe that I will make my wedding arrangements around its opening or closing."

She became very serious and looked from him to Elizabeth in earnest.

"Darcy, I know that you never have given much consideration to the season, but things are different now. And, as I told Elizabeth earlier, there is a difference between what you or she would like to do and what must be done. Elizabeth is not at all known in the *ton*, and you know there will be much speculation and gossip."

"I do not care about that, Aunt."

"I do care, and I am sure Elizabeth will care too after considering the implications. Mrs. Darcy must have her place in London society, just as she must have the proper presentation at court. It is the prestige of her position we are talking about here, the prestige of your sister who will be out in a year or two, and the prestige of your children. This is not something with which to trifle." She was serious, and the inflection in her tone did not bear contradiction as she looked from one to the other.

Elizabeth spoke first. "Lady Matlock, I thank you for your advice and concern. Your ladyship is right, and we will certainly consider these aspects when we plan our wedding date."

"Good! Then when we meet again, we can discuss that as well." She rose to her feet, joined by both Mr. Darcy and Elizabeth.

"I am glad we talked, Elizabeth. You did not disappoint me."

"Thank you, Lady Matlock."

She stroked her cheek in a motherly way, smiling. "You may call me Lady Ellen; I prefer that from my family."

The look of gratitude on Elizabeth's face could not be misunderstood. "It would be an honour, Lady Ellen."

Elizabeth remained inside in the main hall, trying to relax a little after such a formidable conversation and a tumult of emotions, while Mr. Darcy escorted his aunt to the carriage.

Darcy returned shortly and approached Elizabeth, smiling tenderly and wrapping her in such an adoring gaze that she felt her knees weakening as her eyes looked deeply into his.

He came closer and took her hands, kissing them, and lowered his head whispering, "I am so happy you are here. I tried to settle everything sooner than expected so I could spend more time with you."

She fought the sudden knot in her throat and, licking her dry lips, managed to articulate her thoughts.

"You need not have been concerned nor rushed, for I promised I would wait for you."

"Yes, you did." He smiled while his eyes darkened, wearing a more intense expression than Elizabeth had ever seen there before. It made her tremble, the rhythm of her heart rising to a tormenting level.

He gently took her arm and escorted her to the stairs, but instead of climbing them, he pulled her into the library, and she could do nothing except follow him.

"I already spoke to Georgiana. She told me you were in the drawing room with my aunt. Poor Georgie seemed a little worried. I told her I would take care of you and that we would probably be delayed a few minutes. There is something very important I want to ask you."

His deep voice became even more tender, and she could not think properly in order to understand his meaning. "Is something wrong?"

"Not wrong, but very grave indeed." He closed the door and made her sit on the same settee as the day before at his left side. As strong as she thought herself to be, the emotions and her own overwhelming feelings — together with the fear that something bad may have happened with Mr. Wickham — made Elizabeth wary of what would come.

Her lips became even drier, and she started to ask him what had happened; but before she could do or think of anything, he lowered his head and captured her half-opened mouth with his warm, moist lips. At the same time, his left hand glided up her back, around her shoulders, while his right hand gently held her head, fingertips resting on the back of her neck.

She was so surprised that she did not even have the time to breathe. She had thought that, by now, she knew what to expect from a kiss and the kind of feelings she would experience, but this kiss, though gentle and tender, was nothing like the day before. His lips were not just pressing gently as they had previously, but he was actually tasting hers, tentatively at first and then bolder, even demanding; in a moment, her lips were no longer dry but wet with his intoxicating taste.

She unconsciously leaned her head to rest on the back of the couch, pressing against his arm in complete abandonment to his will; she did not know what to expect, but she knew it must be more. Suddenly, her entire body shuddered violently when his tongue slightly touched her lips and then tasted them. She had never expected that to happen while they kissed; she tensed, almost frightened by such an intimate gesture and by the novelty of the new sensations engulfing her; it felt so strange, so wet, so warm...so utterly arousing. She remained still, but did not withdraw from him, not even to breathe.

Gradually, his kisses changed again, turning rather more tender than passionate, and she relaxed instantly. Her hands encircled his waist shyly, and she leaned closer to him, so close that she could feel her body pressing into his chest; his deep moan sent another shiver through her.

The sweet assault on her mouth started again, growing more intense, but this time she knew what to expect, and her mouth did not remain passive. Timidly at first, she learned the rhythm of passion easily so that, when his tongue touched her eager lips again, teasing and tantalising, they parted even more, allowing him almost to conquer her completely. He did so, with an urge that proved how ardently he had waited for a sign of her acceptance, and a moment later, any other thoughts, wishes or feelings vanished except for the astonishing sensation of him invading every sense and his delicious taste spreading into every fibre of her body. Involuntarily she moaned deeply, but not a sound could escape from her imprisoned mouth. Elizabeth was certain she would faint

Mr. Darcy pulled back some time later, but not completely, only to place a few small kisses on her graceful eyelids, her flushed cheeks, and the delicate line of her jaw. He was tempted to trail his kisses to her throat — as she evidently had no intention of stopping him — but he wisely restrained himself and instead placed a cheeky kiss on the tip of her nose, making her open her eyes in surprise.

They stared at each other not only with love but also with longing and passion, immersed in the depths of each other's eyes. Gently but without shyness, she lightly caressed his face, and then her fingers twined tentatively in his hair, making him close his eyes and let out a satisfied moan. He leaned his head towards hers on the back of the couch, and they turned a little to face each other. She moved closer, keeping one hand in his hair and the other around his waist, nestling her head at the junction between his shoulder and neck. They were sitting on the couch, but their position was so intimate it was as if they were lying together for the first time, staring at each other, intoxicated by each other's presence and scent.

"I missed you so much, Elizabeth. I could think of nothing else today than to be with you once more. I hope I did not frighten you with my impetuous and very improper attentions."

He was speaking so close to her hair that she could feel his lips moving at each word.

"Do I look frightened, sir?" she asked teasingly, her breath burning the skin of his neck. "But you did surprise me a little, though it was a most pleasant and welcome surprise, as were the roses and your note this morning."

"I am glad you enjoyed them — both the roses and the kiss."

He became more daring in his words and lifted her face gently. While the intensity of his gaze increased and his hand continued to stroke her cheek and her neck, sliding to her nape, his fingers played in her hair while his thumb caressed the spot below her ear, tracing the line of her jaw and then lowering to her throat. His left hand was resting on her shoulder but travelled up and down her bare arm, making Elizabeth feel half of her was burning in fire and the other half freezing from countless chills. She was waiting, hoping, for him to kiss her again, but he did not.

"Elizabeth, I am sorry I was not here when you met my aunt. I spoke to her last night, but she did not mention any intention of visiting Georgiana today or I would have warned you in my note. Was she very harsh with you?"

She swallowed hard, trying to answer while hiding her disappointment for the absent kiss.

"She was a little harsh, yes, but I understand her reasons. Her only concerns were for you, Georgiana and your family's honour. I cannot blame her for that."

"I trust you made a very good impression from what I could witness."

She began to laugh softly. "I am afraid not. She told me very clearly that she did not consider me prepared to be the proper mistress of Pemberley and that I have many things to learn so I can rise to the expectations of Mr. Darcy's wife. And I could not contradict her. But I hope she believed me — and I hope you believe me — that I would do everything in my power to honour your name."

She felt her emotions and uncertainties overtake her again, but he smiled quite humorously.

"My love, I have not had the slightest doubt about that, not for a long time. Indeed, you will have to become accustomed to many small things, but your wonderful qualities are more important, for they are not things one can learn. You will be the best mistress..."

He leaned a little to place small kisses on her cheek, and his lips stopped near her ear for a small kiss and a whisper. "And the best wife..."

Though hardly able to think, she managed to answer while trying to keep some composure under his attentions, and even to tease him. "But sir, I must warn you: though for the moment I am quite...overwhelmed...by emotions, I am afraid my old habits will come to light again soon. Would it be acceptable for Mrs. Darcy to tease her husband and to contradict him — maybe even to quarrel with him from time to time?"

"I am depending upon that, Miss Bennet. However, I also must warn you that I will have no scruples in using this very efficient method of silencing you..."

He proved his argument, claiming her lips again with his opened mouth, only this time she was not at all surprised; her lips parted in an instant and then, without restraint or hesitation, joined his devouring lips in a wild dance of passion. As she became more accustomed to the sensations aroused in her, she found that she could actually breathe during the kiss, a startling but useful discovery that allowed her to remain in his embrace for what seemed an eternity, and it was still not enough as their desire for each other seemed only to increase. Their lips finally parted after some length of time, for it was necessary for them to regain their composure and normal breathing, until she managed to whisper, "William, will you tell me now what happened?"

"What happened? I do not understand your meaning."

"When we entered the library, you said you had something important and grave to tell me."

"Oh… Well, I just told you what I wanted to say. Perhaps you did not understand me well enough. Shall I try to explain it one more time?"

He did not wait for her answer before lowering his head to capture her lips again, but she moved her head so his lips met only her cheek somewhere near her ear. He did not seem displeased with this as he started to place small kisses on her skin, but she started to laugh and, not without a considerable struggle, extricated herself from his arms.

"Mr. Darcy, as much as I would like to continue to…umm…discuss things with you in this particular manner, I strongly insist that we must stop now. We are acting preposterously — not to mention completely improperly — and are being very inconsiderate to Georgiana! Poor girl, she must be wondering what has become of us. Shall we not go to her and delay this…conversation to other time?"

She was smiling teasingly, but was slightly embarrassed, blushing at her own words, which were encouraging him to persist in what she called improper and preposterous behaviour; he took her hand and kissed it while assisting her to rise in order to exit the library.

"You are not to be blamed for anything, Elizabeth. I am the only one being inconsiderate, for I always tend to forget propriety when I am near you. I know I am not behaving as properly as I should, but I treasure so much these rare moments of privacy with you. Do you not as well?"

"I do; you know that I do… It is just… I do not want Georgiana to suffer; she has been very affected by these last day's events."

"I thank you for your concern, my love. I sent for the doctor when I returned home. I want him to examine her carefully. I am afraid that her emotions might make her recovery even more difficult, and I do not want to risk that. I am equally concerned about her feelings; she did not say a word after we spoke yesterday."

"William, I did talk to her; I had to tell her that I knew about Ramsgate."

"Oh my, I forgot to tell her that."

"Do not worry; we managed to come to an understanding. She is much stronger than we thought where her heart is concerned. Do you know that her major concern was for you? She was afraid to disappoint or to hurt you. I dare say Mr. Wickham means nothing to her now. I am glad I was able to make her see the event a little differently; that was all she needed."

"Do you really think she is well now? I cannot believe you have succeeded in two days where I have failed for all these months. She is more open with you than she ever was with me, but I am so happy and grateful to you."

"I am sure she is well, and she will be even better. She is an admirable young lady; I told her that much. So like her brother..."

She was looking at him with her smiling eyes and quickly rose on her toes and kissed his chin, as she could not reach his lips. He gazed at her, surprised but delighted by her spontaneous display and, as she turned her back to him continuing to walk, he lowered his head and placed a quick but warm kiss on her neck, feeling her skin tremble under his lips.

"Elizabeth, there is another thing I forgot to mention and which must be said before we enter Georgiana's room. I had a very interesting conversation with Wickham today."

"With Mr. Wickham? What interesting things could he possibly have to say? Has he not done enough?"

"Oh, he did say a few interesting things, I assure you. Can you imagine? He tried to persuade me that you only accepted me for my situation and, moreover, that Mrs. Bennet convinced you to do it. And he implied that you and he were... very fond of each other and that you and he had been more than slight acquaintances. He insisted on reminding me that you confided in him and favoured him exceedingly from the beginning of your acquaintance."

Elizabeth stopped in the middle of the hall at Georgiana's door, turning to him in shock at such horrible insinuations. She looked at him with worry, trying to find an answer and expecting to see a dark, offended expression on his face. She was greatly surprised to hear his light tone and see a serene countenance, lightened by obvious good humour.

"Why would he lie about such a thing? He is to be marrying my sister in less than a week! Why would he lie?"

"To offend you and hurt me, of course."

"And... William, may I ask what your reaction was, after all that he said?"

"Well, for a moment I seriously considered strangling him, which would have resolved all our problems!"

"William, please be serious!"

"But I am serious, believe me. However, after I concluded that murdering a man in my own carriage in the middle of town might damage my reputation at some length, I could do nothing but laugh at such a ridiculous attempt. I told him I would share the story with you so that we could laugh together — and I threw him out of the carriage."

She looked at him incredulously, half-laughing and half-frightened. "You did not — "

"Of course I did, I told you I would never lie to you. My only regret at that moment was that the horses were moving at a slow pace."

She put her hand on her mouth to stop her laughter but with little success, and he joined her as they entered Georgiana's room together.

Caroline Bingley never remembered being so frustrated or distressed. The last week had been the worst. Eliza Bennet had arrived in town and was ruining all her anticipated plans and dreams.

Her brother, usually so docile, had now turned against his own sister, offending her with almost every question she tried to address to him. He was undoubtedly changed in a most annoying way. And, worst of all, she had had no opportunity to speak with Mr. Darcy and offer him an explanation for that unfortunate misunderstanding with the letters as he had completely ignored her at the dinner two days earlier, and she had not seen him since then.

She tried to persuade Charles to assure her of at least a short visit to Georgiana — her dear friend, whose company she missed so much — but he had decidedly refused her under the false argument that Miss Darcy was not well enough to receive visitors. How was it, Caroline wondered, that a country nobody like Eliza Bennet was allowed to see Georgiana?

Of course, she did ask Charles that particular question, and he only answered rudely that she should reconsider her manner of addressing Miss Bennet and that Darcy was entitled to decide who could visit his sister and when.

Caroline spent hours trying to understand with what arts and allurements Eliza Bennet had succeeded in imposing herself upon Mr. Darcy for him to bestow such attentions upon her. Apparently, both her brother and Mr. Darcy were under some outrageous spell that must be affecting their sensibilities and binding them to the Bennet sisters! She blamed everything on Eliza Bennet. *It must be her fault!* This thought made her lose her temper, and her vexation increased. She did not know what was happening, but she could tell that it was indeed something very important. The dinner had ended in a strange, hasty way, and afterward, Charles had dropped them at their door and vanished, only to return the next morning, refusing to talk to her. The previous evening he had had dinner out, and from the extra care with his appearance, she was certain he was going to see Jane Bennet, and Mr. Darcy would likely accompany him.

The disaster she could foresee could not be allowed to happen! Something must be done to stop Eliza Bennet in her plan to entrap the master of Pemberley! Caroline Bingley could not just wait and see all her hopes thrown away. But what was to be done? She absolutely had to talk to someone, someone who was easy to manipulate and who could divulge some useful information. She had to visit Georgiana, and if Mr. Darcy was at home, so much the better. She would find a way to make him listen to her!

Chapter 18

Being delighted with Elizabeth's company and happy at the prospect of having a sister so much to her liking, Georgiana never considered that someone in her family might disapprove her brother's choice of wife. Her aunt's coldness and innuendos against Elizabeth were difficult to bear, divided as she was between love for her aunt and loyalty to her intended sister.

Though the conversation had become more neutral at the end of Lady Matlock's visit, Georgiana did not fail to sense the hidden tension behind the politeness. She almost panicked when her aunt solicited Elizabeth to accompany her downstairs, afraid that Elizabeth might be offended or possibly reconsider her engagement. She did not know Elizabeth well enough to appreciate how capably she could stand against Lady Matlock, but Georgiana had found over the years that her aunt was not to be defeated or persuaded when she had decided upon a matter. She was relieved when her brother entered her room and she could suggest that he join the ladies downstairs; however, the delay in his return only increased her suspense.

When Mr. Darcy and Elizabeth finally returned, undoubtedly good humoured and looking somehow... different, Georgiana showed no restraint in expressing her pleasure at seeing them and her curiosity about what had occurred. Curiously, at her question, Elizabeth's face coloured highly while searching for an answer.

"Dearest, it was I who detained Elizabeth, for I wanted to talk to her after Aunt Ellen left," answered Mr. Darcy, a neutral and perfectly sensible reason, which — to Georgiana's utter surprise — made Elizabeth blush even more as she cast a quick glance at him.

A little intrigued, she attributed the strange behaviour to Elizabeth's recent emotions, and indeed, she was right. "Was everything well with Aunt Ellen, Elizabeth? I know she can be a little... severe sometimes, but she is excessively kind and generous. I am sure you will like her very much."

"Dear Georgiana, do not distress yourself, everything went very well. And Lady Matlock has been all kindness and good intentions, I assure you."

"I am so glad to hear that. I sent William to protect you, you know."

Elizabeth started to laugh. "Thank you, but I was in no real danger."

"Indeed she was not, Georgie. I dare say Aunt Ellen was pleased with her. She asked Elizabeth to call her 'Lady Ellen'."

"She did?" the surprise in her voice made Elizabeth laugh again.

"Yes she did. But is that so astonishing?"

"Oh yes it is! You see, the colonel's elder brother has been married for six months, and he was engaged for two years before that. His wife is still addressing my aunt as 'Lady Matlock'."

"Oh..." was all she could answer at this unexpected proof of the lady's approbation.

Before a new topic began, Mr. Darcy announced that he had planned a family dinner for that very day with only Elizabeth's family and Bingley to attend; he was pleased to see how delighted Elizabeth was with this surprise, but he turned his attention to his sister.

"Georgie, as I see you are feeling so well, I was wondering if you would like to join us tonight. I think we will have a very pleasant time, as the Gardiners and Mr. Bennet are delightful company. Moreover, I asked Mr. Gardiner to bring the children too, and I am sure you will love them."

She opened her blue eyes in surprise while her whole face was wearing a happy smile, but very soon, a shadow passed over it. "Oh, William, I would like that so much! But I am afraid I will not be able to join you. My leg is not yet fully healed, and I must keep it stretched out and unmoved, so I cannot sit at the table."

"I know that, dearest, and there is nothing easier to accomplish. We will arrange two armchairs — one at the table and the other under the table for your leg — so you will appear as though you are sitting as normally as the rest of us. Moreover, we will have dinner in the drawing room, so when we finish eating, you ladies will not have to move; instead, the servants will remove the table completely. That way you will stay comfortably with us the whole evening, and I will have the great joy of having my sister near me. What do you think?"

She could not say anything, for big tears rolled down her pale cheeks. "But what will Mr. Bennet, and Mr. and Mrs. Gardiner say about such unusual arrangements? Would they not be offended?"

It was Elizabeth's turn to reassure her. "Georgiana, please believe me that my family will be happy. Moreover, I think they will feel honoured that you decided to make such a sacrifice only to have dinner with them."

"Do you think so?"

"I am sure of it. I know I would feel honoured by such attention."

Her last argument caused Georgiana's doubts to vanish, and she let her excitement burst out in a joyful barrage of questions. She asked about the guests until she became agitated about her appearance and about what she would wear for the occasion. Mr. Darcy suggested letting her stay in Mrs. Annesley's care as it was time for Elizabeth to leave. It was two o'clock, and all of them had preparations to make for the evening.

"ELIZABETH, WILL YOU ALLOW ME a few more minutes before you leave? I have a gift I would like to offer you. Would you mind if I asked you to join me in the library again? I have kept it there for some time."

"No, I would not mind... I mean... If you wish..." she became crimson, making Mr. Darcy smile.

"There is something I want to give you no later than today, Elizabeth, and I want to do it privately. It is also an engagement present; I should have offered it yesterday, but I simply forgot."

They entered, and Mr. Darcy invited her to sit. Elizabeth was sure it was only a mischievous pretext to spend additional private moments with her, and she was torn between the pleasure of sharing this close intimacy with him and the guilt and mortification for accepting and even encouraging such a breach in propriety.

But he indeed went to a locked safe, opened it and returned to her with a velvet box of impressive dimensions. Only then did he take a seat near her. She looked at him with a smile.

"William, please do not think there is any need to give me presents. The ring is the most beautiful thing I ever saw. I thought that you were speaking in jest about the gift, only to — "

"Only to bring you here again?" He laughed, seeing her blush, and placed a kiss on her cheek.

"But you agreed to come, nonetheless."

"Yes..." she could hardly speak when his warm breath was caressing her; she turned her head to him and their lips met, but only for a moment before he withdrew.

"I do not know what is happening to me when I am near you, Elizabeth. I simply cannot think properly; your presence intoxicates me, and I feel as though I am under the power of the finest but strongest liquor."

He kissed her hand and then gently put the jewellery box in her hands on her lap.

"Elizabeth, the present I want to offer you is very special, not because of its value but because of what it means to me..." A little pause followed, as he was searching for words.

"When my mother became ill, I was not quite 12 years old. Her illness was long and difficult to bear, both for me and for my father, for we both loved her more than could be said. She burned out like a candle before our eyes without anyone being able to tell us the reason for it or to help her in any way. My father engaged all the doctors he could find but without any success. She stayed in bed a long time, for her powers became weaker every day. She could not hold little Georgiana when she was barely one year old and could only have her company for a few minutes in the presence of a nurse. More than once, I found her crying in despair at not being able to take care of her own child. I used to stay with her when my father was away on business and to read to her. We spent hours talking together until very late when my father returned and, only then, could I go to my room because I knew I would leave her in his good care."

He stopped a moment with great emotion, and with difficulty he managed to continue as she took his hands in hers, squeezing them both, hoping to give him a little comfort.

"I am sorry, my love, I do not want to speak about these sad moments now, but I hope you will understand why I must. One winter day, it was snowing, and I remember I played in the snow for hours. My father sent for me and said that she had asked to see me; his face was pale and undoubtedly wet with tears. I ran up the stairs wildly, full of guilt for staying away from her so long, and I remember that my soul was burdened and heavy as I came closer, afraid she was dying. I entered her room, but to my surprise, she looked better than ever. Her hair was beautifully arranged and she was wearing a lovely, pale blue dress and a necklace of blue sapphires with matching earrings. She had the same eyes as Georgiana, you know? I was looking at her and thought her eyes were more beautiful than the sapphires."

He swallowed violently, trying to overcome the sadness that threatened to burst into tears; tears appeared in Elizabeth's eyes, grieved by his suffering.

"She smiled at me and asked me to sit near her on the bed. Then she handed me this jewel box. She told me they were not family jewels but something she asked to be made especially for me as a present for my future wife. You know, Elizabeth, a thousand times her words have sounded in my mind over the years, but I never repeated them to anyone until now. *'My dear son, I trust that, when the time comes, you will choose your wife with wisdom and consideration, but choose her with your heart, too. Try to find a woman to deserve you and be worthy of our name but also to have the power of winning your heart and loving you as I want you to be loved. You deserve no less in a wife. And when you find her, let this be the first present you offer her after the engagement ring.'"*

His voice was almost lost, and he cleared his throat to be able to speak further as his eyes moistened; he took her face in his hands, gazing deeply into her eyes, and she put her own hands on top of his. Without knowing what she was doing and only wanting to assure him of her love and devotion, she turned her face so that her lips kissed his palms, first one and then the other. He smiled with mixed sadness and happiness, full of gratitude at this unusual but heartfelt display of tenderness.

"My heart never rejoiced until I met you, Elizabeth. And when it finally did, I was fool enough to try to silence its glee until that day when I came to understand that my heart was no longer mine. It was yours, and all I could do was to hope that you would not break it, and you did not. You treasured my heart and filled it with joy and with your generous love. So, this is my first present for you."

He wiped her tears with little kisses, trying to stem his own and then opened the box; Elizabeth gasped, covering her mouth with her hands in a childish gesture of utter amazement. It was a set of jewellery in gold and rubies — necklace, earrings, bracelet and ring — so beautiful that she did not dare breathe, much less touch them.

"Nobody has touched these since my mother's death. After she gave me the box, she held me near her, very close, kissing my head and telling me how much she loved me. We talked until I fell asleep, and I think my father took me to my room. That night she died...

"My housekeeper, Mrs. Reynolds, told me years later that she knew her end was near, and she demanded to be dressed and arranged so she could speak with me for the last time. She wanted me to remember her like that, not lying in her sickbed."

He rose suddenly from the settee, almost dropping the box, and went straight to the table; he poured himself a glass of brandy and gulped it violently, trying to regain his composure and hide his tears from her. Nobody had seen him cry since he was six years old.

He was startled to feel her behind him. Her hands encircled his waist and, with all her strength, she embraced him and leaned her head against his back.

"William... please, do not run from me, and do not hide from me. I want to share your love, your joy *and* your sadness; I want you to let me so close that we feel the same things, the same emotions. Please, my love..."

He turned slowly in her embrace until he could face her. Her cheeks were wet with tears, her eyes gazing at him from behind long lashes; he pulled her into his arms and held her so tightly that she could not breathe, but they could feel each other's heartbeat. He rested his chin atop her head, placing countless kisses in her hair.

"This is the first time I have spoken of my mother since my father died. I never felt anyone as close to my soul as I feel you are, Elizabeth." No answer was needed. She placed a little kiss on his chest, where his heart was beating, a kiss so warm that he could feel its heat through his clothes.

Closely embraced, they returned to the settee, and he picked up the velvet box, taking her hand and brushing their entwined fingers over the glowing jewels, barely touching them, caressing them. She could not subdue her emotions enough to whisper a single word, her heart aching as she tried to imagine the grief of a mother who knew she would leave forever her son and her baby girl.

"Elizabeth, I wanted so much for this to be a happy moment for us, and I only saddened you. Please forgive me. I am truly sorry."

"Do not say that! Never say that you are sorry for kissing me, for holding me, or for allowing me to see the sadness in your soul, because if you are indeed regretting doing all these things, I must have misjudged you and your feelings. And if you are not regretting them, do not apologise only because propriety demands it. I do not want you to be polite with me."

He was a little surprised at her reaction; in an attempt to lighten the mood, she continued,

"Rest assured, Mr. Darcy, that if you do offend me or I consider that you need to apologise, I will let you know without any doubt."

She bit her lower lip, looking at him with a flirtatious grin that succeeded in making him smile.

"Then I shall depend upon you to censure me whenever it is needed, Miss Bennet. But I spoke the truth when I said I wanted this moment to be one of utter happiness for us."

"And it is, my love, or at least it will be. Now that you have shared your sadness with me, I have taken half of it, and it will be easier for you to bear. I am grateful to you for telling me about your mother, William. I do not know if I am indeed worthy of this gift, but I do know that I love you as she wanted you to be loved."

Her words almost made his heart stop, and all he could do was kiss both her hands and whisper, "Thank you."

Several long moments of silence passed until he could speak again coherently.

"Elizabeth, do you like the jewels? I mean... do you like rubies?"

"Do I like them? Oh William, they are beautiful beyond my imagination! How could I dare to touch them? How could I dare to wear them?"

"How could you not, Elizabeth? Do you not feel they belong to you? As much as you belong to me..."

He took the necklace and leaned back a little so he could gently put it around her neck. Her skin shivered under the cold touch of the necklace and the hot, lingering touch of his hands resting at each side of her neck.

"How... how does it look?" She found the words difficult to express.

"It looks exquisite," he whispered softly, caressing the necklace and her bare skin with the tips of his long fingers.

"This dress is not at all... suited for such beautiful jewellery."

He was sitting behind her, resting his chin at the junction of her neck and her right shoulder, their faces touching, his every word warming her with his hot breath.

"I do not know about the dress... but your neck is perfectly suited... and so are your fingers... your ears... and your wrist..." As hee placed small kisses at each mentioned part, she leaned back against him, surrendering completely to the pleasure of his attentions.

He gently turned her head to him and touched her soft lips with his, lovingly and tenderly, without any urgency or haste.

It was not long before she turned toward him, her hands encircling his neck, both lost in a breathtaking embrace while passion enveloped them, eclipsing every rational thought. Their lips were hungrily joined in a deep, wild kiss and every sense was aware only of the other's closeness.

It was no wonder, therefore, that neither Mr. Darcy nor Elizabeth heard the tumult of voices from the other side of the library door, and never noticed Caroline Bingley officiously entering the room, pushing Miles, who wisely decided to remain outside the door, out of the way.

As it was, their kiss lasted several moments after Caroline wailed in a voice close to hysteria, "Mr. Darcy! I demand to be informed why I am being treated in this outrageous manner. I am a close friend of this family, and I must be allowed to — "

She was close to the settee by now, and to her horror, she saw Eliza Bennet wantonly kissing the master of Pemberley without being in the least disturbed by her presence. Her eyes and mouth gaped in astonishment.

"Mr. Darcy! What are you doing? How can you allow yourself to be trapped in the underhanded schemes of this woman?"

Only days before, had anyone entered unannounced to disturb him, the unpleasant event would have had severe consequences — both for the intruder and for the servant responsible for such a breach of propriety.

This time, however, fully preoccupied with nothing but Elizabeth's presence — and realising it was only Caroline Bingley who came upon them — he felt merely annoyed by the interruption, vaguely asking himself how she dared to come into his house uninvited after everything she had done. Reluctantly, he withdrew from his intended and, with perfect courtesy and the most polite tone possible, acknowledged the third person in the room.

"Miss Bingley... to what do I owe this unexpected pleasure? May I be of any help to you?"

"No indeed, it is I who must help you before this country girl induces you into a forced marriage! You must throw her out immediately before your sister finds out about — "

He looked quickly at Elizabeth, and his happiness turned his annoyance into wicked glee, which made him turn to the visitor with the most innocent expression.

"Oh, that cannot be, Miss Bingley; you must be wrong. I am sure Miss Bennet has no intention of forcing me to marry her."

"No intention? Mr. Darcy, how can you say that? She placed you in this scandalous situation, insinuating herself upon your person! Of course she intended to trap you; even a child would understand that — "

"Well, Miss Bingley, to avoid any uncertainty, let us ask her. Miss Bennet, do you intend to force me to marry you?"

He was so serious that Elizabeth had to bite her lip so as not to burst out laughing, and she forced herself to answer with no less seriousness. "No sir, I have no such intention, I assure you!"

"You see, Miss Bingley? There is no cause for concern. May I help you with anything else?"

She was staring at him in shock, incapable of moving her feet.

"Well then, if you will excuse us, I would like to resume our previous activities. I hope you can find your way out; if not, ask Miles to show you. Have a pleasant day, Miss Bingley."

He turned his back to her and began to speak in whispers with Elizabeth.

Caroline Bingley did not recover from the extraordinary shock until the moment Miles handed her into her carriage and the horses began to move. She was unaware that another surprise was waiting for her.

Charles Bingley was savouring a glass of port in his library, curtains drawn. He had no intention of reading — rather, he wished only to enjoy a few moments of solitude. He was very pleased with his day.

He had just paid a call at Gracechurch Street and had been informed that everything was settled regarding Wickham and the youngest Bennet's wedding. He did not really give much consequence to the whole situation, for it was not the first — and certainly would not be the last — elopement of which he had heard. "And they certainly deserve each other; she will drive him insane in a couple of months, and he will ignore her completely in a lesser time." Still, he was most assuredly angry with them for the distress they had caused Miss Bennet.

However, the news of the completed arrangements had transported Jane into a state of happiness that made her radiate joy and smile constantly, and her smiles were directed at him. Moreover, she thanked him for his help, and he, of course, insisted that he had done nothing at all — which was true, for Darcy and the colonel were responsible for the result. She was so beautiful while speaking to him; they had been in the drawing room together with the whole family when she had suddenly rested her ungloved hand on his arm. Even now, hours later, he shivered remembering the exquisite sensation aroused in him by her touch; looking into her eyes, he had been sure that her feelings were the same.

Desperately, he swallowed the entire contents of the glass, and then poured something stronger. He still could not understand how he had managed not to kiss her at that moment. He could not stand being in this state any longer. He had to find a way to speak to her — privately — and to propose to her. He knew the situation was difficult for the entire family: Lydia and Wickham's elopement, Elizabeth and Darcy's engagement — a pleasant surprise but still stressful — so he did not intend to pressure Jane into a hasty marriage. He only had to make his feelings known to her and to be certain that she returned them — even more, that she would accept the offer of his hand. He closed his eyes, trying to bring her image back into his mind. He almost could smell her scent and feel traces of her touch burning his arm.

Drowsiness gradually overwhelmed him in the dimly lit library…

The sudden slamming of the heavy door and the hysterical voice of his sister made him almost fall from his chair! He rose to his feet, looking around in confusion in an attempt to understand what was happening.

"Charles!! Charles, where are you?! You will never guess what has happened! I told you so many times those Bennets are nothing but the lowest class of fortune hunters, doing anything to get their greedy hands on a man!"

"Caroline, why are you yelling like that? You scared me to death."

"Charles, you will not believe me! I went to Mr. Darcy's house and entered his library, and there he was — on the couch with Eliza Bennet! And they were kissing shamelessly in the most disgraceful and disgusting manner. I think he has lost his mind completely! I warned him that she would force him to marry her, and he asked her if she intended to force him! Can you believe that? This is outrageous! Preposterous!!"

Her voice grew more agitated as she paced the room, never ceasing to wonder at Mr. Darcy's reaction. After a few minutes, recovering from the surprise of his sister's entrance and incredulous tirade, Bingley managed to understand the meaning of her words.

"Darcy was kissing Miss Elizabeth Bennet? And they were alone in the library? This cannot be."

"YES! Now what do you say about Eliza Bennet? I was correct in everything I stated about her; you must grant me that."

She got no answer from her brother. A satisfied grin appeared on her face when her brother started to pace the room, deep in thought, his forehead creased in wonder.

Charles Bingley was indeed deep in thought and very angry… with himself for his own weakness and indecision. How did this happen? I liked Jane Bennet from the first moment I saw her. And I never concealed that, not from her, not from anyone. Darcy did nothing except fight and quarrel with Miss Elizabeth for more than a month; now he is engaged to be married, and he is kissing her in his library! And I have not even dared to kiss Jane's hand. What is wrong with me?

He had always known that Darcy was clever — much cleverer than he was — but now he was convinced beyond any doubt! His only consolation was that he would meet Jane again that very evening at dinner, and happily, they would be in intimate and pleasant company without any annoying disturbances.

"So, Charles, what do you have to say?"

Speaking of annoying disturbances… "About what, Caroline?"

"About what? How can you ask that? About Mr. Darcy kissing Eliza Bennet in the library!"

"Oh, about that… But Caroline, what were you doing in Darcy's library? Did he invite you in?"

"Charles, that is not the point. The only important and very disturbing fact is that Mr. Darcy was kissing that woman in his library!"

"I am afraid I do not fully understand you! Would you have been less disturbed if he had kissed her in the drawing room? Or in any other room?"

The absurdity of the question and the serene countenance on his face as he spoke left Caroline breathless; she turned red with anger and sputtered, "Charles Bingley, how can you say that? Have you forgotten all decency and sense? Will you just remain calm while Eliza Bennet is trapping your friend and forcing him to marry her?"

"Oh, stop talking nonsense, Caroline! Why would she force him when they are already engaged?!"

Only when his sister turned from red to white and her wide eyes stared at him blankly, did Bingley understand where the problem was. "Oh... I forgot to mention that Darcy proposed to Miss Elizabeth Bennet yesterday morning and she accepted him."

While her mind tried to make sense of what she had heard, Caroline's knees betrayed her, refusing to support her any longer. In a most unladylike manner, she fell... to the floor... on her back.

That was how the Hursts found her a moment later when they entered the room and hurried, together with Charles, to help her up. What followed next was more than an hour of abusing Eliza Bennet's character until Bingley could stand it no more and asked them to remove themselves from the library immediately. Mr. Hurst was happy to oblige, leaving him to keep company with his glass of port.

Chapter 19

The moment Miles escorted Caroline out of the room and closed the door after him, Elizabeth burst out laughing, incredulous at what had just happened. She could not believe Darcy's response to Caroline Bingley, but she had no time to say a word before he kissed her again.

She hesitated less than a moment before she kissed him back. Any restraint she may have had vanished. Her mouth was closed and she moaned when he gently bit her lower lip and his tongue touched her, played with her, tantalised her until her lips parted enough to allow him inside. For a few moments she did not move, did not breathe, surrendering completely to his will. Barely thinking, she wondered how it was possible that his sweet invasion aroused such frightening reactions inside every fibre of her body. Then she stopped wondering at all, simply rejoicing in the pleasure of his touch.

His left hand encircled her waist, slowly sliding onto her back, along her spine; the thin muslin fabric offered little protection, and each touch made her skin shiver under his strong palms. His right hand rested on her face, close to her ear. It did not remain still for long, however. His fingers entwined in her hair, and his thumb fondled her earlobe until the sensation made her tremble, and unconsciously she moved closer to him until their bodies touched. It was then Mr. Darcy who moaned deeply, and his lips broke the tormenting kiss to whisper hoarsely, "Elizabeth..."

She waited for the return of the kiss with her eyes closed, her head lying against the back of the couch, her lips ready, moist and parted, waiting for him, inviting him...

But his kiss did not come. Instead, she shivered almost violently when his fingers started to slide down from her face to the line of her jaw, to her throat, to her shoulders, tentatively stroking each spot not covered by her dress, tracing a line of fire everywhere he touched her. Her skin was burning. He was not really caressing her; his fingers were brushing her bare skin so gently that she could not be certain whether he was actually touching her or she was merely dreaming it. She opened her eyes and met his dark gaze staring at her so closely that she could feel the warmth of his quick breath.

His fingers started their tentative movements again and slid down to her neckline, stopping a moment and then resuming their voyage until they reached the edge of her dress. Her eyes were watching him, surprised, embarrassed and wondering, silently asking what he intended to do. However, his stare was darker than ever, and she could not understand his answer.

She closed her eyes again in complete abandon. She had neither the power nor the desire to resist him. She heard him whispering, "My love," but this time his voice sounded different. While she expected his moves to become more passionate and more demanding, she felt nothing but tenderness; his fingers retreated from that dangerous destination and returned to her hair, while his lips returned upon hers — soft, gentle, and with less urgency.

Darcy knew he had reached the limit, and not to cross it was a difficult battle he had to wage against his own will. It was not only his reaction he had to fight but hers as well. Her responsiveness was more than he imagined, and his desire and need for her tempted him to progress to the limits she allowed him.

When he had broken the kiss and looked at her, he knew he could continue as he wanted. It was beyond any doubt that, despite her complete lack of experience or perhaps precisely because of it, her body betrayed her mind, and the temptation was stronger than his rational mind. His only coherent thought was how to take her in the comfort and privacy of his room as the library was not the proper place to make love to her. And then… she opened her eyes and looked at him. His intentions changed in a moment!

Yes, her eyes were revealing her love, passion, and desire; she — herself — was a true picture of inviting abandon, but he could see so much more in her gaze! That desire was not a mere need for physical completion, but a desire burning from her love. She seemed so vulnerable to him and to her own passion. In that instant, he realised that she did not know what to expect or how to fight against it without hurting him. Thus, the way she closed her eyes again, surrendering to him, allowing him to do what he wanted… for him, it was a gesture of trust, more than anything was. This was a trust he could not betray by using her weakness simply to fulfil his wishes, no matter how much his wishes were generated by his powerful love. She was alone with him in his library on the second day of their engagement. Kissing her passionately, caressing her, teaching her the first steps on the path of physical pleasure — it was more than he had dreamed of a week earlier and certainly more than he could demand from her at that moment. His lips had then returned to hers with gentle tenderness, to comfort and assure her that there was nothing of which to be worried or frightened. Shortly thereafter, he knew he had been correct in his assumptions and in his decision when he felt her begin to relax in his arms as the tension in her body began to subside and she responded to his kisses with more trust and passion than she had previously.

They came to their senses some minutes later when the clock announced half past three. There were less than two hours for her to reach her aunt's home, change for dinner, and return with her family.

Elizabeth rose from the settee in a hurry, trying to rearrange her dress, brushing her hands over it to smooth it. She asked for a mirror, and Mr. Darcy showed her one hidden in a corner of the room.

"I must look wild..." she whispered, flustered, avoiding his eyes.

"No indeed. You look beautiful... and do not worry, no... damage was done." He smiled daringly at her, making her blush; but a moment later he lowered his head slightly, staring at her, and put his hand close to her face; mesmerised, she felt — more than saw — his thumb brushing her lips as gently as a breeze's touch.

"Well... almost no damage..."

"What... did something happen?" She sounded worried and hastened to face the mirror, while he leaned his head over her shoulder. She could see for herself that her lips were red and swollen. It was virtually impossible for anyone not to notice. Unconsciously, she touched her lips with her fingertips while he did the same.

"Please forgive me, my love. I was selfish and inconsiderate. I should have known that something like this could happen. Is it painful?"

She tried to smile, not just to hide her embarrassment but also to assuage his worry. "No, it is not painful at all; do not distress yourself. And it is not your fault; how could you have known — ?"

But before she finished the sentence, a sudden understanding struck her and made her blush violently. Lowering her eyes from the mirror so she could avoid his gaze — and fighting the unexpected knot in her throat that stopped her words — she could not refrain from asking. "Oh... I see... Does this happen every time...?" She could not continue, mortified by the implication of his words and by her own daring question.

She was surprised to see him quite easy and smiling, speaking mostly in jest.

"I cannot tell. I have never been in the situation of kissing someone so much that this could occur, so I never have given it any consideration." He added in a lower voice, whispering warmly in her ear. "In truth, I do not think I ever truly desired to kiss a woman before meeting you."

She met his eyes shyly but was still not completely at ease. She forced herself to smile, not knowing what to do with his admission and not being able to think clearly enough to catch his true meaning, whatever that might have been. Darcy placed a quick kiss on her hair, continuing to speak quietly in her ear.

"Let me help you remove the necklace, and then I will pour you a glass of cold water; it might help."

Gently, he took off the necklace, and in doing so, his hands lingered, caressing her neck; then he put the jewellery in the box and handed her a glass of water. "Elizabeth, we must discuss another thing before you leave so we can make plans with your father tonight. Our wedding day…" She gazed at him and only nodded.

"Did you truly wish to take into consideration what my Aunt Ellen said? I would not want you to feel forced to do anything solely because of social obligations."

"No, William, I think Lady Ellen made a very good point in this. Did you…did you have any date in mind?"

"Yes, I have, but again I ask you to tell me if you do not agree. I was thinking that the season starts in the middle of the March. So, if we were to be married in a month…or let us say six weeks, we would still have a little peaceful time to spend together before entering into all that tumult."

"A month?" She looked at him with mixed feelings of surprise and fear. "I do not think we will be able to make all the arrangements in a month. My mother does not even know yet, so — "

"Elizabeth…" His voice was calm and his eyes were full of understanding while his hand stroked her hair. "My love, I can understand if you need more time to become accustomed to all this. I can imagine that it might seem a little frightening to be forced to change your life so suddenly, but do not speak of wedding arrangements, please. I can make all the wedding arrangements in less than a week if necessary. Just tell me what you want as you always have. You told me a little earlier that we must share everything."

"I am a little frightened, William; I cannot conceal that. Everything has happened so fast. Only a week ago I came to London without knowing whether I would ever see you again — then Lydia's elopement — and then our engagement… Sometimes I think that I am only dreaming."

He kissed her temple tenderly. "I know, my love. I want nothing more than to marry you because I do not dare to think of being separated from you again. But more than anything I want you to be happy. And pleased… And content…" He continued in a different tone, less serious but more insinuating as a smile twisted the corner of his mouth. "And I am sure the engagement period will have its own charms… So tell me, please: when would you be prepared to plan our wedding?"

She turned to him and held his gaze for a few moments, and in his looks was everything she needed to decide. If there was one thing in the world she could be certain of beyond any doubt, it was his love. She had nothing to be afraid of as long as he was close to her.

"A month will be too soon, I am sure. However… I think that six weeks will do. And hopefully by that time, Georgiana will be fully recovered. But I warn you, I will have to tell my mother that you insisted on being married so soon."

"Six weeks seems perfect indeed, Elizabeth. And you may tell your mother anything you want; I am convinced she will be on my side. Did Becky not mention that Mrs. Bennet is very fond of me?"

He took her hands, brushing his lips over her palms and her wrists, then pulled her to him in a close embrace, which lasted no longer than a moment before Elizabeth withdrew quite firmly.

"William, I must go. Now!" He met her gaze, seeing her determined and a little reproachful — but smiling — expression and nodded obediently.

"You are right, of course. It is already quite late. I will accompany you to Gracechurch Street."

"No, you will not, sir. You will remain home and prepare for tonight because I am afraid you do not fully understand what a trying evening you will have. And there is no need for Molly to come either."

He tried to protest, but she would not allow him to sway her. "Sir, I trust that by now I can manage to keep myself safe for a short drive in London in the most comfortable Darcy carriage. Would you not agree?"

Her mood was high, and her lips — still a little more swollen and red than usual — twisted in a challenging smile while her eyes laughed in delight at his discomfort at not being allowed to do as he wanted.

"As you wish, madam; I do not dare to contradict such a decided demand."

She walked to the door, her hand still in his, and turned her head to look at him. "A very wise decision, Mr. Darcy. I hope you will remember that in the future. As I said, I cannot promise to obey you unconditionally, but I do warn you in advance, I will make my wishes decidedly known."

They exited the library and were in the main hall as Miles opened the door for them. Mr. Darcy helped her to enter the carriage, and she arranged her reticule and the jewel box in her lap, ready to leave; but before he closed the door, he leaned close to her, whispering so near to her ear that she could feel his lips.

"I will be more than happy to know your every wish and to comply with each one of them. However, I must also warn you that things will be different by then. You must consider that I will not have to be mindful of the propriety of being alone in a room with you or to worry about your family waiting for you... or about your swollen lips..."

His gaze was dark and so intense that she could feel it penetrating her soul as shivers spread over and within her. His words made her melt, and her hands trembled slightly as he politely bestowed a kiss on her now-gloved hand, bowing in the most gentlemanlike manner.

He closed the door, and she turned her head to hold his gaze a little longer, sad to be away from him but somehow relieved for now to put a little distance between them.

Lady Matlock was preparing herself for dinner, her maid arranging her hair as for an important social event. When she had returned home from her visit to Darcy House, she had found in her bedroom a gift from her husband — a flower. One unique red rose, so beautiful that even she — well accustomed to immense bouquets of flowers — was impressed. Near the flower was a little note asking for the privilege of speaking to her.

She smiled then, and she was still smiling now, pleased at the effect she still had on her husband after 35 years of marriage. Her heart melted, and she felt herself blushing a little at her own reaction to him after so many years.

Elizabeth's words when speaking of her feelings for Darcy and the passion in her eyes were the ultimate argument in her favour. Lady Matlock could understand her only too well, for she often felt the same for her own husband.

They had quarrelled quite often — and not without passion — during their life together, but even more passionate were their mutual feelings and their reconciliations. Though her husband had offended her, she could understand it was his temper that had betrayed him. And she knew that she could ask anything of him in exchange for her forgiveness. She decided to speak to him before dinner, and a tentative knock on the door announced to her that he had come.

"Ellen… I do not know what I could say to be worthy of your forgiveness. My behaviour toward you was outrageous; I am ashamed to remember how I offended you."

"Yes it was. And you indeed offended me — in front of our son no less and in the full hearing of the servants. What will they think of me now — or of you?"

"You must know I had not intended to do so. But…" He paused, searching carefully for the proper words. "I was at a loss to see how you could give your consent so easily to that ridiculous marriage. You must know as well as I do that this marriage will ruin Darcy's reputation and he will end up being very unhappy."

She gave him a sound look, and she could see that her husband was indeed sincere; he honestly believed that what he had predicted would come to pass. He was completely honest in voicing his opinion as he strongly believed it was for Darcy's benefit.

"Please take a seat, husband. Let us talk about this rationally, shall we?"

"Yes, thank you."

She looked at him for a few long moments. "Let me explain my meaning, and please try to understand me. When Darcy announced his engagement to us last night, I was as surprised and strongly opposed as you were, and I was equally decided not to allow this marriage to take place. The only difference was that I chose to express myself in a different manner. I, of course, had the advantage of speaking to our son while you were employing your time offending Darcy regarding his choice of wife."

Her voice was as full of irony as it was censure. He said nothing, for nothing could be said.

"After speaking with Robert, I easily understood that Darcy had made his decision and already taken any arguments I might add into consideration. It was not a sudden decision undertaken in the heat of passion but rather a rational one — and not to be changed. Darcy did not come here to ask for our consent. He does not need our consent. He came out of respect and affection to announce his engagement to us, his close family, as soon as he could. I dare say he wanted our blessing, but he does not need that either. Moreover, husband, Darcy anticipated our reaction, and he understood it plainly. He told me as much."

"Ellen, if it was indeed a rational decision that is even worse! That means he has lost his mind; he has forgotten everything he was taught and everything his parents wanted for him."

"Indeed? And pray tell me, how do you know that? When did you specifically talk with your sister or your brother about what they wanted for their son?"

"I did not need to discuss it with them. I simply know. They could not want anything less than what I want for our sons."

"In this we agree, husband. But do you know Miss Bennet that you can say she is not what you would want for our sons — or for Darcy?"

"Ellen, I refuse to answer that question. I do not need to know her; she is completely unfit and beneath us, and everybody will see that. She will never be accepted in society, and I myself will never be able to accept her."

"I see. So you are determined to reject her without even meeting her."

"I am. What I know about her is more than enough. And I will not give my consent to something that goes against everything I believe."

"I am satisfied that I understand your feelings now. But pray tell me, did you give the proper consideration to all the consequences of this kind of attitude?"

"I fail to understand your meaning."

"You fail indeed, husband, for you have allowed your temper to defeat your sense again. Let me enlighten you then. Darcy will not be moved in his decision, so your rejection will estrange him from us, and not only him but most likely Georgiana as well. Moreover, as we will frequent the same circles, you will undoubtedly meet Darcy and his wife at some point, and your attitude toward her will became publicly acknowledged. The hostility between our families will make us the subject of all the talk and gossip of the town for a long time and will damage the names of Fitzwilliam and Darcy much more than Miss Bennet could ever do. Are you prepared to allow that to happen? Do you think that this is what Anne Darcy would want for her son? Because I certainly do not. I will do everything in my power to prevent anything of that kind, for my name and my reputation are also involved as well as the future of my nephew and my niece."

Lord Matlock remained silent, deep in thought, looking from time to time at his wife.

"But Ellen, are you saying that we do not have any choice but to accept this marriage? And to accept *that* Miss Bennet, despite her situation in life and no matter how low her character might be?"

"Yes, indeed, that is what I am saying. We have nothing else to do but handle the situation as well as we can to the great benefit of everyone involved, no matter what kind of person Miss Bennet might be."

His whole countenance darkened, and he froze at that understanding, pacing the room in useless torment, not wanting to accept that he could do nothing to impose his will upon the situation.

Lady Ellen allowed him to suffer a little longer before taking mercy on him and giving him some relief.

"Fortunately, Darcy has proven himself to be wise in his choice, and his future wife's character is not at all as you feared. Earlier today I went to pay a visit to Georgiana, and I unexpectedly met Miss Bennet."

She paused and waited for his reaction, but his surprise did not allow him to say anything.

"And I came to conclude that she is everything Robert and Darcy told me. Her honesty in this situation cannot be questioned, and I strongly believe that Darcy will have no cause to repine. She is witty and pleasant, very determined and outspoken. She will be quite a challenge for him, but at least he will never be tired of her *charms,* as you implied. She has brought about an astonishing change not only in Darcy, but in Georgiana too, and I am indebted to her for that. I indeed approve of her now, and I dare say Anne would approve as well. And society will accept her; I will see to that. Moreover, she will make quite a sensation, I can tell you."

Lord Matlock finally found his voice.

"Ellen, you were trifling with me! Meeting Miss Bennet and concealing it from me — "

"Yes, I did trifle with you! You could not possibly believe that I would forgive your offence so easily, husband! As for Miss Bennet, I will not ask you to change your mind now, nor will I argue with you again on this subject. But I trust you will show decorum and politeness to Darcy and his intended when you meet them, even if you spend no more than five minutes in their company."

"If that is what you want... "

"It is. And trust me, Lord Matlock, sooner rather than later you will have to declare your failure in judging this situation. And do not entertain hopes that I will not take advantage of that or that I will not remind you constantly of that failure among many others. You should have learned to trust my instincts after 35 years of seeing how many times I am right! And now, will you escort me to dinner, please?"

Around six o'clock, two carriages stopped in front of Darcy's town house; one belonged to the Gardiners and the other had been sent by the master himself to bring the rest of the guests.

Mrs. Gardiner had reluctantly agreed to bring the children under a strict condition: immediately after dinner, Mrs. Taylor and the maid would come to retrieve the children while their parents were to remain longer.

The condition had been accepted by everyone, and even Becky was well dressed and her hair done properly for what she was told would be an important event. Elizabeth told them in detail about Georgiana and asked them to behave as well as they could, a promise given without reserve. Lydia had been very upset to attend without her dear Wickham, but a short private talk with Mr. Bennet was enough to bring her to reason.

Mr. Darcy himself was waiting to greet them and — to everyone's surprise — Mr. Bingley was also present; he moved toward Jane in an instant, and she could do nothing but blush under the adoring gaze he bestowed upon her.

While bowing to each lady, Mr. Darcy had no time to offer his arm to Elizabeth before Becky reclaimed his attention, and his only option was to take her in his arms. The best he could do, while inviting everyone in, was to grip Elizabeth's hand, squeezing it briefly, making her blush and respond in the same manner.

If her father had not warned her, Lydia's astonishment would have been loudly expressed; she was certain she had never been in such a house before, and she could not believe the splendour in which her sister would live.

They entered the drawing room — now arranged as a dining room — to find Georgiana sitting at the table.

Though she was not completely recovered and still weak, her appearance made all the guests — as nobody except Jane had seen her before — widen their eyes in admiration. Her pallor only increased the brightness of her blue eyes — blue as two sapphires, just like her mother's; golden curls were dancing on her temples, showing an elegant but unpretentious hair style. For jewellery, a pair of delicate golden earrings and a cross of gold with sapphire stones lying on her delicate neck enhanced the effect of her pale blue dress.

Since her shyness and modesty did not allow her to recognise the look of admiration on the guests' faces, Georgiana's cheeks coloured as her eyes moved from her brother — still carrying Becky in his arms — to Elizabeth, who was at her side in a moment, taking her hand with much affection. "Georgiana, you look beautiful!"

She only blushed and coloured even more, embarrassed by such open praise in front of everyone, but Bingley came closer, bringing Jane with him, and expressed their admiration with such enthusiasm that Georgiana was simply overwhelmed and could do nothing but thank them.

Mr. Darcy unburdened himself of Becky and made the introductions; the only difficult moment for Georgiana, happily noticed by no one but Mr. Darcy and Elizabeth, was the introduction of Lydia, but it passed well enough.

The children were introduced at the end; the boys acted like very proper gentlemen, bowing politely, and Margaret curtseyed with elegance to everyone's admiration.

Becky was the last to be introduced, and when Georgiana greeted her with her gentle voice, the girl looked up in deep admiration:

"You must be a fairy!"

Georgiana burst into laughter, all her shyness vanishing.

"No sweetie, I am not a fairy at all."

"Are you sure? Because you look exactly like Mrs. Taylor tells me fairies look."

"Yes, I am sure, but I thank you for the compliment."

"Well, you are welcome. You know, I am very good at compliments. I made many compliments to Mr. Darcy, too; he can tell you all about them."

"Oh yes, I will tell her," answered the gentleman to everyone's amusement.

Not only was Becky convinced that Georgiana was a fairy, but so too was young Thomas Gardiner. At the age of nine, he had never seen anything or anyone so beautiful in his life as Mr. Darcy's sister. He could not keep his eyes off her the whole evening, his thoughts being deeply sad because he was so young, praying hard to grow up sooner so he could marry her some day.

When the guests became more accustomed to their surroundings and seemed comfortably settled, Mr. Darcy asked Mr. Bennet to favour him with a private talk in the library.

"Mr. Bennet, I would like to discuss a very pressing matter with you before you leave town."

"Please do."

"Earlier today I had a discussion with Miss Elizabeth about deciding upon a wedding day."

"Ahh… I see… I was expecting this. And did you decide something?"

"Yes we did. Unless you have some objection, we would like to marry in about six weeks."

"Six weeks? That would be the middle of February? Well… You seem to be very impatient. I suppose Elizabeth has consented to this?"

"Yes sir, she has. Mr. Bennet, please rest assured that I am prepared to accept any delay of the date if you would prefer. The only reason for our… hurry was that Miss Elizabeth discussed with my aunt, Lady Matlock, the possibility of being in town for the season —"

"Well, Mr. Darcy, I somehow fail to believe that was the *only* reason."

He raised his eyebrow at him, pleased to see how teasing made Mr. Darcy's face colour highly.

"To be honest, I do have a problem with losing my favourite daughter so soon, but then again that will only give me an excuse to come to visit her as soon and as often as possible. Mr. Darcy, if you and Elizabeth have agreed, I shall not oppose you. However, we must hurry with all the arrangements. If not tonight, I expect an express from you with all the details very soon."

"Thank you, sir. If you allow me a suggestion, Miss Elizabeth and Miss Bennet may take care of everything that can be arranged in town, so Mrs. Bennet will have fewer things for which she need be worried."

"Good. Is there anything more, Mr. Darcy?"

"Yes, sir, I am afraid there is. My solicitor had no time to finish the settlements — "

"Mr. Darcy, I can hardly believe that there will be any point of which I would not approve in the settlements. It will be perfectly acceptable for me to sign them when we next meet."

"Thank you, sir. I hope you will not be displeased."

"I am sure I will not be. However, at this point the settlements are my last concern, for I have other pressing matters that I must consider first."

"About the wedding, sir?"

"Yes, Mr. Darcy, about the wedding. I think what you did was very selfish and dangerous for the sanity of an old man."

"Sir, I cannot — "

"Mr. Darcy, did it cross your mind that you are sending me alone to tell Mrs. Bennet not only that Lydia will be married in town but also that her second daughter will be married in less than two months to a man with ten thousand a year? Can you imagine what I will go through?"

Mr. Darcy let a deep breath escape, relieved that he was only teasing him, and replied in the same manner.

"Yes, I can imagine, sir, and I will be forever grateful for your sacrifice."

"Well, you should be. However, you will have your share of delight in this. Do you know that Charlotte Lucas — who is a good friend of Elizabeth — will marry Mr. Collins very soon? You have many reasons to hope that you will see Mr. Collins quite often in the future."

The same grin of satisfaction appeared on Mr. Bennet's face, while Mr. Darcy's expression turned to exasperation.

Mr. Bennet changed the topic to one more neutral. "I must say, sir, you have an impressive library here."

"I am glad you approve of it, and I dare say you will be delighted with the Pemberley library as well. Speaking of which, please consider that you will need no invitation to visit us at any time, both here and at Pemberley. I will be as happy as your daughter to see you, sir."

"Thank you; it is good to know that."

They returned to the drawing room where Mr. Darcy moved closer to Elizabeth and announced the established date to the party. Congratulations came with great delight from all except Lydia — annoyed by all the attention her sister received — and from Bingley, who was growing more and more envious of his friend's happiness and ashamed at his own lack of determination. Turning his eyes to Jane, their eyes met, and he was sure he could read in her the same thoughts. He soon recovered and joined the others in expressing congratulations, taking the opportunity to mention that he, too, intended to return to Netherfield in a fortnight and offering his home to host all the guests who would come for the wedding. The happiness that spread over Jane's bright face was his most desired reward.

Before dinner, Mr. Darcy proposed a tour of the house for his guests, as none of them — not even Elizabeth — had had the opportunity for an 'official tour.' As the children had no interest or curiosity in visiting empty rooms — quite the contrary — they remained with Georgiana, surrounding her with their gaiety.

Mr. Darcy took the lead of the little group but not before he offered Elizabeth his arm, this little gesture of intimacy being the only one allowed for the evening. More than once during the tour, Mr. Darcy found various opportunities to brush Elizabeth's hand with his, briefly, but nonetheless intensely. They were walking so closely together that it was impossible not to touch each other.

The group returned when a servant was sent to announce that the first course was ready to be served, and Mr. Darcy invited Elizabeth to stay at his right, opposite Georgiana, while he invited the rest of the guests to choose their places as they wanted; it being a family dinner, no formal arrangements were made.

Georgiana was thrilled with the evening. The Gardiners were indeed very pleasant, Mr. Bennet very kind and witty, and the children adorable. She was delighted to have the little girls around her and to be the object of their innocent admiration so openly displayed.

Many comments made by Becky made her laugh aloud, to her brother's delight, and she was sure she had not had such a pleasant time in years. Before the children returned home, Georgiana extracted from Mrs. Gardiner the promise that she would allow them to visit her again, together with Elizabeth.

It was very late when the guests left Mr. Darcy's town house, content with a most delightful evening. The next morning, Mr. Bennet left for Longbourn, and a few hours later, he rejoined his family after days of absence, three days full of more events than in his last ten years.

Mrs. Bennet's reaction to the news was everything he had feared. In fact, it was far worse.

MR. DARCY WAS HAVING HIS breakfast alone — hardly touching the food and enjoying a cup of strong coffee to help him awaken fully after a night filled with dreams and little sleep — when a note from Lady Matlock was delivered. He opened it, expecting to see the invitation to tea to which his aunt had previously referred, but instead he read something quite remarkable.

Darcy,

Last night I was considering that it has been too long since I have hosted a ball. And what better occasion could there be than my nephew's engagement?

So this is what I have decided: we will have a ball in a fortnight! And this time you will have no excuse; it would be quite strange to miss your own engagement ball, though from you I could expect it. Fortunately, I am sure you will not stand to see other men dancing with Elizabeth, so if nothing else, this is enough reason for you to attend.

I shared my intentions with your uncle, and although he was not exactly pleased with the idea, he was not opposed to it either. Please tell Elizabeth that I shall meet her tomorrow morning at your house while visiting Georgiana, and that she should not make plans for the next few days; she will be quite busy choosing her gown for the ball.

I have already made appointments at 'Madame Claudette' for the day after tomorrow. Of course, Elizabeth's relatives will be invited to the ball, except that impertinent Wickham character. Oh, do not be shocked, Darcy; of course I know about the youngest Bennet and that rascal. I know everything that is of any interest to me. Do tell Wickham not to dare appear anywhere near me, or I will punish him as I did a few years ago when I caught him… But that is not your business. Just tell him to stay far away, and he will understand, I am quite sure.

And Darcy, for heaven's sake, did you inform Catherine about your engagement? I imagine the announcements will appear in the newspapers in the next few days, and I would not want to be around when the information reaches her. Poor Anne, she will be alone to bear her fury, poor dear!

That will be all for the moment.

Your affectionate aunt.

Mr. Darcy did not know whether to laugh or to be distressed at what he read. Lady Ellen did not consider any contradiction or opposition to her plans. She did not ask their opinion about the ball, only informed them about it. He knew that it was a very considerate gesture and was further proof of her approving of Elizabeth, but he could not help feeling uncomfortable about someone — even his aunt — making decisions for him and his betrothed.

He smiled to himself at her reference to Wickham, and he was more grateful to her for not holding this situation against Elizabeth. But then again, Lady Ellen also had been deceived by Wickham's charming manner until one day more than seven years ago when she changed her opinion entirely without anyone knowing the reason behind it.

The prospect of the ball was more annoying than pleasant for him. He was still angry with his uncle over the way he had insulted Elizabeth and was reluctant to meet him at a social event. He delayed forming a conclusion until he had spoken to

Elizabeth, which would happen in a short time as he was to call at Gracechurch Street as soon as the clock showed the proper time for a visit.

For quite some time, he had not even thought of spending his days on his former schedule; the last time he had gone to his club was before departing with Bingley for Netherfield, but he did not miss any of the enjoyment he would find there. He gave little importance to anything except Elizabeth and Georgiana. Regarding his sister, her recovery was better than he would have hoped a fortnight ago, and even the doctor — who had visited her that very morning — expressed his surprise at her improvement.

Everything had changed for the better for him since Elizabeth had reappeared in his life ten days before. She brought joy into their lives as he had told her that night before their engagement. The bond between them was everything for which he had hoped, and her love for him and her shy passion, which induced her willingly to accept his attentions and return them, exceeded anything he had ever dreamed. The happiness of knowing that in only six weeks she would belong to him forever was almost too much to bear.

"I say, Darcy, you seem very pleased with yourself. I do not even dare to ask what kind of thoughts crossed your mind to make you smile like that."

"Bingley! What a pleasant surprise. I did not hear you entering. Do come in, please. Did you already eat?"

"No, I did not. I simply had to leave the house as soon as I could; Caroline has not ceased yelling since yesterday when she found you in . . . umm . . . private conversation with Miss Elizabeth." He expected to see Darcy embarrassed and ashamed, but his face expressed nothing of the kind.

"I am sorry, Bingley. You have every reason to be angry with me. Indeed, it was my behaviour that put both Miss Elizabeth and Miss Bingley in an unpleasant situation. I will apologise to your sister when I meet her next. In fact, if you do not mind, I would like to come to your house and apologise no later than today."

"Oh, spare me, Darcy. Indeed, you put all of us in a ridiculous situation, but that is not why I am angry with you. And if you want to go to my house and speak to Caroline, you must go alone, for I have no intention of returning before midnight when I am sure she is asleep."

He was so serious that Darcy could do nothing but laugh. "Do not look so miserable; I can offer you more than one room here. After all, it is entirely my fault. And please, do tell me why you are angry with me."

"Why am I angry with you? Why?! Darcy, do you remember the evening we returned to Netherfield after you and Miss Elizabeth were caught in the storm?"

"I do."

"That night we had a very interesting discussion about my feelings for Jane, and you advised me to act prudently and not to display my affection so obviously before

I was sure of my true feelings for her and of hers for me. Am I correct?"

"You must be. I do not recollect the exact words, but I remember that I did give you that advice — and wisely, too, I might say."

"Really? Wisely, you say? Well, Darcy, I followed your wise advice; I acted prudently and patiently, and I did not display my affection in an obvious manner while we remained in the neighbourhood."

"Indeed Bingley, you have behaved very gentlemanlike as you always do. But what is the point of this?"

"Oh, have patience; now I will come to the point. Until that moment, if I recall correctly, you never showed any kind of open admiration for Miss Elizabeth. Then after the ball, we left together and met them both in London one month later at the same time. So how on earth has it happened that I am still in the same kind of relationship with Jane as I was at Netherfield, while you have become engaged to Miss Elizabeth?! Not to mention the fact that she seemed to accept private meetings with you in your house."

He was indeed angry and turned quite red, causing Darcy to laugh as he almost choked on a piece of bread. "Bingley, you are hilarious."

"I am glad you find my anger so entertaining, Darcy, but I am in no mood for you to laugh at me."

"My friend, please believe that I do not laugh at your expense. I do understand your torment, and I will answer you; and trust me, things will not look as bad as they do now." He turned quite serious. "Bingley, I must confess that, although I did not show any sort of preference for Elizabeth, I had come to admire her shortly after I first met her. But of course, for some time I considered her unsuitable as my wife, and as I had no desire simply to flirt and trifle with her, I tried to conceal any admiration for her. However, that day when the storm caught us truly was my lucky day."

He looked at his younger friend gravely before speaking further. "I said that it was lucky because it was then that I understood not only how wrong I was in not considering her worthy to be my wife, but that my behaviour had given her a poor opinion of me. Knowing that, I was able to act so as to improve that impression."

"Yes, as I recall now, you did... and quite an improvement, I might say." Bingley's anger changed quickly to his usually jovial and amiable self, and he listened to his friend's story with amusement.

"As for the engagement... I was simply so fortunate as to find Elizabeth visiting Georgiana two days ago, and we started to speak about that dreadful situation with Wickham and... I do not really know how I came to propose to her, but I did, and she accepted. But Bingley, I must tell you what I see as obvious: Miss Bennet is more than ready to accept any marriage proposal from you as well; I have no doubt about that. I am sure that as soon as you have the opportunity of a few private moments with her, you will propose to her."

"I hope so, Darcy. I intend to call on her this morning."

"Splendid, then we can go together. Bingley, there is one more thing I should like to tell you."

"Yes, Darcy, what is it?"

"Please rest assured that nothing improper happened between me and Elizabeth except what your sister witnessed. I hope you do not think that — "

"Oh, for heaven's sake, Darcy, do not be ridiculous. That never crossed my mind. However, being alone with her and kissing her… is much more than you deserve after calling her only 'tolerable' that night at the assembly. Oh, I will absolutely have to tell that story to your children and to your grandchildren. And to mine too… "

It was Bingley's turn to burst into laughter as Darcy shook his head reproachfully.

ELIZABETH WAS EXPECTING MR. DARCY that morning. He did not say when — or even if — he would definitely come that day, but she was certain that she would see him soon.

Her memories of the previous day were so vivid; still she could not believe everything that had happened. *"My heart never spoke until I met you, Elizabeth… "*

But during the night, other recollections, equally vivid, disturbed her peace and threatened to overshadow her joy. *"I have never been in the situation of kissing someone so much… "*

So he did kiss other women before… She could understand as much from his answer. And she did know about gentlemen's habits — Mrs. Gardiner had talked to both her and Jane quite openly since they were 18 and began to attend balls and parties. Due to that knowledge, her reason avowed that she could not expect a gentleman of Mr. Darcy's situation to lack experience regarding these… matters of the world. But her heart and mind ached at the image of him kissing other women. She could still feel the taste of his mouth and remember the touch of his lips, his tongue invading her and melting her senses… Did he do the same with other women? What was for her a most beautiful and exquisitely pleasant dream of love could have been for him a mere repetition of some previous experiences. *"In truth, I do not think I ever truly desired to kiss a woman before meeting you."*

Then why did you do it? her heart was screaming without finding an answer, and then sleep refused to come for many hours to put an end to her torment.

The first thing she saw when she awoke was the jewellery box; as under a spell, her spirit lightened in an instant. She had risen from the bed and run to the window, delighted to see the sun shining on that cold, January day. Before she called for the maid, she stopped in front of the mirror, wondering at her image.

My eyes are red and I have dark rings around them. I look very bad indeed. How can I be such a simpleton? I cried like a silly girl for… nothing! For something I thought may have happened some time ago. And William believes me to be clever. I am not at all, but quite the opposite. Well, at least thank God nobody will know about that. Papa would tease me forever! A light smile spread over her face, and she shook her head in disapproval of her own folly.

She took the jewellery box in her hands, remembering his words, his caresses, his kisses, his scent… She missed him so much that she painfully felt his absence, and she became angry with herself, guilty of putting their happiness in danger. *He gave me his present and his future, and I allowed an unknown past to cloud my felicity. He gave me so much, and I still demand more.* She threw herself on the bed, burying her face in the pillow. *I don't deserve that he should see me today. Nevertheless, he will come… I just know it.*

Mr. Darcy did come as soon as the time was proper for a visit, and she went to greet him quite hastily, almost ignoring Bingley who, fortunately, needed nothing except Jane's smiles. Mrs. Gardiner was still upstairs with some house business, so the couples were pleased to have a little privacy only in each other's company.

Mr. Darcy sat with Elizabeth on the couch, very close to her, taking her hands in his. "I missed you so much…"

"I missed you, too." She blushed, casting a short glance at her sister and her companion before continuing. "I knew you would come this morning."

He smiled and put her hand to his lips without even considering that they were not alone.

"I knew you were waiting for me to come."

"Will you stay long, William?"

"Not very long, unfortunately. Today I must see about the announcements for our wedding. And my love, I have some… interesting news to share with you."

"Good news?"

"I cannot tell, for you will have to decide for yourself. Apparently, Lady Ellen is quite determined to host a ball for us — for our engagement — no later than a fortnight from today."

"A ball? But how? So suddenly?"

"What can I say? Apparently she had an agitated night."

"Oh, but William, I have no gowns for such an event. When we came to town we did not expect to socialise much and certainly did not expect to attend such an event."

"That is the last thing about which you should worry. My aunt has already made appointments for the day after tomorrow at her usual modiste. However, she intends to visit Georgiana tomorrow morning and asks if you will be able to meet her there. I honestly do not think you can decline."

He tried to sound light and amused, but he was searching her face for any sign of distress.

"Oh… I… I do not know what to say."

"Please, just tell me what you think and feel; do not search for proper words."

"Will Jane and — "

"Of course, Miss Bennet will be invited, and the Gardiners as well. Her eyes brightened, and a smile spread over her face while his gaze darkened slightly, and he spoke before she could express her joy.

"Elizabeth, did you really think that I would accept having your family slighted? Have I done anything to make you believe me so inconsiderate?"

She met his eyes and only then understood how easily her words could hurt him. His expression made her heart ache, and she tightened her grip on his hand, entwining her fingers with his.

"No, you have been nothing but wonderful to me and to my family. It is I who seem to have lost all my ability to think properly these days. I will not even attempt to justify my words, only to ask for your forgiveness."

This time it was Mr. Darcy who melted at her guilt and worry, but he wickedly continued the game a little longer. "Unfortunately... I cannot promise to forgive you so easily... "

His tone was grave and she was startled for a moment, fearing again to have hurt him deeply, but the next moment his thumb started to move slightly, tracing small circles in her palm. "I will have to consider the whole situation carefully... and I will give you the answer tomorrow... after my aunt leaves."

Her palm suddenly demanded all her thoughts, and his touch spread chills up her arms and down her spine; his gaze lowered from her eyes to her mouth, and her lips unconsciously parted under his scrutiny.

Only the noisy entrance of the children — fortunately some moments before their mother — made Elizabeth return to her senses, pulling her hands from his so that Mrs. Gardiner saw nothing about which to complain when she entered the room a few moments later.

LEAVING THE GARDINER'S HOME, MR. Darcy's attention was driven back to Lady Matlock's note as he came to understand that he had not considered the proper way to announce his engagement to his other aunt, Lady Catherine de Bourgh. He knew without any doubt that her reaction would be even more violent and her words more offensive than his uncle's had been.

Lady Catherine had long expressed her desire and hope for an alliance between him and her daughter, and though he had repeatedly spoken with his cousin Anne and ascertained that she was no more inclined to marry than he was, Darcy had never taken the trouble to disillusion his aunt.

As he never had the desire to bind himself to any other woman, the problem had not been an urgent one. He had hoped each year that, seeing that the year had passed without an understanding being reached between him and Anne, Lady Catherine would realise the truth; but of course, that had never happened.

Now, the problem was imperative.

The measures he must take to solve it were clear to him, but so were the impediments. Thus, he spent much of his time searching — with complete success — for remedies to those impediments.

As Mrs. Gardiner and Jane were planning to accompany Lydia to purchase all she needed for her upcoming wedding, Elizabeth asked Mr. Darcy to send Georgiana her greetings and excuses for not being able to visit that day.

She remained at home with her cousins, and especially with Becky, as the elder children were engaged with their daily lessons. The time was most happily spent for her, because not only did she love Becky but also the little girl's favourite subjects seemed to be Mr. Darcy and Georgiana. What other subjects could have been more pleasant for Elizabeth?

Elizabeth found herself blushing from time to time, remembering everything that had passed between her and her intended the previous day, and she blushed even more as she remembered his thrilling, insinuating words meant for no one except herself. And there were less than two months until he... How had he put it?

"I will not have to be mindful of the propriety of being alone in a room with you or to worry about your family waiting for you... or about your swollen lips..."

His words resounded in her mind, and their meaning made her shiver, not without fear of the unknown, of her future life and of what he was expecting from her. She did not doubt his love, but she still doubted other aspects of their union, and in the last few days, she had come to understand and value Lady Matlock's acceptance and implicit support, even if it was a bit overwhelming for her still.

Though Mr. Darcy did not mention it explicitly, Elizabeth could guess that the earl's opinion was not favourable — neither Mr. Darcy nor his aunt spoke about him in front of her — and she also gave some thought to Lady Catherine de Bourgh, Mr. Collins's formidable patroness. She was aware that the lady had her own plans and desires regarding Mr. Darcy — he had informed her of that himself on the night of the Netherfield ball. So Lady Catherine would inevitably be displeased by the news of her nephew's changed marital status.

Becky's endless questions succeeded in diverting her mind from these thoughts, and she soon ceased to pay attention to anything except the girl with brown curls who was throwing herself on the floor, playing leapfrog.

Their pleasant time was interrupted by Mr. Wickham's sudden arrival. Instantly, the pleasant mood turned sour, and Elizabeth hurried to inform Mr. Wickham that Lydia and her aunt were not at home and were not expected for another hour. Yet, he showed no intention of leaving, instead asking for permission to wait as he had some important news to share with them.

Feeling uncomfortable at receiving him alone, Elizabeth had nothing to do but invite him to sit, ringing the bell for some refreshments. Becky's presence kept the conversation at an acceptable level of neutrality, and with great difficulty, the time passed until Lydia's thrilled voice could be heard in the yard. The three ladies entered the house surprised — only one of them pleasantly — to find their guest.

Mr. Wickham's news was regarding his commission. Apparently, Colonel Fitzwilliam had sent him a note to confirm a new position for him in a northern regiment, and he was expected to be there in a fortnight. He expressed his enthusiasm at the prospect of fixing the wedding date for a week hence, and then to depart — together with his beloved wife — to start a new life.

His words were so full of insincerity and forced affability that everyone — except Lydia — fought the impulse to roll their eyes and remove themselves from his presence. Unlike her aunt and elder sister, Elizabeth yielded to that impulse and retired at the first opportunity, not leaving her room until after Mr. Wickham's departure.

To everyone's pleasant surprise, Mr. Darcy returned a few hours later, this time with firmly set plans. First, he settled with Mr. and Mrs. Gardiner that Lydia and Mr. Wickham's wedding would take place in six days, and every detail was to be seen to by then.

Second, he asked for a favour, as an urgent matter required his immediate attention. He intended to make a short trip to Kent two days hence, personally to inform Lady Catherine about his engagement and the subsequent changes it would entail for his future. He was reluctant, however, to leave his sister, so he asked that Elizabeth stay with her for the duration of his trip, which would be no more than a few days. He also pointed out that this would afford an opportunity for Elizabeth to become accustomed to the house in which she would soon be mistress.

It took the Gardiners only a short time to agree to his plan, and Elizabeth was delighted and flattered that he would entrust his house and his sister to her care.

Mr. Darcy's third piece of business was to deliver another note from his aunt to Elizabeth as Lady Matlock was not familiar with the Gardiner's address. She opened it without delay and was very pleased by its contents. Lady Matlock had extended an invitation for Mrs. Gardiner and Jane to accompany her on a shopping expedition to Madame Claudette's *'if Mrs. Gardiner has not already made her own appointments with her personal modiste.'*

The invitation was issued with great elegance and diplomacy. As Lady Matlock did not know the Gardiners' financial situation — and Madame Claudette was not only the most famous but also the most expensive modiste in town — she was offering an opportunity for a dignified refusal in case the expense was too much to bear. Mrs. Gardiner understood the hidden meaning of the note and urged Elizabeth to accept the invitation with gratitude, answering in the same diplomatic way.

My aunt insisted on expressing her deepest gratitude for your generous invitation. As her previous attempts to make an appointment with the famous modiste had unfortunately been unsuccessful due to Madame Claudette's immense popularity and limited time, she would now be happy to accept such an appointment in company with you, Lady Matlock.

Lady Matlock was satisfied when she received the reply, for it contained the complete answer to her unwritten questions.

THE '*VISIT*' TO MADAME CLAUDETTE took more than three hours, and afterwards Elizabeth felt completely exhausted. Lady Matlock had been very polite — if not really friendly — to both her aunt and Jane, whose beauty and sweetness she had openly admired. She very much approved the selections for Jane and Mrs. Gardiner's gowns, but to Elizabeth, Lady Matlock had been simply overwhelming. From the very beginning, she declared that Elizabeth's gown would be a gift, and Elizabeth wisely decided to say nothing except to express her gratitude.

It was then that Lady Matlock truly sprang into action. Elizabeth was given the chance to choose the model of her gown, but the rest was up to her future aunt. In selecting the fabrics to be used, she asked Elizabeth if there were any particular jewels she intended to wear. Upon hearing that Elizabeth was to wear the Darcy ruby set, she nodded in satisfaction and informed Madame Claudette that she was to find 'the best fabric to suit gold and rubies, along with Miss Elizabeth's complexion, hair, and eyes.'

It took her an hour to find something appropriate, though for Elizabeth everything she saw was of the most astonishing beauty. Indeed, she teased, she could hardly be expected to decide!

However, any complaints Elizabeth made were in jest, for in truth she was deeply grateful to her ladyship for all the trouble she was taking with her and for her gracious condescension towards her and her family.

The dresses Jane and Mrs. Gardiner ordered were exquisite, but as for her own... she felt breathless just thinking of the softness of the fabric and the colour — different from anything she had ever seen before. An inner smile lit her face as she thought of Mr. Darcy's reaction upon seeing her, and she imagined how the delicate fabric would feel against her skin when he touched her as they danced.

She had no opportunity to meet him in his house that day, instead spending the time with her aunt and sister before returning directly home when their business came to a satisfactory conclusion. Lady Matlock promised to visit her and Georgiana at Darcy House the next day and have tea with them.

As he had some business to attend to before his departure, Mr. Darcy was not able to call at Gracechurch Street that evening; Elizabeth retired for the night slightly disappointed, hoping that she would have the opportunity to speak to him briefly the next day.

Mr. Darcy called the next morning, together with Mr. Bingley. In addition to escorting Elizabeth to Darcy House, Mr. Darcy brought an invitation from Georgiana for Jane and the Gardiner children to visit her as they had promised a few days before during dinner.

It was quite a large party, then, that reached Mr. Darcy's home an hour later. Georgiana's delight in receiving her visitors raised her spirits, especially when Becky climbed onto her bed to bestow a noisy kiss on her cheek.

Arriving some time later, Mrs. Hamilton and Mrs. Annesley did not hide their pleasure at seeing Miss Darcy surrounded by the children and conversing easily with Miss Bennet and Mr. Bingley, who were seated on a settee near the bed. Mrs. Hamilton expressed her satisfaction in having Elizabeth there and assured her that the whole staff had been informed of her status as future mistress of the house. Elizabeth thanked her and blushed but could not add anything more as Mr. Darcy entered the room and the ladies excused themselves.

Elizabeth had felt his presence even before seeing him, and she could not take her eyes off him from the moment he appeared. Her gaze held fast with his as he approached her and took her hand, whispering in her ear. "I will leave soon. Will you accompany me outside?"

She nodded in agreement, squeezing his hand, happy to feel his closeness and his tender touch after two long days apart from him.

Mr. Darcy made his goodbyes to his sister and his guests, while Mr. Bingley could not help making sport of him.

"Oh, for heaven's sake, Darcy, just go! You will be gone two days, and you make these preparations as if you will be gone for two years. Georgiana will be fine, and so will I — in case you were worried about me."

"No, Bingley, I was not at all worried about you. Do not flatter yourself." He left the room in a very good humour, taking Elizabeth with him.

Her hand was clasped tightly in his, their fingers entwined, and she already felt a shiver travelling from her palms throughout her body, anticipating the moment when they would be alone and he would kiss her. He pulled her after him, however, apparently in a great hurry, passing Georgiana's sitting room and then the hall without stopping. They reached the head of the stairs, and he changed direction to his left, going through another hall, and opened a door, pulling her inside. She cast a quick glance around, not recognising the room, and then turned her eyes to his. "William — "

"Shh... Do not worry, I only wanted to spend a few minutes alone with you, and in this house, there is no other place to have some privacy. Do you mind?"

"No, I do not mind... but this room... ?"

"It is my room."

Her heart stopped for a moment then started to beat again wildly. A shiver ran up her spine as his left hand encircled her waist and the other glided over the back of her neck, pulling her closer to him. Soon she was so close that their bodies touched and she could feel his heart beating.

"My dearest Elizabeth… it has been two days since I last kissed you, and another one will pass before I kiss you again. I cannot bear it any longer; I will die if you do not allow me to kiss you."

His voice was deep and hoarse with passion as he tightened his hold on her, and she could not breathe or speak… or think. But her arms, guided by their own will, rose and found their way around his neck. She did not divert her eyes from his, and her lips parted slightly in a silent acceptance — no, a silent invitation. Her whole face was covered by small, tender kisses until his hungry mouth reached hers, gently and tentatively at first, and then growing impatient, demanding, and possessive.

She was leaning with her entire body against his, her arms clinging to his neck, as her knees became weak with her growing passion. She felt as if she were floating, and indeed his embrace had lifted her off the ground as he moved, taking her with him until he found a chair in which to sit, pulling her into his arms. Her arms were still encircling his neck, and his hands changed their position to hold her better. Their lips remained closely joined, in a desperate attempt to satiate their need for each other.

Mr. Darcy withdrew from her but held her close a few moments as they tried to regain their breath. Her head rested on his shoulder as his hands caressed her back.

"I must go now so I can return tomorrow before dinner."

"Tomorrow? But you said you would be gone two days. Shall I return to my uncle tomorrow night?"

"No indeed." He placed a quick kiss on her ear. "I know what I said, but there is a chance that my business may be concluded sooner than expected, especially when my reward will be an evening spent with you… almost alone in the house… with no one to disturb us… "

Mr. Darcy was almost lost in the delightful anticipation of their next meeting when he felt her startled reaction as she tensed and caught her breath. Only then did the import of his words strike him.

"Elizabeth, I did not mean that… "

He pulled her gently from him so he could see her eyes and then cupped her face, smiling at her. "Please believe me that it was not my intention to suggest anything improper when I spoke of spending the evening together."

He paused and started to laugh before adding. "Or rather, nothing more improper than this."

A smile brightened her flustered face as she fully realised that she was in his room, sitting in his lap, her arms around his neck. What could have been more improper than that?

"Elizabeth, I will not deny that I desire you more than I could have believed possible. I can understand that my passion might appear frightening to you; sometimes I am frightened myself by the intensity of my feelings. It is true that I desperately enjoy holding you, kissing you, caressing you and that sometimes I am too demanding, and I have never allowed you to tell me whether you are displeased with my insistence…"

"I am not displeased. You know that…" Her voice was only a whisper as she averted her eyes.

"I am very happy to hear it. But perhaps you think it is too soon? Would you prefer to postpone these…private encounters until after the wedding? Please tell me the truth."

No answer came, but she shook her head in disagreement.

"Then what is it?" He searched her distressed countenance a few moments in an effort to understand her. "Are you afraid that I will demand…something more from you? That I will insist on having my way… Am I correct in assuming this?"

"William, I am not afraid of you. And I do not believe you would insist on having your way with me. I am more afraid of what I feel when we are together. I know I could refuse you nothing…and I do not want to… I mean…I would rather wait until we are married to…"

Her eyes were moist with tears from distress and embarrassment, and Darcy covered them with light kisses, caressing her cheeks with his thumbs.

"I understand you, my love. I must confess that I am very impatient to have you as my wife, but I am content to wait as patiently as I can until that day comes and to enjoy your company, your closeness, your love…and all the charms of our engagement. I know you have already been more generous than I deserve and that you have allowed me more liberties than propriety would allow, but do not be afraid that I will take advantage of your generosity or that I would do anything against your will."

Her eyes lifted to face him as he spoke, and she nodded, smiling shyly at his last words. Staring so deeply into her eyes that she could feel his dark gaze penetrating her soul, he continued, his voice deep and low but so powerful that it made her tremble.

"You must remember one thing, Elizabeth. I desperately desire you, but my love is a hundred times stronger than my desire."

It had been more than an hour since the noisy family party had returned to Gracechurch Street, leaving Elizabeth with Georgiana at Darcy House. The master of the house had departed for Kent a couple of hours before noon, and Elizabeth was resting on a couch near Georgiana's bed, reading to herself as the younger lady slept peacefully.

A sudden tumult of voices resounded from downstairs, and Elizabeth rose instantly to demand silence for Georgiana, trying to understand who would dare to be so disrespectful.

Before she could take a step further, she was startled by the door being violently thrust open. Georgiana awoke in great distress, and the two of them turned to stare at the imperious guest — a woman of Lady Matlock's age, no less impressive but utterly different in demeanour.

Chapter 20

She entered the room with a most ungracious air, followed by a disconcerted Mrs. Hamilton and a worried Miles, so worried that he did not even notice that he had entered Georgiana's room uninvited.

The guest cast a disdainful glance at Elizabeth and proceeded to the bed with a slight inclination of her head, sitting down without saying a word.

Struggling to speak, Georgiana managed to whisper, "Aunt Catherine, what an unexpected surprise! We did not know you were in town. William departed for Kent this morning to visit you."

"Really? How considerate of him to visit me. I wonder what his reasons might have been. Perhaps it was to explain the fact that he has put himself and our family in a most dishonourable situation!"

The girl stared at her in shocked silence, her face white, incapable of any reply. After a moment of silence, Lady Catherine stiffly addressed her niece. "Well, I see you are still in bed, Georgiana, though you do not seem ill anymore. And that lady sitting there, I suppose, is Miss Bennet? May I inquire what she is doing here? The servants informed me that she is staying in the house. Is this true?"

"Yes, Aunt, this is Miss Elizabeth Bennet. Elizabeth, this is my aunt, Lady Catherine de Bourgh. Elizabeth is keeping me company while William is out of town."

"It is an honour to meet you, Lady Catherine." Elizabeth tried to sound as respectful and warmly polite as possible, in order to diffuse the tension that was causing Georgiana such discomfort.

"Oh, I can hardly believe that you understand the notion of honour, Miss Bennet. I am sure you are merely surprised by my coming and do not know how to defend yourself."

The direct attack took Elizabeth by complete surprise.

"Lady Catherine, I must confess that I do not understand your meaning."

"Do not try to fool me, Miss Bennet. You can be at no loss to understand the reason for my journey hither. Your own heart, your own conscience — if you possess either of these — must tell you why I have come. Or perhaps you entertained some daft hope that I would remain silent and allow you to trap my nephew into a dishonourable marriage."

Elizabeth stared at her in astonishment, hardly able to believe her words or the tone in which they were voiced. She forced herself to remain calm, though her spirit and temper demanded a fierce reply to such an attack.

"Lady Catherine, I repeat that I do not understand your meaning about defending myself, for I do not know myself to be culpable of anything. As to your ladyship's reason for paying this visit, I can easily guess its nature. Evidently, your ladyship is displeased with my engagement to Mr. Darcy."

"Displeased? When I heard the rumour two days ago, I thought it to be only the false report of a most alarming nature, but the situation now seems far more serious. I see you are already settled in his house and — no doubt — in his bed. Are you with child, Miss Bennet? Is that how you forced Darcy to marry you?"

As earnestly as Elizabeth tried to keep her composure, Lady Catherine's last words made her face colour profusely, and the offence bestowed upon her left her breathless with indignation. She lifted her chin and threw a fierce glance at her opponent.

"Lady Catherine, I will not dignify that ludicrous accusation with an answer nor any other consideration. I suggest continuing this conversation outside of Georgiana's room. She is not fully recovered, and I do not think this kind of talk is proper for her."

"Miss Bennet," replied her ladyship, in an angry tone, "my character has ever been celebrated for its sincerity and frankness, and at such a moment as this, I shall certainly not depart from it. My niece must hear what I have to say to understand your scandalous entrapment and her brother's inexcusable weakness! Your arts and allurements drew him into this and have made him forget what he owes to himself and to all his family."

As Elizabeth attempted to exit the room, Lady Catherine followed her, continuing even louder, her anger growing to the point that she could not maintain control of her own words.

"Let Georgiana know and be ashamed that her brother is no better than her father! He was equally weak and incapable of controlling his lust and carnal desires! Anne never would have died if her husband had given her the consideration of leaving her alone! He knew another pregnancy would be fatal for her; still he kept imposing himself upon her to satisfy his wanton desires. He murdered her for his own pleasures and for the selfish desire to have another child. And Darcy is even worse. He has lost his reason in a moment of infatuation and brought his mistress near his own sister."

"Lady Catherine! I cannot imagine that your nephew would approve of your statements, but I will certainly not tolerate further insults. And I will not allow you to distress Georgiana a moment longer! Miles, show Lady Catherine to the drawing room immediately. Mrs. Annesley, please see to Georgiana until I return."

She saw Mrs. Hamilton's approving nod. She was the mistress of the house, and she was acting accordingly.

All the way to the drawing room, Lady Catherine loudly voiced her disapproval, but Elizabeth paid her no heed. Feeling herself in complete control of the situation and keeping her calm demeanour in the face of the elder lady's wild rage, Elizabeth asked Mrs. Hamilton to send a maid with some refreshments as she continued her conversation with Lady Catherine.

"Miss Bennet, do you know who I am? I have not been accustomed to such treatment and such language. I am almost the nearest relation Darcy has in the world and am entitled to know all his dearest concerns."

"Is your ladyship complaining about *my* language? Was it I who offended everyone present? Was it I who offended your ladyship in any way? And as for being entitled to know Mr. Darcy's dearest concerns, if you had delayed this . . . this *visit* only one day, you would have been in a position to ask him about each and every one of your concerns. As it is, you have no other choice than to wait for his return if that is your wish."

"This is not to be borne! Miss Bennet, you ought to know that I am not to be trifled with. I insist on being satisfied. I know that it would be impossible for my nephew willingly to make the decision to marry you without some strong inducement. Has Darcy any reason to make you an offer of marriage?"

"He must have a very strong reason! Your ladyship has just declared otherwise to be impossible."

"And can you, Miss Bennet, declare that there is no foundation for suspecting something dishonest has occurred between you? Have you not been in his house many times? Have you not attempted to persuade him since he was in Hertfordshire? Did you not spend time alone with him in the wildwoods, even going so far as to be caught in the rain? How can you defend yourself in this?"

"I have no intention of defending myself in anything, as neither my behaviour nor Mr. Darcy's requires any defence. I was invited several times to Mr. Darcy's house for the purpose of visiting Georgiana and keeping her company as I am doing today, but your ladyship seems determined to find only dishonour and failure in other people's manners and intentions."

"Well, then it is for the best. This match to which you have the presumption to aspire, can never take place though you believe yourself comfortably settled in the position of mistress of the house. Mr. Darcy is engaged to my daughter. Their union was planned while they were in their cradles; it was the favourite wish of his mother and me. And now, is a young woman of inferior birth, of no importance and wholly unallied to the family to prevent it? Are you lost to every feeling of propriety and delicacy?"

"Lady Catherine, might I suggest that you not raise the subject of propriety and delicacy at this moment?"

She could not help feeling satisfied at the astonished and offended expression on Lady Catherine's face.

"I am well informed of your ladyship's wishes as well as Mr. Darcy's opposition to them. He confessed to me that he has the highest esteem for his cousin but never intended making her an offer of marriage. The truth is that Mr. Darcy is neither by honour nor by inclination bound to his cousin. He made another choice, and his choice was in my favour."

"His choice was forced and cannot be acceptable! You cannot expect to be noticed by his family or friends if you wilfully act against the inclinations of all. You will be censured, slighted, and despised by everyone connected with him. Your alliance will be a disgrace; your name will never even be mentioned by any of us. Do not deceive yourself into believing that I will ever back down. I will not be dissuaded from my purpose. I have not been in the habit of brooking disappointment."

"That will make your ladyship's situation at present more pitiable, but it will have no effect on me. I am afraid I am at a loss to understand what your ladyship's real purpose is."

"My purpose is to have this engagement broken and this marriage forgotten forever. And if you were sensible of your own good, and as honourable as you claim to be, if there is indeed no reason to force this alliance, you would see the wisdom of my demand."

"I fail to see any kind of wisdom in your demand, Lady Catherine, and I am not to be intimidated into anything so wholly unreasonable. I must beg, therefore, to be importuned no farther on the subject."

"Not so hasty if you please. I have by no means done. To all the objections I have already urged, I have still another to add. I am no stranger to the particulars of your youngest sister's infamous intended elopement. And still you are selfishly resolved to have him and determined to ruin him in the face of all his friends, and make him contemptible to the world by forcing him to become the brother of such a girl and of the son of his father's steward!"

"Yes, I am. I am fully resolved to act in that manner which, in my own opinion, will constitute my happiness and Mr. Darcy's. And now, your ladyship can have nothing further to say. You have insulted me in every possible manner. I must beg to be excused; I must return to Georgiana."

She rose as she spoke, and Lady Catherine also rose, following her.

"You refuse, then, to oblige me. But depend upon it; I will carry my point. I still have influence in Town. You will feel my anger and my disdain! And do not believe you can dismiss me. I will not leave my nephew's house! I will return to my niece's room if I desire to do so."

"Lady Catherine! Mr. Darcy has asked me to remain here while he is away and to act as the mistress of this house! All the servants have been informed of my future position. The only will they will answer to is mine. Do not force me to ask the servants to show you out of the house!"

"You would not dare!"

"I most certainly would! I will not allow you to disturb Georgiana any further! You may remain in the house and even demand a room; you are Mr. Darcy's close relative, and you are entitled to be well received in his house, but you will not be allowed to offend anyone. It is your ladyship's choice. Now, if you will excuse me..."

Elizabeth tried to open the door, but Lady Catherine, suffocated by anger and revolting against such a manner of address, pulled the door open forcefully and exited the room in a great hurry.

At that moment Molly entered with refreshments and hot water for tea. Lady Catherine's sudden appearance took her by surprise, as did the lady's shoving her brusquely out of the way. The impact made Molly lose her grip on the tray and she dropped it, spilling the scalding hot water on herself.

"Clumsy girl! With such a future mistress, no wonder the servants cannot stand on their feet."

Lady Catherine left the house angrier than she had ever been. Meanwhile, the pain of her unfortunate accident had made Molly faint, and Elizabeth hurried to her side offering as much help as she could.

Only later, when Molly, with all her clothes quickly removed, had been put into bed and a note for the doctor had been sent, did Elizabeth return to Georgiana's room.

She found her future sister in deep shock, her entire body trembling violently, her face frighteningly pale and her eyes staring blankly. Neither Elizabeth nor Mrs. Annesley managed to extract a coherent answer from her, not even an hour later when the family doctor arrived. It took all of Elizabeth's calm and diplomacy to explain to the doctor what had induced such a state in his patient, but she did not completely succeed.

With a reproachful expression on his face, he demanded that everyone leave the room so he could examine Miss Darcy properly and completely.

Lady Matlock's day had been very pleasant so far. She was content that she had received favourable responses to every invitation to the ball and that everything was progressing to her liking. She cast a quick glance at her husband, who was reading in his favourite armchair, his brows frowning in concentration. The earl had not voiced another objection nor did she insist on changing his opinion regarding Darcy's engagement. She had no doubt that he would eventually come to see things her way. He always did.

Her pleasant day took an unfortunate turn only a few moments later when Lady

Catherine de Bourgh — barely announced — entered the salon.

More than 15 minutes had passed before Lady Catherine ended her tirade of disapproval toward Elizabeth Bennet's despicable character and scandalous behaviour.

All this time, the earl's eyes rested occasionally upon his wife's face, reading her reactions, so he knew what to expect when his sister, her reprimand complete, waited for Lord and Lady Matlock to join her in disapproving Elizabeth and opposing the unthinkable marriage.

"So, Catherine," said Lady Ellen with deceptive calm, "Let me see if I understand you correctly. You suddenly appeared at the door of Darcy's house and hurried upstairs to express your opinion about Miss Bennet? And all of this you did while you were in Georgiana's room?"

"Yes, I most certainly did, for it was there that I found the impertinent girl. She was ashamed, I suppose, because she demanded that we move downstairs so Georgiana could not hear us. But I told her what I wanted to say; she could not doubt my opinion."

"Catherine, how was Georgiana faring throughout this episode?"

"Georgiana? She was doing well enough, I suppose, though I could not understand why she was still in bed. But I had no time to inquire, and she was as silent as ever."

"And where is Anne? Did she remain in Kent?"

"No indeed. She is in the carriage."

Lady Matlock favoured her sister-in-law with a stern, icy glare and then turned her eyes to the earl.

"Husband, I will give orders that Anne be taken care of. She must be exhausted after spending so much time on the roads. I will also ask that rooms be prepared for Anne and for Catherine, as well. I trust you will treat this situation with proper and fair consideration and act accordingly. As for myself, I have an urgent visit to attend to."

"Ellen, you cannot possibly leave without even expressing your opinion." Lady Catherine looked most displeased at her sister-in-law's calm demeanour.

A tense pause followed, and the earl knew his wife was searching for the proper words.

"Catherine, do not force me to give you my opinion! I will only say that I am sorry your excellent father wasted so much money on your education with so little evident success. He should have given all of the money to the poor, and he would have been a hundred times better rewarded."

Before Lady Catherine managed to understand fully the meaning of her words, Lady Matlock proceeded out of the room, fetching her housekeeper, giving her short and precise orders, and then calling for her carriage. Only inside the carriage, alone, her face red with indignation, did she allow her rage to burst forth in whispered words, which she would never admit knowing, much less speaking.

When Lady Matlock reached Darcy House, she was prepared to find evidence of her sister-in-law's presence, but the situation was worse than she could have imagined.

Mrs. Hamilton welcomed her with obvious gratitude and informed her without delay that the doctor was with Georgiana and that Miss Bennet was waiting in the salon.

As Lady Matlock demanded straight and honest answers, the housekeeper related to her everything she had witnessed. Mrs. Hamilton obviously struggled to relate the conversation between Mr. Darcy's intended and his aunt; with her every sentence, Lady Matlock's countenance darkened, and she frowned, almost damaging her perfect features.

"Thank you Mrs. Hamilton. Now I will see my niece."

Mrs. Hamilton was about to remind her that Georgiana was undergoing the doctor's examination and was not to be disturbed when she realised that Lady Matlock's direction was not towards the stairs but the salon. She was going to see her other niece — Elizabeth.

Elizabeth's hands were trembling so that she could not control them. She felt a coldness engulfing her whole body, and her head spun painfully. She was not thinking of her own injury, her own offence, but of poor Molly and most of all Georgiana. Helpless, powerless to undo what had happened, alone in a house she did not know well, pained by the grief suffered by the innocent girls, she could not fight her tears any longer.

She noticed Lady Matlock's presence only when the lady gently stroked her hair. "Elizabeth?"

She tried to wipe her tears before lifting her eyes to face the visitor, but Lady Matlock sat near her, continuing to caress her hair.

"Elizabeth, do not worry, dear. I am here now, and I will help you make everything right, but please do not cry anymore. I do not want to see you affected by the foolish words thrown at you by an uncivil woman. You are too bright for that."

When she finally dared to meet Lady Matlock's eyes, Elizabeth could see an encouraging smile and a tenderness that had not been there until that moment. She forced herself to smile back and to dry her tears.

"Lady Ellen, I am so grateful you are here! Do you know Georgiana is unwell? The doctor is with her now."

"I know, dear; Mrs. Hamilton informed me. And you? How are you feeling, Elizabeth?"

"Oh, do not worry about me; I am well. I am only worried for Georgiana. I do not know what happened to her. Mrs. Annesley said that at first she cried a lot. But when I returned to her, she was in a most disturbing state. She did not say a word, did not even seem to hear us. She was trembling as though she had a high fever, and she was so pale. How will she bear that after her long illness? She is so weak yet… What can we do?"

"Elizabeth, calm yourself, please. Here, I will pour us each a glass of wine, and then we will talk until the doctor has finished his examination."

Her words brought Elizabeth to her senses, and she instantly rose to her feet. "No, please, Lady Ellen, allow me to do it. I shall return in a moment."

She returned with two glasses of wine and handed one to Lady Matlock who took it and then invited Elizabeth to sit near her.

"And now, while we are waiting, I would like to hear everything about what happened here. Mrs. Hamilton has already informed me about some of it, but I want to hear the whole story from you. And please, do not hesitate to give me all the details so I will know what must be done."

Warmed by the wine and encouraged by Lady Matlock's kindness, Elizabeth gained enough courage to relate her entire conversation with Lady Catherine. They were still talking in low voices half an hour later when the doctor returned to give them a complete report.

"Well... What can I say? I am very displeased that my patient, after such a miraculous recovery, was not treated with more care. From what I can see, there is no physical damage, but the shock she suffered makes me wonder at the circumstances behind this. If I had found a girl on the street in such a state, I would assume she had been abused in the worst manner possible. But for something like this to happen to her in her own room..."

Lady Matlock assured him that she would explain in detail all he needed to know, but asked for a full report on all that must be done for her niece.

"For the moment she is under the effect of some medications I gave her. I hope she will sleep until tomorrow morning and will be fine. I can say no more. As long as I do not know what to heal, I am as helpless as you are, Lady Matlock. I would suggest that someone be with her constantly, even during the night."

"Of course," offered Elizabeth. "I will see to that. We will not leave her alone for a moment."

"Well then, Miss Bennet, would you be so kind as to have someone supervise my other patient as well? Molly will need someone to change her bandages at least once during the night, and you must make sure she gets plenty of rest until she is fully recovered. I will return in the morning, but please do not hesitate to fetch me for any necessity."

"I will, sir. Thank you."

The afternoon passed in anxious waiting, but no change occurred. Elizabeth and Lady Matlock did not stir from Georgiana's room, hoping for any sign of improvement, but their hopes were not gratified.

Elizabeth checked a few times on Molly, and at least on that account she could be pleased. The injuries were painful but not at all severe, and the young maid was almost ashamed by all the attention bestowed upon her. She even pretended that she was well enough to return to work, but Elizabeth silenced her with an admonishment, ordering her to rest at least a week and not to leave her bed until the doctor approved.

Returning from Molly's room, Elizabeth's heart pounded at hearing voices in the library and recognising, beyond any doubt, that of Mr. Darcy. She forgot about proper manners and ran to meet him, opening the heavy door with the anticipation of finding comfort and help from him; however, she froze, frowning and not daring to go further at the image of Mr. Darcy's anger overflowing on Mrs. Hamilton and Miles.

"I want someone to explain to me, very clearly, how this was possible? Is this house open to the public? Is anyone allowed to enter at any time? A few days ago, Caroline Bingley barged in on me in the library. Now, my aunt was allowed to move through the entire house and into my sister's room without restraint. Why do I keep 30 servants in this house — only to waste my money?"

No answer came, and he continued, growing more furious. "Mrs. Hamilton, did I not give specific orders that no visitors be allowed to see Georgiana except those specifically approved by me?"

"You did, sir."

"And did I revoke that order?"

"No, sir."

"Well, I am pleased to see that at least you heard me, even if you did not obey me. And how did my aunt obtain the information that Miss Bennet was in the house? Why was she given such details rather than a brief announcement that I was not in town and would return the next day?"

"Sir," interrupted Miles, "the doorman informed her ladyship, but he could not imagine that — "

"Imagine? Miles, what are you speaking of? Was it his duty to imagine things? And what of you, Miles? What important business kept you from interfering and settling the situation? "

Elizabeth could bear no more. "Mr. Darcy, please believe me that Miles, Mrs. Hamilton and John are not to blame. Lady Catherine would not have listened to them."

"Ahh, Miss Bennet, please come in. It is good that you are here."

He approached her and took her hand gently, but his tone was not a bit calmer. "Mrs. Hamilton, did anyone ask Miss Bennet's permission before allowing Lady Catherine into Georgiana's room?"

"No, sir."

"Mr. Darcy, please try to understand that, even if they had asked me, I would have had no reason to forbid your aunt to visit her niece. I never would have imagined that Lady Catherine could — "

"Perhaps. But even so, why did you agree to have that kind of conversation with her? Why did you not ask her to leave and return when I was at home? What could she possibly have said to put Georgiana into a state of shock that required her doctor's intervention?"

At this point, Lady Matlock's calm but determined voice interrupted him as the Lady stepped into the room with elegant grace.

"Darcy, why on earth are you yelling like that? Keep your voice down! Did you inherit that remarkable quality from your uncle and Lady Catherine? Do not blame your staff! You know as well as I do that Catherine cannot easily be stopped. Calm yourself and ask for a bath; you look awful."

His anger, heightened by fatigue and profound worry, was not easily released; his aunt's words did not have the desired effect.

"Lady Ellen, please do not interfere in this. I am the master of the house, and I am in no mood to be censured — not even by you."

Lady Matlock slowly took a few steps closer, looking at him thoughtfully before speaking with the same imperturbable elegance.

"You may be in no mood, but you are in great need of being censured! And do not raise your voice to me, young man; I slapped Robert for far less a few days ago, and you must know that I have always treated you as my son."

He gazed at her, incredulous and disconcerted, moving his eyes from Elizabeth to Mrs. Hamilton to Miles and back to his aunt while he felt as embarrassed as would a small boy; he had not the smallest doubt that she, indeed, would do as she declared if necessary.

"Lady Ellen, you must agree with me that this situation could have been avoided. Miles and Mrs. Hamilton have been in my family's employ for more than 15 years, and they know my aunt only too well. They disobeyed my orders. Miss Bennet did not handle the situation well enough either, but I cannot blame her as she was inexperienced in this matter."

It was Elizabeth's turn to cast him a stern, wondering glare, pulling her hand from his. He turned to her, his voice calmer, smiling at her with a superior, conceited understanding.

"Do not be upset, my dear; I know you had the best intentions. However, you must learn that being kind, generous and attentive are not always enough to be a good mistress. There are moments when you must show determination, toughness and severity; and you certainly must learn how to have your staff obey your wishes."

Elizabeth continued to stare at him, her eyes like flint.

"Thank you, Mr. Darcy, for pointing out my deficiencies so clearly. I shall always keep your meaningful words in mind. And now, if you will excuse me, I must return to Georgiana; *she* might need me."

She proceeded from the room without a backward glance.

Lady Matlock inclined her head, vastly amused.

"Well, Darcy, she just slapped you — harder and more painfully than I would have done! Oh, for God's sake, Nephew, try to discern the particulars before making a complete fool of yourself. Mrs. Hamilton and Miles might help you on that score."

Half an hour later, Mr. Darcy entered Georgiana's room, barely daring to lift his eyes to Elizabeth. She was sitting on the bed, holding Georgiana's hand in hers and caressing it gently while the girl was lost in sleep. On the other side of the bed, Lady Matlock was caressing her niece's hair.

Darcy was torn between the pain of seeing his sister in such a state and the shameful mortification for his unjust words to Elizabeth. He kneeled near the bed and gently, tentatively, took hold of the joined hands of the women he loved most. Elizabeth did not look at him or move her hand in his — nor did she pull her hand away.

Only few minutes later, Georgiana's sleep became agitated, and senseless whispers escaped her dry lips. Darcy moved towards her and called her name until she opened her eyes and, with obvious effort, searched the room to understand who was there. Her brother's presence seemed to calm her, and she turned from Elizabeth to her aunt. She forced herself to smile shyly at them.

"I am so sorry! I gave you so much trouble again. Please forgive me."

"Well, my dear," answered her aunt, "indeed you gave us much trouble. Can you imagine that, because of you, I am still wearing the same clothes as I was this morning? I do not think that has ever happened before."

Instead of raising her spirits, the teasing comment seemed to release a dam in Georgiana. She suddenly turned to her brother and began to cry. "Oh, William, did you know that it was all my fault? If not for me, Mother would still be alive. It was I who took Mother from you."

Before Darcy's surprise allowed him to answer, Lady Matlock's severe voice startled them all.

"Georgiana, do not say that any more. It is the most ridiculous thing I have ever heard."

"It is the truth! Aunt Catherine told me. She said that Father... My mother should not have had me..."

"Georgiana, stop that nonsense this instant! Your words would make your mother suffer more than anything else!"

Lady Matlock turned her back to them, fighting her own tears as Georgiana sobbed. When she regained her composure, she gave her niece a strange look and then addressed her nephew.

"Darcy, please leave us! I must speak to Georgiana privately."

He hesitated only a moment before obeying, his aunt's intense stare worrying him even more. "Aunt — "

"Darcy, please leave — now. You cannot be part of this talk. It is not for you." Lady Matlock's gravity left Darcy with no arguments; he left the room reluctantly, followed closely by Elizabeth, who assumed the demand to leave included her, too.

"Elizabeth, you may stay if you wish. Your company would be most welcome. It will be a talk between the ladies of this family." Elizabeth glanced quickly at Mr. Darcy and then returned to his aunt, thanking her, deeply grateful for being invited to share in their private conversation.

As soon as the door closed, Lady Matlock sat on the bed, her back against the pillow and her legs stretched out in front of her; she invited Elizabeth to do the same. When they were sitting on either side of Georgiana, she gently put her arm around her niece's shoulder and started to speak.

"Georgiana, did you understand the meaning of what Catherine said about your parents? About your father imposing himself on Anne?" The girl nodded, mortified, her face completely white.

"Good. Because I want to talk to you as I would talk to another woman, not to my little niece." Lady Matlock's voice was full of emotion, a slight tremor changing her usual tone. Her effort was obvious.

"Anne was my dearest friend; you must know that. And the most important thing I can tell you about her was that her life was full of love and happiness. Love for William, for you, and for your father. She loved all of you with a full heart until the last moment of her life. She told me that her only regret was that she had no more time to love you a little longer. She called you her treasure and her joy. As for your father… I have no words to tell you how much he loved Anne. Do not let anybody even suggest that your father might have done something against your mother's will. He would rather have died than hurt her! He tried everything humanly possible to save her, and I can certainly say that he gladly would have given his life to save hers. But it was not meant to be. Nothing could help her. She simply died, slowly…"

"But, Aunt, she became ill after I was born. Aunt Catherine said it was well known that she could not survive giving birth to another child. She should not have had me…"

"Oh dear, Catherine knows nothing and speaks only nonsense. She and Anne never confided in each other. And nobody could say for certain that having you aggravated her state. She died more than a year later."

"Perhaps, Aunt, but… if not for me, she would have lived longer. If she had taken better care of herself… If father had taken better care of her…"

"My dearest, I want to confide something very important, something that will help you have a better understanding of the situation. Before having my sons, I was with child twice. Each time, I carried the child until the end, and each time I gave birth to a girl, but both my daughters were born dead. And each time I was close to death myself. The doctors warned me that I must protect myself from having another child because my life would have been in great danger, but I did not listen. Moreover, I concealed the gravity of my condition from Lord Matlock. I loved my husband with all my heart, and I wanted to have a child born from our love. I never considered that wish could cost me my life. God has been good to me, and He made a miracle — two miracles. Now, 30 years later, I am healthy, and I pride myself on my two sons. Every danger I put myself in was nothing compared to the happiness I shared with my husband all these years."

She stopped and kissed her niece's forehead.

"As for your mother, dearest, she never was of a strong constitution although she was full of life. Her laugh was the most beautiful laugh I have ever known. Maybe, instead of thinking that Anne died because of your birth, you should think that your birth was a gift from God, a miracle the Lord sent to her before taking her to Him. And that must be the case, because you look so much like her. I cannot tell you with certainty whether her health would have changed if you had not been born. But I can tell you that your mother would have been less happy without you — as would we all."

Georgiana put her arms around her aunt, leaning her head on her shoulder. On her other side, Elizabeth had long since ceased fighting her tears, pleased that at least Georgiana could not see her. Suddenly, she felt the girl's hand squeezing hers as Georgiana pleaded with her aunt.

"Would you please tell us more about Mother? Elizabeth does not know anything about her, and I can never hear enough."

"Of course I would, dear. I too cannot speak enough about her."

AN HOUR LATER, GEORGIANA FELL asleep, a peaceful, deep sleep, her face brightened by a smile that followed her into her dreams.

Lady Matlock returned to her house, drained and exhausted by the emotions she had endured. Once in her bed, she cried for a long time. She could not sleep until her husband came to her, worried and pained by her grief, and she finally found some rest in his arms.

Although Georgiana's state seemed to be completely improved, Elizabeth did not leave her side. Her thoughts were with her own parents, of the joy and happiness of her life, of her mother...

Sleep surrounded her after midnight as she sat on the chair, her head resting against Georgiana's.

She did not speak with Darcy again, but she dreamed of him — of how he came to her, wrapped her in his arms, kissed her face, and carried her away. The dream was so vivid that she inhaled his scent and heard his heartbeat.

Only when she felt a cool, soft sheet and the warmth of his arms releasing her, did she wake. She opened her eyes slowly and saw his dark gaze, inches away, resting on her.

Chapter 21

The clock had long since struck midnight, but Darcy paced his room, wondering what to do and blaming himself for the day's events.

He could not imagine what Lady Matlock had told Georgiana, but he did trust his aunt, and his gratitude toward her increased at her gesture of inviting Elizabeth to join them. Impatiently, an hour after his aunt had ushered him out of the room, he approached the door and opened it a few inches — only to listen to the tone of the conversion. To his utter amazement, he could hear his sister asking questions in a carefree voice as though nothing had happened. Relieved, he had closed the door and returned to his room. Everything seemed to be fine again but not due to his efforts. He had done nothing to make things right — quite the contrary. Lady Matlock knew what was appropriate in any circumstance while he only pretended to make things right — largely due to his pride and selfishness.

He felt painfully that, in character, he was too much like his uncle the earl and his Aunt Catherine. His temper and manners had offended people in the past, too — albeit unintentionally. He was not able to give sufficient attention to others' feelings, not even to those he loved deeply.

Lady Matlock had left some time ago, and her look towards him as she departed clearly demonstrated that she was displeased with him and deservedly so. She had said earlier in the library that she would slap him if necessary. At that moment, he had been furious with her for humiliating him in front of the servants and Elizabeth. Nobody had ever slapped him in his life or dared to address him in such a manner.

However, when Miles related to him every detail of his aunt's accusations and Elizabeth's reactions to them, his anger grew exponentially against Lady Catherine and himself. He concluded that, though he deserved any humiliation that came his way, it would still not be sufficient punishment for his despicable behaviour.

Each minute that passed made his feelings of guilt stronger. *Elizabeth*... He had not talked to her since she left him hours earlier. He remembered taking her hand in Georgiana's room and her lack of response to his touch. He was grateful she did not withdraw her hand. She understood his grief and did not want to increase it. She generously allowed him the comfort he needed, despite the fact that he had offended her so undeservedly.

Miles's words and the admiration in his voice as he spoke of the manner in which Elizabeth reacted to Lady Catherine's attack made him even more proud of her and ashamed of himself. He had been an arrogant fool, and only that night — spending the last few hours alone in his room — had he fully understood that. Now, he could not cease asking himself whether he deserved her love and devotion.

Her simple gesture of remaining loyal to Georgiana after she had been so abominably abused by his aunt and unfairly censured by him hurt him more than any harsh words she might toss his way. Any other woman would have left the house instantly if she had been so grossly insulted. Instead, Elizabeth had verbally 'slapped' him in the library — an elegant though more painful punishment — and then simply returned to her duties. Georgiana needed her, and that was more important to her than her own pride.

Darcy realised that, as much as he presumed to love and admire her, every moment with Elizabeth confirmed to him that he was doing her a great injustice; she deserved more. Not only was she worthy of him and his name, she was superior to him in many ways.

Darcy knew he could not hope to obtain Elizabeth's forgiveness easily. He even considered that she might postpone the wedding because of his arrogance. Only a few days before she had expressed her fears about the wedding date being too soon. Now, he only proved to her that her doubts were justified. He was not the man she believed him to be.

He left his room and went in search of her. He entered Georgiana's apartment quietly so as not to disturb her, his intention to inquire of the maid after Elizabeth and be certain she was well.

An acute pain twisted his heart when he saw Elizabeth fast asleep in a chair by Georgiana's bed, her head lying near the pillows. Nodding to Mrs. Annesley, who was resting in an armchair in a corner, he lifted Elizabeth into his arms, fearful that she might awaken and reject him. He wanted nothing more than to take her to the comfort of her room, as he could imagine how exhausted she was.

Carrying her with great care so as not to wake her, he felt her arms encircle his neck and her head nestle against his chest. Obviously, she was doing this in her sleep and was clearly not aware of her actions. He shivered at the thought that she might open her eyes, and he would see nothing more than disdain and anger in her eyes. He knew he deserved it, but he also knew he could not bear to see it.

Lowering his head as he walked down the hall to her room, he placed light kisses in her hair and on her forehead. He heard her murmur contentedly and felt her tighten the grip around his neck; whether it was a reaction to him or only a dream, he could not tell.

Darcy entered the room she had been given — one of the family apartments — and gently put her on the bed, wanting to ease his arms from around her without disturbing her, but she seemed unwilling to let him go, instead drawing him closer. Not needing much encouragement, he yielded to her desire. He knelt near her bed, wrapping her closely in his embrace. His right arm was now under her neck and around her shoulders, but his left was still under her legs as he had been carrying her. He decidedly removed his arm — for its position was most improper — and simply rested it at her side.

Full of remorse for everything she had endured that day and overwhelmed with the love that was melting his heart and the happiness of holding her closely, he simply remained still and gazed at her beautiful, sleeping face.

A few moments later, her long lashes moved slightly, and his eyes were suddenly mirrored in hers. No words were spoken; no words were needed for each to understand the other.

His grief increased at the sight of her eyes — usually vivid, joyful, and ready to express any emotion — searching his face gravely. Then, slowly, her right hand rose and gently stroked his face. She smiled.

"How is Georgiana? We must not leave her alone."

"Georgiana is fine, Elizabeth. She is sleeping soundly. Mrs. Annesley is with her now. She will not be alone for a moment; do not worry."

"And you? How are you, William? Are you feeling well?"

He looked at her incredulously. "You ask me how I am?"

"Should I not?"

"No, you should not. I do not deserve your concern. You should be furious with my family and me. When I think of the mortification you have suffered from my own aunt… And I was not here to protect you as I should have been… Even worse, I behaved unforgivably and offended you further."

As his words increased in vehemence, her hand continuously stroked his cheek and temple, until it found its way to his hair. Her caresses gently pulled him closer. He could see the light of the candles reflecting as sparkles in her eyes and a smile spreading on her lips.

His words sounded so childish — and completely honest — that Elizabeth could feel nothing but the deepest tenderness towards him.

"I was and I still am angry, William. I am angry with your aunt for the distress she caused Georgiana. She offended me in front of your sister, Mrs. Hamilton and Miles, and her voice could be heard in Cheapside."

She paused, her countenance solemn and her voice tentative as she continued, her gaze deepening in the darkness of his eyes. "I was also hurt by your presumption and lack of trust. I might not be accustomed to running a household such as yours, but I dare say I can confront anyone who would threaten me or those I care about. Well... that is... I used to think I could until your words prompted my doubts."

"Elizabeth — "

"No, please, let me finish. I do not blame you for saying or believing that; in fact, I am grateful the occasion arose so you could voice your opinion. Now I wonder if we are doing the right thing in marrying so soon. Perhaps we should wait until we know each other better and any doubts are assuaged."

"Elizabeth, I have no doubts. I never have been more certain of anything than my love for you. I have never wanted anything more than for you to be my wife."

"William, neither your love nor your desire to marry me is what concerns me — of that I am certain. But without your trust, would love be enough for us to have a strong marriage? Would it not be wiser to wait until you are certain that I would be able to honour your name and the position as your wife?"

Her words were cutting his heart more painfully than a sword. She spoke without passion or anger but in earnest and with a calmness that frightened him. Only at that moment did he understand how deeply his foolish reproaches had affected her and what torment she felt because of it.

She had behaved faultlessly, but he had made her doubt her own abilities and their future compatibility. He was still grateful for one thing: Now that she had expressed her own fears, he knew how to comfort her.

He took her hand in his as he caressed her nape and the line of her jaw, gliding his fingers over the skin of her shoulder. He could feel her shiver under his touch, but her eyes never lost their sadness.

"My love, I cannot tell you how much I regret my reaction. And I will not even try to apologise; I do not deserve your forgiveness. I put myself at your mercy to decide what you wish me to do next, but you completely misunderstood my meaning. I do trust you, more than I have ever trusted anyone. I deeply value your opinion, and I have the greatest confidence in your intelligence and judgment. I know that you may lack experience, but you excel in good sense. You are everything and more than I ever dreamed of in a wife."

"Is this your true opinion? Then why — ?"

"Why did I lay the blame on you and my loyal servants? Because I am an arrogant fool with a horrible temper. I hurried to place blame on others when no one but me can be held responsible for what happened. I should have told Lady Catherine long ago that I did not intend to marry Anne. I should have insisted that she not entertain such a hope, but I did not. I was content simply to ignore her every time I was in her company. Your and Georgiana's sufferings were due to my lack of consideration."

Her fingers toyed with his hair as her eyes expressed the mixture of feelings his words aroused in her. Darcy knelt near her bed, properly humbled. He silently enjoyed the pleasure her tender ministrations afforded him, allowing his own fingers to entwine in the heavy locks of her silky hair. Smiling bitterly, he shook his head as he continued.

"And the most hateful thing is that I really believed I was correct in my reproaches. I impulsively and foolishly presumed that your generosity and kindness undermined your determination in handling the situation. And I did not hesitate to accuse Mrs. Hamilton and Miles — two people who have never failed to comply with my wishes — of not being diligent enough in preventing the situation.

He paused a moment, breathing deeply, before an important confession.

"However, you must understand it was not you I did not trust, but any and everybody except myself. My selfish pride made me think that everything went wrong because of my absence. To my egocentric mind, it was one more proof that nobody could take care of a situation as well as I could. And your reaction, Elizabeth, was deservedly harsh, though properly directed. As Lady Ellen said, with a few words, you *'slapped'* me harder than anyone has ever done before."

"Slapped you? I know my words were impertinent, especially considering we were in company — but I never thought they would be taken so harshly — "

"You were not impertinent. You reacted reasonably and fairly to my arrogant presumption and unjust criticism. You will rightly hate me when I tell you that, even when you closed the door behind you, I felt no regret for my words. All I thought was, *'She might be offended now, but this will be a useful lesson for her in the future.'* What do you think of me now? I would expect you to yell at me. I deserve nothing less."

Elizabeth could not fully comprehend the meaning of his words as his statements seemed occasionally to contradict themselves. He seemed determined to condemn himself. He called himself selfish and foolish, and spoke scornfully of his 'horrible pride.' What she truly understood though — and dearly hoped she was correct — was that he trusted her more than he trusted any other woman; it was reason enough for her spirits to rise, an open smile lightening her countenance as her eyes began to brighten with mirth.

"Thank you for offering me the opportunity to act in so unladylike a manner, William. But may I please yell at you tomorrow? I am so tired that I can hardly speak. Besides, I dare say there has been enough shouting for one day, and the staff already have been entertained amply by our antics."

She could hardly restrain her laughter, but he remained grave.

"Elizabeth, I know what you are trying to do. Generously, you want to lighten my spirits, but I cannot reconcile myself so easily to my behaviour. Knowing that I have hurt you pains me most. I cannot tell you how I hated myself in the minutes after you left the library when I found how abominably you had been offended. Mrs. Hamilton and Miles's admiration for you only made me more ashamed, seeing how ridiculous all my pretensions of superiority have been. Your admirable rebuttal to Lady Catherine's attack and your gentle care for Molly have raised you more in their esteem in one day than most women could have accomplished in years. And you have been more considerate with them than I ever could have been because I do not possess either your generosity or your kindness. I recognised my error and apologised to Mrs. Hamilton and Miles, but how can I apologise to you? Now, it is I who must ask whether your love will be enough for you to suffer marriage to a man like me."

His words left them both on the brink of tears. His heart was breaking, thinking of all the pain he had caused her. Her soul melted, burdened by his sadness. Both needed release from their pain. And Elizabeth knew that nothing could bring them comfort and alleviate their sorrow better than their mutual trust in the strength of their love. He had done nothing for which she could not forgive him.

"William... please, come closer to me. I want you to hold me — no apologies, no more discussion about this."

He looked at her, afraid he might misunderstand her meaning.

"Please... " Slowly, without taking his eyes from hers, he lay on the bed beside her; she nestled her head on his chest, encircling his waist with one arm. He wrapped her tighter in his embrace, kissing her hair, afraid to believe she had forgiven him.

Darcy could not say how long their blissful peace lasted, as he did not want to think of anything but the undeserved happiness of being allowed to lie next to her. He could hear and feel their hearts beating together.

"Elizabeth, I cannot stop wondering how it is possible for two people to share a love that is so strong yet so different in nature."

"Different? Why would you say that?"

"Because it is the truth. My love is as selfish and arrogant as I am. I demand so much from you and give you so little in return. I want nothing more than to be with you, and I care for few things except this. Your love is generous and kind; you give me not only your heart but so much more. Your affection and your presence in my house are a blessing not only for me but also for so many around me: my sister, Lady Ellen who finally found someone to accept and be pleased with — even for my staff. All of us have gained so much from you."

"I must utterly contradict you. What I have constantly wondered in the last fortnight is how I have been so fortunate as to secure the love of such a remarkable man. It is I who have gained from our love and engagement. I am so deeply grateful for your affection and proud to know you will be my husband! You are truly the best man I have ever known — despite your horrible pride and your bad temper!"

The last words were spoken in jest, trying to hide that she was fighting her emotions. His arms embraced her more closely as his lips placed tender kisses and whispers in her hair.

"Elizabeth, I will use every moment of our life to make you proud of my love. I do hope I can offer you as much happiness as you have given me."

"You need not worry about that. I am happier than I ever could have dreamed or hoped to be. I have always wished to marry a man I could deeply love, but until now, I never imagined what such a deep love would mean. And may I tell you what I think, William? That each of us has given the other what we most needed. We are not different; our love is not different. We are just completing each other in every sense."

"So true, my love! You complete my being and my whole life. And do not think I speak in jest when I say that my love and happiness grow stronger each day."

"I am happy I can make you happy, Mr. Darcy."

Her voice was grave with an inflection he did not hear often. She reached up to his face and kissed him tentatively, barely touching his dry lips. He did not make a single move, waiting for her to do as she pleased.

Slowly, she grew more daring, placing small kisses on his closed mouth, chin, and the line of his jaw; then, to her astonishment, she returned to his lips — still dry and closed — her tongue brushing slightly against them, passionately testing them until, moist and thirsty for her, his lips parted to welcome her warm tongue.

His deep moans made her tremble, and her kiss grew more demanding; it was the first time she initiated kissing him while he remained still, lying on his back, surrendering completely to her desire. Her caresses became as daring as her kisses; her hands lowered from his face to his neck and then to his chest, every touch matching the rhythm of her lips. With wonder, she discovered a new kind of power she possessed over him: the power of having him at her mercy and at the mercy of the pleasure she was offering him.

His groans at her touch only increased her desire to offer him more. Barely conscious of what she was doing, she leaned closer until her body was lying atop his, pressing against his entire length. Only then did she feel him move beneath her, his hands gliding around her waist.

His lips were no longer passive, and the kiss quickly turned into a passionate dance, ending in complete harmony. Every fibre of her body was burning at the feeling of his fingers stroking her, sliding the length of her bare arms up to her shoulders, her neck and then down to her waist again; she did nothing to stop his caresses. She only abandoned herself to the growing pleasure his hands were giving her.

She could hear her own moans, and her mind briefly noted how improper she sounded, but her modesty lasted only a moment. Every rational thought vanished when his hands slid a little lower than her waist, pressing her tightly against him. He did not insist further; his caress returned to her arms, but her body remained pressed against his in the most intimate embrace she had ever experienced.

She moved slightly, brushing against him, and was startled to hear him groan so deeply and loudly that she was certain she was hurting him. His lips withdrew only enough to whisper in the same tone at the edge of passion and pain, "Elizabeth...

We must stop this... now..." but a moment later her mouth was imprisoned again, and his hands resumed their torturous mission, more demanding, embracing her in a restless, moving circle of fire, burning every part of her body.

His arms, tightly entwined around her, took her breath away, and a moment later, her heart nearly stopped when his fingers, gliding up along her ribs, touched the sides of her breasts. The sensation, so new and powerful, froze her, and she was shocked to hear her barely recognisable voice pleading, "William, please..."

She did not know what she was pleading for. She could not decide whether she was asking him to stop or begging for more, but he did not ask for clarification; he chose to do what he believed to be best for her.

Darcy stopped all movement and reluctantly broke the kiss, his lips placing countless light kisses over her face before moving slightly away from her. He cupped her face toward him so he could stare into her eyes, marvelling to see her aglow with passion. Then he gently pulled her head down to rest against his chest while he embraced her again, both of them struggling to regain their senses.

No sound disturbed the tense silence for many long moments. Elizabeth was still lying atop him, and as soon as she recovered enough to think properly, she resumed her previous position beside him, suddenly embarrassed by what had resulted from her own desires and not daring to touch him or meet his gaze. She felt his finger removing a lock of hair from her neck and lingering on her cheek.

"Elizabeth... are you upset with me?"

"Upset with you? Why would I be upset? It was I who started this — "

"Because I was too bold. I should have been grateful and content for your mere forgiveness. Instead, I took advantage of you though I know you are exhausted and what you really need is a peaceful rest."

"No, you did not take advantage... quite the contrary. And I thank you for being so kind to me."

He could barely understand her whispered words, yet it was easy to notice the embarrassment in her voice. He was not certain what he should do next; he knew instinctively that he should leave and let her rest, but he could not bear to leave her in distress. Thus, instead of leaving, he gently took her hands in his; he was content to feel their fingers entwining.

"Elizabeth, you said you are not upset with me. Then will you not tell me what is troubling you?"

"Please do not ask me... I could not bear to speak about it. I am so ashamed to think of what I have done."

He lifted her face to hold her gaze and smiled at her, his thumb brushing against her lips.

"Are you ashamed of kissing me, Elizabeth? I have kissed *you* many times before. Should *I* feel ashamed for that? Because I confess, I do not. The only thing that could give me more pleasure than kissing you is you kissing me as you did. Your sweet passion and tender caresses…"

With great effort, she managed to meet his gaze though her cheeks coloured highly. "Oh please, William, do not remind me of that! And it is not the same as when you kissed me! You are a man, and it is perfectly natural for you to… demand this kind of attention. But a woman must be completely wanton to behave as I did." She diverted her eyes again, shaking her head in shame at her lack of restraint and decorum.

Darcy did not know whether to be amused or worried. Hoping he understood her well enough, he decided on the former. "And pray tell me, what do you know about a wanton woman's behaviour, Miss Bennet?" His efforts to lighten her spirits were obvious, but he did not succeed easily.

"I know enough…"

"Indeed? And would you be so kind as to share your knowledge with me?" His countenance was mirthful at that moment though her distress did not seem to diminish.

In fact, his last question quickly raised her interest and changed her mood. Arching her eyebrow wonderingly at him, she could not lose the opportunity to inquire further.

"Do you pretend yourself ignorant on this subject, Mr. Darcy?"

Her question made his lips twist into a mischievous little smile while his eyes were wearing the expression that always tormented her. "I do not pretend to be ignorant on the subject, Miss Bennet. I was only curious to discover how a proper gentleman's daughter knows 'enough' about this topic. I would also be curious to know under what circumstances you acquired this knowledge."

He was teasing her, and she grew the tiniest bit angry. She had trapped herself in this web of questions that could not have an answer, and she tried to find an escape that might help her throw his teasing back at him. She had no time to find anything as he continued, his lips moving closer to her ear.

"You should know by now, Miss Bennet, that I can hardly be called ignorant on any subject of importance to a gentleman."

She almost chuckled at this statement, but his warm whispers were burning her skin, and she swallowed deeply in an attempt to concentrate on what she wanted to say. She could not lose the opportunity of extracting a little revenge, which he — generously though unwillingly — afforded her.

"You are correct, sir. I should have known that by now; but apparently, I am not as perceptive as other young ladies are. And I dare say it is your fault, too; instead of helping me to improve myself, you only deceived me, grossly and purposely, all these months since we met."

He did recognise her teasing tone — as he had fallen victim to it many times — but her reference to his deceiving her worried him, and he withdrew his face from hers again so he could search her features carefully.

She met his gaze, and the expression of worry on his face drew a hidden smile from her eyes. He was correct when he had said he put himself at her mercy. She had the power to toy with him if she desired, even in those moments when he believed he was in control. And at that moment, she did enjoy the game.

"Elizabeth, I do not understand your meaning. I have never deceived you, at least not willingly."

"Well, from your earlier confession, it appears that your own opinion about the impeccability of your character secretly matches perfectly with Miss Bingley's opinion on the subject. Apparently, both of you agree that you are a man without fault and therefore closer to perfection than any other human being. Perhaps you should reconsider the offer you made to me and ask for Miss Bingley's hand instead. In doing so, you would assure yourself many hours of praise each day, not to mention you would have someone to mend your pen remarkably well any time you should require it."

The emotions displayed on his face as he finally understood her were too much for her to bear, and she burst out in such a loud laugh that she buried her head against his chest, afraid that a servant would hear her from the hall.

Without completely realising what was happening, she felt herself tumbled over, and in the next moment, she was on her back, almost trapped beneath him. He was leaning on his side, holding her playfully and just firmly enough to prevent her from getting up, obviously enjoying his sense of power over her.

Elizabeth continued to laugh, staring closely into his dark eyes. She could feel the weight of his body, and his hands tightened their grip in her hair, pinning her head to the pillow. She was at his mercy, but she deeply trusted him and knew she had nothing to fear.

"So, Elizabeth, are you making fun of me? You believe me to be not only an arrogant fool but a stupid, haughty conceited one, too, am I correct?"

"Sir, I will confess to only half of your accusations. I am, indeed, making fun of you, but I never would dare say any of those horrible things."

"Really? But you do believe that I need hours of praise each day?"

"That I must admit to as well. And if I cannot persuade you to break our engagement, I will be obliged to ask Miss Bingley to teach me the particular compliments you appreciate most."

Again, she burst into laughter while he tried to maintain a serious countenance and a grave tone.

"I dare say, Miss Bennet, you are very impudent for someone trapped in such a precarious situation. I might lose my patience after being laughed at in such an impolite manner. I might be tempted to think of a harsh punishment, and you could do nothing but accept it. You could not possibly consider fighting against me."

"Oh, do not try to frighten me by speaking so menacingly, Mr. Darcy. My spirits always rise in the face of a challenge. And the only one in a precarious situation is you, sir. You can depend on it that I will tease you about this every time I find an opportunity. Moreover, I fully intend to tell Georgiana and Lady Ellen as well."

"No, you will not, because I intend to silence you for as long as I can."

No other answer was possible; her mouth was trapped, and she completely surrendered to his kiss as her hands found their well-known path into his hair.

He leaned slowly covering her body a little at a time, giving her the chance to protest if she wanted to, until he completely lay atop her, careful not to allow his weight to overwhelm her.

She did not protest, as she did not remember any of those feelings of guilt she had declared only a few minutes earlier. This novel and unexpected form of embrace aroused new and mixed feelings inside her; her mind and body were reacting equally strongly and were allowing him to conquer her; she felt dominated and protected at the same time, not capable of deciding whether she was enjoying the sensation of his power or feeling frightened by it. At that moment, nothing seemed as important as the happiness of being overwhelmed by his love, his closeness, his caress, and the novelty of the increasing intimacy they shared.

She knew they again were going dangerously beyond the limits of acceptable behaviour for an engaged couple. Yet, she banished her shame and guilt; she knew that their love — and passion — were also far beyond what most engaged couples shared.

His body seemed stronger and heavier than she would imagine, almost crushing her, and she tried to move beneath him. She heard him groan again and whisper her name, and she understood that her movements caused a strange and powerful reaction in him, though she did not know enough to understand what it was. She did not have time to wonder though, as her mind registered little except his lips, which had begun a moist, warm journey down to her throat and lower, tantalising her with a sweet torture. Her whole body was arching from waves of cold shivers travelling inside her, and she gasped loudly when his tongue tasted her, tracing a line of fire along her throat until he met with the edge of her dress. He stopped there without any attempt to go further, but his kisses covered every bare inch of her soft skin, caressing and tasting, his hunger for her becoming more intense with each passing moment.

In the middle of their ardent interlude, a strange noise from her drew Darcy's attention and made him stop in an instant. He gazed at her wonderingly as her face coloured highly with embarrassment.

"Elizabeth....was that your stomach groaning with hunger?"

She nodded, half amused and half mortified that such a thing could happen at such a romantic and passionate time. He put his open palm on her stomach and then lowered his head to bestow small kisses on her lips, cheeks, and forehead.

He broke their embrace, rising to his feet; their arms withdrew reluctantly from around each other.

"Miss Bennet, this cannot be. After forcing you to suffer offences today, it now seems we have decided to starve you as well."

She began to laugh heartily, rising to a sitting position.

"Do not even think that you will go anywhere outside this room, Miss Bennet. I will have someone bring you something to eat and assist you in preparing yourself for the night. You have to start paying attention to yourself for a change. Or better, you must allow me to give you all the attention you deserve..."

He paused and met her questioning glance, her eyebrow raised in such a sweet challenge that he could not help laughing and placing a tender kiss upon it. "Yes, I understand your silent reproach, Miss Bennet. Allow me to make amends. What I have in mind is a different kind of attention — more proper and useful for your present state of fatigue."

"Why, thank you for clarifying, sir; I was wondering whether you were by any chance flirting with me?"

"No, I am not flirting. I am very worried for you, Elizabeth. Please forgive me for not being more attentive to your needs until now." He stretched out his hand to grasp her palm and kissed it gently.

"Should I send someone to help you undress and ready yourself for the night?"

"No, indeed, there is no need to awaken anyone for me; everyone is tired after this difficult day. I can manage to prepare myself. And you must not disturb yourself either. I will just go to sleep and eat in the morning."

He did not listen to her; instead, he went to the door and looked over his shoulder.

"I will return shortly. I want to find you in your night robe, and you will eat as much as I deem necessary."

DARCY RETURNED A QUARTER OF an hour later, carrying a plate with more food than she could eat in days. She was nestled in the middle of the bed, already dressed in her nightgown, her unpretentious night robe covering her properly. Her hair was flowing freely down her shoulders in a cascade of dark silky curls, and Darcy remained at the door, simply staring at her. Her appearance — so simple in its beauty — took his breath away.

"William, why on earth did you bring so much food? Who do you think will eat all of it?"

"You will, and if you can bear my company a little longer, I would like to join you. I did not have a proper dinner, either."

"Of course, Mr. Darcy! I would love to dine at this late hour in your company. However, if you stay a little longer, we could have breakfast as well. Do you know it is already three hours past midnight?"

"Yes, I know. We will have to enjoy a hasty, late dinner. And I absolutely insist that you tell me one thing: The first time you met Georgiana, I found you eating with her and laughing at something. I must have my share in it, for I have the impression it was something important."

A new cascade of laughter followed his inquiry, and it took much more pleading before she finally agreed to tell him the little story.

More than an hour later, they finished the meal. That dreadful day remained somewhere behind them, all the pain and suffering it brought vanishing slowly, swept away by a new sunrise. They sat in the middle of the bed, their legs curled under them, the tray of food between them. They ate with their bare hands, sharing things they both favoured and exchanging bits of food with each other. The simple pleasure of another intimate moment often mixed with little proofs of their restrained passion. His lips tasted food from hers countless times, made her blush constantly and caused him to long for the moment when they would have the right to share everything forever.

"Elizabeth, you know this is the only time in my life I have had dinner with someone in a private room? Not to mention in bed..."

She lifted her eyes to him, trying to understand the meaning of his words.

"You mean...with a lady?" She blushed slightly at her daring question.

He laughed at this new attempt to receive an answer without asking the question.

"No, I mean with anyone, including my family. Even when Georgiana was ill, I used to stay with her and supervise her meals, but I never actually ate with her, only having some coffee or tea. Moreover, I do not remember having dinner anywhere but in the dining room, not even as a child."

She seemed content with his answer but looked as though she wanted to ask more. She returned her attention to the food, however, without further inquiries until they finally declared themselves satisfied. Darcy took the plate off the bed and then returned to sit next to her.

"My love, you should sleep now as it is almost morning. But I simply have to steal another moment of your time to do something I have desperately wanted to do since that day in the cottage."

Her eyes opened widely at him, a little darkened by fatigue, but sparkling with mirth at the memory of that day.

"What have you so desperately wanted to do since that day, William?"

He leaned slowly to her, whispering near her ear.

"This...among many other things..."

His thrust his fingers in her long hair and buried his face in her silky curls, allowing them to caress his face. His desire for her suddenly became so strong that he was afraid he would not be able to fight against it. He withdrew gently, his hands cupping her face while his long fingers were still entwined in her hair. He gazed at her adoringly and smiled with tenderness.

"I will go now, my love. Come, I want to see you settled in bed, and you must promise you will try to sleep." She only nodded and leaned back slowly until she rested against the pillow.

He could feel her shiver, and it was clear that she shared his feelings. Her passion might have been more innocent than his, but it was no less strong. Pleased at each new discovery of his beloved, he gently stroked her forehead and bestowed a lingering kiss on it, then a light one on the tip of her nose. Carefully, he wrapped her in the counterpane. "Sleep well, my love."

"William?"

"Yes?"

"I was wondering... Could you please stay with me a few more minutes?"

"Of course, if you wish. I will leave after you fall asleep."

"Thank you."

He lay down near her, his arms embracing her closely, and she nestled her head on his chest as she had done earlier. The steady beating of his heart was like soothing music, which brought her long-needed rest. His hand stroking her hair made her feel as if she were dreaming, long before sleep enveloped her.

"Thank you, my love."

"What are you thanking me for, William?" Her hand encircled his waist while the other slid to the junction of his neck and shoulder.

"For everything. For your generous heart... for your care toward me and my family... for allowing me to love you... and for loving me so much... "

She lifted her face to stare into his eyes a moment; then she gently touched his lips with hers, answering simply, "You are very welcome, sir," making him chuckle.

"Now try to sleep... I will put more wood on the fire when I leave, and in the morning, a servant will come to take care of it so you will awake to a warm room. I am afraid this bedchamber might be a little cold since nobody has slept in it for the past few years."

She could not resist asking, "Whose room was this? Mrs. Hamilton told me it was one of the family's rooms."

"It was mine before I took the master suite. Nobody has lived here for the last five years."

"I see... I am happy you decided to offer it to me."

His lips lowered to whisper against her ear.

"Well... I thought it might be helpful for you to get accustomed to sleeping in my room." Though he could not see her face, he felt her stiffen in his arms, relaxing a few moments later. He chuckled again.

"Mr. Darcy, I think you delight in vexing me... as my mother would say."

"I confess I do, Miss Bennet. Teasing you back is even more pleasurable than being teased by you. Now sleep well, my dearest.

Her breath became steady a few moments later as a deep, restful sleep enveloped her, and she unconsciously nestled into his chest. Darcy remained near her, gently stroking her hair, watching her, amazed by the tumult and infinite variety of feelings this young woman could arouse in him. Her sleep seemed filled with dreams;

he could hear her whisper his name a few times while her hands seemed to search for him, wanting to be certain he had not left her. She was obviously feeling the effects of that difficult day. As strong and courageous as she was, she needed his protection, and he was willing to offer it along with anything else in the world she might need from him. Her movement caused her hair to tickle his face and his neck delightfully, and he could not help leaning his lips into it countless times. He was certain that, even in sleep, she could feel his slight touches as her lips were set with a continuous smile.

She moved again, shifting the covers from around her as though she were trying to cool herself. As she did so, her nightgown slid down from one shoulder. Mesmerised, his glance was drawn to her neck and lower, widening at the beauty of a creamy breast becoming free of the fabric, deliciously moving with every breath.

Every fibre of his body was screaming at him to touch it.

He knew he could do it and that she would not oppose him; she was asleep and likely would not know whether his touch was real or merely a dream. He could touch it, rest it in his palm; his fingers could close around it, and he knew it would fit perfectly. His eyes remained fixed on its perfect, light-pink centre, and he licked his lips, which were aching to taste her. Yes, he could do that, too; she would allow it, and her pleasure would be even greater than his. Why should he deny them such joy and pleasure when they could both rejoice in its delight? He was drawn back from his luscious thoughts by her moving again, her hand encircling his waist while her head found a better place on his chest. He heard her whisper against the place where his heart was beating, "I love you, William."

She was sleeping but also keeping him there: in her dreams, in her heart, and in her mind. His heart melted as remorse filled him again. *How can I be so selfish and inconsiderate? Even now, I am thinking of nothing but my own needs and desires. I do not deserve her love…* Gently, he pulled her gown back over her shoulder, covered her with the sheets, and embraced her lightly so he did not disturb her.

"Sleep well, my love."

He smiled to himself, suddenly struck by an amusing and wonderful revelation, which he decided to share with her… as soon as they were married.

Loving Elizabeth was similar to savouring the pleasure of a book. Every page of the book — every moment spent with her — caused him the joy of a new discovery, which only increased his pleasure and happiness. More than once, a wonderful, exciting book with a mysterious plot had tempted him to cheat and peek at the last page. To see the ending earlier was a great temptation, more so since he knew it was in his power to do so once the book was in his hands.

Similarly, his passion and overwhelming desire to have her tempted him to surrender to his need sooner than he should. Moreover, he knew he could do so if he wanted. He could see the final chapter of the first volume of the novel called 'Elizabeth.' Only a few minutes earlier, he had undoubtedly felt her surrendering to him and had known she would refuse him nothing in those passionate moments of incredible intimacy.

The selfish part of him could not help feeling satisfied at his power to dominate her — the power of choosing between what would satiate his desires and urges, and what was best for her.

However, a momentary completion was nothing compared to the long anticipated pleasure of enjoying the culmination at the right moment. The wait and the slow journey — page by page and step by step through that exquisite book — the mysteries slowly revealed to him and the knowledge gained while carefully reading it gave him infinitely more satisfaction than the immediate relief of passionate curiosity. He knew with certainty that the end could be nothing but marvellous. He was sure it would exceed his every dream and expectation. Even more so, he was already anxious to begin reading the next volume, which would start when Elizabeth became his wife.

Darcy rose from his place next to Elizabeth only when dawn appeared tentatively through the heavy curtains; he covered her as well as he could and, after checking on the fire, silently closed the door behind him. They had spent their first night together. Lady Catherine might have been content to know how helpful her visit had been.

Chapter 22

Though he did not sleep more than a couple of hours, Mr. Darcy woke early, well rested and with such a happy disposition that he began to hum a tune while enjoying his bath. Miles's eyebrows rose in astonishment, but he kept his wonder to himself. His master was not a man to share his feelings and surely not with a servant — even after a decade and a half of service.

Sometime later, Mr. Darcy was having his coffee in the library, scanning the newspaper and fully content with the reports he had received about Georgiana's current state of health. Mrs. Hamilton also had informed him that Molly's condition was more than satisfactory.

"Mrs. Hamilton, please do everything necessary for Molly and convey my best wishes and apologies to her. It is a shame that she was hurt due to the savagery of one of my own family members."

"I shall sir. I am sure she will be grateful to hear of your concern."

As Mrs. Hamilton returned to her duties, Colonel Fitzwilliam entered the library, without so much as an announcement or knock, and unceremoniously collapsed into an armchair.

"Good morning, Robert."

"Yes, Darcy, good morning. Although how good it might be is questionable. I just returned home an hour ago and had to escape, so let me pour myself a cup of coffee. Then give me something to eat, because I am starving! And for heaven's sake, tell me what happened yesterday, because nobody is giving me a full report."

"Why did you need to escape, Robert? Did someone chase you, of all people? And why did you not return until this morning? Where have you been?"

The colonel was utterly surprised by Darcy's obviously good mood. His father's house had been an utter disaster, and what few pieces of information he had gleaned had prepared him to find Darcy in similarly low spirits.

"I was out, Darcy. Young, unmarried, unattached men are in the habit of going out on occasion. I had been out since yesterday noon, and when I returned, I found Lady Catherine there — an angry Lady Catherine — arguing with an equally angry Lord Matlock. The worst situation possible! Honestly, it was more dangerous than a military battle! Mother and Anne were in their rooms, or so I was told. I tried to have a rational conversation with my father and my aunt, but I only started another quarrel, so I left. Thank heavens we do not keep the pistols and swords in that room!"

"I see… And what were they arguing about?"

"I asked first. Tell me the whole story, and only then will I oblige you."

"Very well, Cousin. You are entitled to know, but I warn you — it is not pleasant breakfast conversation."

Half an hour later the colonel had forgotten his hunger and determinedly poured himself a glass of brandy, earning a reproachful look from Darcy.

"Do you not think it a bit early for that, Cousin?"

"Oh, shut your mouth, Darcy. Are you sure Georgiana is well now?"

"Yes, the doctor just left. She slept well, and there is nothing to be worried about. I am utterly grateful to Lady Ellen for her assistance last night… If not for her… Pray tell me, how is my aunt today? Did you speak with her?"

"I did speak with her but only briefly. Apparently, she did not feel well this morning, or perhaps she just wanted to avoid the battlefield, though avoiding confrontation is generally not in her character."

"Indeed it is not. I hope she is only tired from the previous day's turmoil."

"I hope so too, Darcy. I will return home to check on her." He swallowed some brandy before continuing. "Now it is my turn. So… I returned home early and, surprisingly, found Father and Aunt Catherine having breakfast. They were hardly eating, rather speaking to each other harshly. Of course, it was easy to guess the reason for our aunt's visit to Town, but I feigned ignorance and tried to start a polite conversation. What followed was a torrent of 'interesting' opinions about you, Miss Bennet and your engagement. Then, suddenly, the earl said, 'Catherine, I cannot help wondering how on earth you can spout off so much nonsense in such a short time. In this, you are truly proficient.'"

Darcy's mouth opened wide as he stared at his cousin.

"The earl said that?"

"Yes he did. Can you imagine? And Lady Catherine answered as she always does, 'You have become as impertinent and improper as your wife.' So Father demanded an apology for speaking in that manner about Lady Ellen or she would be asked to leave the house."

"Hmm… Lord Matlock surprises me, I grant him that. And…?"

"Why would he surprise you? The earl would never allow anyone to speak an unkind word — not to mention be rude — about Lady Ellen. But of course, Lady Catherine considered she was the injured party, and she sent for Anne and their belongings."

"Poor Anne. Have they already gone? I confess I am disappointed because I intended to assure myself a private meeting with Lady Catherine. I cannot allow her to remain under the impression that she can enter my house and spew such offences at my intended. I never would permit that, nor would I ever forget or forgive her for them. I will not permit anyone to disturb my future wife or my sister ever again."

"No, they did not leave. Anne felt suddenly unwell, and the doctor was fetched, but I do not think this would be a good moment to seek a private meeting with Lady Catherine. It would be wiser for both of you to calm yourselves a day or two. Moreover, I do not think Lady Ellen will tolerate another round of arguments in her house."

"Have no fear, Cousin; I do not intend to do anything out of reason, and I certainly do not intend to barge into your parents' house uninvited just to quarrel with Aunt Catherine. I will most likely ask for Lady Ellen's advice and find a proper place and moment for that. But pray tell me, how is Anne? Is she truly ill?"

"I found a moment to speak with my mother and she told me — privately — that Anne was only very tired and did not want to return so soon to Kent. I cannot believe that the whole situation has become so dramatic — quite Shakespearean I might say." He paused a moment to gulp some more brandy and then started to laugh. "'Much ado about nothing.'"

"Quite. However, I am not as inclined to be amused as you are. The greatest part of the damage fell on Elizabeth. The offences she had to suffer from Lady Catherine were beyond any limit."

"Yes, I heard. Miss Bennet cannot have too favourable an opinion of our family. If I were you, I would insist on an elopement, because she might change her mind at any time."

He spoke in jest, but Darcy's countenance turned dark.

"She might, and I could not blame her, especially after my own preposterous behaviour. I am to blame more than our aunt."

"You, Darcy? What on earth did you do?"

"Did Lady Ellen not tell you?"

"No, she did not. Otherwise, why would I ask you to elaborate?"

"Well..." While Darcy, with obvious uneasiness, told him the second part of the story, the colonel turned equally serious. The situation was less amusing and more grievous than he might have imagined an hour before.

"I say, Darcy, I am surprised to see you so calm and relaxed. Miss Bennet has all the reason in the world to be displeased with you."

"I am not relaxed at all, Robert, but, happily, I spoke to Elizabeth last night, and she generously accepted my apologies."

"Truly? Well, that is the first good news of the day. You should thank the Lord for how fortunate you are. The addition of Miss Bennet to the family will be a blessing;

from now on, Lady Ellen will not be the only wise and charming member of this family."

Darcy started to laugh. "You are absolutely right, Robert. And I dare say in a couple of years, with Elizabeth and Lady Ellen's guidance, Georgiana may turn out to be very much like them."

"She will be, Darcy. I am certain of that. She only lacks self-confidence, but she is very intelligent and a quick learner. She will blossom in a couple of years and then, finally, there will be equilibrium in our family; the three ladies' qualities will compensate for the many faults in the men."

"Cousin, you are an exceptional observer. I bow to your wise judgment. Now let us go and have breakfast. It is likely that we will have only each other's company."

Elizabeth could not believe that she had slept so late. Even before she had time to ring for a servant, Betty knocked tentatively at the door. Elizabeth prepared herself in a short time while she was informed that Mr. Darcy and the colonel had already had breakfast and were to be found in the library.

Though she ached with eagerness to see Mr. Darcy as soon as possible, she did not dare let her recollections of the night before occupy her mind. The mere thought of their passionate kisses, her boldness — so close to wantonness — and the intimate moments they shared made her face and neck warm and crimson. She put her memories aside, waiting for a moment of complete solitude to let them envelope her.

She exited the room with the strong feeling of having committed a shameful impropriety; she had spent her first night in Darcy's room. *Well, his former room to be precise... But his embrace, his kisses, and the warmth of his body were so intense that I can still feel them.*

She thanked Betty for her assistance and went, not downstairs to meet the gentleman, but to Georgiana's room to check on her. The pleasure of seeing each other in such good spirits made the previous day's events vanish. As Georgiana was brought breakfast, Elizabeth joined her, and they spent a full hour together. They were finishing their meal when a knock at the door and a well-known voice announced they had company.

The moment he entered the room, Mr. Darcy's gaze fell on Elizabeth, and as if drawn by a spell, he took her hand in his and brought it to his lips.

"Miss Bennet, it is a pleasure to see you."

Elizabeth startled and only then noticed the colonel's figure behind Mr. Darcy. Blushing in deep embarrassment and fighting a lump in her throat, she hardly could articulate a few words.

"Colonel Fitzwilliam! I am delighted to see you too, sir."

He bowed to her, and she rose to her feet with the intention of greeting him, but she could not do so properly as Mr. Darcy's grip on her hand was tight and possessive.

The colonel noticed her gesture and started to laugh.

"Darcy, do you intend to let go of Miss Bennet's hand anytime soon? She might need it to greet me, you know."

Elizabeth's mortification made her cheeks burn. Her first look was to Georgiana to see her reaction to such improper behaviour, but the girl seemed deeply amused, chuckling and hiding her mouth behind her hand. Before she could say anything, she felt her hand clasped between Mr. Darcy's in an even tighter grip.

"No, Cousin, not anytime soon. If you want to take Miss Bennet's hand, you must be content with the left one, as this one is otherwise and permanently engaged."

"Mr. Darcy!" Elizabeth's tone was full of reproach, her eyes shooting darts at him. "I think this is a very improper joke."

Her voice was drowned out, however, by the colonel and Georgiana's laughter, and her embarrassment grew to the point where she became upset with Mr. Darcy for putting her in such a humiliating situation.

Sensing her obvious discomfort, he turned more serious, not letting her hand go but loosening his grip in case she chose to withdraw it.

"I am sorry if I embarrassed you, Elizabeth. I shall have to beg your forgiveness once more. I am sure that my cousin and my sister already know I am incapable of acting properly where you are concerned. And you look so beautiful this morning that I had to take your hand to be certain that you were real."

He sounded and looked completely serious; while his words warmed her with the greatest pleasure, she could not help bursting into laughter at his exaggeration. "Well sir, you find the most perfect excuses. What woman could deny you this little reward after such a public declaration?"

She resumed her seat but did not pull her hand from his, which made the colonel comment — with great difficulty between peals of laughter — "I agree; he deserves this little reward after making himself completely ridiculous in front of his little sister. Miss Bennet, I do not know what you did with the real Darcy or what spell you have cast upon him, but I am praying something like that never happens to me."

"You are more the fool, Cousin," answered Mr. Darcy, his voice utterly serious and his eyes embracing Elizabeth with a tenderness that everybody in the room could sense. "You should pray something like this happens to you. You should pray to someday feel the same love and happiness that I do."

Saying that, he kissed Elizabeth's hand again, staring into her eyes and reading her silent response to his unexpected declaration. The love and gratitude that lightened her face could not be misinterpreted. And Georgiana's whispered words confirmed that. "I do pray for that, Brother. I hope the Lord will allow me someday to be as happy as you are."

Mr. Darcy moved closer, still holding his betrothed's hand, and bestowed a tender kiss on his sister's forehead.

"I am sure He will, dearest. Have no doubt of that."

After years of service in the army, the colonel found himself in the unacceptable and absurd situation of hiding his emotion — which would forever compromise his name in the eyes of his fellow officers; he forced himself to laugh again without really succeeding in deceiving his companions.

"Let us not be so sentimental. And, Darcy, Miss Bennet has already given you permission to keep her hand, so you need not act the silly lover any longer."

Having Georgiana chuckle again at his words allowed him to turn the conversation to an easier and less emotional topic. He inquired and received a favourable report about Georgiana's state of health; she was pleased to tell him that she might be allowed to start using her leg for a few minutes each day, and she expressed her happy anticipation of being able to take a short walk in the room within a week.

"That is wonderful news, dear. Lady Ellen will be thrilled to hear it."

"Thank you, Robert. I cannot wait to tell her myself. But how is Aunt Ellen? I expected to see her this morning as she said she would visit me after breakfast."

"Ahh... she is well; do not worry. It is just that... a special situation has occurred at the house and... " He cast a brief glance at his cousin, asking for his help, as he did not know how much he should relate to the young ladies. Mr. Darcy did not fail to understand his meaning and assisted him.

"Georgie, Robert told me that the situation has been difficult in their house today. Apparently, Lady Catherine had an enormous argument with the earl and — " He sensed the tension in Elizabeth's hand as Georgiana's face tuned white, her eyes opening wide. He knew both his sister and his intended shared the same fears, but it was the former who voiced them.

"Lady Catherine is still here? What did Lady Ellen say? William, what if she comes again? You will not go away, will you?" Both Mr. Darcy and the colonel felt the sharp pain caused by the young girl's distress, so strong that she could barely speak coherently.

Mr. Darcy took hold of his sister's hand and tightened his grip on Elizabeth's suddenly cold fingers. "Georgie, there is nothing to worry about. I will protect both you and Elizabeth against anything and anybody, I promise you. And I will not go anywhere; I will stay here with you."

He wrapped both her and Elizabeth in a protective gaze, and his betrothed tentatively smiled back at him. However, Georgiana's state did not improve much. It was the colonel's turn to intervene.

"Georgie, for heaven's sake, there is no need to be so frightened. She is your aunt, not some foreign enemy. What can she do except shout? Try not to give her so much importance."

"Oh, Cousin, you do not know how angry she was! And what she said... and how she spoke to Elizabeth! I cannot bear that to happen again. The things she said about my father... and about Elizabeth, and — "

"Do not worry, sweetie; she will not return soon. And if she does, you can throw her out of the house; Elizabeth will teach you how to do it."

Everybody's eyes turned to Lady Matlock, who stepped into the room with her usual elegance and perfect appearance. However, the traces of fatigue and the effects of recent events could be seen on her face and in the hint of sadness in her smile. On greeting the new guest, Mr. Darcy and Elizabeth separated their hands, but the gesture had not escaped the lady who smiled and exchanged meaningful glances with her son.

She bent to kiss her niece's forehead and was pleased to see her so recovered. She took Elizabeth's hand and squeezed it affectionately, while Mr. Darcy offered her the most comfortable armchair in the room.

"Thank you, Nephew. So... from what I hear, I dare say you are still discussing yesterday's events."

"No, Aunt," answered Mr. Darcy, "we were having quite a pleasant conversation... until now... But I am afraid Georgiana is still a little worried, though I assured her she has no reason to be."

"I see... Georgie sweetie, let us move beyond this story, shall we? We have a ball and a wedding to plan, and I left my home precisely to get away from that relative of ours. I hoped she would finally leave, but the doctor confirmed that Anne was too weak to bear the voyage back to Kent so soon. She must rest for at least a week; and Catherine, though she was very angry with us, refused to return without her daughter, so she was offered a guest room in the East wing. Dear me, we will be the laughingstock of the *ton* if the servants start gossiping."

Her unusual tirade disconcerted Georgiana even more. "Dear Aunt, I do not understand. What is happening with Anne? And when did Elizabeth throw Lady Catherine out of the house?"

Lady Matlock grinned with an uncharacteristic lack of elegance. "I am acting strangely and talking nonsense, am I not? I beg you to excuse me; it must be the bad influence of a certain rude visitor I have had recently. Robert dear, please be so kind as to entertain your cousins with the ridiculously dramatic story of what took place this morning in our house. And please, could someone ring for some fresh tea? I am in desperate need of a cup or two."

Though neither of them could be certain whether Lady Matlock was speaking in jest or not, they obeyed. The colonel started to re-tell the story for Elizabeth and Georgiana in a much lighter and more amusing manner with proper care not to distress them while Elizabeth, without hesitation, rang for the tea.

The maid entered with a tray, and looked to Elizabeth for further instructions. She thanked her with a kind smile before dismissing her. The place was very crowded with all of them gathered near Georgiana's bed, and the maid would not have had enough room to move around them, so Elizabeth offered to pour the tea herself. Graciously, she offered each a cup and helped Georgiana to sit more comfortably before handing the tea to her. When she was certain that everybody was contented, she resumed her place near Mr. Darcy.

Once more, Lady Matlock marvelled with pleasure at the mix of qualities in Elizabeth. Her natural, unpretentious manner made everyone around her feel comfortable. She was kind and attentive, not because propriety demanded it, but because that was her way. It was as simple as that. However, Elizabeth's harsh words and sharp looks when she had censured Mr. Darcy in the library and the way she stood up to Lady Catherine proved that she had strength rarely found in a young woman. *Mrs. Hamilton was generous in her praise and showed no restraint in expressing her admiration for the future mistress of this great house, and she was correct,* thought Lady Matlock. *Elizabeth Bennet has many admirable qualities.*

However, the most important thing Lady Matlock noticed was the warmth and tenderness in the small interactions between the two betrotheds. When she entered the room, Mr. Darcy had clearly been holding Elizabeth's hand, a gesture completely improper in company. However, she did not disapprove of their overt gestures of tenderness. Instead, their love for one another melted her heart. For Mr. Darcy to break with propriety in front of his sister was a most astonishing event. She remembered her son's words when they first spoke about the engagement: *"I saw how happy Darcy is."*

Lady Matlock savoured her tea and smiled, contented and relieved. She congratulated herself on being wise enough to give this young woman a chance. Elizabeth Bennet was a gem — a natural, unpolished one — and as Mr. Darcy's wife, she would sparkle as a priceless jewel. *I will be around to be certain of that.*

She saw Mr. Darcy trying unobtrusively to touch Elizabeth's hand and arm with slight movements of his hand, hoping the others would be too caught up in their conversation to notice. For her part, Elizabeth was making obvious efforts to remain focused on the topic, but her face coloured highly every time he touched her. Moreover, as Lady Matlock noticed, she did not encourage his behaviour nor did she try to put an end to it.

Soon, Lady Matlock could bear it no longer.

"Oh, for heaven's sake, Darcy, take her hand and be done with it. You are acting like a schoolboy!"

Elizabeth's mortification made her face crimson; she tried to hide her eyes behind her lashes and fixed her gaze on the ground. However, in the next moment, Elizabeth did the most astonishing thing, making the colonel and Georgiana burst into laughter and Lady Matlock smile and nod her approval: She put her hand in Mr. Darcy's strong palm, and he closed his fingers around it with no intention of letting go.

About an hour later, Georgiana showed obvious signs of fatigue and they insisted that she rest alone.

The remainder of the party removed themselves to the salon, Lady Matlock having many details to discuss about the ball. Elizabeth took the opportunity and excused herself to pay a short call on Molly, who was following the doctor's directions to remain in bed for the day.

As Elizabeth walked down the hall to rejoin the others in the salon, she could not miss the shadow of a man waiting there. Though she was convinced the visitor noticed her presence, she determined to pass by him, as it was Mr. Darcy's duty to receive the visitor and eventually to make the introductions.

She was startled by the sound of a deep, severe voice addressing her. "Miss Bennet? Miss Elizabeth Bennet?"

She stopped and turned to face him as the man took a few steps forward. The moment they faced each other, the resemblance she saw left her in no doubt that he was the colonel's father, Lord Matlock.

They gazed at each other, eyes fixed searchingly on the other's face, waiting in silence. They were, after all, two strangers with no one to introduce them properly.

The earl could not hide his surprise at seeing this pretty, unpretentious girl with evidence of fatigue in her eyes. Her hair was simply arranged, her clothing equally simple though tasteful, lending her an overall appearance of natural beauty. Nothing was as he expected it to be.

"I must apologise for this unannounced visit. I know it is very improper of me, but I was very concerned for my wife and my niece. I requested an audience of my nephew as there are some pressing matters I need to discuss with him. I am Lord Matlock." He bowed politely, and she curtseyed.

"I am Elizabeth Bennet. It is an honour to meet you, Lord Matlock."

"I am afraid I cannot say I am pleased to meet you, Miss Bennet..." he paused a little before adding, "I would rather have made your acquaintance under more pleasant circumstances and in a more proper manner."

"In that case, I can only hope that at least our second meeting may be under more favourable circumstances."

He nodded slightly.

"If you will excuse me, I shall go and inform Mr. Darcy and Lady Matlock of your arrival, sir."

"Miss Bennet..." She turned to him in surprise.

"The servant has already gone to announce me. However, I was wondering if you would allow me to have a few words with you."

She hesitated only a moment before agreeing.

"Miss Bennet, thank you for your understanding. I want to offer you my deepest apologies for any injuries you suffered because of Lady Catherine's impromptu visit. I will not deny that I myself was strongly opposed when Darcy informed me of your engagement, and I still have many doubts regarding this union as you and my nephew come from very different circles, but neither of us had any right to offend you, and it was not to our credit that we questioned your character or Darcy's decision."

"Lord Matlock, you are correct in assuming that I was offended and undeservedly accused with a harshness I could scarcely believe, coming from someone of Lady Catherine's station. I feel I deserve an apology, and I will accept yours, though it was not you who offended me, at least not directly."

She spoke with bitter determination and did not try to conceal her hurt feelings against those who had slighted her. She was pointing out the incivility of his own sister, and her reproof was the more strongly felt because the earl knew himself to be guilty of the same uncivil behaviour. Lord Matlock blinked several times, but Elizabeth finally offered a release from the tension that surrounded them.

"But sir, I think you have every right to have and express doubts about me as well as about this — I agree — sudden engagement. As long as your motive is the well-being of your nephew, your concern is justified and legitimate, and I cannot fault you for it."

It was another strike — a subtle allusion to those not so legitimate motives — and the earl could not help but perceive the wit and quickness of the young woman's mind, even under such difficult circumstances.

She was not intimidated by him nor did she try to hide her opinions behind polite and neutral statements. She was conciliatory and reasonable without allowing her pride to be damaged or her self-esteem to be lowered. He could do nothing but bow to her as she continued.

"Lord Matlock, I can only hope that the future will prove all your doubts and concerns without foundation."

"Then let us hope together, Miss Bennet. My nephew's felicity will be the strongest proof of my mistaken judgment. And I would be more than willing to humbly recognise my failure if that should be the case."

"Thank you, sir. I know that I have done nothing to earn more than your politeness and fair judgment, and I could ask for nothing more at this time. However, neither would I accept anything less."

"Miss Bennet, I can already see that I have been mistaken in some of my previous statements about you."

"If that is meant to be a compliment, I thank you, Lord Matlock."

The truce between them had been signed — mutually and silently.

It was not long before Mr. Darcy, Lady Matlock and the colonel appeared, each of them wearing a worried expression. Instantly, Mr. Darcy was at Elizabeth's side, protectively gazing sternly at his uncle.

"Lord Matlock. What an unexpected pleasure." His tone betrayed many other feelings but no pleasure at all. Lady Matlock and her son chose to remain a little behind, allowing the others to resolve the issue between them.

"Darcy! I have come to fetch my wife and to ask for a private conference with you if you would favour me."

"Of course." His voice did not warm in the slightest. "Lord Matlock, allow me to introduce to you my future wife, Miss Elizabeth Bennet. Elizabeth, this is my uncle, Lord Matlock"

She smiled, her eyes giving him the answer he needed and the reassurance to ease his tension.

"Lord Matlock and I have already become acquainted. Apparently, both of us are well qualified to introduce ourselves to strangers and even to carry on enlightened conversation at our first meeting. I can only imagine how charming our second meeting will be."

The earl gazed at her a moment and then turned to Mr. Darcy.

But the master of the house was no longer looking at his uncle, only staring into Elizabeth's eyes, his countenance suddenly lightened, the expression of adoration so evident that it made the others feel like intruders.

In that moment, the earl bowed to Elizabeth, took her hand and — to everyone's astonishment — lifted it politely to his lips. He was kissing the country girl's hand, a gesture of which only his wife knew the value.

"Miss Bennet, I look forward to our second meeting and to our future conversations."

Then he turned his attention to Mr. Darcy. "Nephew, I have apologised to Miss Bennet on Lady Catherine's behalf and my own; our reactions have been preposterous and unforgivable. I also confessed to Miss Bennet that I was opposed to your engagement and that I still have not changed my opinion. But I also expressed my hope that your marriage will prove me wrong and will force me to recognise my failure to judge the situation properly."

Mr. Darcy averted his eyes from Elizabeth and met the earl's gaze, holding it so long that everyone could feel the tension filling the room.

"If that be the case, I think there can be nothing more to say on the subject. Would you care to join us in the library for a glass of port, Uncle? I think the ladies have some ball details to take care of."

Accepting the invitation with obvious relief, the earl dared to meet his wife's smouldering stare, and though she did not say a word, he knew he would be reminded often that he had been wrong once more in a quarrel with her.

WITH MR. DARCY IN THE house, Elizabeth knew she could not remain another night under the same roof; propriety — not to mention her aunt and uncle — would forbid it. So, while the gentlemen were in the library, she sent a note to her aunt, explaining the situation and informing her she would return in time for dinner.

Her belongings were already prepared, and she only waited for Georgiana to awaken so she could make a proper farewell. She retired to her room and changed her clothes; then she reclined on the bed, her eyes closed, exhausted but content with the day's events.

A gentle knock on the door startled her and, convinced it must be either Mrs. Hamilton or Betty, invited her to enter. The visitor's identity surprised her but made her face glow with happiness.

Mr. Darcy entered carefully and locked the door behind him. Before she could say a word, he took her in his arms, so close that she could not breathe. "My love, I missed you so much. I have been close to you the whole day and yet so painfully far away. Not to be able to hold you, to kiss you, to caress you... was torture."

He was whispering in her hair, kissing her lightly at first; then his lips traced their way down to her temple, her eyes, and her cheeks until they met the sweetness of her mouth. Elizabeth tried to oppose him, but soon everything around her vanished, and she surrendered to the hungry passion that seemed to devour them, both trying and barely succeeding in satisfying their desire for each other.

In the dizzying tumult of caresses, wanting nothing more than to feel her as close to him as possible, Mr. Darcy leaned onto the bed, pulling her with him, side by side and heart-to-heart, bodies entwined in an endless kiss. He expected to hear Elizabeth protest, but she did not.

Growing more trustful and daring, his hands possessively started to caress her. His fingers stroked the softness of her neck and then glided down to her throat, brushing for a few sweet moments over the bare skin of her neckline. She moaned, and that enchanting sound only increased his urge to touch her.

His kiss grew more insistent, but his caresses remained gentle and patient. With tender moves, barely touching the soft fabric of her dress, his fingers slid lower over the edge of her the dress, brushing over her breast. He was not even certain that she truly felt his touch, but his doubts vanished when she tensed and moaned deeply, her lips whispering something against his mouth. He waited a few moments, his fingers remaining still on the spot where her heart was beating; then his hand continued its delicious journey until its reached her waist, her hips and finally stopped to rest against her thighs. He felt her shivering, and her hands started to caress him as if trying to mirror his own caresses. She did not say a word as her lips seemed unwilling to part from his.

So he did what he believed she desired: His hand began exploring a different path on the other side of her body, tracing its way back from her other thigh, her hips, encircling her waist for a moment and then lifting and brushing against her breast, this time lingering there, in the slightest caress.

Her back instinctively arched and he heard her whispering his name. Mr. Darcy broke the kiss into countless small kisses over her face while he delighted in listening to her soft moans. As he was lying on his side near her, his right leg lifted then lowered over her legs, trapping them beneath its weight. Having half of her imprisoned, his fingers began a slight and sweet torture of her breasts, only brushing against the fabric, without allowing his hungry fingers to close on their roundness or to touch them as greedily as he wished. Patiently, tenderly, he taught her body another lesson of the pleasure he could offer her. Her body learned quickly — she learned quickly — but only a few moments later, she begged for more, unconsciously moving and arching against his torturing strong hand. A knock on the door and Betty's voice startled them and put an end to their interlude; Elizabeth scarcely could find the strength to assure the maid that she would be ready in no time.

However, many moments passed with neither of them moving, only lying together, staring into each other's eyes, and smiling breathlessly, flustered but still closely embraced.

He quickly and playfully kissed the tip of her nose. "Now that I finally managed to kiss you I feel much better, my love, would you not agree? I am sorry; in my hurry, I forgot to ask if you would allow me to enter your room. I hope you will forgive me."

She started to laugh, burying her head in his chest. "This could hardly be called only a kiss, sir. And may I dare ask what you would have done if I had not allowed you to enter earlier?"

"I do not know, my dearest, soon-to-be wife. I presume I would obey your wish; I do not think I would be capable of doing anything against your will. But I truly hope I will never have to endure such a moment when you will not allow me to come to you."

"I could never refuse your coming to me, William..."

Though the conversion had begun in jest, both felt the depth of their words. It was the first vow of their life together.

Minutes passed in silent bliss; they lay together without kissing or speaking, simply rejoicing in their shared happiness. Mr. Darcy's lips tenderly touched her forehead, and he whispered as he caressed her hair. "Elizabeth, I will go now and let you prepare yourself. I will accompany you to the Gardiners' and stay for dinner if that is acceptable to you."

"Of course. Thank you." She leaned to touch his lips with hers, but he stopped her, gently but decisively. "Elizabeth, if I start kissing you again, I am not certain I will let you go — not now, not later, not ever again."

His voice was husky and grave. She knew he was speaking in earnest, and for a moment, she was tempted to answer: *"I do not want you to let me go."*

She recovered, however, and stroked his face with her fingertips, lingering a little upon his lips. "Mr. Darcy... Please make sure the carriage is ready. I would like to leave as soon as I have spoken to Georgiana."

Chapter 23

The following days passed uneventfully except for the necessary preparations for Lydia's wedding. Most mornings, Elizabeth called on Georgiana, and Becky often accompanied her — as the elder children had their daily lessons — and a few times Jane came along as well. Her gentle sister quickly developed a warm relationship with the shy Georgiana, and Jane's kindness along with Elizabeth's liveliness seemed to draw the young girl from her shell. Her health improved remarkably, and she was soon taking short walks in her room, supported by Elizabeth and watched closely by Mrs. Annesley. In no time, she gained enough courage and strength to stay a few minutes by the window and enjoy the fresh, winter air.

As she spent some of almost every day in the house, Elizabeth started to become involved in household routines with Mr. Darcy's encouragement. She spent at least half an hour each day speaking with Mrs. Hamilton and asking all she could without interfering with the housekeeper's duties. It was during one of these talks that Mrs. Hamilton asked her future mistress whether she would bring her own personal maid with her after the wedding.

"No, Mrs. Hamilton. I must confess that we are five sisters at home, and I did not have a personal maid."

"In that case, we must select one, Miss Bennet. If it is acceptable to you, I will select a few and then fix appointments with each of them so you can choose one to your liking. It should not take more than a week."

"The process sounds very complicated." Elizabeth laughed. "I was wondering... could we not choose someone from among the staff? I imagine you have already interviewed them carefully before accepting them into the house. Perhaps you could recommend one of them."

"But... none of them is sufficiently trained and qualified to be your maid."

"What about Molly?"

"Molly?" The housekeeper's surprise was obvious as she searched for the proper answer.

"Yes. I must confess I have found Molly's behaviour quite satisfactory, and she seems to be intelligent and pleasant. I enjoy her company, and I am sure she could learn in no time, but I am willing to accept your advice and opinion in this matter. Is there anything wanting in Molly?"

"No... No, of course... I am pleased to hear you consider her capable of this position as I have trained her myself since she was very young."

"Well, then why did you hesitate before?"

"It is just... Please forgive me for not mentioning this to you before. Molly is my sister's daughter. As her father died, Mr. Darcy was kind enough to hire her two years ago. I did not dare, until now, thank you for your kindness towards her when she was unwell. My gratitude — "

"Mrs. Hamilton!" Elizabeth touched her arm gently, interrupting her. "There is no reason to speak of this matter any further; I am content to know that Molly is well. And if you indeed want to thank me, talk to Molly. If she is willing to accept the position, please do everything necessary to train her for her new duties after the wedding." Her voice was light but decided, not allowing any other words of gratitude to be spoken.

When Mr. Darcy was informed later, he found the whole arrangement to be satisfactory. He did not know Molly well, for her duties did not entail any interaction with the master, but he was content to know that Elizabeth's closest servant would not be a stranger.

THE DAY LYDIA WAS TO wed Mr. Wickham arrived so quickly that Mrs. Gardiner and her elder nieces barely had sufficient time to make arrangements. At their concerted insistence in daily letters, Mr. Bennet finally agreed to allow the newly wedded couple to visit the family in Hertfordshire before they departed for the North.

Oblivious to anything and everything around her, Lydia took the news that she would be received in her parents' house without any excitement, as if it were the most natural thing in the world. She did not give any thought to the fact that her intended elopement could lower her reputation in the neighbours' eyes or damage her family's name. Quite the contrary, she planned many visits and tea parties to invite all her acquaintances.

"Only think of it; it has been less than a fortnight," she cried, "since I went away, and yet so many things have happened. Good gracious!"

Her aunt rolled her eyes, Jane was distressed, and Elizabeth looked expressively at Lydia; but she, who never heard or saw anything of which she chose to be insensible, gaily continued, "Oh! I am so happy we will visit Mama before we go to the North! I wonder, do the people there know about my wedding?"

"I am sure they know, Lydia — more than we would like."

"Oh, Lizzy, you are so boring, just preaching and talking away as if you were reading a sermon. You are jealous because I am marrying sooner than you are and my husband is so much more charming than your betrothed. You would like to have my Wickham marry you, I am sure of that."

Only Mrs. Gardiner's severe censure and her demand that Lydia start packing for her trip made the latter leave the room; Lydia was convinced she was envied by her sisters and that her own aunt was very unkind. The thought of her dear Wickham was the only important thing to her, and she soon stopped thinking of anything else.

For Elizabeth, the days preceding her sister's wedding were a time of anxiety and displeasure. Mr. Wickham was in the house more than she liked, and more than once she was shocked by his manners. Though his words were polite, his tone and the inflections in his voice were disturbing; if he were not to be married to her sister directly, Elizabeth would have been inclined to think he was trying to impose upon her. He also missed no opportunity to make disparaging remarks about Mr. Darcy, and how "his dear sister Elizabeth" could possibly manage to bear the company of such an unpleasant sort of man for the rest of her life.

Only one day before the wedding, that particular comment was spoken loudly in the Gardiners' salon, and it was too much for Elizabeth to bear. Though Jane, Lydia, her aunt, and even Becky were present, she could control her temper no longer.

"Mr. Wickham, I am grateful for your brotherly concern, but I would suggest you direct it toward your future wife. *She* is the one who might find it difficult to bear married life. As for Mr. Darcy — considering that he paid your debts, bought your commission and made all the arrangements for your wedding, I am sure you must be deeply grateful to him, despite your insinuations to the contrary."

Jane paled at her sister's words, and Mrs. Gardiner cast a reproachful glance at her niece; Elizabeth chose to ignore them. She made to leave the room, but Mr. Wickham hurried to grasp her hand, bowing to kiss it.

"My dear sister, please do not leave displeased with me. I apologise for anything I might have said to offend you, though my concern and care were nothing but genuine."

She pulled her hand from his, whispering so that the others could barely comprehend her words.

"Try to restrain yourself from calling me 'dear sister' and kissing my hand, sir. Neither your gestures nor your presence give me any pleasure. Now if you would excuse me…"

She heard Lydia's voice behind her and suddenly felt Becky's little hand sliding into hers. Squeezing Becky's hand, she entered the music room and did not emerge until Mr. Wickham had left the house.

The wedding was celebrated Monday morning at St. Clement's. They arrived at eleven o'clock to meet Mr. Wickham, Mr. Darcy, Colonel Fitzwilliam and Mr. Bingley.

As no one was inclined to accept the position of Mr. Wickham's best man, Mr. Bingley offered himself. Jane was to stand near Lydia at the altar, and that alone was sufficient motivation for him.

In truth, Mr. Bingley was a daily visitor at the Gardiners' house or at Mr. Darcy's; although he was in Jane's company daily, the busy days of preparation had not allowed him to secure even a few private moments with her. He had even chosen some eloquent words to express his love and admiration and to make her the most perfect proposal — for in his eyes she was the most perfect of women. Fate, however, seemed to be against him. His anxiety and eagerness made him behave with unusual nervousness at his own house, and as Caroline did not cease her abuse of Eliza Bennet and occasionally of Jane herself, he frequently found himself quarrelling with his sister. Only a day before the wedding, he ordered her to move to the Hursts the very next morning if she did not heartily apologise for everything she had said. She could not believe he was speaking in earnest, so she ignored his warning and retired to her room with an air of supreme offence. However, to her utter surprise, Mr. Bingley sent her word to prepare her excuses or her belongings by the time he returned home that evening.

Consequently, his state was not particularly calm when the bride and her party arrived at the church. Jane's bright smile and her eagerness to accept his offered arm were all he needed to change his mood and his countenance.

The ceremony was short, simple and gave little pleasure to anyone except Lydia. All of them went to the carriage, prepared to return to Gracechurch Street. Lydia seemed so happy and sincere in her affection for her "dear Wickham" that Elizabeth's heart bled for her. A deep, painful regret overwhelmed her, and she felt guilty for not trying with greater energy to convince Lydia against this marriage. In that moment, her name, her reputation, and her own felicity seemed of little importance compared to the unhappiness and deception her youngest sister would have to bear.

She could sense Mr. Darcy approaching her long before his hand gently rested on her arm, and he leaned to whisper in her ear, "You did all you could to convince her, Elizabeth. She simply refused to listen."

Elizabeth smiled as she allowed him to show her to the carriage. "Are you a mind reader, Mr. Darcy?"

"Not usually, no. But I do try diligently to be your mind reader, Miss Bennet. And your face reader...and your eye reader... I want to learn how to understand your every wish and concern so I can do everything in my power to comply with them."

His whispers warmed the spot near her ear and sent cold waves over her body while her face turned crimson. A moment later, he continued, his tone more serious. "Elizabeth, you have every reason to be worried for your sister, but do not think we will abandon her to Mr. Wickham's power. Colonel Fitzwilliam specifically asked that Mr. Wickham be supervised at his new commission, and I promise you I will ask for timely reports regarding their state. You will be able to help her in any way you like whenever she is in need."

She squeezed his hand, her eyes speaking more than her words could. "Thank you, William."

The rest of the day was pleasant enough, considering the circumstances. The newlyweds planned to leave for Hertfordshire the following morning, and Lydia could not stop expressing her pleasure in being the first married of all her sisters and being introduced to her former neighbours as Mrs. Wickham. Mr. Wickham only smiled charmingly.

"My only regret," added Lydia, "is that we will not be in town to attend Lady Matlock's ball. I would love to be there, and I am sure my dear Wickham and I would have been the most admired dancers."

There was no response to this statement, so she expressed her displeasure further. "Now that I think of it, I am sure we could delay our departure for a few days and leave after the ball. We would be a welcome addition, I assure you. No other gentleman will be as charming or as handsome as my husband in his blue coat, and all the ladies would admire him."

"Unfortunately, that will not be possible." Mr. Darcy's voice was so severe that Lydia's words stopped in her throat. She looked from him to her sister and then to her husband, searching for support, not oblivious to the sudden tension and discomfort in the room. Mr. Darcy slightly softened his tone.

"Mrs. Wickham, I am afraid you will have to follow the planned schedule if you wish to visit your parents before leaving for the North. If I remember correctly, your husband's commitment will start very soon, and he must be at his regiment a few days hence. Is that not so, Mr. Wickham?"

His effort to be civil was only for Lydia's benefit, as he could not tell her that Lady Ellen had specifically forbidden Wickham to appear, not only at her ball but anywhere near her.

Mr. Wickham's answer was awaited with much impatience by his new wife, and he finally conceded to give it. "You are correct, Mr. Darcy. My dear Lydia, I promise you there will be other balls you will be able to attend at least as pleasurable as this one." Lydia was evidently displeased but did not contradict her husband.

The conversation returned to the previous topics when, suddenly, Mr. Wickham addressed Elizabeth. "Miss Elizabeth, I imagine you are very excited about this ball. The whole *ton* will be present, I imagine."

"I certainly hope not the whole *ton*, Mr. Wickham. I will be content to have my own relatives in addition to Mr. Darcy's and Colonel Fitzwilliam's family. As for the others, I trust Lady Matlock has devised an appropriate guest list; her ladyship's understanding of human character is exquisite."

As he knew he had not been invited, the remark was a pointed reference to his own character that Mr. Wickham did not fail to notice; so did all the others, except for the bride. He pursed his lips, and an offended air pervaded his usually smiling countenance. Mr. Darcy cast a quick but eloquent glance at Elizabeth, turning his head to the window to hide his admiring smile. He was surprised to hear Mr. Wickham persisting in the conversation as it was clearly so disadvantageous to him.

"I wonder that you have come to trust Lady Matlock's taste so implicitly after so short an acquaintance. However, were you not curious to see the guest list for yourself? At least then you could have had time to prepare for some less pleasant encounters and perhaps even avoid them."

"Mr. Wickham, I must thank you again for your concern, though I see no reason for it. As I know very few people in town, it is unlikely that any acquaintance of mine would be on the list. It is also unlikely that I would want to avoid any of the guests."

"As you like. Still, I wonder if Lord and Lady Hothfield are on the list, and I wonder even more what your opinion of them will be. You must know that Mr. Darcy is as fond of them as they are of him."

Elizabeth's annoyance increased at his insistence, and she tried to put an end to the conversation. "Well, on our next meeting, I will satisfy your curiosity and inform you about my opinions of the event, Mr. Wickham."

Neither Elizabeth nor any other person in the room failed to notice Mr. Wickham's gaze repeatedly directed at Mr. Darcy, who was still facing the window. Though Elizabeth sensed the sudden stillness of his body, none of them could see the instant darkening of his countenance.

Sometime later, Mr. Darcy abandoned his position and took a seat close to Elizabeth. He ignored Mr. Wickham, despite the latter's efforts to interfere in various topics of conversation, and barely talked to anyone except his intended. Only later, after the newlyweds had departed for Hertfordshire, did Mr. Darcy's mood improve.

The day after Lydia's wedding was unusually bright and not very cold, and Becky enthusiastically expressed her desire to take a stroll in the park as her cousins had promised her a few days before. Jane confessed to being fatigued and preferred to remain indoors with Georgiana. Mr. Darcy, however, readily offered to accompany Elizabeth and the little girl to the nearest park, content to be in relative privacy with his betrothed.

They spoke in low tones, discussing the future ball, their return to Hertfordshire, and the wedding plans. Mr. Bennet had written to Mr. Darcy once since his return, and the letter was a continuous complaint about Mrs. Bennet's preparations and the unbearable agitation in his house. He was demanding that his sensible daughters return as soon as possible. As a great favour, he accepted the three-day delay until after the ball, but he insisted that Mr. Darcy owed him a whole month of solitude in his library in exchange for the favour.

Both Mr. Darcy and Elizabeth had been pleased the day before to hear Mr. Bingley say that he had asked his housekeeper to prepare Netherfield for his return. He intended to make his way back at the same time as the Miss Bennets, and he put his house at Mr. Darcy's disposal, offering to host all the guests for his wedding. They were even discussing the possibility of taking Georgiana with them if the doctor would agree, though Mr. Darcy was reluctant to expose her to a journey so soon.

As the day was bright, Becky was happy to run and play under the attentive eye of her cousin.

She showed them various little things she had found and asked many questions. An hour later, when she was finally tired and cold, they decided to return home.

As expected, Becky's feet hurt her too much to walk home, so Mr. Darcy lifted her in his arms. Delighted, she continued asking questions about anything and everything. Fortunately, having Elizabeth on his arm, Mr. Darcy seemed to bear the chatter reasonably well.

Worried about his change of mood the previous day, Elizabeth was determined to discover what had upset him so deeply. Mr. Wickham's impertinent remarks were annoying but no more than usual, so it was more likely that his words held a different meaning for Mr. Darcy — and for Mr. Wickham. However, the moment she tried to guide the conversation toward that subject, Mr. Darcy interrupted her decidedly.

"Elizabeth, let us not waste this beautiful morning talking about Mr. Wickham. There is nothing about him that deserves our attention."

His tone alone was sufficient for her to belay her inquiry, though it only left her with more questions. It was the first time he had avoided speaking about a subject in which she was interested.

Still preoccupied, she forced herself to put aside her curiosity and to respect his decision. He deserved her trust; he had proven that, so she decided to trust him and wait for him to tell her willingly. She resumed the topic of their return to Hertfordshire, and they were so deep in their conversation that they did not notice the person who stopped in front of them until Mr. Darcy almost ran into her.

"Lady Matlock!"

"Darcy! Watch your step, boy, or you will hurt somebody!"

He put Becky down to greet her properly as Elizabeth already had.

"Lady Ellen, did you come for a walk in the park?" she inquired.

"No dear, I came to find you both because I have pressing matters to discuss with you. Early tomorrow we must go to Madame Claudette's to try on the dresses for the ball so they can be delivered in time after the final fitting. Mrs. Hamilton told me where you were, and as I had not the patience to wait, here I am. But it is strange; I cannot remember when I last walked in the park in such cold weather. It must have been years ago."

Becky raised her eyes to watch Lady Matlock in such astonishment that she could hardly breathe. Just then, Elizabeth remembered her presence.

"Lady Ellen, allow me to introduce to you my youngest cousin, Rebecca Gardiner."

"Pleased to meet you, Miss Rebecca Gardiner." The girl remained silent, and Lady Ellen turned to Elizabeth. "Does Miss Rebecca Gardiner not know how to speak?"

"Oh, I know how to speak," Becky finally answered, "but you are so beautiful that I forgot the words."

Her little face was so honestly impressed that Lady Matlock smiled.

"Why, thank you, dear! That is the most charming compliment I have heard in quite a while."

"Oh," answered Becky, suddenly talkative again as she felt herself on secure ground, "I am very good at compliments; everybody knows that. But you should know my name is Becky, not Miss Rebecca Gardiner."

Elizabeth decided to interrupt, as a talkative Becky could be a dangerously voluble one. "Lady Matlock, please forgive us. My cousin can become very... forward when she likes someone, and she tends to speak about many things that are not entirely proper."

"Is that so, Becky? Well, I have always liked girls who hold decided opinions and know how to talk about many things."

"Do you let your girls talk about many things?" asked Becky, suddenly ignoring both Elizabeth and Mr. Darcy, her interest completely drawn to her new acquaintance.

"Unfortunately, Becky, I have no girls — only two boys."

"Becky, Lady Matlock is Colonel Fitzwilliam's mother," explained Mr. Darcy.

The girl looked from him to the lady, and back to him, and then her face brightened in revelation. "Oh... You are trying to trick me like my brothers. She cannot be the colonel's mother!"

"Why do you say so, Becky? Lady Matlock *is* the colonel's mother," said Elizabeth.

"She cannot be! Because she is beautiful and the colonel is old! He is as old as Mr. Darcy."

A disconcerted expression spread over Mr. Darcy's face.

"So I am old now, Becky? A few days ago, you said I was pretty!"

"You are pretty! But you are old, too, and so is the colonel."

Lady Matlock could hardly hold back her chuckle.

"Thank you Becky; that is another lovely compliment. But the colonel is indeed my son."

The girl looked at her incredulously, but the lady's countenance convinced her she was sincere, and Becky decided that somewhere there must have been a big mistake.

"I would suggest returning to the house, Aunt, as it is cold and we have been outdoors for some time now."

Mr. Darcy offered his arm to Lady Matlock, but she declined.

"Oh, I can walk by myself, Darcy; do not worry. You should offer your arm to Elizabeth. I am sure you would rather have it that way." He tried to protest but knew it was little use; he bent again to hoist Becky into his arms, but to his surprise, she also refused.

"I can walk for myself, too; do not worry."

Lady Matlock laughed and offered her hand to Becky.

"Then shall we walk together, Becky?"

The girl took the offered hand instantly.

"But Becky," insisted Mr. Darcy, "are you not tired? Why did you insist that I carry you before?"

"Because I am spoiled, and I was too lazy to walk on my feet," answered the girl in complete honesty. Lady Matlock burst into peals of laughter, hurriedly covering her mouth with her gloved hand.

The two of them set off together while Mr. Darcy and Elizabeth followed them, exchanging worried glances.

"So, Becky, do you have any brothers or sisters?"

"I have! I have two brothers and a sister. My sister is very beautiful, and she will be a proper lady, but my brothers are insufferable."

Elizabeth tried to censure her language, but the girl was encouraged by Lady Matlock's laugh and considered it as tacit approval, so she paid little attention to her cousin.

"Oh, Becky, I am sure you are a proper girl, too," offered Lady Matlock.

"No, I am not. I cannot be proper because I like to play too much. Proper girls do not play in the mud; that is what Mrs. Taylor said."

"Well then, you will be a proper girl when you grow up."

"Yes, but I do not want to grow up. When you grow up you are not allowed to do anything."

"Are you sure, Becky? As far as I know, adults are allowed to do many more things than children."

The whole conversation — and the little girl's company — delighted and amused Lady Matlock exceedingly.

"No, you are not allowed to do anything important: You cannot be carried in someone's arms when you are tired; you cannot kiss somebody if you want to; you cannot cry, and you cannot eat quite so many cakes…"

"Now I understand," answered the lady as seriously as she could. "And I must agree with you, Becky."

"You do? I must say I like you very much," declared the girl, obviously satisfied to have another ally."

"Becky!" Elizabeth thought it proper to interfere, as the girl had become dangerously familiar with Lady Matlock.

"Yes, Lizzy? Did I say anything wrong?" She lifted her eyes to Lady Matlock, explaining, "I said I like you, and that is good, you know?"

"I know, sweetie." She turned to Elizabeth, smiling reassuringly. "Do not worry,

Elizabeth. I am delighted to talk to her. She is charming."

Lady Ellen took the little hand and continued to walk towards the house while their conversation grew more animated, and Elizabeth's embarrassment mixed with Mr. Darcy's amusement.

"Do you know my cousin got married yesterday?"

"Indeed? And was she a beautiful bride?"

"Yes, she was. She is always beautiful. But she is very silly, you know? My mother said she married a rascal. What is a rascal? I thought she married Mr. Wickham!"

Her cascade of words surprised Lady Matlock, and she did not know whether to laugh or to change the topic of conversation. She was beginning to understand Elizabeth's earlier warning.

"Is rascal good?"

"No, Becky, it is not good."

"I thought so. Mr. Wickham is not good either, you know?"

"Yes, I know," she whispered to herself, but the girl heard her.

"You do not like him, either? I am so happy! Lydia said he is handsome! Handsome is good, you know, but I do not think he is handsome. The colonel is handsome; I can tell that. And Mr. Bingley is handsome though he has blond hair. But Mr. Wickham has snake eyes."

"Snake eyes? What are 'snake eyes,' Becky?"

"Snake eyes are the eyes of a snake," explained the girl, clearly surprised that the Lady did not understand something so obvious. "I do not like snakes. I am so pleased he left. Lizzy did not like him either, I tell you."

She turned to watch her cousin walking with Mr. Darcy, and whispered again to her companion.

"But I do like Mr. Darcy... and so does Lizzy! She will marry him, you know? I think Mr. Darcy is pretty! And he has dimples, did you see? Lizzy said dimples are good. I like dimples too!"

Lady Matlock could not remember the last time she had laughed aloud in the middle of a park. Elizabeth was torn between joining Mr. Darcy and his aunt in their amusement and hiding from embarrassment at the girl's words. She was pleased when the Darcys' house came into view

She walked silently on Mr. Darcy's arm, paying close attention to the conversation between Lady Matlock and her young cousin. Her mortification at the mention of Mr. Wickham was so high that she believed she could not feel worse. Nevertheless, the name brought a sudden idea into her head, an idea that grew stronger with each passing moment.

She cast a quick glance at Mr. Darcy, and he looked back at her, smiling. He was content and relaxed, obviously enjoying himself and their walk. She knew she should restrain herself. The rational part of her acknowledged that the price for satisfying a mere curiosity might be too high to be worth it, but she could not bear being ignorant any longer. She must find out what it was that he would not talk to her about. The uncertainty made her anxious, eager, and impulsive. She threw away any second thoughts or prudence.

"Lady Ellen, I was wondering... will there be many guests at the ball?"

"Yes, dear. I invited everyone I consider important enough to make your acquaintance at this early stage of your engagement. However, some of them declined the invitation and with good reason. It not being the Season, most of them are not in town, so for them the long distance might make it difficult to attend in this weather."

"I see... " She did not know how to continue her inquiry, her courage slowly falling as both Mr. Darcy and Lady Matlock's gazes rested upon her.

"Elizabeth, are you nervous about the ball?"

"I confess I am a little, Lady Ellen."

"Well, it is understandable, but do not worry. Your relatives and we will be there. Moreover, nobody would dare to be unkind to you in my house, and if they are, I authorise you to throw them out."

Her playful allusion to Lady Catherine made Mr. Darcy smile, but Elizabeth seemed not to notice it.

"Are Lord and Lady Hothfield among the guests, by any chance?"

The effect of her words was immediate; she felt Mr. Darcy's arm stiffen, and though she did not dare meet his eyes, she could feel his intense gaze burning her. However, Lady Matlock seemed pleased by the question.

"Why, yes they are, and I am delighted they have accepted the invitation though they do not usually socialise much. Are you acquainted with them?"

"No. But their names were mentioned yesterday in my uncle's house."

"Indeed? Then perhaps your aunt and uncle have met them before?"

"No, my family is not acquainted with them, either. It was Mr. Wickham who mentioned them and inquired about their presence."

Every word she spoke made Mr. Darcy tense; she was close enough to him to feel his unease though he continued to walk at his usual pace. She raised her eyes to him, but he was not looking at her any more. His stern countenance was unreadable. No feeling or reaction showed on his face; only his lips slightly pursed together betrayed him.

"Wickham? What did he have to say about my guests? And what interest could he have in Lord and Lady Hothfield?" She paused a moment and then offered the answer herself. "Oh, it must have been mere curiosity about Lady Hothfield, and I, for one, can understand it. After being so long the centre of attention, her sudden retirement naturally raised people's curiosity and deservedly so. After all, she was not such a famous actress for nothing."

Chapter 24

Elizabeth was not prepared for that answer, as she was not prepared for the vice-like feeling that instantly and sharply gripped her heart. Her head was spinning so fast that everything seemed to swirl around her.

So it was true. She must have been the actress Mr. Wickham was talking about in Hertfordshire.

As if in a dream, she heard Lady Matlock saying something, but the meaning of the words did not reach her. Then there was the sound of Becky's little voice... and then Darcy's — strong, deep and harsh.

"Apparently, Mr. Wickham was not the only one curious about the Hothfields, Miss Bennet."

She lifted her eyes and met his, only to confirm that he was upset.

He is more than upset; he is angry. She tightened her lips and silently held his gaze, but for the first time she could not read what she saw in his eyes. However, she did not need more proof; everything made sense at that moment. The story was real; *she* was real — real and so close to him all that time, all those years. She was married to an earl older than herself and a friend of the Darcys. How convenient indeed! What else had Mr. Wickham said the day before? 'Mr. Darcy is as fond of them as they are of him.' And he did not deny it. Fond of them! So fond that the mere mention of her name distressed him deeply, and a simple question from his intended made him angry!

They were already in front of Mr. Darcy's house, and Lady Matlock entered with Becky.

Elizabeth did not want to talk to or see anyone; she wanted nothing more than to run as far as she could. She had to think. Yet, what was she to think about? She felt him guiding her inside the house and then upstairs... Becky's voice could be heard, full of joy, and then other voices. They were in Georgiana's apartments: Jane, Mr. Bingley — when had he come? — Lady Matlock... She sat on the first chair she encountered, grateful for the support, for she feared her weak knees would betray her.

Lady Matlock spoke to Jane and then asked her something she did not hear. She only nodded, and she felt his stare burning her. Her eyes desperately needed to meet his, but she did not allow them to. She could not bear to see his angry face again.

"Elizabeth, are you unwell?" She startled violently when Jane touched her arm to catch her attention.

"I… I have a headache, Jane, nothing serious."

"You look so pale! Can we get you something?"

"No, there is no need; and pray, let us not worry the others. It will pass soon."

It was too late though, as Lady Matlock joined them, and Mr. Darcy was already moving toward her chair. "Elizabeth, what is the matter, dear? You do not look well at all."

"Lady Ellen, please believe me there is no reason to be concerned. I am just a little tired, and a slight headache is bothering me."

"Of course, you are exhausted with everything that has happened in the last fortnight. With all the talk about the ball, I am afraid you have given it much more importance than it deserves. We have all been too demanding of you; we must take better care of you and allow you to rest more."

Elizabeth could not even protest as she was surrounded by everyone.

"Mrs. Hamilton, would you please show Miss Bennet to the room she previously occupied? She is not well and needs rest."

Mr. Darcy's voice was heard above the others, and the housekeeper hurried to obey, but Elizabeth would not have it. She did not want to be imposed on, and he had no right to decide what was good for her. She started to protest but found no support, not even from her sister. Not willing to be the centre of a conflict, she reluctantly agreed, casting a quick glance at Mr. Darcy, her displeasure so obvious on her face that he could not possibly fail to notice it.

Both Jane and Mrs. Hamilton guided her to her room and insisted that she drink a little tea. Then they nestled her into bed and covered her in blankets; she had to pretend she was asleep before they finally left the room.

As soon as the heavy door closed behind them, she opened her eyes and remained still, staring into the fire. It was burning steadily, warming the room, but the room was already warm and pleasant; the fire evidently had not been recently made, as was usually the case in a guest room. The air smelled… alive, as though someone usually inhabited it. He had told her no one resided there except her. Then how was it that a fire was laid? Who else stayed in this room? Was it that woman? Could he do such a thing? Was she a regular guest in his house? Could he be that kind of man, to be involved with a married woman, the wife of a family friend?

She had heard previously about such situations, but she never would have believed him capable of such a thing. He was the best of men: honourable and honest. If nothing else, he would never expose his sister and his family to such a scandal. His sense of duty would forbid it, but what of his heart? Was that lady still in his heart? She might have been, considering his reaction when her name was mentioned.

Elizabeth knew only too well that Mr. Darcy must have been closely acquainted with other women before meeting her. Moreover, she knew that many gentlemen kept mistresses or visited "special places" on occasion. Though she did not want to allow her imagination to picture Mr. Darcy doing so, she realised that it was a strong possibility. The thought of another woman in his arms hurt more than she could have imagined; the pain of it was unbearable. The thought of another woman in his heart, in his thoughts or in his dreams was even worse.

She did not doubt his love or his desire to marry her. All his words, embraces, caresses, and kisses made her believe with all her heart and beyond any doubt that she was the only one who mattered to him — the only woman he had ever loved or wanted.

"My heart never spoke until I met you."

"I never desired to kiss a woman before."

He never would have said those words if he had not meant them. His professions of love were true; her own heart could testify to his sincerity. But what was the other woman to him?

She closed her eyes, trying to remember the former Miss Alton when she was still performing. She had made a stunning debut. She took possession of the stage from the first moment she set foot on it. Every performance brought ovations, and after each performance, there were throngs of people waiting for her. How could a man not admire such a woman? Could a man — could Mr. Darcy — love two women at the same time?

She wrapped the blankets around her and hugged her knees to her chest, but the pain would not go away. Her body and soul had fallen into a deep, frozen hole. She was alone, and she was afraid of remaining alone without what mattered most to her. Tears rolled along her cheeks, wetting her pillow, until she finally fell asleep.

Elizabeth opened her eyes slowly and looked around the room, trying to understand where she was. She recognised the surroundings, and the memory struck her. The pain instantly returned. She climbed out of bed, keeping the blankets wrapped around her.

Without the support of the pillow, her head was spinning, and she felt herself falling; she fell for what seemed like forever, finally landing not on the floor but in his arms.

"Elizabeth!"

Still not certain whether she was dreaming, she let him guide her to the armchair near the fire and place her in it. His arms withdrew from around her, and he settled himself on a chair in front of her.

"Elizabeth, what is the matter? Are you still unwell? I shall call for the doctor."

"No! No... there is no need. There is nothing wrong with me except that I am tired. I must return home. Where are Lady Ellen and Jane? And Becky?"

"Lady Matlock returned to her house. Your sister is having tea with Mr. Bingley and Mrs. Annesley. Becky amused herself for a while and fell asleep half an hour ago on Georgiana's pillow. I suspect they will both sleep for a couple of hours."

"But are Jane and Mr. Bingley aware that you are here with me?"

"Yes."

"Yes? What must Mr. Bingley think of me? What about Mrs. Annesley?" She attempted to get to her feet, but he pressed her arm gently.

"Do not worry about that, Elizabeth. I only informed Mr. Bingley and your sister about my whereabouts. Mrs. Annesley knows you are sleeping and that I had to attend to some important letters. I have settled everything."

"Yes, so it seems. Then again, I am not surprised, sir. You are accustomed to settling things to your liking. It must be very convenient for one to be able to do so anytime he pleases."

"I do not understand your meaning, Elizabeth, but I can see you are angry with me."

"Really? How very perceptive you are, sir. You astonish me."

"Elizabeth, would not you rather tell me what is bothering you instead of trying to offend me?"

"I would rather not talk about anything at the moment, sir. I think I am entitled to that. After all, you preferred not to talk to me earlier. Indeed, you became very angry because I asked your aunt a simple question." She bit her lips after the words escaped. She did not want to provoke that kind of conversation. She did not feel strong enough to handle confronting him.

"I see... So I was correct in my assumption." His voice was so low that she could barely understand his words. "I was not angry with you. I confess I was displeased but certainly not because you had asked my aunt a question. Then again, I am convinced you know well enough why I was displeased."

"Indeed I do not, sir. I am afraid you are giving me far too much credit."

He stared at her silently for a few long moments. She was not talking to him; she was fighting with him as she had in their early days.

"Very well then, I shall trust your word and explain to you what upset me. And may I hope you will then tell me the cause of your distress? I cannot bear to have this misunderstanding between us."

"If there is a misunderstanding, I am sure it will soon be cleared up, sir." Her tone was still cold and polite, and he did not fail to notice that she had not promised to reveal the cause of her disquiet.

"Mr. Wickham made that reference to the Hothfields yesterday with a very precise purpose; it was another cowardly attack against me as he knew very well that I could not respond to him as he deserved."

"And why not? As I recall, you have done very well in defending yourself against Mr. Wickham's impertinence before. You even threw him from your carriage if I remember correctly."

"Because it was a private matter — a very unpleasant one — that involved other people's reputations as well as my own. I could not expose them by publicly arguing with Mr. Wickham over their past affairs."

"I see… I noticed your strong reaction at the mere mention of the matter."

"Yes, you do know me well enough to notice my discomfort. But it was his comment, not your question, that was the reason for my displeasure. Earlier, while we walked in the park, you tried to bring up the topic in our conversation, did you not? But you did not really ask me, you merely made a reference to Wickham and his opinions."

"Yes I did. I apologise if my curiosity caused you such discomfort. I never could have imagined that an inquiry about Lord and Lady Hothfield could give rise to your anger. Are you holding yourself personally responsible for protecting them?" It took all of her courage to hold his gaze and appear calm.

"I certainly am not responsible for them in any other way than being a close acquaintance who is considerate and willing to protect their privacy."

"Is it only their privacy you are trying to protect or yours as well?"

He stared into her eyes, searching them in utter surprise, his brow furrowed in wonder and worry.

"Elizabeth, what is it that you specifically want to ask me?"

"Apparently nothing that you are inclined to share with me." She lowered her eyes, swallowing violently as the lump in her throat stopped her breath. She could feel tears gathering in her eyes.

"I believe that statement is unfair, Elizabeth. I dare say there are many things I have shared with you; in truth, I have opened myself to you as I never before have done with anyone. If I choose not to indulge your curiosity once, I do not think I deserve such censure. There are things a man may not want to discuss with his future wife. Though I promise never to lie to you, there are — and will most probably be in the future — things I might not want to talk with you about."

He gently raised her head so he could meet her eyes. He could easily see that she did not agree with him, but he could not allow her to persist in her stubbornness, either. "Elizabeth?"

"Yes, sir. You are correct, of course. You are entitled to choose what you do and do not want to keep secret from me. You may do whatever pleases you; I must beg your forgiveness. I should not have attempted to impose upon your privacy. Now would you be so kind as to allow me some privacy? I am not well." She rose to her feet and moved away, sitting on a settee with her back turned to him so she could hide her face, now wet with the tears she could no longer control. She wanted him to leave.

Mr. Darcy hurried toward her, surprised and irritated by her seemingly irrational behaviour and her refusal to see the justice of his statements. Her persistence seemed childish to him; he knew that most men never shared private matters with their wives, even less with their intendeds, and most women never would have dreamed of making such demands of their betrothed or their husband. He did not want to yield in this first disagreement as he was certain he was right. She was a remarkably intelligent woman but passionate in defending her opinion even when she was in the wrong. It was important that she learn to accept his decisions as a man and as her husband.

Carefully, he moved towards her and stopped a few steps away, his heart melting at the sight of her, burdened by grief, her head down and her hands slightly trembling in her lap. He had not seen her in such a state since the night of the ball in the Netherfield library.

A sudden icy shiver ran up his spine, and memories — both old and recent — invaded his mind; many small things, gestures and words from that night almost two months ago and of that very day, mixed in his head. Everything suddenly became painfully clear, and the meaning of her words struck him as he could now understand her deep, hidden grief. How could he have been so blind and selfish in interpreting her reactions? He had styled himself as her mind reader but had failed miserably at such an important moment.

He knelt before her and cupped her face in his hands, wiping her tears away with his thumbs.

"My love, I was such a fool not to understand the true reason for your torment. It is not *Lady Hothfield*, but *Miss Alton* who troubles you, is it not? Wickham told you about her that night at the ball; I am sure of it. Why did you not ask me before?"

His tender and comforting voice wrapped around her like a melody, and she finally lifted her eyes to meet his. "You said you did not want to discuss this with me, and you were right. It was not for me to insist — "

"Elizabeth, if I had imagined what was really troubling you, I would not have said that. Pray tell me — what story did that scoundrel tell you?"

She fought to restrain her tears. "He told me about you and Miss Alton. He said that you and she had quite a story a few years ago. At the moment, it did not bother me excessively. I mean . . . "

She felt her face burning with embarrassment and lowered her eyes, too ashamed to hold his, but she continued nonetheless. "I know that gentlemen sometimes . . . meet other ladies before they get married and . . . I mean, I imagined that it was possible that you . . . "

He sketched a smile, but her embarrassment only grew.

"But, my love, if you were so rational in dealing with Wickham's story when you first heard about it, why did you let yourself be overwhelmed with distress today?"

She stared deeply into his dark gaze, wondering that he could not understand such a thing. Did he truly believe she would accept sharing his love, caresses, and attention?

"William, I could accept the fact that Miss Alton was a part of your past. But I could not accept it if she were a part of your present, too. I simply cannot bear it. I would rather annul our engagement than be forced to live every day with that burden."

Darcy withdrew from her, frowning.

"Elizabeth, what on earth are you talking about? Are you implying that there is currently a relationship between me and Lady Hothfield?"

"Is there not? Mr. Wickham said that — "

"Mr. Wickham?! Despite the fact that you know well what kind of man he is, you insist on believing him every time. Will this pattern never end?! It cannot be that you value *his* opinion, so your opinion of *me* must be exceedingly low."

She hurried to protest, but he rose from her side and started pacing the room in a state of agitation she had witnessed before. He finally stopped in front of her, lowering his stare so he could lock his gaze with hers.

"What pains me most, Elizabeth, is that you distrusted not only my character but also my love for you, and that is more than I can bear."

His words drained all the blood from her face until she became as pale as he was.

"William, please do not say that. You cannot believe that — "

"I do not know what to believe, Elizabeth. Every time a difficult situation arises, you seem inclined to think the worst of me. Apparently, I have not succeeded in redeeming myself in your eyes no matter how hard I have tried — quite the contrary. I now discover that you gave little consequence to everything I told you about my feelings. Have I ever given you reason to suspect that I have an interest in any other woman or that my affection lies elsewhere? Or perhaps you think that as soon as I finish kissing you, I hurry off to kiss another — behind her husband's back, of course. Pray tell me, of what other horrible things do you believe me capable? And would it be useful to defend myself? Would you believe anything I might tell you? Is my word any good at all compared to Wickham's?"

His voice became stronger, and his face darkened with every word. His eyes were searching her face with such an expression of hurt and anger that she could not bear it and lowered her glaze again; she desperately wanted to say something, to do something… But what could be said? What could be done? She could not fight with him any longer; she had no strength left for that. She felt empty, tired, and alone — frozen in her loneliness. It had served nothing for either of them to have such a conversation; it had only pained them more. He seemed to suffer as much as she did, and she still did not know the truth. He had not denied or confirmed anything. She had gained nothing but stood to lose so much.

"I… I should go now. I do not know what I could say. I never meant to hurt you, William. And you must know that I never doubted your word. I never doubted what you told me. What you did *not* tell me pained me more than I could bear… And it is true that I tend to believe the worst... because I am so frightened that I might lose you. I... I should go now."

Slowly, as though she suddenly aged twenty years, her steps moved to the door. Ceasing to fight the tears rolling over her cheeks, she pressed the door handle and began to open it — the door leading her out of their room.

The next instant, she gasped as he violently slammed the door shut from behind her, trapping her between the heavy wood and his body. With the same violence, he grabbed her arm and turned her toward him, and then his hands fixed her shoulders against the door. She was staring at him, wondering, waiting, and almost frightened by his fierce moves. His dark eyes, troubled by his distress, held hers for a few torturous moments before he finally broke the silence and spoke.

"Elizabeth... " his voice was low and husky, and every word brought him closer to her, his breath burning her face while his nearness took her breath completely. "We are the silliest and most ridiculous fools who ever lived."

She felt his arms lifting and carrying her across the room toward the bed; her last remnants of rational thought told her to protest and ask him what he had in mind, but she had no strength to do it or the will to stop him, no matter what he might do with her. She surrendered completely to his will, wanting nothing more than to forget the loneliness and unbearable suffering she had experienced only moments earlier. She wanted him; she needed him.

He practically threw himself on the bed with her in his arms, almost crushing her with his weight. From only inches away, his eyes fell into hers again, while he shook his head in wonder.

"Elizabeth, what should I do with you? What should I do with me when I am near you? You make me lose my self-control. You make me... you make me want to devour you before my love for you devours me."

She did not answer... did not move... did not breathe. His face leaned closer until his lips brushed against hers, and her mouth parted instantly, welcoming him. The next moment, however, he abruptly and unceremoniously sat up, pulling her with him and withdrawing his arms from around her, his insistent stare fixed on her face. His countenance was calmer.

"Elizabeth, please forgive my wild behaviour! Of course, I will allow you to leave whenever you want to, but perhaps we should try to clarify this misunderstanding first. We cannot simply hope that tomorrow everything will be fine. And we cannot presume that a kiss will wash away any trace of this quarrel."

She nodded in silent agreement, trying to recover from the emotional shocks she had just experienced.

"There is no need for you to apologise, William. Neither of us has been without fault; I can see my mistake now. I should have confided my fears to you. It is just that everything happened so quickly. When Lady Matlock said that Lady Hotfield was… I instantly remembered everything I had been told about her. But my mind was clouded, and I could not think rationally. The only thought that persisted in my head was that you… I cannot explain what I felt… I am so sorry that I hurt you." She bit her lips and closed her eyes tightly to stop another outburst of tears. He watched her, grieved by her obvious pain, but not attempting to comfort her.

"William, please do not believe that I doubted your love or your character. Even if it was true that you and she…" She blushed and swallowed violently to clear her throat. "Even then I know I would not have any right to blame you for deceit because you have never told me that you are not…visiting any other lady. And I know it is customary among the gentlemen of the *ton* to… I know a woman must accept that her betrothed, even her husband might do that. But I cannot bear it, and I am afraid I never could. The pain was so strong that it broke my heart. I am sorry…" She could not fight the tears anymore, but she felt relieved that at least she had told him what she really felt. At that moment, it was for him to decide. And so he did.

His own heart broke, seeing the pain he had unwittingly caused her. And, as he surrounded her with his arms and nestled her head against his shoulder, he did not curse Wickham's malicious manoeuvres as much as he did his own selfish pride and his temper that had once more controlled his reason. It had taken so little for him to become angry when she had suggested an affair between him and another woman instead of thinking how deeply that thought was affecting her. She had been wrong to suspect him, that was true; but again, he had hurried to censure her when all she needed was the assurance and comfort he could offer so easily. He took her face between his hands and kissed her eyelids, wiping away her tears with his lips.

"My love, please do not cry. There is no reason for such distress; you must trust me. It is true that I had a close acquaintance with Miss Alton, and I did admire her very much. But she was never my mistress nor did we ever share that kind of intimacy because I did not want that to happen! As for being involved in a sordid affair with her now — when she is a married woman — I am indeed offended that you could think such a thing."

"William, I — "

"No, please, let me finish; I will tell you the entire story so you will understand. Or would you rather ask me something particular?"

"No… I have no particular questions."

She whispered her words, wishing she had the strength to tell him she needed no further explanation — that she trusted him implicitly. She was ashamed to realise how weak she had been before the green bite of jealousy.

"The story Wickham referred to happened more than four years ago, only a few months after my father passed away. As the estate's responsibilities were trying — quite overwhelming at the time — I spent most of my time at Pemberley, travelling to town only when absolutely necessary, and even then, only rarely indulging in any kind of social event. On one of those occasions, my cousin — the colonel's brother — introduced me to Miss Alton. To my utter surprise, she expressed her pleasure in 'finally making the acquaintance of the handsomest young gentleman in London,' and then proceeded to tell me of the many things she had heard about me. I must confess I was flattered by her attentions at the time, but I did not really give them much consideration. During that time, she was the centre of everyone's attention, and most gentlemen were engaging in constant and expensive efforts to gain her... favours. As I had not the slightest interest in that kind of competition, I merely exchanged a few pleasantries with her at that party or the next when we met again."

"Do you think she was interested in you? I mean... she obviously admired you; she told you as much."

"I cannot tell if her interest was real or not. I am more inclined to believe that she was intrigued by my lack of attention toward her. You must understand, Elizabeth, that there are women — and Miss Alton was one of those — who find great pleasure in having men's admiration and company, just as there are men whose only interest in a woman is the pleasure of an intimate acquaintance. Do you understand my meaning?" He paused and withdrew from her a little so he could meet her gaze; he saw her blushing and nodding silently, so he resumed his story.

"Approximately a week later, I joined the Matlock party at the theatre. As it was the last play Miss Alton was to perform that season, the theatre was crowded, a fact that I found annoying and tiresome. Though the spectacle was exquisite, I was relieved when it ended. My relatives departed, but I remained in the box until the last of the audience left, and only then did I retire. I asked my carriage to follow me, and I took a stroll to enjoy the pleasure of the night, but it was not meant to be. Behind the theatre, I witnessed a quarrel between a man and a woman whose faces I could not distinguish. I refrained from moving forward, as it was not for me to interfere; however, I changed my mind when the man actually hit the woman and she fell to the ground. I approached them and was surprised to recognise the woman as Miss Alton. I hurried to help her. Meanwhile, her companion disappeared, but not before I recognised him; it was Lord Felton, one of the richest and most active members of the *ton* and a close acquaintance of our 'friend' Mr. Wickham. Miss Alton also recognised me and asked that I take her home as discreetly as possible so nobody would see her in such a state."

Elizabeth's eyes opened wide at such a horrible story, and a gasp escaped her lips as he continued.

"We reached her house, and as soon as she was safe inside, I made to depart, but she insisted that I should wait for her return. I thought she needed my assistance in something so I remained in the salon. She returned about an hour later; by then her face was swollen and darkened from the attack, and she looked pitiful."

"Dear God, what a horrible man! Did you do something? Was he punished for his cruelty?"

He bowed his head, impressed by the compassion displayed on her face.

"It was not for me to do anything, Elizabeth. I did offer her my assistance, but she insisted that the matter be kept secret as she was to leave England in less than a month. Lord Felton was a married man, and she did not want to leave such a scandal behind her."

"He was a married man? But then how — "

"That was the question I wanted to ask as well, but I restrained myself. She confessed the whole affair to me, and I understood that she had not been without fault in what had occurred. You see... Lord Felton was one of those men who had tried to gain her favour, and he had offered her many expensive presents, which she gladly accepted without ever officially repelling or encouraging his advances. That evening, he was... claiming his rights... "

Another gasp escaped her, and he could easily see a disgusted, appalled expression changing her countenance.

"Yes, Elizabeth, that was my reaction as well. She did not fail to notice it; to my shock, she suddenly produced a bottle of brandy and began to drink — two, maybe three glasses. From that moment, I cannot say exactly how things happened, but she began to talk. She angrily asked what gave me the right to judge her — though I had not yet said a single word — and that it was easy for me to play the perfect gentleman as life had given me everything. I watched her, stunned, as she paced the room, talking and drinking more brandy. She told me about her family passing away when she was five, about the years she had spent in one orphanage after another, about running away — at the age of twelve — with a group of strolling actors, and about unbelievable cruelties and experiences that easily would destroy a man, not to mention a child.

"Among those actors, she discovered her talent, and they taught her to use it and encouraged her to learn to play and sing. Without apparent remorse, she confessed that the most important lesson she learned was never to let herself be used by men but to use them instead to reach her goal. I will not tell you all the details, but obviously she succeeded in what she proposed to do. Her remarkable talent could not be denied; at the age of twenty-three, she had already become a well-known actress. Ten years later — at the time I met her — she was so famous that nobody gave any importance to... the way in which she had reached that success."

Elizabeth's incredulous stare was exactly what he had expected, and he paused before continuing.

"A couple of hours later — it was far past midnight — she lay on the sofa, and in a few moments, she fell asleep. I fetched a servant to take care of her and left, but I must say I did not find much sleep of my own that night. Such a story was difficult for me to hear."

"I can easily believe you. I have admired Miss Alton occasionally at the theatre, but it never crossed my mind that she might be anything but a beautiful and talented lady, whose fame was fairly justified by her exquisite performance. I must confess... I never thought her to be anything but honourable and worthy of admiration."

"Elizabeth, I hope you will understand me when I say that, even now, I consider her worthy to be admired. I came to that conclusion shortly after that night, as the following morning I received a note from her, expressing her gratitude and politely asking if I could join her for tea in the afternoon. I could not refuse the invitation and returned to her house later that day. A few close friends of hers were already present, and she loudly begged my forgiveness for her behaviour the previous night, again expressing her gratitude for my assistance. She also confessed she had returned through a messenger all the presents she had received from Lord Felton and intended never to allow him near her again."

"That was very wise of her."

"Yes, it was. As I already told you, she was prepared to leave the country for a European tour within a month, but during her remaining time in town, I was often invited to her house for the various small parties she hosted, as her bruised face did not allow her to be seen by a larger circle of acquaintances. I was most surprised for the opportunity to know a completely different type of woman — not the actress glowing on the stage or the adventurous person I had thought her to be after the first night. She was pleasant and charming company, and a very bright lady, quite educated and capable of handling a conversation on almost any subject. Her private performances while she played and sang for only a few guests were an even greater delight than those displayed at the theatre. This new Miss Alton — whose real name was Mary Ann Smith — was less glamorous, less spectacular in her appearance and gowns, but much more friendly, unpretentious, and worthy of admiration. Her behaviour toward me was attentive. In the beginning, she was embarrassed by the facts she had disclosed to me, and she desperately asked for my secrecy as nobody else was aware of her past. Of course, I assured her that her secret was safe with me, and indeed, until today I have never told this story to any other person."

"I see... From what you have told me, I can easily understand how you came to admire each other. She seems a wonderful person... and such a beautiful woman. I am certain any man would fall in love with her. You must have deeply regretted the sudden separation." Her voice was again soft and unsure, and she lowered her eyes.

Darcy's hand gently tilted her chin up until she met his gaze — unexpectedly serene, even smiling.

"Elizabeth, I was not in love with Miss Alton. Even more, I never suspected or fancied myself in love with Miss Alton or any other woman. When I told you the day after our engagement that my heart never spoke before I met you, I was completely in earnest — you must know that."

Her eyes were like two mirrors of her soul; he could easily see all her love for him, every feeling, every fear and every hope. His heart melted in tenderness, and though her distress saddened him, the happiness he felt at such an honest and strong profession of love from his beloved was more powerful than any other feeling.

"Because I want to be completely honest, I will confess to you one more thing. A few days before her departure, she invited me to remain for the night after a party. I was quite young at the time — ten years her junior — and I was flattered at first and tempted to accept. She must have noticed my indecision, because she became quite insistent; in a short time, she turned into a skilful seductress, and I have to confess to you that I was... quite overwhelmed by her attentions."

He felt Elizabeth's body stiffen, and her expression changed in a moment, but he did not want to keep anything from her. Gently stroking her hands, he continued.

"Only a few moments later, I recovered from the surprise and rejected her, gently but firmly, and I declined her invitation. She was surprised and incredulous; she even laughed and told me I could not possibly be serious as no man had ever rejected her. When I insisted in my decision, she asked for my reason, and I told her with complete honesty that I had come to admire and respect her too much to use her as a pleasant diversion, and that neither my duties nor my feelings would allow me to offer her more than that."

"Oh my..."

"She frowned and politely asked me to leave; I did not see or speak to her again until the evening before her departure when I received an invitation from her. There were no other guests when I reached her house, and we talked for less than half an hour. I tried to apologise if my words had offended her, but she interrupted me and expressed her own regret for placing me in such an embarrassing situation. She thanked me again for my support and friendship though she said she did not deserve either. We agreed to put aside the incident and parted on friendly terms."

"And she married Lord Hothfield."

"Yes, but not immediately. Her European tour had been a success, but in London, things were not as good. As soon as she left, rumours about her were spread around town, undoubtedly by Lord Felton and his closest friends, Mr. Wickham among them. Rumours of great seriousness arose, implying that she had stolen jewels from Lord Felton and other men and that she had used her charms to ruin still others — rumours that, of course, were as ridiculous as they were untrue. Not many people believed such malice, but a few of them did. I had no restraint in expressing my favourable opinion of her every time I had the chance, but as I said, I was rarely in town. One of her most fervent defenders was Lord Hothfield, and rumour had it that he involved himself in a physical fight with Lord Felton upon hearing his slander of Miss Alton."

"They fought? But I understood Lord Hothfield is an old man."

"Not old at all, Elizabeth; I mean, he was seven or eight years younger than my father, which would make him around forty-five now. He is a very pleasant sort of man who had the misfortune of losing his first wife and two children a long time ago when my mother was still alive. He had not much family left nor any other close relatives, and I truly believe that his marriage to the former Miss Alton was to the advantage of both."

"William, do you think he knows about — ?"

"About her past? Yes, he certainly does. Apparently, they met later that year in Rome and renewed their acquaintance; they married in France at the end of winter. I confess that my first — and very ungentlemanlike — thought was that she had accepted Lord Hothfield to be assured finally of that respectability she had lacked. You can imagine how many old and new rumours this unexpected marriage gave rise to among the *ton*. I met them the next spring, however, and after the first moment, I ceased to doubt the affection between them. I had the opportunity to speak to her privately for a few minutes, and she assured me she had told her husband everything before the wedding, including how the two of us had met, how she had told me everything about her past... and how I had refused her when she offered herself to me."

"Oh, how astonishing! He must truly love her very much to marry her after such a disclosure."

"I dare say he does and that her affection for him is equally strong and honest. She retired from the stage that year, and they spend most of the time at his estate. Lady Ellen and Lord Matlock, having been on friendly terms with Lord Hothfield for years, reluctantly accepted an invitation two years ago, as they had many doubts about his marriage. However, they returned a fortnight later truly delighted, declaring Lady Hothfield a charming hostess, a proper mistress of the house, and a devoted and loving wife."

His tone changed as he continued his story.

"Despite Wickham's statement, I cannot say I am a friend of the Hothfields but more a close acquaintance. I have met them only three or four times in the last three years, and each time I was happy to be in their company. However, last summer their happiness was put to a most difficult trial: Lady Hothfield gave birth to a child, but the boy survived only two days. I confess that I suffered for them as I would have for a member of my own family. And one morning at the club, while I was having breakfast with the colonel, we heard Lord Felton talking with other gentlemen; in short, his opinion was that the child's death was a blessing, as he surely was not Lord Hothfield's child, and he was wagering as to who the real father might have been."

"Dear God, how can a man be so horrible?" Elizabeth's eyes were full of tears, and he gently stroked her cheek with his fingertips.

"I am sorry to pain you, my love. I told you the story was not a pleasant one; I will finish it shortly. His insinuations were clearly directed to offend me, but nobody understood their meaning except me. However, before I could do or say anything, Colonel Fitzwilliam reacted quite violently as he considered the Hothfields close and dear to his family. His behaviour provoked a real scandal, which only spread further rumours and caused more pain and grief to Lord and Lady Hothfield. Lady Ellen was angry with Robert for his foolish reaction. That was why I avoided any conversation on the subject last night when Mr. Wickham mentioned their names, no doubt intentionally to force a response from me."

By the time he had finished his story, Elizabeth's hands were trembling from the emotion that overwhelmed her. Everything was so completely different than she had expected; she could do nothing but stare at him, her eyes still wet with tears. She whispered, "William…" and then stopped, as no more words came out.

His right arm encircled her shoulders and he pulled her to his chest, his lips gently touching her hair. "Elizabeth, let us not discuss our disagreement further, shall we? As you said, neither of us was without fault, and we reacted passionately and impulsively."

"It was I who reacted impulsively. I must say I learned a very difficult lesson today; I will never presume anything nor will I doubt you again before asking for the truth. I am grateful for your generosity in sharing the blame with me and forgiving me."

Impetuously, before she had time to notice his gesture and even less to guess his intention, his arms lifted her up and — shockingly — she found herself in his lap; she gasped loudly, staring at him in astonishment.

"Well, it is good to know that but hardly believable, Elizabeth; apparently, you have not learned your lesson well enough." His voice was deep and husky, and for a moment, she worried that he was still upset.

"You have already presumed that I have actually forgiven you, which I have not. Quite the contrary, I am adding this offence to the one from the Gardiner's house when you implied I would not invite them to the ball."

"Oh…" Her mouth rounded, her lips suddenly dry, as she saw the glint in his eye and began to understand his meaning.

"Ahh, so you do remember! I am glad. Because I must warn you, I am still determining the proper compensation for such undeserved insults. I really doubt that any other lady would vex her future husband so greatly, especially when his value is ten thousand a year! I seriously intend to complain to my future mother-in-law as soon as we return to Hertfordshire, unless you can persuade me to change my mind."

"I beg your forgiveness, sir. I am afraid your kindness has deeply affected my behaviour. I will try most diligently to improve myself in this regard, for I never would want to merit complaint."

Every moment that passed raised her spirits, all her previous fears vanishing under the spell of his unspoken profession of love and desire, and she readily entered into his little — but dangerous — game of words. From her new position, she experienced more daring than she had previously. The novelty of having her face at the same level as his was thrilling, as her hands encircled his neck and toyed with the curls on his nape.

As soon as she was quiet, he felt his face covered by light, delicious kisses, her soft lips tracing their way from his forehead down to the line of his jaw. He closed his eyes, allowing the exquisite sensation to wrap him until her lips finally reached his and pressed tenderly against them, a tenderness soon dominated by a passionate urge.

Impudently, she pulled him back until he lay on the bed; a moment later, his hands and long legs encircled her, trapping her in a breathtaking embrace. Their mouths were not just kissing but also fighting to possess the other, their tongues dancing together with ever-growing passion.

Her hands daringly slid inside his vest and stroked his chest through the thin fabric of his shirt; he moaned deeply, whispering her name, and his moan grew dangerously louder a moment later when her fingers, greedily, possessively, and shamelessly, found their way under his shirt and touched the bare skin of his back.

"Oh God, Elizabeth..."

The shock was equally strong for her, and for a moment she stopped kissing him, stopped breathing — only to start again, her heart beating more wildly, a moment later. For the first time, her caresses were more daring, passionate, and possessive than his. Her hunger for him seemed more ravenous. She could feel it; he could feel it.

It was not a mere search for pleasure, but a consuming need for the assurance that he belonged to her and only to her, that the place in his arms — and in his heart — was only for her. She wanted to take everything he could give her and offer herself to him — completely.

Her body ached with desire for his touch, and she barely suppressed a scream of delight when his legs that already encircled her pulled her closer between his thighs, rubbing her against him. She could feel him pressing almost painfully, though astonishingly pleasurably, against her. Her body — her hips — shattered in response, trembling but not able to move in the grip of his legs. Her hands — the only free part of her — frenetically stroked his chest, now completely uncovered by his opened shirt, strong and warm under her exploring fingers.

She did scream though — fortunately not very loudly, as her mouth was imprisoned by his — when his hands cupped her breasts as he never had before. His fingers began a sweet, maddening torture through the fabric of her dress, caressing their soft fullness until she thought she could not bear it any longer — but she was wrong.

Reluctant to abandon the sweetness of her lips, his mouth traced a warm path from her chin down to her throat and along the line of her neck, touching her, tasting her, trying to satisfy his appetite with the savour of her skin until he reached the edge of her dress; he did not stop there — not this time. His left hand released the soft roundness of her breast, allowing his mouth to appease its desire. The touch of his lips burned her through the thin muslin until she was forced to bite her lips so as not to cry out again — but her violent trembling she could not control.

However, his hunger only grew — disappointed, unsatisfied, and frustrated by the fabric that kept his lips from their goal; with little thought, his free hand pulled the offending garments from her shoulder, and he heard her whispered entreaty, "William, please..."

His hand remained still on her shoulder, the other still cupping her breast, and he lifted his eyes to meet her gaze. His lips returned to her face, touched her cheek and then rested near her ear, whispering, "What is it you wish, my love?"

Her body was still trapped between his legs, his hand lying where her heart was beating, his thumb never ceasing its torturous stroke. It was difficult to speak; she did not want to speak. She wanted... "I wish you to... Please do not stop. I do not want you to stop."

It was more than an acceptance — more than an invitation — it was pleading. All her previous resolution eluded her, and she closed her eyes, waiting — hoping — for what would come next. She felt him stroking her cheek with the backs of his fingers, and his lips whispered in the hollow of her ear.

"My beautiful, passionate Elizabeth..." Nothing more.

His legs slowly released their grip around her, and his hand lifted her dress back onto her shoulder; she opened her eyes to stare at him, her disappointment so obvious that he could not help smiling and kissing the corner of her lips tenderly.

He adjusted their position so they were lying beside each other, his arms embracing her again as he pulled together his unbuttoned shirt. Gently, he moved her head to cradle on his chest, her hair — now escaped from their pins — tickling his bare neck. He felt her stiffen in his embrace, and as his fingers caressed the line of her jaw, she lifted her face, revealing her wondering gaze. He saw passion — unfulfilled passion — in her eyes, mixed with hurt feelings.

"Elizabeth... If you knew — really knew — how strongly I desire to love you — here, now, and for the rest of my life — you would be frightened. *I* am frightened, and I am struggling so much to protect you. But your wonderful, generous offer only makes my struggle more difficult. It is sheer torture that I can hardly bear."

As soon as he finished, he regretted his words and most of all his grave tone; the expression in her eyes changed in an instant and he could sense that he disturbed her. Her whispered question confirmed his suspicions.

"But, William, I do not understand. Why would you say that? Why would you need to protect me? You said you desire me... Is that something to be feared?"

"No...! No, Elizabeth! I am sorry I distressed you. It is just that..."

She was staring at him, her eyes wide with curiosity, asking him silently the same question, so close to him that her breath — deep and slow — was burning his neck. He could not possibly let her go without explaining his meaning. He could not possibly permit her to be frightened by the thought of intimacy. He must explain his meaning to her; but how could a man explain such a thing to his young, inexperienced betrothed — the respectable daughter of a gentleman?

He averted his eyes a moment, his brow furrowed in concentration, searching for the proper words.

"Elizabeth, do you know... what is supposed to happen?" Her cheeks turned crimson as she nodded.

"Yes... my aunt explained it both to me and Jane some time ago."

He stroked her cheeks again, smiling. "Then I will only tell you this: I cannot speak for other people, but I promise you that, for us, it will be a wonderful thing. Indeed, what can be more beautiful than to share our love, our passion, and our desire to be one body — as we are already one heart?"

"Then why — ?" Her eyes, moist with tears, were still wondering, asking him what her lips did not dare to.

"Why did I stop? Because I want our first time together to be perfect, my love, and it will be perfect. So, I cannot allow it to happen now with a house full of people — my sister, your sister, Mr. Bingley and all the servants — who could disturb us at any time. Not to mention that Becky might awake any moment and ask where we are. Do you understand my reasoning?"

His voice was tender and teasing at the same time, trying to dissipate the tension between them; she blushed and then instantly became mortified at her obliviousness of the reality around them and her complete lack of consideration for the outside world. Was she so wanton that she forgot all rationality, propriety and decorum?

How was it possible for her to lose all her dignity? She practically begged him to dishonour her, his house, their sisters. And he — wisely, prudently, respectfully — refused her. What a horrible indignity for both of them — and it was her fault!

She averted her eyes from him, but it took Darcy only a moment to notice her distress — and to understand it. His hands cupped her face, forcing her to bear his intense gaze. "Elizabeth, when I said my desire was frightening me, I meant that I was very close to throwing away all these considerations. None of my family, your family or the entire world were as important as loving you in that instant; I confess that it was the most difficult struggle I have ever endured. But do you know the most compelling reason to maintain control? I did not want our first time together to occur on the same day we had such a harsh and painful argument."

His thumbs were caressing her cheeks, and she felt her heart shattering with the burden of her love for this man. His words, his tender looks, and his mere presence were always the perfect palliation for any grief in her soul. Then again, he was also the primary *cause* of any grief or pain she had experienced of late. She wanted to say more — to tell him how grateful she was for his caring love and his tender protectiveness toward her — but she could say nothing more than a simple, "Thank you, William."

They lay in silence together for a while longer to recover completely, and he finally rose, pulling her with him so quickly that she almost fell off the bed. She could not restrain her peals of laughter, and he shook his head in mocking censure.

"Miss Bennet, enough laughter! We have duties to which we must attend immediately. Mrs. Annesley might find it hard to believe you have been sleeping so long, or that I would need this much time to read a few letters — not to mention that Mr. Bingley is not to be trusted alone with your sister as he is capable of doing anything to force her to marry him. I will wait for you downstairs as soon as you are ready."

He opened the door, then turned toward her and moved a few steps closer. "Oh, and Elizabeth, one more thing: What I told you earlier about the house being full of people and all the other aspects — these are valid considerations only for the time being. As soon as we are married, all of them will significantly lose their importance. As for our future quarrels — and I dare say there will be many — I cannot think of a better way to reconcile."

He exited through the door, leaving her in the middle of the room staring after him, her lips suddenly dry.

'As soon as we are married…'

Mechanically, she moved to the mirror, trying to adjust her wild appearance and wondering at the astonishing emotions she had experienced in the last few hours. *From despair to felicity…fire and ice… William!*

LESS THAN TEN MINUTES LATER, Elizabeth met Mr. Darcy in the salon; with proper politeness, he kissed her hand and directed her to the drawing room where Jane, Mr. Bingley and Mrs. Annesley were supposed to have tea together.

Mr. Darcy opened the door, but the sight made him stop in the doorway; as for Elizabeth, once more she was given proof that her future husband was correct in his assumptions: Jane Bennet and Charles Bingley were sitting on the couch, engaged in such a passionate kiss that they did not even notice the door open. No, it was not just a kiss; it was a passionate embrace; and the only thought that crossed Elizabeth's mind was that she could not fathom where Jane's hands were.

Astonished and hardly knowing how to react, Mr. Darcy pulled Elizabeth back and slowly closed the door, allowing the couple a few more moments of privacy to recover themselves. Elizabeth's wide eyes diverted him exceedingly, as she clearly could not believe the scene they had witnessed. In truth, it was equally hard for him to imagine sweet, angelic Jane indulging in such activities in a house full of people.

"Well, my dear sir, apparently you were right. However, from what I saw, not only is Mr. Bingley not to be trusted, but neither is my sister. I never would have expected something like that from her — not that I would dare complain, as my own behaviour was much worse. I dare say my aunt would be utterly displeased with both of us."

Her words were half-serious, half in jest, and he laughed at her, placing a light kiss on her half-parted lips.

"Dearest, I must say I am very happy for them. And the fact that your sister is so much in love that she cannot help breaking with propriety is wonderfully charming, would you not agree?"

"Yes, of course I would. I want nothing less for my sister than to be as happy as I am."

"Well, I dare say they will both be very happy. Now let us try to enter again before anyone else appears."

He opened the door once more, this time with such a clamour that it would be impossible for anyone inside the room not to hear. Still, when they entered, the couple was fumbling to withdraw their arms from around each other. They quickly rose to their feet, their faces crimson, vainly searching for the proper words to greet the master of the house until he took pity on them.

"Miss Bennet, Mr. Bingley, I dare say you have some news you would like to share with us..."

It was all the encouragement the newly betrothed needed as Mr. Bingley practically shouted the news in his happiness at having been accepted by his beloved Jane.

The moments that followed were happier than Elizabeth could have hoped. To know her most beloved sister was engaged to be married to a man she loved, and whose worthiness and affection could not be doubted, was a true blessing and was as precious to her as her own blissful felicity.

When the sisters returned home an hour later, Jane was still on a cloud and remained in that state the entire evening, especially since the object of her affection had joined them for dinner.

Jane knew she had done something highly improper and that she should feel mortified by the fact that Mr. Darcy witnessed her shocking behaviour in his house. All she really felt, however, was enormous happiness, so powerful that she was afraid she could not bear it. She kept wondering — and even asked her sister Lizzy in the solitude of their room — whether someone could die of too much happiness. When she and Elizabeth retired to change for dinner — a dinner spent once more in the company of the gentlemen — she tried to relate to her sister everything that had passed between her and Mr. Bingley. She could not remember much, but she did recall that at some point Mrs. Annesley excused herself to check on Georgiana and that Mr. Bingley took the opportunity to move near her. And then... his words sounded like the most beautiful music she had ever heard. He spoke to her of his love, his adoration, his wishes... and then he placed a ring on her finger and...

"Oh Lizzy, is it not a beautiful ring?"

"Yes, it is a most beautiful ring." Elizabeth's eyes were as full of tears as Jane's were, and she was certain she had never seen her sister as beautiful. "Dearest Lizzy, you would be ashamed of me; I was so silly! He told me so many wonderful things, and I could not say a word. I only started to cry. And then he... he..."

She blushed so fiercely that her pretty face seemed if it were on fire and could not hold her younger sister's smiling gaze. She averted her eyes while she tried to find the words to confess to her dear sister everything that occurred within the solitude of the library. She remembered Mr. Bingley's tender, comforting words whispered to her and then his thumbs wiping her tears — tears of supreme joy — and then the bliss of his lips on hers... and everything vanishing around her. She could not even testify whether it was real or the most wonderful dream of her life.

Fortunately, Elizabeth did not inquire further, the memories of her own first kiss and embarrassment too fresh in her mind. When they gathered the rest of the family for dinner later that evening, the Gardiners could guess the news long before Charles Bingley informed them of it. In truth, Jane's radiance easily betrayed her happiness and her new state of mind and heart.

Charles Bingley was the only one who did not notice any change in Miss Bennet's countenance that evening. He had always been certain that Jane was as beautiful as an angel, so he found nothing different in her appearance. In truth, he could hardly think of anything but the taste of her lips and the feel of her arms around him. None of his many dreams about the moment she would accept his offer had been even close to that reality. Jane Bennet was more wonderful than any dream; she not only allowed him to embrace her and kiss her, but she responded to him as he never would have dared to hope.

Her lips were so sweet, so soft; he tasted them, and she permitted him to do so. He simply could not have enough of her — the warmth of her body in his arms, the shocking pleasure of her hands touching him, caressing him tentatively... She was an angel and he was the most fortunate man in the world.

And she was soon to be his wife! Though not as soon as he would like as he was forced to wait a few more days for Mr. Bennet's consent when they returned to Hertfordshire. Then he would have to bear the agony of the engagement. His only hope for relief was that Longbourn and Netherfield were remarkably close to each other.

More than once during the evening, Mr. Darcy noticed — and easily recognised it, as it had happened to him countless times — Mr. Bingley's fixed stare at Miss Bennet and the lady's constant blushes. He breathed in sincere relief, knowing that his friend would have no reason to envy him or be angry with him for some old and long-forgotten advice.

Even more, he made a resolution to support his youngest friend as much as he could. Perhaps an invitation for Jane Bennet to join them in town for the season would be convenient for all the parties involved. Yes, he decided, it most certainly would be.

Several days later, Jane and the Gardiners had been ready for quite a while and were entertaining Mr. Darcy and Mr. Bingley in the salon as they waited for Elizabeth to make her appearance. She was at that moment being assisted in her preparations by a modiste purposely sent by Lady Matlock.

At first, Darcy had found Lady Matlock's many preparations and endless preoccupations with Elizabeth's appearance useless and quite tiresome; he knew how to appreciate a lady's fashionable, high quality gown, elegance and good taste, but he had never found Elizabeth wanting in this. She had always been charming, and her tastes were quite to his liking no matter what she wore.

He even tried to have a private talk with his aunt, but Lady Matlock was not to be moved. She insisted the ball would be a very difficult event for Elizabeth, and half of the ladies in attendance likely would want to tear her apart and treat her poorly as a consequence. So, she explained to Mr. Darcy that it was imperiously necessary for Elizabeth to look *"astonishingly and intimidatingly wonderful"* the moment she entered the ball room. *"Astonishing"* and *"intimidating"* were notions that distressed Darcy deeply. He was afraid that all those professional preparations would transform her natural, lively charms into those artificial arrangements so often seen on the young ladies of the *ton*. However, when Elizabeth entered the room, it was several moments before he could breathe again. When he could think rationally, he could do no more than admit that Lady Matlock had been correct once again.

Elizabeth's beauty had been by no means altered but helped to blossom until she became truly stunning. He could not fix his gaze on any particular part of her; he could not have related the colour of her dress or her shoes. He barely noticed the ruby necklace glittering on her creamy skin or the earrings gleaming from behind the dark curls playing near her ears.

All he could see was that she was glowing; she simply radiated light around her, and neither the jewels nor the exquisite gown were brighter than her sparkling eyes and shining smile.

Not only Mrs. Gardiner and Jane, but also Mr. Bingley and Mr. Gardiner gasped loudly at the vision before them. Elizabeth started to laugh, though her face turned red from the pleasure of the silent compliment. Her eyes, however, were captured by Mr. Darcy's intense stare.

"Lady Matlock's choice was exquisite; I hardly recognised myself in the mirror. This dress is the most wonderful thing a woman could ever hope to wear."

With comments and compliments for all three ladies, the gentlemen escorted them to Mr. Darcy's spacious carriage. Remaining a little behind, Mr. Darcy bent his head to whisper in her ear.

"Elizabeth, it is not the dress. I have never seen anyone more beautiful than you."

The warmth of his closeness against her skin made her blush, and she turned to him, smiling in delight.

"I am glad you approve. Your opinion is all that matters to me."

"Then I shall try to make my opinion as clear as possible throughout the night, my dear."

She stared at him in surprise but had no time to ask for more as they had reached the carriage; he handed her in, placing himself near her.

Elizabeth's emotions reached an alarming state as they neared the Matlocks' residence. It would be her first time in their house, and though her first and only meeting with the earl had been rather pleasant and given her no reason to worry, still she never had met the colonel's brother and his wife and did not know what to expect from them. Even more alarming, Lady Catherine was still in the house as her daughter was not fully recovered. Elizabeth felt cold shivers of fear at the mere thought of a public confrontation, though Mr. Darcy assured her that Lady Catherine was being hosted in the opposite wing of the house and would not be present at the ball. The earl himself had assured him of that.

Above everything, however, Elizabeth's distress was generated by the knowledge that she would have to face members of the *ton*, and it was probable that many of them did not hold her in any regard. She looked at her aunt and her sister, happy and a little relieved to have them so close, not realising that they were experiencing their own fears and emotions at being in such exclusive company under the scrutiny of so many eyes. Their position as relatives of Mr. Darcy's future wife would undoubtedly make them the centre of everyone's curiosity, and their major concern was to be at their best — in appearance and behaviour — for Elizabeth's sake.

Unlike the ladies, neither of the gentlemen was occupied with such worrisome thoughts as they gave little importance to anything except the charming ladies at their sides. Society's opinion was of little consequence to either of them.

THE HOUSE HAD THE SAME impressive elegance as Lady Matlock, and Elizabeth tightened her grip on Mr. Darcy's arm as though afraid of their being separated. He smiled at her, covering her hand with his, protectively and comfortingly. Her courage rose a little and then fell again as she entered the enormous ballroom, already filled with people who instantly turned their eyes to her as every attempt at conversation ceased. However, in spite of any fears she might have experienced, her countenance expressed nothing of the kind, the sparkle of her eyes and the slight blush of her cheeks only increasing her beauty.

As the butler formally announced their entrance, Lord and Lady Matlock greeted them warmly and left no doubt about their approval of their nephew's choice. Any rumours of opposition on the earl's part vanished in an instant along with the hopes of some attendees who were anxious to see Darcy embarrassed by his unworthy betrothed.

In truth, many young heiresses and their mothers took it as a deep, personal affront that the man who had paid little attention to any of them had chosen the unknown daughter of a country gentleman to be his wife.

Mr. Darcy had been declared either to have poor taste in women or to be so foolish as to let himself be trapped by a fortune hunter. His future fate had been considered unfortunate, as it was easy to predict that the Matlocks, not to mention Darcy's other relatives, never would accept someone so beneath their position. Therefore, the news that Lady Matlock was in fact hosting a ball for the couple had come as a great surprise and had caused more vexation among the former aspirants to Mr. Darcy's hand than ever had been occasioned before.

Of course, none of them would miss the opportunity to see with their own eyes the lady who had spoiled their hopes, or to enumerate her faults as the basis for at least several months' discussion over tea. Consequently, preparations for the ball had far exceeded what was usual, and the modistes in town had been paid handsomely to have the most fashionable dresses ready in a short time.

The entrance into the ballroom of Mr. Darcy's intended had rendered pointless all of their hard work and preparation. The gentlemen present immediately noticed and approved Miss Elizabeth's complexion, the admirable line of her neck and bare shoulders, and her exceedingly pleasant features, as well as the lines of her curves, masterfully covered and simultaneously revealed by her gown. The ladies, however, needed considerably more time to notice her figure, so consumed were they by thoughts of the exceedingly fine dress Miss Elizabeth was wearing.

The heavy, cream-coloured silk fabric — embroidered with small, satin roses of the same colour as the incredible ruby jewels she wore — fell in waves around her body, creating an astonishing effect of elegance and grace. It was undoubtedly quite expensive, as all the ladies noticed. Her entire appearance was far beyond what they had expected and beyond what they themselves were wearing. After that bitter realisation, their eyes focused on Elizabeth's face, only to meet her bright smile and scrutinising gaze.

LADY MATLOCK MADE IT HER personal responsibility to introduce Elizabeth to the other guests, allowing Colonel Fitzwilliam to take proper care of the Gardiners, Miss Bennet, and Mr. Bingley.

Soon after their arrival, Mr. Bingley and the Gracechurch party were joined by the Hursts and Miss Bingley, whose efforts at politeness toward Elizabeth were under tight regulation. Her cold reception from the Matlocks and Mr. Darcy, as well as the iciness of her brother's manners, made Caroline more indignant, and the bitterness in her tone and expression became unpleasantly obvious. Her previous dislike of Eliza Bennet was painfully supplemented by the sense of her own position — beneath that of everyone else present. To the famous members of the *ton*, she was no more than an unknown young lady, unworthy of notice. She previously had been introduced to a few of them, but none showed any sign of remembering her or any willingness to renew the acquaintance. She had prepared with special care for the evening, not only to prove to Mr. Darcy that she had not been crushed by his poor choice, but also with the hope of gaining the interest of other worthy gentlemen. However, neither Mr. Darcy nor any other young man seemed to have any interest in her, at least for the moment. Fortunately, the evening was only beginning, and she could still hope.

Colonel Fitzwilliam was in quite a good mood and enchanted by Elizabeth's appearance and amiability. Despite her evident emotion — which made her face slightly and charmingly flushed — and her hand clenching Darcy's arm, she was displaying a pleasant self-confidence and admirably proper but unpretentious manners.

A few moments before, she had been introduced to the colonel's elder brother — who had been polite and seemed delighted to make her acquaintance — and his wife, the Lady Beatrice, who barely spoke. She made it clear to Elizabeth and to everyone that she did not intend to bridge the gap between the daughter of an earl and that of a small country gentleman. Still, not for a moment did Elizabeth lose her smile and her amiable tone. Her only little revenge — which brought a barely hidden grin to the lips of Mr. Darcy, the colonel and Lady Matlock — was in addressing the latter with a familiar *"Lady Ellen,"* making the face of Lady Beatrice turn white as, with an even sterner expression, she hurriedly excused herself and departed, dragging her husband with her.

My poor brother, he must do something with that wife of his! Oh... but this night is going to be exceedingly entertaining, thought the colonel, turning to his cousin.

"Darcy, pray tell me, which sets did you fix with Miss Elizabeth? I want to secure at least one for myself."

"Of what are you speaking, Cousin? There is nothing for you to secure, as I intend to claim all the sets for myself." Darcy's countenance was serious and his tone firm, which made the colonel burst into laughter.

"Oh, very amusing, Darcy! You are quite diverting; I grant you that. Now let us be serious, as I want to ask Miss Bennet to dance as well, and I have no time to waste."

"Cousin, you missed my meaning. I was speaking absolutely seriously. I would love to allow you a set with Elizabeth, but then there will be others who will demand the same favour, and I have not the slightest intention of being separated from my intended for so long."

"Oh come, Darcy! You are making yourself ridiculous," Lady Matlock spoke up while Elizabeth laughed softly, smiling gratefully at the colonel.

"Sir, I am sure Mr. Darcy is only teasing you. I would be pleased to stand up with you for any set except the first and the last."

Though they had not previously discussed what sets they were to dance together, she saved those two for him without hesitation. Instantly, Darcy's delighted eyes met hers, silently sharing the happy memories of their last ball, when they had stood face to face for the first and last set; for a moment, they forgot about anyone and anything else in the room. The colonel cleared his throat to draw their attention, smiling ironically at his cousin.

"Now, to resume our conversation, may I have the supper set then? And after it, I will return Miss Elizabeth to you safely so you can enjoy your meal. Would that be acceptable, Darcy?"

"Of course, sir, it would be my pleasure," answered Elizabeth, barely suppressing her laughter as Mr. Darcy sulked.

"I was not teasing Robert, but neither of you seem to take my opinions seriously; I am truly displeased. You must have considered, Elizabeth, that I will be forced to invite other ladies to dance while you enjoy the pleasure of dancing with the colonel."

She was holding his arm tightly, and his free hand was covering hers, squeezing it furtively from time to time; her face was lifted to his, their gazes locked during their humorous exchange. His declared jealousy and disinclination to allow other men to approach her, though in jest, warmed her with pleasure, and her eyes clearly communicated this. Her cheeks were crimson as were her lips, and he had to fight an impulse simply to pull her into his arms and claim those lips, whose softness and sweetness he knew so well.

As if understanding his inner struggle and desire, her lips instantly became dry as a wave of redness spread over her neck and bare shoulders. He could feel the thrill shiver through her arm and could not restrain from slightly tightening the squeeze of her hand.

Lady Matlock's voice broke the spell, but her words only increased Elizabeth's surprise.

"Elizabeth, let me introduce you to Lord and Lady Hothfield. This is my future niece, Miss Elizabeth Bennet."

"Miss Bennet, we are delighted to meet you at last." The earl bowed to her while his wife smiled politely.

It took Elizabeth a few moments of staring at the couple in front of her before she regained her composure and curtsied with proper elegance to them both. Though she had no remaining doubts about Darcy and the former Miss Alton, facing her so suddenly was not as easy as she had hoped. She felt Mr. Darcy's eyes on her, and her cheeks coloured even more; she needed all her strength to return their polite greeting.

"Lady Hothfield, Lord Hothfield... It is an honour to meet you."

"Elizabeth, you are indeed right," said Lady Matlock. "It is truly an honour and the most pleasant surprise to have them with us tonight. Lady Hothfield, I do not recall seeing you in town during the little season; am I mistaken?"

"You are not mistaken, Lady Matlock. We have not left our home since last spring."

Neither Lady Hothfield's tone of voice or appearance was as Elizabeth had expected. Though she was still remarkably beautiful and of perfect elegance, Lady Hothfield was less spectacular and less glamorous than even Lady Matlock. Elizabeth was certain she would not have recognised the former famous actress had she come upon her alone. The lady seemed simply content to be on her husband's arm and to carry on a neutral conversation discreetly without drawing anyone's attention to herself as had usually happened in the past.

"The honour is ours; I am sure, Lady Matlock. As you know, any invitation from you is a true delight for me and for my wife." Then, turning to Elizabeth, the earl continued, "Miss Bennet, allow me to congratulate you on your engagement and to compliment you on your beauty. We were truly impressed the first moment we saw you. Mr. Darcy is a very fortunate man."

Elizabeth blushed and thanked him with a tentative smile; she felt Mr. Darcy slowly taking her hand and placing it back on his arm, then covering it with his own hand, and she felt grateful for that small but thoughtful gesture.

Colonel Fitzwilliam approached them with the Gardiners, Miss Bennet, and Mr. Bingley, and introductions were made, followed by a light and pleasant conversation.

Though trying hard to contribute to the topic of conversation and to pay polite attention to everyone around her, Elizabeth could not help casting repeated glances at Lord Hothfield and his wife. She could also feel that lady's eyes falling upon her more than once. Their eyes met and held for a few moments; Elizabeth blushed as if caught doing something wrong, but Lady Hothfield smiled at her: an open, warm smile; then to Elizabeth's surprise, she moved closer, the smile never leaving her face.

"Miss Bennet, I just wanted to add my praises to my husband's words. You look very beautiful tonight."

"Thank you, Lady Hothfield." Mostly to hide her persistent nervousness, she added. "But I do not deserve such praise; it is this wonderful dress and the exquisite jewels that look beautiful. My only merit is in wearing them."

Obviously surprised by her humility, Lady Hothfield was silent for a moment, and then her smile grew wider. "Your modesty only increases your charm, Miss Elizabeth. I insist in saying you look beautiful and very happy tonight."

Worried about Elizabeth's comfort and still holding her hand on his arm, Mr. Darcy could not find a proper moment to intercede in their conversation. He was searching his intended's countenance, ready to support her if needed.

"In this I cannot contradict you, Lady Hothfield. I am indeed very happy."

"I am glad to hear that, Miss Elizabeth. I hope there is nothing that might shadow your happiness or the pleasure of enjoying this ball."

Neither Elizabeth nor Mr. Darcy failed to understand the hidden implication of that apparently neutral comment. Clearly, Lady Hothfield had noticed Elizabeth's discomfort and insistent stare, and she could easily suspect the reason for it. Miss Elizabeth was not oblivious to Mr. Darcy's past acquaintance with her. The former Miss Alton paled for a moment, not daring to presume how much the younger lady really knew and what her opinion might be. Yet, any fear or distress found a well-deserved relief a moment later, as Elizabeth decidedly put an end to any misunderstanding.

"No, indeed, Lady Hothfield, there is nothing to shadow my present felicity; I am grateful for your concern but there is no reason for it. I truly hope your ladyship will enjoy this evening as well."

"Thank you, I am sure I will." Lady Hothfield intended to return to her husband when Elizabeth's low voice, almost a whisper covered by the others' conversation, stopped her.

"Lady Hothfield, may I dare to be so bold as to tell you how much I admired your performance a few years ago?" She was surprised but evidently not displeased.

"Thank you, Miss Elizabeth. You are very kind."

Lord Hothfield joined them, moving very close to his wife and taking hold of her hand. "Are you feeling well?"

"Yes, very well, thank you. I have been having a pleasant conversation with Miss Elizabeth."

"I am glad to hear that; unfortunately, I must bring it to an end as there are a few acquaintances we have neglected for too long. Though they are not nearly as delightful as your present company, we must fulfil our duty to them, too. Miss Elizabeth, Mr. Darcy, I hope we will have the opportunity to speak to you again tonight."

They curtseyed and departed, arm in arm, as the earl lowered his head to whisper something into his wife's ear. Elizabeth followed them with her eyes and then turned to Mr. Darcy. "She is beautiful."

"Yes, she is. Marriage seems to suit her very well." He pressed her hand against his lips, whispering, "Thank you. You are wonderful."

"No, I am not. But please, sir, feel free to praise my qualities as much as you want. I am delighted to hear you." Her voice was as low as his, as they were surrounded by their families, and everyone's attention was on them.

"My only desire is to delight you, Miss Bennet."

She blushed and could barely hold his intense gaze, trying to devise a teasing answer. However, she had not the time for pertness as the music for the first set started and they directed their steps to the dance floor.

Standing face-to-face with Darcy and allowing herself to be surrounded by the music and the exquisite pleasure of all those little touches and caresses a dance allowed, Elizabeth suddenly became aware of nothing except her happiness, a blissful happiness that she had every reason to believe would only grow with each passing day. Having his love, she wanted and cared for nothing more. She needed nothing more.

The evening progressed admirably, and Elizabeth grew more comfortable as time passed until she completely regained her spirit and wit, easily making new acquaintances and having pleasant conversations with the guests. She had felt contented and relieved when she heard her aunt and uncle expressing their delight with the ball more than once; as for Jane — her pleasure and happiness were obvious. Undoubtedly, she heartily enjoyed the two sets she danced with Mr. Bingley, and she had her card full for every dance — a fact that made Mr. Bingley less pleased and consequently more jealous, his musings and repeated glances in Jane's direction diverting Elizabeth exceedingly. She would wager that Mr. Bingley was thinking of efficient ways to secure Jane to himself as soon as possible.

Her amusement grew during the next dances as she stood up with the colonel and then other gentlemen whose names she barely remembered, her eyes constantly drawn toward Mr. Darcy. Joining Mr. Bingley, he was sharing opinions with his old friend, and Elizabeth could barely contain her laughter at their concerned and displeased faces. Neither seemed pleased with the admiration received by their betrotheds, and neither seemed inclined to dance. In the end, they were forced to do so, as Lady Matlock approached them and exchanged a few words. Consequently, the next set saw both of them on the dance floor. Mr. Darcy danced with Miss Bingley; his friend stood up with a young lady who had been introduced to him and whose name sounded quite strange, so he was forced not to use it the entire half an hour.

Of course, not all the guests were so readily enchanted by Miss Elizabeth Bennet; in truth, some of the ladies — Lady Beatrice among them — declared her to have no beauty nor the proper manners required of a member of the *ton* and treated her with icy politeness. Therefore, awkward moments still occurred, and Elizabeth had to face various malicious comments, the worst made by Miss Bingley. In the middle of conversation during supper, she asked Elizabeth how her sister was enjoying married life and how her brother-in-law was managing to adapt *"his old habits to his new commission."*

Though surprised by the question, after casting quick, worried glances at Jane and Mr. Darcy, Elizabeth kept her calm admirably and gave her the most neutral answer she could, explaining that her brother-in-law likely had not yet undertaken his new commission, as they were still visiting her family in Hertfordshire. Lord Hothfield, though not guessing anything about Elizabeth's reason for embarrassment, showed an honest curiosity about her family's home, and asked for more details about the country. She was happy to indulge him, and as Mr. Bingley and Mr. Darcy were ready to add their favourable impressions of the area, the conversation pleasantly turned, and Caroline Bingley was left out of it, having no alternative but to concentrate on her plate of food.

Lady Ellen was delighted with Miss Elizabeth Bennet's first public appearance. She closely observed her and was enchanted by the natural elegance with which Darcy's future wife behaved during the entire night. More than anything, Lady Matlock was delighted with the subtle — but eloquent — proofs of adoration Elizabeth displayed toward Darcy and the way he reciprocated them: stolen glances and smiles, blushes, slight touches of the hands unnoticed by the others, private comments when they found a moment of seclusion in a room full of people. To have her nephew — whom she considered a son — engaged to a woman who could share his love and seemed worthy of his deep affection and devotion was the fulfilment of her strongest desire.

If her heart ached, knowing her older son was far less happy in his marriage, she turned her hopes and thoughts to the colonel for whom she was determined to secure as blissful felicity as Darcy had.

The ball ended with the unanimous opinion that it had been yet another astonishingly successful event hosted by Lady Matlock, whose reputation was not to be easily equalled among the *ton*.

Mr. Darcy and Elizabeth's family were the last guests to leave. After making their goodbyes, she had almost reached the carriage when Elizabeth suddenly returned to her hosts, followed closely by a surprised Mr. Darcy.

"Elizabeth, is something wrong?" asked Lady Matlock.

"No, nothing is wrong… It is just that… Lady Ellen, I only wish to thank you again. I cannot find the proper words to express my gratitude for everything you have done for me from the first moment I had the honour of meeting you… I…" she smiled, as her emotions were too strong to let her speak further, and impetuously she leaned and placed an affectionate kiss on her ladyship's cheek.

Not accustomed to such openly displayed proofs of affection even from her own sons, Lady Matlock was taken by surprise but not displeased in the slightest. She patted Elizabeth's cheek and returned her smile.

"No need to thank me further, my dear girl. It was my pleasure to see all those long, shocked faces the moment you entered the ballroom — all those mothers and daughters, so prepared to criticise the unknown, insignificant country girl who trapped Darcy. I was only afraid some of them might die when they saw you."

"The dress your ladyship helped me to select and the exquisite jewels that matched it had an extraordinary effect, Lady Ellen," laughed Elizabeth, while the lady shook her head in disagreement.

"Of course the dress and jewels had an effect, my dear, which was precisely my intention when I insisted upon your wearing them. But you wear them with a perfect elegance and grace that are not often observed, you may well believe that — not to mention that you and Darcy are an astonishing pair. I can only imagine how beautiful your children will be. But we will have time to talk about all this in the next couple of days before your departure for Hertfordshire. Now go; do not keep your relatives waiting too long."

The morning after the ball, Elizabeth woke after only a few hours of sleep. She still felt as though she were flying from happiness, as if she were in the midst of the most wonderful dream; she could not wait to share her impressions with her sister and aunt.

As she rose from bed, a gentle knock on the door startled her, and her heart fluttered when the maid entered with an enormous bouquet of red roses; their beauty astonished her. Eagerly, she found the note hidden among the blossoms and held her breath as she read it.

My love, there are only a few hours until we meet again, but what I want to tell you is private and very urgent, and I could think of no better way to do it than through these roses.

I awoke this morning with a painful longing to see you, to touch you, to hold you, to delve deeply into your eyes. I miss you so much that I cannot bear it for long. My only consolation is to know that in exactly one month from today I will not have to long for you anymore. In a month you will be mine; from that moment, every night when I fall asleep, I will have you close to my heart, and every morning when I wake up, I will have you in my arms. I have already started counting the days until our wedding. But, my love, will I be strong enough to bear such exquisite torture for so many days? I must beg for your help. I must beg you to share this torture with me so it is an easier burden to carry. And I know you will not refuse me, for I have never doubted your generosity as I have never doubted your love.

W

Elizabeth read and re-read the letter, each time her heart melting with growing passion for the man who had written it. However, what tormented her exceedingly and made her burn and shiver at once was the phrase whose meaning she did not dare to admit. *"In a month you will be mine; from that moment, every night when I fall asleep, I will have you close to my heart, and every morning when I wake up, I will have you in my arms."*

Could his words be implying what she thought they were? Was he prepared to put aside what propriety demanded for a husband and wife of his situation and share a bed with her?

She threw herself on the bed and pulled the letter close to her heart, closing her eyes, repeating his words in her head again and again. And, though she knew how improper her thoughts were, she could not help imagining herself sleeping blissfully in his arms every night.

Chapter 25

Elizabeth and Jane Bennet were allowed to remain in town for only three days after the ball. Mr. Bennet had long come to the end of his patience, and his second letter to Mr. Darcy and to his brother Gardiner left no doubt regarding his wishes: he wanted his two sensible daughters at home and to be spared any further talk of laces, dowries and jewels for at least the next ten years.

Mrs. Bennet also insisted that her daughters return home for precisely the opposite reason. She longed to have someone to talk to about laces, dowries and jewels; furthermore, to have the future Mrs. Darcy accompany her on the numerous visits she paid every day would inspire tremendous jealousy in all her neighbours. She had been informed by Mrs. Gardiner of Elizabeth's success at the ball, and her excitement while passing along all the details to Mrs. Long and Lady Lucas hardly allowed her to pause for breath. Her triumph over those two ladies and many others in Meryton filled her life with more anxiety and happiness than she ever could have imagined. Not only had she two daughters very soon to be married, but also Lady Catherine de Bourgh's nephew was soon to be her son-in-law, and that was a fact she could not repeat often enough to anyone who had the misfortune to be around her.

Another problem that concerned Mrs. Bennet was Elizabeth's trousseau as Mrs. Gardiner informed her sister that she, together with the bride-to-be, were purchasing everything needed for the happy event. She could not put aside the fear that neither her daughter nor her sister Gardiner knew the best shops, and that Mr. Darcy would be displeased by their lack of taste. Finally, after many exchanged letters, Mrs. Gardiner was struck by a wonderful inspiration — she mentioned in her next letter to Longbourn that Elizabeth had been assisted in her purchases by none other than Lady Matlock and that all her gowns had been ordered at Madame Claudette's. That news occasioned the second most pleasant shock of Mrs. Bennet's later years — the first pleasant one being, certainly, the news of Elizabeth's engagement.

Although the weeks spent in London had been by far the happiest and most fortunate time of their lives, both Miss Bennets shared their father's anxiety to return home, as they truly missed their family. Their departure from London was eagerly anticipated, especially as it would not require a separation from the gentlemen who had captivated their hearts. Mr. Bingley had ordered that Netherfield be prepared for his return, and he addressed a permanent invitation to Mr. Darcy, who did not consider refusing it.

Still, both Mr. Bingley and Mr. Darcy were forced to face a similar problem — both regarding the closest member of their families — their sisters.

Georgiana had openly expressed her wish to accompany her brother to Netherfield, and Mr. Darcy was tempted to concede to her desires. He hoped that she and Elizabeth would have time to become close friends, and the remainder of their engagement seemed to be the perfect opportunity for such a friendship to develop. Selfishly, he was already determined not to share his wife's attentions with anyone immediately after the wedding. The month before the season would be spent at Pemberley — the two of them alone. Therefore, it was all the more important that Georgiana spend as much time as possible with her new sister now, as they would have little chance to be in each other's company after the wedding. For that reason, he was inclined to take his sister with them to Netherfield.

But Georgiana's doctor, though pleased with his patient's progress and not opposed to her travelling, expressed some concern about a journey so soon and for such a long distance. He advised them to delay the journey for a fortnight, a suggestion that saddened Georgiana. However, her disappointment found some release after long talks with Elizabeth — who was visiting her daily — and with Lady Matlock. Together they convinced Georgiana that it would be much better and wiser to have a little more patience. Lady Matlock insisted that she would join the Netherfield party ten days before the wedding, and that it would be the perfect opportunity for Georgiana to accompany them. The Gardiners were due to arrive at Longbourn at the same time — ten days before the wedding. Until then, Mrs. Gardiner accepted Georgiana's request to allow Becky and Margaret to visit her and keep her distracted from her loneliness.

Unfortunately for Charles Bingley, things had not been as simple regarding *his* sister. Dealing with Caroline proved to be a difficult task for him, but later, over a glass of brandy with Mr. Darcy, he admitted that he had not chosen the most favourable moment to address her.

The day following the ball, Caroline had likely been in the worst mood of her life. She felt humiliated, betrayed, abandoned and full of rage against the person who had brought her to such a state: Eliza Bennet. To see that little nobody being accepted by Mr. Darcy's family and the guest of honour at a ball hosted by Lady Matlock in the presence of the most influential members of society was her darkest nightmare come true. She had desperately tried to engage in conversation, at least with those ladies whose resentment toward Eliza Bennet was barely hidden, but she had failed miserably in that as well. Apparently, the ladies of the *ton* were unwilling to share anything with her — not even their grudge against Mr. Darcy's future wife. Eliza Bennet might have been an opportunist and a fortune hunter to some of them but she, Caroline Bingley, was nobody — was nothing.

She had not slept a single hour after the ball and could eat nothing at their late breakfast, unlike her brother who seemed to be in an extraordinarily good mood — so good, in fact, that she felt sick upon seeing him.

"Caroline," she heard his joyful voice, "I am returning to Netherfield in three days' time. If you want to join me, you should start packing."

His words marked the beginning of a quarrel that lasted half an hour; Caroline angrily accused him of not asking her opinion when he made the decision to remove from town. As Bingley's patience was not what it used to be, he answered in the same manner: that he was not obliged to ask anyone's opinion when making such a decision, as he was his own master.

"Caroline, as I told you previously, you are not forced to join me. You can remain in the house, at least for the moment, as the lease has been paid for the entire year, and I have not decided what I will do with it."

"What you will do with it? Charles, have you completely lost your mind? How can you say such a thing? Can you think of nothing except being near the Bennets? What did they do to you that you have lost all reason and common sense?" Rage made her voice rise higher, and her face turned dark red while she could hardly breathe.

"Caroline, speaking to me this way will not convince me to change any of my plans. And now, if you will excuse me, I have an appointment to attend."

He rose from his chair and made one last attempt before exiting the room. "Caroline, you are my sister, and I do love you. I can understand your feeling disappointed these days, but you must consider that Darcy never showed you anything more than consideration for being my sister. Regardless of Miss Elizabeth, his choice still would not have been you. You must understand and accept that before you expose us all to ridicule."

"I will never accept that. I will never accept Eliza Bennet."

"That is very unfortunate for you; first, she does not need you to accept her for she will be Mrs. Darcy. Secondly, I suspect you will be in the Bennets' company quite often, and I will not tolerate any uncivil behaviour toward any of them."

"Quite often? What are you saying Charles? What are you planning?"

"Nothing more than I have already declared, Caroline. My strongest desire is to secure Jane Bennet's hand in marriage. As soon as I do that, all my plans will follow her wishes and happiness. You should start to accustom yourself to that, regardless of how difficult it might be."

She threw her fork on her plate and left the table, pushing her brother aside and exiting the room before him. She did not want to return to Netherfield. She hated more than anything to be in the company of all those country people. No, something else was worse than that; more than anything, she hated Eliza Bennet and her family.

However, in her room later, after screaming a few times and frightening the servants, she reconsidered her decision. She might have hated to go there, but would leaving Charles alone be a better option? Could she remain calm while stupid Charles destroyed what was left of their future and hopes? Something must be done. Anything. No matter what it might cost. She yelled for her maid and ordered her belongings to be packed.

More yelling and harsh orders for the packing of belongings could be heard at Matlock House in Lady Catherine's apartments. Lady Catherine de Bourgh had left town two days after the ball as she could not bear to hear about Miss Elizabeth Bennet a moment longer. She dragged her daughter Anne with her all the way back to Rosings though the doctor advised them to delay the journey and allow him to supervise the patient a little longer.

Anne de Bourgh did not look well at all, and she did not seem to display any improvement during her stay in town. She barely left her bed, and her pallor and weakness became worse, a fact that worried Lady Ellen and made her suggest they should ask the opinion of other doctors. However, Lady Catherine gave no consideration to her suggestions or her daughter's state. She repeatedly claimed that this was Anne's usual state of health, and if she felt worse, it was only because of her nephew's engagement to an upstart.

As for Mr. Darcy himself, her ladyship had not an opportunity to see him. She avoided visiting his house again but she did send him a note, demanding a private conference with him. His answer was brief, cold and of an impertinence that left her ladyship breathless.

> *Lady Catherine, my education, as well as my respect and affection for our family, forbid me to express my opinion freely regarding the events caused by your ladyship's presence in my house. Except for that, I consider any other topic of conversation between us to be of very little interest to me; and so will I remain for as long as necessary until Miss Elizabeth — soon to be Mrs. Darcy — is treated with all the respect due my wife. A letter of apology would be a promising start.*
>
> *For the moment I will only add, God bless you and my cousin Anne.*

Lady Catherine left London fully convinced that she would never speak to — and maybe not even see — her nephew again. Accepting that Bennet girl and apologising to her were beyond her imagination.

DURING THE LAST FORTNIGHT, LADY Matlock found a surprising delight in spending time in the company of her niece, as well as Elizabeth, Jane, and the Gardiner girls. For more than 30 years, her closest family had consisted of her husband and two sons, so the company of three young ladies and two little girls gave her many pleasurable moments. She concluded more than once to herself and to her husband, that Darcy's alliance with Elizabeth Bennet also brought great benefit to her, more than she could have imagined when she had decided to accept the country girl into her family. Her delight with Elizabeth grew with each visit, as did her gratitude for the remarkable changes and improvements in her niece Georgiana. Lady Matlock did not fail to express her approval — starting with the very first morning after the ball — when the report she gave to Georgiana, Mrs. Annesley and Mrs. Hamilton was so favourable that Elizabeth's cheeks were constantly flushed with the honour of receiving so many compliments.

The only moment of serious disagreement occurred when Lady Matlock insisted that Elizabeth order all the gowns needed for the wedding at Madame Claudette's, and that she herself be allowed to pay for them as a gift. Elizabeth expressed her gratitude and welcomed Lady Ellen's advice regarding her purchases but decidedly refused to accept such a payment arrangement, saying that she would feel as if she were taking advantage of Lady Matlock's generosity. She tried not to give offence and insistently repeated that the most important gifts were Lady Matlock's kindness and affection. In the end, she won the little argument, supported by Mrs. Gardiner, who was in possession of a very generous amount of money from Mr. Bennet — more than sufficient for any necessary purchases, even from the most famous modiste. Therefore, Elizabeth, under the supervision of her present and future aunts, ordered the wedding gown and three other dresses.

Another event, which was embarrassing for Elizabeth and most diverting for Lady Matlock and Mrs. Gardiner, occurred when the nightgowns were to be selected. Elizabeth's mortification made her far less talkative than usual, and she could not decide on anything as her cheeks were burning and she could barely express her approval or disapproval. Her companions selected a few models of the latest fashion, which Elizabeth declared she would never dare to wear in front of a man, even if he was her wedded husband. As both ladies tried to hide their amusement and exchanged knowing glances, Elizabeth could do nothing but conceal her embarrassment and try not to think of the moment she would wear the gown, daring or not.

When the order had been completed and Madame Claudette gave them the final bill, it was no more expensive than any other good modiste in Town. Neither Elizabeth nor her aunt failed to understand that Lady Matlock had an arrangement with

Madame Claudette, but to insist upon the subject would only generate embarrassment for both parties. Elizabeth contented herself with thanking her future aunt once again, and the matter was put to rest. The last days in London were full and quite agitated for Elizabeth. Although she was in the same house with Mr. Darcy the entire day — sometimes in the Gardiners' house, sometimes in his — she had few opportunities to speak to him aside from some polite conversation. Mr. Darcy seemed determined to share her time with everyone, and he used his own time to finish a variety of business matters with his solicitors. He was near her all the time, though she barely saw him. She concluded, however, that it was a wise decision of his to keep his distance as she had many things to occupy her attention.

She split her time between purchasing the remaining necessary items for the wedding, visiting Georgiana and making plans with her, and talking with Mrs. Hamilton and Molly. They insisted on asking her opinion about everything — what she expected from her future maid so Molly could be trained, her favourite courses so the chef could learn to prepare them, her favourite colours so they could make any changes to fit her tastes — according to their master's orders. However, Elizabeth tried to assure everyone that she considered Mr. Darcy's house and his staff perfect in every way and did not intend to make any changes, but everybody seemed so willing to please her that simply refusing to express any preferences would appear rude and inconsiderate. She finally agreed with some minor alterations and made a few suggestions and requests for Molly.

It was not as easy for Elizabeth when it came to her future apartment. She visited the rooms with both Mrs. Hamilton and Molly and was immediately thrilled and overwhelmed by their beauty. Mrs. Hamilton carefully presented each piece of furniture, but Elizabeth could hardly listen to her words; she simply allowed her eyes to be spoiled by the exquisite surroundings. The rooms were impressive but not at all intimidating, quite the contrary — they were very inviting. She felt a sudden urge to lie on the bed, close her eyes, and let herself become part of the rooms. *"I thought it would be good for you to become accustomed to my room."* His voice sounded so clear that she startled and looked around, only to realise that he was not there and the words were resonating only in her mind. "Miss Bennet, please let me know what you want us to change. If you cannot decide now, a simple note will do very well. I assure you, everything will be settled as you wish when you return to London. Master said — "

"Mrs. Hamilton!" She gently touched the lady's arm to stop her effusions, and her smile grew, seeing the housekeeper's surprised face. "I know what Mr. Darcy said, but I beg you not to worry about anything. I promise I will tell you if or when I want something to be changed, but for the moment, my honest conviction is that everything is perfect. It would be silly of me to make changes simply to prove I am the mistress, would it not?"

"As you like, Miss Bennet. We are at your disposal." The housekeeper's countenance lightened and relaxed, pleased with another proof of the future mistress's wisdom and generosity. Elizabeth's constant approval was a compliment not only to Mr. Darcy as the master of the house, but also to the housekeeper and the servants, a compliment that Mrs. Hamilton was eager to carry downstairs, as the entire staff deserved to be aware of it and to be content knowing their efforts were so well appreciated. Molly, too, felt more relaxed and confident in her ability to learn in a short time how to serve her future mistress as she deserved. Of one thing, both Mrs. Hamilton and Molly were certain: that Mrs. Darcy would have their unconditional devotion and affection.

They had reached the main hall when they met — with no little surprise — the master, who was clearly in search of them. His gaze fell on Elizabeth, searching her face insistently. She blushed and averted her eyes, but she could not help glancing at him again, only to look down once more.

"So, am I to understand you have finished visiting the mistress's rooms?"

"We have, sir."

"Very well, Mrs. Hamilton, I am certain that you took notice of everything Miss Bennet wanted to be done in her apartments."

"I did, sir. However, Miss Bennet made few requests. She declared herself to be pleased with the present arrangements."

He moved closer to Elizabeth, and his voice changed instantly as he addressed her directly.

"Is it true? I must say I am glad that you approved them, but — "

"I think the rooms are perfect as they are. I do not wish to change anything, at least for now."

"Very well then. Mrs. Hamilton, thank you for your help. I will take care of Miss Bennet from here." He spoke to the housekeeper, but his eyes never left Elizabeth's.

"Very well, sir." Mrs. Hamilton departed in haste, followed closely by Molly.

Mr. Darcy took another step toward Elizabeth until he was close enough to whisper to her, "Did you enjoy the rooms, Elizabeth?"

"I did, thank you. I think they are perfect." She could not understand why her lips were suddenly dry and she found breathing difficult.

"So there is nothing much for you to do for the time being?"

"Not particularly. Everything is settled, including my belongings."

"Indeed, then there is only one thing that must be taken care of before our departure tomorrow."

"Is there? I confess I do not know what that might be. I thought I had already — "

In a gesture that admitted no resistance and no argument, he took Elizabeth's arm and guided her through the door of her future room, closing it behind them.

She should have expected it. His dark stare was a clear sign of his intentions. Still, his gesture surprised her, and she wanted to warn him that the house was full of servants walking about, but her lips were soon incapable of speaking. His hungry kiss left her breathless and mindless to any rational thought, and she was barely able to stand. She was grateful when she felt herself lifted and carried to the couch, his mouth not releasing her lips for a moment from their sweet but demanding captivity. His arms embraced her closer, so tightly that she could not say which were the beats of his heart or which beats stemmed from hers. The servants and the whole outside world were soon forgotten.

THE JOURNEY BACK TO HERTFORDSHIRE was the most pleasant trip Charles Bingley had ever made — at least that was what he declared to his companions a few minutes before Mr. Darcy's carriage stopped in front of the Bennets' residence. While Jane could do nothing but blush and nod silently, Elizabeth and Mr. Darcy heartily and loudly approved of his amiable behaviour.

Early that morning, Mr. Darcy had arrived in Gracechurch Street to join the family for breakfast and to collect his intended and his soon-to-be sister. He had informed them that Charles Bingley, Miss Bingley, and Mr. and Mrs. Hurst were awaiting them at the Bingley house. Though she tried to hide it, Jane's face betrayed her disappointment, as she was obviously hoping to have that gentleman's company before their departure. Their engagement was still secret as they had not yet secured Mr. Bennet's consent, though it was apparently not quite so 'secret' since, besides Elizabeth and Mr. Darcy, the Gardiners and Georgiana were informed, and Lady Matlock had mentioned more than once that *"something seemed different in Miss Bennet's countenance."*

However, Jane's disappointment did not last long. When Mr. Darcy's spacious carriage arrived in front of Bingley's house and Miss Bingley and the Hursts were finally ready and gathered in their own carriage, Mr. Bingley closed the carriage door, wished them a pleasant trip, and turned to enter Mr. Darcy's carriage instead, leaving his sister in utter surprise.

He took his place near Mr. Darcy, facing Miss Bennet, and breathed deeply.

"Well, good morning everyone! Though it is very cold indeed, I dare say this will be a fine day for a journey, don't you think?"

Jane's face lightened instantly, and a smile spread over her face as she agreed with him wholeheartedly. As for Elizabeth, she cast an intense glance of gratitude toward her betrothed, who was undoubtedly responsible for such satisfactory though perhaps not entirely proper arrangements. However, considering that she would be married very soon to Mr. Darcy and that Mr. Bingley intended to ask for Mr. Bennet's consent the moment they arrived at Longbourn, she was certain that her parents would not be displeased with their travelling together.

The party stopped only once at an inn for some hot tea as the weather was cold indeed and the carriage did not offer enough warmth. However, their carriage was considerably more pleasant than the other, as Caroline Bingley's disposition was insufferable even for her sister. Consequently, the short rest was welcomed by Mrs. Hurst, and she even managed to have a polite conversation with the Bennet sisters while Mr. Hurst chose liquor rather than tea to warm himself.

When they re-entered the carriage, a change occurred. Without hesitation, Mr. Darcy sat next to Elizabeth, and Mr. Bingley got what he had not dared to ask for — the place beside Jane. While Elizabeth seemed quite content with the new arrangements, Jane could not control her rapid heartbeat and constant blushes; she wanted Mr. Bingley to be close to her, but feeling his closeness and the slight touches of their bodies from the carriage's movement embarrassed her greatly. She could not tell whether she wanted the journey to end as soon as possible or last forever.

As the weather worsened and the horses moved at a slower pace, Elizabeth began to complain of being cold, though both she and Jane were wrapped in blankets. Mesmerised, Jane watched Mr. Darcy take off Elizabeth's gloves and hold her hands in his, stroking them gently to warm them while his right arm encircled her shoulders, pulling her closer to him until the blanket covered them both. Her sister accepted his attentions with a smile and leaned her head against his shoulder, oblivious to the presence of the others in the carriage.

Though Jane knew that such an intimate display was highly improper, she could see nothing improper in Mr. Darcy's tender concern; quite the contrary — her heart melted at such a proof of affection toward her sister from a gentleman whom so many had considered proud and unpleasant. To her shock, for the first time in her life, she envied her sister. The envy was full of affection and tenderness, but envy it was, nevertheless.

To conceal her embarrassment, Jane began a conversation about the differences in weather between Hertfordshire and London, and another half an hour passed pleasantly until the other three noticed with surprise that Elizabeth had fallen asleep. Her head was nestled against Mr. Darcy's chest, her hand in his, her cheeks red with the warmth that enveloped her. They smiled to each other in understanding and stopped talking loudly so that Elizabeth could continue her nap.

It did not take long for Mr. Darcy to follow Elizabeth's example, and Jane found herself practically alone with Mr. Bingley. She dared to meet his eyes only for a moment and smiled shyly at him; she then turned her attention to the window, wrapping the blanket around herself.

"Miss Bennet... Jane... are you cold? May I offer you my coat? That blanket seems to be as thin as your pelisse. You must be chilled." Mr. Bingley's voice was more of a whisper in order not to disturb their companions, and he leaned closer to her so she could hear him — so close that she could feel his warm breath on her ear. She turned her head to whisper back, their faces almost touching.

"I thank you, sir; you are too kind, but I could not possibly take your coat. You would freeze without it."

"You must not think of me. I shall be fine. Please take my coat."

"Sir, I would not feel comfortable knowing you are risking your health." He looked at her, and then a sudden smile lightened his face; his warm breath warmed her ear once more.

"You are right, of course. I could not risk becoming ill before I have the opportunity to speak to your father. We must find a way not to endanger either of our health."

Earnestly, his eyes not leaving her blue, wondering gaze, he unbuttoned his coat, opened it, and then daringly pulled the blanket from around her. She was staring at him, her surprise turning to worry; he resumed his place, leaning closer to her so that he could cover her back with the free part of his coat; then his arm wrapped around her shoulders and he adjusted the blanket to cover them both.

Before she realised what was happening, Jane found herself enveloped in his arms, her hands resting defensively between their chests, not daring to breathe as her every breath made her body move and rub against his. She remained still, desperately trying to decide what she should do until his whisper made her shiver again.

"Are you comfortable enough? You will be warm very soon, I assure you."

"Sir, it is not about whether we are comfortable or not. We… We cannot stay like this. My sister and Mr. Darcy will awaken soon."

"Yes, they probably will." Meaningfully, he directed his glance towards the other pair and then back to her again; she blushed, understanding his reason and searched for an explanation.

"It is not the same thing… We are not… They are engaged."

Jane was struggling between the desire to remain in his embrace and the necessity of doing what propriety required. She was amazed that Mr. Bingley, until that point unwilling to do anything against her will, seemed determined not to release the grip of his arms around her. "And we are not engaged, Jane? It is true I do not have your father's consent, but do you think he will refuse me?"

"No, of course not… But… They are to be married soon."

She hoped her last argument would convince him, but while his countenance became more serious, his hold remained the same. "I am more than willing to marry you whenever you want, Jane. I could want nothing more than to elope and marry you tomorrow."

Her eyes opened even wider, trying to see if he was speaking in jest, but even with her lack of experience, she could see that the intensity of his gaze confirmed his passionate words.

"Jane… I will let you go, of course, if that is what you desire. I do not want to do anything against your will. But I beg you, do not tell me I am not allowed to express my care and my love for you in the same manner that Mr. Darcy does with Elizabeth. Unless you do not wish me to…"

The expression in his eyes and the tone of his whispered voice changed in a moment, and she was taken by surprise when she finally felt his arms loosen around her, allowing her to make the decision. Their gazes were still locked, and it was easy for her to see his uncertainties, hopes, and desires. He was waiting, and for Jane in that moment, the struggle was over.

Her cheeks red, she leaned, nestling her head against his neck, still shaking her head in disapproval for what she was doing, but her soul was bursting with happiness as she realised she had no reason to envy her sister's felicity.

"I will die of shame when I face Mr. Darcy. And I will die of shame when I meet you again tomorrow, Charles. This is the most improper thing I have ever done."

He breathed deeply, his heart starting to beat again as joy overtook him and his lips lightly touched her silky, blonde hair.

"That is not quite true, Miss Bennet. The most improper thing was to be alone with me in Mr. Darcy's library and allow me to kiss you the way I did."

He could feel her holding her breath, as still as a statue in his arms, and he continued, as his free hand searched for hers. "And Jane — that was the happiest moment of my life."

He felt her moving and saw her face lifted to his as her lips whispered, "But still — I will die of shame tomorrow."

However, she proved herself wrong, as shame was the last feeling she experienced! Less than a quarter of an hour later, Mr. Darcy awoke and asked about their location, as it was late in the afternoon. At that time, though startled at his voice, Jane managed to keep her countenance — as well as her present position. A few minutes later when Elizabeth opened her eyes, she saw her sister's crimson cheeks and smiled at her. Elizabeth's heart ached for a moment, as dark, painful memories of their journey to London less than a month before came vividly to her mind; now, they were returning home filled with blissful happiness.

It truly was the most pleasant journey of their lives as Mr. Bingley had stated.

IT WAS DARK WHEN MR. Darcy's carriage stopped in front of Longbourn; the rest of the party was eager to reach Netherfield as soon as possible. Neither Caroline Bingley nor the Hursts were in the mood to bear the Bennets after such a long journey, and besides, no invitation had been extended to them in any case.

As Elizabeth had presumed, her mother found no reason to be displeased at seeing all of them descend from the carriage; in fact, Mrs. Bennet saw little else than the grandeur of the carriage and paid little attention to anyone except her soon to be son-in-law, Mr. Darcy. She embraced her daughters lovingly but quickly, congratulated her second daughter, exclaiming far more loudly than was proper, how smart Elizabeth had been in securing such a husband. Her duty done, she thereafter bestowed the whole of her attention upon the gentleman. Mr. Darcy could not hide a smile, thinking it was the first time Mrs. Bennet had ever treated him with more solicitude than

Bingley, and he remembered Becky's words: *"She must be very fond of you."*

The elder Miss Bennets retreated to their rooms to change clothes before dinner. Though the gentlemen were also in need of proper dinner attire, since the hour was late and everyone was hungry, it was decided that they would forego the formalities — for once — so they immediately could enjoy the most extraordinary dinner Mrs. Bennet had ever prepared. Truly delighted to be in the presence of the young gentlemen again, Mr. Bennet insisted they join him in the library for something stronger to whet their appetites, an invitation they accepted with pleasure.

Seizing his opportunity, Mr. Bingley lost no time in asking Mr. Bennet for a few private moments. Mr. Darcy was allowed to remain in the room but politely retreated to a corner, looking with great interest at Mr. Bennet's bookshelves. However, a few minutes later, Mr. Bingley's enthusiastic voice could not be ignored, especially when he unexpectedly appeared immediately next to Mr. Darcy's ear, shouting joyfully that they would be brothers after all. Half an hour was spent in pleasant conversation until dinner was ready. All three decided it was wiser to delay telling Mrs. Bennet their news as Mr. Bennet was afraid her poor nerves could not bear so much felicity in one evening.

Dinner was a pleasant affair for everyone despite their fatigue and the excitement of the day. Mr. Bingley did not have the opportunity to speak to Jane privately, but from his few whispered words, she understood that the next step had been taken; she barely touched her food, her heart and mind occupied with happy thoughts of her future.

Elizabeth could not have been more pleased with the behaviour of her betrothed. Although her mother's attentions were overwhelming and difficult to bear — even for a man with more patience than Mr. Darcy — the gentleman was all kindness and politeness; he took every opportunity to praise Mrs. Bennet's courses at dinner, the talent of her chef, and her own skill in running the household. Such compliments from a distinguished, handsome gentleman with ten thousand a year, a house in town and more than one beautiful carriage were almost too much for Mrs. Bennet's vanity to bear.

Realising the day had been exhausting for all, the gentlemen announced they would take their leave shortly after dinner. Both Elizabeth and Jane escorted them outside to their carriage, wishing for a few private moments, though nothing more than a tender squeeze of hands could be expected. To Mr. Darcy's surprise, however, Elizabeth grabbed his arm and delayed him in the darkness of the hall, while Jane and Mr. Bingley were already in front of the main entrance.

"Thank you for the patience you showed toward my mother."

"Well..." he lowered his head so he could whisper to her, "you have every reason to be grateful. She asked me three times about the number of rooms in my London house and the colour of Lady Ellen's ball dress."

She blushed, trying to force a smile. "I am sorry... I know she can be very tiresome at times, and — "

"Elizabeth . . . " his voice was by now even lower and his lips so close to her ear that they almost touched her. "I was only teasing you. I enjoy your mother's company infinitely more than the company of some of my own relatives."

"Oh . . . " she could not find more to say as he was taking her hands in his and entwining their fingers. His lips were so close to her face that her desire to feel them upon hers was making her dizzy.

"There is another problem that is tormenting me greatly."

"A problem? Is something wrong?"

"Yes, there is. During our entire journey, and the whole evening since we arrived, I have wanted nothing more than to kiss you."

She startled and held her breath. "William, we cannot . . . I cannot . . . My father is just inside and . . . "

He lifted her hands to his lips and kissed them tenderly, smiling. "I know, my love . . . I must fight against those kinds of feelings or else I will completely lose my mind before the wedding."

His voice was half in jest, and they had already reached the doorway to join Mr. Bingley and Jane when Elizabeth stopped him once again.

"Mr. Darcy?" He turned to face her, surprised by the sudden change in her tone. "My mother never would forgive me if she knew that I was jeopardising your sanity a month before the wedding."

He knew she was teasing him back and was about to tell her that he would ask Mrs. Bennet's assistance for the problem, but he was mistaken — she was not teasing him. The proof came a moment later, when he suddenly felt with delight her soft lips pressing, and then moving gently against his.

For the first time, the thought occurred to him that Mrs. Bennet did after all have quite a good influence over Elizabeth.

More than a fortnight passed in the greatest excitement and agitation for the Bennet household. Mrs. Bennet did not have a single moment of peace or silence in all that time, and neither did anyone else around her — family, servants or neighbours.

The news of Jane's engagement almost made her faint, and for a couple of days, she did not know how to divide her attention between her two prospective sons-in-law. Eventually, she decided with much determination in favour of Mr. Darcy since he was twice as wealthy and of much more importance than Mr. Bingley. However, she made a private resolution that, after Mr. Darcy married Elizabeth and they departed the area, she would then be able to re-direct all her affection and energy to her second favourite. Her original favourites, Lydia and Mr. Wickham, were long forgotten.

Despite her countless tasks with wedding arrangements, she had time to pay calls on her neighbours and receive even more calls in return.

Mr. Darcy and Mr. Bingley were daily visitors at Longbourn; though directly involved in the events, Mr. Darcy's business regarding the wedding finished quickly as soon as he and Mr. Bennet had discussed and agreed upon the settlements. From that moment on, his only efforts were exerted in keeping his countenance civil and polite toward all the visitors who bestowed endless attention on him and, occasionally, on Mr. Bingley.

Mr. Bingley's amiable nature helped him display patience and forbearance tolerably well toward Mrs. Philips, Mrs. Long and Lady Lucas, but it was a trying time for Mr. Darcy. He managed to secure relatively private time with Elizabeth only when he asked her to join him for a short turn around the garden, but even then, they were accompanied by Mr. Bingley and Jane. However, even if Mr. Bingley did allow him some privacy on a few occasions, Mrs. Bennet always managed to require Elizabeth's presence in the house for one reason or another. So, for most of the time spent at Longbourn, Mr. Darcy enjoyed Mr. Bennet's library, his port and his conversation.

About ten days after their return from London, an important event occurred in Meryton: Miss Charlotte Lucas married Mr. Collins in a ceremony full of affability. The Bennets attended the wedding together with Mr. Bingley and Mr. Darcy, though the latter had a harsh discussion with Mr. Collins just two days prior to the event.

It so happened that, as soon as he found a few moments alone with Mr. Darcy in the salon of Longbourn, Mr. Collins wasted no time in bringing to his attention the fact that Lady Catherine de Bourgh was very displeased with his choice of wife, and that her ladyship had the lowest opinion of Miss Elizabeth Bennet. The clergyman went so far as to suggest that Mr. Darcy reconsider the idea of marrying his cousin. It was at that precise moment that Kitty — who later anxiously reported what she saw — happened upon them in the salon and was shocked at Mr. Darcy's violent reaction and Mr. Collins's hasty departure from the house.

The following day Mr. Collins returned with Miss Lucas and bowed humbly in front of Mr. Darcy, requesting a private meeting to express his apologies. His grovelling being satisfactory, Mr. Collins had the pleasure of Mr. Darcy's gracious attendance at his wedding after all.

ELIZABETH AWOKE AFTER ANOTHER NIGHT of restless sleep, her mind preoccupied by all manner of thoughts and worries. The Gardiners, the Matlocks and Georgiana were due to arrive in a couple of days, and although she dearly missed them all, Elizabeth knew that their presence would require all her remaining time and energy. She would have no time for anything else.

I will not have any time at all to be alone with him.

Although they met every day, she missed the opportunity to be with him privately. Their eyes constantly searched for each other in a room full of people; they even had a few moments alone in the evenings just before he took his leave... but nothing more.

She did not even have the chance to thank him for his generosity in the marriage settlements. She tried to do it one evening in the hall, but he refused decidedly and silenced her with a hasty, brief kiss. *I miss him so much,* was her only thought as she dressed and slipped out of the house before anyone awakened.

It was early in the morning and quite cold; the air was frigid and so was the ground. Elizabeth started trembling the moment she left the house, but she needed time alone — a time of solitude and peaceful silence before the rest of the house awakened and the general agitation began once more.

She started walking slowly at first, looking around at the garden, the house, and the paths she knew so well and loved so dearly. Everything that had been part of her life for twenty years would be left behind in less than a fortnight.

She was looking with excitement and happiness towards her future life, but she could not avoid feelings of melancholy for all the changes that would transform her from Miss Elizabeth Bennet into Mrs. Fitzwilliam Darcy. Then more pleasant thoughts filled her, knowing that he would be with her, and the thought brought a smile to her lips. Her cheeks reddened with the mere remembrance of what they had shared so far and the anticipation of everything they soon would share.

Unconsciously, her steps took her to the path that led to the cottage, but the road was frozen and slippery, and she did not even attempt to reach the hill. The sound of a horse galloping startled her at first and then worried her as it grew stronger, but long before she could discern the rider's face, his posture betrayed his identity; if she needed further proof, her heart pounding wildly told her without any doubt that it was Mr. Darcy.

The horse halted, and he hurriedly leaped from his back to pull her into a close embrace. Suddenly, before she could say a word, a trail of small, tender kisses covered her eyes, her cheeks, and down to her jaw line until their impatient lips finally met and passionately joined. They eventually drew slightly apart, their foreheads leaning against each other.

"Elizabeth, what are you doing here so early?"

"I came for a short walk before breakfast. And you? Am I to understand that you are displeased by my being here? I was tempted to think quite the opposite a few moments ago." She was biting her lower lip, staring into his eyes with obvious happiness and no less impudence, demanding an answer.

"Quite the opposite would be a very correct assessment, I grant you." Another passionate kiss followed his words, her impudent smile merging with his. He broke the kiss to speak further, keeping her in his arms. "I have been riding here every morning at this hour since the day we returned. These paths where we met that day in the rain have become my favourite places. And I confess I was secretly hoping that I would meet you here again at some time."

"Secretly? But why did you not tell me? I would have found a way to come." Her eyes were staring into his, full of love and longing.

"I could not possibly ask you to wake up early only to meet me."

"I would have come for I greatly miss being alone with you."

"Well, I can be patient, knowing that in a fortnight we will be alone for as long as we want."

She smiled and nodded in agreement, but he did not fail to notice the trace of a shadow that darkened her eyes for a moment. "Elizabeth, is something amiss? You seem upset."

"No, I am not upset. How could I be? I am happier than I ever could have dreamed. It is just that I feel a little sadness, thinking that soon I will depart from these places, from my family…"

"My love, you know that you will be able to see your family whenever you desire. You can invite them to visit us at any time, and we will come to visit them as often as you wish it. I hope you are not worried on that score."

"No, and I thank you for your concern. I am so anxious to see Pemberley, yet so sad to leave these grounds as well. I came out to walk today precisely to enjoy the beauty of these surroundings."

"In that case, Miss Bennet, I believe I have just thought of a better proposition for you — would you not rather admire all these places from a more beautiful prospect?"

"I do not understand you, William…"

"Well, then I will speak more clearly. Let us ride together along all the paths you love most. We will admire them together, you can tell me about your favourite places, and I can tell you about Pemberley if you wish."

She stared at him with wide eyes, but then her brow furrowed.

"I cannot ride your horse! I do not like riding and… I am not a good rider at all; I prefer walking."

"You do not need to be a good rider; I will be with you. There is nothing to be afraid of."

"I am not afraid!" He raised his eyebrow, an ironic smile hidden in the corner of his mouth.

"Then may I dare ask what you call it, for it does not seem like courage either."

"It is not a matter of courage, it is…well, I certainly cannot ride with you on the same horse! It would not be proper."

His arms encircled her waist tightly while his mouth whispered against her cheek, close to her ear, "I would be very much obliged if you would do me this favour. As I recall, the first evening we returned to Hertfordshire, you said you were very grateful to me, do you remember?"

She nodded silently, and he continued with the same persuasiveness that weakened her knees. "This would be a wonderful opportunity to show your gratitude by indulging me. Will you not do that for me?"

She swallowed, shivers running through her, while she tried to voice an argument. "It is very ungentlemanlike to use that to persuade me. You are forcing me to do something against my will. I do not want to ride. I am not prepared for this."

He smiled, placing small, warm kisses on her temples and on her cold, crimson cheeks.

"I know it is very ungentlemanlike, but I am not forcing you to do something against your will. I am begging you to do something to please me. You are free to refuse if you feel too frightened to do it. I told you there is no need for you to express any kind of gratitude to me."

His words, full of sweetness, and his tender look changed her mood instantly as she did not fail to notice his meaning. He was teasing her and using his powers of seduction to gain the advantage.

Immediately, she quelled her misgivings, and her voice was unexpectedly sharp as it issued from her soft lips, almost touching his as she spoke.

"You are mistaken, Mr. Darcy. I am not at all frightened. I said I was not prepared as my gown is not proper for riding, and I am not at all accustomed to your horse — not to mention that it is highly improper to ride upon the same horse even if we are betrothed. But let it be as you desire since it seems you are accustomed to having things your way. Would you be so kind as to help me into the saddle?"

She was up in a moment, seated side-saddle, and in the next moment she felt him close behind her, his arms embracing her and taking the reins at the same time; instantly, the horse started to move restlessly and she gasped, wrapping her arms tightly about his waist and hiding her head on his chest. Darcy laughed as he pulled her closer, and the ride started at a slow pace. Then he softly coaxed her chin up with one hand, forcing her to meet his eyes.

"Elizabeth, try to relax a little. Trust me, you will like this as much as I do, I promise."

"You tricked me into this, William."

"Yes, I did, my love, and I rejoice in my success." His voice changed again, deeper and lower. "Having you in my arms in these secluded places, your warmth much more powerful than the winter's coldness, your beautiful eyes gazing at me... This is happiness, Elizabeth. Can you not feel it? Look around you and tell me: is it not more beautiful to admire this from up here?"

Reluctantly, she unlocked her eyes from his and cast a glance around them. A loud gasp and then a deep sigh answered his questions, and he could feel her adjusting her position so that her arms were still around his waist, but she was allowed a better view. Soon, in the comfort of his arms, she regained her composure and allowed herself to enjoy the wind playing on her face, the soft sway of the steady ride, and the newly discovered beauty of those well-known surroundings.

He tried to direct the horse to the cottage, and she smiled in undoubted agreement. The place was dear to both of them; she wanted as much as he to spend at least a few minutes there, but when he realised the road was frozen and dangerously abrupt, he immediately turned back. He did not even consider risking her safety, not even for such a romantic reason.

They returned to the main road, and it was with no little regret that he whispered to her, "When we return in the spring, perhaps for your sister's wedding, we will go there; I promise."

"I would like that very much."

"And even more, I will ask your father to allow me to have the cottage repaired and some improvements made. It can be used very well for fishing parties. I am sure Mr. Bennet would like the idea, and so would Mr. Gardiner."

"I am sure they would. And if they did not..." She paused, her gaze a mix of sharpness and sweetness, her lips twisted in a challenging smile. "I am sure you will be more than able to convince them to like it. You seem very proficient in persuading people as to what they like and dislike."

"Are you complaining about something, Miss Bennet? Are you not enjoying our ride?"

"Quite the contrary, sir, I am enjoying it very much. You seemed to know better than I did that I would find great delight in something I have always disliked. Do you have any other suggestions for me?" The moment she finished her question she blushed and averted her eyes from his intense, dark gaze. However, she could not avoid hearing his answer, which was as husky as she expected.

"No, I do not have any other suggestions for the moment. However, I will think very diligently on the subject, and I will gladly share any ideas with you... most likely after our wedding."

She tensed and turned her attention to the road, not knowing what she could say in the embarrassing silence provoked by her imprudent words. Her position made her feel altogether vulnerable. She was practically trapped between his strong thighs, his hands around her, his body pressing against hers. How could she answer him? How could she even look at him?

"Elizabeth... you must learn not to ask questions if you are not certain you can bear the answers."

She laughed, though she was still embarrassed, her cheeks crimson and her eyes filled with mirth as she dared to meet his gaze again.

"Thank you for your advice, sir. I will try to follow it. I have always tried to follow your wise counsel as you well know."

"Indeed you have, Miss Bennet. I have no complaints."

The witty, teasing dialogue gave them equal pleasure, and Elizabeth did not even notice when the horse, under Darcy's guidance, quickened its pace.

"Elizabeth, when we arrive at Pemberley, will you allow me to teach you how to ride?"

"Well, I do know how to ride — a little. But I would not be opposed to improving my skills. And I have to do so in any case. I promised Lady Ellen as much the first day we met."

"Lady Ellen? On the first day?"

"Yes. She informed me that the mistress of Pemberley must be a very skilful rider. But do you know what her supreme argument was that instantly convinced me of the wisdom of her idea?"

"No, and I confess I am eager to know it."

"She told me Miss Bingley is a proficient rider, and I would need to learn how to ride a horse so I might protect you from her."

He looked at her, his mouth open in obvious incredulity. "Lady Ellen told you that on the first day you met? Well, my aunt is an impressive as well as an insightful woman. And she always knows what arguments to use in order to convince people to have her way."

It was Elizabeth's turn to chuckle. "Apparently you have somehow learned this quality from her, sir."

"When it comes to you, Miss Bennet, I certainly hope I have."

His face lowered to hers, and their lips joined in a brief, tender kiss.

The wind started to blow more strongly, but neither seemed affected by the frozen breeze. Still, Darcy turned the horse back to Longbourn, and the quick pace soon turned into a gallop, but Elizabeth did not protest. She leaned her head against his chest and closed her eyes, feeling safe and protected by his strength and warmth. For the first time in her life, she enjoyed the pleasure of riding.

Chapter 26

"There can be no doubt of that. It is settled between us already that we are to be the happiest couple in the world."

—Elizabeth Bennet, *Pride and Prejudice* (Chapter 59)

A week before the wedding, the number of guests had grown considerably at Longbourn as well as Netherfield. If Mr. Darcy had anticipated a difficult time with his relatives in attendance, the reality proved much worse. However, to his utter surprise, the unpleasantness did not come from Mrs. Bennet or her youngest daughters, but from Caroline Bingley's constant rudeness and insistence on ingratiating herself with Lady Matlock and Georgiana. This was especially so after Mr. Bingley's engagement was announced, as Caroline felt acutely that her last advantage of being the mistress in her brother's house was jeopardised.

Their wedding had been scheduled for three months' hence, and the thought of being a guest in Jane Bennet's house in such a short time and losing all her rights frightened Caroline. It did not make her wiser, however — quite the contrary; she became more bitter and malicious.

As for Mrs. Bennet, her sister Gardiner's suggestions — aided in no small part by the importance of such a personage as Lady Matlock — persuaded her to show unexpected restraint and more decorum than before. Of course, her true character and usual manners were quickly perceived by Lady Matlock, but considering the short time she had spent in Mrs. Bennet's presence, her ladyship ended by declaring to Darcy that Elizabeth's mother was 'tolerable enough and *"quite enjoyable in some ways."*

"I have to say, Nephew," she confessed one evening in a private conversation with Mr. Darcy, "that Mrs. Bennet is perhaps not the most proper example of decorum and propriety, but at least she is... entertaining, unlike Caroline and the Hursts, not to mention some of our own relatives."

The earl also tolerated his time in Hertfordshire better than he had anticipated, more so because he was not forced to bear the presence of the women except at mealtimes. His acquaintance with Mr. Gardiner allowed him to approve the colonel's appreciation of the gentleman. In addition, Mr. Bennet's immense knowledge of books added to the generally favourable opinion he formed.

However, the earl still was not completely content with his nephew's decision and choice of wife. He had met Elizabeth Bennet only occasionally after the ball, and his many concerns and doubts about her and about the marriage had not yet been laid to rest. He needed the proof of time for that. Still, he admitted that on those few occasions when they had been together, he had seen nothing in Miss Elizabeth that might indicate her unworthiness, and her affection for Darcy seemed sincere. He also admitted to his wife that the Bennet family was bearable enough, at least if he were not forced to spend excessive time in their company.

Fortunately, the time until the wedding passed quickly, and the happiest day of Mrs. Bennet's life finally came. At least a hundred times did she ask anyone who was willing to give an opinion whether everything was perfectly arranged to satisfy the taste of Mr. Darcy and the pretentiousness of Lord and Lady Matlock. And though everybody — from Hill to Mrs. Gardiner and Jane — tried to convince her that there was nothing to worry about, she continued to ask, since she did not actually listen to the answers. The extraordinary fact that Longbourn was to host the wedding breakfast and that so many important members of the *ton* would attend made her deeply distressed.

When Lady Lucas tried to offer advice, mentioning that she had already gone through similar preparations, Mrs. Bennet rolled her eyes in exasperation. How could she even dream of comparing Charlotte Lucas's wedding to that clergyman with her daughter's wedding to Mr. Darcy? It was not to be borne! According to Mrs. Bennet, Lady Lucas had simply lost her reason.

The wedding ceremony turned out to be the greatest success of Mrs. Bennet's life, gratifying all her maternal feelings and her vanity as well. She had the unforgettable pleasure of being congratulated for the elegant arrangements by Lady Matlock herself, and she was so surprised that she forgot to breathe; at length, she recovered enough to thank her ladyship for her kindness.

Moreover, everybody repeatedly admired not only the bride but the bridesmaid as well, and indeed Jane was more beautiful than ever before and looked charming standing by her sister, together with her betrothed, Mr. Bingley. Everyone in attendance agreed that the wedding ceremony was the most beautiful they had ever witnessed in Meryton, and Mrs. Bennet's nerves could hardly bear so much praise. When Mr. Darcy's carriage stopped in front of Longbourn, Mrs. Philips, Mrs. Long and Lady Lucas agreed that it was the most imposing vehicle they had ever seen; they immediately began to speculate about Elizabeth's pin money and the other carriages

Mr. Darcy must possess.

When the time came for the newlyweds to depart, the most difficult moment for Elizabeth was to say goodbye to her father. Mr. Bennet had said more than once that he would miss her exceedingly, and his distress was so evident that Elizabeth felt tears in her eyes. Georgiana also seemed affected by the idea that she would not see her brother and sister for several months as she was scheduled to return with the Matlocks and remain with them for a time.

When the newlyweds finally took their leave, Elizabeth's heart was so overwhelmed by emotion that she had to struggle to keep her countenance. Her husband handed her into the carriage as she tried to capture everyone in her memory with one last, loving glance.

Mr. Darcy closed the carriage door, and the horses started immediately, apparently as impatient as their master was. They took off at a fast pace as Elizabeth was still looking through the window and waving her hand to everything that would remain behind her: her family, her home, and her past life. Tears threatened to spill from her eyes, and she pulled her head back into the carriage, trying to conceal them from the worried glance of her husband.

He was sitting opposite her, but in the next moment, he was at her side, his hands taking hers.

"My love, are you unwell?"

She tried to force a reassuring smile. "I am well, William. Please forgive me."

"Elizabeth, there is nothing to forgive. Would you not rather tell me what saddens you? It would be much easier to bear. You taught me that some time ago."

His arms embraced her closely, and his gloved hands reached for hers. She did not answer, but instead moved closer into his embrace. They did not move, nor did they even talk for a while, only sharing her sadness silently.

Elizabeth was the first to move; she unexpectedly pulled her hands from his, and he turned his gaze to her in wonder. She did not lift her eyes, however, as she was too preoccupied with her new task: She took her gloves off and then his. Her bare hands reached for his and their fingers entwined instantly, gently caressing each other. He raised both her hands to his lips, placing small, warm kisses upon them, and when their eyes met again, she was smiling.

"Thank you for your patience, William. I am feeling much better now."

She searched his face intensively for a moment and then added, "I dare say you are not at all displeased to be leaving, sir."

He stared at her for a moment and then opened his mouth with the intention of protesting. He returned her smile, and a hint of guilt could be perceived in his tone. "I have to admit I am relieved that the festivities are finally at an end. I had not imagined it could be so fatiguing though I did not really do anything for it by way of preparation. I do not dare to presume how tired your mother and Mrs. Gardiner must be, and also Miss Bennet."

She smiled, pleased to have the opportunity to speak of her family a little more.

"Yes, they are, but I dare say for Mama it was a most entertaining experience. Without a doubt, I am certain she enjoyed it immensely. And she was exceedingly rewarded when Lady Matlock kindly congratulated her on all the arrangements."

"Did she? It was very kind indeed. Should I have congratulated her myself, do you think? It did not cross my mind —"

She started to laugh heartily. "Yes you should have, sir. But you seemed to pay little attention to anything the entire day."

"Elizabeth, I have something to confess to you: I did not even notice the arrangements! I hardly noticed whom I was talking to; all I know is that Miss Bennet and Bingley stood with us at the altar. Except for that, my mind was most pleasurably engaged — thinking of you."

"I see…" She could find nothing else to say.

"I still cannot believe you are finally my wife. I have dreamed of this day for so long…"

His eyes locked with hers, and the intensity of his gaze made her shiver in anticipation of his kiss. She closed her eyes, and her lips parted slightly, waiting. He only brushed her dry lips briefly, however, his kisses moving further to cover her face.

She breathed deeply, feeling his hand stroke her arm and lift to her neck; his fingers stopped on her neck, but it was not the caress she had anticipated. He was playing with the ribbon of her bonnet until he untied it and threw it to the opposite side of the carriage. His lips reached her ear and he whispered huskily, fondling her ear lobe.

"I do not like bonnets… or gloves. I think I will forbid you to wear them."

She laughed, and her lips whispered back while trying to reach his, "It appears to me that you will be a very demanding husband, sir. We are barely married, and you have already started to forbid me something of great importance for a lady. Should I have known earlier your true character — "

She had no time to continue as his mouth captured hers with a possessiveness that admitted no opposition. She never considered deterring him, not even when his caresses, gentle and tender at first, grew more daring and demanding than ever before. These were the kisses and caresses of a husband, not just of a betrothed — and she was his wife.

His fingers unbuttoned her pelisse and pulled it apart, exposing her to his eager hands, which travelled without restraint along each part of her body. His kiss grew more passionate, possessive, and demanding, as if his lips were driven by an urge impossible to control or appease.

Elizabeth focused all her strength on a struggle to conceal her moans, mortified that the footmen who escorted the carriage would hear her, though the struggle seemed to be futile. Fortunately, their closely joined mouths kept their mixed groans within the privacy of the carriage, but only for the moment. His hands returned from their passionate journey, and tentatively at first, his fingers engulfed the soft roundness of her breasts; her back arched instinctively, welcoming his touch. Not surprisingly, he needed no further encouragement. His moves became almost violent in their eagerness, as violent as the maddening pleasure that left her trembling beneath his caress. One of his hands released the object of his previous desire and slowly glided down along her body toward her legs, which parted slightly under the delicious insistence of his touch; deep moans escaped her mouth and, to conceal them, she bit her lips — and his. With increased possessiveness, his fingers slid down, stroking, tantalising, burning her almost painfully through the thin fabric until countless shivers shattered her body… and she knew nothing more.

Elizabeth could not tell if an eternity or only a few moments passed until she finally opened her eyes and met his gaze only a few inches away from her. She struggled hard to breathe again — as did he; his forehead leaned against hers as several moments elapsed before he drew back and looked into her face. She felt her cheeks flush and her lips — pained from her bite and swollen from his passion — could not say a word; silently, her eyes stared at him shyly, wonderingly, begging him to say something to break the unbearable tension.

She wanted to ask him what happened to her, but how could she dare voice the question?

Finally, carefully arranging her pelisse around her, he managed to speak, his worry and uneasiness obvious in his countenance.

"I am sorry, my love. I completely lost control. I am afraid I acted like a savage."

"You must not apologise. We are married now. You may do whatever you please."

She felt mortified by her own words and reactions, which had encouraged him to act in that manner, and she could barely meet his eyes.

"Yes, we are married… still, that does not excuse my behaviour. We are in a carriage with two footmen escorting us! I should have —"

She turned her head to the window, unable to hold his gaze any longer. He seemed so full of remorse, so willing to apologise… and his words only made her feel more ashamed of herself and her feelings. She was certain he had done something entirely wrong. So how was it possible for her to enjoy it so much? She felt him leaning closer to her, and his hand turned her face toward him.

"Elizabeth? I cannot bear to see you upset with me…"

Her words finally came out in a cascade of mixed emotions, which flustered her face even more. "William, I am not upset with you… I am just… I do not know what happened to me. And you apologised, so it must be something bad. But all I know is that you kissed me as you have done before. Well… no, not as before; still, you only kissed me and I…" She averted her eyes from him again, unable to continue speaking.

If she could have held his gaze a moment longer, she would have witnessed the change in his countenance, lightened by his sudden understanding. However, she only felt his arm encircling her shoulders and pulling her gently against his chest. She hid her face inside his opened coat and remained still while his hand tenderly stroked her hair and his comforting words warmed her ear.

"My love, I did not mean to imply that kissing you or touching you is wrong, especially now that we are married. I only meant that I should not have forced myself upon you now in the carriage."

She only nodded without lifting her face from his chest. He continued with a lower voice even closer to her ear. "And I certainly did not mean that what you felt or what I felt was wrong."

She stiffened in his arms and whispered, her eyes still not meeting his, "Do you know what I felt?"

His voice grew huskier as he whispered back, "I know that you just discovered the flavour of passion, the exquisite pleasure of a shared love."

Again the surprise of his statement found her unprepared while his words and the inflexions in his voice made her head spin. 'The pleasure of shared love…' How could the incredible sensation she just experienced be voiced aloud? Yet, he seemed to know exactly how to describe it.

"You seem to know so much about that…" She startled violently at the sound of her own words, shocked and frightened at daring to say such a thing to him, and on their wedding day no less. She expected him to be upset or even angry, and justifiably so; no lady would raise such a subject in front of her husband. She hardly moved in his arms, waiting for his reaction, which came a moment later.

With no less surprise did she feel his lips lying upon the top of her head and his hand lifted to stroke her cheek. The amusement in his voice could not be concealed.

"My dearest Elizabeth… yes, it might be said that I do know more than you about 'that'… and about many other things in life. And I dare say that is how things should be — first because I am a man and second because I am older than you. In fact, I am quite old, as Becky said."

He paused a moment, and then added in a different tone, the tone of his voice meant only for her. "But my love, I have to confess that my feelings and sensations when I am with you, when I merely look at you, or when I am only thinking of you are as completely new for me as they are for you. The pleasure — the happiness — aroused in me by your presence, by your touch, by your kisses, or simply by your smiles is more powerful than anything I have ever experienced in my life."

How could she respond to such a statement? Someone who felt less, perhaps, would find the proper words. Her hands silently encircled his waist tightly, and she placed a long, lingering kiss on his chest — a light kiss through his clothes upon his heart. After a few long moments spent in blissful silence, his lips started to move slightly over her hair. Her face lifted to him and soon their lips joined in another kiss. Yet this time the kiss was significantly shorter in duration; he withdrew a few inches, stared at her a little, and then chuckled boyishly.

"Mrs. Darcy, this will not do. We can never manage to end our journey benignly if we continue in this way. It is your responsibility to keep me under good regulation until we arrive in London."

"I... I shall try, Mr. Darcy." She endeavoured to regain her composure, still feeling the disappointment of their short, broken kiss. For her, it was difficult to understand why he would be opposed to them simply kissing each other, even caressing each other once they were married, but she decided not to deliberate it further and to oblige him. He might have a good reason for doing so.

"Very well, sir, but if I were you, I would not trust me in this. As I already have proved to you, I am far from able to keep my own behaviour under good regulation. But I will try. Perhaps some conversation would do, do you not think so?"

"Yes, I think it would." He smiled openly at her light teasing and kissed her hand. "Do you have a favourite topic, Mrs. Darcy?"

"I do not know... books, perhaps?"

"Oh, please no... I could not possibly have such a serious conversation on our wedding day."

She looked at him for a few moments, good-humouredly, her spirits raised to playfulness again. She exceedingly enjoyed their teasing conversations, and it helped her to keep her mind — and obviously his — occupied during the long hours they had to spend in the carriage.

"Then perhaps you would be so kind as to tell me some details about the Season? I must confess I have very little knowledge about what I should expect."

He stared at her, a puzzled expression on his face. "About the Season? What is there to say? There will be some balls, some dinner parties and, fortunately, the theatre and the opera — that is all."

His annoyed countenance made her laugh heartily. She could well believe that for him the Season had little attraction.

"Well sir, if we end the topic so soon, I am afraid I will not be able to keep an interesting conversation going until we reach London. Do you have other ideas?"

He did think of various topics for them to discuss, and they spent the rest of the journey talking about anything that crossed their minds, Pemberley being their favourite subject. However, none of the topics proved sufficiently interesting to keep them from overlooking their earlier passion and re-enacting the kisses quite regularly.

By the time they reached Darcy's town house, Mrs. Darcy's hair was in great disorder, apparent even under her bonnet, and Mrs. Hamilton did not fail to notice the mistress's swollen lips. It was fortunate that rain had started hours earlier and that the short trip from the carriage to the house rendered them considerably wet, allowing them to go directly to their rooms to change their clothes. By the time they returned downstairs for dinner, their appearance was completely proper, and all the servants agreed that Mrs. Darcy looked even more beautiful than she had when she was Miss Bennet.

Around eight in the evening, Mr. and Mrs. Darcy finished a light, pleasant dinner and retired to their apartments. Though neither the house nor even Darcy's room was unknown to Elizabeth, she climbed the stairs on her husband's arm with increasing anxiety, growing more uneasy with every passing moment, barely understanding her own state of mind and heart.

"Elizabeth... do you think an hour will be enough time for you?"

His voice startled her, and only then did she realise they were in front of her bedchamber.

"Yes... yes... I think it will be sufficient..." she managed to agree with a reasonably calm voice.

"Very well then. I shall see you again shortly..."

He guided her into her rooms, and after Molly took over her care, he departed through the door that separated their apartments. Elizabeth remained standing in the middle of the room, looking at the closed door without remembering when exactly he had said he would return.

She was brought to reality by Molly, who announced her bath was ready. Elizabeth did not have the patience to enjoy the pleasure of settling into the tub of warm water as she was used to doing. He had said he would come in an hour — she finally remembered — and suddenly she thought of so many things she needed to do in a short time. She emerged from the tub and asked for her nightgown.

Molly had done everything that Mrs. Hamilton instructed her to do so everything would be perfect for her mistress's preparations on such an important night. *And everything would be perfect,* thought Molly, *if not for the extreme anxiety and nervousness of my young mistress.*

With the assistance of her young maid, Elizabeth prepared for the night, and then took her place at the dressing table. Molly started to brush her hair, carefully arranging her heavy curls. She kept staring into the mirror as if she were seeing someone else's reflection.

"Shall I bind your hair, Miss Bennet? Oh, I am sorry, I mean, Mrs. Darcy. Please forgive me."

"Do not worry Molly. We shall become accustomed to this new title together. I still very much feel myself to be 'Miss Bennet'."

She stopped and blushed at the meaning of her own words though she did not mean it *that* way.

"I can easily understand that, Mrs. Darcy." Molly tried to smile, suddenly full of emotion herself.

"Thank you Molly. I think my hair looks perfect now."

"Indeed it does, Mrs. Darcy; your hair is beautiful. You are sure you do not want it up in a braid?"

"No, no, let it be. Mr. Darcy — " She stopped again, mortified at what she had started to say: *Mr. Darcy prefers it down and loose.* What kind of explanation might there be for the fact that Mr. Darcy had already seen her with her hair down and loose and thus had an opportunity to form a preference at all? "Everything is well as it is, thank you. I think... I think you may go now, Molly."

"As you wish... If you need me, I will be downstairs waiting for your call... "

"No, Molly, you must not wait. I do not think I shall need your services this evening. I... I shall call you in the morning, when I require your assistance." *Will I still feel like Miss Bennet in the morning? Will he be with me in the morning?*

She felt her cheeks burning and became furious with herself as every word and thought seemed improper. If she continued to blush this much in front of Molly, how would she react when he was before her and they were alone?

"Very well, madam. I will wait for you to call me early in the morning."

"Good night... umm... Molly?"

The maid was just opening the door and turned to cast a last glance at her mistress. "Yes, Mrs. Darcy?"

"Please be honest with me. Do I look well?" She was standing in the middle of the room, her hands at her sides, waiting for the maid's answer as if it were the most important verdict in the world.

"You look wonderful, Mrs. Darcy. I swear I never saw a more beautiful lady."

"Indeed you look wonderful, Mrs. Darcy."

Mr. Darcy's voice startled both women, and Molly almost knocked him over as he stood in the doorway. Ashamed, she tried to pass by him and exit as quickly as she could, barely whispering her excuse with a shy "good night."

Mr. Darcy started to laugh. "Good night, Molly." He grinned and turned toward Elizabeth, expecting to see her amused countenance with laughter brightening her eyes and twisting her lips, but she was only staring at him, and her face was slightly pale. Moreover, she was biting her lower lip and wringing her hands in front of her, her eyes fixed upon his figure, her chest heaving with each deep breath she took as she inhaled and exhaled rapidly.

Mr. Darcy's entrance took Elizabeth by surprise. She had hoped she would have a few minutes alone after Molly left, but apparently, he had come earlier than he suggested. Perhaps he was as anxious as she was.

She tried to keep smiling as he was standing in front of the door; it would not do for him to see her distressed. He had not longed for this night only to face a fearful bride. She swallowed violently, trying to remove the lump in her throat, and then, finally, she smiled at him, as he was wearing only his trousers and a thin shirt.

Mr. Darcy moved closer until they were touching each other; his strong palms found a spot at the junction of her neck and shoulders and rested there, burning her skin through the silky fabric. His fingers glided slowly along the back of her neck, playing in her heavy curls, and his thumbs gently stroked her throat, moving up to the line of her jaw. Needing support, her arms encircled his waist; she wanted to lean her head against his chest, yet his hands forced her face upwards, his eyes delving into hers until she could hardly bear the intensity of his stare and the novelty of the feelings she saw there.

She was convinced she had witnessed all of his feelings, all of his moods — until this moment of their wedding night. Suddenly, she knew she had been wrong.

"You are so beautiful, Elizabeth. I cannot get enough of just looking at you. How is it possible for you to become more beautiful each day and for me to love you more? Do you know how much I love you — how much I desire you?"

"I am glad you are pleased, William. The nightgown was chosen by Lady Ellen and my aunt; we were told it was the latest fashion, but I was not certain — "

"Elizabeth...*you* are beautiful...! Did you really think I would give any importance to the gown?"

His deep voice interrupted her, while his thumb brushed her lips and his face lowered closer to hers. His intentions were clear, and she held her breath, waiting for their lips to join, certain that his kiss would make all her fears vanish. But the kiss did not come, and his face stopped inches from hers.

She opened her eyes, searching his face for a sign of his intentions.

Darcy's intention had indeed been to kiss her, but his worry was stronger than his desire. He had left her less than an hour ago, joyful, pleased with his company, teasing him sweetly and flirting with him during dinner. He had no doubt that she was as anxious and desirous of his presence as he was for hers; in fact, she had told him as much. He had been fantasising that she would throw herself into his arms the moment he entered her room, that she would lift her soft inviting lips to his without a moment's delay. Instead, he found her practically petrified in the middle of the room, looking as though his arrival was distressing for her. Her reactions to him were more reserved than ever before.

He desperately, painfully wanted to embrace her so close to his heart that she would not be able to breathe, to capture her lips and not free them until the need for air forced them to break apart. Instead, he moved slowly towards her, a tentatively inquiring smile on his face.

Was she unwell or perhaps only overwhelmed by the idea of what was to come?

"My beautiful bride, what is troubling you?"

The tenderness in his voice and his obvious worry were her sweetest comfort. It was her turn to reassure him.

"It is nothing, William, I am only a little nervous..."

To prove her words, her hands rose from around his waist and joined his hands, entwining her fingers with his.

He startled. "My love, your fingers are so cold! You are freezing. This nightgown may be the latest fashion, but it is too thin, and this room is chilled. Come, we must warm you; I would not want my wife to catch a cold on the first day of our marriage."

His hands brushed up and down her arms, then on her back before he pulled her into a tight embrace while his hands continued to stroke her gently through the silky fabric. Against her will, his caress made her shiver even more.

"Mrs. Darcy, are you cold, or are you afraid of me? Should I leave?"

His voice was half-worried and half-teasing, but she failed to notice the humour. She only heard his words and startled. "No, please do not leave. I am sorry I am acting so foolishly. I am not cold or fearful; I am just... well... I... You said you wanted this night to be perfect, and I do not know what to do to make it perfect. Will you not tell me what you want me to do? Please?"

Her distress was obvious, her countenance more unsure than ever, and he did not know whether to be worried or simply amused by her insecurities. What was she imagining he would demand from her?

"What do I want you to do?" He stared at her with his eyes wide open, trying to find the proper words; then his face lightened as his voice turned more serious, even demanding. "For the moment, I want you in bed... this instant!"

Without waiting for any response, he impulsively lifted her from the floor, walking through the room with the sweet burden in his arms. Elizabeth startled, her heart pounding forcefully, so wildly that she could hear its echo in her ears. She closed her eyes, waiting for him to lay her on the bed and renew all those attentions as he did many times before. Instead, she felt herself being put down on the bed in a sitting position, while he wrapped her in sheets as silky as her gown; his arms withdrew from around her, and she immediately felt cold and lonely without his touch.

Opening her eyes, she saw him standing with his back to her, and she could not figure out what he was doing and why he was not joining her. Soon, the room darkened with only two candles in a far corner and the blazing fire; she understood — she had been cold, and he had made the room warmer for her.

His voice brought her back from her reverie.

"Elizabeth, would you like a glass of wine?"

She hesitated only a moment. "If you wish... A little wine would be fine, I think."

She barely recognised her hesitant voice and did not say another word until he returned with a bottle of wine and a glass. She had not noticed that there was a bottle of wine in her room.

With controlled gestures admitting no resistance, he filled the glass with a practiced hand, handed it to her, and then climbed onto the edge of the bed, half turned toward her so they could face each other. He continued to stare at her, an ambiguous smile twisting the corners of his mouth.

She searched his face for any kind of hint as to his wishes but could not figure him out. His gaze showed passion; his hands were slowly moving to touch the fabric of the gown, brushing her leg — first tentatively and then more daringly. His smile was the thing that disconcerted her most. Nervously, she hid her emotions behind the glass and violently gulped a mouthful of red wine.

His hands reached for her hair, which was almost covering her face, and arranged her heavy locks behind her ears.

"Elizabeth, are you feeling better now?"

"Yes, I am. Thank you, William."

"I am glad. Is the wine to your liking?"

"Yes, very much." Only then did she notice that he had not taken a glass for himself.

"Will you not pour some for yourself? I thought we would drink together."

"We will… That is why I filled the glass — so there would be enough for both of us."

"Oh…" She could think of nothing else to say — just held the glass in her hands, her eyes locked with his, waiting… waiting for him.

"Then… shall I tell you what else I want you to do now?" His left hand played with her hair while his right one slowly moved along her throat and down to her neckline. His fingers reached the line of her gown, stopped there a moment, and then moved again, stroking the fine fabric and her bare silky skin.

He could feel her shivering and moved closer until he could sense her irregular breathing.

She startled, blushed violently and clenched the glass tighter, but she did not avert her eyes. He was so close to her that only a few inches separated their foreheads. She did not want him to move away from her again. She smiled at him: reassuringly, lovingly, shyly. She reached to stroke his face, and he turned so he could place a kiss in her palm.

"Yes, please tell me. I do love you so much, William. I want nothing more than to make you happy."

She leaned in a little, and her lips brushed his.

It was an invitation he did not fail to understand, but he also realised that she remained tense.

He hesitated a little, his desire tempting him to reciprocate; she was clearly offering herself to him, but his own desire was of little consequence. The only things that mattered to him were her wishes and desires.

"Elizabeth, I *am* happy; I do not think a man could be happier than I am."

His lips brushed back against hers, and he placed a feathery kiss on the spot near her ear.

She shivered again, and the glass trembled in her hand. His palm covered her fingers around the glass, holding them steady. He raised the glass to her mouth, and she took another swallow, the dizzying liquor spreading inside her body before it was her turn to direct the glass towards him.

"It is very good. You should taste a little."

He decidedly took the glass from her hand, whispering huskily, "Yes, I should." He did so a moment later, laying the glass aside and tasting, not from the glass but from her lips, his tongue tantalising them to part for him, and they did so, welcoming his tender invasion. Her lips were incomparably sweeter then the wine.

His arms could not wait a moment longer to embrace her gently and tenderly with the same care he showed her when he kissed her for the first time.

"Elizabeth… the only thing I want you to do for me is to love me… and to allow me to prove my love for you. There is nothing to fear and nothing to worry about tonight. It will be perfect because we are here, together, veiled in so much love, so much passion… so much desire… "

His face was only a few inches from hers, and her eyes delighted in admiring his handsome features as her heart rejoiced, understanding the heartfelt meaning of his words. All her uncertainties and restraint vanished one by one until they were gone as if they had never existed.

"Mr. Darcy, I will be happy to comply with your every wish… and particularly this one." Her fingers reached to caress his eyelids, his cheeks, and the contour of his mouth; her lips eagerly followed the path of her fingers.

He closed his eyes, abandoning himself to the pleasure of her soft lips covering his face with light kisses, gently at first, and then more daring. His lips and his soul smiled as he revelled in the proof of not only her love but also her maidenly passion. His hands reached the belt of her night robe and untied it, but she did not even seem to notice, her lips never leaving his face. Only when he slowly, patiently pulled the robe off her shoulders and removed it from around her did she react. Her eyes found his, and they locked, silently speaking to each other. Her hands encircled his neck and she leaned back against the pillows, pulling him with her until she felt trapped under his warm weight, but she did not want to escape. Her body wanted to surrender to him — as her heart had surrendered so long ago — and feel the heat of passion. She wanted their love to be complete in every way and in every sense.

His strong palms cupped her face, and he buried his fingers in her hair, fixing her head on the pillow; she was indeed trapped. She started to laugh, remembering him holding her in the same way the night they slept together. "You remember," he whispered, smiling with heartfelt delight.

"How could I forget?" she replied. "I remember everything, starting with that day in the cottage; I remember every word, every touch, every look… " He lowered his face over hers, kissing her smile, her cheeks, her temples, the spot near her ears, and then her chin and down to her throat while she continued to whisper, "… and every kiss."

He stopped and met her eyes again, his fingers removing a lock from her forehead. "You know, Elizabeth... that day in the cottage... when I saw you wrapped in that dirty, smelly blanket, your hair in such disorder, your beautiful face dirty... I was frightened of how much I wanted you. I was certain I had never desired anything as much in my life and never would again. But I was wrong. There is something I want much more than I wanted you that day. It is you, now."

She smiled at him, flustered and mortified by what she intended to say; yet, the words came out nevertheless.

"But William... you said there is nothing to be frightened of, and now we are married. Whatever you want from me, you may have..."

"My dearest Elizabeth..." were the last words she heard from him, words he continued to whisper over and over until his lips passionately fell upon hers again.

His kisses — countless kisses that spread from her lips to her cheeks, her eyes, the line of her jaw and back to her lips again — were as patient and gentle as they had been on the first day of their engagement. There was no urgency, no release, and no overwhelming passion — only love, tenderly bestowed.

His hands travelled gently along her body, exploring each part of it; the soft fabric of her nightgown flowed through his fingers, brushing over her skin and sliding down from her shoulders and lower until she remained enfolded only in his adoring gaze.

Her eyes were closed; she did have enough courage to look at him, but she could feel his gaze burning every inch of her bare skin. Her body remained uncovered but a moment until his hands draped her in sweet caresses and his lips covered her with the softness of his kisses, softer than any silk and warmer than any velvet.

His lips departed from the sweetness of her mouth, into a maddening exploration of her beauty. More daring and more hurried than his lips, which rested for a moment near the hollow of her ear to whisper his love, his hands did not stop until they reached the perfect roundness of her breasts. He groaned loudly at the exquisite pleasure of touching her unrestrainedly for the first time; he greedily cupped the long-desired softness in his palms. His restless fingers traced tantalising circles closer and closer to the pink centres, which hardened under his touch, begging for more. He gave her more when his lips blazed a path along her neck, claiming their right to savour the taste of her skin.

His right hand continued the eager exploration, allowing his hungry mouth to satiate its urge. A trail of warm kisses encircled her breast until they finally closed upon the soft hardness and captured it. He heard her moans grow louder as her body shivered violently beneath him; her fingers were tightly entwined in his hair, pulling him closer to her, more painfully as the pleasure overwhelmed her.

Never did he experience a more gratifying sensation than in those moments when he was showing her, teaching her, offering her the complete pleasure a man can offer his beloved. Her body was delightfully undulating under his eager hands, yielding to them, surrendering to his hunger. Several moments later, his mouth released its captive only to conquer the soft hardness of her other breast; he wanted to touch, to kiss, to taste every part of her body, now, before she became a woman — to have her maidenly flavour forever in his mind and his senses, as this night would remain forever unforgettable to him.

Amidst his ever-growing passion, he did not realise that he was not only thinking but also whispering his desire to her, and her body shivered in the torturous anticipation of his promise. It was a promise he would not break.

With infinite and tender patience, his ardent love wrapped her, overwhelmed her, conquered her. She let herself be overcome by his passion and by her own desire. Her body arched for his touches, begging for more, begging for everything, as he seemed willing to give her all. Each spot of her skin that bore the exquisite torture of his lips, his tongue, and his fingers longed for their return while each part of her body that remained unsatisfied demanded his touch. The fire that had seized her grew stronger each moment in places his caresses had not yet reached, but he seemed to know her desires better than she did. His hand slid slowly with gentle determination to her thighs and rested upon them, but only for an instant. His fingers glided between them, parting them with burning strokes, brushing along them — tender, yet strong fingers, admitting no resistance, drawing all her senses to the place that was still aching for his touch.

Unexpectedly, his lips returned to her mouth, and hers joined them in eager joy; her lips had missed his, and he could feel it. While the kiss grew wilder, their tongues danced in sensual domination of the other. His fingers climbed to the warmth between her legs until he was possessively cradling the only part of her body he had not yet conquered. Countless chills shivered throughout her body, and she screamed against his mouth as her legs instinctively gripped his hand. However, his caresses were not rejected, not when every stroke left her wanting more, every daring, impudent, demanding touch seemed to be the answer to the deepest need inside her, and every caress of his fingers sent waves of pleasure through her body.

Every sensation she had ever experienced before was a pale prelude to what he was offering her that night. Every time the pleasure became unbearable, he gave her more.

His lips left her mouth— already longing for his kisses — and returned to a familiar path; they tarried on their journey at her breasts once more, and then resumed the track lower to reach their goal. The novelty of his lips pressing against her inner thighs and his tongue tasting her skin while drawing nearer to his fingers, made her quiver again; her body was begging, full of eager anticipation for what might come, while her incredulous mind, clouded by desire, refused to believe that something like that could happen. No anticipation could prepare her for the shock of feeling the softness of his lips on *that* place or for the unbearable pleasure that followed and seemed to last an eternity, throwing her into the midst of a violent storm of fire and ice.

When her senses returned to her, she felt his weight upon her and his warm, naked form covering her, imprisoning her. She could feel his breath as his face was a hair's breadth from hers. She opened her eyes and found the message of his eyes, deeper and darker than ever.

She had dreamed many times about the moment she would become his wife — and the moment had arrived at the end of a journey more wonderful than any dream. Their eyes locked in perfect understanding, and his hand lifted to her face, caressing her with a tenderness that melted her heart. His eyes were speaking of his love, his lips, smiling adoringly, were professing his feelings, while his body — strongly, powerfully, possessively — broke the final barrier, confirming their complete union.

For a few moments, her body stiffened, and her beautiful face furrowed in pain; her soft cry cut his heart, tearing him between tenderness and passion. His heart ached for her and wanted nothing but to comfort her. He knew he should stop, but his body would not listen. The glorious feeling of taking her as his wife — of being inside her — was more than he had ever experienced; the pleasure that overwhelmed him was more than he could have imagined. He could not fight it; he tried, but failed. His body seemed to have a will of its own, demanding the long-awaited completion. He managed to control himself briefly, slowing his movements for a few moments and allowing her to become accustomed to him.

His eyes searched her face, which was still wearing a faint trace of pain; her eyes were closed, and he wanted to see them, to read them, so his lips grazed her long eyelashes, forcing them to open. Meeting his gaze seemed to relax her, and he could feel her moving slightly beneath him; despite his struggle, his body started to move too, slowly, as if by itself.

His lips lowered to her beloved face and moistened her dry mouth, silencing her moans for a moment. He knew he had caused her pain, and he wanted to tell her how much pleasure and happiness she was giving him. He whispered everything to her, each word followed by a brushing of his lips against her neck, her ears, her cheeks, her trembling chin and her eyes hidden behind their lashes.

She listened to his words without understanding them, but her mind and body slowly relaxed under the comfort of his lips and the warmth of his voice. Her mind soon fell into a whirl of light and ceased its struggle to understand what was happening to her and how it was possible for such painful, tormenting pleasure to exist. Her body belonged to him, as did her heart; his love was conquering her, possessing her, and filling her with his passion, taking her as his wife; yet, he was her prisoner, too. She could feel him inside her, joined with her in perfect completion. She heard his whispered professions of love, his words of passion and gratitude and sorrow for the pain he caused her — and indeed the pain was stronger and sharper than she had imagined — but he did not know also how astonishingly pleasant the pain was, and she wanted him to know; she ought to show him as much. Tentatively at first, her body struggled to learn the rhythm of shared passion, moving slightly beneath him, with him, toward him; unconsciously, her legs encircled his waist, pulling him even closer to her, and she could not repress a cry when, with a husky groan, he thrust deeper and harder inside her. His lips captured hers again as the rhythm of their joined bodies grew wildly fervent — passion mixed with happiness becoming perfect love — until it was not him and her anymore, but them.

An eternity seemed to pass until he reached the long desired moment, shattering in release and spreading warm waves inside her trembling body, his hoarse groans mixed with the soft cries escaping her swollen lips.

Countless moments passed before they could breathe steadily again; yet, not then — not even later — did either of them pull apart. They remained closely bonded, bodies and souls entwined in a perfect whole, with their two equal parts belonging to each other in that moment of blissful felicity.

THERE WAS NO NEED FOR words later. They lay on their sides, closely embraced, their naked bodies not wanting to part from each other. Elizabeth's head was nestled against her husband's strong chest, her face close to his heart, her fingers caressing his warm skin while her long hair cascaded in dark, silky waves and covered them both. His hands continued tenderly to stroke her smooth back, her arms and her head; his fingers played with her hair until she fell asleep, exhausted from the emotion and unbearable happiness she had experienced. The last sounds she heard were the rain outside and the beating of his heart — calm, reassuring and steady. She placed her lips against that spot and allowed sleep to surround her.

Enraptured by the beauty of the woman who was finally his wife — truly his wife — and her soft, warm body lying almost atop him, her soft breasts pressing against his chest and her smell intoxicating his senses, Darcy did not sleep, nor did he want to. He was not tired — quite the contrary — his body, which had longed for her for so long, could not be satiated by their lovemaking. His urge was only increased now that, as a starved man, he tasted her exquisite flavour. He wanted nothing more than to love her again and again until he satisfied his hunger.

This time, however, he was more capable of controlling his desires. He could be patient for her sake — and for his. He could afford to be patient now that he knew for certain he would not have to wait long and his waiting soon would be rewarded. He would let her sleep as long as she needed, and when she awakened, he would be there to teach her more about passion and pleasure.

His gaze rested upon her curves, which were revealed through the thin sheet, remembering the feeling, the taste, and the form of every inch of her naked skin. He had touched her, kissed her, tasted her, caressed her as he had never done before in his life — nor had he ever imagined he would do so with a woman, at least not before meeting Elizabeth.

He could recall precisely the day that he started to dream about her. It was an evening at Lucas Lodge that she refused to dance with him. Since then, countless times every night, she was present in his dreams, and he had loved her in every dream. What a poor imagination he had and how easily the reality had surpassed it! This night had proved it beyond any doubt. And it was only the beginning; he was certain of that. There was still so much he wanted to offer her and so much he could receive from her — so much passion and pleasure for them to share.

His eyes returned to her face, and he stroked it tenderly with the back of his fingers. His thumb slightly brushed her lower lip. It was swollen and bitten; she had done it in that wonderful moment when she reached the edge of her pleasure. He licked his lower lip and felt a little mark there, too, where she had bitten his lips at that same moment.

As if sensing he was staring, she moved, turning half on her back, offering to his greedy eyes the splendid view of her breasts — creamy, soft, and perfect in their roundness, their pink centres slightly hardened, begging for his touch. Unconsciously, before his mind understood what happened, his right hand lowered and his fingers brushed around them in tantalising circles, and he released a groan so loud that he was afraid he would wake her. She sighed and then moaned softly under his caress, but in the next moment, she resumed her previous position, her breast pressing against his chest as she clung to him tightly.

He chuckled and a smile of delight spread over his face; she looked so young, so innocent, so... sleepy that his tenderness conquered his passion. He kissed her hair, and she smiled in her sleep, whispering his name, her hands and her legs circling him tighter.

His thoughts returned to more than a month ago — their first night together after the dreadful fight with his aunt — when she finally had fallen asleep in his arms after generously and lovingly forgiving him for his unfair behaviour. That night, he had not believed it possible that his love, passion, and happiness would grow each day. Yet grow it did, and it reached the highest peak that night.

How is it possible for a man to feel so much for a woman?

A FORCEFUL THUNDERCLAP AND RAIN hitting the window with increasing intensity startled Elizabeth, and she opened her eyes, a little confused about where she was. A moment later, all the wonderful memories of the night flooded her. She sighed deeply with an inner smile spreading over her lips, and her cheeks turned hot and crimson as she felt her naked body under the covers. Then she remembered: She did not put her nightgown back on simply because after... *after he took me as his wife,* they remained united, closely embraced. He had only pulled the bedclothes over their bodies; she had fallen asleep with her head on his bare chest, and she blushed again remembering how wonderfully strong and warm his chest felt. *Not just his chest — all of him. He is so warm and strong and yet so tender... my husband!* Astonishingly, the sensations made her tremble as she recalled the exquisite feeling of having him inside her, and her body suddenly, shockingly burned and ached with her desire for him. His arms, his hands, his lips, his tongue... his entire body... that part of his body... different from what she knew, from what she imagined but so amazingly, so wonderfully suited to her... inside her. *My husband...* Elizabeth stretched her arms and turned on the other side to be closer to him, but the bed was empty and cold. *He went to his own room,* she thought, and a cold sense of loss and disappointment made her shiver.

She could not help calling him in a low voice. "William?" though she knew he could not hear her from his room. Why had he left?

"Yes, my love?" His voice was light and full of joy, and her heart pounded as she sat up, pulling the sheet around her.

He was there in the dark, kneeling near the fireplace, naked, and the firelight was dancing on the firm planes of his body. Her eyes opened widely, and she desperately struggled not to allow her gaze to fall below his waist.

"The fire died, and I was afraid the room would become too cold by morning. It will be ready in a moment."

Mesmerised, she watched his strong, tall figure, lit only by the fire, move closer to her until he reached the bed and leaned near her, embracing her gently.

"I am sorry I did not cover myself. I thought you were sleeping. I hope I did not embarrass you too much."

She put her arms around him, whispering with great effort to sound as light and teasing as he did. "No... not *too* much. I think I can bear it well enough." Then her tone became grave, and she tightened her grip on him. "I thought you had gone."

"Gone? Where would I have gone?"

"To your room."

His fingers tipped her chin so he could search her eyes. "Do you want me to go to my room?"

"No..."

"Then I shall not. I shall never leave you as long as you want me near you. I shall hold you in my arms every night, and your beautiful face will be the first thing I see when I wake up each morning."

"We shall sleep together every night?"

"Not just sleep, my beloved. We shall make love each night until we fall asleep in each other's arms... and then we shall wake up and make love again as many times as we want."

Her eyes were locked with his, and he did not fail to see the change in her expression as he spoke. He could not hide his amusement and hurried to reassure her, as he thought he could understand her distress.

"My love, that is how I would like for it to be if you approve: to share our beds and our rooms. I told you as much long ago when we spent our first night together and the next morning in my letter with the roses. However, if you are displeased with this arrangement, I would gladly do as you wish. As for what I said about our lovemaking, you must not be frightened. I hope you know I would never force my will upon you, nor would I do anything without your consent."

Her fingers pressed his lips, silencing him, as her eyes laughed at him. "Do I look displeased, Mr. Darcy? Or frightened? Or do I appear inclined to refuse you my consent in anything?"

Her face was glowing, and her eyes were sparkling with unconcealed delight, her cheeks slightly flushed under his intense stare; her lips — intensely red from their shared passion — were twisted into a bright, teasing smile. His hands slid through her hair, framing her face so he could admire her fully.

"No, Mrs. Darcy, you do not look displeased or frightened. You look beautiful... and quite happy."

Her fingers moved and found their way into his hair, mirroring his gestures while she leaned even closer to him and the sheet slipped down from around her.

"That is because I *am* happy, Mr. Darcy. I dare say I am the happiest woman in the world."

Darcy leaned down against the pillows, pulling her with him; her body was warm and daring, emanating passion and unconcealed desire. She moved until she laid atop him, and in an instant, his arms and legs imprisoned her.

"I cannot disagree with that, my dear wife; however, I believe that you cannot possibly be happier than I am."

Elizabeth lowered her head until it was a few inches from his. Her eyes deepened into his adoring gaze, their hearts beating together in perfect rhythm while her lips whispered warmly only a moment before he captured them.

"It is settled then, my dear husband: We are to be the happiest couple in the world."

THE END

Lightning Source UK Ltd.
Milton Keynes UK
UKOW05f2201190813

215622UK00002B/435/P

9 781936 009183